Civilized Civil War
How Developed Countries are Vulnerable to Foreign Instigated Violent Internal Conflict

Aaron L. Hirschi

Table of Contents

Copyright

Disclaimer:

All statements of fact, opinion, and analysis expressed are those of the author and do not reflect the official positions or views of the Office of the Director of National Intelligence (ODNI), the Department of Defense (DoD), the US Army, or any other agency of the United States Government. The public release clearance of this publication by both the DoD and ODNI does not imply endorsement or factual accuracy of the material. Nothing in the contents should be construed as asserting or implying US government authentication of information or endorsement of the author's views by ODNI, DoD, or the US Army. This material has been reviewed by the ODNI and DoD to prevent the disclosure of classified information.

Author's Note:

When the idea came to me for writing this book just before the Ukrainian War started in 2022, I didn't fully appreciate the challenge of matching the concepts presented in the book to the ever-shifting geopolitical realities of the current world. As the world is still in transition from the 1990s globalist era into a new era of multipolar power politics between rival spheres of influence, the issues surrounding these events remain in a constant state of flux. I tried, partly in vain, to keep real world examples as up to date as possible to help crystalize and better articulate key themes, points, and trends to make the thesis more compelling. However, as time moves on, circumstances around some examples have changed either by resolution or an issue becoming obsolescent. This challenge is further exacerbated by the challenges of publication.

I completed the book in 2023, but still had to overcome more challenges. Since I am still an employee of the U.S. government's national security apparatus, this book had to be submitted to the pre-publication security reviews of both the Department of Defense and the Office of the Director of National Intelligence which took nearly three months. Only after they had both approved the manuscript that I was finally able to seek out and persuade a publisher to take a risk in publishing a first-time author which added an additional six months of time.

As a result, for the sake of simplicity, the analysis of the book is focused on a snapshot in time before the publication date. Some edits were included to highlight some obvious changes, such as the end of the Assad Regime in Syria, to acknowledge changing developments, but largely keeps to the first few years of the 2020s. The concepts of the main thesis remain true even as specific contemporary examples fade into the past.

Introduction:

Since 2020, the idea of another civil conflict happening among the nations of the West, especially in France and America, has gained traction in popular political discussions. From French generals warning of civil war in 2021 to political pundits using hyperbolic vitriol to emphasize certain policy positions, civil war discussion has reentered the Western political zeitgeist for the first time since the 1930s. In isolation, this trend would appear to be a symptom of a hyper-partisan political era with no serious risk of this transpiring in the foreseeable future. There is, however, a theoretical way for such a calamity to happen, even if it is only the remotest of possibilities. A foreign power in this new era of multipolar state rivalry could possibly use its power, wealth, and influence to instigate a civil war via gray-zone warfare.

Gray-zone warfare is an "in-vogue" catch all term for nation states carrying out actions to undermine their rivals' societies without actually resorting to open warfare and current technology now gives rivals access to every aspect of their opponents' societies. In the West, gray-zone warfare is usually referencing the antics of either Russia's actions in Europe or China's actions in the South China Sea and against Taiwan. For the United States, the gray-zone activities waged by the People's Republic of China against the American homeland are of the greatest concern. China uses a multitude of methods and tactics to weaken US and Western nations' resolve to challenge China's ambitions ranging from diplomatic maneuvering to using America's own laws against itself to impede security protections. Part of my work has been to map out China's gray-zone efforts in an attempt to see if one could build a singular comprehensive picture of their strategic intent and capabilities. In evaluating their efforts, and more importantly their potential capabilities, I have discovered how China could potentially execute its most dangerous form of gray-zone warfare within a nation such as the United States. If properly executed, this could induce sufficient chaos within a target nation, such as the United States, to force it to tear itself apart from within. China could accomplish all of this while avoiding blame or attribution. The ultimate gray-zone escalation for China is to set and manipulate circumstances to induce civil war within the US or any of its allies.

At first glance, this ultimate escalation in gray-zone warfare seems impossible, but an in-depth analysis indicates that as long as China's involvement remains undetected this scenario is plausible. The key for China's success relies on finding ways to legally subvert critical segments of American society while simultaneously appearing innocuous until it's far too late to reverse the destabilization. Exposing such activity prior to its execution would disrupt all such actions and create enough diplomatic, economic, and potentially military fallout to deter China from pursuing this action any further.

Western governments have a major weakness in seeing how China conducts its strategies. The West creates clear boundaries of government power, both as a singular entity as well as dividing powers within the government. Each element of a Western government pursues and studies problems and challenges within a confined set of rules and jurisdictions. Sometimes, these jurisdictions overlap but overall, there are clear distinct lanes of administrative control. China is a totalitarian regime where all things, both public and private, are subject to the authorities and whims of the Chinese Communist Party. China is able to use its superior bureaucratic flexibility to circumvent Western laws, policies, and regulations in order to exploit Western societal weaknesses without Western governments even knowing it is happening. The West watches the military threat, the espionage threat, voting manipulation threat, and so on, but China also pursues actions that bypass all government jurisdictions and scrutiny. There are many private activities within Western societies that their governments do not watch or consider relevant, particularly if these are done by economically or socially influential private individuals. Perfectly legal non-threatening actions are easy to overlook but can be susceptible to subversion and will after a sufficient number of years, allow China to embed itself into crucial parts of the Western societies. This can induce enough instability to provoke civil conflicts. This book attempts to wargame what and how such a possibility could be achieved and avoided if caught in time.

Western governments are designed to go after very specific types of threats while also being constrained by institutional checks and balances in order to prevent the rise of authoritarian power. Part of these checks and balances is having an alert electorate to supervise both democratic-republican style government and the health of the society. China however has delegated all power and responsibility exclusively to the totalitarian Chinese Communist Party. The Chinese Communist Party is waging a whole-of-society effort to fight to achieve its grand strategic goals. In the West, the electorate is separate and independent of the state. If the electorate is not made aware so they can actively participate in countering China's gray-zone warfare, then the West will remain the underdog and be at greater risk.

The research in this book will demonstrate how a gray-zone induced violent uprising can be a genuine plausible threat to Western countries when major foreign powers directly manipulate one or both sides of a nation's political factions. In a sufficiently volatile political situation, few would conceive that the work of a foreign power was deliberately aggravating all political camps within that Western nation. The best way to help improve everyone's ability to detect such happenings is to walk through a potential worst-case scenario in which a major foreign power successfully induces civil conflict within a Western nation.

The book will also analyze how such a conflict would likely be fought differently from the industrial-age warfare of the 1860s Civil War, world wars of the 20th Century, or the civil wars of the Middle East. The interconnectedness of developed nations creates opportunities for very precise targeting with advanced weapons requiring a much smaller fighting force with a relatively tiny industrial footprint. The key for a foreign adversary to "win" a hypothetical civil war within the West is to convince disaffected factions to directly fight their government institutions in old classical industrial age total warfare. This would destabilize the economy and social cohesion of the targeted Western nation-state.

This book will first lay out the case for why and how China could instigate such a disastrous scenario and then the rest of the book will wargame a civil war scenario if a great foreign power succeeds in its gray-zone instigation. This wargame will be a viable scenario of a foreign induced civil war in a developed Western country. The analysis will, as objectively as possible, break down and evaluate each level of war to include strategic, operational, and tactical considerations. This scenario applies to the developed nations of the West and for objectivity and to avoid any bias, I will use nameless states and generic factions. This also will demonstrate that there are many common applicable threads across all Western states as to make this scenario plausible in Europe or North America or Australasia. The instigating foreign power in such a scenario would achieve the greatest victory possible by avoiding direct confrontation while helping to convince the combating factions to fight without restriction against each other in spirit of the industrial-age concepts of total war. Such an outcome would cripple the targeted Western country for the rest of the century and turn it into a willing vassal. If on the other hand, the Western nation fails to detect this gray-zone intrigue and civil war becomes unavoidable, this scenario will also show how the forces loyal to the Western nation can still achieve victory. By rejecting the methods of total war and traditional forms of insurgency and adopt the more refined sophisticated means of modern warfare that target just the domestic implementers and supporters of this gray-zone subversion, the targeted nation will avoid total defeat.

Section One: Only China can Subvert the West

Chapter 1: China is the Only Qualified Subverter

A civil war in a modern Western society requires circumstances so dire and so extreme that in the current era of economic wealth, such an event requires an outside initiator possessing the drive and capability to instigate one. Few would believe any nation would undertake such a high-risk venture in trying to shift the global balance of power. A nation would only risk this covert declaration of war if that nation's own existence, or its ruling faction, was in danger of extermination. Is there a circumstance that could compel a foreign adversary to take such a risk and if so, who could be potential candidates? Determining the motivation circumstance depends on who is the instigator.

Subversion on a scale as to instigate civil war in a highly developed country requires resources, time, and extensive connections in the West to be successful. The named requirements help narrow down the list of adversarial candidates considerably as only a few countries are powerful enough to have all the necessary means. The simplest way to identify a plausible adversary is to gauge each major anti-Western nation's strength by the four principal instruments of national power: diplomatic, informational, military, and economic (DIME). A great world power must be able to exert several, if not all of these instruments on a global scale while still having the resources to subvert Western countries over a period of decades. Only China has sufficient rivalry and clout to be a proper candidate in the contemporary era. China also has a long history of using subterfuge and infiltration to weaken enemy countries further demonstrating it has the skill and understanding to properly execute such an extreme plan. Theoretically, China could destabilize a modern Western country with only gray-zone warfare but could it do this realistically?

The People's Republic of China's national power is one of controversy because many differing interests either want to portray China as a paper dragon,[i] strong in appearance but weak in reality, or portray China as the irresistibly rising hegemon[ii] that will supplant the United States as the unchallenged global colossus. The interesting point is that both sides of this argument are correct and wrong. China is a nation not only with many strengths but also with glaring weaknesses that could cripple China and the Chinese Communist Party (CCP). As will be explained later, China is a paper dragon but does have iron claws that could potentially deal a fatal blow to a rival before China would succumb to its internal weaknesses. China is weaker than it portrays itself but is still very dangerous. Overall, China sufficiently possesses the motivation, resources, and the patience to wage a covert strategy to subvert Western countries to weaken them and perhaps eventually instigate a civil war.

The case of Russia successfully instigating a covert war to promote domestic instability in the West is weak because Russia struggles to maintain its DIME especially after incurring the costs of the Ukrainian War. Most acknowledge Putin must balance his ambitions of great power status with the diminished resources (economic and political) that are needed to keep economic stability at home while trying to assert military strength in a badly executed war. After this war is finished, Russia will need years of restructuring. China, has built in the last 40 years a sufficient level of resources, coupled with a consistent and cohesive grand strategy, to continuously build on all elements of DIME without endangering its domestic stability; or at least, retain it as of this writing in 2024.

To quickly summarize, China's DIME remains strong allowing it to take risks the Russian regime cannot. The CCP is patient in a way never demonstrated by Vladimir Putin. China waits until circumstances arise that will give it a natural advantage. If the circumstances do not arrive naturally, the Chinese regime will gently nudge over a period of years the necessary components into place to create the best opportunities. The United States witnessed this firsthand from the Tiananmen Massacre in 1989 to China's attainment of World Trade Organizational membership in December of 2001. China waited a decade to allow the international anger to subside and used various economic marketing strategies to exploit Western greed to blind critical eyes of the CCP's anti-Western policies.[iii], [iv] The CCP's patience enables them to wait until its DIME is strong enough to confront or co-opt an issue then move on to the next target of opportunity.

The DIME parameters for the purposes of this book require a nation rich enough to spend large quantities of resources over decades to subvert the political, economic, and cultural institutions of its rivals while still having the resources to either maintain or strengthen its DIME. Although this book postulates a hypothetical case, it is only of use if there is a realistic basis. China's DIME makes the country a realistic foreign backer to corrupt Western social factions into betraying their own country or countries for personal power or wealth.

China's economy is only second to the United States in raw numbers while its trade with the world's nations has grown into the trillions of dollars.[v], [vi] The CCP keeps prioritizing foreign investment both within China and having domestic firms invest in foreign countries.[vii] Circulating large sums of money into coffers of the world's ruling elites has built large quantities of good will that strengthens China's diplomatic power while also controlling the portrayal of China's rulers overseas.[viii], [ix]

The Chinese military, the People's Liberation Army (PLA), remain largely a regional power, however it is methodically changing this reality. Unlike Russia, China is co-opting elites in other countries on a colossal scale with its economic and diplomatic elements of the DIME to expand its military presence. Russia may get Syria, Venezuela, Cuba, and perhaps one or two African spots but China is building its military presence in South Asia, Central Asia, Southeast Asia, and the entire continent of Africa. This effort is slow and methodical to prevent overreach either militarily or diplomatically. Yet, the PLA's presence grows in Cambodia, Djibouti, Tanzania, Iran, Equatorial Guinea, and Tajikistan.[x], [xi], [xii], [xiii] Always seeking nations that are poor, weak, or controlled by strong autocratic regimes, the large money investments only have to placate the elites of the invested nations, not necessarily the people.

China's success is by using its DIME on co-opting ruling elites, not necessarily winning hearts and minds of the general populations of those countries. This means the Chinese DIME does not have to commit large resources or risks that the West must undertake. Any abuses or corruption will incentivize the local elites to cover up or censor such activities, putting the onus on China's newly acquired proxies rather than China itself.[xiv] This method means any serious resistance to Chinese influence must come at considerable financial or political cost.

This pattern of co-opting elites with largess while also investing large quantities of resources or money into foreign economies all demonstrate China is in fact using the art of subversion right now in developing countries. The CCP possesses the experience, skill, and foresight to carry out these complex means of indirect subjugation with many decades of experimentation and approaches under its belt.[xv] The CCP's actions in the world make the hypothesis of a foreign-instigated civil war or wars in the West both plausible and valid.

To understand the nature of a foreign power's support to a corrupt Western elite, the observer must understand exactly who is carrying out such actions, why they would perform such a risky move, and how exactly could the CCP or some other possible future major power instigate a civil war in the West? To answer these questions, the following chapters will explain the relevant political history, policies, and organizational structures of the CCP that make up the components of modern China. This will reveal both the limits and capabilities of the CCP and will demonstrate the plausibility that under the right circumstances they have both the ability and motivation to carry out such an extreme operation.

---

[i] Michael Beckley, *Unrivaled: Why America Will Remain the World's Sole Superpower*, (Ithaca: Cornell University Press, 2018) 2.

[ii] Fareed Zakaria, *The Post-American World*, (NY: WW Norton & Company, 2008) 92-96.

[iii] Joseph Fewsmith, "China and the WTO: The Politics Behind the Agreement," The National Bureau of Asian Research, November 1999. https://www.iatp.org/sites/default/files/China_and_the_WTO_The_Politics_Behind_the_Agre.htm

[iv] Magdalena Trzclonka, "US Economic Sanctions against China as a Reaction to Human Rights Abuses During the Tiananmen Crisis," Jagiellonian University, March 2018. https://www.researchgate.net/publication/323613399_US_Economic_Sanctions_against_China_as_a_Reaction_to_Human_Rights_Abuses_During_the_Tiananmen_Crisis

[v] Prableen Bajpai, "The Fastest Growing Trillion-Dollar Economies in 2021," NASDAQ, February 5, 2021. https://www.nasdaq.com/articles/the-fastest-growing-trillion-dollar-economies-in-2021-2021-02-05

[vi] ChinaPower Team, "Is China the World's Top Trader?" CSIS, China Power, March 28, 2019. https://chinapower.csis.org/trade-partner/

[vii] Michael Enright, "Developing China: The Remarkable Impact of Foreign Direct Investment," Hinrich Foundation, 2017. https://www.hinrichfoundation.com/research/book/developing-china-impact-of-foreign-direct-investment/

[viii] Robert Spalding, *Stealth War: How China Took Over While America's Elite Slept*, (Penguin Random House, 2019) 6-9.

[ix] Chris Fenton, *Feeding the Dragon*, (NY: Post Hill Press, 2020) 66-76.

[x] Craig Singleton, "Beijing Eyes New Military Bases across the Indo-Pacific," Foreign Policy, July 7 2021. https://foreignpolicy.com/2021/07/07/china-pla-military-bases-kiribati-uae-cambodia-tanzania-djibouti-indo-pacific-ports-airfields/

[xi] Farnaz Fassihi and Steven Lee Myers, "Defying US, China and Iran Near Trade and Military Partnership," NY Times, July 11, 2020. https://www.nytimes.com/2020/07/11/world/asia/china-iran-trade-military-deal.html

[xii] Nathan Beauchamp-Mustafaga, "Where to Next: PLA Considerations for Overseas Base Site Selection," Jamestown Foundation China Brief, Vol. 20, Issue: 18, October 2020. https://jamestown.org/program/where-to-next-pla-considerations-for-overseas-base-site-selection/

[xiii] Michael Tanchum, "China's New Military Base in Africa: What it Means for Europe and America," European Council on Foreign Relations, December 14, 2021. https://ecfr.eu/article/chinas-new-military-base-in-africa-what-it-means-for-europe-and-america/

[xiv] Dickens Olewe, "Why African Countries Back China on Human Rights," BBC News, May 2 2021. https://www.bbc.com/news/world-africa-56717986

[xv] Timothy L. Thomas, "New Developments in Chinese Strategic Psychological Warfare," Foreign Military Studies Office, Center for Army Lessons Learned, 2005, page 6. https://apps.dtic.mil/sti/pdfs/ADA434978.pdf

Chapter 2: Who in China is the Threat?

In geopolitics, arguments are simplified by referring to respective polities by the names of the nation state, in this case China. However, the reality is more nuanced and to understand who is actually making the decisions, one must talk about the Chinese Communist Party (CCP) itself rather than the nation or even government of China. The CCP rules China uncontested and dictates all actions via state institutions but many people do not realize the CCP is not the state but a separate entity.[i] The CCP, like a parasite, latches onto the state and controls all government functions but still is independent of all laws, regulations, or government oversight. To understand the CCP and the mentality it forges among its members is to understand the intentions and actions of China.

Communist derived dictatorships have the unique characteristic of having a dual system of governance where the communist party and state institutions operate in parallel and are linked. This is not an equal partnership but instead the communist party dominates the state with the communist party itself being immune to all actions from the state. Communist parties operate as a separate entity, like a secret society, that directs all activities but the decisions, and sometimes the persons making the decisions, are hidden from public view. The party exists to rule and impose the utopian collectivist ideals of Marx, at least theoretically, onto the subjugated populations by using the state apparatus to execute all actions.[ii] Therefore, understanding who the CCP is and how its intentions, members, and apparatus that are shaped by historical and modern factors that few Westerners appreciate is critical to understanding "who" is the threat in China.

One of the most unique factors of the CCP which sets it apart from the Soviet controlled parties is the impact of China's dynastic period and its failures during the 19th Century. Otherwise known as the "Century of Humiliation," China experienced its downfall from being the most powerful kingdom on Earth for centuries to becoming a weak and broken society overcome by European imposed modernity.[iii] Unlike Japan, which took advantage of the circumstances of the forced Western trade dealings to modernize and become a rival power to the West, China stubbornly refused to reform. The traditionalist Empress Dowager Cixi actually led a coup against the reformist Emperor Guangxu and destroyed his Meiji-like 100 Days' Reform Movement that kept the Qing Dynasty in its old stagnant ways. The Qing Dynasty's refusal to adapt to the changing times would culminate in the disastrous Boxer Rebellion in 1899-1901.[iv], [v] These events shattered the collective psychological will of China, leading to the first attempt at a republic in 1912.

Imagine believing you have complete understanding of the world and in your intellectual confidence, believe all your past achievements prove your superiority and can never be supplanted by any rival. Your success allows you to impose your will on anyone you please because you have achieved supreme power and wealth. Then later in life, you quickly discover not one but a dozen others have surpassed your achievements and can impose their will upon you and any attempt at resistance brings extreme physical pain. The shock of a dramatic reversal of fortune combined with experiencing a brutal humiliating defeat when attempting to assert oneself would devastate anyone's mind. This is especially hard when there is no mental escape from such disaster. No social media, no echo chambers to reinforce a sense of self-worth, no ability to insulate one's mind from objective reality. Instead, one has to face every negative facet of humiliating defeat, derision, mockery, and subjugation without any means of psychological escape. This is what China experienced in the 19th Century as a nation and such experiences leave lasting impressions on a nation's beliefs.

After the failures of the dynastic system, China still suffered from failed projects of republican government, foreign invasion, and anarchic civil war for the first 50 years of the 20th Century. The CCP arose from pain, suffering, corruption, and the avarice of the powerful during this time, portraying itself as a new movement promising justice for the aggrieved Chinese population. Exploiting the population's craving for stability and revenge against the established power made its talk of revolution very appealing. However, events within China were not the only influences that forged the CCP's foundations.

The Soviet Union and its COMINTERN took interest in China in the 1920s by backing the fledgling CCP. The Soviet Union would train the CCP in the arts of organization, psychological warfare, propaganda, Leninist Doctrine, and subversion.[vi] Of course, the Soviet Union intended to eventually create a subordinate communist party in China that would become a vassal like the future parties of the Warsaw Pact but unforeseen circumstances would prevent this outcome.

The final social factor that influenced the CCP was the Chinese nationalism that arose within the party itself. Until the rise of Mao Zedong, the CCP was in fact, like their Russian counterpart, an urban and intellectually centric party. The Soviet ideology of communism arising from the workers of a late-stage industrial capitalist state was still the dominant doctrine. This doctrine failed to consider the unique circumstances of China which barely evolved beyond a feudalist system. This meant the first leaders of the Chinese Communist Party attempted to impose a Leninist-Stalin style ideology on a society too economically primitive to adequately build upon Soviet doctrines. Then Mao Zedong took control of the CCP.

Mao created his own unique take on Marxist concepts and argued a revolution can come from the peasantry instead of the urban classes and factory workers. Of course, contradicting doctrinal orthodoxy that provides the justification for Stalin's legitimacy would not be popular in the Soviet Empire. Regardless, Mao's new ideological doctrine incorporated China's economic circumstances while emphasizing the historic plight of China itself created a popular rallying force to make the CCP a true contender for political domination of China.[vii], [viii] The CCP's victory in the Chinese Civil War in 1949 assured Mao's concepts and the nationalist fervor would dominate China's mindset for the next 30 years. During this time, ideological purism of the Party's utopianist and radical beliefs of being China's only savior dominated all policy. This fanaticism further deluded the young CCP it could act as a god in its actions as a state to create heaven on Earth. This fanaticism shaped the Party's view of foreign interference, to eventually include the Soviet Union itself, as an unhelpful interfering threat to the CCP's existence. The result created a permanent victimhood complex within the Party which perpetuated it amongst the general population to keep paranoia, fear, and resentment of outside influences as means to maintain legitimacy and control. This leads to the final major influencing factor of the modern CCP, its own past experience of governing.

Mao Zedong secured absolute control of the CCP's ideology and policy making by the end of the Chinese Civil War in 1949. As the sole authority and absolute ruler, no one could veto any proposal of Chairman Mao, regardless of flaws or myopic thinking. Mao spent the first decade of CCP rule over China engineering a socialist utopia based on the communist beliefs of people being inherently good and just needed enlightened guidance to work together in harmony. There were multiple plans and efforts during this time but the largest and greatest impacting was the Great Leap Forward.

Mao promised China and the world the CCP could industrialize the nation within a decade and have the same industrial output as Great Britain while drastically improving the quality of life for the peasantry and party cadre alike.[ix] This came in the form of communes designed to destroy all Chinese traditional norms, values, and beliefs so the CCP could act as a hive-like entity to fulfill everyone's needs and wants. The CCP under Mao intended to become mother, father, preacher, teacher, messiah, and God all at once. The Great Leap Forward was to be the supreme test of the CCP being able to change China like a god creating a new world.

This failed so thoroughly, Mao was in danger of being ousted. Instead of producing overly abundant surpluses of wheat and steel, the Great Leap Forward created famine and near economic collapse.[x] The CCP had been governed by blind faith in its ideology regardless of real-world facts. For instance, Mao just assumed all steel was alike and didn't bother to learn the differences of type and manufacture until after the Great Famine had begun. [xi] Chairman Mao, despite being the supreme leader, never allowed himself to admit any wrongdoing and instead blamed it on "rightists" within the CCP sabotaging his efforts. This set a major precedent that influences the CCP's behavior and character to this day. The priority of saving face.

Saving face or miànzi (me-an-ze), was one part of ancient Chinese culture the CCP and Mao failed to eliminate and instead twisted the concept for their own interests. Miànzi is the need to preserve the honor and social standing of whichever group or organization a person has fealty towards. [xii] In the dynastic era, this could mean loyalty to the emperor, governor, clan, or guild. In the CCP, miànzi means subordinates must protect their superior's reputation, even if it means taking the blame so the social cohesion is not disrupted. Chairman Mao's effort to avoid blame was so strong, one could argue this was the indirect cause of the CCP's next major blunder, the Cultural Revolution. Mao feared losing power above all else because his messiah complex couldn't tolerate the idea someone could surpass him. The only way any potential rival could weaken Mao in the late 1950s was for Mao to lose face and bring dishonor to the CCP. Mao ensured he retained his position by going on the offensive and compelling his subordinates to lose their reputations with self-criticism campaigns and forced removals from office.[xiii] This began a long period of purges and upheaval which ultimately protected both the power and reputation of Mao Zedong with the culmination of the Cultural Revolution in 1966.

The Great Leap Forward was the first major event of CCP rule to psychologically scar both the Chinese population and members of the Party but the 1960s would witness the rise of another major shock in the Cultural Revolution. Mao justified his continued rule over the CCP and China in spite of his miscalculations and errors by shifting blame to his subordinates by declaring the CCP was not yet pure of heretical and counterrevolutionary thinking.[xiv] His solution to protect his power while maintaining legitimacy was to put the CCP in a state of perpetual revolution. Mao believed revolutionary fervor was always in the young, especially the idealistic students. The idea being his young followers remained pure from the corrupting influences of political power and willingly embraced the utopian collectivism envisioned by Mao without critical judgement. To achieve a true collective, or even hive-mind, the CCP would have to continue to cleanse itself of corrupting influence. Of course, in practice this meant eliminating all rivals to Chairman Mao. Like the more brutal emperors of the old days, Mao became an absolute monarch and neutered the Party.

This action was done socially and politically through the Red Guard students and youth organizations but was ultimately enforced by the radicalized People's Liberation Army (PLA) commanded by Marshal Lin Biao. Lin Biao loyally built the personality cult of Mao and was rewarded the Vice Chairmanship of the CCP and became the Vice Premier of the People's Republic of China.[xv] Although this event may seem unimportant to outsiders at first, from the perspective of the members of the CCP, it was profound. From 1966 to 1971, China was in fact a military dictatorship that completely supplanted the Chinese Communist Party apparatus from political power.[xvi] Vice Chairman Lin Biao, with help from Mao's wife, used Mao's personality cult to his advantage to make the PLA completely loyal to Mao, not the Party. The PLA protected Mao and key loyalists while letting the Red Guard fanatics seek out and purge all enemies, both real and imagined. Mao had created a military-first policy and let his youth conduct his revolution.[xvii]

Mao's permanent internal revolution continuously increased the chaos and anarchy within the country to the point that many CCP members feared a new civil war would arise. Luckily for the CCP, events turned the situation around in its favor. Lin Biao was killed in 1971 in a plane crash after a suspected coup attempt against Chairman Mao, weakening the grip of the hardline elements of Mao's inner circle. Then shortly thereafter, Mao himself believed order needed to be restored, and Chairman Mao "rehabilitated" several members of the pragmatist wing of the CCP to bring back stability, including Deng Xiaoping.[xviii] Mao would die soon after and the radical elements that grew in power under Mao, otherwise known as the Gang of Four, would be purged in a successful power play by Deng Xiaoping. The Cultural Revolution period left two major impressions on the CCP.

The first impression and lesson learned from these events is how reliant the CCP is on the PLA.[xix] With Mao's endorsement, the PLA quickly took the reins of power away from the Party but the PLA was also critical in returning the reins of power back to the CCP's Central Committee and the executive Politburo. The CCP learned the PLA must be placated but never to such an extent that it can again become a dominating force outside party control. The PLA needed to be given some power and strong social standing but still controlled. Maintaining this balance is a major consideration in all of the CCP's decision-making processes and why in the present CCP, the uniformed members of the PLA occupy only a few positions in the Politburo and no positions in the supreme executive body of the Standing Committee.[xx]' [xxi]

The second impression and lesson of the Cultural Revolution is understanding the danger of ideological puritanism and being ruled by a single figure. Mao's actions more often harmed the CCP than helped but because of miànzi, Mao can never be truly condemned by the CCP. The CCP gained power and legitimacy through Mao's efforts and reputation. If Mao was wrong, then by the concepts of miànzi, the CCP is also wrong. So, the Party had to protect its reputation to preserve its power but at the same time change how it governs to prevent another absolute ruler from taking the CCP's power away again. Deng Xiaoping devised a compromise of a dilution of executive power to be spread more evenly among the Party's internal factions and govern by consent. Dictatorship by committee would maintain party cohesion while also allowing more pragmatism into policy making.[xxii] However, because of miànzi, Deng would not formally institutionalize the leadership structure because it would be admitting Mao and the CCP were flawed.[xxiii] This meant an ambitious CCP member under the right circumstances could attain a Mao-like level of power. Nevertheless, Deng Xiaoping and his faction of pragmatists set the precedent that the Party must maintain its power above any ideological considerations and would set the modern CCP as pragmatic authoritarians.

The modern CCP stems from all of these factors. The CCP exists for the sake of itself and its leaders and is only concerned about the welfare of China when it benefits the CCP. The numerous interactions with foreign influences of European communist concepts, imperial colonialism, Japanese invasion, civil war, and the ideological shock of their adored leader being the cause of China's troubles have created an ideological Frankenstein's monster of a political party. The modern CCP will adopt, incorporate, or dispense with any element of political ideas, policies, or beliefs that aids in keeping power. As will be explained in more detail later, the modern CCP is all at once a political party of communism, fascism, and absolute monarchism. Instead of seeking an ideologically pure utopianist totalitarianism, the CCP now adopts practical syncretic totalitarianism with Chinese characteristics. So, when people ask if China is actually ruled by communists or fascists or is Xi recreating dynastic monarchism, the answer is yes! A pick and mix system of selecting ideas or concepts from the entire range of the authoritarian spectrum based on the criteria of being able to further perpetuate centralized control of China and the CCP's new fledgling imperial ambitions. This modernized CCP still faces challenges and its first challenge came in the form of the 1989 Tiananmen Square Massacre.

Deng Xiaoping and his faction wanted to modernize China without endangering the Party's hold over the country. Deng's pragmatic faction had to balance the needs of the ambitious party apparatchiks with the stability of new prosperity. The desire to make up for the lost decades of being a backwards nation held by absolute rule spurred the Party accelerate reform efforts in the 1980s. This soon created the exact opposite problem for the CCP of potentially losing control. The simultaneous events of student protests for a reformist leader and the collapsing Soviet Empire were too much for the CCP. The combination of previous experiences and historical precedents resonated among the leaders of the CCP which created a strong sense of paranoia and fear of being overthrown. This paranoia came to the point of being neurotically sensitive to criticism and over reactive against any sign of weakness. This can still be seen today with Chairman Xi Jinping's lack of a sense of humor with Winnie the Pooh. Deng and a powerful faction from Shanghai decided to crush the protests to send signals to the world and its population that the CCP will not fall like its Soviet counterpart, the Communist Party of the Soviet Union or CPSU.[xxiv] This massacre became a new lesson to the CCP that further political devolution from the central authority in Beijing was too dangerous and all political reforms halted ever since.[xxv] These experiences and lessons embraced by the CCP created its current mental state and shapes the perceptions of its members.

These influences in the CCP's short but incredibly complex history reflect in the modern Party's organization and function. The CCP is designed first and foremost to survive and perpetuate. The Party's system and organization incorporates all of the life lessons of the 20th Century. This means that no matter what is said in public or what ideological concepts are being proselytized, the Party is pragmatic in practice. Meaning the needs of its members supersede the needs of China and this effort is done through a system of reward and punishment. The Party, unlike political elites in the West, formally integrates its patronage network into the Party itself to protect its members from outside scrutiny, including that from the Chinese citizenry.[xxvi] There is no need to obfuscate mechanisms of bribery and embezzlement from the state as these mechanisms also enforce state loyalty. The patronage system is designed to do two things. The first is to dilute the power of the Politburo and make the executive leadership reliant on the Party as a whole to maintain collective unity. The second is to ensure the Party is protected from its subordinate members. With leadership authority spread amongst the Central Committee and the provincial secretariats, there is sufficient personal incentive among mid-level subordinates and junior leaders to remain loyal to senior executives. This patronage is based on loyalty to one's superiors whose fortunes rely on the good will of the Party. Combined with the CCP's People's Liberation Army, there is little incentive amongst the upper social strata of China to rebel.

The patronage system is further protected by the administrative hierarchy of the Party itself. The organizational structure has many similar characteristics to the old monarchic system of Imperial China.[xxvii] Although the Central Committee in Beijing is the supreme authority of the Party, the day-to-day operations of the state and country at large are managed at the provincial and city level. Like baronetcies of old Europe or the prefectures of the Qing Dynasty, provincial Party leaders are expected to govern and produce economic output by any means to the satisfaction of the national level party leadership. This means provincial secretaries wield considerable power, like the mandarins of the old system with both formal and informal means of income, tribute, and authority.[xxviii] Being a CCP member at the provincial, or in some cases very important cities like Shanghai, functions in the same way a mandarin or imperial noble acted in the Qing Dynasty. Apart from the secular jargon and titles, the CCP's modern aristocracy more closely mirrors the prior dynastic bureaucracies than the CCP would like to admit. This creates a complex system with many overlapping and conflicting interests that are only resolved through informal networking among key Party members.[xxix] These informal networks provide the second foundation that supports the official Party apparatus by reducing friction between competing Party interest groups. These informal networks rely on the old tradition known as guanxi.

Guanxi (goo-one-shee), usually translated as "relationships", describe the dynamics in personalized networks of influence and the concept is central to social advancement in Chinese society. Guanxi are transactional based relationships where favors or gifts are used as a means to buy trust with others. The more earnest a person wants to demonstrate their reliability or value is reflected in what favors or tangible assets they "gift". If guanxi is successful, then the more senior or influential person in the transactional relationship is obligated to protect or help out the gift givers.[xxx] Over time, large personal networks form in which a person is obligated to support this network's members in addition to the person's business and family obligations.[xxxi] Guanxi creates much complexity in the CCP because a member's formal Party rank alone will not advance that member's career. A Party member must also have the right guanxi. This creates strange social dynamics that could potentially result in circumstances where junior officials are more important than their official superiors because of personal connections. This means there is a formal hierarchical chain of command and an informal one simultaneously. Such a situation makes the CCP opaquer to outsiders and threatens confusion within the Party itself.

CCP members must not only accomplish Party objectives but must do so while improving their guanxi network's status and social standing. This often creates strong rivalries along with adding greater complexity to Party and government bureaucratic processes. Not only does a person have to know the laws, regulations, and policies over an issue but he must also know which guanxi networks must be sated to get things done. Figuring out these connections is made even harder because most political guanxi are not obvious. Losing face or miànzi is still a critical factor in any decision. Overt guanxi could expose members to political attack or embarrass a senior official. So many guanxi transactions are hidden from casual observation. Hosting award dinners for meritorious deeds or efforts that disguise personal favors as accomplishments for the Party would be one example. Of course, such social norms make the CCP very vulnerable to economic and political corruption.[xxxii] Or more accurately, provides more covert avenues for the corruption that is inherent in any totalitarian system.

All of these elements make up the composition of the modern CCP. The CCP as an organization is structured to seek power while being paranoid about potentially losing power to not only the possibility of revolution from the Chinese populous but also internal coups from their own members. Guanxi, miànzi, and corruption are all required elements for individuals to be successful members of the Party. Combining all these ingredients has created a political party of power-hungry nihilistic opportunists. The Party is the only entity in China that matters to the CCP and the only individuals that matter are the senior leaders of the CCP. This organization, which attempts to rule China like a god but in practice rules as a demon, is the actual threat to the West from China.

[i] Richard McGregor, *The Party: The Secret World of China's Communist Party,* (NY: HarperCollins Publishers, 2012) 8-15.

[ii] Andrew Erickson, Editors: Thierrry Balzacq, Peter Dombrowski, and Simon Reich, *Comparative Grand Strategy,* (NY: Oxford University Press, 2019) 74-75.

[iii] Fei-Ling Wang, *The China Order: Centralia, World Empire, and the Nature of Chinese Power,* (Albany, NY: State of University of New York Press, 2017) 135, 137-139.

[iv] Young-Tsu, Wong, "Revisionism Reconsidered: Kang Youwei and the Reform Movement of 1898." The Journal of Asian Studies 51, no. 3, 1992, page 513-544. https://www.jstor.org/stable/2057948

[v] Jason Qu, "Self-Strengthening Movement of Late Qing China: an Intermediate Reform Doomed to Failure," Asian Culture and History, Vol. 8, No. 2, 2016, 148-154. https://www.ccsenet.org/journal/index.php/ach/article/view/62542

[vi] Wang, *Centralia,* 161-165.

[vii] Wang, *Centralia,* 176-178.

[viii] Dr. Li Zhisui, *The Private Life of Chairman Mao,* (NY: Random House, 1994) 70.

[ix] Ibid, 332.

[x] Wei Li and Dennis Tao Yang, "The Great Leap Forward: Anatomy of a Central Planning Disaster," Journal of Political Economy, Vol. 113, No. 4, August 2005, 844-848. https://www3.nd.edu/~nmark/ChinaCourse/TheWeeks/Li_Yang_GLF_JPE.pdf

[xi] Dr. Li Zhisui, *The Private Life of Chairman Mao,* (NY: Random House, 1994) 272-287, 290-291.

[xii] David Smith, "Guanxi, Mianzi, and Business: The Impact of Culture on Corporate Governance in China" International Finance Corporation Global Corporate Governance Publication 26, 2012. https://www.ifc.org/wps/wcm/connect/topics_ext_content/ifc_external_corporate_site/ifc+cg/resources/private+sector+opinion/pso+26+cg+and+china

[xiii] Dr. Li Zhisui, *The Private Life of Chairman Mao,* (NY: Random House, 1994) 233-234, 328-329, 387-388.

[xiv] Ibid, 470-472.

[xv] Ibid, 513-516.

[xvi] Yuhua Wang, "The Political Legacy of Violence During China's Cultural Revolution," British Journal of Political Science, 4-5, 16-17. https://doi.org/10.1017/S0007123419000255

[xvii] Jung Chang and Jon Halliday, *The Unknown Mao,* (NY: Anchor Books, 2006) 493-496.

[xviii] Dr. Li Zhisui, *The Private Life of Chairman Mao,* (NY: Random House, 1994) 575-578.

[xix] Richard McGregor, *The Party: The Secret World of China's Communist Party,* (NY: HarperCollins Publishers, 2012) 111-112.

[xx] James Char, "What a Change in China's Officer Rank and Grade System Tells Us About PLA Reform," The Diplomat, March 2021. https://thediplomat.com/2021/03/what-a-change-in-chinas-officer-rank-and-grade-system-tells-us-about-pla-reform/

[xxi] Richard McGregor, *The Party: The Secret World of China's Communist Party,* (NY: HarperCollins Publishers, 2012) 118.

[xxii] Fei-Ling Wang, *The China Order: Centralia, World Empire, and the Nature of Chinese Power,* (Albany, NY: State of University of New York Press, 2017) 182-183.

[xxiii] Joseph Torigian, "Elite Politics and Foreign Policy in China from Mao to Xi," Brookings, January 22, 2019. https://www.brookings.edu/articles/elite-politics-and-foreign-policy-in-china-from-mao-to-xi/

[xxiv] Richard McGregor, *The Party: The Secret World of China's Communist Party*, (NY: HarperCollins Publishers, 2012) 148-149.

[xxv] Melissa Murphy, "Decoding Chinese Politics: Intellectual Debates and Why They Matter," Center for Strategic and International Studies, January 2008, 10-11. https://csis-website-prod.s3.amazonaws.com/s3fs-public/legacy_files/files/media/csis/pubs/080129_murphydecoding.pdf

[xxvi] Richard McGregor, *The Party: The Secret World of China's Communist Party*, (NY: HarperCollins Publishers, 2012) 8-15, 70-72, 74-79.

[xxvii] Ibid, 32-33.

[xxviii] Susan V. Lawrence and Michael F. Martin, "Understanding China's Political System," Congressional Research Service, May 10, 2012, 4-6. https://www.justice.gov/sites/default/files/eoir/legacy/2013/06/13/chinas%20political%20system.pdf

[xxix] Global Leader Monitor, "China: National Supervision Commission Granted Power to Maker Supervision Regulations," Library of Congress, January 10, 2020. https://www.loc.gov/item/global-legal-monitor/2020-01-10/china-national-supervision-commission-granted-power-to-make-supervision-regulations/

[xxx] Xiao-Ping Chen and Chao C. Chen, "On the Intricacies of the Chinese *Guanxi*: A Process Model of *Guanxi* Development," Asia Pacific Journal of Management, v. 21, 2004, 307-309. https://citeseerx.ist.psu.edu/viewdoc/download?doi=10.1.1.453.8461&rep=rep1&type=pdf

[xxxi] Kenneth G. Lieberthal and David M. Lampton, *Bureaucracy, Politics, and Decision Making in Post-Mao China*, (Berkeley: University of California Press, 1992), 56-57.

[xxxii] Richard McGregor, *The Party: The Secret World of China's Communist Party*, (NY: HarperCollins Publishers, 2012) 137-147.

Chapter 3: Why Would China Want to Instigate Civil War in the West?

Understanding who the CCP and its members are shows this organization is composed of people willing to carry out highly risky ventures to retain power. An action such as instigating a civil conflict in a Western state is plausible for the CCP's members if they feel existentially threatened. Yet this is insufficient to explain why China is a plausible instigator. Understanding why the CCP would carry out such a risky endeavor of interfering in Western states is just as important a question to answer as who the actual threat is. Essentially, the simple reason is the CCP is an organization designed to accumulate and maintain political power. Nothing else fundamentally matters. Human nature may encourage CCP members to rationalize their avarice and vanity by cloaking their ambitions in idealism or national interests but none have demonstrated a willingness to voluntarily reduce the CCP's power for the betterment of China. Power is the spur driving the CCP's actions and plans. Yet this simple motive is only a partial answer. Risking the CCP's power by carrying out subterfuge against the West only makes sense when the CCP is in danger of losing the power it currently holds. The danger for the CCP is determined by the global strategic realities outside its control and the CCP's own actions that create negative consequences. This section will explain the strategic obstacles hindering the CCP's power ambitions and why this is directly tied with the CCP's actions against the West. So, why would causing rebellion in the West by sowing internal division within these nations' societies protect CCP power?

The previous chapter of the book showed the contemporary CCP's need to adopt many conflicting characteristics in order to survive its tribulations of the 20th Century. The CCP's 21st Century ideology is not easily categorized into one political ideology. It is a hodgepodge of authoritarian beliefs and methods to balance the ideological fanaticism of puritanical Maoism with the moderating force of Deng Xiaoping's pragmatism. The chaotic failures during the CCP's first 30 years of its Maoist reign contrast sharply with its follow-on 30 years of successes from Deng Xiaoping pragmatism. This gave the Party a stark contrast of methodology to evaluate what works best for CCP survival. This new modern system of mixing idealism and pragmatism has the side effect of creating contradictions and organizational weaknesses the CCP must continuously monitor and control but cannot actually fix or correct. Having a system that cannot inherently correct itself endangers the CCP more and more as time progresses because the faults will accumulate to the point the CCP cannot keep the system functioning. Such an eventuality would make the CCP desperate enough to carry out high risk ventures in any existential crisis.

The Hybrid Ideological System:

So why can't these systemic contradictions be permanently corrected? The reason is the contradictory policies are actually mutually reinforcing each other in the short-term, making the CCP appear strong and healthy but at the same time, these same contradictions degrade the system's integrity over a period of time measured in generations. To understand why this occurs, each major element of the CCP's mixed ideology will be evaluated. Once each component is understood and how each connects to the others, then the strengths and weaknesses of the CCP's belief system become apparent. In the previous section, this mixed ideology was simplified by breaking it down by the various authoritarian political systems from which the CCP derives its current system. The mixed ideology is a Frankenstein's Monster of syncretic authoritarian and totalitarian ideas. This ideological monster incorporates elements of communism, fascism, and absolute monarchism to create the ultimate hybrid system of centralized control.

The first element of the ideological hybrid of the modern CCP is in its origins and founding beliefs in communism. Socialist utopian ideologies differ from the previous historically pragmatic dictatorial monarchies by promising the people "heaven on earth." Communism swept through the world of the 20th Century by the promise of endless prosperity brought about by enlightened leaders who would bring fairness, equity, and collective justice to the world.[i] In other words, communism ironically proselytized it could make the spiritual promises of Christianity in the afterlife come true in a tangible materialist way on Earth. A secular religion that made the Party a replacement for God and the state its loving disciple. These promises helped build legitimacy with many peasants and rural communities before the end of the Chinese Civil War and victory over their rivals, the Kuomintang (KMT), in 1949 established the CCP's authority over the whole mainland.

As soon as the Party secured its hold over China, the regime immediately began to implement its materialist promises to drastically improve the quality of life while eliminating all of the old social structures the CCP claimed was responsible for all of China's misery.[ii] These actions and declarations helped the Party monopolize all instruments of political power while establishing a tangible form of political legitimacy with the majority of the population. Instead of getting the people's consent to achieve legitimacy like in the West, the communist system offered a transactional social contract promising to carryout social justice and economic advancement in exchange for total political submission by the Chinese population.[iii] This gave the CCP an immediate advantage but created a perpetual weakness. The CCP's entire legitimacy is based on promising a materialist utopia being achieved by collective central control of the CCP. Failing this promise eliminates all legitimacy of the CCP in China.

What is worse for the CCP is the cultural force of miànzi prevents the CCP from changing this promise. In the Soviet Empire, the Communist Party of the Soviet Union was able to maintain legitimacy even after criticizing Stalin amongst the apparatchiks and quietly removing his policies impacting the Soviet population. China's CCP cannot do this. Miànzi links the founder of the People's Republic of China, Chairman Mao, and the CCP's reputation which stems from Mao himself. If Mao was illegitimate then the Party loses face and legitimacy as well. Even though the CCP doesn't actually follow Mao's mantra in practice anymore, Mao's political teachings still keep social consistency. Any viable philosophical political alternative to the CCP would likely be Western-centric in nature which inherently contradicts the dogmas of Mao that legitimize one-party totalitarian rule. Retaining the teachings of Mao's philosophy keeps out Western concepts of legitimate rule, even as the CCP adopts Western management ideas to better govern.[iv] No matter how contradictory communist and Maoist teachings are to the modern CCP's behavior, this philosophy maintains the Party's foundation for its secular version of the Mandate of Heaven.

This is why China cannot become like another Singapore which had an autocratic leader, Lee Kuan Yew, implement a free market means of attaining prosperity while holding onto political power. Contradicting the CCP's mantra of being a materialist stand-in for God where the Party is the source of all good decisions and success could be politically fatal in a culture of miànzi. Free markets mean people without the Party, can be successful and create new centers of power in China. This is why China may have reformed economically but never to the point where anything can be independent of the Party's decisions. The CCP must and will continue to wield the power of veto over all major life decisions in China. The collectivist ideal of communism remains the bastion of legitimacy even if the Party has abandoned many of its economic prescriptions.[v]

Communism is the binding agent that holds both the Party and the population together. It is the driver of cultural cohesion but not for the economy. Ironically, the centralized planning of all economic actions and endeavors being the bedrock of communist ideology was the main element removed from contemporary Chinese communism. The pragmatic reforms of the 1980s and 1990s introduced market elements into the overly centralized and inefficient communist economy but not in the way many shallowly perceive. In the popular perception's narrative, China adopted a more Western-style market-centric economy with reforms that accelerated China's wealth and economic growth. This is a half-truth. The reality is some market elements are allowed to operate in China but all concerns, either private or public, are still to be bound to the interests of the state and political policy. This is the 2nd element of the CCP's hybrid ideology and it drives the Party's economic policies to being more akin to fascism than capitalism.

The popular perception by the West of the mixed economic model of modern China is often credited exclusively to Deng Xiaoping. The idea being the enlightened despot wanted to mimic the Western bloc's 1980s-style capitalism and stopped the state interfering in economic decisions is still the common version of events most people are told.[vi] However, the reality is Deng Xiaoping never had any intention of ceding control from the central authority of the Party nor did he implement some of the most important economic reforms. This misconception must be addressed to fully understand the CCP's strategies and fears towards the West.

Far more credit for China's current economic system belongs to two masterminds of the CCP in the 1990s: Chen Yuan, then Vice Governor of the People's Bank of China, and Zhu Rongji, then Vice Premier of China.[vii] In the early 1990s, after the shock and backlash from the Tiananmen Square Massacre subsided, the CCP debated what would be the most effective strategy to bring in crucial foreign investment while preventing the creation of an independent capitalist class. The Party finally settled the debate with Chen Yuan's proposal of having the Party allow private businesses to exist and allow market mechanisms to determine most of these companies' decisions but the Party would have veto over who could run any company.[viii] This authority would apply to both state-owned and private business concerns. By determining the personnel at the top of every business, the CCP would be able to still rule the economy without having to directly manage it. In theory, the mixed socialist-market economy would grow wealth for China while maintaining a one-party authoritarian state.

Chen Yuan and Zhu Rongji created a system which doesn't neatly fit into a singular category. "Chinese socialist-market economics" is so termed because Yuan created a shape shifting economy that bends to the needs of the CCP. The system is socialist because the needs of the state and CCP override all other considerations. If the CCP requires something, the private sector's business leaders are compelled to set aside the priority of profit to help the Party. When the CCP doesn't have a particular goal for a company or industrial sector, it allows the companies to run everything for profit. The CCP turns the market on and off like a switch, hence sometimes market, sometimes centrally planned economy.[ix] So, even though Chinese businesses may appear to the casual observer to be vibrant independent enterprises, the reality is business is subordinate to politics. China is a model corporatist state and the Chinese economic "miracle" was successfully tricking foreigners into financially sustaining this system, camouflaged in free market bells and whistles, with foreign direct investment and one-way trade agreements.[x]

Corporatism, in drastically simplified form, is the economic system of the "right-wing" portion of the socialist political spectrum. Rather than fully socializing the political-economic system, Chinese corporatism is having the government support politically loyal businesses and industries without having to manage them directly. Corporatism is socialism without micromanaging daily business decisions. Instead, the system focuses on being able to hire and fire members of corporate boards and CEOs to retain loyalty and control. A glaring example of the CCP exercising its corporatist power is the fate of Jack Ma, former CEO of Alibaba. Alibaba is, at least on paper, a private enterprise that was built in part by Jack Ma's entrepreneurial efforts and good business sense. In 2020, Jack Ma was compelled to cede control of his own company by CCP directive. Jack Ma was no longer trusted by the CCP at that time and that mattered more than Ma's ability to generate profits.[xi]

This system also depends on hiding the CCP's decision-making process from outside scrutiny and eliminating any transparency that could potentially expose the Party's internal weaknesses to outsiders. Besides, open CCP interference in business decisions would frighten foreign investors knowing they couldn't rely on any business-centric dealings being honored when the Party can override them behind the scenes. The façade of corporate boards being separate from CCP organizations is the vital lynchpin to the current system's functionality and cannot be changed without diminishing CCP power. Overt control of the businesses and industries bring legal and diplomatic difficulties that would discourage investors. This a major reason why the CCP does everything it can to hide its influence in economic affairs with seemingly no formal Party participation on corporate boards. Instead, the CCP uses a separate political committee, not on any official organization chart in any Chinese private business, to make political decisions the corporate board must obey. A specific example of the CCP hiding its influence but getting caught happened in December 2021. The United States government and others have long accused the Chinese telecommunications giant, Huawei, of complicitly aiding the CCP in its surveillance and espionage efforts. Huawei has always denied being politically influenced because such activities would alienate clients and investors. After years of denials, a major data leak of internal files revealing Huawei's efforts to assist the CCP and the PLA in using its communication backbone to support surveillance activities was released to the public.[xii] Huawei is a private company but the documents demonstrate the CCP retains the power of veto and control over the telecom. Huawei may not be state-owned but its leaders are.

Just as damning is the actual root origins of the modern Chinese economic system. The CCP is not known for its originality but for stealing other's ideas and improving upon them. Although China's thefts of technology are the most famous example, its current corporatism is also a Chinese modified idea from another country. In this case, Nazi Germany. The modern world seems incapable of avoiding Godwin's Law, even in book form, but the reality is Nazi Germany has had a disproportionate influence on the world and not just in the West. Although the modern leadership doesn't realize it, the People's Republic of China uses an economic system that closely parallels the Nazi Pre-World War II economic system. Seeing the past often reveals truths in the present, namely the CCP co-opted the Nazis' means of economic control.

In both Nazi Germany and People's Republic of China, key economic positions of businesses and regulatory agencies were members of the political party or close confidents of senior party officials. Although notionally independent, the "will" of the party overrides any other legal or financial consideration.[xiii], [xiv] Neither the CCP nor the Nazis allowed private entrepreneurs to make plans or actions independent of the political parties' need for social economic development. CCP provincial parties will mandate businesses and enterprises to carry out investments and projects to boost GDP numbers even if these actions are fiscally unsound. The need to please the central leadership and meet the Party goal of continuous GDP growth drove many bad fiscal decisions within China's provincial leadership.[xv] Likewise, in the desire for ersatz materials in preparation for war, the Nazi Party mandated private companies invest and develop high risk technologies to manufacture domestic substitutions for critical supplies Germany had to import. The political demand forced German industry to reduce its dependence on imports of vital materials even before the ersatz substitutes were ready. This created shortages and price hikes just before the invasion of Poland. The Nazi officials, in their effort to please their leadership, sacrificed economic well-being that weakened the very regime they were trying to sustain in the long run.[xvi]

The only way for private business interests to survive in either system is building relationships between business leaders and key party officials. In China, this is guanxi, but a parallel system was just as common in Nazi Germany. However, no guanxi or personal networking in Germany can override the needs of the ruling party, which is determined by the national leadership, be it Fuhrer or Chairman of the CCP. The example of Jack Ma in China where a connected entrepreneur is sacrificed for Party interests is repeated with Evergrande's CEO Hui Ka Yan. In 2021, when property developer Evergrande Group became a risk to the Chinese housing market, the CCP compelled Hui to sell off his own personal wealth to cover some of Evergrande's liabilities.[xvii] The same occurred in Nazi Germany. Before the war in 1939, industrialist Krupp von Bohlen und Halbach was a very powerful and influentially connected individual within the Nazi economic structure. However, Krupp's attempts to use his influence to stop Nazi Party directives to have his conglomerate invest large sums of money into developing synthetic rubber for the military buildup failed. This project was not only cost prohibitive but also beyond the technical means of Krupp's firms. The Nazi Party required him to invest in the development anyway and Krupp was forced to comply at considerable financial loss because obeying the ruling party was the only means of survival.[xviii]

These parallel methods of the Nazi and CCP controlling business leaders also extend into the financial sector. In the summer of 2015, the Chinese stock market experienced a major shock when it crashed far more quickly than expected. Falling nearly 9% in a single day, the CCP feared a fiscal calamity that could have popped several market bubbles within China, triggering a potential recession. Instead of market forces correcting the fiscal imbalances, the CCP commanded the national government to directly intervene and implement "Announcement 18" to severely punish any major shareholder or manager if they attempted sell shares.[xix] These actions stopped the fiscal hemorrhaging but revealed the Chinese stock exchange was not governed by any true market but was and is a political mechanism to raise capital for CCP-favored interests. In 1936, the Nazis blocked foreigners from selling stocks and only allowed the purchase of government bonds because the Nazi Party had just expropriated Jewish businesses and investments without compensation. Fearing a run on the stock market, the Nazi-controlled Foreign Exchange Board implemented state mechanisms designed to prevent any economic consequences for destroying the Jewish business community.[xx]

The Nazi economic parallels with modern China's economic mechanisms are almost mirrored. The thin veneer of market capitalism is used to allay foreign fears which has successfully camouflaged China's fascist model for nearly 40 years. The one true Chinese innovation of fascist economics was inverting the strategic goals for the economic system. Nazi Germany's corporatist economy was built for a war of conquest in Europe but the CCP designed its corporatist economy to create a peacetime global mercantilist trade empire. Given the economic growth of China and its rapid expansion of global influence, the CCP must be given credit for making a superior authoritarian economic system over the Germans. This reality does highlight an interesting philosophical quandary in some quarters of the West. China's Western supporters among certain leftist elements and in some circles of self-proclaimed libertarians, often praise China's means of economic success.[xxi] One must appreciate the irony that these groups view Hitler as one of the worst persons in history yet are ignorantly praising a system the tyrant helped pioneer.

The final element of the CCP's hybrid system is incorporating features of absolute monarchism. As of 2024, the CCP's has existed for over 103 years and for 53 of those years it has been under the control of a singular leader. Mao Zedong was the central figure and supreme authority from 1935 – 1976, and Xi Jinping from 2012 – present day. Each of their reigns have facets of governance mimicking the emperors of previous dynasties. Both encourage near religious reverence to the supreme leader of China by adopting symbols, social and political rules requiring unquestioning loyalty. Despite the CCP stating it brought modernism into China, the CCP continues many imperial policies and traditions.

The Confucian concept of the Mandate of Heaven established legitimacy for the ruling elite. It states, "a just ruler embodies true order and the heavens bestow the emperor the divine right to rule". If an emperor was overthrown, then this act was by divine will because the ruler had become unjust and lost heaven's blessing.[xxii] Instead of eliminating the ancient concept, Mao simply replaced the ancient philosophy with his own, the Mandate of the People. The mandate stated Mao and the CCP would above all else serve the people with the scientific precision of Marxist socialism. By replacing Confucius with Marx and heaven with the state, Mao secularized a cult of personality and deference to his unquestionable rule in the name of serving all.[xxiii]

The notion of an absolute ruler from which all political legitimacy of the state is derived challenges the notions of collective actions and collective leadership. Yet, Mao governed like an emperor with a strong imperial army, in this case the PLA, to enforce his will on the bureaucracy and the populace. Mao's guidance to both the CCP and the public was to believe in his messianic vision and only Chairman Mao could bring China to greatness, negating the CCP itself.[xxiv] An absolute monarch with a cult of personality backed by loyal marshals of the military is more akin to the Qing Dynasty than to Marxist visions of a proletarian dictatorship. Although contradictory to Marxism, the concept of the strong ruler given divine right, either by the people or by heaven, to rule China became a cornerstone for the modern CCP. Although Deng eliminated such a possibility for the remainder of the 20th Century after Mao's death, the CCP's institutional structure remained unchanged. The foundations for the making of a new supreme leader were never abolished, making the rise of an ambitious leader after Deng's death almost inevitable. China discovered this ambition in Xi Jinping. Xi Jinping became the first CCP leader since Mao to try to become a new "emperor."

No one should believe Xi Jinping's policies and actions help strengthen collective party leadership.[xxv] Xi Jinping is using the tradition of miànzi to justify Mao's rule in order to strengthen Xi's own position. Party propaganda relies on the continued deification of Chairman Mao because he made himself the principal source of political legitimacy for the CCP's rule during the first decades of the People's Republic of China. Xi makes concerted efforts to tie his policies and ideas to Mao's in order to greatly enhance his own importance in the eyes of the Party and the general public. To this end, President Xi is using old slogans, symbols, and policies from the Maoist era in an attempt to portray the time of an absolute ruler as a golden age of moral and social strength.[xxvi], [xxvii] These symbols and teachings are being updated with technology to better reach 21st Century Chinese audiences, such as the "Chain on Aspirations" App for CCP members to download on their phone. Mao used loyalty pledges, self-criticism sessions, and requiring Party members to work with the people doing hard labor as a psychological means of shaping CCP member's loyalty.[xxviii] The "Chain on Aspirations" App records and tracks all loyalty pledges while another called the Xuexi Qiangguo or "Study to Make China Strong" App is Xi's modern version of Mao's Little Red Book.[xxix] Indoctrination of baseline Party doctrine combined with the specific teachings of the current Chairman are modernized versions of the political tools used to strengthen the imperial dynasties.

In practical matters, Chairman Xi consolidated several offices and re-organized multiple ministries that took away many fiscal powers of the provincial party leaders. Xi further centralized his authority over the military by creating new loyalty enforcement mechanisms in the guise of anticorruption such as the Politics and Law Commission to oversee all legal and judicial issues for Xi's reorganized Central Military Commission. These new enforcement mechanisms for the Party don't work to make the bureaucracy more functional but to ensure loyalty to Xi Jinping.[xxx] The threat of investigating corruption is effectively used as a cudgel against any senior official to ensure loyalty is retained because corruption is rampant. Instead of eliminating corruption, Xi Jinping finds it a useful incentive to keep senior party and military leaders loyal, even at the cost of military or security effectiveness. Changing the chain of accountability where the leaders of all major institutions of political power answer to one supreme leader is an action worthy of an emperor.

The three guiding elements of modern CCP governance have benefited the Party immensely for the last 30 years as it hid the Party's continuous avarice for power as simply economic reform but the system's weaknesses have never gone away. The Party never truly changed, just its methods. There is no real name for this type of hybrid system of dictatorship. The one commonality of this Frankenstein monster amalgamation is that each element incorporates some aspect of centralized control. The best catch-all to describe this ideological jumble is "centralized-absolutism". Central absolutism doesn't consider utopia for the masses or wealth for the nation, the only relevant objective is the power of the CCP and its leaders over every facet of society to remain unchallenged and absolute. Centrally planned economics can be ignored if the central authority can benefit from the market and the market can be halted when the central authority needs to direct its resources to cut-off any potential threat. Central absolutism is the amalgamation of every form of totalitarianism devised by mankind culminating in having an all-of-society conforming system acting like a hive to serve the needs of the central authority, the CCP leadership.

These three elements mutually reinforce each other's functions to maintain a strong grip on political power for the Party. Each element of the hybrid ideological system acts as a separate pillar of totalitarian control: communism supports the ideas, fascism supports the finance, and absolute monarchism supports the leader. All of these require the system to have carte blanche on all decisions and actions within China. Yet, there are weaknesses. The pillars are each formulated from different types of authoritarian government creating categorical and ideological inconsistencies that make identifying the flaws of the system difficult and imprecise. Accusing the modern CCP of being exclusively communist will just have China refer to its private endeavors and when its domestic radical leftists say China is too capitalistic, the Party can point to its legal and organizational controls. This obfuscation by mixing ideas and processes creates a veneer of benign technocracy over the system which fools the casual observer into believing the CCP uses Western-style markets and legal processes outside of communist dogma. Since each elemental pillar requires the other two to exist, reforming or scaling back one or more of these governing elements is impossible without endangering the CCP. The CCP cannot liberalize any part of a system that requires central control to function without fatally crippling the whole system. Meaning any problems arising from within the system will likely be missed or ignored but are unlikely to weaken it for a long period of time.

Measuring Strength and Weakness of the System:

This system provides many obvious advantages to the CCP which has consistently been demonstrated for the past 30 years. The system provides sufficient material goods and well-being to keep the general population docile while the Party's authority gradually expands in parallel with China's economic growth. However, despite the appearance to the contrary, the system's design still has many inherent vulnerabilities. The fatal flaw is that it cannot fix itself. When a weakness is found, the CCP usually only carries out a superficial quick fix to delay rather than eliminate the problem because a real fix means the CCP must change and cede some power; an unacceptable option even in the direst circumstances. So, what exactly are the strengths and weaknesses of the system the three elements have built for the CCP?

Central absolutism provides the CCP the same advantages as enjoyed by previous historical authoritarian regimes. Unlike Western-democratic republics, the CCP does not have to consider the concerns of the various power bases within society. Nor does the Party have to balance conflicting interests between social elements or seek compromise among differing political views. Being the only authority simplifies planning and reduces the number of steps to formulate and carry out policy. There are no checks to the Party's power so actions are executed quickly without having to consider the concerns or consequences for the Party's subjugated citizenry. Central absolutism gives dictatorial China the advantage for short-term or immediate actions over the Western government systems and making China appear efficient, incisive, and superior compared to the actions of outsiders. Unlike pure monarchism, communism, or fascism, the CCP's central absolutism provides far greater bureaucratic flexibility by being ideologically amorphous since they are not bound by the rigid dogmatic processes that hindered the Qing, Nazis, and the Soviet Union. The greatest advantage of the modern CCP is its political maneuverability in near real time.

Central absolutism's weaknesses, on the other hand, are not as easily apparent. Trying to evaluate the health or strength of China or the CCP is hindered by active deception. Not only aimed at the public but also within the Party itself. Individual members and departments compete with each other which means hiding their own mistakes while unattributably exposing their rivals'. The reality of the three elements of the modern ideology is it hides everything, even from itself. The Central Committee of the CCP is unlikely to have an accurate picture of its own performance or health. In times of prosperity, inaccuracies are likely to be less impactful because prosperity compensates for any individual mistake. In times of chaos, the inaccuracies are likely to grow more acute as individuals fear being sacrificed in the name of miànzi and will deceive and coverup more problems.

This mess of ideological contradictions, lies, and Party power struggles means measuring the scale of China's strengths vs weaknesses will vary depending on what element of China's DIME is being evaluated, the source of the information, and how the metrics for that information is measured. Meaning both sides of the China debate on whether China is a true global power or a paper dragon can each provide sufficient information to reasonably justify their side of the argument. Demonstrating the problem of accurately assessing the true ability of the CCP and China is by comparing two competing analyses to see how each comes to their differing conclusions on China's power and threat level to the West. Two authors, retired Brigadier General (BG) Robert Spalding and Dr. Michael Beckley, both wrote thorough works referencing China and its potential dangers to the West. Each is authoritative and each comes to different conclusions analyzing different criteria. Dr. Beckley's *Unrivaled: Why America will Remain the World's Sole Superpower* addresses China more indirectly but concludes China cannot ultimately compete with the United States. BG Spalding's *Stealth War* concludes the opposite, stating China is destroying the West in order to become the new unipolar hegemon by the mid-21st Century. Both of these conclusions are contradictory yet both are correct and the reason two contradictory conclusions can mutually exist is that the authors evaluated two different components of the CCP system. BG Spalding evaluated the CCP's power of direct action while Dr. Beckley studied the power of America's national durability and its potential competitor countries. In other words, BG Spalding looked at China's short-term strengths and Dr. Beckley looked at China's long-term strengths. Time is the key. Central absolutism's ability to carry out plans and activities intended to last decades or more differs greatly from central absolutism's ability to carry out actions requiring immediate or near-term results.

Short-term Gains:

The core strength of the central-absolutist system is it helps the Party and government of China to act immediately on a singular issue to achieve results in a relatively short amount of time. Individual considerations can be ignored or overridden, including political rivalries, to accomplish tasks. Whatever problem is currently worrying the Party, the system can devote all resources and social elements to its solution. Contrasting this ability with the West, the democratic republics must balance legal, ethical, and cultural concerns into all decisions. Western systems are designed to be slow to not only limit state power but also make the process reversible if a national decision becomes unpalatable to the voting public. Central absolutism gives the CCP the flexibility of using any authoritarian means, to act quickly. This gives the world the perception that China wins because it is faster at executing short-term actions. In terms of time for a nation's grand strategy, any time less than a decade is short-term. China amazes the world with its ability to react with almost violent haste to any perceived crisis. Central absolutism can link every element of the DIME together into a common mission that no Western government can match. Having no considerations for other interests or people's liberties combined with the legal means to execute actions without review or challenge means the Chinese system is very efficient at executing immediate actions.

BG Spalding's analysis and warning about China's activities against the United States all reference Chinese actions to carry out immediate goals. In the cases cited by BG Spalding, these malicious actions are establishing processes and organizations to extract wealth, knowledge, technology, and political influence from the United States in the here and now. These actions compliment and support China's long-term strategic objectives but all of BG Spalding's examples of nefarious CCP activities are each singular immediate steps on the CCP's journey to reach China's apex objective of becoming the global hegemon. None of the actions appear to be systemically executed as part of one cohesive grand plan but what is needed for the Party at the moment an action is tasked to their personnel.

For instance, BG Spalding highlights China's use of slave labor to keep costs of manufactured products lower to undercut international business rivals.[xxxi] The need to use slave labor meant the CCP quickly devised a series of legal and policy rules to allow both state-owned and private enterprises to take advantage of illegal internal migrants and prisoners to work for little cost. The CCP only had to consider how the Party could benefit from the decision. The decision required provincial parties to coordinate with law enforcement, companies, and relevant ministries to ensure all facets of society executed their individual tasks to give the CCP the means to make China the sweatshop of the world.

More examples BG Spalding provides include commodities and raw material monopolies such as rare earth mineral mining.[xxxii] China currently holds a monopoly on extracting rare earth minerals vital to the function of advanced electronics and other technologies. Despite the name, rare earths are abundant in the planet's crust but require considerable effort to extract without ecological damage. China adopted policies to make the mining operations as cheap as possible to undercut any overseas rival extraction operations. CCP's success in creating a monopoly didn't come from exceptional business acumen but using political power to suppress social inhibitors that restrain Western companies. In this case, the CCP eliminated all environmental considerations or concerns and used the trade friendly systems of the West to undercut foreign competitors.[xxxiii]

Both of these examples are a small sampling of China's anti-American activities BG Spalding provides. However, all of the examples are derived from the CCP addressing an individual need that could be quickly acted on by the Chinese state. This advantage applies to everything the CCP does, not just against its foreign rivals. The CCP also uses its advantages in domestic programs to strengthen the Party within China itself. The Three-Gorges Dam was not an economically viable project but it was a demonstration of national might and CCP pride. Fulfilling the Party's pride was the central objective with economic considerations as an afterthought. The central-absolutist system reacted very fast at initiating and completing the endeavor regardless of diverging opinions on the dam's viability.[xxxiv]

The CCP's advantage of quick action is also observed in its pursuit of hypersonic weaponry. Even though the United States was the lead in hypersonic-related aeronautics for decades, the CCP's determination meant large numbers of resources and personnel were dedicated to steal Western knowledge to short-cut China's time to catch up to the United States.[xxxv] Then China brute forced its way into developing prototypes with far more testing with less consideration for things like defense industrial base competition, legal considerations, or worrying about budgeting due to other political priorities of a divided legislature like the US Congress.[xxxvi] Simplifying the goals with few, if any, checks or balances allowed China to exceed in this one specific field of military technology, even at the cost of other programs, military or otherwise, because the Party wanted to upstage the United States and Russia.[xxxvii]

In each instance, the CCP is able to command any and all necessary contributors, regardless of if they are directly state owned or not, across Chinese society to prioritize the needs of the Party. This concept is not fully appreciated in the West where there are clear delineations between private and public roles. The US Congress cannot compel private individuals or businesses to immediately support the police, military, or other bureaucracies without some legal process yet in China all persons and groups must serve the interests of the state and the Party on demand.[xxxviii] At first glance, the advantage of commanding the whole of society appears superior to Western systems because many people only think in the moment, not considering consequences that are not immediate. China's success at imposing its will when it deems the action necessary has created a small but influential envious fanbase within the West itself. These individuals may downplay elements of China's authoritarianism and pretend the West could adopt some facets, not willing to acknowledge the negative aspects of China's absolute authority are inseparable from the positive. [xxxix] In fact, analysis indicates the West still utilizes the overall superior system for wealth creation, innovation, and improving quality of life for individuals.

Long-term Costs:

China's central absolutism easily deceives the casual observer and those who want to believe in the superiority of technocratic rule. China's supporters and apologists cite many actions, statistics, and timelines showing China's rise and seemingly brilliant ability to achieve all announced goals in remarkable time. So, what is China's systemic weakness? For this analysis, Dr. Beckley's *Unrivaled* provides some clues.

Dr. Beckley's thesis is America's fundamental strengths have not changed and argues the key indicators of true national power still favor the United States for the foreseeable future.[xl] Dr. Beckley contends China's growing power is misperceived because China's advocates only take gross measures of China's DIME without deducting the resource costs to sustaining that DIME. For instance, China's economic rise is usually measured in just GDP but Dr. Beckley contends, 'creating an index that gives equal weight to a nation's gross output and its output per person,' provides a greater understanding of a nation's net resources than GDP alone.[xli] For all the boasting China does about its economic growth, theU.S.is more economically and militarily efficient than China.[xlii] Dr. Beckley's argument is well supported by his evidence but creates a divergent theory from BG Spalding. So where is the disconnect between Dr. Beckley's thesis of China remaining weaker than the US and not a long-term threat and BG Spalding's of China being a true existential threat? The disconnect is the separation of China's long-term processes and development from the short-term actions that benefit China in the immediate period of time.

Central absolutism focuses on the immediate problems. For all the claims to the contrary, China does not have an inherently superior means of executing long-term plans or actions than the West. The complexity of the world means no polity or ideology can properly account for all the variables needed to execute a multi-generational plan without some miscalculation. This is seen in the historical example of Japan in the late 20th Century. In the 1970s to the 1980s, Japan appeared to be the juggernaut to usurp the United States as the dominant economic power of the world. The world was envious at the work ethic, communal culture of cooperation, deference to efficient hierarchy, and the perceptions of exceptional technocratic planning and foresight.[xliii] Japan was becoming the leader in many technology sectors, Japan was acquiring large swaths of American real estate, and Japanese keiretsus (corporate conglomerates) worked seamlessly with the Japanese government in devising a long-term economic grand strategy that projected out decades of planning ahead. Then the economic bubble of Japan burst and the fictional persona of the Japanese juggernaut ended. Like central absolutism, the Japanese economic system had no means of acknowledging or addressing internal problems nor could Japan always calculate what was truly needed to meet long-term goals.

Japan could anticipate immediate challenges but what about the follow-on challenges? Japan had its starting point A (short-term challenges) and identified its long-term goal at point C (long-term objectives), but couldn't truly plan for how to get to point C. The mid-term challenges of point B were always too nebulous to foresee clearly and then trying to connect the immediate policy actions of A did not always yield advantageous consequences for the challenges at point B meaning Japan's planners could not always control the implementation of their strategy. Getting from point A to B to finally C cannot be directed along a planned line without the flexibility to deviate from the plan. This means empowering more elements beyond the state within the society that can react more quickly to changing circumstances. Or alternatively, have an effective means to cheat to avoid costs of miscalculation. If Japan couldn't carry out a methodical long-term economic grand plan, why is China more successful? As Dr. Beckley and others point out, China's success is more superficial than what is popularly perceived and its central absolutism is causing more problems than solutions. As the CCP plans and acts in decided haste, the system accumulates more problems as these actions evolve in the mid-to-long term consequences in their implementation.

For all of its power, the CCP is still built on rotted foundations. Central absolutism does not have a self-correcting mechanism to eliminate internal problems or change course for better outcomes. The lack of transparency in a system designed for a Party whose members seek power above all, including from each other, means the CCP's actions are carried out with a tunneled vision with little consideration of secondary and tertiary consequences of those actions. Furthermore, the system functions in a culture of miànzi and guanxi which only further obfuscates the true consequences of Party actions. Social structures are skewered to revolve around the Party's system which not only enables widespread corruption but also makes such activities socially acceptable. In non-totalitarian countries, society is structured around customs, traditions, and rites that act as social inhibitors for the betterment of keeping cohesion and order in society. In China, traditional culture is skewered to create cultural inhibitors on the general public to discourage defiance of the Party. With roles reversed there is neither customary nor statutory protection from the CCP. The CCP is controlled by humans with all their sins, fallacies, and avarice. With nothing to check the Party, the CCP's corruption and abuse grows exponentially and contributes to the many mistakes created by the CCP's decisions made in the moment.

This corruption and inefficiency of bad governance are cumulative effects of bad decisions and the full force of impact will not be realized for years and possibly decades but will slowly kill China's body politic. Party members and leaders focus on their own individual portions of power and often only think of how they can personally advance regardless of negative effects these actions may have on the public or country at large. This nihilistic pursuit of self-indulgent advancement among members can be observed everywhere within modern China. Enough time has passed for observers to evaluate China's plans and actions of the 1990s and to identify the secondary and follow-on consequences of decisions made in the previous two decades, showing the follies of the modern CCP.

China's Hidden Technocratic Follies:

The most glaring example of Chinese actions reconsidered as short-sighted later is Deng Xiaoping's One-Child Policy. The CCP feared the population exceeded the nation's ability to sustain itself and immediately acted to make China's population smaller in the hope a smaller population would keep China more stable. In the 1970s, when China was as poor as certain parts of Africa, the CCP's fears appeared justified and easy to rationalize, so little debate or study was carried out before this major decision was executed. Now, decades later in contrast to the CCP's long-term planning in the late 1970s, China is desperate to reverse the policy. The One-Child Policy worked very well as the dictatorship directed all elements of society into compliance with ruthless zeal. China now has one of the lowest fertility rates in the entire world at 1.15 children per person as of 2021.[xliv] Again, miànzi prevented the CCP from completely reversing the One-Child Policy all at once because that would be admitting to a mistake. Instead, incremental policy changes are caveated with rationalizations such as greater health, wealth, and education being created is given to the general population so the Party can justify alterations while appearing incisive during the entire time the policy was enforced. The lack of a strong social safety net or family support means the inherent costs to have children are now interfering with the CCP's new effort to reverse its population decline. As of 2024, China has been unable to change their demographic decline which is now exacerbated by the CCP's draconian quarantine restrictions to contain a virus the Party unleashed with its incompetence. Central absolutism cannot adjust to the consequences of the decisions made in the past attempting to solve short-term problems. This repeats itself in every aspect of China's political system.

In China's real estate market is another example of the CCP's desire for too much instant gratification and later regret. Construction of infrastructure, housing, and utilities all require large amounts of raw materials, durable capital goods, and abundant manual labor. As stated earlier, the contemporary CCP uses economic growth and prosperity as the cornerstones of its political legitimacy and the Party quickly appreciated how a poor country with abundant labor could exploit real estate as a means of economic growth. Beginning in the 1990s, the CCP's Central Committee set growth targets for their provincial party leaders to generate GDP as quickly as possible. Provincial leaders would direct large-scale building projects to construct cities, railways, airports, dockyards, business parks, canals, highways, bridges, and tunnels with near reckless abandon. Over time, the provincial budgets became more dependent on real estate transactions while at the same time still needing to please the Central Committee with good GDP growth performance.[xlv] At first, in the short-term portion of the plan, the legitimate need to build modern infrastructure to help China function was constructive and provided legitimate economic value to the Chinese market place but this changed as the years progressed. Raw GDP targets meant the provincial parties of the CCP couldn't invest in only economically valid projects. The provinces had to keep building year-round for those provinces to meet the ever-growing Party set GDP and full employment quotas, eventually making real estate responsible for nearly 25% of China's GDP.[xlvi]

Any disruption to these projects, such as lacking new loans to support the construction, would endanger the careers of provincial and city party leaders because failing to achieve Beijing's objectives meant a loss of face or miànzi, ending their careers. To keep economic momentum, at least statistically, the provinces and key cities would encourage shadow banking by requiring local enterprises take on loans to construct economically detrimental projects. In many cases, local government authorities would take on the debt to secure the continuing GDP growth numbers even as bank debts increased.[xlvii] For years, this problem was not acknowledged by the CCP's senior leadership as these individuals used guanxi to build personal networks to corruptly benefit financially from the state-backed real estate and construction investments. Miànzi meant these networks of guanxi could not be acknowledged because if one's superior is corrupt and found out, then all of the superior's subordinates are also culpable. This means there is little incentive to self-report or to inform authorities, with some exceptions based on political convenience. Only when the problem became too big to ignore, did the Chinese regime act with more aggressive audits but now must deal with a system dependent on debt driven real estate growth.[xlviii]

The midterm consequences of these policies led to the creation of ghost cities and poorly constructed infrastructure that ignored safety to meet Party deadlines. Additionally, overabundant numbers of highways leading to nowhere, rail lines hardly used, and empty airports are now commonplace all over China.[xlix] The CCP's power to make quick decisions without allowing contrary views led to excess waste of resources on a national scale unseen before in human history. Yet, these actions met the requirements of the ambitious local party leadership who can keep the CCP national leadership satisfied so the Party can continue to justify its legitimacy at home and create envy abroad. The leadership did not care for years of the inefficient allocation of resources because that was not the Party's problem, only the nation's problem. Now however, the market bubble surrounding these artificial GDP growth projects is becoming too large to manage and endangering social order. Local provinces use of shadow loans and GDP driven investments has swelled local government debt to equal nearly half of China's GDP.[l] Chairman Xi fears a real estate collapse could trigger an economic calamity on a scale that could endanger the Party's leadership. This danger exists partly due to another unforeseen consequence of the real estate market, the Chinese people's faith in property over other investments.

The corruption driving these provincial land investments is also driving Chinese banking and finances. Although the rule of law has improved over the years, most people within China have more faith in tangible goods than the CCP-controlled stock market. The state can still arbitrarily freeze accounts, limit withdrawals, manipulate currency value, and prevent the selling of assets to prop up politically valuable investments. The main form of investment among private Chinese households is buying up real estate and housing.[li] China, through its GDP growth efforts, convinced a large portion of the population to speculate on the real estate market as the primary means of building up wealth which is made easier by the existing social status prominence of being a home owner.[lii] This encouraged many families to spend their liquid savings and even take out loans to buy properties, even ones of dubious legal nature.[liii] Of course, the wealthy and politically-connected can offshore as much of their personal wealth as possible by buying real estate overseas to avoid the substantial demands of the CCP. The unwillingness of the CCP to cede any real control over the financial system keeps encouraging the population into tying their investments to an overinflated property market. The CCP's actions on real estate for short-term gains of China's exponential GDP growth is now impeding the mid-term goals of turning China into a services-based high-tech economy. To make matters worse, the CCP's decision-making is not limited to one industrial sector but permeates every facet of Chinese society.

Another example of short-term gain with long-term pain is the CCP's environmental policies. For most of the CCP's existence, the environment was irrelevant and was just one more thing to exploit. To achieve the large energy demands of China's growth and to also increasingly make global economies more dependent on China, the CCP mandated mining and extraction of raw materials as cheaply and quickly as possible. Abundance of coal meant areas like Inner Mongolia became blanketed by coal dust as numerous mines were built with no consideration to worker safety, clean water, or breathable air.[liv] The CCP did however, accomplish its goals of being able to sustain the energy demands for China's decades long economic expansion. A similar decision was made regarding rare earth minerals. China built a monopoly on rare earth extraction by building multiple mines using very cheap labor and no environmental standards in order to undercut all potential foreign competitors. Rare earth extraction is extremely polluting if not done correctly which means Western countries cannot compete as regulations and demands for a clean environment make it impossible to match Chinese prices without substantial subsidy from Western governments.[lv] The CCP knew the West's desire for cheap rare earth minerals would override any security concerns, at least for a while, and consequently justified these actions in the eyes of CCP leadership. Even now, the priority of the CCP is to maintain the monopoly with greater oversight by the CCP as the Chinese government consolidates its holdings into a singularly large state-owned enterprise.[lvi] The priority of rapid modernization at the cost of sustainability created such major negative consequences in the decades that followed that the CCP now implements more environmental rules to correct its prior mistakes. The negative effects of those miscalculations are still present and cannot be ignored especially since the provinces whose prosperity was built on dirty industry cannot just simply change its economic landscape overnight.[lvii]

China produces a large amount of food for the world as part of the CCP's policies to build up world dependencies on China, however China at the same time has lost a sizable portion of its arable land to pollution and poor water management.[lviii] Even though the CCP is scrambling to reallocate water and other efforts to improve food security at home, local factions impede and slow major projects as each competes to protect provincial resources from being pilfered by rival provinces.[lix] In the meantime, the CCP endangers regional food production to sustain its own power demands, even at the cost of endangering its own Belt and Road ambitions in Cambodia, Laos, and Thailand. In keeping with CCP demands for immediate results, China is building multiple irrigation networks and new dams on the Mekong River to support energy demands even as fish and fresh water supplies are diminished in South East Asia.[lx] This does have the strategic bonus of undermining China's traditional enemy, Vietnam whose economy relies on the Mekong for food, employment and ecological sustainment.[lxi] However, instead of cowering the Vietnamese, it is only hardening their defiance. The long-term negative consequences of having numerous dams on key rivers is not just impacting Belt and Road member countries.

In China, many hydroelectric projects have been undertaken to support energy and manufacturing requirements, often without regard to the terrain or ecological impact. In 2020, at the height of the China-based pandemic, China experienced severe storms and flooding in the central valley where numerous dams had been constructed.[lxii] Unfortunately for the common Chinese citizens in the region, the numerous smaller dams on the tributaries created pressure on the larger dams which risked collapsing. The CCP's priorities of power and energy ignored the ecological impact of how thousands of dikes, dams, and levees on water ways would knock the water flows out of equilibrium.[lxiii] To avoid cataclysmic damage, the CCP destroyed multiple smaller dams, sacrificing the smaller towns and villages to protect the major industrial centers.[lxiv]' [lxv] Such consequences of poor decision making are rife as the CCP's system encourages a culture of avarice and indifference to anyone not protected by being a part of a guanxi network.

The central-absolutist concepts of immediate actions for quick results also impacts the government bureaucracies themselves but are kept hidden from the international media. The most obvious example of socialist bureaucracy is healthcare. Socialist countries often pride themselves on their healthcare systems, even if these systems are overrated. Cuba boasted for decades about its healthcare system and the doctors Cuba sent overseas. Even the mixed economies of Europe cite healthcare as a key accomplishment. The fact is healthcare is a central theme in most states' discussions of social welfare yet China doesn't talk about its healthcare system and one must wonder why?

The CCP adopted the central-absolutist hybrid of totalitarianism because the inflexibility of communist utopianism nearly caused China to collapse by the 1970s. Embracing the fascistic concept of allowing some property rights helped balance CCP finances. The Party's immediate success with implementing this hybrid in policy was also applied to as many systems as possible. China's medical system is a hybrid in being a publicly owned government industry but the CCP requires each major medical treatment facility to return an annual profit.[lxvi] Officially, the Chinese medical system offers free healthcare but only for general medicine and routine procedures. Specialist procedures must be paid for by families of patients and are very expensive. To help improve efficiency, the CCP created a ranking system for hospitals broken into three separate tiers. Tier 1 are the health clinics and general care facilities where many services are basic and are either cheap or free. Tier 2 are the general hospitals treating common ailments and the Tier 3 hospitals provide the highly specialized healthcare, medical training, and medical research.[lxvii] The CCP believed this would simplify administration and more efficiently allocate patients and fairer fiscal apportionment to the types of hospital.

In practice, the CCP system inadvertently created a hybrid that incorporated the worst elements of socialist and private healthcare, not the best. The Party mandate of basic care being provided cheaply or for free to stay in keeping with their socialist principles while demanding hospitals be self-financing by charging for advanced care has created a hybrid monster of a system that distorts the concept of medicine. In order for hospitals to turn a profit, the doctors must over-diagnose and over-prescribe medical treatments to get patients to pay for expensive treatments, whether the patients are healthy or not. Tier 1 hospitals will work with Tier 3 to find ailments that require the most expensive treatments in order to make profit and can endanger their patients' health. Compounding this problem is the corruption and guanxi that is prevalent in Chinese society. Due to corruption, many patients do not trust Tier 2 hospitals out of fear that the bad or mediocre specialists who graduated by bribery reside at these general hospitals. For this and other reasons, Chinese patients who are sick will try to get more severe diagnoses from doctors, often via bribery or guanxi favors, in order to get referred to more prestigious hospitals.[lxviii]

This situation creates an imbalance where prestigious hospitals are overwhelmed with patients and an entire tier of hospitals minimally attended due to the reputation of corruption of the CCP, doctors, and the healthcare system in general. To make matters worse, genuinely sick patients are often given treatments that are financially cheap because costs are too high for patients who can't afford to bribe. This is a major reason why traditional Chinese medicine is so popular again in China even though it increases the risk of patients dying due to suspect standards and reliability. [lxix] Traditional Chinese medicine is much cheaper but hospitals only make profit from selling contemporary Western pharmaceuticals. This has encouraged the Chinese pharmaceutical industry to bribe doctors to prescribe medicines to patients regardless of the actual diagnosis.[lxx] For these reasons, the medical establishment is deeply distrusted in China by Chinese citizenry. Anger and frustration by patients due to the corruption and mismanagement has made it almost a tradition for doctors in China to be at risk of physical assault and death threats. Such dysfunction helps explain why China does not even bother to pretend that its national health system is something worth boasting about to other nations. This application of the CCP's hybrid system has created a truly unique cultural phenomena where the social status of doctors in Chinese society is just above that of loan sharks and pimps.[lxxi] The CCP's hybrid authoritarianism repeatedly creates artificial imbalances that gradually destabilize all systems without major intervention to patch the faults. In spite of Chinese propaganda to the contrary, many institutions and social structures in China limp along as barely functional.

The long-term consequences for the impulsive and reactive nature of the CCP's central absolutism where immediate problems are tackled for the sake of making the problem go away rather than permanently solve the issue means the Chinese state institutions are brittle. Chinese systems and bureaucracy fail more often than is generally known, creating many opportunities for corruption and criminality to covertly thrive within the system the CCP created. Crime in China, especially property and fiscal crime, is far more prevalent than is officially acknowledged because the system only cares for the welfare of the Party, not China or its people.

The massive economic boom China experienced over the last several decades was partly due to the use of cheap labor. A sizable portion of this cheap labor are treated only slightly better than historical slaves yet their exploitation goes unnoticed because these people are mostly from the illegal migrant population. Unlike the West, China doesn't have freedom of movement because it would weaken the CCP's power over the general population since it could no longer control employment rates in the cities. In order for a Chinese citizen to move within the country, they must go through the Hukou system to get permission from local CCP authorities and, like a passport, go to the specified locations for the assigned amount of time.[lxxii] The wealthier cities and provincial districts for decades demanded labor willing to work for little money but couldn't always rely on the local constituents providing sufficient manpower to meet CCP GDP quotas. In spite of the official law, many politicians and bureaucrats took advantage of millions of poorer Chinese from smaller towns, rural districts, and remote areas who were desperate for work due to the inability of their poor hometowns to sufficiently provide a means to build up their families' standard of living. These exploitative officials would turn a blind eye to these poor migrants who violated the Hukou and illegally travelled to major cities to work in the richer parts of China to support families back home. Since millions of illegal migrant workers are considered criminals by the CCP and the Chinese government, companies take full advantage and make these migrants slaves.[lxxiii]

In China, corruption is prevalent but is tolerated as long as it's hidden so no local party leader risks losing miànzi or alternatively, a profit loss for the local CCP. This environment has created a unique set of criminal enterprises that are not seen in Western countries. Working in the cities doesn't always deliver the required income to support families and the migrants' home communities. With so many participating in the underground economy, many migrants cannot find stable income as competition is fierce and rates of return can be small. So, instead of trying to get work with state-owned enterprises or major manufacturers in cities, some entire villages decided to turn their whole communities into criminal enterprises. Criminal townships arose in the 1990s to support their neglected communities because one of the great ironies of totalitarian societies is caring about the collective whole of society means neglecting individuals.[lxxiv] If all individuals, except party leaders, are just cogs for the collectivist machine then the laws will be made to ensure collective survival at expense of expendable cogs. In practice in China, whole towns and villages get neglected by the Party for a variety of reasons, being too remote, no arable land, local party leaders are out of favor, etc.

Unlike the triads of Hong Kong or coastal China, these crime towns often specialize in one type of property crime such as car theft or wire fraud. One specific example studied by Hong Kong University was cake delivery. In Chinese cities, there are many small food and baking shops run by urban families who receive mass produced baked goods for delivery and these shops then turn around and sell these cakes and baked goods to local clients. In the case of the criminal town selling cakes, the criminal delivery drivers would deliver the baked goods and while the shop keepers helped unload their paid-for goods, the delivery drivers would either swap the account books or receipts to indicate the shop keepers underpaid for deliveries over a period of time.[lxxv] Then the delivery drivers would confront the shop owners to demand payments. If dozens of delivery drivers duplicate this activity over several cities, a small village of a few thousand could make considerable profit as the delivery drivers share the proceeds with family members.

The importance of highlighting this corruption is demonstrating how central absolutism can help the CCP complete its objectives quickly but does so in such a sloppy and haphazard way, that CCP actions create many negative side effects on Chinese society. All societies have policy processes that produce negative effects but China has no mechanism to correct the CCP's mistakes and just neglects them. The criminal towns arose throughout China because the provincial leaders wanted GDP growth at all costs and ignored the details of who might suffer or benefit from such top-down micromanagement. Hence, central absolutism often ignores the messy details, allowing the problems to fester and compound into greater economic inefficiencies. These inefficiencies' effects will not be noticed for years as these tend to be minor at first and grow slowly.

The criminal towns grew gradually and are mostly ignored by the CCP. The Ministry of Public Security (MPS), China's civil police force, did not help remedy the situation any better than the CCP provincial officials. The dual nature of Chinese policing means police must answer to both the national police authorities as well as local party officials. Local police, especially in smaller districts, receive payments based on performance to the local party leadership. The party leadership of the area is far more important than the government ministry because the CCP overrides the state. Since local party leaders of criminal villages and towns receive a portion of all illicit income, many police units are complicit in the town-wide criminal enterprises.[lxxvi]

These examples reflect the CCP's practice of implementing a "just good enough to function" mentality to governance. Corruption and cumulative inefficiencies of top-down control creates indifference within the bureaucracies that is only stirred to action when a problem is immediate or too politically risky for the leaders to ignore. Ironically, the system that boasts about its plans and strategies created a culture that lives in the moment among both bureaucrats and the general population because nothing is certain in this unreliable system. This attitude stems from the CCP's systemic mismanagement during Mao's reign which created shortages and unreliable government services. The Chinese population's culture encourages people to hoard and take as much as possible when one has access to something to ensure survival because a system that discards the value of individuals often leaves many behind. There is debate on whether the CCP's actions exacerbated or are the root cause of this behavior as scarcity of goods and services among the peasant classes was also a recurring theme during the dynastic period.[lxxvii] Regardless, the quality and reliability of a system in China does depend on a person's personal connections and avoiding anything that risks undermining someone more senior in the CCP.

Ironically, the ruling CCP is more concerned with people or groups it cannot control directly because the CCP must expend more effort to influence these outside groups to mitigate any potential threat. Contrarily, Chinese citizens who are not members of the Party are the least important and draw less concern from the Party. This is reflected in the quality of services given to foreign investors as opposed to the poorer quality given to the Chinese citizenry. The Chinese regime demands greater scrutiny and more reliability for supply chains, products, and services going to its overseas customers than domestic consumers in order to keep foreign technology and financial capital flowing into China.[lxxviii] Contrasting this with domestic performance, in 2008 more than 300,000 infants became ill because over 22 Chinese companies conspired to add melamine to powdered milk to boost protein levels to meet government standards. The corrupt inspections system and the lack of local leader concern allowed the widespread poisoning of China's children.[lxxix] This generated so much distrust in local government and business reliability, that a whole new industry of milk tourism arose where Chinese citizens known as daigou would go to Hong Kong and Australia to bulk buy powdered milk to sell back to Chinese mainlanders for large profits.[lxxx] Even over a decade later, the CCP's reputation for callous indifference and corruption pervades the minds of the Chinese general public.

Nor did this milk scandal bring any meaningful reform. Another major scandal happened again in 2018 when hundreds of thousands of vaccine doses sold to the public were discovered to be faulty and multiple officials had been bribed in the attempt to hide this criminal cost-saving measure.[lxxxi] Outside observers seemed surprised because new penalties for fraud and new safety standards were implemented earlier by the Chinese government to combat such occurrences. This perspective comes from the assumptions that the state and rule of law are the final arbiters of authority in China but that is not the case. The laws are only enforced by what the Party deems convenient. If party officials benefit from guanxi or the greater CCP is not embarrassed or at risk for losing revenue, then the laws can be bent, ignored, or discarded. It cannot be over emphasized, central absolutism turns the rule of law on and off based on the interests of the Party, not China or its citizens. The vaccine scandal resulted in many being arrested or removed but this is more to do with miànzi than any true concern for the general welfare. The Chinese public understands this and continues to have more faith in foreign made goods rather than Chinese.

If the CCP was truly concerned with the welfare of China, it would likely support more grass root efforts to reduce corruption but the Party relies on this corruption to maintain cohesion among its own ranks. A classic example is fixing the severe environmental degradation caused by CCP monopoly building and trade manipulation yet grass-root activism is discouraged. To improve the CCP's reputation, international image and reassure China's population, the Party did create new environmental regulations. However, in 2016 the environmental activist Liu Shu was arrested for 'revealing state secrets' by exposing politically connected industries dumping heavy metals into water ways in the Dongting Lake.[lxxxii] The guanxi between the Party and the industries once again showed the CCP will only concern itself with China when the Party is actually threatened.

These examples of China's domestic negligence and the inherently inflexible nature of the CCP's modernized ideology of central absolutism demonstrate how China, in spite of all its economic good fortune, remains a paper dragon relying on a corrupt and brittle system. In the era of Mao, the Chinese Communist Party brought itself to the cusp of self-destruction as it blindly attempted to create a utopia based on theories and delusions which completely ignored the context of human nature. Deng Xiaoping was pragmatic enough to know the CCP's system needed external lifelines to sustain its control as the inefficiencies of an overly centralized country eventually accumulate to the point of impeding the entire society's ability to function at all. The modern CCP's added capitalist veneer gave them a life support system, the West.

For all the talk of China's revolutionary economy, the many faults are unintentionally hidden or minimized by the West's investments into China. Despite decades of development, China still has not created a fully organic entrepreneurial and innovation-based society for the technology-centric economies of the 21st Century. When Chinese entrepreneurship or invention becomes too successful, this risks the CCP's power so the system penalizes too much success. Jack Ma can attest to this and in 2021, China cracked down on private education by deliberately imposing regulations to stymie any teaching outside of CCP control. One victim was the New Oriental Education company which had reached a market value of $33 billion before the CCP reduced its value to $3 billion after imposing the new regulations.[lxxxiii] The CCP uses its many regulatory mechanisms to manipulate business environments, contracts, and uses China's currency to manipulate markets and can arbitrarily impose capital controls, seize accounts, and halt transactions with little to no warning. The Chinese public must constantly readjust their lives to fit into the political diktats of the moment and are never certain about anything.

Under Xi Jinping, the desire for singular control is a short-term problem that is typically found in an absolute monarchy but is now actively undermining the CCP's long-term strategies of the 1990s to alure foreign money and knowledge. Xi is loyal to the CCP but only to a CCP which is exclusively commanded by himself and, despite his collectivist proclamations to the contrary, pushes for rules that enhance his authority and make dissent against Xi impossible. In economic terms, the CCP's interest in keeping its interference in private businesses lowkey is paramount to CCP long-term strategy yet Xi is requiring the CCP's United Front organizations to become more involved with China's private sector. The United Front helps propagate CCP social mores and ideological indoctrination among the general population. Before Xi's era, the United Front kept a low profile, mainly focusing on the state-owned enterprises and major conglomerates but now are being directed to strengthen ideological fervor within the private businesses of China. President Xi dictates the United Front must ensure work in the private economy upholds party principles of 'trust, unity, service, guidance, and education . . . and continuously increase political consensus.'[lxxxiv] Despite what Xi hopes, increasingly micromanaging daily business decisions with political considerations will impact business performance. Again, the full impact of such actions is not appreciated for years and the negative consequences will not likely significantly manifest until a major crisis exposes them.

China's central-absolutist government attempts to have society behave entrepreneurially, innovatively, and yet wants total conformity and nothing outside the CCP's control. This schizophrenic back and forth goal-making is contradictory and cannot co-exist simultaneously. Without internal checks or forms of accountability, this system of trying to have its cake and eat it too has produced endemic corruption that cannot be corrected. The practical consequences of central absolutism is that both party member and citizen will put all of their energies into pleasing the Party, not bettering society or improving national wealth. The paper dragon has created a society encouraging mediocrity. Why bother to innovate or invent if the CCP takes the fruits of one's labor? The CCP may occasionally reward some token exceptions but for many, just impressing the Party to ensure personal success is enough.

In 2010, one-third of all scientists in six of China's top scientific institutions plagiarized or falsified their research.[lxxxv] In 2013, major drug companies were discovered to have made fraudulent breakthroughs in medicine while bribing people for market access with questionable products and research.[lxxxvi] In China, young students' future and status is heavily determined by the Gaokao exam and the desire to succeed at all costs has created highly organized cheating rings among students, parents, and bribed teachers to attain success.[lxxxvii] Nor is such duplicitous activity limited to research or academia. The notorious telecommunications giant Huawei has been widely successful throughout the world selling its communication devices and infrastructure at cheap prices enabling the company to become one of the most important industry leaders in the world. However, closer examination of Huawei software and equipment by UK's Cyber Security Evaluation Centre identified shoddy quality standards and multiple deficiencies. The UK oversight board also identified technical issues with Huawei's engineering process and had been slow to correct these deficiencies.[lxxxviii]

Regardless of whether these specific examples are eventually corrected, in each case the problems of corruption or lax standards kept recurring over the years in spite of new laws or regulations. Central absolutism does not reform itself; it only corrects problems on a case-by-case basis and will only do so as long as such actions protect the Party. So how does the CCP's brittle system survive year after year even though it encourages mediocrity and China's own population actively participates in the corruption? The West covers all the losses.

China's system paused its death spiral in the late 1970s by reforming just enough to encourage foreign participation in the Chinese economy. As China grew, more and more foreign investment filled the CCP coffers and technology was supplied to the regime. After years of success, China grew wealthy on the Western clients that happily gave large quantities of capital and know-how to short-cut China's path to economic development. The capitalist veneer is used as much to keep Western investment in China as it is to placate the Chinese population. Even after decades of technical and financial accumulation, the CCP still needs the West as its life support system to compensate for the inherently corrupt and inefficient domestic system. China doesn't need to plan out brilliant strategies of long-term investment like the Japanese attempted to do in the 1980s. Instead, China leeches off the avarice of easily manipulated Western investors, financial elites, academics, and innovators to compensate for the dictatorship's systemic faults. Without the ability to have internal reforms, the system will increasingly become more centralized over time as the human condition will demand more power as CCP factions compete for more power amongst themselves. Xi Jinping demonstrated this himself repeatedly in 2021 when he ordered a crackdown on Chinese technology firms to dictate content in an effort to help improve equity among the Chinese populace. [lxxxix] This was in response to correcting the social stratification the CCP had created from previous policies. Central absolutism does not allow for any solution except for centralized control by the Party.

The West, as will be shown in the next section of the book, sustains China while at the same time helps China keep the West addicted to China's exploitation. China promises access to its markets but in practice, focuses its enticements on providing cost-savings for products bound for Western firms' already established markets in the West with use of slaves and cheap commodities. This benefits Western consumers in the short-term at the cost of economic development in the future but the CCP's system of keeping the West supporting the regime also emphasizes co-opting the Western elites that own the firms or institutions that invest in China. This partnership between China and Western elites is relatively cheap as the profits that leave China go to a relatively small group of Westerners. This system of mutual dependence keeps China alive. If the elites of the West decide to break free of Chinese influence and de-couple its freer market systems from China's economy, then the systemic death-spiral of the CCP that was paused in the 1970s would quickly resume. A successful decoupling of Western economies dooms the CCP to destruction, likely within a few decades of such an act.

This would be the reason for China encouraging instability and create the circumstances for civil wars in the West. The CCP would not risk its existence by directly subverting Western elites and encouraging civil strife unless its existence was already threatened. Although very difficult, the West could survive without China and build an economic system separate from CCP influence but China cannot survive without the West, and indeed the world, to leech off of to sustain its paper dragon economy. So how does a paper dragon survive? The West's beneficence in trade has given the paper dragon iron claws to threaten any nation attempting to free itself from China's parasitic system. China hopes to eventually drain dry all of the major powers of their economic and technological advantages long enough to paralyze the world and compel them to be vassals or the lucky ones becoming just tributary states in a Chinese-centric world hegemony. China is not competing with the West on the world stage to prove which systems are superior because as Dr. Beckley demonstrated, the United States would win in a fair global competition. Instead, the CCP intends to destroy all other alternatives before China's own system collapses. China intends to win global control by making itself the only option left standing by engorging itself off of the world's other economies.

[i] Kerry Brown, "The Communist Party of China and Ideology," China: An International Journal, vol. 10, n. 2, August 2021, 54-56. https://www.academia.edu/3581321/The_Communist_Party_of_China_and_Ideology?pop_sutd=false

[ii] Dr. Li Zhisui, The Private Life of Chairman Mao, (NY: Random House, 1994) 201-209.

[iii] Ibid, 268-279.

[iv] Jinghan Zeng, The Chinese Communist Party's Capacity to Rule: Ideology, Legitimacy and Party Cohesion, (NY: Palgrave Macmillan, 2016) 96-104.

[v] Huiming Guo, "Adhere to the Four Cardinal Principles and Socialism with Chinese Characteristics," Learning and Education, v.9, DOI: 10.18282/l-e.v9i3.1580, December 2020, 73-74, https://ojs.piscomed.com/index.php/L-E/article/view/1580

[vi] Editors, "Deng Xiaoping, Chinese Leader," Encyclopedia Britannica, Feb 15, 2022. https://www.britannica.com/biography/Deng-Xiaoping

[vii] Richard McGregor, The Party: The Secret World of China's Communist Party, (NY: HarperCollins Publishers, 2012) 36-47.

[viii] Ibid, 62-64.

[ix] Ibid, 66-69.

[x] Ibid, 39, 52-53-, 58-60.

[xi] Li Yuan, "Why China Turned Against Jack Ma," New York Times, December 24, 2020. https://www.nytimes.com/2020/12/24/technology/china-jack-ma-alibaba.html

[xii] Eva Dou, "Documents link Huawei to China's Surveillance Programs," The Washington Post, December 14, 2021. https://www.washingtonpost.com/world/2021/12/14/huawei-surveillance-china/

[xiii] Gunter Reiman, The Vampire Economy: Doing Business Under Fascism, (DE: Mises Institute, re-printed September 2020 (1939)) 16-17.

[xiv] Richard McGregor, The Party: The Secret World of China's Communist Party, (NY: HarperCollins Publishers, 2012) 77-79.

[xv] Wei Chen, Xilu Chen, Chang-Tai Hsieh, and Zheng Michael Song, "A Forensic Examination of China's National Accounts," Brookings Institute, March 7, 2019. https://www.brookings.edu/bpea-articles/a-forensic-examination-of-chinas-national-accounts/

[xvi] Gunter Reiman, The Vampire Economy: Doing Business Under Fascism, (DE: Mises Institute, re-printed September 2020 (1939)) 195-197.

[xvii] Bloomberg News, "Evergrande's Hui Forced to Trim Stake in Defaulted Developer," Bloomberg, December 10, 2021. https://www.bloomberg.com/news/articles/2021-12-10/evergrande-s-hui-forced-to-sell-part-of-stake-in-defaulted-firm

[xviii] Gunter Reiman, The Vampire Economy: Doing Business Under Fascism, (DE: Mises Institute, re-printed September 2020 (1939)) 127-130.

[xix] Arthur R. Kroeber, Victor Shih, "How Will China's Stock Market Drop Affect the Rest of Its Economy?" Foreign Policy, July 31, 2015. https://foreignpolicy.com/2015/07/31/china-stock-market-economy-assets-investors/

[xx] Gunter Reiman, *The Vampire Economy: Doing Business Under Fascism*, (DE: Mises Institute, re-printed September 2020 (1939)) 176-178.

[xxi] Andy Stern, "China's Superior Economic Model," The Wall Street Journal, December 1, 2011. https://www.wsj.com/articles/SB10001424052970204630904577056490023451980

[xxii] Luke Glanville, "Retaining the Mandate of Heaven: Sovereign Accountability in Ancient China," Millenium: Journal of International Studies, v.39, 324-325. DOI: 10.1177/0305829810383608

[xxiii] Fei-Ling Wang, *The China Order: Centralia, World Empire, and the Nature of Chinese Power*, (Albany, NY: State of University of New York Press, 2017) 49-51, 167-170.

[xxiv] Dr. Li Zhisui, *The Private Life of Chairman Mao*, (NY: Random House, 1994) 176-186.

[xxv] Tsukasa Hadano, "Xi Jinping Moves Closer to Reviving 'Chairman' Title to Match Mao," Nikkei Asia, November 19, 2021. https://asia.nikkei.com/Politics/Xi-Jinping-moves-closer-to-reviving-chairman-title-to-match-Mao

[xxvi] Elizabeth C. Economy, "China's Neo-Maoist Moment: How Xi Jinping Is Using China's Past to Accomplish What His Predecessors Could Not," Foreign Affairs, October 1, 2019. https://www.foreignaffairs.com/articles/china/2019-10-01/chinas-neo-maoist-moment

[xxvii] ChinaFile Editors translation, "Document 9: Current State of the Ideological Sphere," CCP Communique translated, November 8, 2013. https://www.chinafile.com/document-9-chinafile-translation

[xxviii] Masha Borak, "People can Pledge Loyalty to the Communist Party of China on Blockchain," South China Morning Post, October 30, 2019. https://www.scmp.com/abacus/culture/article/3035406/people-can-pledge-loyalty-communist-party-china-blockchain

[xxix] Samuel Wade, "Xi Study App Highlights Party Influence Over and Through Tech," China Digital Times, February 21, 2019. https://chinadigitaltimes.net/2019/02/xi-study-app-highlights-party-influence-over-and-through-tech/

[xxx] Timothy R. Heath, "The Consolidation of Political Power in China Under Xi Jinping: Implications for the PLA and Domestic Security Forces," RAND Testimony before the US-China Economic and Security Review Commission, February 7, 2019. https://www.rand.org/pubs/testimonies/CT503.html

[xxxi] Robert Spalding, *Stealth War: How China Took Over While America's Elite Slept*, (Penguin Random House, USA, 2019) 31-33.

[xxxii] Ibid, 78.

[xxxiii] Michael Standaert, "China Wrestles with the Toxic Aftermath of Rare Earth Mining," Yale School of the Environment E360, July 2, 2019. https://e360.yale.edu/features/china-wrestles-with-the-toxic-aftermath-of-rare-earth-mining

[xxxiv] Yumiko Kojima, Kyoko Murai, Howard Pang, and Elena Vitale, "The United States, China, and the Three-Gorges Dam," Princeton Journal of Public and International Affairs, vol. 9, Spring 1998. https://jpia.princeton.edu/sites/jpia/files/8.pdf

[xxxv] Aaron Mehta, "Is China Already Inside America's Hypersonic Industrial Base?" Defense News, June 9, 2020. https://www.defensenews.com/pentagon/2020/06/09/is-china-already-inside-americas-hypersonic-industrial-base/

[xxxvi] John Grady, "STRATCOM: China's Pursuit of Nuclear and Hypersonic Weapons Adds Urgency to US Deterrence," USNI News, August 26, 2021. https://news.usni.org/2021/08/26/stratcom-chinas-pursuit-of-nuclear-and-hypersonic-weapons-adds-urgency-to-u-s-deterrence

[xxxvii] Bloomberg News, "China's Hypersonic Test Showed Unprecedented Capability, FT Says," Bloomberg, November 21, 2021. https://www.bloomberg.com/news/articles/2021-11-22/china-launched-missile-from-hypersonic-weapon-in-july-ft-says

[xxxviii] Ashwin Kaja, Yan Luo and Timothy P. Stratford, "China's New National Security Law," Global Policy Watch, July 7, 2015. https://www.globalpolicywatch.com/2015/07/chinas-new-national-security-law/

[xxxix] Matt Welch, "Thomas L. Friedman Wants Us to 'to be China for a day,' to 'authorize the right solutions'," Reason, May 24, 2010. https://reason.com/2010/05/24/thomas-l-friedman-wants-us-to/

[xl] Dr. Michael Beckley, *Unrivaled: Why America will Remain the World's Sole Superpower*, (Ithaca, Cornell University Press, 2018) 16-18.

[xli] Ibid, 17-18.

[xlii] Ibid, 31-32.

[xliii] Adam Theirer, "'Japan Inc.' and Other Tales of Industrial Policy Apocalypse," Discourse Magazine, June 28, 2021. https://www.discoursemagazine.com/culture-and-society/2021/06/28/japan-inc-and-other-tales-of-industrial-policy-apocalypse/

[xliv] Dennis Normile, "China's Population May Start to Shrink this Year, New Birth Data Suggest," Science, January 18, 2022. https://www.science.org/content/article/china-s-population-may-start-shrink-year-new-birth-data-suggest

[xlv] Major Tian, "The Role of Land Sales in Local Government Financing in China," CKGSB (English), September 3, 2014. https://english.ckgsb.edu.cn/knowledges/the-role-of-land-sales-in-local-government-financing-in-china/

[xlvi] Daniel Lacalle, "China's Property Bubble Collapse Gets Worse," BBN Times, February 21, 2022. https://www.bbntimes.com/financial/china-s-property-bubble-collapse-gets-worse

[xlvii] Louis Kuijs, "China's Local Government Debt – What is the Problem?" World Bank – East Asia and Pacific on the Rise Blog, March 24, 2010. https://blogs.worldbank.org/eastasiapacific/china-s-local-government-debt-what-is-the-problem

[xlviii] Bloomberg News, "Shadow Banking Risks Exposed by Local Debt Audit: China Credit," Bloomberg, January 6, 2014. https://www.bloomberg.com/news/articles/2014-01-06/shadow-banking-risks-exposed-by-local-debt-audit-china-credit

[xlix] David Barboza, "Building Boom in China Stirs Fears of Debt Overload," New York Times, July 6, 2011. https://www.nytimes.com/2011/07/07/business/global/building-binge-by-chinas-cities-threatens-countrys-economic-boom.html

[l] Bloomberg News, "China Hidden Local Government Debt is Half of GDP, Goldman Says," Bloomberg, September 29, 2021. https://www.bloomberg.com/news/articles/2021-09-29/china-hidden-local-government-debt-is-half-of-gdp-goldman-says

[li] Wade Shepard, "How People in China Afford Their Outrageously Expensive Homes," Forbes, March 30, 2016. https://www.forbes.com/sites/wadeshepard/2016/03/30/how-people-in-china-afford-their-outrageously-expensive-homes/?sh=4ef2ad41a3ce

[lii] Juwai, "Why are Chinese so Obsessed with Buying Property?" Juwai IQI Asia News, June 26, 2017. https://list.juwai.com/news/2017/06/why-are-chinese-so-obsessed-with-buying-property

[liii] Youqin Huang, Shenjing He, and Li Gan, "Introduction to SI: Homeownership and Housing Divide in China," Cities, vol. 108, January 2021. https://www.ncbi.nlm.nih.gov/pmc/articles/PMC7546956/

[liv] Simon Denyer, "In China's Inner Mongolia, Mining Spells Misery for Traditional Herders," Washington Post, April 7, 2015. https://www.washingtonpost.com/world/asia_pacific/in-chinas-inner-mongolia-mining-spells-misery-for-traditional-herders/2015/04/07/16b3a252-d643-11e4-bf0b-f648b95a6488_story.html

[lv] Michael Standaert, "China Wrestles with the Toxic Aftermath of Rare Earth Mining," Yale School of the Environment E360, July 2, 2019. https://e360.yale.edu/features/china-wrestles-with-the-toxic-aftermath-of-rare-earth-mining

[lvi] Shunsuke Tabeta, "China Consolidates 3 Rare Earth Miners into 'Aircraft Carrier'," Nikkei Asia, December 24, 2021. https://asia.nikkei.com/Business/Markets/Commodities/China-consolidates-3-rare-earth-miners-into-aircraft-carrier

[lvii] Naomi Xu Elegant, "How China's Top Coal Province is Defying Xi Jinping's Carbon Neutral Pledge," Forbes, January 20, 2021. https://fortune.com/2021/01/20/china-coal-power-plants-xi-jinping-carbon-neutral/

[lviii] Tina Ma, Siao Sun, et al., "Pollution Exacerbates China's Water Scarcity and its Regional Inequality," Nature Communications, v. 11:650, 2020. https://www.nature.com/articles/s41467-020-14532-5.pdf

[lix] Hongzhou Zhang and Genevieve Donnellon-May, "To Build or Not to Build: Western Route of China's South-North Water Diversion Project," Wilson Center New Security Beat, August 21, 2021. https://www.newsecuritybeat.org/2021/08/build-build-western-route-chinas-south-north-water-diversion-project/

[lx] Philip Citowicki, "China's Control of the Mekong," The Diplomat, May 8, 2020. https://thediplomat.com/2020/05/chinas-control-of-the-mekong/

[lxi] Abby Seiff, "China is Choking Off Asia's Most Important River," Foreign Policy, April 2, 2022. https://foreignpolicy.com/2022/04/02/china-is-choking-off-asias-most-important-river/

[lxii] Alice Su, "'Man Cannot Win Against Nature': Amid Catastrophic Floods, China's Dams Come into Question," LA Times, July 28, 2020. https://www.latimes.com/world-nation/story/2020-07-28/china-floods-three-gorges-climate-change-dams

[lxiii] Anjani Trivedi, "The Big China Disaster that You're Missing," The Japan Times, September 1, 2020. https://www.japantimes.co.jp/opinion/2020/09/01/commentary/world-commentary/big-china-disaster/

[lxiv] AP, "China Blasts Dam to Release Floodwaters as Death Toll Rises," Times of India, July 19, 2020. https://timesofindia.indiatimes.com/world/china/china-blasts-dam-to-release-floodwaters-as-death-toll-rises/articleshow/77047326.cms

[lxv] AP, "China Blasts Dam to Divert Floods that Killed at Least 25," Chicago Tribune, July 21, 2021. https://www.chicagotribune.com/nation-world/ct-aud-nw-china-flooding-20210721-fv2qifqznndk3d4ghkq2y7vkt4-story.html

[lxvi] Borge Bakken, Yujing Fun, and Zelin Yao, Crime and the Chinese Dream, (Hong Kong University Press, 2018) 21-22.

[lxvii] Ibid, 24-25.

[lxviii] Ibid, 27-29.

[lxix] Judy Xu and Yue Yang, "Traditional Chinese Medicine in the Chinese Health Care System," Health Policy, 90, 2009, 135-137. https://www.ncbi.nlm.nih.gov/pmc/articles/PMC7114631/pdf/main.pdf

[lxx] Borge Bakken, Yujing Fun, and Zelin Yao, Crime and the Chinese Dream, (Hong Kong University Press, 2018) 30-32.

[lxxi] Emily Rauhala, "Why China's Doctors are Getting Beat Up," Time, March 7, 2014. https://time.com/15185/chinas-doctors-overworked-underpaid-attacked/

[lxxii] Congressional Research Office, "China's Hukou System: Overview, Reform and Economic Implications," CRS In Focus, January 7, 2016. https://crsreports.congress.gov/product/pdf/IF/IF10344/3

[lxxiii] Peter Bengsten, "China's Forced Labor Problem," The Diplomat, March 21, 2018. https://thediplomat.com/2018/03/chinas-forced-labor-problem/

[lxxiv] Borge Bakken, Yujing Fun, and Zelin Yao, Crime and the Chinese Dream, (Hong Kong University Press, 2018) 40-42.

[lxxv] Ibid, 42-44.

[lxxvi] Ibid, 62.

[lxxvii] Emily Conrad, "The Great Hoards of China," The World of Chinese, April 16, 2021. https://www.theworldofchinese.com/2019/04/the-great-hoards-of-china/

[lxxviii] Dirk Dusharme, "Made in China: From Scary Bad to Scary Good Part Two: Chinese Quality is Improving, Fast!" Quality Digest, May 30, 2018. https://www.qualitydigest.com/inside/management-article/made-china-scary-bad-scary-good-part-2-053018.html

[lxxix] Bloomberg, "China's Lethal Milk Scandal Reverberates a Decade Later," The Strait Times, January 33, 2019. https://www.straitstimes.com/asia/east-asia/chinas-lethal-milk-scandal-reverberates-a-decade-later

[lxxx] Rebecca Puddy and Rhett Burnie, "China's Thirst for Baby Formula Creating Problems for Australian Shoppers and Staff," Australia Broadcasting Corporation News, December 10, 2018. https://www.abc.net.au/news/2018-12-11/abc-investigation-uncovers-chinese-baby-formula-shoppers/10594400

[lxxxi] Andy Extance, "Vaccine Scandal and Heart Drug Recall Show China's Pharma Struggles," Chemistry World, July 31, 2018. https://www.chemistryworld.com/news/vaccine-scandal-and-heart-drug-recall-show-chinas-pharma-struggles/3009330.article

[lxxxii] Yang Fan, "China Jails Environmental Activist for 'Revealing State Secrets'," Radio Free Asia, October 11, 2016. https://www.rfa.org/english/news/china/activist-10112016122729.html

[lxxxiii] Garfield Reynolds, "China Divorce from Capitalism Steals Joy from Stocks," Bloomberg Markets Live, August 31, 2021. https://www.zerohedge.com/markets/china-divorce-capitalism-steals-joy-stocks

[lxxxiv] Scott Livingston, "The Chinese Communist Party Targets the Private Sector," Center for Strategic & International Studies, October 2020. https://csis-website-prod.s3.amazonaws.com/s3fs-public/publication/201008_Livingston_CCP%20Targets%20Private%20Sector_WEB%20FINAL.pdf

[lxxxv] Jane Qui, "Publish or Perish in China," Nature 463, 142, 12 January 2010. https://www.nature.com/articles/463142a#citeas

[lxxxvi] Mara Hvistendahl, "Corruption and Research Fraud Send Big Chill Through Big Pharma in China," Science, v. 341, issue 6145, 445-446. https://www.science.org/doi/10.1126/science.341.6145.445

[lxxxvii] Sophie Williams, "From A Wireless Receiver Shaped Like a Belt to A Camera Hidden in A Pen: Chinese Authority Exposes the James Bond-Style Cheating Devices Used by Students During the University Entrance Examination," Daily Mail, June 7, 2017. https://www.dailymail.co.uk/news/peoplesdaily/article-4580428/High-school-exam-cheating-devices-exposed-China.html

[lxxxviii] George Calhoun, "Why are Huawei's Customers Satisfied with Defective Products?" Forbes, June 4, 2020. https://www.forbes.com/sites/georgecalhoun/2020/06/04/huawei-is-happy-with-crappy--why-are-their-customers/?sh=5a006b7936c3

[lxxxix] Andrew Browne, "Xi Jinping's Tech Crackdown Ignores Bigger Problems Facing China," Bloomberg New Economy Daily Newsletter, August 21, 2021. https://www.bloomberg.com/news/newsletters/2021-08-07/tech-sector-crackdown-ignores-china-s-bigger-problems-new-economy-saturday

Chapter 4: Tianxia – All Under Heaven

China's system is brittle, corrupt, and vulnerable to severe shocks. Without the safety net of foreign wealth and knowledge to sustain the regime, it would collapse under its own weight. Despite the propaganda to the contrary, the CCP knows it needs overseas support to retain and grow its power. The Party's grand strategy revolves around two mutually reinforcing goals of keeping foreign capital and knowledge flowing into China while simultaneously making China's trade partners co-dependent and addicted to the Chinese economy. The CCP ensures enough profit is made for its trade partners in the short term even though China will eventually deplete their trade partners' wealth in the long run. By keeping the trading nations addicted to China's economy, any attempt to break away or become more independent from China will result in severe economic stress and pain for the defiant trading partner. This is the quintessential driver of China's means and methodology to become the dominating global hegemon.

The final grand objective for the CCP is ultimately being the uncontested global hegemon, a new Pax-Sinica centered on the absolute control of the Chinese Communist Party. This lofty ambitious goal is driven by the CCP's lust for power but the justification presented to the Chinese people is rooted in ancient tradition and philosophical thought. Learning from its own mistakes, the contemporary CCP no longer rejects China's dynastic history like Mao did; as long as the history being told conforms to the Party's narrative. Citing the annals of China's golden ages, the Chinese public endorses the idea of their country's historical exceptionalism that brought centuries of advancement and prosperity. The CCP particularly endorses the old legal and philosophical justifications declaring China can only be governed by absolute rule of a strong central authority. Tying the good fortunes of China's past with autocratic rule of enlightened mandarins led by an emperor helps justify why the CCP must rule likewise for contemporary China. Linking China's political philosophy of the past with the Party's current interests establishes a chain of legitimacy since the time of the first emperor. The CCP's grand objective of Sino-centric global rule is no longer driven just by socialist revolution but by a corrupted new version of an old political concept. This concept is defined by the simple term Tianxia (tee-yen-sha) or "under heaven".

"Tianxia" is a very old political concept. In dynastic times, this concept is linked with the "Mandate of Heaven". The Mandate of Heaven justifies an emperor's legitimacy to rule as long as he is just, wise, and governs effectively. Tianxia on the other hand, is the justification for the existence of the position of emperor. In the post-dynastic era, the term "Tianxia" is the name for the political strategic objective of the CCP. All-under-heaven is the root of the Tianxia concept which means more than just political borders or territory. The political phrase means everything including the earth, peoples' hearts and minds, and cultural beliefs will be subject to the rule of a strong centralized state in the name of harmony.[i] The ancient argument being that without a strong ruler, the world descends into chaos which only brings hunger, misery, war, and despair. The only way for complete harmony is to have order imposed by one singular authority so there is no conflict about who controls what. Transforming enemies into friends and making multiple conflicting factions into a peaceful singular body politic requires strength and unity of vision. This does not necessarily mean taking the world by force, in fact direct overt force is discouraged and is only to be the last resort. The logic being summed up by military strategist Sun Tzu himself as "Your aim must be to take All-Under-Heaven intact. Thus, your troops are not worn out and your gains will be complete. This is the art of offensive strategy."[ii] Too much destruction increases the risk of chaos so Tianxia not only justifies the CCP's strategic objectives, Tianxia also prescribes the strategic methods for accomplishing the goal.

Even though Tianxia has a long history of being used by dynastic rulers, the CCP still needed Tianxia to be updated to better justify Chinese rule in contemporary times. One of the leaders in this endeavor is the Chinese philosopher Dr. Zhao Tingyang. Dr. Tingyang argues Tianxia, in contrast to many Western political concepts, offers a realistic and viable global political system of order that will help the world evolve beyond nations struggling for power. He argues the concept doesn't offer utopia nor dystopia but is an optimal system conducive to the constraints of reality by eliminating extremes of social excess and deficiencies.[iii] A world in equilibrium whereby global standards and goals are universally set and accepted to direct Humanity's development. An example of how the Tianxia world order would function would be to reduce the wealth differences between nations and have equity more evenly distributed. Poverty itself would not go away but the extremes of poverty such as chronic hunger and gross economic stratification can be eliminated. A realistic and rational goal not bound to radical idealism; a world bound by a 'universalism of compatibility'. Goals universally acceptable without the instability of radical changes or social experiments.[iv]

He advocates abandoning the old-world order established by the West with the United Nations and idealist social advocacy in embracing freedom, free markets, universal rights, etc. because he argues it to be far too hyperbolic, farfetched, and naïve. Dr. Tingyang argues Western societies are trying to create an ideal universalism while Tianxia creates a realistic harmonious environment and system for various nation-states and their competing interests. The West creates disharmony by trying to create an 'end of history' moment, as advocated by Francis Fukuyama's idea of universal liberalism, which runs contrary to history or reality. Interestingly, by rejecting world systems created by idealism that ignore the constraints of reality, Tianxia is also rejecting the Marxist worldview as well. This aligns with the interests of the modern CCP because the CCP always prioritizes Chinese global control over any universalist workers' revolution. Tianxia is to allure world leaders by appealing to realistic goals that include and factor in the interests of all nations, not just Western idealism.

Using Confucian principles as a basis, Tianxia is intended to harmonize the conflicting interests of nations by uniting under a common set of standards that mutually protect all nations' sovereignty. The mutually beneficial interests of this non-Western system would create interdependent relationships that would reduce or eliminate the need for open conflict or drastic divisions. This interdependence would provide economic benefits made by a streamlined and common standard of international trade and commerce. The benefits of this Tianxia system would discourage any nation from leaving the new international system but would still prevent having the world powers imposing universal beliefs on the smaller member nations thus being less intrusive on domestic political affairs. This system would be confederated in that no one could unilaterally act within this system, such as military action or sponsoring terrorist activity without severe cost to the violator. Tianxia would have a common core of standards and protocols for common security and stability as well as preventing violations to the public aka world wellbeing.[v] Ironically, much of what Dr. Tingyang advocates has many commonalities with arguments made by the European Economic Community in the Cold War era of the 20th Century.

Of course, in the abstract this system appears reasonable and less intrusive to its members than the current world system. The modern system has a plethora of organizations such as the UN and its multitude of agencies, or the International Monetary Fund, or World Bank, which often directly interfere with nations' internal affairs for a variety of reasons. However, when one looks at the details of the proposed system of Tianxia, there is a problem. Although there is no demand for a direct world government per se, Tianxia requires a common-world policy making apparatus. Tianxia is focused on order and harmony above idealism but still requires standardized rules for everyone to follow. What body would create the standards of trade, technology requirements, arbitration, and indeed who would define what is the common good? Although not explicit, Dr. Tingyang's system mimics very closely the old dynastic imperial tributary system with China actually having more direct control over the economies of the vassal states. The Imperial Empire of China did not directly rule over all of its holdings. Some kingdoms paid Imperial China in tribute to protect their ruling elites' wealth and power by keeping trade with China open. In modern Tianxia, China would be the lynchpin for international trade and finance. By making China indispensable to the global economy, China would naturally be the dominating "partner" in all world common-policy making by virtue of being the new "middle-kingdom" of the international economy.

The strategic objective of the CCP is to not rule the world in the classic means of territorial conquest or direct acquisition of nations. Instead, the CCP would turn the world into a global collective of vassal states that serve the "international community" that is directed by Beijing. If all countries are harmonized by becoming dependent on China, these nations must balance their interests with the needs of the common good that is defined by the new Sino hegemony. Economic domination means setting standards of technology, both hardware and software, trade, and monetary systems. Such processes would be slow in human terms. Integrating trade and economic dependencies would require decades and must be done without provoking the other major powers interfering. So Tianxia would ultimately mean a globalist neo-Confucian ideal where the common good is sought and order is maintained by a central authority empowered to define and enforce the common good by trade-backed fiat. A confederated empire of trade and cultural domination rather than military domination or at least, not using the military as the primary means of control like the Soviet Empire, is the ideal end state for the CCP.

Tianxia is the grand objective of the CCP. China's system of central control and corruption degrades China over time which means it needs to continually sustain itself by extracting external sources of wealth and influence. CCP-ruled China cannot function on its own so it must leech off as much of the global community as possible to exist while helping the CCP acquire more power and control. Tianxia is the perfect ideological blueprint for the CCP. It forgoes any Marxist obligation to an internationalist workers revolution and replaces it with the notion of a Sino-centric world system that will recreate the dynastic imperial tributary system on a global scale. More Marxist governments and parties would be great for China, but their creation is no longer the main objective. So, how is the CCP going to achieve this grand objective? In this, the CCP faces a historical dilemma dealing with radical changes.

One of the primary tenants of the proposed Tianxia world order is it would make the new international system risk averse. Dr. Tingyang argues the most rational principle for an orderly international system is to create governing rules that eliminate the ability of nations to execute radical actions because these are far less likely to have an optimal outcome for the world. Instead, the system would adjust using 'Confucian Improvement' where nonaggressive strategies are devised to find an optimal compromise that doesn't threaten any nations' vital interest.[vi] Again, this argument appears benign but in strategic terms, this means creating a world system where resistance to the Chinese-led system becomes impossible. The CCP's history shows its system is vulnerable to shocks or sudden changes and Tianxia is a means to avoid them. The Great Leap Forward, the Cultural Revolution, the purging of the Gang of Four, and the Tiananmen Square Massacre each debilitated and paralyzed China's system.

Although the CCP is still in power, one must point out that each of these aforementioned historical events threatened the existence of the CCP. The Great Leap Forward of the 1950s kept China an economic third-world backwater for the rest of Mao's reign and still took an additional two decades of economic repairs to put China on its path to becoming an economic powerhouse. The Cultural Revolution actually removed the CCP from power with Mao and the PLA becoming the sole arbiters of authority in China. Fate or luck saved the CCP by having an actual competent leader in the pragmatic Deng Xiaoping to successfully outmaneuver and defeat the 'Gang of Four's' attempt to seize power in the wake of Mao's death. The Gang of Four were Mao's most committed ideological fanatics in his inner circle and intended to continue Mao's "eternal revolution". Had Deng's struggle for power against the Gang of Four failed, China would likely have suffered a fate similar to modern North Korea as a totalitarian impoverished society ruled by key Maoist personalities rather than the CCP itself. Yet still the Party's foundation was so weak that the Politburo panicked and sent in troops to crush students during peaceful demonstrations at Tiananmen Square in the 1980s. The CCP knows it is at its greatest peril during times of tumultuous upheaval because historically these are times when tyrants are overthrown.

Given lessons of the dynastic past and the Party's own history, the Chinese regime is inherently cautious and methodical when it comes to power maneuvers. So, Tianxia must not only establish a world system that is dominated by China but must also function slowly where the Party can monitor and maneuver against any potential enemy without disrupting economic and social harmony. However, this is only sufficient once the CCP accomplishes its grand objective and Tianxia is actually established. The CCP must still use a grand strategy for how to actually achieve Tianxia while avoiding a hostile backlash to China's grand ambitions from other nations. Overt conflict is inherently risky for any fledgling empire but it is especially dangerous for a system that relies primarily on economic growth for political legitimacy rather than ideological fervor. The solution for the CCP came in 1999 in a PLA's analysis of the United States' performance in the First Gulf War in 1991.

In 1999, the PLA published a book, *Unrestricted Warfare*, which lays out a grand strategy for not only the PLA but the CCP itself. Written by PLA officers Qiao Liang and Wang Xiangsui, *Unrestricted Warfare* coined the name for Tianxia's grand strategy as "Grand Warfare."[vii] The PLA analysts argued the United States' military had entered a new revolutionary phase of warfare that would transform the political use of force into a new form previously unseen in history. The analysis was complex and delved into the many facets of the Gulf War and its immediate aftereffects on military thinking. For the purpose of this analysis, the key relevant points for the purpose of the CCP's Tianxia are the lessons the US military did and did not learn from the First Gulf War. The first point the PLA analysts state is the US military understood and fully appreciated the implications of the military technological revolution where information synchronization, near real-time intelligence, and long-range precision fires would alter how modern armies would fight future wars.[viii] The second point is the US military also understood the need to change doctrinal and organizational orthodoxies to better incorporate information sharing to function in a faster operational tempo in data-centric battles but was less successful at implementing these reforms due to inter-service rivalry and the differing mission parameters between services. However, the most important point the PLA concludes is that the US military was too myopic and did not appreciate the full scope of revolutionary change the Gulf War created.

The PLA authors decry the fact that the US military thinkers only thought about the Gulf War's lessons in strictly military terms. War is fundamentally a political act where one polity compels another polity to acquiesce by force. The PLA thinkers understood that force does not and should not be limited to the force of arms. The PLA concluded the United States invented many of the ideas of this new revolution of war but failed to fully develop these concepts to their maximum potential.[ix] New advanced weaponry and more effective joint coordination were not the sole reasons for the American-led Coalition to achieve its overwhelming victory. The foundations of victory were laid down before combat operations even began. The United States used its diplomatic power to build an international consensus to take back Kuwait while simultaneously restraining Israel from attacking Iraq and convincing wary Arab allies to establish bases and logistical support for the military operations. Then the United States convinced the coalition partners to share the burden of the financial costs of the war while using economic institutions to restrict Iraqi finances. When military actions actually began, the US and its allies fully utilized information and psychological warfare to maintain political support for the war at home while demoralizing Iraqi forces on the ground. The US-led Coalition had, in a very short span of time, utilized every element of the DIME. All instruments of political power, not just the military, were used to gain a quick overwhelming victory against the Saddam regime. This was the true revolution in military affairs born out of the Gulf War, not just the new era of military technology but to also exploit and apply new capabilities derived from advanced technologies to the entire DIME to overwhelm a targeted country across all domains of warfare; this was 'unrestricted warfare' which the PLA analysts would name more eloquently as 'grand warfare'.

In the past, total war meant using military power to target every aspect of a rival society to physically devastate the opponent to the point of either surrender or annihilation. In the post-Gulf War era, the PLA analysts argued for a new form of 'unrestricted warfare'. The new unrestricted warfare would:

transcend all boundaries and limits . . .extending over a broad and all-inclusive range that covers ground, air, sea, space, and cyber realms. Such a strategy takes all things into consideration that are involved in each aspect of the security index of the interests of the entire nation . . .factors on the economy, culture, foreign relations, technology, environment, natural resources, nationalities, and other parameters before one can draw out a complete 'extended domain'.[x]

Instead of destroying an entire nation with raw military might, a nation can be defeated by using every aspect or critical component of a society as attack vectors to achieve total victory without total destruction. Grand warfare would be formulated in two components of two different methodologies: the military method would use force of arms and the non-military method would carry out warfare in every other dimension of political affairs to include diplomatic, informational, and economic.[xi]

The post-Gulf War US military thinkers understood the technical revolution for the military method but failed to notice the second non-military method of using the rest of the DIME for war. In fairness, this critique is born out of cultural bias. As stated earlier, authoritarian societies do not make legal or social distinctions between public and private. Western militaries are given the public role of national physical defense and will focus on this role exclusively as part of the social contract that maintains checks and balances on state power while keeping the private citizens free to pursue their own legitimate goals within the society. In China, the state is all encompassing which gave the PLA analysts the unique foresight to identify the full potential of unrestricted warfare as the Chinese state can wield any institution or person as it deems fit. In fact, the PLA analysts' division of grand warfare into two separate methods of unrestricted warfare easily fit into already established Chinese military thinking. Sun Tzu himself had created two separate means of military strategy that easily incorporates and overlaps grand warfare's contemporary methodology.

Sun Tzu identified two types of forces in war, the regular or direct military force known as 'zheng', and the extraordinary or indirect force known as 'qi'. Zheng is the traditional means of war using armies to attack and defeat an opponent. Qi are the means of an attack to strike when and where the enemy has not anticipated.[xii] Grand warfare combines zheng and qi which in Western geopolitical parlance means using all political instruments of the DIME simultaneously to defeat China's opponents in the most comprehensive and cost-effective way possible. *Unrestricted Warfare* is the PLA's report that helped China identify the modern qi that can be used against the West. Since the West traditionally views war only as using violent means of compulsion, its societies will be blind to other forms of indirect non-military attack that China can exploit for victory. If properly utilized, the CCP can wage war against the West indirectly without the West realizing its being attacked. Qi can be waged in times of official peace and lay down the foundations for a victory in a direct military confrontation before open hostilities even begin. This unrestricted grand warfare is the strategy China is using to achieve the objective of Tianxia with the zheng and qi being the methods to execute China's grand strategy. China cannot supplant the United States until the world truly believes China is stronger than the United States in all elements of the DIME. If the United States becomes so dependent on China that America cannot risk waging war to defend itself, then America becomes subservient to China. Zheng and qi create the circumstances to ensure America is defeated in any overt confrontation but preparing modern qi takes time. The following chapters deal with how China is preparing zheng and using qi to ensure victory before any open confrontation even begins.

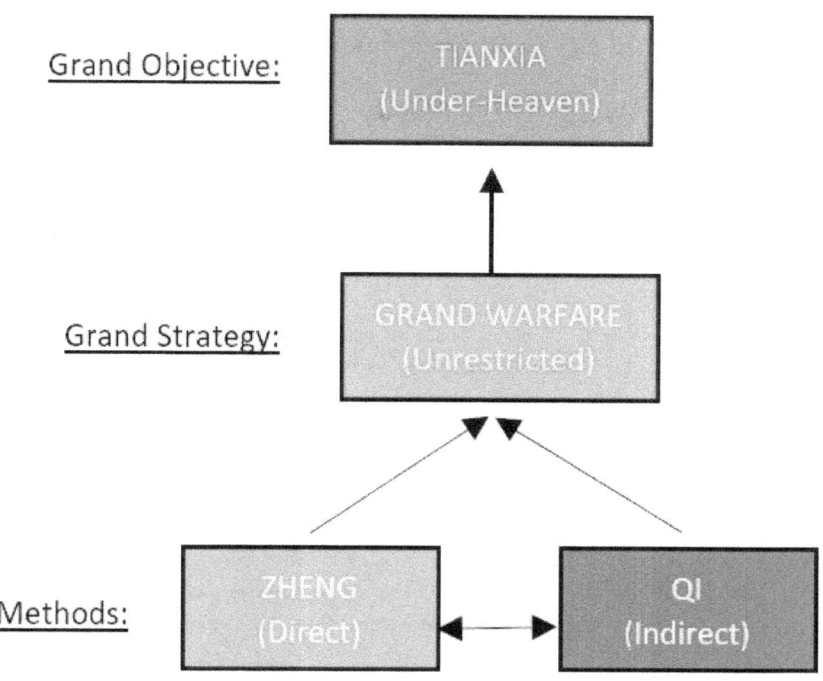

Grand Objective: TIANXIA (Under-Heaven)

Grand Strategy: GRAND WARFARE (Unrestricted)

Methods: ZHENG (Direct) — QI (Indirect)

[i] Fei-Ling Wang, *The China Order: Centralia, World Empire, and the Nature of Chinese Power*, (Albany, NY: State of University of New York Press, 2017) 7, 44-48, 50-52, 65-67.

[ii] Sun Tzu, *The Art of War*, translated by Samuel B. Griffith (NY: Oxford University Press, 1963) 79.

[iii] Zhao Tingyang, "'All-Under-Heaven' (Tianxia): Between Idealism and Realism," Journal of Global Ethics, v. 17, n. 1, June 25, 2021, 27-28. https://doi.org/10.1080/17449626.2021.1964579

[iv] Ibid, 28.

[v] Ibid, 35-36.

[vi] Zhao Tingyang, "'All-Under-Heaven' (Tianxia): Between Idealism and Realism," Journal of Global Ethics, v. 17, n. 1, June 25, 2021, 36-37. https://doi.org/10.1080/17449626.2021.1964579

[vii] Qiao Liang and Wang Xiangsui, *Unrestricted Warfare*, (VT: Echo Point Books & Media, originally published in 1999) 97-98.

[viii] Ibid, 13-17.

[ix] Ibid, 82-86, 94.

[x] Ibid, 5, 54, 97.

[xi] Ibid, 98.

[xii] David Lai, "Learning from the Stones: A 'Go' Approach to Mastering China's Strategic Concept, Shi," Strategic Studies Institute, US Army War College, May 2004, 4-6. https://man.fas.org/eprint/lai.pdf

Chapter 5: Zheng – Direct Force (Military Means)

The CCP's greatest chance of successfully becoming the global hegemon by the mid-21st Century is by peacefully co-opting the global economy and gradually wearing down opposition by economic addiction. Any breakdown with the West that could lead to war would seriously imperil CCP rule due to its fragile foundations. The power of central absolutism relies on rival nations to be cooperative and remain passive victims from which the Party can continue to parasitically leech wealth to sustain China. Tianxia is the gradual zombification of the world's nations to China's encroachment and this 'peaceful' conquest is the least risky and most optimal course of action to ensure the Party's survival. However, as the People's Republic of China gains more power and prominence, the more likely other nations will begin to recognize the CCP's methods and ultimate intent. Especially since national governments become increasingly overconfident and hubristic with growing success, making intentions even more difficult to hide as they get closer to accomplishing their goals. China's government is no exception to this behavior. The CCP leadership are not deluded and understand they must prepare for the worst contingencies which means their military power is as critical as economic power in their pursuit of global hegemony.

The People's Liberation Army's (PLA) mission is to be the CCP's ultimate enforcer when all other instruments of power fail. Unlike other major armies, this military is the armed forces of the Party itself and not China. Its soldiers are pledged to protecting the CCP first and foremost with China being a secondary priority. The PLA, as a matter of self-preservation, will carry out hostilities if ordered to do so by the senior military command authority, the Central Military Commission. Note the Central Military Commission is a CCP organization and not a state one.[i] For all of the CCP's attempts to obfuscate its role in China's economy, it has no compunction in boasting about its control over the military. In fact, the oath taken by PLA military personnel states emphatically:

I am a member of the People's Liberation Army. I promise that I will follow the leadership of the Communist Party of China, serve the people wholeheartedly, obey orders, strictly observe discipline, fight heroically, fear no sacrifice, loyally discharge my duties, work hard, practice hard to master combat skills, and resolutely fulfill my missions. Under no circumstances will I betray the Motherland or desert the army.[ii]

The lessons learned from the Cultural Revolution and the Tiananmen Square Massacre on instilling loyalty to the Party remains a vital lynchpin to the CCP's continued existence.

The Party understands that a weak military means China cannot physically compel its enemies to adhere to CCP interests, leaving pockets of resistance to build and promulgate if war ever comes. Alternative indirect means of war on their own such as cyberattacks, covert operations, and small-scale attacks have limitations which cannot sufficiently subdue a determined opponent if the fight is existential in nature. Indirect means are meant to inhibit or cripple an adversary's ability to resist but not destroy it. Without having overt direct power to confront and physically destroy an opponent, China would simply provoke adversaries to escalate beyond the CCP's ability to stop them. A lethal overpowering military remains a critical instrument of power for not only rendering a threat harmless but also for psychologically convincing the world that resistance is futile and capitulation is the better choice.

This is why China invests so heavily in modernizing their ability to use direct force, the zheng, even as China pursues 'peaceful' policies of Tianxia throughout the world. Like the other instruments of political power in the DIME, zheng covers a wide range of options based on the scale and severity required. Large-scale military operations are at the most extreme end of the spectrum of military actions but there is a large number of smaller scale actions China would more likely use to keep potential damage to China's Tianxia efforts to a minimum. These smaller scale options fall under the category of combat-related gray-zone warfare. Such actions are for the moment confined to the far western portion of the Pacific, Indo-Chinese border, and Central Asia. The actions are performed in places the PLA can sustain and reinforce its forces while also having the ability to overwhelm its opponent with superior numbers and firepower if there is a need. These combat-related gray-zone activities are referred to by the PLA as the "peacetime employment of force" in which the PLA confronts an opponent, in the most important case Taiwan, without escalating into open war.[iii]

Taiwan is the most important strategic location because it is the most likely point of contention where American and Chinese forces could potentially clash in open warfare. Again, the Party hopes for peaceful assimilation of Taiwan back into Chinese control because of the severe economic and political costs of war. China states this openly and conveys this messaging to the West to try to help allay fears of war and often is noticed by think tanks and pro-peace organizations. [iv] Ultimately, China hopes Taiwan's elites, like so many in other nations, will let avarice take hold and blind them to Taiwan's gradual submission to CCP control in exchange for easy money-making ventures while using cultural institutions and personalities to persuade the Taiwanese population.[v], [vi] Yet, the CCP knows a stick will make its economic carrots more attractive.[vii] For this reason, Taiwan is the main effort of the PLA's "peaceful employment of forces." Gray-zone zheng actions are meant to intimidate the militarily weaker Taiwan into conceding to Chinese political demands without destabilizing the region by using open war. The wide variety of military gray-zone options are all based on using China's overwhelming naval and air advantage to intimidate Taiwan into complying with CCP interests such as avoiding independence.[viii] Each action is provocative to cause consternation and also create sufficient fear to deter Taiwan from escalating the incidents into an existential war.

Numerous examples have occurred since the end of the Cold War. At sea, the PLA Navy harasses Taiwanese or American vessels in Taiwanese territorial waters to demonstrate sovereign control over the Taiwanese strait. In the air, the PLA has arbitrarily changed the boundaries of their proclaimed East China Sea Air Defense Identification Zone. This area of airspace is deemed critical to Chinese national security and declared off-limits to foreign aircraft. Any aircraft in violation could be shot down for violating Chinese airspace or so the declaration would state. Such actions discourage civil aviation and Taiwanese air defense patrols must cede certain air corridors, making Taiwan more vulnerable to air attack, even briefly.[ix] Naturally, all of these actions are intended to intimidate politicians in the United States, Taiwan, and to a lesser degree, Japan from changing their defense posture to an aggressive one against China.[x]

For the purposes of this analysis, the only scenario of concern is the CCP deciding to resort to a full-scale invasion of Taiwan. The fundamental assumption of this book's thesis is the CCP wants to avoid direct confrontation with the West for as long as possible to maximize the probability of successfully implementing its Tianxia policy. If war happens with the United States in a Taiwan confrontation before the CCP can effectively insulate itself and China from the negative effects of such an event, then the Party will likely collapse even if there is a military victory. The CCP remains risk averse for this reason and will only carry out overt action when it is overwhelmingly confident in the outcome before hostilities commence. At the moment, the CCP is indicating it is unlikely to be confident of success because the PLA doesn't have the ability to achieve absolute victory.[xi], [xii]

To ensure success, China is preparing both its direct (zheng) and indirect (qi) forces to help set the stage and shape the battlefield for victory. Such preparations will involve the same tools the CCP can use to subvert and instigate civil war in targeted Western countries as well. In order to analyze the scenario of the civil war, one must understand the warfare tools of zheng and qi China would use in a war. Each method will be briefly analyzed and shown how each integrates with the overall grand warfare as espoused by *Unrestricted Warfare*. The first is the most obvious and public, the direct force of military action otherwise known as zheng.

Taiwanese sovereignty is the main issue over which the CCP is willing to openly start a war. Taiwan is the lynchpin for multiple strategic objectives vital to the continuing existence of the Party. Firstly, the Chinese government has committed a considerable amount of political capital backing the assertion Taiwan belongs to China.[xiii] The CCP failed to completely defeat its rival in the Chinese Civil War, meaning there exists another political system that has the historical and cultural background to potentially challenge the CCP's legitimacy as the rightful governing authority for China.[xiv] Both the governments of Taiwan and China have declared the island was part of China as the island was annexed by the Qing in the 17th Century and taken back after the fall of Japan. When the KMT fled to the island in 1949, Taiwan's political lineage has a contiguous connection to mainland China going back to the formation of the Republic of China in 1912 and its founder Sun Yat-Sen. A totalitarian state cannot have an opposition, especially one that has potential legitimacy in the eyes of the Chinese population.

Secondly, the CCP has already committed its reputation and linked its future to Taiwan's fate. In the early 21st Century, the Chinese regime passed an anti-secession law clearly referring to Taiwan and rejecting any notion that any territory claimed by the CCP as rightfully Chinese can legally leave the grasp of the CCP.[xv], [xvi] In a culture of miànzi, the Party must honor its commitments to demonstrate to its subjects and subordinate party members, the leadership of China is strong in both will and political power. In totalitarian and authoritarian systems, some form of "might makes right" always exists for its leadership because there are no legal checks or balances to peacefully remove the leadership cadre of a regime. The only way is through usurpation and that only happens when regime rivals sense weakness. If the CCP leadership fails to act in asserting its sovereign control over claimed territory or cannot follow through on declared threats, the leadership will be at risk of being deposed. By committing themselves, the CCP leaders portray themselves as a regime of confidence and strength but simultaneously limit their options if a crisis does unfold. Even if the CCP are unprepared or disinclined, they are politically compelled to act against Taiwan if sufficiently provoked.

Finally, Taiwan does not just represent a test of the CCP's reputation, it is also a major test of China's ability to become the global hegemon. Even though centuries old, the PLA Navy still study the 19th Century US Navy Admiral Mahan's analysis on naval strategy and the importance of controlling the vital sea lanes. Although warfare has changed, the fundamentals of strategic domination remain the same. Admiral Mahan stated that one of the principal elements of sea power is controlling key strategic points to achieve victory in war and domination during peace. Having control of key geographic areas or terrain help a sea trade dependent nation like China avoid having its trade and military from being corralled and blocked. A nation losing the ability to trade on the sea and ceding to foreign navies the freedom to maneuver in their own territorial waters perpetually keeps that nation weak and vulnerable.[xvii] If the United States remains the only guarantor of protecting the sea lanes, then the United States wields overwhelming economic and military influence throughout the Indo-Pacific region.

Taiwan has become a bastion of democratic-republicanism and an outpost for Western influence thus preventing China's uncontested access to the Pacific. By keeping Taiwan separate from China, the West has incontestable domination over the open Pacific and enables the US Navy to be the exclusive guarantor of the major sea lanes that feed the world economy. With Japan and South Korea in the north and a potential ally in the Philippines to the south, Taiwan acts as part of a natural barrier that could help encircle and contain Chinese forces in the event of hostilities.[xviii] China needs Taiwan as a geographic foothold to break out and gain direct uncontested access to the open Pacific. If China can succeed in this action, then China can dictate military dominance in the Pacific while convincingly persuade many nations that it can be a legitimate alternate guarantor of securing the sea lanes and trade in the world's busiest shipping lanes.[xix] If such events occur, global opinion would likely conclude the United States is in decline because it lost its most prominent military command of the most vital waters in global commerce.

One more tertiary strategic implication to consider but one that is rarely acknowledged is Taiwan's role in the global technology economy. Many observers understand the economic implications of war in the Middle East or war in Ukraine and Russia because each war impacts vital commodities that can disrupt entire continents but few appreciate the criticality of semiconductors. Unless one looks at the microchip and CPU industry, few know Taiwan now holds the most advanced semiconductor corporation and fabrication foundries on Earth. As the COVID plague era demonstrated, the disruption to microchip supply chains can cripple major manufacturing and technology industries. Despite all of China's boasting, the nation is still behind the West, Japan, Korea, and Taiwan in semiconductor and microchip technology. They can supply many of the supporting chip elements, assembly of boards, and less advanced chips but China lacks the ability to manufacture the cutting-edge microprocessors that drive advanced technological systems and developments.[xx] If China were to seize the Taiwan Semiconductor Manufacturing Company (TSMC), then China goes from a technology underdog to the dominating technology power overnight. The most advanced chips, designs, and processes would all be in the hands of the CCP and its subordinate companies. Some might dismiss this as overblown fear but China often uses economic intimidation to cudgel business partners and international institutions into complying. These semiconductors are the life's blood of all advanced technology industries in the same way oil is to the manufacturing industry. If China controls these chips, then China will have direct access to all advanced technological development globally. This bonus factor does further incentivize China to try to take Taiwan back peacefully to avoid the risk of destroying TSMC but no incentive will deter China from resorting to war if the Party believes Taiwan cannot be subjugated peacefully. These are the major strategic incentives for China in taking back Taiwan from Western influence. Yet, power trumps all other considerations and China will sacrifice global economic wellbeing in the short term if it needs to destroy the TSMC as a price to conquer Taiwan.[xxi] All of these considerations make the issue of Taiwanese freedom from the CCP not just an academic moral debate but a central strategic interest for United States and its Pacific allies.

Even with all of these motivations, the potential disruption to global commerce and economic stability of China is, as of 2024, too risky for it to launch an invasion of the island. To invade the CCP needs one of two conditions. The first being the Taiwanese openly declare independence or the CCP is convinced Taiwan can only be reacquired with force while also being confident of a quick military victory. The biggest concern in the CCP's calculation is on whether the United States and its allies would actually militarily intervene if all-out war broke out between Taiwan and China. The answer would likely depend on who the president of the United States is at the time of the war. The CCP, like Westerners, have their own presumptions, cultural biases, and perceptions. Autocrats have difficulty predicting the decisions of the United States because they cannot conceive there are multiple groups whose influence on policy waxes and wanes depending on political circumstance and popularity. China and others often look at what government institutions and senior leaders say without considering Western domestic population expectations. American interest groups and advocates make cases supporting both sides of this argument. Some believe peaceful coexistence can be achieved without confrontation, like the Atlantic Council, which often advocates for engagement with China.[xxii] Some even broach the argument that the United States should cede the Western Pacific security role to China to avoid a potential nuclear conflict.[xxiii] Contrast this with American leaders making statements that America will unambiguously defend Taiwan; so no amount of messaging from the West is likely to alleviate CCP paranoia about Western intervention.[xxiv] With the CCP assessing everything from a power perspective, the West would be safer in assuming the CCP and the PLA will likely target the US, Japan, and others before open hostilities commence to ensure China's victory.

The CCP understands how the international system works and reacts to military actions. The international community, despite its title, only acts to serve the interests of the various parties represented within the community. Tyranny, atrocities, carnage, and suffering is addressed only when it is convenient to do so. Moral courage is found only when it is safe for international and supranational organizations to do so. These organizations are lumbering and beholden to many various interests, all linked to the political elites of the member nation-states. Since these organizations balance the interests of so many conflicting parties, international bodies can only consider the immediate future since they are only empowered to reach agreements on issues brought up to the bodies. In a quick decisive war where one side, particularly an economically powerful one, gains the upper hand and can seize its intended target before any counteraction can be organized, then the international community will often accept the outcome. In such a situation, challenging an aggressive power after the fact will be more costly in both financial and political terms. Instead, the international community will make platitudes, virtuous gestures, and shed crocodile tears but ultimately accept the situation as a fait-accompli. China has seen the precedent the UN and others have set and takes it to heart. The most recent and pertinent examples being both Russia's invasion of Crimea and Georgia where some relatively minor sanctions were imposed but nothing to seriously impact Russia's trade with Europe.[xxv], [xxvi] In fact, China saw many in Europe trying to forgive Russia after Crimea and push for getting sanctions lifted for short-term economic benefits proving that all geopolitical sins are forgiven provided there is an economic incentive to do so in international politics.[xxvii] That forgiveness of course all changed with the 2022 Invasion of Ukraine which also demonstrated the inverse of this rule of passive acceptance.

Russia showed that quick conquests, no matter how aggressive or egregious, can be forgiven because it only minimally disrupts the international system. No doubt President Putin was counting on this when he intended for a quick one-month war in Ukraine which has instead degenerated into a protracted quagmire. Only when the war was certain to be a protracted long fight after Russia's failure to quickly capture Kyiv did the international community at large decided to find the "moral" courage against the Russian invasion.[xxviii] Protracted conflicts disrupt the international system and there is little political cost in actively condemning or working against such an aggressor state because the aggressor state is now costing the international interest groups more by prolonged uncertainty and supply chain disruption. If China moves before it's ready, it risks severe economic shocks as global commerce is disrupted and uncertainty grips investors and foreign elites. The longer the conflict, the more open resistance and condemnation China will experience. Furthermore, if the conflict becomes protracted and the PLA's reputation suffers humiliation, then the risk of factional infighting will grow as fear of defeat would expose the current CCP leadership to a party-led purge. Unlike Russia, China's leadership must consider the one additional factor of having "no backup trade partners" if the war fails. Relatively speaking, Russia is an economic pygmy on the global market and can slowly shift to alternate trade partners in Asia after Europe became hostile, even if the results have been mixed.

[xxix], [xxx] China has no alternates. China is the be-all and end-all for authoritarian economies across the globe. If war breaks out and becomes a drawn-out bloody affair then China will not be able to find alternate sources of income. Russia certainly cannot reciprocate and be a place holder for Japan, Korea, the Anglosphere, and the European Union. Fear of defeat in war leading to political defeat at home stays the aggressive hands of the CCP leadership for now.

So, the CCP and People's Liberation Army (PLA) will continuously prepare its forces until the CCP leadership is confident victory is assured even before the first shot is fired. This will take some time and despite all the propaganda of China's military, the PLA is still not considered an equal to the United States or even a world class military. The last few decades have yielded many technological modernizations for China based on its successful espionage of Western technology but there are still major gaps.[xxxi], [xxxii] Lessons learned from Russia's invasion prove that having both a proficiently trained force and the logistical means to sustain it, are vital and exceed the value of having high-class weaponry. China doesn't have any major military allies in the region and the PLA's training is conducted by leadership with little to no actual combat experience. The effectiveness of PLA soldiers and their training is unknown, but the few instances of the PLA engaging with their rivals on the Indian border indicate that China might be suffering from the same affliction as the Russian Army.[xxxiii], [xxxiv] The reports and training outcomes might be written to show what the senior leaders want it to show rather than reflect what is actually happening. The quality of the PLA's performance under fire will remain an uncertainty until actual combat but it must be concerning enough for China to continue developing its forces until at least 2027 according to US analysts. A symbolic year for the PLA as it would mark the 100th Anniversary of the Shanghai Massacre when the KMT nearly annihilated the CCP.

The PLA being combat ready also requires logistical support with excellent reliability and timely delivery. Russia's poor logistical planning and corrupt mismanagement prevented a quick victory in Ukraine, but Russia was still able to relocate logistical supply trains and lines of communication when their commanders decided to change their strategic objectives to more limited aims in Eastern Ukraine. China does not have this luxury. On a global map Taiwan doesn't appear too far away but 150 km of water between the mainland and the island a major exposed gap that any PLA army will have to bridge to sustain combat forces on the island.[xxxv] Even if China overwhelms the air and sea defenses, the PLA troops still have to land on the island, secure a population of 23 million people, and have access to critical supplies while doing so. If the invasion force is cut off from the mainland due to high ship losses or becomes encircled, then the PLA will have little ability to regain the momentum of the invasion. An amphibious invasion must continuously push forth until it can break out and establish secure key points deep within enemy territory, allowing the beachheads to be secure and become a reliable bridge to overseas supplies.[xxxvi] This means China can only invade with overwhelming firepower and sufficient numbers to absorb the high attrition the initial invaders will suffer. Building up sufficient amphibious platforms, professional troops, and sufficient air and sea support takes time and China is patient.

Still, all of this preparation does not guarantee victory. Ukraine was invaded when it was unprepared yet it still brought a major military power to a standstill with Western aid. If Taiwan can inflict sufficient losses on the PLA to stall the invasion long enough for Western aid to arrive, even if it is only weapons and ammunition supplies, then China would likely suffer defeat. In such circumstances, China would likely have to resort to nuclear weapons which the Party almost certainly wants to avoid to save their own skin. China's economy cannot sustain itself if its major ports are near nuclear detonations and the international loss of face and fear from foreign investors and traders. This is why China and the CCP do not rely on just the military for solutions against their opponents.

Unrestricted Warfare is a book that updated the CCP on both its zheng and qi and one that the Chinese leadership have embraced to ensure victory. China is still building up its direct forces in the form of the PLA but is also using its indirect force to exploit Western weaknesses.[xxxvii] The indirect elements of China's operations act as force-multipliers for any future conflict as the West remains focused on military solutions. China's qi focuses on the informational, economic, and diplomatic elements of the DIME to debilitate Western and Taiwanese responses to China's actions. The West's weakness is that it doesn't fully appreciate or understand the implications of China's "grand warfare". The West enables China's qi to be more effective than it would otherwise be against nations fully cognizant of the indirect attack concept. The Western concept of private vs. public activities prevents general understanding that all activities are considered by the CCP to be public (for use by the state). These acts of qi are the iron claws the West has given to the paper dragon China.

China is using qi now against its rivals and competitors to weaken Western competition but not debilitate it to the point of open conflict. Qi focuses on exploiting areas and activities the West ignores or doesn't implement countermeasures against because the West doesn't fully understand the operational and strategic impact. In the case of a CCP-induced war with the West, these indirect means of qi can be escalated to the point of outright social disruption before combat operations would begin. Successfully initiating qi to war-levels will paralyze a civic society to the point of being incapable of fully mobilizing its military assets for weeks or months. In such circumstances, the indirect force of qi will prevent any Western military reaction from responding long enough for the PLA, China's direct force of zheng, to defeat and conquer Taiwan. Chinese victory relies on unrestricted warfare in both forms of zheng and qi to win a war in the Pacific but will also rely on the same mechanisms for any action that escalates conflict beyond the Pacific and Taiwan. The zheng is straightforward but the qi is not obvious to Westerners and their classic biased views on traditional warfare. To fully grasp China's modern unrestricted warfare, the qi must now be examined to ultimately understand how civil war in the West can be instigated.

---

[i] Congressional Research Service, "China's Political System in Charts: A Snapshot Before the 20th Party Congress," CRS Reports, November 24, 2021, 15-16. https://crsreports.congress.gov/product/pdf/R/R46977

[ii] Dennis J. Blasko, *The Chinese Army Today: Tradition and Transformation for the 21st Century*, (NY: Routledge Taylor & Francis Group, 2006) 51.

[iii] Roderick Lee and Marcus Clay, "Don't Call It a Gray Zone: China's Use of Force Spectrum," War on the Rocks, May 9, 2022. https://warontherocks.com/2022/05/dont-call-it-a-gray-zone-chinas-use-of-force-spectrum/

[iv] Zheng Wang, "Ukraine's Wrong Lessons for Taiwan," National Interest, May 1, 2022. https://nationalinterest.org/feature/ukraine%E2%80%99s-wrong-lessons-taiwan-202113?page=0%2C1

[v] Jason Li, "China's Surreptitious Economic Influence on Taiwan's Elections," The Diplomat, April 12, 2019. https://thediplomat.com/2019/04/chinas-surreptitious-economic-influence-on-taiwans-elections/

[vi] VOA, "China Steps Up Efforts to Influence Taiwan with Soft Power," Voice of America News, September 14, 2019. https://learningenglish.voanews.com/a/china-steps-up-efforts-to-influence-taiwan-with-soft-power/5079784.html

[vii] Bryce Barros and Mary Ogbuehi, "What the United States Can Learn From Chinese Economic Coercion in South Korea, Australia, and Taiwan," Alliance for Securing Democracy, April 19, 2022. https://securingdemocracy.gmfus.org/what-the-united-states-can-learn-from-chinese-economic-coercion-in-south-korea-australia-and-taiwan/

[viii] Michael Green, Kathleen Hicks, et al, Countering Coercion in Maritime Asia: Theory and Practice of Gray Zone Deterrence, (NYC: Center for Strategic & International Studies Rowman & Littlefield, May 2017) 21-25.

[ix] Ibid, 52-55, 148-151.

[x] Adam Liff, "Has Japan's Policy Toward the Taiwan Strait Changed?" Washington Post, August 18, 2021. https://www.washingtonpost.com/politics/2021/08/18/has-japans-policy-toward-taiwan-strait-changed/

[xi] John A. Tirpak, "In CNAS-Led Taiwan Wargame, No Air Superiority, No Quick Win," Air Force Magazine, May 17, 2022. https://www.airforcemag.com/in-cnas-led-taiwan-wargame-no-air-superiority-no-quick-win/

[xii] Chris Pleasance, Ross Ibbetson, and Chris Jewers, "China 'will be Ready for a Full-Scale Invasion of Taiwan by 2025'," Daily Mail, October 6, 2021. https://www.dailymail.co.uk/news/article-10063831/China-ready-scale-invasion-Taiwan-2025.html

[xiii] Rear Admiral Alfred Thayer Mahan, Mahan on Naval Strategy, (Annapolis, MD: Naval Institute Press, 2015) 53-61.

[xiv] John Culver, "The Unfinished Chinese Civil War," The Lowy Institute – The Interpreter, September 30, 2020. https://www.lowyinstitute.org/the-interpreter/unfinished-chinese-civil-war

[xv] Xinhua News, "Anti-Secession Law Adopted by the National People's Congress," China Daily, March 14, 2005. https://www.chinadaily.com.cn/english/doc/2005-03/14/content_424643.htm

[xvi] Kerry Brown, The Chinese 19th Party Congress: Start of a New Era, (London: World Scientific Publishing Europe Ltd., 2018) 20-21.

[xvii] Rear Admiral Alfred Thayer Mahan, Mahan on Naval Strategy, (Annapolis, MD: Naval Institute Press, 2015) 30-37, 97-107.

[xviii] Felix K. Chang, "China's Encirclement Concerns," Foreign Policy Research Institute, June 24, 2016. https://www.fpri.org/2016/06/chinas-encirclement-concerns/

[xix] National Defense University, "The Chinese Navy: Expanding Capabilities, Evolving Roles," Center for the Study of Chinese Military Affairs, 2011, 215-221. https://ndupress.ndu.edu/portals/68/documents/books/chinese-navy.pdf

[xx] Rhett Hatch, "Why China's Semiconductor Industry Remains Behind," National Interest, January 31, 2022. https://nationalinterest.org/blog/buzz/why-china%E2%80%99s-semiconductor-industry-remains-behind-200143

[xxi] Christopher Vassallo, "The 'Silicon Shield' is a Danger to Taiwan and American," National Interest, May 15, 2022. https://nationalinterest.org/feature/%E2%80%98silicon-shield%E2%80%99-danger-taiwan-and-america-202363

[xxii] Robert A. Manning, "The United States Can Negotiate with a China Driven More by Power than Ideology," Foreign Policy Magazine, December 4, 2020. https://foreignpolicy.com/2020/12/04/us-negotiate-china-power-ideology-coexist/

[xxiii] Lami Kim, "Should the United States Defend or Ditch Taiwan?" National Interest, June 3, 2022. https://nationalinterest.org/feature/should-united-states-defend-or-ditch-taiwan-202772

[xxiv] Christina Lu, "Biden Vows to Defend Taiwan," Foreign Policy Morning Brief, May 24. 2022. https://foreignpolicy.com/2022/05/24/biden-taiwan-china-defense-policy/

[xxv] UN Press Release, "Security Council Fails to Adopt Text Urging Member States Not to Recognize Planned 16 March Referendum in Ukraine's Crimea Region," United Nations, March 15, 2014. https://www.un.org/press/en/2014/sc11319.doc.htm

[xxvi] Steven Pifer, "Five Years after Crimea's Illegal Annexation, the Issue is no Closer to Resolution," Brookings Institute, March 18, 2019. https://www.brookings.edu/blog/order-from-chaos/2019/03/18/five-years-after-crimeas-illegal-annexation-the-issue-is-no-closer-to-resolution/

[xxvii] European Union Committee, "The EU and Russia: Before and Beyond the Crisis in Ukraine," House of Lords, February 20, 2015, 27-31. https://publications.parliament.uk/pa/ld201415/ldselect/ldeucom/115/115.pdf

[xxviii] Rick Noack, Emily Rauhala, and Griff Witte, "As Over 100,000 Rally for Ukraine, Germany Announces Vast Defense Spending Increase that May Upend European Security Policy," Washington Post, February 27, 2022. https://www.washingtonpost.com/world/2022/02/27/europe-germany-defense-russia-ukraine/

[xxix] Natasha Turak, "How Much Can – and Will – China Help Russia as it Economy Crumbles?" CNBC, March 16, 2022. https://www.cnbc.com/2022/03/16/how-much-can-and-will-china-help-russia-as-its-economy-crumbles.html

[xxx] Bobo Lo, "Turning Point? Putin, Xi, and the Russian Invasion of Ukraine," Lowy Institute, May 25, 2022. https://www.lowyinstitute.org/publications/turning-point-putin-xi-and-russian-invasion-ukraine

[xxxi] Office of the Secretary of Defense, "Military and Security Developments Involving the People's Republic of China," Department of Defense, November 2021, 29-34. https://media.defense.gov/2021/Nov/03/2002885874/-1/-1/0/2021-CMPR-FINAL.PDF

[xxxii] Testimony of LTC (R) Dennis J. Blasko, "PLA Weaknesses and Xi's Concerns about PLA Capabilities," US-China Economic and Security Review Commission, February 7, 2019, 5-8. https://www.uscc.gov/sites/default/files/Blasko_USCC%20Testimony_FINAL.pdf

[xxxiii] Ross Ibbetson, "India Says its Soldiers were Mutilated after Being Beaten to Death by Chinese Troops in Brutal Himalayan Border Battle – and reveals the Nail-Embedded Sticks Used in Brawl," Daily Mail, June 18, 2020. https://www.dailymail.co.uk/news/article-8435033/India-says-soldiers-mutilated-beaten-death-Chinese-soldiers.html

[xxxiv] Zaid Hamid Best Comedian, "Exclusive Video from Beijing Military station after soldiers posted there were transferred to Ladakh Border to face Indian Army," Facebook, September 19, 2020. https://www.facebook.com/ZaiduHamid.BC/videos/2680500612201596/?extid=lndNLVfSyZecNl11

[xxxv] US Army War College, "The Chinese People's Liberation Army in 2025," Strategic Studies Institute, July 2015, 83-93. https://press.armywarcollege.edu/monographs/9/

[xxxvi] Ian Easton, "China's Top Five War Plans," Project 2019 Institute, January 6, 2019, 2-5. https://project2049.net/wp-content/uploads/2019/01/Chinas-Top-Five-War-Plans_Ian_Easton_Project2049.pdf

[xxxvii] Qiao Liang and Wang Xiangsui, Unrestricted Warfare, (VT: Echo Point Books & Media, originally published in 1999) 116-119.

Chapter 6: Qi – Indirect Force (Non-Military Means)

When properly executed, the forces of zheng and qi balance each other's strengths and cancel out the weaknesses to achieve victory by the effective use of resources at minimal risk. In books of military theory and academic discussion, experts discuss various formulae on how to achieve this success in an ideal setting. Of course, reality intervenes and disrupts all "ideal" models for executing any plan. In the book *On War*, General Clausewitz referred to real-world variables that disrupt the ideal plan as "friction".[i] The authors of *Unrestricted Warfare* themselves warned that grasping the ideal theoretical potential of the concept is only the first step to understanding the use of "grand warfare" and users must further understand the limitations imposed on "grand warfare" by the reality of the circumstances.[ii] This is why the Chinese implementation of qi can never be fully executed to perfection because friction exists for the non-military indirect force as much as it does for lethal force. In fact, one of the reasons China's qi is so successful is that the CCP doesn't contort to an elaborate preconceived "ideal" plan.

The CCP has been using qi, the category of non-combat gray-zone warfare, for decades but many of the qi-related actions are not necessarily executed as part of a contiguous grand unified plan. As stated earlier in the book, to implement a plan from start to finish with every step assigned a specific set of tasks to achieve the final objective requires both perfect information and perfect understanding. As much as the CCP desires to be God-like, they of course don't come close. Reality of circumstance prevents the PLA and CCP from anticipating all events and whatever qi plans exist are likely only for short term goals and foreseeable needs. There is an overall grand objective, global hegemony, which shapes and directs the zheng and qi efforts but these plans are ad hoc. Ad hoc in this instance typically means carrying out plans within a decade, a typical strategic short-term span of time where at least some of the issues can be foreseen with some accuracy. Any attempt by the Party to stick to a top-down derived plan for all actions is doomed to failure.

Few examples of history better demonstrate the dangers of planning-hubris than the German Army in the beginning of World War I with their doomed inflexible adherence to the Von Schlieffen Plan. This planned invasion for defeating France was based on historic concepts and actions of the early 19th Century and failed to update to the contemporary circumstances of 1914. The German high command's inflexibility in adhering to the 'scythe-sweep' maneuvering in North France doomed the German Army's hopes for a quick war precisely because it required a very strict timeline to be achieved in a rapid sequence. Ignoring issues such as communications between units, Allied resistance, or problems with the terrain contributed greatly to Germany's failed initial invasion of France.[iii] Grand plans and elaborate schemes fail in reality because too many things exist beyond the planners' control. This is often why many conspiracy theorists tend to exaggerate and overstate the powers of the group they accuse of nefarious activity. Too often these theories are portrayed as being executed by people with infinite perception and understanding with the ability to plan out every action with every consequence being mapped out and considered. Such assumptions blind observers to the true actions of these nefarious actors.

In reality, planners of intrigue such as the CCP rely on advantageous circumstances, opportune moments, and exploiting corruptibility wherever it's discovered when actually implementing qi. The CCP's pragmatism allows its bureaucracy to have the flexibility to wage qi with the necessary initiative without having to adhere to a set planned timeline for long-term objectives. Planning is for the immediate actions only, bound by the long-term strategic goals that keep all actions of qi focused in a single general direction. Observers of qi will see the CCP's activities in practice can sometimes be contradictory, incomplete, or self-defeating because unlike a story of fiction, the execution phases of a plan do not neatly bookend each other with seamless sequential transitions. Reality forces the qi to manipulate multiple activities at once and at differing stages of accomplishment. All of this friction makes qi difficult to identify and its effectiveness difficult to gauge.

Qi can and often is evaluated in multiple ways depending on the observer. The crux of modern qi is that it is unrestricted warfare covering all aspects of human activity. The authors of *Unrestricted Warfare* broke down each aspect of human activity into what the PLA call separate human social "dimensions" that can be exploited by China to achieve its political objectives. The authors identified 24 dimensions which they further simplified for ease of reference by putting these dimensions into three separate categorizes: military, trans-military, and non-military. The dimensions under the trans-military and non-military categories apply to the indirect force of qi. However, *Unrestricted Warfare* is not the only source of indirect warfare instruction that shapes CCP and PLA thinking. Other CCP doctrinal concepts have been published which adopt other terms and doctrinal concepts such as the "Three Warfares Doctrine" of using legal, psychological, and media warfare to combat the West. Each western analyst and academic who study these sources interpret intent and actions slightly differently and these interpretations are situationally dependent based on what the observer assumes about the CCP methods, motives, and responses to resistance. The complexity of implementing qi is compounded further by how indirect forces are supposed to be executed. To successfully implement unrestricted warfare requires incorporating actions across each dimension in every applicable domain of air, space, land, sea, and cyberspace so that each action amplifies the impact directed against the target. Successfully exploiting every human dimension requires action at every level of warfare from the strategic level to the operational and finally the tactical levels to keep the target off-balance and unable to respond in a cogent fashion.[iv]' [v]

Qi is done so China can win an open war before the first shot is fired but if the CCP chooses, these same indirect forces could go further and be the tools to instigate civil war. This is an act of escalation requiring infiltration of an enemy's social institutions, culture, and economy on a greater scale than what is required for just supporting a future open war. So, comprehending the extent and pervasiveness of the indirect forces of qi currently in the West will explain how China could induce civil war if sufficiently provoked. Other experts such as BG Spalding, Professor Kerry Gershaneck, Dr. Peter Navarro, and Dr. Michael Paul Pillsbury go into greater depth on how specific dimensions of unrestricted warfare for qi work but not how indirect forces of qi would start or work for manipulating a civil war in a Western nation. The following chapters will examine the two categories of qi's indirect force, the trans-military and non-military, coined by the authors of *Unrestricted Warfare* to demonstrate how China's decades of qi activities have placed China into a position of strategic surprise for not only open war but for turning the West against itself. For the sake of simplicity, real-world examples of qi used against the United States will reference events and incidents up to 2023. Given the rapidity of these changing qi actions, some or many of the example threats may have been addressed or morphed since the publication of the book. The defined period provides a set piece of examples for ease of reference and comprehension.

The division and categorization of trans-military and non-military dimensions of unrestricted warfare are somewhat arbitrary and will vary depending on the source of study because all the dimensions have subjective definitions and qualifiers. For this analysis, the book will reference the unrestricted warfare category chart created by the BlackOps Partners Corporation. As seen below, the corporation updated the original dimensions of the *Unrestricted Warfare* book with more dimensions incorporating additional social and technological fields China is targeting in the present day. The chart also added the official "Three Warfares Doctrine" of the PLA to the chart to be as comprehensive as possible to the breadth and scope of unrestricted warfare the CCP wages with its modern qi. A quick observation shows a single act of unrestricted warfare could overlap and cover multiple dimensions at once.

Dimensions of Unrestricted Warfare[i], [ii]

Military (zheng)	Trans-military (qi)	Non-military (qi)
Biological Warfare	Espionage Warfare	Economic Warfare
Chemical Warfare	Information Warfare	Financial Warfare
Ecological Warfare	Intelligence Warfare	Business Warfare
Space & EMP Warfare	Influence Warfare	Trade Warfare
Electronic Warfare	Resource Warfare	Resource Warfare
Guerrilla Warfare	Data/AI/Quantum Warfare	Regulatory Warfare
Terrorist Warfare	DarkNet Warfare	Legal Warfare
Conventional Warfare	Technology Warfare	Education Warfare
Kinetic / Smart Warfare	Cyber Warfare	Smuggling Warfare
Nuclear Warfare	Political Warfare	Media Warfare
	Drug Warfare	Propaganda Warfare
	Infiltration Warfare	Cultural Warfare
	Industrial Warfare	Ideological Warfare
	Psychological Warfare	Religious Warfare
	Diplomatic Warfare	Poisoning Warfare
	Subversion Warfare	Environmental Warfare

[i] BlackOps Partners Corporation, "Unrestricted Hybrid Warfare" Infographic. https://blackopspartners.com/insight/
[ii] Qiao Liang and Wang Xiangsui, *Unrestricted Warfare*, (VT: Echo Point Books & Media, originally published in 1999) 123.

[i] Carl von Clausewitz; Edited by Michael Howard, *On War,* (Princeton, NJ: Princeton University Press, 1989) 119-121.
[ii] Qiao Liang and Wang Xiangsui, *Unrestricted Warfare*, (VT: Echo Point Books & Media, originally published in 1999) 145-148.

[iii] Gerhard Ritter, *The Schlieffen Plan: Critique of Myth*, (London: Oswald Wolff Publishers Limited, 1958) 9-13. http://www.gwpda.org/memoir/Ritter/ritter1.pdf

[iv] Major Joao Vincente, "'Beyond-the-Box' Thinking on Future War: The Art and Science of Unrestricted Warfare," US Air Command and Staff College, April 2009, 14-16. https://apps.dtic.mil/sti/pdfs/ADA539664.pdf

[v] Qiao Liang and Wang Xiangsui, *Unrestricted Warfare*, (VT: Echo Point Books & Media, originally published in 1999) 127-145.

Chapter 7: Dimensions of Qi: Trans-military

Sun Tzu's indirect force (qi) in warfare encompasses all actions that do not involve direct military confrontation. Dividing qi into *Unrestricted Warfare's* trans-military and non-military categories better illustrates how Sun Tzu's classic war strategy can be integrated with the PLA's unrestricted warfare theory. *Unrestricted Warfare* identified the various human elements of an enemy polity that a modern version of Sun Tzu's qi would need to attack in order to gain strategic victory against a contemporary opponent. For this reason, the Sun Tzu's qi will be examined under the two separate non-open warfare categories of trans-military and non-military as named in the *Unrestricted Warfare* book. So, what qualifies as trans-military force?

According to the authors of *Unrestricted Warfare*, trans-military actions occur in a conflicting situation where, "a nation wages a campaign using a combination of traditional and new techniques to actively undermine an opponent's military capability without direct confrontation."[i] A broad simplified category meaning to fight a country by proxy without using overt or blatant violence. When examining all of the human dimensions listed in the trans-military category, it is easiest to remember that each of these dimensions can directly assist the military waging war without actually involving or being a part of the military itself. Unfortunately, this category of dimensions doesn't have clear cut lines that distinctly separate it from non-military or military categories of human dimension.

Since military theory involves human beings and institutions, the metrics to gauge what qualifies as what category is subjective based on preference and priority of the person evaluating these targeted dimensions. This subjectivity is further complicated by the impact objective reality will have on implementing unrestricted warfare as well. Few human activities are conducted with just one factor or objective in mind. More often than not, strategic activities involve balancing multiple organizations trying to manage multiple tasks with mutually supporting objectives. Real world complexity means an activity carried out by China's indirect forces will rarely fit neatly into one targeted human dimension in one category of unrestricted warfare. The subjectivity of evaluating each activity combined with real world complexity means any example of trans-military action will overlap multiple targeted dimensions in multiple domains in several categories of unrestricted warfare.[ii] For quick reference, the list of referred trans-military dimensions is:

Espionage Warfare	Resource Warfare	Cyber Warfare	Industrial Warfare
Information Warfare	Data/AI/Quantum Warfare	Political Warfare	Psychological Warfare
Intelligence Warfare	DarkNet Warfare	Drug Warfare	Diplomatic Warfare
Influence Warfare	Technology Warfare	Infiltration Warfare	Subversion Warfare

If examined closely, many of these dimensions have similar themes with potentially overlapping actions and outcomes. Information warfare can influence subversion, psychological, cyber, technology, and influence warfare for example. Another is espionage warfare and infiltration warfare have many opportunities to mutually support and overlap each dimension's objectives.

A list of real-world examples of China's trans-military activities against the West is the most effective way to demonstrate the case that China has both the scale and capability necessary to induce civil conflict within the West. The problem is conveying the information in a concise and consistent way given the subjectivity of the cited dimensions targeted by unrestricted warfare which can bleed into multiple categories. Instead of listing examples by dimensions arbitrarily, the examples will be organized by 'war fronts' where the Chinese conducts multiple trans-military dimension activities to accomplish specific strategic objectives. This way, examples that have multiple associated dimensions will not be tangled in categorical confusion and will be easier to visualize the current dilemma the West faces. These examples will also highlight the scale of how much the West willingly enables China to be strategically successful.

Special Military Category Carve Out – Terrorism - Front:

The first example is not from the trans-military category but is a perfect example of the malleability of these unrestricted warfare categories. Usually, terrorism is categorized in the military dimensions but deserves special mention because it demonstrates how China's actions related to terrorism can bleed into other trans-military dimensions of unrestricted warfare. China is not normally associated with terrorism in either political discourse or in popular perception. State terrorism is usually the tool of weak third world nations that cannot muster any direct force of sufficient strength to oppose a stronger foe like Iran against Israel or Pakistan against India. Yet, China is complicit in terrorism albeit with more subtlety than the Iranian mullahs.

China enables terrorism in three different ways and all of them give China plausible deniability. Even though terrorism is in the military category of unrestricted warfare, the Chinese state uses terrorism in peace time as part of its indirect force. China doesn't directly sponsor anti-Western terror organizations but instead aids them indirectly by financially supporting the elites of terrorist states without requiring the elites to restrain terrorist activity. No strings attached aid and investment helps third party countries weaken Western credibility and influence in regions without China ever getting directly involved.

In March of 2021, Iran and China signed a $400 billion dollar investment deal where China would build economic investments in Iran in exchange for oil over the next 25 years.[iii] Although this "Comprehensive Strategic Partnership" remains vague in detail, the partnership will very likely aid the Iranian Revolutionary Guard Corps (IRGC) given its tremendous influence within the Iranian economy.[iv] The IRGC leads all state-directed terrorist activity for the Iranian theocracy. The IRGC's Al Quds special force units aid Shia militia attacks on US personnel in Iraq and Syria,[v] logistically support Hezbollah,[vi] and conduct terrorist activities against Israel.[vii] The IRGC is prolific in its use of terror cells but China never has nor will bring up this issue in public or allow it to hinder any political discourse. Iran happily targets Western interests with violence in the name of protecting Muslims while keeping quiet about the Uyghur genocide in China and without taking any direct orders from China. This demonstrates the CCP's successful use of economic incentives to have third-party states carry out anti-Western terrorism without directly getting involved.

China seems to focus this effort on its policies dealing with influencing Asian regions near its periphery of direct influence. Investing in terror states to co-opt the ruling elites is also replicated in Chinese dealings with Pakistan, North Korea, and potentially Afghanistan. Not all actions of qi are directed against the West, as supporting the Pakistani military and intelligence elites is done with greater focus on counterbalancing India than the United States. China uses its investments to further its objectives of Tianxia in Pakistan with the creation of the China-Pakistan Economic Corridor. China is helping build critical trade and industrial infrastructure in this corridor to improve all economic lines of communication and interconnectivity throughout Pakistan that will connect to China and other Belt and Road Initiative linked countries.[viii] Despite some practical difficulties, the Chinese regime appears committed to seeing this effort through even with the Pakistani's government's duplicitous relationships with anti-Indian terrorist organizations. China rarely mentions or condemns anti-Indian terror activities yet are openly vocal about Baloch terrorism in southern Pakistan. Balochistan is a major province in Southwest Pakistan where a sizable segment of the indigenous population resents Pakistani rule and strives for greater autonomy. Baloch insurgents now regard China as enablers of Pakistani oppression and target Chinese interests in Pakistan. China has been openly critical of the Pakistani government's efforts in subduing Baloch activities in the past and have insisted Pakistan increase counterterrorism efforts to protect Chinese investments.[ix] China's singular condemnation of terrorist acts being limited only to the Baloch insurgents demonstrably proves China condones terrorism as long as it's directed against its rivals.

The Democratic People's Republic of North Korea (DPRK) is not often thought about when it comes to terrorist attacks in modern times but the DPRK does have a long history of such activity. During the Cold War, North Korea conducted a series of assassinations and bombings to intimidate and cripple South Korea's government. In 1983, 21 people died in Rangoon as North Korean terrorists attempted to decapitate the South Korean government by bombing an official diplomatic event at the mausoleum of Aung San who won Burmese independence from the British. Several South Korean cabinet members were killed as a result.[x] More recently, Kim Jung Un assassinated his half-brother in Malaysia.[xi] In neither of these cases was China under suspicion, but China is the principle economic lifeline to this rogue regime. This implies the DPRK would likely assist in any future plausibly deniable terrorist activity to support China if the CCP insists on Kim's support.

Even though China uses its support of terrorist regimes to keep some political distance from terrorist groups, China has no problem with directly conducting acts of intimidation and inducing psychological terror without physical violence. From 2017-2021, the CCP directed "Operation Fox Hunt" to stalk and intimidate Chinese dissidents living within the United States. Nine Chinese nationals were arrested in the northeastern United States for attempting to frighten targeted Chinese citizens into returning home and surrender to the government for various 'crimes' against the Chinese regime.[xii] Although these Chinese operatives were not accused of any physical violence, the continuous surveillance and threats effectively terrorized persons on US soil with minimal political repercussions. This incident demonstrates how China will use nonviolent terrorism as the lack of any bloodshed will dampen any interest from the sensationalist hungry Western media.

A final type of terrorism China could potentially use against the West is the encouragement of lone wolf nationalist fanatics to carry out violence within the West. Lone wolves' propensity for violence is encouraged through various media and propaganda echo chambers which makes any official connections or causal links directly to CCP almost impossible. A Chinese lone wolf terrorist named David Wenwei Chou murdered a pro-Taiwanese independence activist in California on May 16, 2022.[xiii] David Chou was a member of the CCP United Front, a political activist organization directly controlled by the CCP with a history of conducting political subversion and influence operations outside of China.[xiv] Despite this connection, there is no definitive proof the CCP ordered the murder which only amplifies the sense of terror opponents of China will experience. There is little political risk to the CCP if it decides to keep encouraging individuals to deal with the Party's enemies without expressly ordering violence and will likely do so.

The CCP currently uses these three forms of terrorist support that indirectly supports the regime and can support either military or nonmilitary objectives. In peacetime, the CCP can help other anti-Western regimes with funding to disrupt Western countries' presence in regions China wants to gain greater influence while also undermining US government credibility by conducting very public demonstrations against dissidents within US territory. Although Chinese agents were arrested, there was no major political or economic penalty against the CCP itself. China's other efforts of indirect warfare such as political, economic, and cultural influence offsets and deters Western governments from being more proactive against Chinese induced intimidation.

Terrorism's multitude of styles, flavors, and scale makes it one of the most flexible forms of qi available to the CCP. Despite being traditionally in the military category and academically put in with the direct (zheng) forces, terrorism can support economic, political, influence, subversion, espionage, and legal dimensions of indirect force depending on the CCP's needs. For this reason, the terrorist front is an important overlapping dimension that connects the zheng forces with the qi forces.

Isolate the West from the World - Front:

China's strategic objective to become the global hegemon by means of Tianxia requires it forgo the internationalist revolution of old communist movements and revert back to dynastic imperial ambitions. Contemporary China's foreign policy now has more in common with the mercantilist policies of the British Imperium of the 19th Century than with Mao Zedong's revolutionary zeal. Central absolutism abandons all pretense of building a global internationalist system for the "workers and proletariat" and instead pursues a practical Machiavellian policy of expanding the CCP's power abroad. To achieve the goal of Tianxia requires China to compete with and eventually defeat Western influence in the developing world. As stated earlier, central absolutism is only successful in the long-term if there are no other viable alternative systems to compete with it. If China's system must contend with a functioning rival, the CCP will eventually wither and die on its ever-accumulating corruption and inefficiency. Latching on to other countries for economic exploitation extends the CCP's lifespan at the cost of its rivals' economic vitality. Tianxia is to eventually rig the international system into favoring China exclusively by making China the center of all critical global economic functions. This new Chinese Imperium requires aggressive diplomatic maneuvering that uses fiscal incentives and penalties to gradually co-opt and then turn most of the world's nations into compliant vassals.

For the trans-military role of qi, the diplomatic dimension can be used to disrupt or block the West's ability to encircle or contain China. Successful diplomacy can convince nations to either remain neutral or become outright hostile to the West in order to deprive China's rivals of additional allies and resources in the event of a major confrontation. In the current state of world affairs, China has the diplomatic advantage in most circumstances. Unlike the time of the Cold War, the West is attempting to advocate for the world to adhere, at least rhetorically, to the liberal international system idealized by the post-World War II set of agreements that embrace global democratic values, liberty, and human rights. This means the West must attempt to build diplomatic relations with nation states within the boundaries of these ideals. During the Cold War, the United States and its European allies often exercised a practical ruthless foreign policy over an idealistic one which would and did support any dictatorship that opposed Soviet influence. Now, the West cannot just back anti-CCP elites, it must attempt to carry out trade, diplomacy, and military agreements that have at least some endorsements of the other nations' general population to have legitimacy. China on the other hand is given a much freer diplomatic hand. As a continuing critic of democratic systems, the Chinese regime doesn't have to feign concern of other nations' populations' opinions or sentiments. China is overtly controlled by a ruthless technocratic oligarchic elite and focus their diplomacy on just co-opting other nations' elites.

Chinese diplomacy of targeting other nations' elites simplifies the Party's foreign policy goals as foreign elites are a relatively small group of people making them relatively cheap and easy targets for bribery in the form of business deals and preferential contracts. Non-Western nations' elites prefer China's diplomacy because the CCP doesn't have any of the moral, ethical, or behavioral standards that hamper corrupt elites' dealings with the West. China's approach also appeals to the common character fault of politicians of all political systems everywhere. Most politicians seek the easy policy answer that provides instant gratification to satisfy immediate needs but often at a detrimental cost that will have to be paid later. Few politicians seek the hard policy answer that painfully fixes a problem to ensure long-term stability and prosperity.

China has created a series of programs and policies intended to offer nations with poor economies or corrupt politicians a wide range of Faustian bargains that provide an infusion of investments and hard currency for the long-term cost of ceding elements of sovereignty to China. The most famous is the Belt-and-Road-Initiative (BRI) that has expanded China's economic presence across the world to become the single largest trade rival to the West. Over the last two decades, BRI grew from a few nations participating in Asia to having over 140 nations being signatories to a variety of BRI projects and initiatives. The focus being investments that on face value bring infrastructure and direct investment into developing or stagnant economies to alleviate poverty while elevating China's status. From 2000-2017, China initiated over 10,849 investment projects with the majority being in Africa, Asia, and Latin America in value of nearly $1 trillion over 20 years.[xv] On initial glance, this economic program appears to mutually benefit all parties where global economic prosperity rises and China earns greater prestige for its benevolence but in most cases, this is not true. Many of these investments lack any financial viability with the CCP initiating projects at major losses but try to sustain them to build political and financial influence within the targeted countries. Yet some projects are so costly that the CCP or host nation must cancel them as they become too much of a drain. Over an eight-year period, China canceled over $18 billion in projects which seems small but one must remember how far such large sums of money can go in places like Sudan, Ethiopia, Cameroon, Kazakhstan, and Bolivia.[xvi] In spite of such failures, China continues to persist in order to build its long-term political foundations of Tianxia throughout the globe. A key part of this effort is making the political elites of participating nations dependent on the financial goodwill of China to make them more susceptible to the CCP's influence. One of the most effective and widespread tools for this influence is the use of debt-traps.

About 81% of China's BRI investments to participating nations comes in various forms of loans.[xvii] Many loan agreements between the CCP and BRI member nations' elites are often kept secret to hide the level of obligation the bribed elites must give to China in exchange for continued financial support. If the participating nations fail to meet their financial obligations to the CCP, then China will often require major concessions in sovereignty in forms of land use, basing, or resource ownership to permanently bind those nations to China's control. Although China is the most famous nation at the moment for using such tactics, these are not novel or original. For all of China's proclaimed progressive ideals for the world,

China's BRI adopts more than a couple of policy methods perfected by the British Empire during its heyday in the 19th Century. A textbook case of a debt trap occurred in 1874 when Egypt's government and their nominal master, the Ottoman Empire, became bankrupt. Egypt's principal source of income came from its shares in the Suez Canal Company which it sold to Britain in addition to pledging to pay Britain 5% of the shares' value annually instead of dividends. This gave Britain considerable control over Egypt's finances but Egypt still owed debts to France and Italy. So, Egypt became indentured to Britain to pay off all of its debts. When the ruler tried to expel the British by force in 1879, the British Empire simply installed the ruler's more cooperative son as a compliant puppet.[xviii] China learns from the best and China is recreating a new version of the British Empire with "Chinese characteristics".

With its economic influence and trade growing successfully, China is not restraining itself but instead is now expanding its ambitions as the CCP gains global diplomatic clout. Now China is expanding its global hegemonic goals with two new politically centric programs that will help build the alternate global institutions of Tianxia in the form of the Global Development Initiative (GDI) and the Global Security Initiative (GSI).

While the BRI is a mechanism to entice developing nations to welcome Chinese economic investment, the GDI is a more nebulous concept that seems to cover everything else the BRI does not.[xix] China often does this initially to probe where nations will have hard limits to Chinese influence within their territory while maintaining the deniability of keeping the GDI aspirational for the moment. Once enough time has transpired, the Chinese regime will develop more concrete goals that are tailored to address any misgivings elites of prospective partner nations might have in order for them to agree to the GDI. Once committed, the Chinese regime will gradually nudge and push these partners into greater commitments until these nations become politically and economically trapped into vassalhood. Although experts will not commit to any final assessment of what the final design of GDI will ultimately be, CCP focuses its rhetoric on helping developing nations with financial aid and climate programs to appear benign. With no certainty, one possibility is China could use the GDI as a seeding initiative to build eventual Chinese controlled international bodies that could be alternatives to the IMF or World Bank. No certainty at this time of writing but all initial Chinese programs start deliberately small and benign to get the CCP's figurative foot into the diplomatic door.

BRI and GDI are programs designed to increase the strength of China's economic and diplomatic elements of its DIME but the GSI is for advocating the expansion of China's military instrument by having its own international security initiatives. China is still bound to the Western created international system which is held together with both security and economic bodies that keep the world participating in the liberal international system. The international system's main security body is the United Nations Security Council which has no direct military authority but uses mainly Western nations and alliances, particularly NATO, to provide enforcement mechanisms. China has no comparable alternative system at present but in order for China to have one, it must first establish a diplomatic narrative to justify creating a new foundation for Chinese-led security bodies. The GSI, like the GDI, is a nebulous aspirational set of narratives that pledges to support global peace while emphasizing greater respect for national sovereignty and "indivisible security" to allure prospective non-Western nations to support China's efforts.[xx] These aspirations appeal to other nations' elites because China pledges to build peace between nations without interfering in the internal policies of the member nations. This can be interpreted as elites can behave as they please as long as they conform to the new Chinese-led international standard. A classic agreement the dynastic Chinese Empire granted its vassals. There are no concrete commitments or institutions as of yet but the CCP is psychologically preparing the global population that a future alternative to the current international system would be better and China is best suited to build that alternative.

With these two initiatives being in the early stages and the BRI's impact varying by region, it remains difficult to assess exactly what China's ideal vision of a globe of Tianxia compliant vassals would look like. Even if one could, how could such a system of vassals be used as part of the indirect force of qi against the West itself? Despite not being well known among the West's general public, several nations have either already become Chinese vassals or are on the verge of being one in the near future. Evaluating what China is doing in these countries and the potential consequences for future CCP victims will identify how diplomatic qi can help cripple the West's influence overseas. The most obvious place to analyze is the first nation to become a full-fledged vassal of the new Chinese Imperium, Cambodia.

From the perspective of national sovereignty, Cambodia's geopolitical situation is one of tragedy. Being subjugated and incorporated into France's Indochina in 1887, the country has spent the last century and half struggling to be free of foreign control. Cambodia was under control by the French, then Japanese, then the French again, and then briefly independent but under a military dictatorship which would then be overthrown by the China-backed Khmer Rouge. After a brief period of chaotic rule, the Soviet-backed Vietnamese government invaded and overthrew the Khmer Rouge and Cambodia remained a Soviet-puppet until the end of the Cold War. In 1993, the monarchy was restored and Cambodia was now officially free and a sovereign nation but not in practice. As a perfect example of realpolitik over idealism, the People's Republic of China sheltered the Cambodian Royal Family in the 1970s and gave them residence in China until the Cambodian monarchy restoration in the 1990s. The royal family under the leadership of King Sihanouk had connections with China since the 1960s and had built a strong repour with the CCP. As part of the UN transition from Soviet puppet to an independent state, Cambodia's government retained many of the Marxist-Leninist technocrats and administrators from the 1980s. With a pro-CCP monarchy combined with a bureaucracy designed by the Soviet Union, Cambodia's government was bound to China. China has been the principal patron of Cambodia sine King Sihanouk's coronation and is continued by his son because China ensured every aspect of the Cambodian nation is owned or influenced by Chinese investments and money.[xxi]

Vassal states, unlike occupied territories, have reciprocal relationships with their overseer state but only as junior partners. The elites of vassals enjoy autonomy on domestic matters, indulge in their corruption, can develop their nation's wealth at the cost of sovereignty over critical lands, resources, and foreign policy. This is the case with Cambodia. The elites are not dictated to on a daily basis or are compelled to defer to China on every issue but must comply when China believes its interests are at stake. It started with small concessions. In exchange for its first investment loans, Cambodia cut all ties with Taiwan and then over time allowed Chinese state-owned enterprises (SOE) more latitude to the point of practically owning the Cambodian economy.[xxii] By 2019, Cambodia was the sixth most-indebted nation to China on Earth with debt owed being the equivalent to 30% of Cambodia's GDP.[xxiii]

From this debt, China is given free reign over Cambodia's economy and use massive infrastructure projects to configure the geography of Cambodia to best suit Chinese interests, usually at the cost of locals' economic well-being. One example in 2017 at Tbong Khmum Province, China started on a major road and bridge construction project where local villagers were compelled to sell their land and many became a source of cheap labor for the Chinese SOEs. This was part of a larger national project where China built over 3,000 km of roads which Cambodia continuously pays for with Chinese loans.[xxiv] Another instance of Chinese mercantilism involved the creation of the Special Economic Zone of the city of Sihanoukville. Since its creation, Chinese firms built over 100 factories with the added escapism of new casinos and hotels all owned by Chinese enterprises sustained by Chinese built hydroelectric dams. China uses these special zones to bring in their own workers and managers under the pretense of Chinese claims that everyone being Chinese keeps work simpler because everyone understands each other. Even if true, another major motivator is to simultaneously keep providing the sizable Chinese population employment opportunities and colonizing the host nation to ensure economic dependence remains. By 2020, Cambodia hosted over 250,000 Chinese workers yet most of the income generated goes back to China as locals are only given menial jobs and Chinese workers spend most of their money in Chinese-owned stores and casinos.[xxv]˒ [xxvi] Also, many of these Chinese treat the local Cambodians like serfs. In 2018, a riot occurred when Chinese workers attacked and attempted to kidnap two Cambodian female masseuses which prompted swift retaliation from local shop keepers and taxi drivers.[xxvii] Such encounters are commonplace but the Chinese Empire isn't limited to just industrial and employee exploitation.

China also uses its power to extract Cambodia's resources. Cambodia is a large producer of agricultural goods such as bananas and a large freshwater fishing industry. As part of China's effort to maintain economic dominance while simultaneously expanding economic output, China has constructed multiple dams to buildup electric power output in southern China and southeast Asia. However, to meet these CCP objectives, China willfully ignores the impact on the Mekong River or the ecological damage that could endanger the food production of Laos and Cambodia.[xxviii] This disregard occurs because whatever corrections that need to be done will be done by Chinese firms to make more profit while making sure the CCP's political influence in Cambodia never diminishes. This national indenturing of the country also helps sustain a servile elite that gains personal wealth at the cost of allowing China to remain parasitically attached to Cambodia. This is the true fate and future idealized by the CCP for the rest of the Earth.

Cambodia is one of the first nations on Earth to reach the ultimate fate of China's Tianxia but many nations are on a similar course. As of the early 2020s, Sri Lanka,[xxix]˒[xxx] Zambia,[xxxi]˒ [xxxii] and Djibouti[xxxiii] are the most at risk of becoming fully vassalized while Nepal[xxxiv] and Kyrgyzstan[xxxv]˒ [xxxvi] are in danger of following close behind. States in earlier phases of Tianxia vassalage have their sovereign states' elites remain largely independent but are actively being co-opted and subverted include Equatorial Guinea,[xxxvii] Zimbabwe,[xxxviii] Bangladesh,[xxxix] Pakistan,[xl] Iran,[xli] and now because of the Ukrainian War, Russia is now vulnerable to becoming subverted into servitude in the coming decades.[xlii] China's mercantilist diplomacy is mainly focused on bilateral dealings but these dealings with most of the world's nations allows China to assert itself in international bodies and defy the international communities' desires or objectives. Whatever pretense of international peace or brotherhood the CCP espouses, it will only embrace actions that benefit the Party as Climate Envoy John Kerry discovered. China made it clear that China will use "climate change" policies in a pragmatic way and ignore any Western desire of a collective effort.[xliii] Although environmental issues are the most prominent international efforts China ignores, China also uses its economic and diplomatic influence to intimidate nations from having policies contrary to the CCP's wishes as demonstrated when China successfully dictated to the World Health Organization to keep Taiwan out during the Wuhan originated COVID-19 pandemic in 2020.[xliv]

One will also observe that China is getting more belligerent and aggressive in its foreign policy and diplomacy. Part of the reason is China's success is making the CCP arrogant and brash but also the CCP knows it's on borrowed time. Central absolutism puts CCP power ahead of everything else and sooner or later that becomes apparent in all foreign dealings. If the West can remain competitive long enough, the negative aspects of Tianxia will outgrow the positive and prospective vassals will make efforts to distance or break away from the CCP's influence. Chinese exploitation of local workers,[xlv]˒[xlvi] the proactive racism towards Africans,[xlvii]˒ [xlviii] building infrastructure solely for Chinese interests, underdelivering on projects,[xlix] and making China the exclusive owners of all critical industries eventually make all these debt-trap endeavors unpalatable.[l]˒ [li] Examples such as practicing a form of eugenics where Chinese workers in African countries father many children with local women and deliberately abandon them once the workers return to China are commonplace.[lii] As such abuses become more widespread and more difficult to hide, China's global momentum will slow down so it must aggressively gain dominance in global commerce and diplomacy to defeat their rivals before time runs out.

Monopolize All Critical Technology - Front:

Tianxia is not limited to just diplomacy and trade deal expansion. A critical part of the CCP's imperial efforts, as well as qi, is making sure China monopolizes the critical technologies that form the bedrock of the modern world economy. If China can dominate the cutting-edge technology fields of the global market and become the principal manufacturing center of these capabilities then, like the oil sheikhs of the 20th Century, the CCP will control the life blood of all the major powers' economic well-being. The qi of China must deprive its rivals of independent means to sustain their economies and armies. In modern times, having the most advanced technology is as equally critical for a world power's DIME as food or energy production. With this understanding, the CCP commits a considerable amount of its indirect forces towards conquering the high-technology industries of the West.

As stated earlier in the book, trying to plan out every step to achieve the long-term objectives of a national grand strategy is impossible because there are too many uncontrollable variables that impact the outcomes of societies, but the CCP can plan out short-term goals. In the case of the CCP, they've retained their Maoist habits of using 5 and 10-year economic plans to direct national strategic efforts to achieve the Party's goals. Although not the only one, the most prominent 10-year tech related plan is Xi Jinping's "Made in China 2025 Initiative" from 2015.[liii] Xi understands China's economic dependence on other nations does benefit the Party with considerable income but at the cost of constraining the CCP's policy options. Any aggressive actions that cause trade disruption by either war or strife could result in mutual economic destruction with the West. Xi Jinping's ambitions to make China technologically self-sufficient while also making it the tech center of the planet has compelled the CCP to devote a considerable number of resources and money to achieve this overly ambitious goal.

Technology is everywhere and the West is still the lead in most fields of the industry, so China is using every possible dimension of indirect warfare to defeat the West's advantage. China does conduct legitimate research on its own and cooperates with global academia on scientific programs, but a sizable portion of its technological prowess comes by illicit means and shortcuts. China will use all means to gain the technological advantage including espionage, theft, insider trading, spies, hacking, manipulation, or just purchasing the technology to beat its competitors. This means China is using cyberwarfare, infiltration warfare, technology warfare, smuggling warfare, intelligence warfare, psychological warfare, and the big data warfare dimensions for this front of the indirect war. The scale of this front of qi is difficult to appreciate but the United States government's Commission on the Theft of American Intellectual Property has conducted impact studies since 2013 on the loss of American technological, industrial, and scientific knowledge to Chinese efforts. In the 2017 report, the commission concluded the United States alone had an estimated $1.2 trillion in economic losses over a three-year period. This includes losses from counterfeit products, patent infringements, intellectual property (IP) theft, and loss of trade secrets.[liv] In fairness, these total losses include all foreign actions against US interests but China is the single largest violator. Even so, this large number still doesn't give proper appreciation as to the scale of the problem for the West or how thorough China has been. This part of qi is the single largest element of China's indirect war and no single book can give a comprehensive picture, so below are individual examples of illicit activities to help better gain proper perspective.

A small sampling of the technology front of the indirect war (qi):

· In 2004, the Canadian telecommunications equipment manufacturer Nortel lost critical intellectual property relating to 4G wireless technologies to Chinese affiliated hackers but Nortel ignored the hack and allowed cyber incidents to occur until Nortel's bankruptcy in 2009 after Chinese firms were able to supplant Nortel in the wireless equipment market.[lv]

· In 2009, China carried out a phishing campaign against 30 organizations including Google, Adobe, and defense firms and gained network access to collect a wide variety of information including intellectual property and personal information on Chinese dissidents.[lvi], [lvii]

· At least four Chinese nationals established a front company to steal trade secrets from the GlaxoSmithKline pharmaceutical company from 2012-2016.[lviii], [lix]

· In 2017, a joint report by BAE Systems and PricewaterhouseCoopers found a sophisticated Chinese hacking group were using smaller vulnerable third-party IT service providers to use as vectors to breach large technology firms for IP theft but specific firms were not disclosed for confidentiality reasons.[lx]

· Again in 2017, FBI Special Agent Ed You testified to Congress on how Chinese firms used their country's lax regulations, generous financial incentives, and data mining ability to convince American and other nations' DNA-sequencing firms to host US genomic data within China. This data is being used as a basis for China to gain an advantage in the creation of precision medicine that could in the near future dominate the pharmaceutical industry as medicine is custom made to a patient's physiology.[lxi]

· A 2018 investigation by the US National Institutes of Health led to the dismissal of 54 scientists from NIH-funded institutions for failing to disclose their financial ties with China.[lxii]

· In 2018, a Chinese national named Hongin Tan was arrested after he was discovered to have stolen over $1 billion worth proprietary information from the US petroleum company he was employed at and sending the information back to China.[lxiii]

· The cybersecurity firm FireEye, announced multiple Chinese-affiliated hacker groups targeted numerous cancer-research programs and other advanced biotechnologies in American universities and companies from 2014-2018.[lxiv]

· In 2019, Chinese hackers were identified using Airbus subcontracted suppliers to try to gain access to proprietary data on jet engines; this was the last of 4 major cyber-attacks over the course of a year.[lxv]

· In 2019, iDefense cybersecurity research firm stated Chinese hackers conducted cyberoperations against 27 universities across the globe to develop advanced naval, maritime, and oceanographic technologies.[lxvi]

· IP theft from China became so prominent that in 2019, FBI Director Christopher Wray disclosed nearly 1,000 espionage investigations were active against Chinese attempts to steal IP or trade secrets.[lxvii]

· A major cyber security firm named Cybereason discovered China-linked hackers compromised 10 of the world's largest telecommunication companies in 2019 stating Chinese hackers exploited their access since 2017. This activity enabled the hackers to have low profile access to target the networks the telecom companies provided to clients to conduct cyber espionage.[lxviii]

· In 2020, the FBI failed to convict a Chinese national professor, Bo Mao, for the alleged attempt to aid Chinese technology firm, Huawei, in acquiring a US-made circuit board for reverse-engineering. Despite the plea deal, federal authorities indicated he played a small role in a larger espionage endeavor.[lxix]

· The federal government announced in 2020 that Huawei was aiding the CCP with providing confidential information and allegedly installing backdoors in client networks to enable Chinese cyber espionage which was denied until 2021.[lxx] In 2021, a major leak at Huawei appeared to corroborate Western governments' accusations that Huawei actively aided the CCP's regime.[lxxi]

· Another federal indictment of two Chinese government hackers occurred in 2020 who were accused of conducting cyber-attacks against Western industries such as software developers, solar energy manufacturers, pharmaceuticals, and defense firms over a 10-year period.[lxxii]

· In 2021, Department of Justice indicted four Chinese Ministry of State Security affiliated hackers being accused of using a front company to embed malware into Western companies and universities to acquire proprietary data, including medical research.[lxxiii]

· Also in 2021, a Chinese spy for the Ministry of State Security, Yanjun Xu, was convicted for spying and technology espionage since 2013 that included targeting GE Aviation on critical jet engine components.[lxxiv]

· In 2022, the cybersecurity firm, Cybereason, declared that a Chinese cyberoperation it dubbed Operation CuckooBees used malware and stole IP from US, European, and Asian companies for years.[lxxv]

This tiny sampling of Chinese illicit means of stealing Western technology and IP are so common occurrence that it would require a separate book just to lay out the extent and history of Chinese theft over the last 20 years. Yet, China does not limit itself to traditional means of espionage but also uses its large financial resources to find legal pathways to exploit the West's unwieldy legal and regulatory framework to maintain an edge in technology acquisitions. This broad array of methods and techniques are categorized under the US government's jargon term of non-traditional collection. Non-traditional collection are means of using citizens and organizations not directly tied to the Party, government, intelligence, or military services but instead serve businesses, schools, or labs deemed "private" or "non-state".[lxxvi] Since the West distinguishes between private and public entities but China doesn't, China can recruit students, scientists, teachers, engineers, and entrepreneurs on an ad-hoc basis to carry out economic espionage whenever the CCP wants them to.

The most prominent example was the Chinese government's Thousand Talents Program. In the 1990s, the CCP understood China was technologically backwards and would require considerable time and investment for China to catch up to the West. However, China lacked the knowledge base and skilled labor needed to build an advanced technology industry to become a major global economic power. China decided to embark on a large-scale recruitment program of science and technology specialists from abroad to teach and develop China's research & development, testing, and engineering sectors. Officially, these programs would recruit foreign experts to China to work on joint ventures while Chinese students, engineers, and scientists would go overseas to collaborate on projects in Western countries.[lxxvii] In practice, China uses its citizens overseas to collect on IP and research to send back to the CCP whenever the Party requires them to do so. Also, the recruitment talent programs offer large grants and other financial rewards to foreigners who establish programs and ventures in China to include bringing back Western IP or proprietary research at the cost of their Western partners.[lxxviii] Although this specific program no longer exists, the Thousand Talents was the most prominent in its heyday as it was directly managed by the CCP, not the government, and successfully recruited over 7,000 highly skilled foreign specialists to work for China.[lxxix] However, the US government and others increasingly put pressure on this program as it blatantly violated research integrity regulations and became too much associated with espionage to be viable for the CCP's operations.[lxxx] China has since created many alternate programs that carry out the same purpose without the reputational hindrance the Thousand Talents had earned. By spending large amounts of money in Western research centers, the CCP co-opts many companies and universities who become addicted to quick cash and cheap abundant research labor that makes Western research leaders' work easier at low cost. So much so, that many of these co-opted entities decry any attempt by Western governments to constrain CCP influence within Western science and technology sectors.[lxxxi], [lxxxii], [lxxxiii]

Non-traditional collection is not just limited to poaching talent but also remaining in Western countries and to continuously smuggle out IP and technology back to China and bypass any export regulations. China has taken advantage of Western governments' traditionally slow bureaucracy and narrow jurisdictions to quickly exploit regulatory loopholes as well as the lack of coordinated effort by the Western bureaucracies to effectively enforce these regulations. A US Government Accountability Office study in 2022 noted the multiple bureaucracies that enforce different export jurisdictions lacked any institutional support to coordinate and synchronize their attempts to protect research institutions.[lxxxiv] Although not specifically mentioned, there is a high probability that many research institutions and their affiliates' lobbying helped slow down effective implementation to compound the problem. Since there is no coordinated strategy, each bureaucratic institution approaches the issue in a piecemeal fashion, allowing the CCP to continue to exploit export control weaknesses with little consequence. So extensive is the problem that a major law firm, Covington & Burling LLP, posted a cheat sheet on what export control risks need to be mitigated when doing business with China. This written report has a wide range of things a company shouldn't do when companies deal with China. Examples include not transferring export control information to Chinese nationals even if they are located within the United States, export technology data via emails, share drives, or a posting to a cloud shared with Chinese partners. Also, the cheat sheet warns about doing ventures with businesses that might potentially obfuscate the identity of their actual China-based owners.[lxxxv]

This point must be repeatedly emphasized, China's central absolutism will inherently become more centralized over time because there are no self-correcting mechanisms to correct its faults. More power will become more centralized and daily life more micromanaged by the state over the coming years to maintain control over a system prone to failure caused by its corrupting contradictions. Keeping the West addicted to China's financial offerings to gradually migrate all technology innovation centers to China by the means of qi warfare keeps China from weakening. By luring creativity and innovation that is nurtured elsewhere in the world over to the totalitarian nation, the West will continuously sustain China's new Tianxia imperium. China hopes that in time, the West's ability to technologically compete will be bled dry and cede technology development to China as resisting becomes too costly. If successful, then China will eventually have an economic de-coupling with "Chinese characteristics" where trade continues but all critical dependencies will be one-way with China in complete mercantilist control. Many in the West want to maintain the status quo because companies make cheap profits for short term quarterly results but going forward this will not happen because China itself wants to eventually change the economic relationship of business partners to dealing only with business vassals.[lxxxvi]

Turn the West into Maple Street - Front:

The science fiction television series, *The Twilight Zone*, would depict unusual stand-alone stories with twist endings and a moral. One of the most poignant stories is in the episode called "The Monsters Are Due on Maple Street" where a street of middle-class homes is cut off from the rest of the world and isolated by a mysterious malevolent force. With no means of outside communication, the various people on Maple Street form into cliques for survival but quickly turn on each other as their fears and paranoia are exacerbated by faulty assumptions, self-interest, and poor information. This group of people were once part of a functioning cohesive society but by severing the common linkages, likeminded people within this isolated street formed simpler smaller tribes united by common emotionally based biases and fears. Although this was allegorical, the story is an example of a common tool used in politics in all societies, both republics and tyrannies, to maintain social divisions in order to more easily control segments of the population. Most examples of this are governments or social elites using this tactic on their own population but China now weaponizes this tactic for their qi and unrestricted warfare.

Although China does use this tactic on its own people, examples being the Uyghurs and Falun Gong,[lxxxvii] the CCP also understands the power of these tools against foreign adversaries as well. A critical part of the qi portion of unrestricted warfare is to sow disunity to cause sufficient chaos to either cripple or destroy a rival society. Economic and military actions are not sufficient to completely defeat an enemy, the enemy's spirit must also be broken to achieve total victory. The added benefit of using social division as a tool is that trying to prove it's being done deliberately by the CCP is almost impossible. Proving the CCP is actively undermining Western cultures would require actual defectors and CCP internal documents which are unlikely to come to light anytime soon. Such activities don't need to be directly managed by the CCP who would just financially assist domestic third parties who already want to cause chaos in the West. There are many ways to achieve chaos and what makes the situation worse for the West is many of the social divisions are naturally occurring, China just inflames the divisions to a more socially disrupting level.

One of the most direct and debilitating methods is another technique China learned from the British Empire, spreading the rampant use of strong narcotics to diminish social stability in a rival state. A society corrupted by rampant drug use must divert considerable resources to the problem, regardless if it is criminal prosecution or rehabilitation. Overdoses and large numbers of addicts diminish social cohesion and can enable anarchy which divides cities and communities. Too much coddling of drug abusers and of those who sell to them reward poor behavior at the cost of those who are law abiding and productive. In effect, such efforts build resentment as sobriety is penalized while personal irresponsibility is rewarded without negative consequence. Draconian actions on the other hand can also provoke resentments as activists will argue select groups are overly targeted. Either way, social divisions grow and Western societies' internal conflicts are exacerbated.

Although there is no dispute China is the primary source for the majority of synthetic opioids and the precursor agents coming into North America, there is argument on whether or not the CCP is complicit in the drug trade. Fentanyl was not regulated in China until 2015, but rampant corruption within the Chinese bureaucracy and the ease of which to bypass Chinese regulations provides enough obfuscation to give the Chinese government plausible deniability.[lxxxviii] President Xi declared all forms of fentanyl were under regulatory control in 2019 but as of 2022 remains the main supplier of the synthetic drugs.[lxxxix], [xc] Given China's greater counternarcotics success with certain south Asian nations, it is clear the CCP is selective on its enforcement. As part of qi, the Party doesn't have to direct drugs or manage drug facilitation, it just has to ignore the activities as drug markets will spread social chaos on their own. This form of social attack is a perfect model of indirect unrestricted warfare as it is nearly impossible to prove such drug activities are explicitly part of the CCP's policies toward the West but the consequences of synthetic drug smuggling indicate China's benefit at the cost of the West.

Numerous examples of drugs causing social decay are found throughout the United States particularly in cities on the west coast such as San Francisco and Seattle.[xci] In many ways, San Francisco's problems indicate it is now a third-world city. Rampant crime,[xcii] poor sanitation,[xciii] incompetent government,[xciv] and extreme stratification of wealthy vs poor[xcv] could be used to describe Caracas, the favelas in Rio de Janeiro, or Karachi but these problems also describe 2020s San Francisco. Poor income neighborhoods such as the Tenderloin district are left abandoned by the city as the poor can be ignored while city officials pretend to care. The city allocated nearly $72 million to drug treatment but no actual plan to implement effectively.[xcvi] Such actions create obvious divisions as the incompetent city government placates wealthy areas while pledging resources to the poor without actually delivering results deepens resentment and exacerbates anarchy. Have this situation repeated in enough American cities, the drug problem begins to impact the country at a strategic level at the cost of billions of dollars and loss of social cohesion.

Although illegal narcotics are the most overt means of creating social division by China, there are more covert means of qi that cause greater social instability. Interfering with domestic political issues is by far the most cost effective while at the same time also the most difficult for the West to prove. Regardless of nation, there are social and political issues with genuine desire and belief on both sides of every issue, but no matter how committed, each side will eagerly take resources to strengthen their cause without inquiring too deeply about where the resources come from. In qi, playing both sides of an issue in a rival nation's political discourse to cause social chaos can paralyze a rival government. This means the CCP could, through third parties, contribute to legitimate and illegitimate activist and political organizations to increase hyperbolic demagoguery and encourage animosity.

In terms of foreign interference with domestic politics, Western governments only seem to be interested in political interference during elections because such activity could be detected and acted upon if discovered. This is the only form of foreign interference that is something Western bureaucracies can actually confront but the CCP doesn't appear to give the West much opportunity. The US government stated in the past that China does not conduct election interference within the United States but other weaker nations, such as Taiwan and Australia, have declared the CCP has carried out election interference operations.[xcvii], [xcviii], [xcix] From the perspective of executing qi effectively, this lack of action makes sense because attributing any interference from the CCP would backfire and unite Western political factions. Instead, the CCP would be best at maximizing its psychological warfare elements by keeping such actions in the more nebulous realm of political activism.

Political activism is often done through non-profit organizations controlled and sponsored by private individuals or groups. The checks and balances to prevent state abuse of power in the West has led to the creation of unique rules for these political groups that makes investigation of any foreign interference or subversion difficult. Many fear non-profits are used for fraud and other illegal financial crimes because these activist groups often rely on small numbers of people or groups to provide a sizeable portion of their funds which would discourage internal controls or accountability.[c] Furthermore, in the case of political manipulation, much of the money would not be used illegally but instead used to fund more radical elements within activist organizations that could indirectly encourage chaotic behavior such as violence or just simple political obstruction. To make this element of qi more advantageous to the CCP is the lack of interest by Western governments or nonprofits to investigate such activities. Terrorism is a far more well-known threat that can use nonprofits to support their activities and yet actions against suspected terrorist-linked activist groups are limited.[ci]

So even if Chinese subversive activities are suspected in politically active non-profits, the facts would be very difficult to establish and almost impossible to prove malicious activity. In 2020, Newsweek claimed a study that nearly 600 groups within the US assisted the Chinese government indirectly through various means, including activist nonprofits, troll farms, and political lobbying.[cii] Furthermore, China is accused of supporting the most radical elements within social activist organizations to encourage divisions and violence beyond what was originally intended by the activists.[ciii], [civ] In other Western countries, other analysts indicate China used nonprofit think tanks in southern and central Europe to help support Belt and Road projects within poorer European countries and environmental lobbyist groups may have received support from the CCP to discourage domestic energy development.[cv] Other nonprofits can also be manipulated to undermine Western credibility while inhibiting the West's economy. Environmental activism is used by the CCP to diminish the political impact of China's poor environmental record while the US Congress and others are concerned the CCP is using Western activists and organizations to undermine Western energy and environmental policies. [cvi], [cvii] The added complication to all of this activity is that such nefarious subversion is likely going to only be reported by these groups' partisan rivals so, no matter how legitimate the concern of political interference maybe, the CCP's financial contributions guarantee the nonprofit organizations will simply accuse its detractors of political falsehoods and unfounded persecution.

The brilliance of using legitimate political activism to exacerbate social chaos synchronizes perfectly with Sun Tzu's qi and the PLA's unrestricted warfare. The ideal method of psychological warfare is to isolate targets into distinct groups and then play on those group's fears, biases, and ambitions.[cviii] Eventually, the groups will act on their own, fueled by demagoguery financed by the CCP through third parties. The CCP itself will not direct anything; it will simply send the resources to the most radical elements because totalitarian societies have difficulty evaluating the actual impact of any subversion in a free society. So, the CCP will likely avoid directing any activism itself and allow radicals within the West who understand the society to evaluate the best psychological approach.[cix] With all of this activity, the Maple Street Front of creating social division is still incomplete. Drugs and psychological subversion of politics are all means of targeting demographics and groups but the CCP also intends to target individuals as well.

Never before in warfare or political intrigue have governments been given the ability to target individuals, outside of national leadership, for ruin on a grand scale. If individual people can be destroyed psychologically, financially, and socially then those individuals will be too distracted or distraught to concern themselves with anything China does. Over the past century, major social events have occurred that have changed nations with monikers like the "Great Leap Forward" or "The Great Resignation", now the CCP potentially can unleash another great social change in its act of qi to cripple the West. A CCP inspired future event which in this book will be given the moniker "The Great Embarrassment".

The "Great Embarrassment" would be an event launched by the CCP's qi by using all the personal data China has accumulated over the years and publicly release all the data at once on as many Westerners as possible to expose all their "sins". Over the past decade, China has been linked with cyber breeches at the Office of Personnel Management,[cx] medical insurance companies like Anthem,[cxi] and credit score companies such as Equifax.[cxii] These cyberbreaches' severity is compounded with Chinese affiliated hacking groups developing malware to create backdoors such as the Winnti hacking group, into Massive Multiplayer Online (MMO) games while Chinese firms buy controlling interest in major video game companies that could collect personal data.[cxiii], [cxiv] All of this combined with mass credential theft from major social organizations means the CCP likely has more data on Western citizens than most believe.[cxv] All of this data does not even factor in the data collected from mobile apps such as TikTok that is used by millions globally.[cxvi] With all of the promise of using machine learning and big data analytics, the concept of compiling, correlating, and then affiliating all of this data to Western citizens is both possible and probably being done. It is not difficult to imagine qi supporting zheng in an overt war, by the CCP releasing damaging information on millions of Western individuals in bulk in a very short amount of time will cause immense social chaos. Illicit affairs, tax avoidance, embezzlement, criminal liaisons, hidden medical conditions, and private comments on loved ones are just some of the data that could be unleashed in the "Great Embarrassment". Such an event, if successfully executed with all other activities, would truly create a Western-wide Maple Street.

---

[i] Ibid, 127.

[ii] Ibid, 124.

[iii] TOI Staff, "Iran, China Sign Huge 25-year Strategic Deal; Could Reduce US Regional Influence," Times of Israel, March 27 2021. https://www.timesofisrael.com/iran-china-sign-major-25-year-strategic-cooperation-agreement/

[iv] Frederic Wehrey, Jerrold D. Green, et al., "The Rise of the Pasdaran: Assessing the Domestic Roles of Iran's Islamic Revolutionary Guard Corps," RAND Corporation, 2009, 55-56 & 59-64. https://www.rand.org/content/dam/rand/pubs/monographs/2008/RAND_MG821.pdf

[v] Ashley Lane, "Iran's Islamist Proxies in Middle East," Wilson Center, May 20, 2021. https://www.wilsoncenter.org/article/irans-islamist-proxies

[vi] Missiles of the World, "Missiles and Rockets of Hezbollah," CSIS Missile Defense Project, August 10, 2021. https://missilethreat.csis.org/country/hezbollahs-rocket-arsenal/

[vii] Jonathan Lis and Ben Samuels, "Mossad Foils Iranian Plot Assassinate Israeli Consulate Worker, US General," Haaretz, April 30, 2022. https://www.haaretz.com/israel-news/2022-04-30/ty-article/mossad-foils-iranian-plot-to-assassinate-israeli-consulate-worker-u-s-general/00000180-8a65-d4ee-a7a8-cb75e18f0000

[viii] David Sacks, "The China-Pakistan Economic Corridor – Hard Reality Greets BRI's Signature Initiative," Council on Foreign Relations, March 30, 2021. https://www.cfr.org/blog/china-pakistan-economic-corridor-hard-reality-greets-bris-signature-initiative

[ix] Jack Lau, "China Calls for 'Resolute' Action from Pakistan Against Terror Attacks on Chinese Nationals," South China Morning Post, May 12, 2022. https://www.scmp.com/news/china/diplomacy/article/3177532/china-calls-resolute-action-pakistan-against-terror-attacks

[x] William Chapman, "North Korean Leader's Son Blamed For Rangoon Bombing," Washington Post, December 3, 1983. https://www.washingtonpost.com/archive/politics/1983/12/03/north-korean-leaders-son-blamed-for-rangoon-bombing/ddec34cc-9c12-4fc6-bf75-36057091aa4e/

[xi] Reuters Staff, "Murder at the Airport: The Brazen Attack on Kim Jong Nam," Reuters, April 1, 2019. https://www.reuters.com/article/us-northkorea-malaysia-kim-murder/murder-at-the-airport-the-brazen-attack-on-kim-jong-nam-idUSKCN1RD185

[xii] Emily Crane, "Chinese Prosecutor and Ex-NYPD Detective Are Among Nine People Charged with Acting as Spies To 'Stalk and Harass' US Residents In A Bid To Pressure Them To Return Home To China," Daily Mail, July 22, 2021. https://www.dailymail.co.uk/news/article-9815147/Nine-people-charged-stalking-residents-China.html

[xiii] Mary Hong, "California Church Shooting Suspect Had Ties to CCP Front Group," The Epoch Times, May 18, 2022. https://www.theepochtimes.com/southern-california-shooter-has-ties-to-the-communist-regimes-united-front-work_4474258.html

[xiv] Kerry K. Gershaneck, Political Warfare: Strategies for Combating China's Plan to 'Win without Fighting', (Quantico, VA: Marine Corps University Press, 2020) 43-46, 52-53.

[xv] Ammar A. Malik, Bradley Parks, Brooke Russell, Joyce Jiahui Lin et al., "Banking on the Belt and Road: Insights from a global dataset of 13,427 Chinese Development Projects," William and Mary Research Lab AIDDATA, September 21, 2021, 18. https://docs.aiddata.org/ad4/pdfs/Banking_on_the_Belt_and_Road__Insights_from_a_new_global_dataset_of_13427_Chinese_development_projects.pdf

[xvi] Ibid, 72-74.

[xvii] Ibid, 12-18.

[xviii] Niall Ferguson, Empire: The Rise and Demise of the British World Order and the Lessons for Global Power, (NY: Perseus Books Group, 2004) 192-196.

[xix] Fikayo Akeredolu, "Don't Sleep on China's Global Development Initiative," The Diplomat, July 12, 2022. https://thediplomat.com/2022/07/dont-sleep-on-chinas-global-development-initiative/

[xx] Carla Freeman and Alex Stephenson, "How Should the US Respond to China's 'Global Security Initiative?" United States Institute of Peace, August 4, 2022. https://www.usip.org/publications/2022/08/how-should-us-respond-chinas-global-security-initiative

[xxi] Chansambath Bong, "Cambodia's Disastrous Dependence on China: A History Lesson," The Diplomat, December 4, 2019. https://thediplomat.com/2019/12/cambodias-disastrous-dependence-on-china-a-history-lesson/

[xxii] John D. Ciorciari, "China and Cambodia: Patron and Client?" International Policy Center of the Gerald R. Ford School of Public Policy, IPC Working Paper Series 121, June 14, 2013, 8-10. https://www.researchgate.net/publication/272300796_China_and_Cambodia_Patron_and_Client

[xxiii] Sun Narin, "Ordinary Cambodians Can Only Look On, As Cambodia Ranks Among Most Indebted Countries to China, VOA Cambodia, December 20, 2019, 1-3. https://www.voacambodia.com/a/ordinary-cambodians-can-only-look-on-as-cambodia-ranks-among-most-indebted-countries-to-china/5212914.html

[xxiv] Ibid, 4-5.

[xxv] Editors, "How Chinese Money is Changing Cambodia," Deutsche Welle, August 22, 2019. https://www.dw.com/en/how-chinese-money-is-changing-cambodia/a-50130240

[xxvi] Lindsay Murdoch & Kate Geraghty, "The Next Macau? China's Big Gamble in Cambodia," Sydney Morning Herald, June 20, 2018. https://www.smh.com.au/world/asia/the-next-macau-china-s-big-gamble-in-cambodia-20180615-p4zlqg.html

[xxvii] Ibid.

[xxviii] Stefan Lovgren, "Southeast Asia Maybe Building Too Many Dams Too Fast," National Geographic, August 23, 2018. https://www.nationalgeographic.com/environment/article/news-southeast-asia-building-dams-floods-climate-change

[xxix] Abdur Rahman Mohammad Thamim, Abu Rushd Muhammed Shaikh et al., "Sino-Lanka Relations: A Critical Study on Chinese Importance in Sri Lankan Economic Development," International Journal of Research and Scientific Innovation, vol 7, Issue 9, November 2020, 213-217. https://www.rsisinternational.org/journals/ijrsi/digital-library/volume-7-issue-11/209-227.pdf

[xxx] Sumathi Bala, "Sri Lanka 'Can't Get Out of Crisis Without China," Analyst Says," CNBC, July 20, 2022. https://www.cnbc.com/2022/07/20/china-can-play-critical-role-to-help-sri-lanka-with-its-debt-problems-analysts-say.html

[xxxi] Institute Report, "African Growing Enterprise File," Institute of Developing Economies Japan External Trade Organization, Chapter 8, 2009. https://www.ide.go.jp/English/Data/Africa_file/Manualreport/cia_08.html

[xxxii] Alexandra Wexler, "After Default, Zambia's Outsized Bet on Copper Could Play into China's Hands," Wall Street Journal, April 27, 2021. https://www.wsj.com/articles/after-default-zambias-outsized-bet-on-copper-could-play-into-chinas-hands-11619514520

[xxxiii] Indu Saxena, Robert Uri Dabaly, and Arushi Singh, "China's Military and Economic Prowess in Djibouti: A Security Challenge for the Indo-Pacific," Journal of Indo-Pacific Affairs, November 18, 2021. https://www.airuniversity.af.edu/JIPA/Display/Article/2847015/chinas-military-and-economic-prowess-in-djibouti-a-security-challenge-for-the-i/

[xxxiv] Kamal Dev Bhattarai, "China's Growing Political Clout in Nepal," The Diplomat, May 22, 2020. https://thediplomat.com/2020/05/chinas-growing-political-clout-in-nepal/

[xxxv] Bruce Pannier, "Central Asia: Getting Pulled From All Directions At The Crossroads of Eurasia," Radio Free Europe, December 24, 2021. https://www.rferl.org/a/central-asia-influences-china-russia-islam/31600167.html

[xxxvi] Dante Shulz, "China-Kyrgyzstan Relations," Caspian Policy Center Research, February 25, 2022. https://www.caspianpolicy.org/research/security-and-politics-program-spp/china-kyrgyzstan-relations

[xxxvii] Article, "Why Equatorial Guinea May Host China's First Atlantic Naval Base," The Maritime Executive, January 7, 2022. https://maritime-executive.com/article/why-equatorial-guinea-may-host-china-s-first-atlantic-naval-base

[xxxviii] Alex Vines, "What is the Extent of China's Influence in Zimbabwe?" BBC News, November 20, 2017. https://www.bbc.com/news/world-africa-42012629

[xxxix] Manjari Chatterjee Miller, "China and the Belt and Road Initiative in South Asia," Council on Foreign Relations Discussion Paper, June 2022, 15-17. https://cdn.cfr.org/sites/default/files/report_pdf/Miller-ChinaBRISouthAsia.pdf

[xl] Uzair Younus, "Pakistan's Growing Problem with Its China Economic Corridor," United States Institute of Peace, May 26, 2021. https://www.usip.org/publications/2021/05/pakistans-growing-problem-its-china-economic-corridor

[xli] Maziar Motamedi, "Iran Says 25-year China Agreement Enters Implementation Stage," Al-Jazeera, January 15, 2022. https://www.aljazeera.com/news/2022/1/15/iran-says-25-year-china-agreement-enters-implementation-stage#:~:text=Iran%20says%2025-year%20China%20agreement%20enters%20implementation%20stage,year%20%5BMajid%20Asgaripour%2FWest%20Asia%20News%20Agency%20via%20Reuters%5D

[xlii] Martin Chorzempa, "Export Controls Against Russia are Working – with the Help of China," Peterson Institute for International Economics, June 27, 2022. https://www.piie.com/blogs/realtime-economic-issues-watch/export-controls-against-russia-are-working-help-china

[xliii] Catherine Wong, "China 'Tells US Envoy John Kerry It Will Follow Its Own Climate Road Map," South China Morning Post, September 3, 2021. https://www.scmp.com/news/china/diplomacy/article/3147540/china-tells-us-envoy-john-kerry-it-will-follow-its-own-climate

[xliv] Colum Lynch, "China Launches Counterattack Against US Effort to Restore Taiwan's Status at WHO," Foreign Policy, May 15, 2020. https://foreignpolicy.com/2020/05/15/china-taiwan-united-states-world-health-organization-observer/

[xlv] Report, "You'll Be Fired if You Refuse: Labor Abuses in Zambia's Chinese State-Owned Copper Mines," Human Rights Watch, November 4, 2011. https://www.hrw.org/sites/default/files/reports/zambia1111ForWebUpload.pdf

[xlvi] Muhammad Azam, "How China's Presence In Balochistan is Intensifying Regionalist Tendencies," Foreign Policy, March 2, 2022. https://thediplomat.com/2022/03/how-chinas-presence-in-balochistan-is-intensifying-regionalist-tendencies/

[xlvii] Celine Sui, "Chinese Racism is Harming Africans," Foreign Policy, April 15, 2020. https://foreignpolicy.com/2020/04/15/chinas-racism-is-wrecking-its-success-in-africa/

[xlviii] Yaqiu Wang, "From Covid to Blackface on TV, China's Racism Problem Runs Deep," Human Rights Watch, February 18, 2021. https://www.hrw.org/news/2021/02/18/covid-blackface-tv-chinas-racism-problem-runs-deep

[xlix] Sebastian Seibt, "Djibouti-China Marriage 'Slowly UnRavelling' as Investment Project Disappoints," France 24, April 9, 2021. https://www.france24.com/en/africa/20210409-djibouti-china-marriage-slowly-unravelling-as-investment-project-disappoints

[l] Abu-Bakarr Jalloh and Fang Wan, "Resistance Growing to Chinese Presence in Zambia," Deutsche Welle (DW), April 9, 2019. https://www.dw.com/en/resistance-growing-to-chinese-presence-in-zambia/a-47275927

[li] Munza Mushtaq, "China's Control over Sri Lankan Infrastructure Reignites Fears," Nikkei Asia, June 30, 2021. https://asia.nikkei.com/Spotlight/Belt-and-Road/China-s-control-over-Sri-Lankan-infrastructure-reignites-fears

[lii] Ismail Akwei, "Babies: Unwanted Seeds Sown in African Women by Fleeting Chinese Workers," Face-2-Face Africa, February 9, 2019. https://face2faceafrica.com/article/babies-unwanted-seeds-sown-in-african-women-by-fleeting-chinese-workers

[liii] China State Council, *Made in China 2025 Economic Plan*, Translated by the Center for Security and Emerging Technology, May 19, 2015. https://cset.georgetown.edu/publication/notice-of-the-state-council-on-the-publication-of-made-in-china-2025/

[liv] Commission Report, "Update to the IP Commission Report - The Theft Of American Intellectual Property: Reassessments Of The Challenge And United States Policy," National Bureau of Asian Research: Commission on the Theft of American Intellectual Property, February 2017. https://www.nbr.org/program/commission-on-the-theft-of-intellectual-property/

[lv] Natalie Obiko Pearson, "Did a Chinese Hack Kill Canada's Greatest Tech Company?" Bloomberg, July 1, 2020. https://www.bloomberg.com/news/features/2020-07-01/did-china-steal-canada-s-edge-in-5g-from-nortel

[lvi] Kim Zetter, "Google Hack Attack Was Ultra Sophisticated, New Details Show," Wired, January 14, 2010. https://www.wired.com/2010/01/operation-aurora/

[lvii] Pooja Prasad, "Adobe Investigates Corporate Network Security Issue," Adobe Blogs, January 12, 2010. https://web.archive.org/web/20100114065445/https://blogs.adobe.com/conversations/2010/01/adobe_investigates_corporate_n.html

[lviii] Press Release, "Fourth Defendant Pleads Guilty to Stealing Trade Secrets from GlaxoSmithKline to Benefit Chinese Pharma Company," Department of Justice, January 3, 2022. https://www.justice.gov/usao-edpa/pr/fourth-defendant-pleads-guilty-stealing-trade-secrets-glaxosmithkline-benefit-chinese

[lix] Nate Raymond, "Ex-GlaxoSmithKline Scientist Admits Stealing Trade Secrets for Chinese Company," Reuters, January 4, 2022. https://www.reuters.com/legal/government/ex-glaxosmithkline-scientist-admits-stealing-trade-secrets-chinese-company-2022-01-03/

[lx] Michael Kan, "Chinese Hackers Go After Third-Party IT Suppliers to Steal Data," ComputerWorld Magazine, April 4, 2017. https://www.computerworld.com/article/3187361/chinese-hackers-go-after-third-party-it-suppliers-to-steal-data.html

[lxi] Congressional Testimony, "Prepared Statement of Edward H. You Supervisory Special Agent Biological Countermeasures Unit Countermeasures and Operations Section Weapons of Mass Destruction Directorate Federal Bureau of Investigation," US Congress, March 16, 2017. https://www.uscc.gov/sites/default/files/Ed_You_Testimony.pdf

[lxii] Jeffrey Mervis, "Fifty-Four Scientists Have Lost Their Jobs As A Result Of NIH Probe Into Foreign Ties," Science Magazine, June 12, 2020. https://www.science.org/content/article/fifty-four-scientists-have-lost-their-jobs-result-nih-probe-foreign-ties

[lxiii] Megan Gates, "An Unfair Advantage: Confronting Organized Intellectual Property Theft," ASIS International Security Magazine, July 1, 2020. https://www.asisonline.org/security-management-magazine/articles/2020/07/an-unfair-advantage-confronting-organized-intellectual-property-theft/

[lxiv] Eduard Kovacs, "Chinese Cyberspies Continue Targeting Medical Research Organizations," Security Week, August 21, 2019. https://www.securityweek.com/chinese-cyberspies-continue-targeting-medical-research-organizations

[lxv] Reuters Staff, "Hackers Tried to Steal Airbus Secrets via Contractors: AFP," Reuters, September 26, 2019.

[lxvi] Laura Widener, "Chinese Hackers Target At Least 27 Universities In US, Canada, Asia to Steal Maritime Technology," American Military News, March 5, 2019. https://americanmilitarynews.com/2019/03/chinese-hackers-target-at-least-27-universities-in-us-canada-asia-to-steal-maritime-technology/

[lxvii] Steven T. Dennis, "FBI Chief Says China is Trying to 'Steal Their Way' to Economic Dominance," TIME, July 24, 2019. https://time.com/5633390/fbi-christopher-wray-china-counterintelligence/

[lxviii] Scott Ikeda, "Chinese Hackers Demonstrate Their Global Cyber Espionage Reach with Breach at 10 of the World's Biggest Telecoms," CPO Magazine, July 8, 2019. https://www.cpomagazine.com/cyber-security/chinese-hackers-demonstrate-their-global-cyber-espionage-reach-with-breach-at-10-of-the-worlds-biggest-telecoms/

[lxix] Jeff Mordock, "Bo Mao, Chinese Professor, Sentenced to Time Served in Huawei Theft Case," Washington Times, December 14, 2020. https://www.washingtontimes.com/news/2020/dec/14/bo-mao-chinese-professor-sentenced-time-served-hua/

[lxx] Jon Brodkin, "US Says It Can Prove Huawei Has Backdoor Access To Mobile-Phone Networks," Ars Technica, February 11, 2020. https://arstechnica.com/tech-policy/2020/02/us-gave-allies-evidence-that-huawei-can-snoop-on-phone-networks-wsj-says/

[lxxi] Eva Dou, "Documents Link Huawei to China's Surveillance Programs," Washington Post, December 14, 2021. https://www.washingtonpost.com/world/2021/12/14/huawei-surveillance-china/

[lxxii] Press release, "Two Chinese Hackers Working with the Ministry of State Security Charged with Global Computer Intrusion Campaign Targeting Intellectual Property and Confidential Business Information, Including COVID-19 Research," Department of Justice, July 21, 2020. https://www.justice.gov/opa/pr/two-chinese-hackers-working-ministry-state-security-charged-global-computer-intrusion

[lxxiii] Press release, "Four Chinese Nationals Working with the Ministry of State Security Charged with Global Computer Intrusion Campaign Targeting Intellectual Property and Confidential Business Information, Including Infectious Disease Research," Department of Justice, July 19, 2021. https://www.justice.gov/opa/pr/four-chinese-nationals-working-ministry-state-security-charged-global-computer-intrusion

[lxxiv] Press release, "Jury Convicts Chinese Intelligence Officer of Espionage Crimes, Attempting to Steal Trade Secrets," Department of Justice, November 5, 2021. https://www.justice.gov/opa/pr/jury-convicts-chinese-intelligence-officer-espionage-crimes-attempting-steal-trade-secrets

[lxxv] Cybereason Nocturnus, "Operation CuckooBees: Cybereason Uncovers Massive Chinese Intellectual Property Theft Operation," May 4, 2022. https://www.cybereason.com/blog/operation-cuckoobees-cybereason-uncovers-massive-chinese-intellectual-property-theft-operation

[lxxvi] John C. Demers Senate Testimony, "Statement of Assistant Attorney General John C. Demers: China's Non-Traditional Espionage Against The United States: The Threat And Potential Policy Responses," Department of Justice Record, December 12, 2018. https://www.justice.gov/sites/default/files/testimonies/witnesses/attachments/2018/12/18/12-05-2018_john_c._demers_testimony_re_china_non-traditional_espionage_against_the_united_states_the_threat_and_potential_policy_responses.pdf

[lxxvii] Staff Report, "Threats to the US Research Enterprise: China's Talent Recruitment Plans," Permanent Subcommittee on Investigations, US Senate, November 18, 2019, 15-17. https://www.hsgac.senate.gov/imo/media/doc/2019-11-18%20PSI%20Staff%20Report%20-%20China's%20Talent%20Recruitment%20Plans%20Updated2.pdf

[lxxviii] Ibid, 23.

[lxxix] Ibid, 20.

[lxxx] Ibid, 27.

[lxxxi] Jane Lanhee Lee, "Stanford Professors Urge US to End Program Looking for Chinese Spies in Academia," Reuters, September 13, 2021. https://www.reuters.com/world/us/stanford-professors-urge-us-end-program-looking-chinese-spies-academia-2021-09-13/

[lxxxii] Tom Bartlett and Karin Fischer, "The China Conundrum: American Colleges Find the Chinese-Student Boom a Tricky Fit," The Chronicle of Higher Education, November 3, 2011. https://www.chronicle.com/article/the-china-conundrum/

[lxxxiii] Matt Schiavenza, "The Tenuous Relationship Between American Universities and Chinese Students," The Atlantic, May 30, 2015. https://www.theatlantic.com/education/archive/2015/05/american-universities-are-addicted-to-chinese-students/394517/

[lxxxiv] GAO-22-105727, "Export Controls: Enforcement Agencies Should Better Leverage Information to Target Efforts Involving US Universities," GAO, June 2022, 18-22. https://www.gao.gov/assets/gao-22-105727.pdf

[lxxxv] Eric Carlson and Peter Lichtenbaum, "China-Related Export Control Risks," Covington & Burling LLP, January 2016. https://www.cov.com/-/media/files/corporate/publications/2016/01/china_related_export_control_risks_january_2016.pdf

[lxxxvi] Ryan Hass, "Why has China Become Such a Big Political Issue?" Brookings Institute Policy Article, November 15, 2019. https://www.brookings.edu/policy2020/votervital/why-has-china-become-such-a-big-political-issue/

[lxxxvii] Thomas Lum, "China and Falun Gong," Congressional Research Service Report, May 25, 2006. https://www.justice.gov/sites/default/files/eoir/legacy/2013/06/13/China%20and%20Falun%20Gong.pdf

[lxxxviii] Kathleen McLaughlin, "Underground Labs in China are Devising Potent New Opiates Faster than Authorities can Respond," Science Magazine, March 29, 2017. https://www.science.org/content/article/underground-labs-china-are-devising-potent-new-opiates-faster-authorities-can-respond

[lxxxix] DEA Intelligence Report Executive Summary, "Fentanyl Flow to the United States," DEA, January 2020. https://www.dea.gov/sites/default/files/2020-03/DEA_GOV_DIR-008-20%20Fentanyl%20Flow%20in%20the%20United%20States_0.pdf

[xc] Vanda Felbab-Brown, "China and Synthetic Drugs Control: Fentanyl, Methamphetamines, and Precursors," Brookings Foreign Policy, March 2022, https://www.brookings.edu/research/china-and-synthetic-drugs-control-fentanyl-methamphetamines-and-precursors/

[xci] Kerry J. Byrne, "Second-hand Fentanyl Fumes Threaten Seattle Bus Drivers," New York Post, May 7, 2022. https://nypost.com/2022/05/07/second-hand-fentanyl-fumes-threaten-seattle-bus-drivers/

[xcii] Lee Ohanian, "Why San Francisco is Nearly the Most Crime-Ridden City in the US," Hoover Institution, November 2021. https://www.hoover.org/research/why-san-francisco-nearly-most-crime-ridden-city-us

[xciii] Eric Ting, "Don't Look Now But San Francisco's Poop Problem Seems to Be Getting Better," SF Gate, July 13, 2021. https://www.sfgate.com/bay-area-politics/article/San-Francisco-poop-problem-stats-streets-feces-new-16311073.php

[xciv] Joe Eskenazi, "The State of San Francisco Corruption," Mission Local News, March 15, 2021. https://missionlocal.org/2021/03/san-francisco-corruption/

[xcv] Andrew Chamings, "Study: San Francisco and Oakland are the most Gentrified Cities in US," SF Gate, July 6, 2020. https://www.sfgate.com/local/article/San-Francisco-Oakland-most-gentrified-cities-in-US-15389147.php

[xcvi] Trisha Thadani, "A Disaster in Plain Sight," San Francisco Chronicle, February 2, 2022. https://www.sfchronicle.com/projects/2022/sf-fentanyl-opioid-epidemic/

[xcvii] National Intelligence Council, "Foreign Threats to the 2020 US Federal Elections," Office of the Director of National Intelligence, March 10, 2021. https://www.dni.gov/files/ODNI/documents/assessments/ICA-declass-16MAR21.pdf

[xcviii] Rod McGuirk, "Australian Minister Accuses China of Election Interference," The Diplomat, April 27, 2022. https://thediplomat.com/2022/04/australian-minister-accuses-china-of-election-interference/

[xcix] Joshua Kurlantzick, "How China is Interfering win Taiwan's Election," Council on Foreign Relations, November 7, 2019. https://www.cfr.org/in-brief/how-china-interfering-taiwans-election

[c] Kayla Matthews, "Why Nonprofits Are More Vulnerable to Fraud Than For-Profit Businesses," NonProfitPRO, October 24, 2019. https://www.nonprofitpro.com/post/why-nonprofits-are-more-vulnerable-to-fraud-than-for-profit-businesses/

[ci] Financial Action Task Force, "Risk of Terrorist Abuse in Non-Profit Organizations," OECD, June 2014. https://www.fatf-gafi.org/media/fatf/documents/reports/Risk-of-terrorist-abuse-in-non-profit-organisations.pdf

[cii] Didi Kirsten Tatlow, "Exclusive: 600 U.S. Groups Linked to Chinese Communist Party Influence Effort with Ambition Beyond Election," Newsweek, October 26, 2020. https://www.newsweek.com/2020/11/13/exclusive-600-us-groups-linked-chinese-communist-party-influence-effort-ambition-beyond-1541624.html

[ciii] Michael Gonzalez, "This BLM Co-Founder and Pro-Communist China Group are Partnering Up. Here's Why." Daily Signal, September 15, 2020. https://www.dailysignal.com/2020/09/15/this-blm-co-founder-and-pro-communist-china-group-are-partnering-up-heres-why/

[civ] Scott McKay, "Is China Backing the Rioters in Our Streets?" The American Spectator, September 18, 2020. https://spectator.org/china-backing-rioters/

[cv] Bryce Barros and Etienne Soula, "Here and Now: Chinese Interference in the Transatlantic Space." Alliance for Securing Democracy, February 9, 2021. https://securingdemocracy.gmfus.org/here-and-now-chinese-interference-in-the-transatlantic-space/

[cvi] Wen Sheng, "China Becomes a Leader in Global War Against Climate Change," The Global Times, July 25, 2021. https://www.globaltimes.cn/page/202107/1229548.shtml

[cvii] Bonner R. Cohen, "House Committee Probes Environmental Group's Ties to China," The Heartland Institute, August 9, 2018.

[cviii] Field Manual, *FM 3-05.30 Psychological Operations*, (Washington DC: US Army HQ, April 2005) Chapter 6-2.

[cix] Ibid, Chapter 1-5.

[cx] Incident Descriptor, "Cybersecurity Incident OPM 2015," OPM, https://www.opm.gov/cybersecurity/cybersecurity-incidents/

[cxi] Press Release, "Member of Sophisticated China-Based Hacking Group Indicted for Series of Computer Intrusions, including 2015 Data Breach of Health Insurer Anthem Inc. Affecting Over 78 Million People," Department of Justice, May 9, 2019. https://www.justice.gov/opa/pr/member-sophisticated-china-based-hacking-group-indicted-series-computer-intrusions-including

[cxii] Press Release, "Chinese Military Hackers Charged in Equifax Breach," FBI, February 10, 2020. https://www.fbi.gov/news/stories/chinese-hackers-charged-in-equifax-breach-021020

[cxiii] Michael Hill, "Winnti Group Targets Video Game Developers with New Backdoor Malware," Infosecurity Group, May 21, 2020. https://www.infosecurity-magazine.com/news/winnti-video-game-developers/

[cxiv] Dace Aitel and Jordan Schneider, "If You Play Videogames, China May Be Spying on You," Wall Street Journal, October 28, 2020. https://www.wsj.com/articles/if-you-play-videogames-china-may-be-spying-on-you-11603926979

[cxv] Ravie Lakshmanan, "Researchers Link Multi-Year Mass Credential Theft Campaign to Chinese Hackers," The Hacker News, August 17, 2022. https://thehackernews.com/2022/08/researchers-link-multi-year-mass.html

[cxvi] Sandy Buglass, "TikTok Engaging in Excessive Data Collection," Infosecurity Group, July 18, 2022. https://www.infosecurity-magazine.com/news/tiktok-engaging-in-excessive-data/

Chapter 8: Dimensions of Qi: Non-military

The trans-military categories of qi are methods of warfare that are destructive to an enemy without resorting to overt organized violence. These target elements of a society that play a supporting role to the military dimensions of warfare such as building alliances, having technological superiority, and a confident unified population suitable for military recruitment. In contrast, the non-military category of unrestricted warfare deals with attacking the society itself by weakening its overall strengths to the point the targeted society is paralyzed in both form and function.[i] *Unrestricted Warfare* notes that such actions must be done simultaneously with the trans-military activities to effectively carry out the indirect attacks of qi. For ease of reference, the identified combined human social dimensions by the PLA authors and BlackOps Partners for the non-military category are again referenced here:

Economic Warfare	Financial Warfare	Business Warfare	Trade Warfare
Resource Warfare	Legal Warfare	Education Warfare	Smuggling Warfare
Media Warfare	Propaganda Warfare	Culture/Race Warfare	Ideological Warfare
Religious Warfare	Poisoning Warfare	Environmental Warfare	Regulatory Warfare

Again, these cited dimensions have a lot of overlap and all can be used simultaneously on the same objectives. Like the qi category of trans-military, the non-military dimensions will be consolidated into "fronts" for simplicity to show how multiple dimensions are used to achieve broad strategic objectives. This keeps the analysis more concise while also giving the necessary examples to demonstrate the extent of China's efforts into using indirect forms of attack to cripple the West.

Critical Infrastructure and Lines of Communication - Front:

Many of the problems in the West stem from consequences of too much success. After World War II, the West undertook a major capital-intensive modernization effort to create the infrastructure and transportation networks necessary to sustain highly industrialized capitalist-oriented societies. Midway through the Cold War, much of the fundamental physical infrastructure, including phonelines, power grids, water works, port upgrades, airports, railheads and major highways were completed. These expensive but critical facets have supported Western nations' tangible needs and wants with minimal disruption for about three decades.

Then in a short span of time, the Cold War ended, the information technology revolution started, and the movement to globalize the economy all occurred in the 1990s. The Cold War's end and the globalized trade movement created new markets and incentives for people to look and invest abroad while the information technologies being developed became the basis of economic growth which required far less capital investment. The emphasis on information technology and new economic markets led to years of neglecting the maintenance and growth of the infrastructure where economic development is now outpacing the Western nations' ability to adequately support it. After years of neglect and prioritizing foreign investment over national security, Western critical infrastructure is vulnerable to CCP meddling to the point where China could potentially paralyze rival Western states in a war scenario. To gauge the severity of these vulnerabilities, the US government carried out studies evaluating key infrastructure and industry vulnerabilities as directed by Presidential Executive Order 14017 and these reports highlight serious deficiencies.

Since the West emphasized globalized trade, seaports and maritime transportation are now more important to the US economy than at any previous time in its history yet the United States allowed itself to become completely dependent on foreign industry for maritime trade. The merchant marine that transports the bulk of goods to and from the United States is largely managed by 10 foreign merchant shipping companies. [ii] More threatening to the West is the fact China is the second largest merchant ship-owning country in the world.[iii] To compound this problem, the shipping industry streamlined cargo containers to reduce cost by increasing modularity in cargo storage capacity but these common cargo containers are not manufactured in the West. Instead, China manufactures 96% of all dry cargo containers and 100% of refrigerated cargo containers used in merchant shipping.[iv] This means that if the United States had to conduct a major military mobilization, it would require the use of foreign ships to transport critical supplies overseas while China's considerable influence in the maritime shipping industry could hamper any force projection effort.

What makes this problem worse are America's seaports. The growth of products and imports has outstripped the ability for the US to build the supporting infrastructure. 90% of all imported goods come into just 25 container ports, with Los Angeles and Long Beach being the largest two ports in the United States handling nearly half of all commercial imports.[v] The COVID lockdowns of 2020 created a crisis afterwards as major bottlenecks accumulated when few ports could offload cargo that had built up in warehouses and dockyards for months. Despite the United States being one of the most developed parts of the world, it has relied on port commercial infrastructure designed to handle a country of the Cold War era's economic size. Bottlenecks contributed to inflation and shortages and will likely continue to do so as many in the US government and state governments alike push for more immigration and consumer market growth without consideration of expanding the infrastructure to support population and market expansion.[vi]

Even when the cargo and materials get out of the port, there is the problem of interior lines of communication and shipping being neglected in the United States. To keep transportation services cheap while complying with the complex regulatory framework of the United States, railroads are streamlining the industry to be as efficient as possible. However, this means a reduction of employed persons and increasing use of automation to keep down costs. Fewer people also mean using fewer routes requiring the use of longer trains to carry the products. This means there are only a few critical junctures an enemy will need to target to disrupt national supply flows.[vii] For this system to work, the rail networks must rely more on "smart" systems that communicate with other freight companies and routing systems to maintain supply chain flows. Logically, this means transportation companies must invest more into building cyber networks to manage this process but as a consequence, leave these already bottleneck-prone routes vulnerable to cyber disruption.[viii]

All of these dangers to the United States supply distribution system are also becoming more vulnerable out of the political desire to decarbonize the economy. The urge to electrify systems to meet carbon reduction goals before completing the construction of the necessary infrastructure could potentially lead to disaster. If cargo lifting equipment such as cranes and forklifts or long-haul trucks become electric vehicles but there is no parallel expansion of the centralized power grids, then any power disruption will completely paralyze all supply and commodity shipments at the same time as power to cities are shut off.[ix], [x]

Adding more electrified vehicles to the power grid is not the only problem facing the United States' energy requirements. The American energy industry is a highly-skilled specialized workforce that remains mostly unionized so the cost of labor for this industry is high.[xi] Combine this with the political imperative to modernize the American power system with the use of solar and wind energy and upgrades are vulnerable to China.[xii] China dominates the global solar industry and already has made major inroads into supporting the United States' power demand by providing most of the solar cells demanded by the West's green ambitions.[xiii] The Department of Energy's recommendation to break away from this vulnerability by providing considerable government subsidies to domestic manufacturers over a very short timeline seems to rely more on hope than any practical reality.[xiv] At the same time, the Department of Energy also recommends more foreign investment into the green energy industry to offset the labor costs of the American market. These two recommendations will come into conflict as the CCP will exploit the slow processes of the American bureaucracy and legal system to use third parties to maintain access to the American solar market for the foreseeable future.[xv]

Also, the costs of transitioning the grid to a less-carbon intensive system doesn't address the current issue of upgrading the grid that already delivers that power to the consumer. There are too many components to switch out all at once so the large electric infrastructure is a combination of old and new systems. Analog and digital components work together in a hodgepodge fragmented system with various levels of cybersecurity. With no common standards or ability to track and protect all the software, industry control functions, and hardware means the CCP has years to target and exploit the power grid's vulnerabilities.[xvi] The United States has already experienced cyber disruptions to its critical infrastructure from private criminal actors who are small in scale compared the capabilities of China. In February 2021, a hacker attempted to gain access to a Florida water treatment plant to poison the town of Oldsmar. The attack failed, but given the variety of infrastructure in the hands of small municipalities and companies not equipped for such attacks, means a coordinated effort by a major political power like China across hundreds of municipalities simultaneously is more likely to succeed.[xvii] In that same year, the Colonial Oil Pipeline and much of the East Coast was paralyzed with a ransomware attack which caused hoarding and other panicked reactions. Although the hackers did not gain access to the pipeline itself, the risk that the hackers could, was enough to prompt the shutdown.[xviii]

The large complex systems that make up the United States infrastructure means there are many vectors for China to disrupt supplies and utilities. The Colonial pipeline attack also demonstrates that China doesn't need to actually succeed in all attacks, just the attempt being made public in the right circumstances can have the proper detrimental effect. China having direct or indirect access to either the energy supply chain or power grid itself makes nations hostage to Chinese aggression. This problem is not limited to the United States but impacts the entire West. European politicians seem oblivious to the lesson that a nation or polity in general should not put its energy requirements into the hands of potential adversaries. The Russo-Ukrainian War should have been a reflective moment but instead, the European Union is enabling China to be a major partner in its green energy development to lessen its dependence on Russia. Instead of building energy resilience, the EU is simply replacing its energy and utility dependence on one tyrannical regime with another more powerful one.[xix]

Economic Domination – Front:

The foundation for China's objectives of Tianxia and global hegemony center on economic domination. The CCP uses every single facet of unrestricted warfare to accomplish this goal. This front can be broken down into two separate groups of action. The first is undermining and subordinating the West's economies to China's dominance and the second group of action is using the large consumer market of China to lure Western direct investment making the West addicted and dependent on China's economic power. The key for the CCP is controlling the lifeblood of the modern global economy by being the leader in developing advanced technology and manufacturing. As seen in the trans-military portion of qi, the CCP concentrates on technology but the Chinese regime doesn't neglect any other aspect of their rivals' economies. This effort of qi is as broad as their technological acquisition efforts and use both licit and illicit means to gain advantages over the West's economies.

The first section of this front looks at the various means China is currently using to undermine the West's economic independence by using financial and legal means to tether Western prosperity to the whims of the CCP. Again, these efforts are complex and extensive to the point that China's influence reaches virtually into every facet of Western economies. Below is a small sampling of China's economic and business efforts in the West to better visualize the extent of economic qi. Unlike the technological espionage, this form of qi is indistinguishable from regular commerce which means most activity will not look nefarious unless evaluated in the wider context of unrestricted warfare. The duality of this form of qi makes it difficult for many Western businesses and entrepreneurs to accept that China is using economic activity as a political and potentially military weapon.

A small sampling of China's economic-related actions (qi) within the West:

· China acquisitions cover both great and small services to impact everyone's daily life and in 2016, Chinese Haier group bought GE's household appliance division.[xx]

· In 2017, the US Department of Energy failed to adhere to its own technology licensing transfer rules which enabled the Chinese firm Dalian Rongke to transfer newly developed advance battery technology from the US back to China, removing a US competitive edge in developing battery technology.[xxi]

· In the previous decade, China encouraged investors to buy up real estate in North America and Australia, causing a surge in housing prices leading to potential housing bubbles in places like Vancouver, Ontario, and Melbourne.[xxii]

· Before America's banning, America's rural wireless providers had China's Huawei telecommunications company's equipment installed in 25% of their networks as of 2018. Despite the ban, it will likely take many years to remove so much Chinese equipment from America's communication networks.[xxiii]

· Meanwhile China also encouraged investors into buying up commercial real estate to the point that Los Angeles became dependent on China with over $5 billion poured into real estate investments. A similar story is found in other cities like Seattle. As China clamped down on tax evasion, Los Angeles became directly impacted as Chinese real estate investments receded by the evading investors.[xxiv], [xxv]

· In total, at the height of China's real estate investments in the last decade, nearly $100 billion was invested into the United States alone before the political backlash in the US and China's tax evasion crackdown began to reverse the number of Chinese land investments.[xxvi]

· As of 2019, China purchased many hectares of farmland in the West but in national terms remains small: Chinese firms own less than 1% of all US farmland while also purchasing arable lands in Europe such as Ukraine and France.[xxvii], [xxviii], [xxix]

· Instead, China acquires agriculturally focused assets that don't take up as much land but are critical to farm production such as China's Shuanghui's 2013 acquisition of Smithfield Foods which controls America's pork supply, ChemChina's $43 billion purchase of Swiss farm chemical and seed corporation Syngenta, and agricultural trading companies such as Noble Agri and Nidera.[xxx], [xxxi]

· In 2019, the Federal Retirement Thrift Investment Board (FRTIB) that overseas many federal workers pensions attempted to invest its monies into Chinese firms and as of 2022, were stopped by fears of the US Congress over China's influence. This was done despite protests by FRTIB that claimed having security concerns were discriminatory.[xxxii]

· In 2020, British Telecom assessed it was so dependent on Huawei hardware for its cellular network that removing all the Chinese components would cost $700 million and not be secured until 2027.[xxxiii], [xxxiv]

· Even though China's purchase of American farmland is small on a national scale, China strategically purchases this land to be adjacent to valuable facilities such as military installations in North Dakota.[xxxv]

· In 2022, the FCC denied China Unicom the right to provide telecommunication services in the US but acknowledged that China can still operate the data centers that manage the information of both individuals and US companies, leaving the information vulnerable to Chinese exploitation.[xxxvi] Even as Chinese owned data centers are discouraged, many Chinese firms collocate their data with officially US-owned data centers which makes extricating China from US domestic data management more difficult.[xxxvii]

· China understands overt acquisitions are easy targets and will often use venture capital investments that are much harder to trace back to Chinese-owned enterprises. With the West becoming more cognizant of the potential threat, China uses limited partnerships by investing money into Western-own venture capital firms to gain access to technology firms and new tech startups. This gray area of regulations allows China to have continued access to Western technology firms despite the regulations.[xxxviii]

· Since the West distinguishes between private and public enterprise, the regulatory clamp downs on critical industries doesn't apply to most of the West's economy, enabling Chinese investments in many industries and services. China has invested over a quarter of a trillion dollars into the United States' various industries in the past decade.[xxxix]

In the West, the differentiation of public vs private activities makes many of these examples appear as benign economic transactions and activities. China exploits this cultural blind spot to help keep the West complacent as many in the West fail to understand the CCP can command any Chinese citizen or company to do its bidding, even at the cost of their own well-being and safety. So, every investment and acquisition done by China can be used in its qi and in the event of hostilities between the West and China, would almost certainly intend to use all Chinese assets in the West as weapons.

Of course, these are just examples of China garnering economic influence within Western countries' territory. The other major group of economic domination is the use of China's own domestic market to keep the West economically tethered and dependent on China. China's allure as a major market entices investors from all over the world. The promise of being able to trade goods and services with potentially hundreds of millions of customers can blind anyone with the promise of wealth and financial stability. The less glamourized incentive is the promise of foreign investors having the costs of doing business being drastically reduced by the lax regulatory requirements and in some cases, slave labor.[xl]

Once foreign investors become addicted to China's economic wealth these lax regulatory standards will be reversed whenever the Party needs to ensure the Chinese government always remains in control. Companies are allowed to conduct business freely so long as it doesn't interfere with CCP control and the Chinese-owned firms retain dominance in the Chinese markets. There are many Western firms who attempted to become investors and participants in China's economy but ultimately failed because of the CCP interference. While others admitted to just not sufficiently adapting to unique Chinese customer expectations. Despite many foreigners' hopes, Chinese political interference happens whenever the Party needs something and this is never spelled out in any legal contract or document. China will always ensure Chinese firms have the controlling stake in a domestic market and will compel foreign businesses to enter into joint ventures with Chinese firms subsidized by the Chinese state to ensure China always has a controlling stake.[xli]

Failure to comply with the wishes of the CCP will unleash a variety of punishments. The CCP can change a foreign company's permissive regulatory environment into one of red-tape, fees, and time lost. These tactics are often so debilitating, that many groups that advise foreign companies entering into China are advised that it will be cheaper for them to just create a joint venture with a Chinese firm from the start. Sort of like the mafia, these organizations recommend paying the "protection racket" of joint ventures as cheaper and healthier than being independent.[xlii] In China, the CCP will remind the investors it is always the master, not the market.

In spite of this loss of control and being junior partner in all ventures, most firms that stay in China have made profitable returns in the past two decades. Since many Western firms' gauge success by quarterly results, the easy money, access to cheap abundant labor, and lax laws (when in the CCP's favor) provide short term gains which helps convert many Western business leaders into advocates of the CCP and China.[xliii] Even the largest foreign companies in the world become enticed by the CCP and will more often than not become trapped and effectively extorted into complying with the CCP's wishes. Two glaring examples involve the American tech giants. Before Google abandoned its efforts to establishing a market presence in China, the company collaborated with the CCP to build a highly sophisticated censoring search engine under the project name "Dragonfly". Google abandoned the project by 2019 but these events can give the impression Google only abandoned the project due to enormous political pressure in the West after the project was leaked by *The Intercept*.[xliv] Not to be left out, Apple signed a $275 billion deal with China which obligates them to use Chinese firms to support Apple's product supply chain.[xlv] Consequently, Apple appears to have readily accepted using Chinese suppliers that use Uyghur slave labor in Apple product assembly.[xlvi], [xlvii]

The CCP's qi also use less publicized means of exerting control on foreign corporations and businesses. Many foreign firms' fortunes are tied to China's, so the Chinese regime has imposed multiple national security laws that compel foreigners to comply with CCP requirements. Even if such compliance would be illegal in the foreign company's home country, companies will still obey because if one wants to do business in China, one must contort to the CCP's central-absolutist regime. President Xi Jinping pushed multiple new laws to strengthen the CCP's enforcement powers within China while also increasing the Party's hold over foreign investors. From 2015-2017, China passed the National Security Law, the Cyber Security Law, and the National Intelligence Law then later in 2021, China passed a Data Security Law. The combination of these laws helps the CCP control not only all information originating from China but also gain access to foreign data within China.

In the 2015 National Security Law, Article 8 explicitly links national security with economic and social development and Article 11 states all citizens and organizations, regardless of function, are obligated to preserve national security. Article 77 and 79 states the duties of citizens to report all activities that endanger the state and to provide full support to all relevant security organizations when required.[xlviii] Given most foreign companies are joint ventures, the law will override any proprietary non-disclosure agreements if national security is involved and the CCP will make the determination about what constitutes a national security threat.

In 2017, both the Cybersecurity Law and the National Intelligence Law were enacted. Under the Cybersecurity Law's Article 9, all companies using networks must submit to security checks to make sure all data storage complies with security protection standards and that no element of a company's network is off limits.[xlix], [l] If this wasn't comprehensive enough, the National Intelligence Law mandates all Chinese citizens cooperate with China's intelligence services at all times as stated in Article 7.[li] One major implication is that any Chinese citizen working with foreign investors is obligated to report or disclose anything the CCP deems pertinent to national security. Since all aspects of Chinese society are deemed part of the public sphere and there is no private sphere, every company, regardless of type will be scrutinized. Not being satisfied with this broad power, new controls on electronic data were imposed by the 2021 Data Security Law. It mandates all companies within China must comply with the Chinese government's data security standards. The law remains deliberately vague so any company or person could easily be interpreted as being in violation if the CCP thinks it advantageous to do so.[lii] This law also holds foreign companies hostage by Article 26 which states the Chinese regime can retaliate against any foreign company whose nation economically punishes China, incentivizing major foreign firms into lobbying against new anti-China laws or actions in their home countries.[liii]

Given all these rules, one must ask the question of how Anglosphere and European companies comply with Chinese law while not violating privacy and data protection laws of the companies' home countries? How do companies shield their countries' citizens' personal data when China demands full access? Also, do these companies block China's access to their overseas networks or are they complicit with the Chinese regime installing backdoors for "inspections"? How do they stop the CCP from using the data and credentials on these inspected networks to access other company networks in America or Europe? These questions are unlikely to be completely answered anytime soon.

Where China can't control foreign companies through financial or legal means, the CCP uses its dominance over the fundamental commodities that support these companies. Semiconductors are the contemporary lifeblood of every industry and these critical components need numerous unique materials.[liv] China, by use of subsidies and little environmental standards, was able to drive out most competition in the critical mineral extraction and refinement markets. If any country tries to separate or de-couple from its economic dependence from China, it risks severe shortages of critical minerals and resources needed to sustain the defying country's industries.[lv] China still controls nearly 70% of global export of rare earths used in technological manufacturing and while rare earths are actually abundant,[lvi] they are just difficult to process and their extraction is polluting and labor intensive. This discourages foreign competitors who are unwilling to spend the extra money for greater independence from China. With so many tools available to the CCP, it is easy to see how China uses the methods of qi to subvert foreign economies to remain dependent on China, even if it is detrimental in the long run.

Thought Control – Front:

An important objective of China's indirect forces is to destroy the decision-making ability of rival countries. If the CCP can create self-doubt, political division, and co-opt at least a portion of opponent country's population and politically influential elites, then China can paralyze their enemy's ability to act before any open war begins. Disrupting the West's ability to act decisively against China requires focus on multiple dimensions of unrestricted warfare to include propaganda, cultural, ideological, educational, and legal warfare simultaneously. The CCP understands they cannot realistically subvert the entire society and government of the United States or all of Europe. Instead, China's activities are meant to create enough societal influence to neuter any major actions by the West to confront China. If qi is successful, then all Western attempts to mobilize their societies to act against China in a united cohesive effort will be watered down, delayed, or stopped altogether. China doesn't expect to have an army of fifth columnists and Manchurian candidates to take over Western institutions, but to just cause enough chaos and public division on China to render Western governments impotent. These efforts are termed as malign-influence operations by the US government.[lvii]

Unlike the "Turn the West into Maple Street" Front where the Chinese use psychological warfare and malign-influence operations to turn Westerners against each other, the "Mind Control" Front is designed to nullify criticism of China or make China's ways and values more appealing to Western populations. Like all other forms of qi, this indirect force uses both overt and covert means to subvert perceptions of China that work in conjunction with the other fronts to achieve success more easily. Of course, the most obvious are the CCP and Chinese government official mouth pieces and propaganda organizations.

China Daily, China Central Television (CCTV), *Xinhua News*, and the various instruments of China's Ministry of Foreign Affairs set the narratives the CCP wants to convey to the world. However, the mistrust in the West makes direct propaganda from Chinese state-controlled media ineffective and instead will use money, educational institutions, and co-opted third parties as the principal means to convey China's preferred narratives in the West itself. These are useful for ensuring just enough doubt is planted within Western societies to create sufficient domestic resistance against any policy or narrative that might conflict with China's interests.

China's wide range of activities show how much the CCP values information control and how much they rely heavily on financial incentives and manipulating cultural sensitivities to get the Party's way. After China's state-controlled media conveys the CCP's narrative, the CCP's other subversive organizations manipulate their foreign opponents' beliefs and opinions to conform to this preferred narrative. Although there are many more, the best-known Chinese malign-influence organizations include the 50-Cent Army, the United Front Work Organization, and the Confucius Institutes. China's 50-Cent Army is a name derived from numerous rumors describing how the Chinese regime hires Chinese citizens, not state employees, to post comments on social media in large numbers to undermine to critics and astroturfing political positions that better conform to China's interest. Paid commentators, in either money or social credit, can help infiltrate forums, online communities, and comments sections to divide and fragment various social groups and constituencies. Using false information and accusations help create confusion, intimidation, or self-doubt among anti-CCP advocates who would then either self-censor or leave social media after intense bullying. These activities are not all directed by the CCP, many indoctrinated or nationalist citizens also volunteer, making direct CCP-affiliation to astroturfing difficult to prove.[lviii], [lix]

One study indicated that one out of every 178 social media posts in China in 2019 were posted by pro-government shills but that was identified by analyzing only the most overt messages. Subtler or more nuanced messaging could likely expand the extent of the CCP presence in social media. More importantly, this demonstrates the scale of the CCP's commitment of resources into eliminating criticism because this study assessed the overwhelming number of entries were by humans and not bots, showing large numbers of persons participating in China's anti-criticism efforts.[lx] The efforts in China are easier to gauge because it is a state-controlled internet but one can extrapolate the scale of effort used in Western social media to be extensive as well. Bots are likely far more prominent in Western social media because many Chinese netizens are unlikely to be sufficiently aware of all the Western cultural nuances. Bots can more easily overwhelm a comments section or forum with endless postings of pro-CCP statements. However, these overt actions could also be potential distractions to divert Western governments' resources away from targeting more nuanced and covert operations since some studies indicate social media botting and trolling doesn't appear too effective in changing minds. [lxi]

The more classical physically present institutional subversion by the CCP is more directed at Western institutions of government, academia, culture, and entertainment instead of the general public. These require more focused and time-consuming efforts to successfully inject CCP influence. Most of these efforts are done by the CCP's United Front Work Department using both explicit and subtle means to influence Western groups and organizations.[lxii] United Front sets up many cultural and nonprofit organizations to provide the aura of harmless respectability with the official narratives of improving international harmony and friendship. In academia, the most prevalent organization being the United Worker backed Confucius Institutes where over 110 organizations were established in American universities with the proclaimed goal of building good relations with China by building bridges with student exchanges.[lxiii] Although these organizations did provide language courses, cultural studies, and student exchanges, these institutes encouraged demonstrations, taught selective history, and offered financial incentives to discourage anti-CCP discourse.[lxiv] By 2019, most of the institutes closed down after these organizations' brazen pro-CCP activities became too contentious to continue unchallenged. However, like all matters of qi and unrestricted warfare, the Chinese regime began reintroducing the same kind of organizations under different names and structures but with the same goal.[lxv] Many academics will actively protect these propaganda tools because of the financial incentives the CCP uses and over the years it is now bearing fruit in the form of producing appeasers. These are just some of the overt means the CCP uses to control the minds of Westerners regarding China. The more subtle means use financial incentives to co-opt Western domestic cultural, news media, and entertainment companies to diminish anti-CCP voices.

Understanding something takes time and China's efforts to co-opt Western entertainment was no different. The CCP learned to entice foreign businesses to invest in China quickly in the 1990s but China's influence didn't permeate the entertainment sector until the late 2000s. China's flagrant copyright infringement combined with entertainers enamored with the Tibetan independence cause in the 1990s by films like *Seven Years in*

Tibet kept the CCP out longer than in most industries. However, by the late 2000s, China was learning to ingratiate themselves with movie and music company executives, producers, and artists by offering to comply with copyright rules, stroking egos, and offering to invest in productions. [lxvi] Of course, China also appreciated the influence of organized sports and its impact on Western escapism. Eager to win over sports organizations, the CCP sponsored major sports stars to come to China such as Michael Jordan's trip to China in 2004 and getting Yao Ming drafted into the NBA.[lxvii] After nearly two decades, of pouring money into ventures, projects, and companies, the CCP have become one of the most important investors and owners of Western entertainment. Rarely does China micromanage or oversee the making of entertainment and instead lets the co-opted leaders of these industries run the day-to-day operations. All the CCP requires is the ability to review and veto anything that might cause China or the Party to lose miànzi.

Whether sports, movies, or music, the money of China has produced numerous grovelers in the entertainment industry that come to the rescue of the reputation of the CCP. For instance, basketball is one of the most important sports in China so the NBA was successfully targeted with financial inducements to buy its loyalty. The NBA panicked in 2019 when the Chinese firms Tencent, CCTV, and Vivo suspended their deals after Houston Rockets' General Manager Daryl Morey tweeted support to Hong Kong democracy advocates forcing the NBA to apologize to China and condemn Mr. Morey.[lxviii] LA Lakers player LeBron James assisted the NBA by stating Mr. Morey's statement was out of ignorance.[lxix] At the same time in the video game industry, Activision Blizzard suspended their *Hearthstone* video game e-sports champion, Chung Ng Wai, and took away his prize money of $10,000 for publicly calling for Hong Kong's independence from China.[lxx] In the movie industry, Disney remained quiet and complicit when its Chinese citizen star of the live version of *Mulan*, Crystal Liu Yifei, condoned the CCP's crackdown on Hong Kong protestors.[lxxi] This was not Disney's only controversy either. As the largest studio company, its behavior is often mimicked by the rest of the movie industry. To placate the CCP's contempt for blacks,[lxxii], [lxxiii], [lxxiv] Disney shrank down John Boyega's picture in all *Star Wars* advertisements in China.[lxxv] To compound Disney's bad publicity was the revelation it also used filming locations in the Uyghur persecuted areas of Xinjiang Province where alleged concentration camps are located to purge the Turkic groups.[lxxvi] Although in the new *Top Gun: Maverick* movie released in 2022 there is an indication the CCP's influence in the entertainment industry might be weakening because the movie showed the previously censored flag of Taiwan on Tom Cruise's jacket. Due to the considerable amount of money in Western entertainment, China is unlikely to leave soon but instead become more discreet in its activities.[lxxvii]

China's malign-influence operations don't neglect traditional news media either. China often uses either its own government agencies or third-party firms to pay for advertisements and other means to exert influence on private news firms. In the Department of Justice's records of foreign agent registration is one for the *China Daily* submitted on April 30, 2021, which shows the Chinese state media company contributed large advertisement campaigns to the LA Times, Financial Times, Time Magazine, and Foreign Policy.[lxxviii]

In academia and general media, articles are made to either downplay China's culpability or divert attention by using Western culturally sensitive issues as distractions. As stated earlier in the book, China attempts to co-opt Western activist groups by claiming to be supporters of certain global issues to increase pressure on Western governments. Without any direct control or manipulation, simply convincing Western audiences the world needs to work with China to solve issues can encourage these groups to disrupt any attempts to counter China's influence. One example of China's propaganda success was when environmentalist groups criticized President Biden for challenging China by proclaiming cooperation with the CCP is the best way of solving the environmental crisis, even though there is little evidence China does anything substantive on the issue.[lxxix] Environmentalism is a topic China is routinely criticized for and the CCP has no intention of allowing a political issue hinder its power. So, instead of making environmentalism about saving the planet, China often uses class warfare and economic inequality arguments to convince utopianist environmental movements non-state-controlled economies in the West are to blame and the solution is creating more centrally planned economies instead. This shift in goals in the environmental movement has been noticed and criticized from within as committed environmentalists criticized their peers for hindering the cause by trying to punish economies and businesses more than finding actual environmental solutions.[lxxx] This is the kind of subtle shifts in argument the CCP often pursues because it is impossible to prove the CCP influenced this change of activist focus but still the CCP profits from the activists attacking their economic competitors instead of condemning CCP negligence.

The largest observed effort of China using its media influence in the West is the continuing efforts to downplay their culpability with the Wuhan-originated COVID-19 Virus. In one instance, the CCP created a fake Swiss biologist account to post articles on media sites that the virus came from somewhere else.[lxxxi] Meanwhile, China exploits the culturally sensitive racial issue in the West to shame Western governments and academics from actually investigating the COVID virus' origins. In one example, the Chinese government stated "white-supremacists" were pushing conspiracy theories that COVID might have come from a Wuhan Lab leak and that COVID actually came from the United States.[lxxxii] The CCP calculates the emotional reaction by using racially charged terminology would garner activist groups in the West into siding with China. And if these are too subtle, the Chinese state-controlled *People's Daily* stated the West, particularly the United States, should be held culpable because the virus was made by a US Army lab and the US should compensate the world in a bid to deflect their own incompetence.[lxxxiii]

Beyond media manipulation is the CCP's interest in Western think tanks and nonprofit groups. Since Western policymakers often rely on "subject matter experts" from think tanks for input on policy decisions, the CCP poured considerable monies for favorable think tank articles to persuade policymakers and their advisors to concede to Chinese interests.[lxxxiv], [lxxxv] To make matters more difficult, many pro-China or anti-interventionist articles could actually be written out of sincere belief but Chinese financing obfuscates any effort to determine what is sincere and what is astroturfed. For instance, many in US politics believe the United States is militarily overextended and commits too many resources to the international system and call for a more limited defensive role. Some go as far as advocating for other powers like China to have a more prominent role in global governance.[lxxxvi] This can be interpreted as sensible restraint or appeasement of America's main adversary but the true intentions cannot be proven either way. Other articles complain that hindering or blocking China hurts America's businesses. Some of these articles are so conciliatory towards China, it is very difficult not to construe some of them as advocating American capitulation into vassalhood and one wonders if the CCP itself wrote some of these articles.[lxxxvii]

True information and disinformation operations are conducted in places democratic governments either don't look or it is politically dangerous for a Western government to look. What makes all of China's efforts especially effective is that the single greatest enabler of China's malign influence operations in the West, the Western governments themselves. Western government bureaucracies were mostly designed and built during the industrial age around the beginning of the Cold War in the 20th Century. These organizations are designed for one-size fits all solutions because the ability to receive, understand, and disseminate important information in the execution of policies was very limited. So, these organizations became specialized in specific missions and tasks to better focus on issues. This creates stove-pipe information channels where agencies rarely inform each other and budgets were provided based on this organizational design. This encouraged turf wars, to hoard information, discourage sharing of information or to jointly work on policy implementation issues. Consequently, Western government bureaucracies are slow to react to situations, lack the flexibility to handle unforeseen obstacles, and discourage initiative or innovation as it could endanger the senior leadership whose power relied on a fixed way of doing things. This means China could carry out malign information operations in multiple areas at once with only one bureaucracy looking at one effort at a time, failing to see all of China's efforts. Even then, the information flows would be slow to the point that China could quickly change tactics before the bureaucracies could act. One positive consequence of the 9/11 Terrorist Attack was the beginning of changing bureaucratic culture to a more joint-collaborative organizational one but that itself is taking at least a generation to create.[lxxxviii] However, this only addresses the problem of information flows and sharing, not the Western governments' lack of understanding of how to deal with disinformation even if they were made more efficient in reacting to it.

The one size-fits all systems of Max Weberian bureaucracy actively seek ways to justify themselves by simple metrics. Metrics are tangible and presentable to lawmakers and voters to enable them to see the bureaucracy doing something; but these metrics use simplified models and criteria to make them understandable and easy to act upon in black and white yes or no answers. However, the complexities of the real world mean simple actions don't always match with the more realistic complex solutions required to fix real world problems. The CCP is not foolish, its malign influence propaganda and disinformation are not complete lies or fabrications, but more often than not, they use partial truths, emphasize irrelevant real facts, play on emotions, or sometimes, because it can favor the CCP even tell the complete truth. When the Western governments are wrong or incompetent, China telling the truth in those circumstances helps the Party. When disinformation is conducted, more often than not, the Western governments will make several mistakes that only undermine their efforts to counter Chinese influence. The first mistake is the governments' attempt to shut down or censor the Chinese malign influence by shutting down the disinformation. This is an easy metric to gauge and score for the bureaucracies but all China has to do to defeat these actions is state a truth or have an anti-Western government third-party state a truth for China and wait to have the Western governments try to shut down or censor that truth. Then China, without overtly pointing this out, will make sure large segments of the West's populations notice the Western governments censoring or removing accurate information. This will convince a portion of the population that the Western governments are hiding their own incompetence or corruption. So, Western government overreaction fulfills the CCP's qi objectives of keeping the public focus on Western failings instead of China's malign influence.

The second biggest problem is the modern West's false belief in the concept of authoritative sources of information. More often than not, Western governments will use social media firms, technology companies, and the traditional news media to either silence or "fact-check" reports, opinions, or articles deemed disinformation. The problem is assuming the "authoritative sources" are actually reliable and trustworthy enough to seek accurate information without having their own agenda. Since all organizations are run by humans, this clearly doesn't happen. The worst part of this is that the very organizations entrusted by Western governments to counter disinformation are the major news media conglomerates who are more often than not the least capable in dealing with misinformation. First of all, many of these media organizations have taken advertisement money from Chinese interests and are owned by companies that will be financially impacted by any trade disruption with China like the *New York Times* employing former *China Daily* workers.[lxxxix] Secondly, the media have a financial incentive to create as much sensationalism as possible to gain ratings and views by causing social division and exacerbating problems which helps more than hurts the CCP. Finally, one last problem with using these organizations is that they are often bad at their job.

Pew research studies have shown the news media is one of the least trusted professions and institutions in the United States with many convinced news media is biased and self-serving.[xc] Given the history of journalistic performance, there is a lot of precedent to justify the American public's misgivings. News media has a long history of self-serving behavior to include creating or purveying their own misinformation. The tradition goes back to the 19th Century with William Randolph Hearst and Joseph Pulitzer's "Yellow Journalism" rivalry. This yellow journalism became so bad that each side's newspapers printed completely untrue or exaggerated stories from Cuba to portray Spanish rule far more brutally than was true to garner more support for Cuban liberation from the Spanish Empire.[xci] Or Hearst's attempts to destroy Orson Welles for *Citizen Kane*.[xcii] There are many contemporary examples of news media failings to legitimize the general public's skepticism towards anything journalists say.

In 2003, the *New York Times* journalist Jayson Blair was fired after being caught plagiarizing a story but the lack of any oversight had allowed him to write fraudulent stories for years before being caught.[xciii] In 2004, the British media had to fire Piers Morgan for using a fake photo of a British soldier allegedly abusing an Iraqi by using forced perspective when the reality was the soldier was standing guard next to the Iraqi.[xciv] At the same time in the United States, CBS' Dan Rather published a false memorandum alleging President George W. Bush went AWOL and Rather was forced to resign, yet the news industry still rewards the man with honorary awards years after the fact.[xcv]'[xcvi] Not to be outdone, NBC's Brian Williams indulged in some exaggeration of his own when he claimed on the Late Show that he had been in a helicopter hit by a grenade in the Iraq War to show his bravery.[xcvii] Such incidents aren't limited to prominent news anchors either. In 2012, Politico published a list of 10 journalists caught faking news stories since 1921 as part of its story of the *New Yorker*'s firing of Jonah Lehrer who was fabricating quotes from Bob Dylan.[xcviii] Not to be out done, in Germany the news magazine *Der Spiegel* had to admit one of their top journalists, Claas Relotius, had submitted fake news stories for years.[xcix] In 2019, a journalist from *Newsweek* was dismissed after posting a false news story about President Trump in Afghanistan.[c] More recently in the pursuit of sensationalism, CNN misrepresented a teenager named Nick Sandman as a racial instigator and had to reach a legal settlement due its inaccurate allegations.[ci] These are just some examples of the news media's transgressions and social media companies often use the same news media and activist groups as the references for fact checking. However, in a lawsuit against Facebook in 2021, the company admitted their fact-checkers are third party groups providing their educated opinions, not facts, to avoid a defamation suit. This further demonstrates that having an authoritative title doesn't mean the information provided by that authoritative source is true.[cii] Europeans trust their media more than Americans[ciii] but this could be attributed to cultural differences as the First Amendment allows for more independent sources of information and European culture broadly speaking is inclined to defer to authority, whether wrong or right, after centuries of autocratic rule instilling deference to "one's betters".

Western governments at large are asking the public to trust social and news media who are considered by much of the public to be feckless, corrupt, sloppy, incompetent, deceiving, and self-serving. Yet, even though Western governments rely on these news and social media services to counter foreign maligned influence and then ask the public to blindly trust these dubious organizations, these governments don't practice what they preach. For instance, in the US government the Executive Branch runs a bureaucracy filled with agencies that act as the authoritative sources for government policy issues; but the US Congress still mandates oversight of these institutions to keep accountable anything stated or done by the Executive Branch to better protect democratic-republic mechanisms. So, if the US government doesn't trust its own authoritative sources without oversight, why would the public trust the unaccountable news and social media firms who have a proven history of unreliability?

Governments and the media look for the overt disinformation from China and others because it is easy to identify and target but rarely is this China's main effort. The purpose of unrestricted warfare is to cause social division within the West without China being blamed. By the governments focusing on "fake news" posted by social media personalities or declaring who qualifies as an authoritative source, the governments inadvertently create resentments and mistrust as their targeting is done by a black and white standard that ignores nuance. So, social divisions and mistrust between the public and the Western governments grow just as the CCP's qi intends. No one notices any potential CCP involvement because China's enablers are the oblivious Western institutions and companies themselves whose battle for information control within Western society enables qi to work. As long as Western governments seek only to quash overt misinformation and continue to rely on the least reliable institutions of media within the West to persuade or sometimes compel social compliance, Western governments will continue to be China's greatest enabler of misinformation and malign influence.

---

[i] Qiao Liang and Wang Xiangsui, *Unrestricted Warfare*, (VT: Echo Point Books & Media, originally published in 1999) 123 - 127.

[ii] US government report, "Supply Chain Assessment of the Transportation Industrial Base: Freight and Logistics," Department of Transportation, February 2022, 21-22. https://www.transportation.gov/sites/dot.gov/files/2022-03/EO%2014017%20-%20DOT%20Sectoral%20Supply%20Chain%20Assessment%20-%20Freight%20and%20Logistics_FINAL_508.pdf

[iii] News article, "China has Become the World's Second-Largest Ship-Owning Nation," Institute of Shipping Economics and Logistics, 2019. https://www.isl.org/en/news/china-become-the-worlds-second-largest-ship-owning-nation

[iv] US government report, "Supply Chain Assessment of the Transportation Industrial Base: Freight and Logistics," Department of Transportation, February 2022, 21-22. https://www.transportation.gov/sites/dot.gov/files/2022-03/EO%2014017%20-%20DOT%20Sectoral%20Supply%20Chain%20Assessment%20-%20Freight%20and%20Logistics_FINAL_508.pdf

[v] Ibid, 11.

[vi] Pia Orrenius, "Benefits of Immigration Outweigh the Costs," Spring 2016, https://www.bushcenter.org/catalyst/north-american-century/benefits-of-immigration-outweigh-costs.html

[vii] US government report, "Supply Chain Assessment of the Transportation Industrial Base: Freight and Logistics," Department of Transportation, February 2022, 17-18. https://www.transportation.gov/sites/dot.gov/files/2022-03/EO%2014017%20-%20DOT%20Sectoral%20Supply%20Chain%20Assessment%20-%20Freight%20and%20Logistics_FINAL_508.pdf

[viii] Ibid, 17-18.

[ix] Ibid, 27.

[x] Jeff St. John, "When will EV Trucks Be Ready for Large-Scale adoption? It's Complicated," Canary Media, March 17, 2022. https://www.canarymedia.com/articles/electric-vehicles/when-will-ev-trucks-be-ready-for-large-scale-adoption-its-complicated

[xi] US government report, "America's Strategy to Secure the Supply Chain for a Robust Clean Energy Transition," Department of Energy, February 24, 2022, 37. https://www.energy.gov/sites/default/files/2022-02/America%E2%80%99s%20Strategy%20to%20Secure%20the%20Supply%20Chain%20for%20a%20Robust%20Clean%20Energy%20Transition%20FINAL.docx_0.pdf

[xii] Ibid, 1, 5.

[xiii] International organization report, "Special Report on Solar PV Global Supply Chains," International Energy Agency, July 2022, 7-8. https://iea.blob.core.windows.net/assets/d2ee601d-6b1a-4cd2-a0e8-db02dc64332c/SpecialReportonSolarPVGlobalSupplyChains.pdf

[xiv] US government report, "America's Strategy to Secure the Supply Chain for a Robust Clean Energy Transition," Department of Energy, February 24, 2022, 9. https://www.energy.gov/sites/default/files/2022-02/

America%E2%80%99s%20Strategy%20to%20Secure%20the%20Supply%20Chain%20for%20a%20Robust%20Clean%20Energy%20Transition%20FINAL.docx_0.pdf.

[xv] Ibid, 29.

[xvi] Ibid, 41-43.

[xvii] Jeremy Rasmussen, "Lessons Learned from Oldsmar Water Plant Hack," Security Today, April 5, 2021. https://securitytoday.com/articles/2021/04/05/lessons-learned-from-oldsmar-water-plant-hack.aspx

[xviii] Sean Michael Kerner, "Colonial Pipeline Hack Explained: Everything You Need to Know," TechTarget, April 26, 2022. https://www.techtarget.com/whatis/feature/Colonial-Pipeline-hack-explained-Everything-you-need-to-know

[xix] EU Commission Report, "Sino-European Innovative Green and Smart Cities," EU CORDIS, July 22, 2022. https://cordis.europa.eu/project/id/774233/reporting

[xx] Tomas Kellner, "Done Deal: GE Sells Its Appliances Business To Haier For $5.6 Billion," GE News Release, June 6, 2016. https://www.ge.com/news/reports/done-deal-ge-sells-its-appliances-business-to-haier-for-5-6-billion

[xxi] Courtney Flatt and Laura Sullivan, "The US made a Breakthrough Battery Discovery-then Gave the Technology to China," August 3, 2022. https://www.npr.org/2022/08/03/1114964240/new-battery-technology-china-vanadium

[xxii] Wolf Richter, "Chinese investors are inflating housing markets in the US, Canada, and Australia," Business Insider, June 10, 2018. https://www.businessinsider.com/china-investors-inflating-housing-markets-in-us-canada-australia-2018-6

[xxiii] Mike Bano, "Huawei Equipment Currently Deployed by 25% of US Rural Wireless Carriers, RWA says," Fierce Wireless, December 11, 2018. https://www.fiercewireless.com/wireless/huawei-equipment-currently-deployed-by-25-u-s-rural-wireless-carriers-rwa-says

[xxiv] Roger Vincent, "As China Puts the Brakes on Overseas Investment, Los Angeles' Development Boom Takes a Hit," LA Times, April 1, 2018. https://www.latimes.com/business/la-fi-chinese-property-sale-20180401-story.html

[xxv] Mike Rosenberg, "Foreign Investors Pouring Billions into Seattle Commercial Real Estate," The Seattle Times, November 12, 2016. https://www.seattletimes.com/business/real-estate/foreign-investors-pouring-billions-into-seattle-commercial-real-estate/

[xxvi] Andrew Soergel, "China is Buying its Way into the US Economy," US News, May 17, 2016. https://www.usnews.com/news/articles/2016-05-17/china-is-buying-its-way-into-the-us-economy

[xxvii] Caitlin Welsh and Jamie Lutz, "Foreign Purchases of US Agricultural Land: Facts, Figures, and an Assessment of Real Threats," Center for Strategic and International Studies, September 8, 2021. https://www.csis.org/analysis/foreign-purchases-us-agricultural-land-facts-figures-and-assessment-real-threats

[xxviii] Marine Jobert, "China Buys Up Agricultural Land in Central France," Euractiv, April 10, 2016. https://www.euractiv.com/section/agriculture-food/news/china-buys-up-agricultural-land-in-central-france/

[xxix] News report, "China to Invest in 3 Million Hectares of Ukrainian Farmland," Reuters, September 22, 2013. https://www.reuters.com/article/china-ukraine-idUSL3N0HI04620130922

[xxx] Caitlin Welsh and Jamie Lutz, "Foreign Purchases of US Agricultural Land: Facts, Figures, and an Assessment of Real Threats," Center for Strategic and International Studies, September 8, 2021. https://www.csis.org/analysis/foreign-purchases-us-agricultural-land-facts-figures-and-assessment-real-threats

[xxxi] Fred Gale and Elizabeth Gooch, "China's Agricultural Investment Abroad is Rising," USDA Research Service, April 24, 2018. https://www.ers.usda.gov/amber-waves/2018/april/china-s-agricultural-investment-abroad-is-rising/

[xxxii] John McCrank, "Federal Pension Fund Says Bill Banning China Investment is Discriminatory," Reuters, November 22, 2019. https://www.reuters.com/article/us-usa-trade-tsp/federal-pension-fund-says-bill-banning-china-investment-is-discriminatory-idUSKBN1XW20E

[xxxiii] Dan Swinhoe, "BT Begins Ripping out Huawei Hardware from UK Mobile Network," Data Center Dynamics, May 18, 2021. https://www.datacenterdynamics.com/en/news/bt-begins-ripping-out-huawei-hardware-from-uk-mobile-network/

[xxxiv] Press Release, "Rubio Releases Hold on Federal Retirement Thrift Investment Board Nominees," Office of Senator Marco Rubio, June 2, 2022. https://www.rubio.senate.gov/public/index.cfm/press-releases?ID=0C8BDC8A-57DE-41FC-BCCC-949EF30B3A03

[xxxv] Lars Erik Schonander and Geoffrey Cain, "China is Buying the Farm: State-owned Companies have Bought many Acres near US Military Bases. What is Beijing up to?" Wall Street Journal, September 8, 2022. https://www.wsj.com/articles/the-chinese-are-buying-the-farm-north-dakota-hong-kong-land-food-shortage-supply-chain-usda-11662666515

[xxxvi] Sebastian Moss, "FCC Revokes China Unicom Americas' Permit to Provide Telco Services In US, But Warns Data Center Services Could Continue," Data Center Dynamics, January 31, 2022. https://www.datacenterdynamics.com/en/news/fcc-revokes-china-unicom-americas-permit-to-provide-telco-services-in-us-but-warns-data-center-services-could-continue/

[xxxvii] Dan Swinhoe, "FCC Seeks To Exclude Three More Chinese Telcos From US Networks," Data Center Dynamics, March 19, 2021. https://www.datacenterdynamics.com/en/news/fcc-seeks-exclude-three-more-chinese-telcos-us-networks/

[xxxviii] Elisabeth Braw, "How China is Buying Up the West's High Tech Sector," Foreign Policy Magazine, December 3, 2022. https://foreignpolicy.com/2020/12/03/how-china-is-buying-up-the-wests-high-tech-sector/

[xxxix] Statistic report, "Foreign Direct Investment (FDI) From China In The United States From 2000 To 2021," Statista Research Department, August 2, 2022. https://www.statista.com/statistics/188935/foreign-direct-investment-from-china-in-the-united-states/

[xl] US government fact sheet, "Forced Labor in China's Xinjiang Region," Department of State, July 1, 2021. https://www.state.gov/forced-labor-in-chinas-xinjiang-region/

[xli] Marcus Lu and Miranda Smith, "American Companies that Failed in China," Visual Capitalist, February 9, 2022. https://www.visualcapitalist.com/american-companies-that-failed-in-china/

[xlii] China Briefing, "China Joint Ventures as Strategic Investment," Dezan Shira & Associates, October 27, 2009. https://www.china-briefing.com/news/china-joint-ventures-as-a-strategic-investment/

[xliii] Speech Transcript, "Attorney General William P. Barr Delivers Remarks on China Policy at the Gerald R. Ford Presidential Museum," Department of Justice, July 16, 2020. https://www.justice.gov/opa/speech/attorney-general-william-p-barr-delivers-remarks-china-policy-gerald-r-ford-presidential

[xliv] Jeb Su, "Confirmed: Google Terminated Project Dragonfly, Its Censored Chinese Search Engine," Forbes, July 19, 2019. https://www.forbes.com/sites/jeanbaptiste/2019/07/19/confirmed-google-terminated-project-dragonfly-its-censored-chinese-search-engine/?sh=25d8923a7e84

[xlv] Matthew McMullan, "Report: Apple Agreed to a $275 Billion Deal with China," Alliance for American Manufacturing, December 15, 2021. https://www.americanmanufacturing.org/blog/report-apple-agreed-to-a-275-billion-deal-with-china/

[xlvi] Katie Canales, "7 Apple Suppliers in China Have Links to Forced Labor Programs, Including the Use of Uyghur Muslims from Xinjiang, According to A New Report," Business Insider, May 10, 2021. https://www.businessinsider.com/apple-china-suppliers-uyghur-muslims-forced-labor-report-2021-5?op=1

[xlvii] Press release, "Xinjiang: Chairs Issue Statement about Forced Labor in Apple's Supply Chain," Congressional-Executive Commission on China, June 8, 2021. https://www.cecc.gov/media-center/press-releases/chairs-issue-statement-about-forced-labor-in-apple%E2%80%99s-supply-chain-in

[xlviii] Translation, "National Security Law of the People's Republic of China," China Law Translate, July 1, 2015. https://www.chinalawtranslate.com/en/2015nsl/#_Toc423592306

[xlix] Lauren Maranto, "Who Benefits from China's Cybersecurity Laws?" Center for Strategic and International Studies, June 25, 2020. https://www.csis.org/blogs/new-perspectives-asia/who-benefits-chinas-cybersecurity-laws

[l] Translation by Rogier Creemers, Paul Triolo, and Graham Webster, "Cybersecurity Law of the People's Republic of China," New America, June 29, 2018. https://www.newamerica.org/cybersecurity-initiative/digichina/blog/translation-cybersecurity-law-peoples-republic-china/

[li] Translation, "National Intelligence Law of the People's Republic of China," National People's Congress, June 27, 2017. https://cs.brown.edu/courses/csci1800/sources/2017_PRC_NationalIntelligenceLaw.pdf

[lii] Yvonne Lau, "Here's What Beijing's Sweeping New Data Rules Will Mean for Companies," Fortune, September 1, 2021. https://fortune.com/2021/09/01/china-data-security-law-beijing-management-regulation-internet/

[liii] Translation, "Data Security Law of the People's Republic of China," National People's Congress, June 10, 2021. https://web.archive.org/web/20220618154704/http://www.npc.gov.cn/englishnpc/c23934/202112/1abd8829788946ecab270e469b13c39c.shtml

[liv] SIA comments, "Comments of the Semiconductor Industry Association (SIA) On the Notice of Request for Information on 'Critical and Strategic Materials Supply Chains," Semiconductor Industry Association, July 22, 2014. https://www.semiconductors.org/wp-content/uploads/2018/06/OSTP-comments-on-critical-and-strategic-materials-september-2014.docx.pdf

[lv] Stew Magnuson, "China Maintains Dominance in Rare Earth Production," National Defense Magazine, September 8, 2021. https://www.nationaldefensemagazine.org/articles/2021/9/8/china-maintains-dominance-in-rare-earth-production

[lvi] Govind Bhutada, "Visualizing China's Dominance in Rare Earth Metals," Visual Capitalist, January 13, 2021. https://elements.visualcapitalist.com/chinas-dominance-in-rare-earth-metals/

[lvii] Statutory Code Reference, *50 U.S. Code § 3059 - Foreign Malign Influence Response Center*, Cornell Law School Reference, December 20, 2019. https://www.law.cornell.edu/uscode/text/50/3059#e_2

[lviii] Rongbin Han, "Defending the Authoritarian Regime Online: China's "Voluntary Fifty-Cent Army," ReserachGate Reposting of The China Quarterly, December 2015, 9-11. https://www.researchgate.net/publication/272490419_Defending_the_Authoritarian_Regime_Online_China%27s_Voluntary_Fifty-cent_Army

[lix] Gary King, Jennifer Pan, and Margaret E. Roberts, "How the Chinese Government Fabricates Social Media Posts for Strategic Distraction, not Engaged Argument," Harvard, April 9, 2017, 17. https://gking.harvard.edu/files/gking/files/50c.pdf

[lx] Ibid, 11 & 26.

[lxi] Tom Robertson, "Why the Pentagon's Disinformation Campaigns Crashed and Burned," The National Interest, September 22, 2022. https://nationalinterest.org/blog/techland-when-great-power-competition-meets-digital-world/why-pentagon%E2%80%99s-disinformation

[lxii] Government report, "China's Overseas United Front Work: Background and Implications for the United States," US-China Economic and Security Review Commission, August 24, 2018. https://www.uscc.gov/research/chinas-overseas-united-front-work-background-and-implications-united-states

[lxiii] Ibid, 12-13.

[lxiv] Ibid, 13-14.

[lxv] Lin Yang, "Controversial Confucius Institutes Returning to U.S. Schools Under New Name," Voice of America News, June 27, 2022. https://www.voanews.com/a/controversial-confucius-institutes-returning-to-u-s-schools-under-new-name/6635906.html

[lxvi] Chris Fenton, *Feeding the Dragon: Inside the Trillion Dollar Dilemma Facing Hollywood, the NBA, & American Business* (NY: Post Hill Press, 2020) 9-11, 63-67.

[lxvii] Ibid, 80-84.

[lxviii] Manish Singh, "Chinese Firms Tencent, Vivo and CCTV Suspend Ties with The NBA Over Hong Kong Tweet," TechCrunch, October 8, 2019. https://techcrunch.com/2019/10/08/chinese-firms-tencent-vivo-and-cctv-suspend-ties-with-the-nba-over-hong-kong-tweet/

[lxix] News report, "Lebron Addresses Backlash to Hong Kong Comments," Reuters, October 15, 2019. https://www.reuters.com/article/us-basketball-nba-lal-lebron-backlash/lebron-addresses-backlash-to-hong-kong-comments-idUSKBN1WV01F

[lxx] Daniel Victor, "Blizzard Sets Off Backlash for Penalizing Hearthstone Gamer in Hong Kong," NY Times, October 9, 2019. https://www.nytimes.com/2019/10/09/world/asia/blizzard-hearthstone-hong-kong.html

[lxxi] Rebecca Davis, "Hong Kong Protesters Push Boycott of Disney's 'Mulan' After Star States Support for Police Crackdown," Variety, August 15, 2019. https://variety.com/2019/film/news/disney-mulan-crystal-liu-yifei-china-hong-kong-protest-police-crackdown-1203304483/

[lxxii] Jenni Marsh, "China Says It Has A 'Zero-Tolerance Policy' For Racism, But Discrimination Towards Africans Goes Back Decades," CNN, March 18, 2021. https://www.cnn.com/2020/05/25/asia/china-anti-african-attacks-history-hnk-intl/index.html

[lxxiii] Sarah Zheng and Aaina Bhargava, "How Racism and Discrimination Affect Black People in China and Hong Kong," South China Morning Post, December 2, 2020. https://www.scmp.com/lifestyle/article/3112105/how-racism-and-discrimination-affects-black-people-china-and-hong-kong

[lxxiv] Xianan Jin, "How COVID-19 Exposed China's Anti-Black Racism," Open Democracy, March 2, 2021. https://www.opendemocracy.net/en/pandemic-border/how-covid-19-exposed-chinas-anti-black-racism/

[lxxv] Maane Khatchatourian, "'Star Wars' China Poster Sparks Controversy After Shrinking John Boyega's Character," Variety, December 4, 2015. https://variety.com/2015/film/news/star-wars-china-poster-controversy-john-boyega-1201653494/

[lxxvi] Juwon Park, "Disney Criticized for Filming 'Mulan' in China's Xinjiang," AP News, September 9, 2020. https://apnews.com/article/ap-travel-virus-outbreak-ap-top-news-international-news-south-korea-c60ffb94e1e5c56eae4e5bcb50571839

[lxxvii] Rhoda Kwan, "Taiwan Cheers 'Top Gun: Maverick' For Defying Chinese Censors," NBC News, June 3, 2022. https://www.nbcnews.com/news/world/taiwan-cheers-top-gun-maverick-defying-chinese-censors-rcna31571

[lxxviii] Government form, "3457 Supplemental Statement Pursuant to the Foreign Agents Registration Act of 1938, as amended," Department of Justice, May 24, 2021. https://efile.fara.gov/docs/3457-Supplemental-Statement-20210524-34.pdf

[lxxix] Open Letter to President Biden, "Cooperation, Not Cold War To Confront Climate Crisis," Friends of the Earth, July 7, 2021. https://foe.org/wp-content/uploads/2021/07/Cooperation-Not-Cold-War-To-Confront-the-Climate-Crisis-129.pdf

[lxxx] Alec Stapp, "What Many Progressives Misunderstand About Fighting Climate Change," The Atlantic, September 25, 2022. https://www.theatlantic.com/ideas/archive/2022/09/capitalism-clean-energy-technology-permitting/671545/

[lxxxi] Suranjana Tewari, "China: Swiss Embassy Urges Media to Remove Scientist Fake News," BBC, August 11, 2021. https://www.bbc.com/news/world-asia-china-58168588

[lxxxii] Tyrone Clarke, "Beijing Claims US 'Likely' COVID-19 Source, and 'White Supremacists' Are Bullying Anti-Lab Leak Scientists," Sky News Australia, July 6, 2021. https://www.skynews.com.au/world-news/china/beijing-claims-us-likely-covid19-source-and-white-supremacists-are-bullying-antilab-leak-scientists/news-story/9ea5987d422088c1c03fa006fb30306e

[lxxxiii] Zhong Sheng, "U.S. Practice to Claim Compensation For COVID-19 Outbreak A Shame for Human Civilization," People's Daily, May 3, 2020. https://web.archive.org/web/20200504222940/http://en.people.cn/n3/2020/0503/c90000-9686646.html

[lxxxiv] Craig Singleton, "Follow the Money: Exposing China's Influence Operations at Academic Institutions and Think Tanks," Foundation for the Defense of Democracies, November 24, 2020. https://www.fdd.org/analysis/2020/11/24/china-influence-institutions-think-tanks/

[lxxxv] Special Report, "China's Influence and American Interests," Hoover Institute, November 29, 2018. https://www.hoover.org/sites/default/files/research/docs/diamond-schell_oct2020rev_ch5.pdf

[lxxxvi] Special Report, "A New Direction: A Foreign Policy Playbook on Military Restraint for the Biden Team," Quincy Institute for Responsible Statecraft, December 3, 2020. https://quincyinst.org/2020/12/03/a-new-direction-a-foreign-policy-playbook-on-military-restraint-for-the-biden-team/

[lxxxvii] Joshua Kurlantzick, "Let China Win. It's Good for America," Washington Post, January 15, 2016. https://www.washingtonpost.com/opinions/let-china-win-its-good-for-america/2016/01/14/bfec4732-b9b6-11e5-829c-26ffb874a18d_story.html

[lxxxviii] US Law, "Implementing Recommendations of the 9/11 Commission Act of 2007." US Congress, 2007. https://www.congress.gov/110/plaws/publ53/PLAW-110publ53.htm

[lxxxix] Isabel Van Brugen, "Several New York Times Staff Previously Worked for CCP-Controlled Media: Report," The Epoch Times, April 10, 2021. https://www.theepochtimes.com/several-new-york-times-staff-previously-worked-for-ccp-controlled-media-report_3768622.html

[xc] Jeffrey Gottfried, Mason Walker and Amy Mitchell, "Americans See Skepticism of News Media as Healthy, Say Public Trust in the Institution Can Improve," Pew Research Center, August 31, 2020. https://www.pewresearch.org/journalism/2020/08/31/americans-see-skepticism-of-news-media-as-healthy-say-public-trust-in-the-institution-can-improve/

[xci] Milestone reference, "US Diplomacy and Yellow Journalism, 1895-1898," Department of State. https://history.state.gov/milestones/1866-1898/yellow-journalism

[xcii] Featured Article, "William Randolph Hearst's Campaign to Suppress Citizen Kane," PBS American Experience, April 2021. https://www.pbs.org/wgbh/americanexperience/features/kane-william-randolph-hearst-campaign-suppress-citizen-kane/

[xciii] Michael E. Ross, "Jasyson Blair: The Fraud and the Fallout," NBC News, February 19, 2004. https://www.nbcnews.com/id/wbna3679328

[xciv] News Report, "Editor Sacked over 'Hoax' Photos," BBC, May 14, 2004. http://news.bbc.co.uk/2/hi/uk_news/politics/3716151.stm

[xcv] News Report, "CBS News Admits Bush Documents Can't Be Verified," NBC News, September 20, 2004. https://www.nbcnews.com/id/wbna6055248

[xcvi] Becket Adams, "Disgraced Fake Newsman Dan Rather Gets Journalism Awards Named in His Honor," Washington Examiner, December 16, 2020. https://www.washingtonexaminer.com/opinion/dan-rather-gets-journalism-awards

[xcvii] News Report, "Brian Williams' Credibility Questioned After Fake News Story," CBS News, February 6, 2015. https://www.cbsnews.com/news/brian-williams-credibility-questioned-after-fake-iraq-story/

[xcviii] Kevin Robillard, "10 Journos Caught Fabricating," Politico, July 31, 2012. https://www.politico.com/story/2012/07/10-journos-caught-fabricating-079221

[xcix] Kate Connolly, "Der Spiegel Says Top Journalist Faked Stories for Years," The Guardian, December 19, 2018. https://www.theguardian.com/world/2018/dec/19/top-der-spiegel-journalist-resigns-over-fake-interviews

[c] Mark Moore, "Newsweek Fires Reporter Jessica Kwong Over 'Inaccurate' Trump Thanksgiving Story," NY Post, December 2, 2019. https://nypost.com/2019/12/02/newsweek-fires-reporter-jennifer-kwong-over-inaccurate-trump-thanksgiving-story/

[ci] Keith Coffman, "CNN Settles Defamation Lawsuit with Kentucky Teen in Lincoln Memorial Case," Reuters, January 7, 2020. https://news.yahoo.com/cnn-settles-defamation-lawsuit-kentucky-031509289.html

[cii] Jordan Boyd, "Facebook Quietly Admits Its Third-Party 'Fact-Checks' are Opinions," The Federalist, December 13, 2021. https://thefederalist.com/2021/12/13/facebook-quietly-admits-its-third-party-fact-checks-are-opinions/

[ciii] Katerina Eva Matsa, "Across Western Europe, Public News Media are Widely Used and Trusted Sources of News," Pew Research Center, June 8, 2018. https://www.pewresearch.org/fact-tank/2018/06/08/western-europe-public-news-media-widely-used-and-trusted/

Chapter 9: The "So What?"

Over the past few decades, China has successfully embedded its influence into almost every facet of Western society including economics, technology, academia, entertainment, culture, and politics. However, this can also be said of every other major trading nation with the West so China's prevalence in of itself doesn't mean very much. There are two major differences from all other nations trading with the West. The first is China is obviously the wealthiest non-Western nation in the world and has the financial, informational, and diplomatic resources to have a disproportional level of impact on the West if any major events disrupt Sino-Western relations. The second difference is one that has been repeatedly emphasized in previous chapters, which is the CCP effectively controls every facet of its society without actually having to directly manage or own everything. The CCP system allows some economic freedom but with the understanding that freedom is immediately suspended when the Party needs something done. The central-absolutist system provides the veneer the CCP needs to make outsiders believe private institutions and citizens of China can truly pursue independent endeavors. Yet, when the Party requires support, it has the money, resources, and legal means to compel every element of their society and economy to sacrifice their personal interests and well-being for the good of the Party. Since the CCP can command anything in China, China's qi can invert global trade and cultural exchanges into weapons against the West if the situation becomes dire enough for the Party to survive. So, how could all of these "fronts" of unrestricted warfare be used if the CCP actually decided war was the best course of action? To truly appreciate China's indirect force, all of these efforts of qi will be summarized below to show the combined impact if used in a time of war to appreciate why China's qi forces matter.

The Fronts of Qi Lines of Effort Summarized:

1. Terrorism→Increase funding to terror sponsors→have United Front send more 'lone wolves' to West→conduct synchronized attacks within the West and abroad→distract Western militaries elsewhere & increase domestic anxiety within Western nations.

2. Isolate West→Use BRI and other mechanisms to leverage corrupt co-dependent ruling elites in non-aligned countries→to restrict freedom of navigation and freedom of transit to Western powers→disrupt flow of raw materials→disrupt and temporarily paralyze lines of communication and supply chains to cripple economic capability and military maneuverability of the West.

3. Monopolize Technology→Turn espionage into sabotage to paralyze high tech industries→deliberately flood tech markets with cheap goods to crash industries→order Chinese national scientists, researchers, and academics to halt collaboration and in some cases actively disrupt ventures→temporarily paralyze Western technology development and industry creating economic chaos→disrupt or halt supplies of medicine and medical tech→disrupt technical support to Western government civil functions and cripple technical supply and support to Western militaries.

4. Maple Street→Flood the West with free fentanyl for social disruption→use connections with activist groups to provoke social disruptions and riots→use demonstrators to block military facilities to disrupt deployments→release the "Great Embarrassment" online with Western citizens' compiled medical, employment, social media, and credit information to incite social chaos in the West.

5. Critical Infrastructure→Cyberattacks on water and power→cyberattacks on ports, shipping, and traffic control systems to create supply chain bottlenecks and paralysis→use merchant ships to deliberately obstruct access to ports to create backlogs→chronic water, fuel, electricity, and perishable goods shortages paralyze targeted Western nations.

6. Economic Domination→Use ownership within Western countries to gain access to internal records and networks to sabotage or erase critical data such as financial records, payroll data, and pension funds→use co-ownership to enable saboteurs access to critical facilities like food distribution and packing centers→sudden selloff of assets causing real estate and stock market crashes→deliberately leak confidential proprietary information of Western companies to public for humiliation and loss of market share→sabotage or destroy data centers and other repositories of corporate and economic information→Destroy private, state, and federal pensions→trigger economic depression, chaos, and hatred towards failed Western governments.

7. Thought Control→Use co-opted media, lobbyists, nonprofit policy organizations to preemptively blame Western governments for deteriorating situation→plant false stories to distract Western governments from subtle malign influence→create social divisions to create hesitancy and risk aversion within Western governments to capitulate to China→encourage political experts and media personalities to advocate non-confrontation with China.

If China decides that war or any escalation toward hostilities occurs with the West, this means the CCP concluded there will be an economic catastrophe for China anyway or the CCP is politically in danger of destruction if no war occurs. It would be a gambit to keep power. This means China will have accepted there will be financial and economic losses and is willing to cripple the West to achieve strategic victory for the CCP. These actions of qi would be devastating but are not like nuclear weapons, there is no finality from the use of qi, just paralysis. So, if China believes an open war is coming, it will use its indirect forces of qi in the months and weeks leading up to a fight to eliminate as many of the West's strengths as possible before the actual war begins. China knows it is a paper dragon and cannot directly confront the United States and the West in a classic nation-state war and expect to win. Instead, China has learned Western weaknesses and have invested into exploiting and targeting those weaknesses so in the eventuality of conflict, the weaker China can still defeat the West. China could cripple the West's economies, instill social chaos, political animosity, cause military paralysis, and do all of this before firing a single shot in open war. These are the iron claws that the West itself has forged and given to the paper dragon of China to gut the stronger West before China itself is burned.

In such a scenario, the West might be too busy to deal with China and cede Taiwan and the western Pacific with minimal opposition. Such an event would give the CCP unparalleled legitimacy in China and earn the belief in most of the world that China has truly supplanted the United States even if the world will take years to recover from such a confrontation. As seen with investment rules in China itself, the CCP doesn't allow any foreign company or nation the level of access to China that China has in the West. The CCP will not allow itself to become vulnerable in the same way. Now of course, this is in a theoretical setting and in practice the forces of qi will not be as well synchronized or executed to its full potential. Western governments are, however haphazardly, now trying to counter some of the Chinese tools of qi with new legislation and restrictions to reduce China's ability to cripple the West, but China only needs qi to be partially successful to be paralyzing to the West.

Despite Western attempts to restrain Chinese malign influence and restrict access to critical aspects of their economies and infrastructure, China still retains access to virtually all major social institutions and critical industries. Years of warnings to the Western public and industries have only made some small headway yet there is still resistance. How is China maintaining its access to the West's vulnerabilities and why is there still resistance from within Western societies to any effort to de-couple China from as much of the economic and political fabric of the West as possible? The answer can be found in the PLA's own book *Unrestricted Warfare* in one of the less discussed later chapters. In chapter seven, the authors talk of methods to adequately prepare for unrestricted warfare with one combination of suggested methods not often discussed by Western analysts but is key to answering how China keeps itself tethered to the West in spite of growing animosity. The authors refer to this combination of methods to secure victory in unrestricted warfare as "Supranational Combinations [Chao Guojia Zuhe]".[i] Here lies the answer, by co-opting the elites of the West and manipulate them to do the CCP's bidding but mainly these are not the political elites of the individual Western nations but the social, financial, and cultural elites of the Western societies who have influence over the political elites. The best way the PLA concluded to access and subvert these elites is through the institutions of internationalism or the supranational bodies.

---

[i] Qiao Liang and Wang Xiangsui, *Unrestricted Warfare*, (VT: Echo Point Books & Media, originally published in 1999) 153-161.

Chapter 10: The Supranational Lifeline – the Lynchpin of China's Influence

The whole idea of the PLA concepts of unrestricted warfare is to fully exploit all of an opponent's weaknesses by "going beyond limits" of traditional warfare of military actions.[1] However, keeping the access to the opponent's societal weaknesses is fragile when executing total societal warfare because sooner or later some actions will be noticed. How can the CCP and Chinese government keep having access to the multitude of human social dimensions of unrestricted warfare, both the trans-military and non-military, necessary to successfully implement qi? *Unrestricted Warfare* authors pointed out that the key to keeping these societal doors open was found in the West's own international system of supranational trade organizations, nonprofits, and governing bodies.[2]

Unrestricted Warfare highlights the West's effort to defer more policies and decision making to Western dominated supranational bodies that can exert greater influence on the rest of the world. This began in the 1990s after Western elites became enamored with the concept of "post-history" after the end of the Cold War. After the Soviet Union's collapse, the social, political, and economic elites of the West believed the end of the Cold War was also the end of major inter-state warfare and competition. A more interconnected world unified by free trade and a cosmopolitan set of universal political ideals would create a new "global village" in a proclaimed neoliberal utopia that was crystalized in Professor Francis Fukuyama's *The End of History and the Last Man*. After the Cold War, Professor Fukuyama argued nations would accept the new global liberalism and adopt more Western democratic systems as the basis for an integrated world economy. The world did change but new challengers arose from Asia and one of the unforeseen consequences of these new challenges was how global trade growth would also transmogrify the West's social, political, and economic elites themselves.

As more businesses offshored their investments to keep down costs and increase profit margins, the traditional economic ties that bound many of the elites to their Western society became weaker and the desire to support international agendas became more dominant over time. The PLA saw this as the Western elites' method to grow and expand Western influence covertly. The PLA also observed globalism had insulated these same elites from their nations' democratic systems of accountability as more power was given to nonaccountable supranational technocrats, CEOs, academics, and diplomats making them more susceptible to corruption and co-option. China's timing in opening itself up to the world and foreign investors was perfect to exploit the new globalist trade growth. The CCP used the West's new love of globalism to ingratiate itself by playing on Western hopes that huge investments in China would give the Western elites the access to Chinese markets that would eventually co-opt China to the Western-led globalist neoliberal order. [3], [4] So certain of this, many leading thinkers and business leaders advocated for China's membership into the WTO and most favored trade status with the United States.[5] Instead of the West co-opting the CCP, the more politically-oriented and better skilled CCP elite co-opted many members of the West's elites instead.

International organizations and nonprofits are dominated by the wealthiest countries in the world, which means China and Western countries. The disproportionate level of power and wealth enables these nations to exert exceptional influence over all the other nations.[6] The multitude of international organizations are mostly specialized with narrow jurisdictions managed by appointed technocrats with few accountability mechanisms, leaving most activities of international organizations opaque. All of the hundreds of countries that participate have their own agendas and interests which further muddle any ability to monitor international bodies. To bypass any effort of transparency, a nation like China just has to lobby for their preferred candidates to attain key appointments to silence any criticism or investigation of corruption.[7] China demonstrated this most overtly with the outbreak of COVID-19 from Wuhan.

When the CCP failed to contain the virus, China instead successfully worked its power to stifle any international condemnation and deflect any criticism of the Party or the Chinese government. The CCP exploited the World Health Organization's (WHO) reputation as an internationally recognized authoritative body to ensure all news focused on China's positive contributions to mitigating the virus, keeping Taiwan isolated, and make the public forget about the virus' origins in China. The WHO put more energy in ignoring Taiwan than coordinating quarantine and anti-viral efforts and even discounted Taiwan's contributions to combating the pandemic lest it offended the CCP.[8], [9] The head of the WHO in 2020, Dr. Tedros Adhanom Ghebreyesus, was an Ethiopian government minister who had many links to China and he proactively protected his CCP allies. [10], [11], [12] How can one tell? The WHO put an inordinate amount of effort campaigning to abolish the term "Wuhan Flu" or "China Virus" as "racist" to reduce China's affiliation with its virus and officially named COVID-19 in three months of the pandemic outbreak.[13], [14] However, when a similar effort was attempted to change the name of the STD "Monkeypox" in 2022, there was little to no actual effort to persuade medical or media establishments to eliminate the term months after the media began to use the term. COVID replaced "Wuhan" or "China virus" in less than three months but Monkeypox was the common use term in both media and authoritative bodies for the rest of 2022.[15], [16], [17] Those affected by Monkeypox don't matter to the WHO, the victims are just a demographic to be pandered to for virtue signaling but the CCP are actual masters who are to be obeyed. So, how does this kind of influence in supranational bodies translate over to the susceptible members of the Western elites themselves?

International governing bodies are overwhelmingly funded by Western governments whose legislatures are lobbied in one form or another by social and economic elites in every Western country. These bodies are also assisted by international nonprofit and activist organizations who rely on private donations for their upkeep with the majority of those funds provided by the social and political elites. Although China does directly approach individual nation's elites, companies, and national nonprofits as shown earlier in this analysis, the global connections between Western elites through their international nonprofit and nongovernmental organizations help circumvent any national-level countermeasures against Chinese influence.

International organizations are technocratic in nature, with no real means of transparency[18], [19] making these supranational organizations the most effective way for China to covertly seek out, engage, and co-opt wealthy or influential members of the West's elite class.

Although money is the principal means of co-option, this is insufficient to manipulate the West's unwitting elites into letting their guard down to being puppets. Blinding some members of the elites by political idealism helps in the creation of what Lenin described as "useful idiots."[20] These are individuals who can be manipulated into carrying out their puppet masters' objectives even if it is detrimental to their own interest. The manipulation often uses the controlled elites' ego to make them believe they are carrying out goals that will lead to their own victory or advantage. The CCP will find common overlapping goals with some targeted Western elites, then pitch those commonalities, exaggerate these commonalities, and then let their puppets believe the CCP are allies or partners in common cause, not realizing they are just unwitting tools oblivious to the CCP's true goals. By using the right symbols, terminology, slogans, and feigned actions on topics of interest within these opaque supranational bodies, the CCP has easily co-opted some "useful idiot" elites. The most conspicuous example of this is China using the issue of environmentalism to co-opt individual members of international activist nongovernment organizations, including members from prominent organizations like the World Economic Forum (WEF).[21]

The WEF is a prominent example because it is very popular in two respects. One, the WEF is one of the leading influential internationalist political advocacy groups in the world attracting international businessmen, academics, and former politicians. Secondly, the WEF is favored as the preeminent organization accused by anti-globalist movements of being a modern incarnation of the Illuminati bent on creating an autocratic unitary world state. Whether one believes the most extreme, some say conspiratorial, assumptions about the WEF being the nefarious organization of evil or not, the WEF does in fact proclaim beliefs that are more authoritarian than democratic. The WEF does its image no favors with many of their stated agendas and policy recommendations, provoking many in the West to accuse this organization of being fascist in their beliefs. Since the CCP moved away from a Marxist economic system in the 1980s, their unique system of central absolutism incorporates a more fascistic economic system similar to Hitler's Germany or Mussolini's Italy than anything related to Maoism. So, if the WEF are truly fascistic in nature, then the WEF would share common interests with the CCP and be an ideal target as a pool to recruit some of the "useful idiots" among Western elites to manipulate. To determine this, one must first answer the question of what is fascist? Fascist is the most overused, misapplied, and probably the least understood political term in contemporary Western politics. Fascist is an actual term to describe a political and economic belief system but now the word is used as an aspersion to brand anyone who disagrees with another's political opinion regardless of what that opinion is.

So, what is actual fascism? Benito Mussolini's thoughts on the subject are the best place to find the answer since he actually founded the first state built on that belief system. The challenge is Mussolini himself didn't spell out a crisp clearcut definition either. Instead, one can piece together the distinct characteristics of original fascism from Mussolini's autobiography where he discusses his political and social doctrine of fascism. Benito Mussolini started out in politics as a devoted socialist who over time came to the conclusion that the egalitarian idealism of socialism was detached from reality but still believed the state should control all means of production.[22] Fascism was a socialist factional rejection of idealist international socialism on pragmatic grounds. In the first decades of the 20th Century, Mussolini observed failed socialist revolutions and academically insulated utopian thinkers ignoring the realities of common workers which made him conclude communism and international socialism did not acknowledge true human nature.[23] For the sake of convenience, the following is a drastically simplified comparison to contrast the ideological differences for the sake of showing commonality with modern activities of the CCP and like-minded supranational nonprofit and nongovernmental organizations susceptible to China's manipulation like the WEF.

International socialism and communism fundamentally believe in the Rousseauian concept of the "Noble Savage" with human nature being inherently good and naturally egalitarian when in its natural primitivist state. All evil and bad actions are from systemic corruption inherent in complex civilized societies. Nations and cultures are artificial constructs arising out of human desires for accumulation of material goods. Therefore, utopia can be achieved when mankind returns to its natural anarchist state which can only be achieved by a global society with as few elements of civilization as possible to eliminate systemic corruption. The final goal is a global stateless society of equal persons united by syndicalist views of economic sharing and group effort like an ant colony.

After years of real-world observations, Mussolini concluded mankind was inherently selfish, tribalistic, warlike, and hierarchical, which convinced him that international socialism was unworkable and delusional.[24] Yet, he still thought capitalism and democratic republicanism as being just as unworkable. Mussolini instead argues Fascism is the practical justification for socialist totalitarianism which ignores the delusions of communism by embracing humanity's true nature.[25] Fascism is necessary because only a strong state can impose sufficient order to subdue humans and their chaotic, violent, and selfish natures to maximize a society's potential. As humans are inherently hierarchical and tribalistic, nations and cultures are also inherently part of human nature, so fascism embraces nationalism and rejects abolishing classes or seeking equality because egalitarianism doesn't truly exist.[26] In short, Mussolini rejected Rousseauian concepts of humanity and embraced Thomas Hobbes. Fascism can be considered an updated technocratic version of Hobbes' *Leviathan*. A strong state that imposes order, embraces national distinction, and uses a version of Social Darwinism where a strong leader directs a strong state to achieve a nation's full potential.[27] This pragmatic argument with a focus on nationalism is what distinguishes fascism from communism, even though both embrace totalitarian economics. Fascists are generally more willing to be economically pragmatic than their Marxist rivals and will turn on market mechanisms in their economic system when they decide it is necessary but turn these mechanisms back off when they threaten the state's power. This is what is done in China and in other examples like Francisco Franco's early period of Falangist Spain. This is why fascist systems have more property rights than communism because it acknowledges the necessity of rewarding individuals, even if only on occasion.

Like democratic republicanism, there is a political spectrum for totalitarian utopianism. Both communism and fascism represent two wings of an ideological system that advocates that the state directs the means of production and dictate all major elements of society towards one unitary goal of utopia. The fascists represent the "right-wing" of totalitarian utopianism that embraces the Hobbesian view of human nature best managed by a strong nation-state while acknowledging some inherent individual agency. The communists represent the "left-wing" of totalitarian utopianism by embracing Rousseauian concepts of a malleable human nature that can be programmed to embrace egalitarianism through the means of abolishing all nation-states to create a utopian global community.

With this simplified explanation, does the WEF advocate anything that mimics Mussolini's and the CCP's current system of corporatist economics? The best way is to compare actual statements Mussolini made with the articles written by the WEF's founder, Klaus Schwab. In Schwab's book *COVID-19 The Great Reset*, the WEF calls for more state intervention in economic life while deferring greater authority to international bodies for greater global governance. The claim being it will improve coordination and enforcement of common rules set by authoritative experts as the best way to mitigate disasters in the future under the concept of "Stakeholder Capitalism".[28] Along with pandemics, environmental issues were used to justify to increased global centralization to better manage emergencies meaning the state should also direct private business decisions:

Governments thus have tools at their disposal to make the shift towards more inclusive and sustainable prosperity, combining public-sector direction-setting and incentives with commercial innovation capacity through a fundamental rethinking of markets and their role in our economy and society.[29]

Comparing that statement from WEF's leader with the one below by Mussolini:

I have wanted the Fascist government, above all, to give great care to the social legislation needed to carry out our part of agreed international programs for industry and for those who bear the future of industry. . .Until now it has been too individualistic. . .the government alone is in the right position to see things from the point of view of the general welfare. This government is not at the disposition of this man or that man; it is over everybody.[30]

The WEF also argues that states need to be directed by common international enforcement to re-engineer new social norms to make all nations' societies conform to a common set of standards for sustainable well-being:

Additionally, several institutions and organizations, ranging from cities to the European Commission, are reflecting on options that would sustain future economic activity at a level that matches the satisfaction of our material needs with the respect of our planetary boundaries. . . If we collectively recognize that, beyond a certain level of wealth defined by GDP per capita, happiness depends more on intangible factors such as accessible healthcare and a robust social fabric than on material consumption, then values as different as the respect for the environment, responsible eating, empathy or generosity may gain ground and progressively come to characterize the new social norms.**[31]**

Compared to Mussolini's stated goals:

The state, as conceived of and as created by Fascism, is a spiritual and moral fact in itself. . .it is the state which educates its citizens in civic virtue, gives them a consciousness of their mission and welds them into unity; harmonizing their various interests through justice, and transmitting to future generations the mental conquests of science, of art, of law and the solidarity of humanity.[32]

The WEF's leaders declare the new post-pandemic social contract will now require businesses to partner with the states and international bodies to help build this more socially responsible economic system by incorporating the social, political, and ecological considerations with the assistance from international activist bodies:

Better alignment between public policy and corporate planning will be a particular focus of attention in terms of greater government interference. . . The bottom line: the maximization of profit and the short-termism that often goes with it is rarely or, at least, not always consistent with the public goal of preparing for a future crisis. . . it is now incumbent upon them to serve all their stakeholders, not only those who hold shares. . .Companies will not necessarily adhere to these measures because they are genuinely "good", but rather because the "price" of not doing so will be too high in terms of the wrath of activists, both activist investors and social activists.[33]

Whereas Mussolini stated:

Fascism desires the state to be a strong and organic body, at the same time reposing upon broad and popular support. The Fascist State has drawn into itself even the economic activities of the nation, and through the corporative social and educational institutions created by it, its influence reaches every aspect of the national life and includes, framed in their respective organizations, all the political, economic, and spiritual forces of the nation.[34]

The WEF argues the advanced technology and the interconnectedness of the world requires a new form of global governance[35] but as seen above, the WEF's proposed ideology of Stakeholder Capitalism adopts many facets of an ideology that has been tried before. As the biblical saying goes, "there is nothing new under the sun." However, like China's current system, the WEF's ideology is not classical fascism but instead seems to mix and match segments of previous political ideologies into a mutated syncretic form to be conducive to 21st Century culture and economic circumstances. The commonalities with fascism include using pragmatic arguments by acknowledging greed and other negative human facets which will always be a challenge to be confronted instead of appealing to egalitarian idealism. Also, like fascism, the WEF doesn't call for the abolition of capital and instead advocate private companies be compelled to partner with the government to address political and social issues.[36] This system also acknowledges hierarchies and classes will continue to exist.[37], [38] Despite the name, capitalism in "Stakeholder Capitalism" appears to only be a stated term to act as a veneer for a classically corporatist system.

Nevertheless, there are significant differences. Although the arguments are pragmatic in nature, the WEF argues a global egalitarian utopia is the final goal. The WEF rejects fascist notions of nationalism and embrace more Rousseauian concepts of an international global community becoming one nation and individual nations would be subsumed to the greater good.[39] This new global order would be dominated by expert and technocratic communities that would advise and direct international authoritative bodies on policies and actions. Instead of nation states, the world state would be representing economic fiefdoms governed by these enlightened elites. These fiefdoms would become the stakeholders of a global stakeholder "capitalist" system. A system that has private economic fiefdoms controlled by technocrats partnered with state institutions to act on behalf of the public good is similar to the old feudal system of landowners swearing fealty to the central authority. Frankly, a syncretic form of corporatist feudalism would be a more accurate description of the WEF's proposals as there is little free market in its descriptions. Again, this concept is not original to the WEF and has been discussed in various forms since Aldous Huxley's *Brave New World*. In fact, an interesting but very obscure computer game from 2007 named *Culpa Innata*, by Momentum Digital Media Technologies, sets its story in a future utopian-disguised dystopia that remarkably matches WEF's declared 2020 aspirations. The final distinction from classical fascism is the WEF's belief that advanced automation and artificial intelligence (AI) will overcome the deficiencies in centralized state economic planning of the past. Unlike historical fascism, the WEF hopes advanced AI can learn the extreme complexity of society well enough to make economics predictable enough to centrally manage.[40], [41]

The economic system advocated by the WEF has considerable overlap with China's Tianxia concepts because the WEF advocates for more politicization of economic decisions and stronger governments with broad powers to enforce social and economic policies. The WEF uses the global impact of potential disasters as the main justification for their proposed system. They argue that global disasters, such as climate change, are too big for any nation or group of nations so it must be handled by global bodies. Only strong central authorities can act in sufficient time to mitigate global disasters. The fear of climate change is the main driver that unites not just WEF members but many other wealthy and connected Western elites. China has repeatedly used climate change initiatives and proclamations to ingratiate themselves to these Western elites who are convinced a strong centralized international system is necessary to save the world.[42], [43] The WEF's ideology, the West's social and financial elites' ties to environmental actions, and sympathetic international nonprofit and nongovernmental organizations create the perfect conditions to recruit "useful idiots" who are easily swayed with the right sloganeering and virtuous proclamations of saving the planet.[44] The WEF is a prime example of how China can use overlapping interests to gain and maintain access to the West's most influential people, but it is far from the only nongovernmental international body targeted by China. The other group of corruptible elites driven by greed are just bribed under the veneer of international activism.

China's indirect forces of qi go after the individual Western societies directly but these international bodies, nonprofits, and supranational supporting elites are the means of keeping access to those societies open. Yes, China uses businesses to indirectly lobby governments to let their guard down but it is through the opaque indirect influence in international bodies where China can bypass Western scrutiny. Using emotional blackmail, the CCP uses these elites' activism and virtue social climbing to disguise its main efforts of malign influence. Even in individual cases within countries, pro-CCP corporations use the verbiage and authoritative references of supranational bodies and their environmental declarations declaring sympathy to the CCP.[45] The supranational linkages are rarely scrutinized and have so much political and social clout, that it becomes very difficult for Western security services to confront this primary means of CCP malign influence. Co-opting supranational groups is the means the CCP maintain access to the West and enable China to wage qi uncontested.

Political Spectrum of Totalitarian Utopianism

[1] Ibid, 155.

[2] Ibid, 156-157.

[3] Henry S. Rowen, "Why China Will Become a Democracy," Hoover Digest, January 30, 1999. https://www.hoover.org/research/why-china-will-become-democracy

[4] Asia Program, "Permanent Trading Privileges for China: A Debate," Wilson Center, January 1, 2001. https://www.wilsoncenter.org/article/permanent-trading-privileges-for-china-debate

[5] Robert Kagan, "Why the Rush to Favor China?" Carnegie Endowment for International Peace, March 20, 2000. https://carnegieendowment.org/2000/03/20/why-rush-to-favor-china-pub-236

[6] James Raymond Vreeland, "Corrupting International Organizations," Annual Review of Political Science, 2019, v. 22, 205-222. https://www.annualreviews.org/doi/abs/10.1146/annurev-polisci-050317-071031

[7] Per Larsson, "Corruption and International Organizations: The United Nations and the World Bank," Institute for Security & Development Policy, Policy Brief No 53, February 3, 2011. https://isdp.eu/content/uploads/publications/2011_larsson_corruption-and-international-organizations.pdf

[8] Yu-Jie Chen and Jerome A. Cohen, "Why Does the WHO Exclude Taiwan?" Council on Foreign Relations, April 9, 2020. https://www.cfr.org/in-brief/why-does-who-exclude-taiwan

[9] News Report, "Why Taiwan has Become a Problem for WHO," BBC News, March 30, 2020. https://www.bbc.com/news/world-asia-52088167

[10] Press Release, "Director-General leads WHO delegation to the Belt and Road Forum for Health Cooperation," World Health Organization, August 15, 2017. https://www.who.int/news/item/15-08-2017-director-general-leads-who-delegation-to-the-belt-and-road-forum-for-health-cooperation

[11] Joel Gehrke, "'Covered Up for China': Criticism of WHO Director Grows for Failures in Early Stages of Pandemic," Washington Examiner, April 10, 2020. https://www.washingtonexaminer.com/policy/defense-national-security/covered-up-for-china-criticism-grows-of-who-director-for-failures-in-early-stages-of-pandemic

[12] Peter Hasson, "China Helped Put This Man In Charge Of the World Health Organization—Is It Paying Off?" National Interest, March 23, 2020. https://nationalinterest.org/blog/buzz/china-helped-put-man-charge-world-health-organization%E2%80%94-it-paying-136002

[13] Morgan Gstalter, "WHO Official Warns Against Calling It 'Chinese Virus,' Says 'There Is No Blame in This'," The Hill, March 19, 2020. https://thehill.com/homenews/administration/488479-who-official-warns-against-calling-it-chinese-virus-says-there-is-no/

[14] Victoria Forster, "Coronavirus Gets A New Name: COVID-19. Here's Why That Is Important," Forbes, February 11, 2020. https://www.forbes.com/sites/victoriaforster/2020/02/11/coronavirus-gets-a-new-name-covid-19-heres-why-renaming-it-is-important/?sh=14a81be1548e

[15] Fact Sheet, "Monkeypox," World Health Organization, May 19, 2022. https://www.who.int/news-room/fact-sheets/detail/monkeypox

[16] Kai Kupferschmidt, "Moving Target: The Global Monkeypox Outbreak is Giving the Virus an Unprecedented Opportunity to Adapt to Humans. Will it Change for the Worse?" Science Magazine, September 15, 2022. https://www.science.org/content/article/will-monkeypox-virus-become-more-dangerous

[17] News Report, "WHO Plans to Rename Monkeypox Over Stigmatization Concerns," NBC News/Associated Press, August 14, 2022. https://www.nbcnews.com/health/health-news/plans-rename-monkeypox-stigmatization-concerns-rcna43012

[18] Robert O. Bothwell, "Corporate Philanthropy and Social Responsibility in Latin America," The International Journal of Not-for-Profit Law, v4, issue 1, September 2001. https://www.icnl.org/resources/research/ijnl/trends-in-self-regulation-and-transparency-of-nonprofit-organizations-in-the-u-s

[19] Nives DolSak and Aseem Prakash, "NGOs are Great at Demanding Transparency. They're Not so Hot at Providing it," Washington Post, February, 2016. https://www.washingtonpost.com/news/monkey-cage/wp/2016/02/22/ngos-are-great-at-demanding-transparency-theyre-not-so-hot-at-providing-it/

[20] Robert W. Pringle, Historical Dictionary of Russian and Soviet Intelligence, (Lanham, Maryland: Scarecrow Press, Inc: 2006): 2.

[21] News Report, "Chinese Premier Meets with Executive Chairman Of WEF," Xinhua News, June 27, 2023. https://web.archive.org/web/20230808004228/http://www.china.org.cn/world/2023-06/27/content_89640616.htm

[22] Benito Mussolini, My Autobiography with the Political and Social Doctrine of Fascism, (Garden City, NY: Dover Publications: 2006) 227-228.

[23] Benito Mussolini, My Autobiography with the Political and Social Doctrine of Fascism, (Garden City, NY: Dover Publications: 2006) 200, 230-231, 235-240.

[24] Benito Mussolini, My Autobiography with the Political and Social Doctrine of Fascism, (Garden City, NY: Dover Publications: 2006) 153, 200.

[25] Ibid, 231.

[26] Ibid, 202-205, 231.

[27] Ibid, 206-207.

[28] Klaus Schwab and Thierry Malleret, COVID-19: The Great Reset, (Geneva, CHE, World Economic Forum: July 2020): 22-27, 44-47, 79.

[29] Ibid, 49.

[30] Benito Mussolini, My Autobiography with the Political and Social Doctrine of Fascism, (Garden City, NY: Dover Publications: 2006) 203-204.

[31] Klaus Schwab and Thierry Malleret, *COVID-19: The Great Reset*, (Geneva, CHE, World Economic Forum: July 2020): 47-48.

[32] Benito Mussolini, *My Autobiography with the Political and Social Doctrine of Fascism*, (Garden City, NY: Dover Publications: 2006) 237.

[33] Klaus Schwab and Thierry Malleret, *COVID-19: The Great Reset*, (Geneva, CHE, World Economic Forum: July 2020): 140-141.

[34] Benito Mussolini, *My Autobiography with the Political and Social Doctrine of Fascism*, (Garden City, NY: Dover Publications: 2006) 238-239.

[35] Report, "Digital Transformation: Powering the Great Reset," World Economic Forum, July 2020, 9. https://www3.weforum.org/docs/WEF_Digital_Transformation_Powering_the_Great_Reset_2020.pdf

[36] Benito Mussolini, *My Autobiography with the Political and Social Doctrine of Fascism*, (Garden City, NY: Dover Publications: 2006) 206.

[37] Report, "Digital Transformation: Powering the Great Reset," World Economic Forum, July 2020, 6. https://www3.weforum.org/docs/WEF_Digital_Transformation_Powering_the_Great_Reset_2020.pdf

[38] Klaus Schwab and Thierry Malleret, *COVID-19: The Great Reset*, (Geneva, CHE, World Economic Forum: July 2020): 177-180.

[39] Report, "Digital Transformation: Powering the Great Reset," World Economic Forum, July 2020, 7. https://www3.weforum.org/docs/WEF_Digital_Transformation_Powering_the_Great_Reset_2020.pdf

[40] Ibid, 9.

[41] Klaus Schwab and Thierry Malleret, *COVID-19: The Great Reset*, (Geneva, CHE, World Economic Forum: July 2020): 116-121.

[42] Press Release, "China's Transition to a Low-Carbon Economy and Climate Resilience Needs Shifts in Resources and Technologies," The World Bank, October 12, 2022. https://www.worldbank.org/en/news/press-release/2022/10/12/china-s-transition-to-a-low-carbon-economy-and-climate-resilience-needs-shifts-in-resources-and-technologies

[43] Liu He, "Three Critical Battles China is Preparing to Fight," World Economic Forum Speech, January 24, 2018. https://www.weforum.org/agenda/2018/01/pursue-high-quality-development-work-together-for-global-economic-prosperity-and-stability/

[44] Isaac Stone Fish, "A Communist Party Man at Davos: Xi Jinping Tries to Charm Capitalist Elite," The Atlantic, January 18, 2017. https://www.theatlantic.com/international/archive/2017/01/china-davos-xi-jinping-trump-globalization/513521/

[45] Peter Schweizer, *Red Handed*, (NY: HarperCollins Publishers: 2022): 141-148.

Section Two: The Foreign Induced Civil War

Chapter 11: Civil War Set-up and Wargame

Up unto this point, this book demonstrated that China has the motivation, the resources, and the skills to infiltrate, subvert, and disrupt Western nations from within, but what about the civil war itself? Currently, most concerned observers see Chinese foreign policy in just two states of being: either China advancing its grand strategy of Tianxia with nonviolent cooption or China's preparation for war in the West Pacific and India. Neither of these foreign policy positions account for inducing civil war outright, so there must be a third state of foreign policy outlook in between those two positions that could account for sparking civil conflict.

The circumstances for China to induce civil war have been mentioned throughout previous chapters but will be reiterated here. Chinese actions to subvert and coopt other nations into its new imperial expansion will be noticed by other nations sooner or later, especially by the wealthier Western nations China intends to supplant as the dominant hegemony. These nations will start to resist China's mercantilist Tianxia policies with greater economic controls, more security measures, and separating critical economic links from China to avoid being subsumed under Tianxia.[i]' [ii], [iii] China's central absolutism is filled with uncorrectable contradictions that accumulate over time and Tianxia is the lifeline that keeps the CCP alive as foreign wealth and resources counterbalance the mismanagement and gross corruption that eats away at China like gangrene. Severing economic and cultural linkages will deprive the CCP of these lifelines and the centralized structure of China will begin stalling out under its own inefficiencies which could lead to the fall of the CCP itself. This situation endangers the CCP's existence but China knows trying to wage an open aggressive war is, as Russia can attest, fraught with considerable risk. Inducing civil war to eliminate your rivals as credible alternatives to China's Tianxia is far less risky, especially since the tools of Tianxia already allow access to every aspect of its Western trading partners for targeted exploitation.[iv] As the West becomes more mistrustful of China and acts to corrects its mistakes of blindly dealing with the CCP, China will use more of its influence with the Western elites to stymie these efforts of reducing dependency on China.[v]' [vi] Overtime, if these anti-Tianxia efforts become more successful, China would likely then shift from a peaceful cooption to using "useful idiot" puppets to cripple Western institutions, provoke division, and encourage some to change the West into more authoritarian regimes receptive to Tianxia.

The most likely series of events leading to civil war in the United States and perhaps Europe, is China using its forces of qi to support co-opted economic, cultural, and informational elites into turning Western nations into what academics' call "anocracies".[vii] An anocracy is a political state where a nation's democratic institutions have sufficiently decayed to allow more corrupt elements of that nation's elite to subvert and gain a disproportionate amount of political power at the cost of the electorates'. These nations are not outright dictatorships but are instead vulnerable to becoming one. As the corrupt influential elites siphon more political power, disenfranchised elements become more aggressive as part of a backlash, with sufficient effort by China to deepen and widen this social divisions, could push these nations into civil war. Given the mixed messaging from the West on how they want to approach China, China is likely preparing and executing at least some contingencies to make the West conciliatory to Tianxia.[viii]' [ix]

Wargame Parameters:

War is fraught with uncertainty, especially civil wars with so many variables and outliers that could push the fortunes of the rival factions one way or the other means a definitive prediction is impossible. Instead of walking through a hypothetical war with fronts, battles, and campaigns for victory, this book will analyze and wargame what are the optimal conditions for victory for both sides of a foreign induced civil war in contemporary Western nations. Using generic terms and locations, the following analysis will be as generally applicable as possible without specified nations, factions, or groups. However, this scenario will be analyzed with the limitation of the hypothetical nation having a federalized system of government for sake of simplicity and the fact that the United States would likely be the principal target in such an event.

To properly analyze all facets of this wargame scenario, each side will be evaluated separately for its strengths and weaknesses and how each side would be best optimized to win a civil conflict. These evaluations will be done for the strategic, operational, and tactical level in order to understand each sides' objectives, lines of effort to achieve those objectives, and the tasks necessary to complete those lines of effort. Finally, this analysis will culminate with a walkthrough of the beginning of what an optimal opening salvo of the civil war from the perspective of the anti-foreign influence forces. This will give the reader a clear picture of how such a conflict would start if the leaders of the anti-foreign influence forces executed an optimal campaign. This means the analysis comes with a caveated warning, that the best one can do to evaluate a hypothetical war is to analyze how everything works to its maximum potential which only happens on paper. The real world is unforgiving and bombards events and plans with sources of friction, disruption, and failure so, if a civil war does occur, it will be messier than this analysis describing the optimal circumstances.

The scenario will consist of two factions that will broadly represent the pro-foreign influence forces and the national resistance forces. Throughout the scenario evaluation, the foreign-malign influenced forces from this point onward will be termed the Foreign-Backed Elites (FBE) denoting the key means of foreign control used to subvert the hypothetical unnamed Western nation. On the other side, the anti-foreign influence faction will be termed the National Resistance Forces (NRF). These two factions will be simplified representations of the various forces at work in such a political struggle but will largely reflect the key requirements needed for each side to achieve its objectives.

The circumstances of the wargame will be set in a situation where the FBE have sufficiently subverted the nation's institutions to disenfranchise the anti-foreign influence elements of the elite and electorate. The FBE's have successfully created an anocracy but still need to consolidate their power to achieve full autocratic rule and therefore must keep the pretense of a democratic state. The NRF uses this time of transition between anocracy and overt tyranny to formulate into a cohesive but decentralized nebulous force. The foreign nation backing the FBE will not overtly support them because it would undermine FBE legitimacy and will instead funnel finances to co-opted elites and their financial networks to sustain FBE loyalty. FBE themselves will use its undue influence to manipulate the nation's institutions to do the FBE's bidding with little direct input from their foreign benefactors. The foreign power controlling the FBE will also, unbeknownst to the FBE leaders, interfere and attempt to influence the NRF to play both sides. The foreign power will be bipartisan in its efforts to cripple its Western rival because its objective is to cripple the Western nation while the FBE's objective is to achieve total power over the Western nation which doesn't truly interest the foreign benefactor.

The final point for this analysis is to understand the perspectives of the warring factions on how to achieve victory. In reality, the unknown and unpredictable danger for both sides is having their leaders underestimate their opponents while overestimating their own capabilities. This often happens because of preconceived notions of how wars are fought or failing to appreciate the complexity of a problem leading to disaster. History is filled with examples as factions misapply lessons from previous conflicts or learn the wrong lessons because they failed to incorporate context into their analysis. In a civil conflict, the leaders of the more powerful faction are dismissive of the underdog while the weaker faction confidently cites historical victories of the underdog without understanding how or why these victories occurred. An optimal path to victory means leaders and organizations not only have access to accurate information about their opponents and themselves but also have the ability to properly understand the information to use successfully. This rarely happens and readers must beware that a perfect scenario doesn't happen because warring factions rarely have all the information they need and more rarely understand the information well enough to achieve victory quickly. Wars are uncertain and the overconfident often blunder into defeats as the Battles of Manassas/Bull Run, First Battle of Fallujah, and the Battle of Kyiv can attest. Beware of those who say war is easy and victory is quick.

---

[i] News Report, "US to Cub More Tech Exports to Keep Chips from Military-Sources," Reuters, October 3, 2022. https://www.reuters.com/technology/us-expected-announce-new-limits-chinas-ai-supercomputing-firms-nyt-2022-10-03/

[ii] J. Stewart Black and Allen J. Morrison, "The Strategic Challenges of Decoupling," Harvard Business Review, May-June 2021. https://hbr.org/2021/05/the-strategic-challenges-of-decoupling

[iii] Derek Scissors, "Partial Decoupling from China: A Brief Guide," American Enterprise Institute, July 7, 2020. https://www.aei.org/research-products/report/partial-decoupling-from-china-a-brief-guide/

[iv] US Army, *Army Techniques Publication 7-100.3: Chinese Tactics*, (Washington DC: Army Publishing Directorate, August 9, 2021): 1-9, para. 1-33 & 1-34.

[v] Andrew Silver, "Scientists in China Say US Government Crackdown is Harming Collaborations," Nature, July 8, 2020. https://www.nature.com/articles/d41586-020-02015-y

[vi] Shi Jiangtao, "Decoupling from China 'the Wrong Answer', Says German Leader," South China Morning Post, October 12, 2022. https://www.scmp.com/news/china/diplomacy/article/3195722/decoupling-china-wrong-answer-says-german-leader

[vii] Barbara F. Walter, *How Civil Wars Start and How to Stop Them*, (NY: Crown, Random House, division of Penguin Random House: 2022): 11-14.

[viii] Michael D. Swaine and Jake Werner, "How Biden's New National Security Strategy Gets China Wrong," National Interest, October 13, 2022. https://nationalinterest.org/feature/how-biden%E2%80%99s-new-national-security-strategy-gets-china-wrong-205323

[ix] Press Release, "Congress Passes Investments in Domestic Semiconductor Manufacturing, Research & Design," Semiconductor Industry Association, July 2022. https://www.semiconductors.org/chips/

Chapter 12: The Foreign-Backed Elites' Optimal Strategy

In the Western ways of war, professional militaries break down the execution of warfare into three levels in order to simplify organizational management and properly delegate tasks to subordinates to accomplish their missions. These levels of strategy, operations, and tactics don't have precise boundaries between each other but help approximate the requirements needed at each echelon of command to achieve its objectives. The strategic level is where the leaders of the polity develop their ideas on how to employ their political and military power in a coordinated fashion to achieve that polity's final objectives.[1] The political and military objectives overlap in a civil war because the outcome of the fight means one side is out of power and is no longer a recognized polity or potential polity. Unlike most wars of interstate conflict, civil wars are usually winner take all and those civil wars that end in some brokered deal more often than not result in only in a pause in the fight.

The Strategic Objective:

The Foreign-Backed Elites (FBE) faction in this civil war gaming evaluation have achieved a dominating political position within the Western nation and have successfully excluded their rivals, the Nationalist Resistance Forces (NRF) from the legal political process. However, the FBEs have not achieved total domination over their nation's population or government because the institutions were based on liberty and democratic processes. To minimize risk of a larger rebellion and to maintain legitimacy, the FBE must subvert institutions slowly while attacking any dissent to keep opposition on the defensive. The FBE are powerful, but vulnerable in this transitory state of keeping covert autocratic power while gaining sufficient influence and power to eventually exert control overtly. The FBE faces several strategic challenges to accomplish this goal.

Firstly, the FBE faction would be an alliance of cliques of various corrupt elites from all elements of society. Influential and wealthy financial, industrial, and technological business owners and investors partnered with corrupt legal, cultural, and academic elites united by common financial or political interests. These interests would be linked to a common idea such as an ideal global state or even a more mundane idea such as keeping their ill-gotten political and financial advantages. Whatever the case, the FBE are not led by a singular ruler or strongman but are a loose confederacy where internal rivalry and competition threaten the FBE's cohesion. This alliance of elites uses their lobbying and financial incentives to co-opt political elites who in turn appoint technocrats, "experts", and regulatory officials who are conducive to the autocratic FBE. Maintaining cohesion requires competent leadership with a clear vision and intent to achieve victory against their NRF opponents.

The second major strategic challenge is the foreign backers themselves. The FBE are controlled indirectly by the foreign power but most members of the FBE faction don't know it. The foreign benefactors will manipulate certain members of the FBE to convince their confederates that the FBE is an independent force with its own self-serving objectives while in reality are serving the interest of the foreign adversarial power. The foreign benefactors' ultimate strategic objective is to use the FBE to divide, cripple, and ultimately weaken the Western nation to the point of becoming the foreign benefactors' vassal. These benefactors don't care what ultimately happens to members of the FBE and will actively undermine their FBE puppets from time to time to draw out the conflict and weaken the Western nation. This will further disrupt FBE strategic objectives as the foreign benefactors will be carrying out a duplicitous campaign of aiding and undermining the FBEs which includes covertly aiding the NRF.

Finally, the last major strategic challenge is from their opponents, the NRF. The FBEs must minimize the scale of rebellion while still trying to obtain absolute power without losing legitimacy. If the FBE fail in this, the Western nation's population will notice the attempt by the FBE to convert the country into an outright autocracy. The NRF will continuously undermine the FBE's legitimacy in the eyes of the public and attempt to coopt the institutions the FBE uses against subversion in order to break the FBE hold on the levers of power. The FBE must destroy these dissenting segments of the Western nation without being overtly brutal or aggressive that would have the FBE and allies lose their legitimacy with the general population.

With all of these challenges in mind, the FBE's strategic objective must be:

To successfully lay all blame for social disruption, violence, and angst on the NRF in order to destroy these rebels while maintaining political legitimacy to gain absolute political power over the Western nation.

By accomplishing this strategic objective, the FBE secure a complete monopoly on the Western nation's instruments of political power while placing all blame for any oppression, corruption, or violence on the NRF.

Optimal Warfare:

The FBE have to maintain a delicate balance of growing their power without antagonizing the general population into open rebellion before the FBE is ready. The FBE are usurping power slowly to avoid being noticed by the general population who do not pay significant attention to power dynamics within the Western nation. This leaves the FBE's ambitions vulnerable to disruption from NRF elements before the FBE can secure absolute control. Overreacting with open draconian force and violence would likely provoke a major backlash and split the FBE faction itself while relying on information warfare and propaganda alone would be insufficient to stop a motivated resistance force. The FBE must devise a strategy that hides their illicit usurping of democratic institutions while bringing sufficient force to bear on the NRF to neutralize them as a threat as rapidly as possible. The best way is to provoke the NRF into carrying out actions that would justify the FBE controlled national institutions to brutally retaliate in the eyes of the public. The FBE would also make sure to manipulate the NRF into fighting in a way that gives maximum advantage to FBE forces to guarantee NRF defeat. This must be done quickly because the general public would only support the FBE-backed government's efforts during a perceived existential crisis which cannot last indefinitely.[2] So, what is the optimum form of warfare that suits FBE's requirements of rapidly destroying their opposition, maintain public support, and acquire more overt autocratic power at the same time?

In the heyday of America's counterinsurgency actions in Afghanistan and Iraq, academics, theoreticians, and military minds endorsed William Lind's theoretical framework of "sequential emergence" where a new type of warfare emerges from a previous generation of warfare. This is akin to social generations that evolve and attune their actions and beliefs to their contemporary circumstances and issues. "Sequential emergence" attempted to explain the paramilitary insurgencies facing US forces in Asia and how these differed from precious insurgencies because of new technologies, especially communication technologies.[3] The idea being counterinsurgency operations had to be performed differently than in the past but this book rejects this concept for the theoretical basis to identify the optimal form of war that both the FBE and the NRF would choose.

"Nothing new under the sun" is the biblical phrase but this book argues this is mostly true for concepts, not all ideas. Science, technology, and greater understanding give rise to new techniques and applications all the time but the fundamental thoughts and concerns of civilization remains largely unchanged. Lind's concept of generational warfare implied generational warfare introduced new concepts but often confused implementation techniques with fundamental concepts. The concepts of psychological warfare, information warfare, deception, and "hearts and minds" are not new concepts. Technology, media, and international norms of war did change the times, the applications, and the techniques, but not the concepts. Instead, this book will use the "xGW Framework Theory" postulated by Daniel H. Abbott and his colleagues as the preferred framework to identify the optimal way for the rivals to fight in a hypothetical future civil war in a Western nation.

Mr. Abbott succinctly describes xGW Framework as, ". . .warfare exists along a gradient of violence, which is more focused on one end and more diffused on another". Using a scale of violence to discriminate the forms of warfare is more accurate for effective analysis because it takes observers out of their contemporary time to better appreciate the fact that the human race was always thinking about how to best kill one another and take more power. Abbott, and his fellow advocates, identify six gradients of warfare based on violence that has existed since the first polities arose in pre-known history, hence the x=number of the gradient and GW stands for Gradient Warfare.[4]

1. Zero Gradient: a war of genocide for one faction to completely exterminate their opposition, like Rome with Carthage;

2. First Gradient: defeating an opposing force by concentrating their greatest warriors to fight and win in one place for battle, like in the Middle Ages;

3. Second Gradient: achieving victory by concentration of firepower to overwhelm an under-armed opponent, like Europe's colonial wars;

4. Third Gradient: warfare that uses operational and tactical superiority to outmaneuver an opponent, even if the opponent has superior numbers or equipment, like Germany's invasion of France in 1940.

5. Fourth Gradient: similar to Lind's "Fourth-Generation" warfare that uses paramilitary and psychological actions to either degrade an opponent's incentives to continue fighting by losing domestic political support or degrade an opponent's military advantage, forcing them to fight either in 2nd or 3rd gradient warfare, like Mao's PLA in the Chinese Civil War or the Taliban against America's counterinsurgency in Afghanistan;

6. Fifth Gradient: a war of political compulsion where deception, political trickery, covert systemic attacks using only dispersed and diffused violence on critical nodes of the opponent's power. A covert war fought in shadow and cloaked in invisibility, like the actions of the Nizari-Ismaili Order of Assassins.

The scale of violence distinguishes the different forms of war humanity has fought with itself while also demonstrating that the techniques may change, actions may occur faster, and more information is available, but the fundamental concepts of warfare remain unchanged.

From these categories, the FBE's best course of action would be to conduct a second, third, or combination of these two gradients of warfare. In the Western nation, the FBE has pushed the society into an anocracy where the corrupt members of the FBE wield the power of the state, even though it is indirect. The militaries of the nation-state, especially major powers, are designed and organized for second and third gradient warfare. For example, the United States government's bureaucracy was built in a post-World War II era where it faced the military might of the Soviet Union.

The West's militaries grew out of old imperial doctrines of the 19th Century and incorporated industrialized warfare efficiently. In the informationalized modern battlespace, the military is still best organized on a strict hierarchy of command designed to deliver maximum firepower onto an opponent by outmaneuvering and outthinking them on a battlefield.[5] Space and cyberspace are just two new domains to be added into the planning of overwhelming organized violence. As seen in Iraq and Afghanistan, fourth and fifth gradients are ill-suited for the government because the government's instruments of the DIME are akin to an axe while fourth and fifth are like scalpels by being small and precise. Provoking the NRF into an open overt war where the FBE can blame the NRF allows the FBE to 1. Maintain public support 2. Use the government institutions to bear the brunt of the NRF fighting while the FBE are themselves largely untouched 3. The FBE coopted government can justify greater centralized control for more overt and direct tyranny to fight the war as their foreign benefactors intend.

Strategic Plan: Catalonia 2.0

Starting in 2009, a small town rekindled an old conflict by voting to secede and called for the independence of the region of Catalonia from Spain.[6] This occurred at a time when the central government in Spain was weak and vulnerable. The Great Recession of 2008 was crippling the economy and the ruling Spanish Socialist Party was a minority government in parliamentary terms where it is must partner with other parties to pass legislation. From 2009-2011, the minority government faced multiple non-binding unofficial referendums in Catalonia without consent of the government or approval of Spain's lower house of their legislature which made these referendums technically illegal. The independence movements were organized by the Popular Unity Candidates who continued to carry out independence referendums in defiance of court rulings.[7]

Eventually, the dominant independence parties at the time, the Asssemblea Nacional Catalana and the Democratic Convergence of Catalonia, organized grassroots support at multiple municipalities to promote secession which eventually culminated with province-wide demonstrations on September 11, 2012.[8] By this time, Spain elected a new conservative government with a clear majority and the Catalonian provincial government was now led by Artur Mas of the Convergencia I Unio (CiU) Pary who became the face of the secessionist movement. As the leader of the Catalonia provincial government, Mr. Mas organized five Catalonia political parties into backing a province-wide referendum on independence despite the Spanish government declaring it illegal backed by court rulings.[9] Although the Artur-led Catalan government declared it a "citizen participation vote" instead of a referendum to avoid legality, the Spanish government still declared it illegal and pursued legal action.[10] For next three years, the legal actions against Artur and Catalonia disrupted both the ruling Catalonian parties and the Catalan economy. Eventually, Artur was convicted and barred from running for office for two years.[11]ˌ [12]

Regardless of the outcome after this period, these events showed how a government can use their opponent's actions against them. The referendums were illegal which gave the national government's decision to reject Catalan demands or acknowledge grievances legitimacy amongst Spain's general population. Secondly, the referendums identified all of the secessionists' leaders, organizations, and sources of legitimacy. By allowing the Catalan movements to flourish unopposed for several years, the Spanish government could group all the opposition under one large organizational umbrella to focus all its legal authority. By the time the Catalans finally carried out its provincial-wide referendum in 2014, the Spanish government had enough time to insulate the rest of the country's economy from Catalonia from any disruption. The Spanish legal apparatus successfully disrupted the Catalan political parties and kept the detrimental effects largely confined to the province's economy. Consequently, Spain was able to remove the leaders of the referendum efforts without loss of public support. From 2009-2015, the Catalonian independence movement suffered a major political defeat and helped the Spanish government retain legitimacy and popularity with both the bureaucracy and the general public by portraying the Catalans as obstinate, illegitimate, and fanatical.

Unlike the Spanish government, the FBE need to use their opposition, the NRF, as a means to establish authoritarian control over the Western nation while having a foreign adversarial power acting as a covert contributor. By provoking NRF sympathetic portions of the national population into wanting to secede, the FBE will be able to easily identify its opponents and use various legal means to exacerbate and provoke greater resentments to want secession. This means the FBE could justify a far more aggressive and violent action against the NRF and legitimately expand greater authoritarian control. The FBE preferably would want a specific part of the country where all opposition to the FBE government gather in one concentrated place for elimination. Once an attempt at secession is done, the FBE could declare this action illegal and use military force to suppress and brutalize the NRF opposition. Since the secessionists had concentrated into one or a couple of provinces, the full effectiveness of the government's second and third gradient designed military can eliminate large swaths of NRF opposition quickly. This strategy applies best to the United States, France, Belgium, Spain, and Australia with less effectiveness in Canada, the United Kingdom, or Germany.

The Strategic Plan of Catalonia 2.0 would likely go approximately along the following path:

àFBE anocratic government continuously adds onerous legislation and regulations to anger dissenting population;

àThe resentful portion of the population fears growing disenfranchisement with the anocracy and the assertive ones join the NRF;

àLegal and political provocations cause the dissenting portions of the population to pursue parallel mechanisms of commerce, finance, and trade to escape FBE legal impositions;

àPart of the FBE's rules include use of power systems networks that require considerable interdependence throughout the country such as smart grids and renewable energy because renewables require large quantities of land and foreign materials for import;

àNRF builds sufficient political capital to push for secessionist referendums in one or several provinces of the Western nation while the FBE decry illegal activities as antidemocratic, treasonous, or illegitimate;

àFBE has insulated the critical infrastructure, commercial, and financial institutions as much as possible from NRF dominated economic areas so when conflict erupts with the NRF, the economic impact will be minimal on the FBE or the national government's forces;

àFBE deliberately escalates provocations to ensure NRF secession referendums are successful and the foreign adversary manipulating the FBE will covertly back secessionist personalities and social media via third party financing to deceive NRF leaders into believing a transition to independence will go more smoothly than it will in practice;

àNRF succeed in referendum despite legal and political warnings from national authorities;

àFBE loyal elements either use false flag operations or provoke NRF into carrying out violent acts against national security forces;

àFBE can now use the secession and violence to declare the secession an insurrection and promptly declare martial law, arrest remaining opposition in other parts of the Western nation, shut off power, water, and other utilities based in neighboring provinces;

àNRF forces launch military action against larger better equipped FBE national armed forces and suffer multiple tactical and operational defeats;

àFBE blockade NRF secessionist provinces reducing food, munitions, medicine, IT services, and power to critical levels;

àFBE controlled media hide abuses by FBE forces while exaggerating atrocities of the NRF;

àThe FBE national government will receive support from the adversarial nation because it doesn't want the precedent of provincial self-determination;

àThe combined economic might of the FBE controlled nation and the adversarial nation that secretly controls the FBE discourages most of the world from trading or recognizing the NRF seceded portions of the Western nation;

àMore and more 5th Column members within the NRF-controlled areas will increase sabotage while discrediting the NRF as oppressive fascists;

àThe brutality of the fighting and the complicity of national media on portraying all acts of the NRF as villains keeps the majority of the population sanguine with FBE actions;

àEventually, the NRF regions are forcefully rejoined back with the Western nation under a more overt autocratic government as the NRF itself is largely defeated with the Western nation population blaming the secessionists for the war and suffering;

àFBE are victorious and turn the anocracy into their pro-foreign benefactor autocracy.

The strategic plan is what is optimized for the FBE's goals and doesn't consider the added complexity of the foreign benefactor's interests. The foreign adversary would certainly prolong the conflict as much as possible while keeping the FBE perpetually dependent to weaken the Western nation as much as possible to turn it into a vassal. To this end, the foreign adversary will continuously play both sides but ultimately back the FBE to bind the corrupt elites permanently as servants to their foreign benefactors.

Secession is the best means of compelling the NRF to fight the autocratic FBE on the FBE's terms because it would stay as a 3GW government against government fight. If the NRF can be tricked into becoming a classical government for secessionists with clear institutional processes such as provincial governments, legal processes, and organized groups of force such as militias, provincial guard units, or police forces then the FBE-controlled national government can use its inherent advantages of third gradient warfare. Secession fixes the targets because the secessionist NRF government now has to have power plants, utilities, IT hubs, datacenters, military bases, command and control nodes, and food distribution sites. Additionally, the NRF's legitimacy relies on adhering to certain Western concepts of civilized war as FBE media would show any ruthless actions. This would further inhibit the NRF's ability to fight with full effect as it restrains its forces from committing brutalities that the FBE will no doubt conduct to hasten victory. The more violence carried out by the FBE, the quicker the NRF will be defeated because the NRF cannot hide.[13] The NRF cannot disperse its forces like guerrillas because a guerilla force cannot protect territory, only armies can do that. By committing NRF to territories by secession, the FBE compels the NRF to fight in the open.

This will not be a simple one and done FBE provocation that will cause the rebellious segment of the population to rally around an armed uprising. There would be many little incidents to cause frustration to build up resentments and multiple false starts. The false starts would come in guise of media and provocateurs sensationalizing a divisive political issue beyond what is actually occurring, warning that this will lead to civil war. These false starts will help condition people to accept the concept of civil war is inevitable, that open rebellion is the only answer, and peaceful reconciliation is not an option. The FBE will instigate multiple false alarms, each one more grandeur in scale and provocation, but will not actually occur until the FBE are confident their side holds most of the cards.

Carrying out an overt war combining the second and third gradients is the most optimal strategic plan for the FBE to achieve their objectives. Organized resistance almost certainly would first arise against the FBE while the Western nation was still an anocracy and the FBE still trying to assert complete control over the Western nation's institutions. By provoking an open war, the Western nation's government and institutions would be weakened by directly engaging the NRF while the FBE, which are a cabal of loosely aligned private elites, would remain unscathed. The FBE would be able to lobby for greater institutional changes towards complete autocratic rule while having the legitimacy of open war to justify the changes. This plan supports the key strengths of the FBE's situation and enables the FBE's centers of gravity to be protected from the NRF's retaliation.

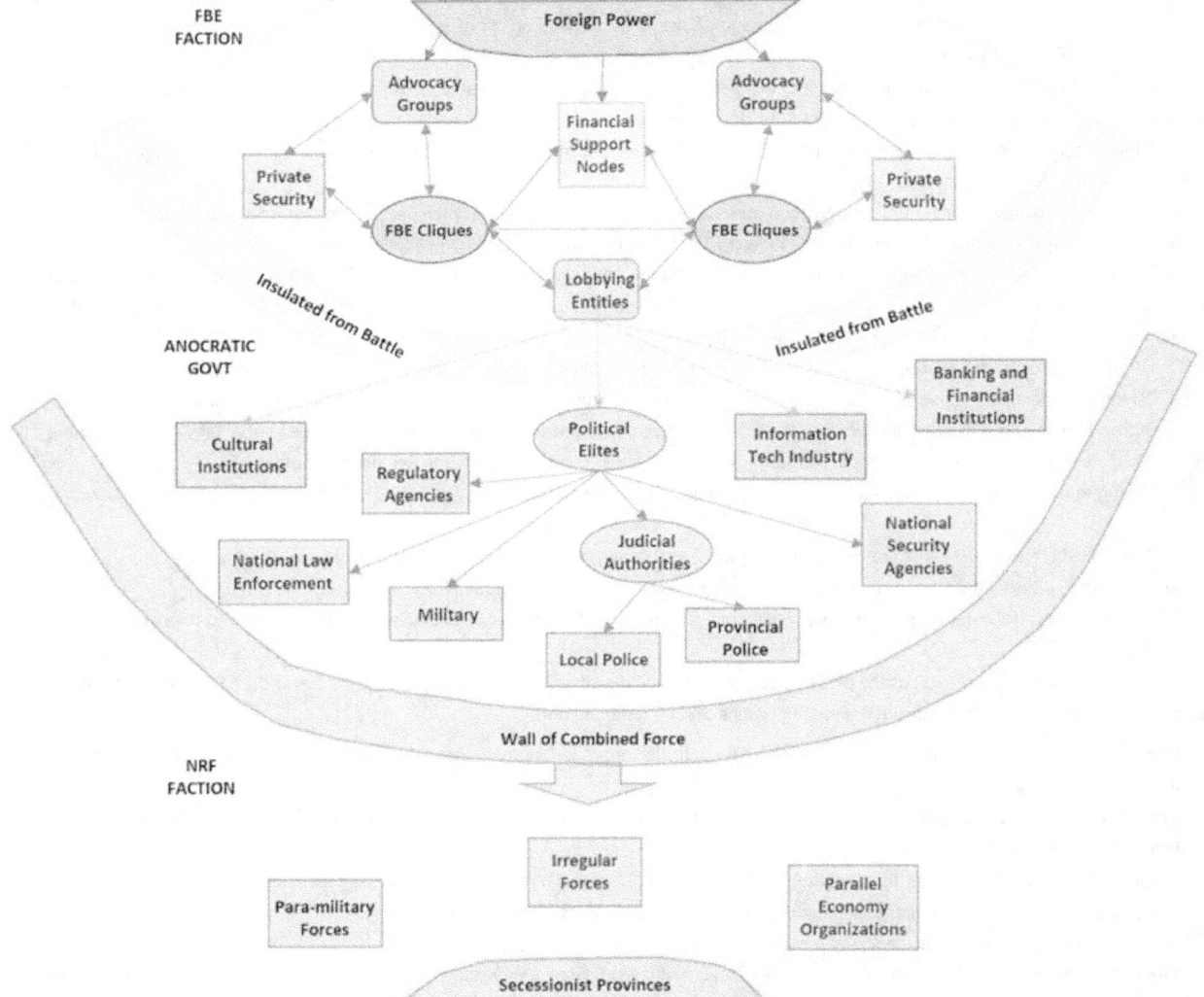

Centers of Gravity:

Carl von Clausewitz's devised several concepts within his book *On War* on how to evaluate the critical elements of warfare that is understood by most Western scholars. One of the most prominent is the concept of "center of gravity". The center of gravity doesn't have a single universally accepted definition but Clausewitz states centers of gravity (COG) are critical hubs of concentrated power a fighting forces depends upon to wage conflict and achieve victory.[xiv] This simple means of evaluating the strengths and weaknesses of fighting factions helps the casual observer understand the differences between the two factions and why each side has a different optimal strategy and means of war.

This civil war scenario is unusual because there are technically two forces operating within the FBE faction. The coopted national elites and their foreign benefactors each have differing objectives and means to achieve those objectives yet only the national elites will be involved in directly combating their NRF opponents. So, the FBE's COGs will be the ones the coopted national elites need to achieve victory. These COGs are critical for the FBE's victory but losing them will almost certainly guarantee defeat. Neither faction has to completely destroy every single COG nor are all COGs equally weighted in importance. Some shape the battlespace more easily while others drive the main effort of the fighting force. Each COG of the FBE will be identified and have its strengths and weaknesses evaluated. These COGs are not just for fighting the NRF once an attempt at secession has been made; but are also critical in covertly convincing the Western nation's society to move from an anocracy to an autocracy ruled by the technocratic and economic elites of the FBEs.

Primary Center of Gravity: The Leaders of the Foreign-Backed Elites

The unique situation of a foreign induced civil war creates a critical node that outweighs all others, the node that links the foreign adversary with their complicit accomplices in the Western nation. Using unrestricted warfare means attacking the entire society and, in this scenario, the foreign adversary was in danger of losing access to the Western nation's critical weak points. The corrupt social elites of the Western nation are the one common node that can maintain connections between the foreign adversary and the exploitable social elements of the Western nation. The coopted elites themselves are the primary COG for the FBE faction as these elites are the only lynchpin that helps the foreign adversary destabilize the elites' homeland.

The elites are the informal leaders of this subversive effort to subjugate the Western nation to their foreign benefactors, but the elites themselves have no one single leader. These elites are not a monolith cohesive organization like the CCP but are more akin to a loose confederacy of aligned cliques united by common cause and interest. No one single member of the elite will fully know or comprehend how they are being manipulated by their foreign benefactors, but instead each clique will do its part in carrying out the actions of the FBE faction when told to do so. Although some of these coopted persons will likely be from the political elites such as politicians and technocrats, as seen in Australia with former MP Sam Dastyari, [xv] the majority of the coopted elites come from private and nonprofit entities. The adversary nation's unrestricted warfare exploits the blind spots of the Western nations' laws while the security forces still look out for older industrial age methods of foreign direct interference of attempting to infiltrate the Western government itself. Most Western nation capabilities are designed to protect the state's government from direct infiltration and subversion as these policies derive from the old Cold War and antiterrorism efforts. The foreign adversary spent decades wooing and coopting elites from the financial, industrial, and cultural sectors of the society where there are fewer legal inhibitors between private individuals.

The FBE faction would have multiple cliques from the Western nation's economic, academic, activist, and cultural sectors. Nonprofit and international advocacy organizations link the various cliques under common "just causes" to coordinate strategy and facilitate monies for illicit purposes. These links enable the FBE to influence each other as well as the Western nation's government's perceptions that pro-national forces are the enemy. These elites operate within organizations and financial networks that were established decades ago allowing the FBE the ease to use a multi-channel network system to direct actions without an explicit chain of command.[xvi]

Strengths:

The FBE leadership are already established within institutions that have existed for generations, meaning they can forgo concerns of building new links and networks to coordinate efforts against the NRF. The combined wealth and social positions of these institutions, both private and public, insulate them from day-to-day management as there are already processes and procedures for most actions. There are enough self-governing mechanisms to enable the various cliques of the elites to issue broad objectives and "suggestions" to direct their agendas. There would be little reason to become directly involved, especially in any actions of open violence.

This also means the elite cliques of the FBE have little risk of exposure to legal actions or criminal charges from the Western government. Governments are hierarchies of command which look downwards at the mid and lower-level echelons of society for miscreants and subversives. The idea behind republics is that the lowly voter would hold the upper echelons of the political elites and their benefactors to account. However, in an anocracy, this accountability mechanism is broken and the FBE can exert influence beyond legal means with little risk of repercussion.

The informality of the grouping of elite cliques means the NRF will have difficulty detecting and targeting a chain of command. As seen in the optimal strategic plan, the FBE themselves rely on the covert nature of their control within the anocracy and use their proxy organizations and lobbying groups to direct the anocratic forces. The diluted networking of the FBE keeps their influence nebulous to outside observers and instead tries to cause the NRF to focus on the official technocratic and political leaders of the anocracy who directly manage the instruments of national power. The foreign adversary knows direct control of the political elites beyond a few corrupt ones would be discoverable and likely lead to open war. Instead, the majority of complicit political elites will be "useful idiots" carrying out actions on behalf of the FBE without fully realizing the complete intention or consequence of said actions. Most of these people will likely be corrupt and mercenary in motivation to satisfy immediate personal desires rather than any grand scheme. Since the political elites don't directly control the illicit funding to corruptly coopt the anocracy's institutions nor control the conceptual or intellectual direction of the FBE, they are also expendable pawns. The FBE will happily use the political elites not just as the middlemen between the FBE and the bureaucracies, but also as shields against NRF targeting efforts.

The broad strokes of strategic level planning and decision making allow the FBE members to remain insulated within "ivory tower" style settings protected from the harsh realities of the fight. Their anocratic advisors, specialists, and politically appointed managers handle the details and execution of the critical tasks set by the FBEs. The elite cliques are already established in the heart of the power-broker networks of the Western nation without needing to directly manage anything beyond the twin decisions of setting the political objectives and where to allocate the monies to ensure the loyalty of the anocratic machine. The opaqueness and nebulousness of the FBE's decision-making process within these established power networks also keeps this COG of ruling elite cliques difficult to find and destroy.

Weaknesses:

The elites that control the FBE faction have numerous advantages because they are not formally part of the government or bound to a legally empowered institution. The majority of the elite cliques making up the FBE derive their influence from private organizations that have fewer legal obligations of accountability or scrutiny. The FBE uses corrupted or easily misled politicians to carry out their orders and act as a front to hide from NRF and public scrutiny. These manipulated political elites also act as expendable foils where anger and discontent can be focused on and deflect any negative consequences away from the FBE. The FBE have no single leader, no Fuhrer or Party Chairman they have to answer to which means there is no obvious head the NRF can try to cut off. This loose assembly of private businessmen, academics, and social engineers are linked only by common interests that are tied to their foreign benefactors and can operate and coordinate with little risk of being targeted, at least at first. Yet, despite the largess of financial and political influence the FBE inherently possesses within the anocratic system, their weaknesses, if properly exploited, could leave them surprisingly vulnerable.

The first problem is the FBE's limited understanding of politics and war which arises as a consequence from all the inherent advantages the FBE possesses over the NRF. With few exceptions, the majority of FBE members already started out their careers with social advantages, connections, and influence which they used to gain more wealth and power. Even the self-made members of the FBE quickly conformed to the expectations and roles of up-and-coming social elites. These individuals had to work with and comply with established systems to grow their wealth and influence which meant these elites had powerful safety nets that protected rising elites from any serious hardship or failure. The members of the FBE have always been raised in or close to a metaphorical ivory tower insulated from reality.

There is no one concept that can fully explain the ecosystem that such a corrupted Western elite would operate in but there are simplified models that can at least outline how the structure of this ivory tower functions. A political theoretician around World War II named James Burnham proposed a theory that comes close to encapsulating the organization and mentality of groups like the FBE which he called, "The Theory of Managerial Revolution." James Burnham was a former Trotskyist who, like Mussolini, grew disillusioned with the presumptions of socialism that humanity would progress into a collectivist utopia.[xvii] Instead, he argued industrialization of the early 20th Century made both societies and economies so complex that a new class of managers was created to act as highly specialized experts to run the everyday operations on behalf of the owners. These managers would work in tandem with government technocrats as more state intervention and regulation grew to manage the highly complex economic and social processes that made modern societies function. [xviii] Burnham concluded that this group of technocratic experts and managers would become the true power brokers of post-capitalist societies by usurping the political classes and the private owners of the means of production. Instead of socialist idealists or the proletariat taking power in a collectivist revolution, these socialist factions would simply be used as tools to help the new managerial class achieve a new oligarchic autocracy to accumulate absolute power. Burnham, like Mussolini, concluded human nature was more avaricious and self-serving than socialist movements assumed and societies embracing more collectivist systems would only result in becoming self-serving autocracies.[xix]

Burnham published his theory at the start of World War II and cited Fascist Italy, Nazi Germany, and the Soviet Union as models of technocratic managerial rule. This technocratic rule doesn't necessarily require the state to own the means of production directly, the only requirement is for the managerial class to control access to the means of production.[xx] Having access to the means of production was effectively the same as owning it. Burnham conceded he did not know what the final incarnations of the new technocratic system's ideologies would look like and deferred speculating on them, saying Nazi German and the USSR would be the most likely models. Burnham's theory lost credibility with much of the academic world because of his prediction that the new oligarchic system of managerial autocrats was superior in directing all of its power than capitalist states. By this logic, he predicted Italy and Germany would defeat the capitalist West in World War II which of course didn't happen. However, one of Burnham's greatest critics, George Orwell, warned in his criticism that a common flaw among all political futurists is having the expectation of their theory unfolding quickly for the convenience of the predictor. Orwell warned that Burnham had a very good chance of being right but would unfold over a longer period of time.[xxi] Despite Orwell's differences with Burnham, Orwell was sufficiently convinced at the plausibility of Burham's concept of managerial oligarchy that Orwell incorporated many facets of this theory into his book *1984*. When the main character, Winston Smith, receives a copy of the forbidden book of the "Brotherhood" called "The Theory and Practice of Oligarchical Collectivism", its contents mirror features in Burnham's theory.

After several generations since Burnham first proposed this theory, the organizational structures of the world's mixed economies have crystalized into set structures to help identify what the final incarnations of managerial autocracy would look like. The overt totalitarian states like China have adopted variations of central absolutism by making the owners and managers of the means of production one class united under a political party. The wannabe autocrats of the West wish to make the managerial, expert, and technocratic classes the new elite in a dominating partnership with state institutions akin to a new form of feudalism which one managerial elitist clique calls "Stakeholder Capitalism". Both forms of technocratic managerial ideology do show Burnham was completely incorrect on one facet of his theory. Burnham argued the technocrat and managerial classes would usurp and replace the owners of the means of production in the same way the merchant class displaced the feudal aristocracy. In practice, the owners and select members of the politically connected wealthy class simply bought and coopted the managerial class into merging into a new melded "elite" class that segregated themselves from the rest of the "common" wealthy class in the West. In places like China, the technocratic elites allowed their peers to become wealthy owners but still had to operate in symbiosis with state officials.

The members of the FBE are an inverted mirror of the elites of their foreign benefactors. A totalitarian monolithic organization, like the CCP, unites the political elites of the foreign adversary nation under a strict hierarchy with a clear chain of command. These foreign elites gained their power via climbing the political and government ladder rather than the FBEs whose influence came from building private fiefdoms in key industries, universities, or financial institutions. The FBE's members are private entities who became involved in politics after building wealth or social influence in the private sector while the foreign elites involved themselves in wealth and social influence after attaining power in government service. The foreign benefactor's national leaders have the advantage over the FBEs because they understand the dynamics of power and geo-strategic thinking far better than the corrupt Western elite puppets. The FBE elites, for all the inherent power of their positions, are politically naïve and amateur compared to the foreign benefactors which helps explain why the FBE remain the pawns.

The next critical weakness of the FBE is a facet of these managerial elites Burnham did not consider, which was the capability of the managerial elites degrading with each succeeding iteration. One of the flaws of European hereditary feudalism that is commonly understood was its ruling class had become more incestuous over the centuries as bloodlines were means to secure power and wealth. Mad, impaired, or enfeebled rulers were more likely to have heirs die young or impair their own abilities to govern which did help encourage more constraint on royal authority in some kingdoms. Genetic degradation meant each new successor generation would have more shallow ability than his predecessor, directly leading to that particular ruling family's loss of power.[xxii] A similar effect occurs in technocratic rule but it is degradation by adhering to procedural orthodoxy rather than bloodlines.

The first generation of managerial elites achieved political influence by building the policies, procedures, and organizations necessary to implement technocratic managerial governance. Many of these elites had to earn or metaphorically fight to obtain their power and influence because there was no established hierarchical structure to shield these first-generation elites from failure. Their success required the first-generation to predominantly have leadership and effective management ability with at least some competence but what about their successors? Since these positions within the managerial and technocratic elite are not secure by hereditary or legal entitlement, this makes the leaders of the managerial elites more vulnerable to usurpation. This incentivizes the majority of the elite to appoint their advisory and deputy managerial members based on acts of loyalty, sycophancy, or deliberately appointing those without any real ability in order for the leadership to secure their hold on power. As succeeding generations of managerial technocrats gain leadership positions, each new generation would adhere to established orthodoxy of the previous generation of leadership to earn sufficient accolades to climb the ranks. This means each succeeding generation becomes more rigid in terms of thinking and more insulated from reality as each new generation builds upon an established system that acts as a safety net from failure. Each new generation will be less capable than the previous. However, the years of constructing the established managerial support structure means each leadership generation's advisory and deputy level members can use this system as a crutch to manage the system without having to deal with the challenges of leadership. After several generations, the managerial elites' diminished leadership skills are severe to the point of them relying exclusively on their advisory groups and experts on all issues, hence becoming trapped in their ivory tower of theory and remote governance. These newer leaders only learn the skills of climbing the now built managerial ladder which often derives from their specialized role of management in fields such as legal, finance, investments, banking, academic, or business administration. The ranking system discourages any maverick or innovative behavior which would endanger their superiors. The FBE leaders are the descendants of this system. They are now glorified advisors debating among themselves, insulated in their ivory tower echo chambers, with little interaction with the real world. This makes them perfect for foreign manipulation as most of the FBE is trapped in their reality bubble of theoretical utopianism. Despite their lack of real world understanding and delusions, most are very smart by academic standards so how can such highly intelligent, but greedy, people be so unwittingly controlled?

This generational degradation creates the FBE leaders' final weakness of having no "common sense", which worsens with every succeeding generation of FBE technocratic managers. In 2021, a study conducted by the British Medical Journal on distinct aspects of cognition between aerospace engineers and neurosurgeons to evaluate old adages such as "it's not rocket science" to determine if people in professions dealing with extremely complex problems are cognitively superior to the general population. The study concluded members of advanced professions were not necessarily brighter than the general population, which lies at the heart of the problem of overeducated, but aloof, rulers.[xxiii] The human brain is a general-purpose machine designed to function against the harsh realities of nature and surviving in an unforgiving world. As civilization arose, more jobs became specialized as the complexities of tasks and fields of study became so great that people had to devote their working lives to understanding these professions. Specialization meant devoting their minds to understanding that particular facet of life but usually at the cost of remaining ignorant about many other aspects of life. No one questions the genius of Mozart on everything related to music but no one would have asked him to perform surgery just because he was a reputed genius. Although there is no doubt that there are exceptionally intelligent persons than those in the general population, the majority of these smart people are considered so because of their understanding of their profession better than most of the population. Being a genius doesn't necessarily mean being smarter than most people in most aspects of life.

These elites are smart in that they've attained a level of proficiency from intense training the FBE members require, to excel in a specialized field necessary to achieve rank within their cliques, but the problem is the lack of the extent of their understanding. True leaders, especially political ones, are most effective when they not only understand a specific element of society but have a generalist understanding of how the world functions in reality. Specialization is important but effective leaders must also broaden their experiences and interact with the real world to observe and understand how theory and practicality interact. This is why in military ranks the most senior leaders are referred to as "generals". Yet, most members of the FBE are raised from the beginning in an environment of privilege and excess, only interacting with others like them: wealthy, pampered, overeducated but minimally exposed to the realities of the world. This weakness means regardless of wealth or the extent of their support edifices within societal institutions, the majority of FBE leaders will be more akin to the likes of Caligula, King John I of England, or Louis XV of

France. The FBE are not leaders, they are overindulgent libertines who've never heard the word "no". This leaves the FBE vulnerable whenever the NRF creates situations where one of the FBE members has to take direct command in a real-world situation. As seen with President Putin and the initial invasion of Ukraine, trying to take the lead on something one doesn't know anything about can lead to disaster.

Secondary Centers of Gravity: Lifelines of the FBE Leaders

The remaining COGs are the critical support mechanisms that enable the FBE to maintain control while also growing its power covertly within the Western nation's institutions. Each of these centers of gravity focus on specific elements of control: the means of funding the FBE, the means of hindering opponents, and the means of social control. The primary COG is the driver of anocracy to autocracy but these COGs are the means to attain this objective. Without these COGs, the FBE will be incapable of subverting the Western nation or influencing political institutions. These COG will be reviewed in brief summation here as each will be analyzed in more detail in the Operational portion of this book.

Shadow Financing:

The FBE's members are mostly very wealthy individuals tied to various associations and companies that collectively yield billions of dollars, but little of this money can be overtly spent on political subversion or government manipulation. Subverting a country is expensive and while the foreign benefactor will bribe or facilitate money, the majority of the funding will be raised by the FBEs themselves. For one, the foreign benefactors are from an authoritarian society with its unique understanding of cultural norms and most Western social and political cultural norms are alien to them. Trying to directly figure out where and how to direct funding to create and exacerbate social divides is likely to be less effective while also increasing the risk of discovery. Instead, the FBEs who are raised within Western society will know the best ways of destroying Western institutions and culture. The key for this COG is how to generate a self-funding system while keeping it hidden from the NRF, the general public, and the uncorrupted elements of the Western nation's government?

Strengths:

Western nations' open societies with private enterprises give the FBE a multitude of options to fund their endeavors. If one channel of funding is exposed or disrupted, the FBE's financial network can create new channels and links quickly. Most of the transactions can used for dual purposes enabling subversion while backing legal endeavors. Any attempt by the NRF to disrupt funds that also support legitimate efforts increases the reputational risk with the general public, enabling the FBE-backed financial organizations to portray themselves as victims instead of foreign-backed pawns. Aside from business ventures, the use of nonprofit and philanthropy organizations provides the greatest advantage as these organizations' finances are better shielded from outside scrutiny due to their tax status. FBE funding in the guise of humanitarian or compassionate actions makes financial disruption harder for the NRF who cannot risk too much loss of reputation with the general population. A recent innovation in the world of money and finance has been to combine philanthropy with profit.

A real-world case is the creation of the "Environmental, Social, and Governance" (ESG) investment portfolio. The idea being investors can demonstrate their virtue by investing in companies and ventures that generate profit while improving global sustainability.[xxiv] ESG brings political and social activism which, unlike profit reports, doesn't have a clear and definitive metric for achieving their goals. The goals will be set by what the investors and the companies will consider ESG suitable but these definitions are normative with lots of gray area in the defined metrics. This is the type of process the FBEs could use to funnel funds for illicit or subversive purposes. This is not to say that ESG investments are actually corrupt or misused per se, but it is an example of financial investment that could be easily corrupted for nefarious use by some of its participants.

Weaknesses:

Networked systems have many advantages and covert funding has all of these advantages as well. However, despite simplified models portraying networks as just nodes and links, the real world's networks are not so simple. No matter how much effort is done for creating network redundancy of systems, adding numerous nodes, or multiple links there will always be key nodes and links. Funding networks are mainly protected by their anonymity, if a key node or link is discovered by the NRF then these can be targeted and destroyed quickly. Despite expectations by either the FBE or NRF factions, stopping the funding of the FBE is not and cannot be the goal, all the NRF have to do is disrupt the pace of the financing. Military and political operations need resources but these also need to be coordinated and synchronized in effort to be effective. If there is disruption to the resourcing, even if it is just one critical segment, then the FBE's operational decision-making process is thrown off. Many military commentators like to refer to this using John Boyd's OODA Loop or "Observe, Orient, Decide, Act" which is a descriptive method to carry out operations.[xxv] If the funding is disrupted, then the gap between the "decide" step and the "act" step widens which gives the initiative to the NRF and endangers FBE's ability to maintain control.

Information Control:

The FBE are fighting in a period of transition between anocracy and autocracy when sufficient organized resistance manifests itself. The FBE have controlling influence in the Western nation's anocracy yet they do not have either full legal control of the Western nation nor the general public fully pacified into accepting autocracy. Although many in the FBE will be overconfident and complacent at this period, the more prudent FBE members will understand the transition period just prior to fully implementing an overtly foreign-backed autocracy is the most vulnerable to disruption. The FBE don't have the legitimacy or sufficient broad support to be too aggressive against dissidents and they will be expected to behave within cultural expectations of the Western republican forms of political discourse and process. Showing their hand too quickly before the public is conditioned will destroy any legitimacy as well as the personal reputations of many FBE supporters. So, a key means to achieve the FBE's strategic objective of attaining absolute legal power means changing the discourse and the institutional norms to make the FBE members always appear as paragons of virtue even as they usurp the electorate. Rushing things too quickly causes severe social disruption and would reveal the FBE's ultimate intentions because their pattern of action becomes obvious.[xxvi] Disrupting the general population's lives too much causes disdain as the masses have learned to function and fit into the established world around them. Rapid change induces chaos which provokes greater resistance so, the FBE must "nudge" the population into accepting autocratic rule incrementally.[xxvii]

Nudging is done by controlling information, both true and false, into creating narratives that make the majority acquiesce to autocratic arguments and policies in tiny increments. These nudges are done by always convincing the public its interests are at the heart of every incremental change. Both sides of the civil conflict will use the same information control methods because these are universal even though the execution will be different based on the resources available to each side. This means an outsider will not be able to judge the moral character of either side based solely on the information operations the warring factions carry out because the absolute objective truth serves neither side, only itself. The absolute truth would reveal the weaknesses of both sides, destroying morale and support, which means both sides will need to use deception as a critical tool for victory.

Strengths:

The FBE would start out in the civil conflict as the dominating force with superior resources and being able to influence all established institutions. This means the FBE can exploit the inherent conditioning of modern Western societies of accepting "authoritative sources" as truth. Many in the West like to believe members of contemporary society are more astute than their ancestors because they are, generally speaking, more literate and have greater access to information. In reality, the majority of people are not wiser, they are just as gullible with only the guise of the manipulators being changed. In the past, regimes used a priest class that dabbled in unusual ceremonies, rites, and incantations to keep the ignorant masses complicit. In modern times, regimes and institutions rely on "authoritative experts" to explain the world to the masses using math and buzzwords instead of incantations. From the layman's perspective, how are incantations of tea leaves and chicken bones different from statistical models, algorithms, and empirical studies? The public don't understand any of these subjects and unless one is versed in these fields, the common person has to take the word of the "expert" because most common people cannot disprove what the state-approved expert says. Much information is manipulated or interpreted by "reputable" persons or groups who only point out misinformation that contradicts those groups' interests. Consequently, many Westerners happily embrace the "credential fallacy" where someone being in a certain profession, endorsed by a certain institution or hold a certain title, can simply proclaim something as fact and the majority of the casually observing general public will believe them even if the statements cannot be independently verified.

Even when facts and events go completely against the FBE's interests, the FBE faction can use their credentialled experts, which include cultural and social experts as well as scientific, to use emotional manipulation to convince people a false narrative is a fact. Authoritarian systems rely on exploiting the negative emotional states that easily transmit among masses of people. Negative emotions are easily accepted by the general public because these appeal to the baser instincts of self-interest while higher or positive emotions require development and building of trust. As a rule of thumb, the standard set of emotions autocratic governments use for exploitative manipulation are guilt, fear, anger, hatred, and greed. FBE's mouthpieces' have the advantage of the fact the society being usurped is decadent and hedonistic. This makes the society selfish, impatient, ill-equipped for harsh life, and inattentive to things that don't directly impact the masses' daily lives. Such a vulnerable society with so many resources available to the FBE means pacifying the majority of the population peaceably is relatively easy. Selected experts can act as the FBE's "priest" class.

Weaknesses:

Controlling authoritative information does not necessarily mean the FBE or their designated experts actually understand what is really happening or have substantive advice on solving problems. This weakness is carried over from the FBE leaders being too often confined to their intellectual ivory towers within the FBE's echo chambers of discussion and planning. The experts themselves are often selected for their credentials and loyalty rather than their understanding or competence. The experts who act as authoritative figures to direct information control also impact the perceptions of their FBE superiors as the FBE faction's nature restricts information flow through only approved channels. To keep control of a faction that is trying to centralize all power into the hands of foreign puppets, the FBE must limit who is considered authoritative and reputable. This system requires information be directed from the top-down and the experts must adhere to the FBE's messaging and directives which encourage sycophancy. Sycophancy amplifies the echo chamber as group think becomes the norm as it protects the experts from being purged which reinforces risk aversion. This risk aversion means further insulating the expert priest-like class from reality and confine their ideas only to the dogmas that protect the ideological foundations of the FBE. Western society's love of the "credentialed expert" makes this worse.

The modern West embraces a contradictory view of knowledge and wisdom. Right now, most people view academics, theoreticians, and people who have gone through years of academic study and training as the apex individuals of understanding the world. While that may be true in the scientific and technological fields, this assumption is not true of the social and political fields. Academia is built around theories about how the world works and these theories are the foundation to build models of the world to explain how these theories apply to the world. Models are simplified constructs about specific aspects of the world with many of the real-world variables removed and models only consider the criteria that act as the basis for the theory. These models show how a theory can work in a perfect setting where it can attain its maximum potential. In scientific fields, variables can be eliminated in laboratory conditions with focus on very narrow parameters to test a theory. In the fields of the humanities, there is no way to control the world settings to fully test and realize the potential maximum of a theory. Instead, most experts in humanities look for how the world can fit into their theories rather than having the theories fit into the world. No matter how complex, sophisticated, or well-thought out a theoretical model of the world is designed, it is still an overly simplistic and comparatively childish conception that doesn't match the real world at all. This is why academia is foundational and not the apex of knowledge in the social sciences. They provided the baseline understanding so people who go out into the real world have stronger frames of reference and apply their experiences to that framework to have a greater and more grounded understanding of the world at large.

The real world is filled with variables with endless sources of friction, conflict, fluctuating fortunes, and contextually changing circumstances. All of this real-world friction interferes with all theoretical plans or idealized systems preventing all social theories, be they economic, political, sociological, or psychological from reaching their theoretical full potential. The real-world places limits on the potential of all human efforts so people must learn to balance between all the variables to function, which is the limitation of many experts. Experts confined to the walled off ivory towers of academia, think tanks, or punditry only understand the potential of something, not the limitations. Understanding limitations can only be done by acquiring experiences in how the real world inhibits idealized systems and concepts and then use that understanding to modify plans into working actions. This is known as wisdom or "common-sense". This is why so many experts in the West get so many things wrong, even though they are academically smart. As Clint Eastwood's character Dirty Harry stated in the movie *The Enforcer,* "A man has got to know his limitations," and most experts lack the real-world experience to do so. The FBE experts suffer from the same weakness as most Western social experts as they are only exposed to the dogmas of their theories showing the full potential of a concept under ideal circumstances. This means the information controllers will be easily susceptible to NRF deception and psychological warfare.

Social Control: Nimbyists and the Atomized, the New Sepoys

The United States government was designed by the Founding Fathers to minimize the risk of the state becoming tyrannical by avoiding the two ways nations become tyrannies. The first means is the tyranny of the majority in which dictatorships arise when states' elites indulged popular demands in exchange for absolute power as seen in the fate of ancient Athens. The second means is the more traditional dictatorship of the minority in which a select segment of the population lorded over the majority based on unique characteristics such as religion, ethnicity, or political party affiliation as seen in Sparta, North Korea, People's Republic of China, and Ba'athist Syria and Iraq. Since that time, most Western systems have implemented checks and balances of various arrangements to prevent these two means of tyranny from forming.

Dictatorships rarely need the majority of the population to support them to hold power, only a dedicated segment of the populace whose livelihoods and fortunes are bound to the tyrannical state as seen in Venezuela or North Korea. These groups protect the dictatorship by inhibiting discontent amongst the rest of the oppressed general population. These enforcers and informers among the public are not military or security forces, but the economic and social support mechanisms that enable dictatorship institutions to function. There are two types. The first are the cadre of the system who become the mid and low-level ranking members of the state or economic apparatus itself. The second are the expendable fodder or pawns who allow themselves to be used by the dictatorship to suppress opposition in exchange for some immediate transactional benefit. These are social mercenaries who assist the state in fighting opposition but are not important enough to be part of the state or if they are, only peripherally. These loyalist servants often act as agents of chaos to keep and maintain social divisions between segments of the subjugated population to prevent any organized resistance against the state itself. The British Empire excelled at this means to keep conquered territories and nations under control with the most famous being the Sepoys of India where the British used Muslim and Hindu Soldiers as counterweights against each other.[xxviii] Variations of this method are used in most dictatorships with the most famous recent example being Saddam Hussein's Iraq where Saddam recruited his secret police from Christian and Turkoman minority populations because only the Ba'athist Party offered protection against the antagonistic majority of Iraqis.

Dictatorships often prefer to recruit their expendable agents from the most isolated or socially ostracized elements of society because they are completely dependent on the goodwill of the leadership to survive. The most famous example was the Nazi Brown Shirts who actively recruited from the unemployed and militias of the post-World War I era who couldn't be integrated into the Weimar Republic.[xxix] Other examples include Venezuela's Colectivo militias consisting of impoverished persons who enforce the Dictator Maduro's reign in exchange for social and economic privileges or rewards.[xxx] One final example was Mao's Red Guards who used indoctrinated students who believed Party traitors threatened the Marxist revolution and the students' future. Being an elitist organization by nature, the FBE needs a similar support base within the general population to execute FBE directives and provide sacrificial pawns to ensure FBE control without any risk to the FBE members themselves. Yet in an anocracy with an advanced economy the recruitment pool is different and requires less overt violent means of suppression.

Economies in the developed world are sufficiently advanced to the point where segments of the population are insulated from the harshest of life's circumstances. This circumstance gives these elements of the population the privilege to overindulge in self-gratification in both a material and psychological sense to the point of being libertine. These spoiled individuals are raised from birth to live in such a sheltered environment that being denied anything is virtually unknown and creates a sense of entitlement. The indulgent lives are fragile and susceptible to external disruption, making them easy to coopt by the FBE. Broadly speaking, these segments can be broken down into two groups of being indulged in all aspects of life and those who are indulged in only one.

The first being people born into the middle and upper classes who value their hedonism but also value the need to be socially accepted and glorified. Whether one believes the need comes from a spiritual compulsion or social pressure, these individuals largely understand that displaying such selfish behavior destroys their social credibility and will therefore work diligently at being perceived to being virtuous. So, to protect their lifestyles, these individuals will proclaim loyalty to ideas, slogans, platitudes, and give money to FBE-backed organizations without the inconvenience of actually sacrificing or doing anything substantively virtuous. The whole point is to ensure these entitled individuals can continue in their libertine lifestyles without criticism. In exchange for their loyalty to FBE-linked efforts, a select few of these entitled individuals are recruited into the FBE cadre and the rest will be given tiny slivers of social power to criticize and persecute those who defy the FBE social requirements with public shaming and harassment. This recruitment pool of individuals for FBE cadres mostly comes from the sheltered middle-class who crave the slightest attention or affirmation of their perceived power, no matter how small, making them easy to control and manipulate. This group of modern socially solipsistic "sepoys" within Western society are colloquially referred to as Nimbyists or "Not-In-My-Back-Yard"-ists.

Nimbyists are decadent and self-absorbed people whose libertine lifestyle makes them believe the world only exists to fulfill their wishes and demands which makes their sense of ethics completely mercenary. To protect their privileged life, the Nimbyists will adopt a public persona of supporting FBE-backed policies and philosophical decisions to be imposed on the rest of the population but not necessarily their own. Nimbyists will happily let everyone else sacrifice for the greater good while Nimbyists keep their privilege and wealth intact for being dutiful moral enforcers of the FBE's public pacification. This keeps Nimbyists immune from logical or moral condemnation because the justice, ethics, or righteousness of an argument or position is not and will never be important. Only preserving their decadent and indulgent social status within the anocracy matters;

so, Nimbyists will change their moral or social activist "principled" position on any issue at any time in order to protect their special privileges. This means rational debate is useless because what is right was never relevant to begin with. "Rules for thee, but not for me" to always justify the Nimbyists' privilege is the only standard. These modern Western cadre and sepoys of the upper classes' efforts of shaming or scaring others into complying with FBE efforts perfectly synchronize with the FBE's second group of sepoys and cadre recruited from the underclasses of Western society who will be termed the "Atomized".

In macroeconomics, a popular metaphor is the "economic pie" which represents the total wealth of a nation. In the metaphor, one way to improve the quality of life is by expanding or growing the pie by generating new wealth so even if the allocation of slices remains the same, everyone will get more pie because market economics are not a zero-sum game.[xxxi] Regardless of the metaphor's validity, the point is the size and scale of a nation's wealth can change and grow over time. In contrast, the amount of power within a society is fixed. There is only so much social and political power to go around amongst the various factions of a nation so power is a zero-sum game. Democratic republics exist to dilute this power to avoid any one group concentrating it to the point of tyranny while the FBE's anocracy is designed to make the diluted power of a democratic society gravitate to the corrupted elites into a more concentrated form to eventually become an autocracy. The dilemma for the FBE is how to co-opt loyal political "foot soldiers", fodder, and advocates without having to share too much power and undermine their own objectives of centralized control? Unlike totalitarian states, the FBE cannot openly proclaim full ownership and control of all economic activity to be ruled by a technocratic elite because the FBE haven't fully subverted the Western nation yet. The most optimal answer is to redefine what power or being "empowered" means to the FBE's expendable puppets. Taking inspiration from the "ignorance is strength" slogan of the fictional totalitarian INGSOC Party of the book *1984*, the FBE educate and condition vulnerable and impressionable segments of the society to be conditioned to focus on a single issue as the entire aspect of their lives. Single-issue focused groups become tunnel visioned to the point of not understanding either society or political empowerment in the broader context of the real world while at the same time binding the psyches of these FBE pawns to only one anchor in their life.

If properly conditioned, these human pawns will believe that their be-all and end-all existence is on the issue they've been indoctrinated to embrace. These corrupted single issues derive from active social problems within the Western nation from which the indoctrinated will be drawn into. These indoctrinated people will then sever all ties and relations that are not directly connected to that single social issue. Like a cult, these pawns will become increasingly isolated from their peers, family, former friends, and any employers that don't blindly embrace their single-issue. The more indoctrinated and the more insulated people will only find common cause with fellow single-issue driven fanatics spurred on by their manipulating FBE masters to become like a cultish tribe. These insulated people would have only their issue and their financial backers as the only anchors in their lives. Since the financial backers will be the FBE-influenced institutions and activist organizations, the insulated have been broken away from larger society into solitary fragments wandering in the social periphery, hence becoming atomized. These "Atomized" will accept poor standards of living, have no expectations of performance by their leaders, and never expect a true solution to their single-issue social problem. If the issue were resolved, then the Atomized would have no meaning in their lives since the FBE conditioned them to only love that single facet of life they must forever "fight" to protect. The Atomized will only have the FBE-controlled state as their social anchor and thus will be loyal to the FBE even if the Atomized proclaim to fight against elites to protect whatever single-issue they represent. In this way, the state becomes mother, father, mentor, and provider as the Atomized cannot take care of themselves because they are conditioned to be co-dependent on the FBE. The FBE's Nimbyists help the Atomized by endorsing pro-single-issue propaganda, donate funds to the Atomized, and crowd-shame any criticism against the Atomized. In turn, the Atomized will attack, both physically and verbally, any opponent of the FBE faction directly as the "boots on the ground" efforts to extinguish any mobilized opposition.

Strengths:

These controlled social elements come directly from the civilian population which reinforces political legitimacy for FBE policies and actions. Instead of a religion or common cultural heritage, the FBE combines single-issue activism of the Atomized endorsed by greedy hedonistic Nimbyists as the new moral code of which the state is the only arbiter of moral authority. These FBE groups create a solipsistic morality in which ultimately the state is the new center of the world. For these groups, the FBE institutions can use mass psychological emotional manipulation for ease of control as both Nimbyists and the Atomized use emotional rationalizations to justify their behavior. With Nimbyists motivated by greed and the Atomized by anger, the NRF will not be able to convert or deprogram many as the NRF cause would drastically reduce the importance these modern sepoys' role in society. The best part is that the FBE and their political benefactors of the foreign adversary will be able to create these groups across all ethnic, economic, and political lines. Even if the NRF identifies some of these groups, they will likely be blind to others that will be active for single issues that NRF leadership support. This is a truly nonpartisan means of manipulation as the FBE can cross all political lines. Finally, these expendable groups are relatively cheap. As Nimbyists just want to hold onto what they have and the Atomized only understand power through their single issue, the FBE only has to delegate tiny slivers of power to these expendable underlings to maintain loyalty. In fact, the Nimbyists and Atomized would likely adore the FBE for these tiny crumbs of power since they have been blinded to not see the overabundance of power the FBE consume themselves.

Weaknesses:

The ease of control the FBE can exert on these groups is also a weakness. The Nimbyists and the Atomized are fanaticized by psychological and political blinders which makes them inflexible in their outlooks and assumptions. This makes them prone to denial and deception techniques employed by the NRF in which the NRF just has to use the right verbiage, personas, and framing of context to trick the Nimbyists and the Atomized into carrying out actions that harm their FBE masters.

The second major weakness is that the FBE's patronage will attract more followers into the Nimbyists and Atomized for the sake of survival if nothing else. This means these controlled assets are a danger if they grow to the point of becoming a separate power base. This risk is compounded by the fact that fanatical enforcers will always need an enemy to justify their existence. If the FBE allows them to become so large as to run out of external enemies, these servile enforcers will turn on the FBE and their other servile groups and consume one another. To mitigate this risk, the FBE would need to keep finding new single-issues and new groups to continuously divide up the slivers of power more and more into tinier gangs of Atomized to keep control. This means the FBE would have to "make up" new social issues to create new divisions to create new Atomized. Even then, sooner or later these groups will fight each other for their slices of power as they fragment into more subgroups, causing their single issues to overlap.

A real-world example of a group trying to become a single-issue activist movement the FBE could coopt is the small but vocal element to de-stigmatize pedophilia. This group would create new major social divisions if it went socially mainstream. This movement is attempting to portray them as unfairly oppressed for having a sexual desire that shouldn't be morally judged thus creating pedophilia as a single-focus activist issue. One example of this, as cited in some academic and social activist publications, is the effort to try to pressure people to address pedophiles as "Minor-Attracted Persons" (MAPS) as a less derogatory term.[xxxii], [xxxiii], [xxxiv], [xxxv] This example is chosen because it is nonpartisan, in that no sensible person of any political persuasion endorses this effort, so it would not likely be chosen by the FBEs. However theoretically, such a movement would in fact be an ideal choice for the FBE. This movement, if it succeeded, would create a very small minority that depends on the FBE-backed state for protection which means these deviants would have to be fanatically loyal to the FBE. In exchange for being new enforcers, the FBE would mainstream child exploitation to exacerbate social divisions to make way for autocratic rule and in this case, would cause significant social division and chaos. Although one would think the FBE leadership would have boundaries, the leaders who would willingly aid and abet a foreign totalitarian adversary in undermining their own country have no morals. Instead, the FBE leaders would no doubt regard children as expendable raw material for gaining political power.

Finally, since these groups act as agents of chaos, the FBE would have to prepare for their elimination once autocracy had been achieved. These elements disrupt societies and will not have any value in the dictatorship once it has fully taken control. This was seen in Nazi Germany with the purging of the Brown Shirts, the purges of the Red Guard and the Gang of Four in China, and Stalin's purges after Lenin's death. Order is the reason why dictatorships always revert to socially conservative systems after attaining power because such societies bring stability while constant change endangers the powers that be. The FBE must purge these elements once open autocratic dictatorship is achieved otherwise its new power will be threatened with social anarchy.

[1] Department of Defense, *Joint Publication 3-0: Joint Operations* (Washington DC: Joint Chiefs of Staff: 17 January 2017): I-12.

[2] Hans Binnendijk and David Gompert, "Another American Civil War? Take Heed or Take Cover?" National Interest, September 4, 2022. https://nationalinterest.org/feature/another-american-civil-war-take-heed-or-take-cover-204583?page=0%2C2

[3] Daniel H. Abbott et al, *The Handbook of 5GW*, (Ann Arbor, MI: Nimble Books LLC: 2010): 7.

[4] Ibid, 8-10.

[5] Ibid, 43-46.

[6] News Report, "Catalan Town Votes for Independence from Spain," Stabroek News, September 14, 2009. https://www.stabroeknews.com/2009/09/14/news/guyana/catalan-town-votes-for-independence-from-spain/

[7] Giles Tremlett, "Catalan Independence Boost after Barcelona Vote," The Guardian, April 11, 2011. https://www.theguardian.com/world/2011/apr/11/catalan-independence-boost-barcelona-vote

[8] News Report, "Huge Turnout for Catalan Independence Rally," BBC News, September 11, 2012. https://www.bbc.com/news/world-europe-19564640

[9] News Report, "Spanish Parliament Rejects Catalan Independence Vote," April 9, 2014. https://www.bbc.com/news/world-europe-26949794

[10] Al Goodman, "Political Parties Announce Date for Vote on Catalonia Independence," December 12, 2013. https://edition.cnn.com/2013/12/12/world/europe/spain-catalonia-vote/index.html

[11] News Report, "Catalan Trial: Artur Mas Independence Vote Case Draws Crowds," BBC News, February 6, 2017. https://www.bbc.com/news/world-europe-38878688

[12] Esteban Durate and Thomas Gualtieri, "Former Catalan Leader Convicted Over 2014 Vote on Independence," Bloomberg, March 13, 2017. https://www.bloomberg.com/news/articles/2017-03-13/former-catalan-leader-convicted-over-2014-vote-on-independence?leadSource=uverify%20wall

[13] Daniel H. Abbott et al, *The Handbook of 5GW* (Ann Arbor, MI: Nimble Books LLC: 2010): 23.

[xiv] Carl von Clausewitz, Edited by Michael Howard and Peter Paret, *On War*, (Princeton, NJ: Princeton University Press: 1989): 485-486, 595-596.

[xv] Justina Crabtree, "Senior Australian Politician Resigns Over China Ties Scandal," CNBC, December 12, 2017. https://www.cnbc.com/2017/12/12/australia-politician-sam-dastyari-quits-over-china-ties.html

[xvi] Daniel H. Abbott et al, *The Handbook of 5GW* (Ann Arbor, MI: Nimble Books LLC: 2010): 18.

[xvii] James Burnham, *The Managerial Revolution: What is Happening in the World* (London: Lume Books: 1941, reprint 2021): ii-v, 11-14.

[xviii] Ibid, 70-81.

[xix] Ibid, 56-57.

[xx] Ibid, 65-67.

[xxi] Ibid, vii, xvi.

[xxii] Sebastian Ottinger and Nico Voigtlander, "History's Masters: The Effect of European Monarchs on State Performance," National Bureau of Economic Research, May 2022. https://www.nber.org/system/files/working_papers/w28297/w28297.pdf

[xxiii] Inga Ushur, Peter Hellyer, Keng Siang Lee et al., "'It's Not Rocket Science' and "It's not Brain Surgery'—'It's a Walk in the Park': Prospective Comparative Study," British Medical Journal, November 8, 2021. https://www.bmj.com/content/375/bmj-2021-067883

[xxiv] Kyle Peterdy, "ESG (Environmental, Social, and Governance: A Framework for Understanding and Measuring How Sustainability an Organization is Operating," Corporate Finance Institute, Updated October 26, 2022. https://corporatefinanceinstitute.com/resources/esg/esg-environmental-social-governance/

[xxv] Daniel H. Abbott et al, *The Handbook of 5GW*, (Ann Arbor, MI: Nimble Books LLC: 2010): 40-41.

[xxvi] Robert Greene and Joost Elffers, *The 48 Laws of Power*, (New York: Penguin Group, 1998): 296-297.

[xxvii] Jay J. Van Bavel et al, "Political Psychology in the Digital (Mis)information Age: A Model of News Belief and Sharing," Social Issues and Policy Review, June 24, 2021, vol 16, issue 1, 310-311. https://spssi.onlinelibrary.wiley.com/doi/abs/10.1111/sipr.12077

[xxviii] Niall Ferguson, *Empire: The Rise and Demise of the British World Order and the Lessons for Global Power*, (NY: Perseus Books Group, 2004): 120-123.

[xxix] Uwe Klubmann, "The Ruthless Rise of the Nazis in Berlin," Der Spiegel International, November 11, 2012. https://www.spiegel.de/international/germany/how-the-nazis-succeeded-in-taking-power-in-red-berlin-a-866793.html

[xxx] Inigo Camilleri de Castanedo, "Colectivos: Maduro's Venezuelan Militias," Grey Dynamics, January 1, 2022. https://greydynamics.com/colectivos-maduros-venezuelan-militias/

[xxxi] James Pethokoukis, "Why We Shouldn't Grow the Economic 'Pie'," American Enterprise Institute, August 27, 2014. https://www.aei.org/economics/why-we-shouldnt-grow-the-economic-pie/

[xxxii] Angel Saunders, "Teacher Fired for Telling Students to Call Pedophiles 'Minor-Attracted Persons' Instead," MSN.com, September 12, 2022. https://www.msn.com/en-us/news/us/teacher-fired-for-telling-students-to-call-pedophiles-minor-attracted-persons-instead/ar-AA11K8Ix

[xxxiii] Emily Crane, "Prof Who Said Pedophiles Should Be Called 'Minor-Attracted Persons' Agrees to Resign." NY Post, November 25, 2021. https://nypost.com/2021/11/25/prof-who-referred-to-pedophiles-as-minor-attracted-persons-to-resign/

[xxxiv] Brittney McNamara, "Video Shows Toddlers Understand Consent," Teen Vogue, May 18, 2017. https://www.teenvogue.com/story/video-shows-toddlers-understand-consent

[xxxv] Tracy Clark-Flory, "Redefining Pedophilia with Pedophiles' Help," Salon.com, August 17, 2011. https://www.salon.com/2011/08/17/pedophilia/

Chapter 13: The National Resistance Forces' Optimal Strategy

The National Resistance Forces (NRF) face major obstacles in combating the FBE. Initially, the majority of NRF members would be politically disenfranchised or perceived to be disenfranchised persons which means they are already scattered and their financial and combat power is limited. Secondly, these disenfranchised elements would be scattered amongst the more compliant and apathetic general population who are unwilling to take any risks regardless of how corrupt, incompetent, or inefficient the anocracy becomes. Finally, the NRF would be more limited in its range of available actions because this faction is trying to reclaim what they believe are the true values of their Western nation. This means for reasons of propaganda and political legitimacy, the NRF cannot wage total war or unlimited violence against the FBE or their anocracy puppets without sacrificing the institutions and traditions the NRF proclaim to protect. So, the NRF would start out with limited resources, manning, and have to restrict its combat actions to maintain political legitimacy. These limits may appear insurmountable, but if the NRF avoids major combat and keeps its operations a mostly covert "invisible" war against the FBE, then the limited resources will be sufficient.

The Strategic Objective:

The NRF will have to formulate a strategic objective that mitigates the NRF's disadvantages while also bypassing the strengths of the FBE's war strategy. Isolating political opposition is part of the transition phase of the FBE's effort to change the Western nation's system from an anocracy to an overt autocracy. This means, unlike totalitarian regimes, the FBE are restricted in their initial actions of violence in order to prevent a revolt from the general population before the FBE's autocratic state is set up. Since the only way for the FBE to eliminate the NRF in this critical juncture is by provoking the NRF into making the first move to justify draconian actions, the FBE would have to cede the initiative to the NRF. The FBE must manipulate the NRF into making critical missteps from the outset which would enable the FBE to use all of its strengths to maximum effect. As stated previously, the anocracy of the Western nation's power is the vast apparatus of government and its supporting private institutions that can bring overwhelming force on an open battlefield of 2GW and 3GW warfare. In short, the FBE will be at its best if the NRF attempt to fight this new civil war like America's Civil War, army vs. army.

Instead, the NRF leadership would have to avoid "fighting the last war" mentality and prevent its faction from giving in to the temptation of fighting the FBE in the old ways which are easily trainable and familiar, but not optimal. This is the first strategic challenge, finding a way to fight in a self-restricting way to avoid FBE's most effective tactics while still undermining the FBE's COGs. This means not only devising means of fighting but also the means of staying organized in a cohesive but decentralized fashion. The more concentrated the NRF's forces become, the slower they operate and the easier they are to be identified and destroyed by the FBE's anocracy. Instead, the NRF's initial diffusion amongst the general population is best embraced because it will help protect the NRF even though this limits the NRF's ability to organize to effectively conduct offensive action.

The ability to project adequate force against the FBE without destroying the Western nation's democratic heritage is the second strategic challenge. Even if the NRF leadership can sufficiently organize a nation-wide resistance force that remains sufficiently dispersed to avoid the less nimble FBE; it will not be sufficiently combat effective. The NRF leadership must organize their forces to hide the bulk of their resources while simultaneously being capable of hurting the FBE COGs. Having a force of sufficient lethality while evading the FBE means no single element can be very large making no major military engagements practical. The NRF will have to be able to optimally target the FBE's critical nodes of control and minimize the stability of the democratic institutions the FBE have corruptly latched onto while still avoiding most of the FBE's combat power.

The final strategic challenge is the NRF's need to maintain political legitimacy of not only itself but of the Western nation's pre-anocratic institutional traditions. War is tumultuous by nature and if the NRF fail to target their FBE opponents with precision, the NRF risk accelerating the Western nation's transition to autocracy. In most civil conflicts, the rebellions usually fail because they didn't plan sufficiently for a post-war society or they destroyed all the institutions that kept order within the society by imposing their own autocracy to restore order. There would likely be factions within the NRF who believe the FBE has corrupted the Western nation's institutions beyond repair and will directly attack these to attempt to destroy them. This is extremely dangerous as it creates power vacuums that usually are filled in by the most ruthless elements that are willing to exert any means for control. The NRF must try to maintain the institutions, no matter how corrupt, as much as possible so that the victorious NRF has a foundation with which to begin orderly repairs of the Western nation's society. The American Revolution was exceptional in history because the Founding Fathers in a way fought a counterrevolution to maintain the old institutional traditions of the British Empire. America fought its mother nation because it was becoming too much like Britain's continental neighbors. The French Revolution on the other hand tried to change everything and destroyed many old institutions creating near anarchy and then tyranny. When the dust settled, the French replaced their monarch for an emperor.

With all of these challenges in mind, the NRF's strategic objective must be:

To successfully prevent the FBE and their foreign benefactors from subverting the Western nation into an autocracy while avoiding destruction of the democratic-republican values and institutions in the process.

Accomplishing this strategic objective requires the NRF to use all of their cunning and patience to avoid being tempted into falling into predictable fighting patterns and habits. Achieving victory means bypassing the FBE's strategy of Catalonia 2.0, keeping the FBE's anocratic institutions at bay by fixing them into attacking the NRF's periphery, and directly targeting and isolating the FBE's leadership simultaneously. The FBE has the challenge of maneuvering all of its combat power into delivering large fatal blows, but the NRF has the greater challenge of synchronizing hundreds of tiny cuts simultaneously across all the FBE's critical nodes of control.

Optimal Warfare:

The NRF would be at a major material and personnel disadvantage. The NRF would have to build a power base capable of opposing the FBE without alienating the home nation's general population. This problem is made more complicated by the unique characteristics of general populations that are only found in the developed Western nations. Historically, most civil wars occur in polities with populations adapted to harsh living conditions and poor economic activity. This means the opposition factions in those deprived nations can rally popular support by arguing how the state fails its citizens. An unstable poor nation provides an ideal source of manpower and material supplies to resistance or insurgent forces. In the case of Western nations, the general population is instead softened by generations of economic growth, improved standards of living, and being insulated from true brutality.

Most social issues that are decried as hardships, oppression, or injustice in the Western nations are over how many privileges or abuses one political faction accuses another of doing in a nation of abundance. Overwhelmingly, even the most disenfranchised still has access to medical care (even if mediocre), electricity, smart phones, shelter, food, and water. Contrast that with nations where civil wars have occurred in the last 100 years where famine, no utilities, torture, and murders in mass are commonplace. Unless the NRF could demonstrate otherwise, Western governments, even the most corrupt ones, don't skin opponents alive,[1] cut out their hearts,[2] set them on fire,[3] starve cities into surrender,[4] use roving death squads,[5] and carry out mass executions.[6] These are circumstances that can entice a population into supporting open rebellion but there is none found in the West. In other words, despite whatever complaints are made, the majority of the population in Western nations have too much to lose in participating in an open war of resistance.

This an inversion of the problem faced by the FBE who must subtly nudge the general population into accepting autocracy because the Western system prevents any easy transition to dictatorship. Too much change too quickly will drastically affect the safe, indulgent, secure lives of the general population which would shock them out of complacency. The NRF must also not shock the general population either because any attempt to induce wide reaching hostilities will destroy the comforts the general population enjoys. If the NRF instigates such drastic impositions on the general population by starting an overt 3GW or even 4GW style war, the NRF, not the FBE, will be blamed and alienated by the general public. So, the NRF will have to build its support base and material resources while causing as little disruption to the general population's daily lives as possible. A civil conflict, no matter how low key, will cause unavoidable disruption but the NRF can minimize it while trying to get the FBE to be blamed. Then there is the NRF's other major challenge of actually getting at the desired targets in a civil conflict.

A foreign induced civil war in a developed nation creates a challenge not faced by most historical rebellions which is that the national government institutions are not the enemy, at least not the true enemy. Instead, the FBE would be subverting these institutions to act as the fighting fodder to grind down the NRF while being insulated from any retaliation. If the NRF are successfully deceived by the FBE into just fighting government agencies and supporting corporations, then the FBE will have achieved half of their strategic objective. Wear and tear of government agencies exhausted by fighting the NRF will allow the FBE-backed political leaders to justify radical changes to more authoritarian institutions as traditional institutions are discredited for failing to stop the rebellion. The NRF's true targets of the FBE are shielded by corrupt elements within government institutions but are not typically government themselves. A traditional form of civil war of army vs army means government institutions fighting rebel institutions but most of the FBE and its support structures are private in nature. Yet, this very structure that shields the FBE from traditional forms of civil conflict can also provide a critical weakness the NRF can exploit.

The FBE are conducting a campaign of manipulation to use others to fight on their behalf while also building their own political influence outside traditional democratic-republic political processes. To accomplish this, the FBE must remain separate from the state so as not to be bogged down in legalities. Instead, the FBE leeches onto the state via corrupt or incompetent interlocutors who direct government actions with financial and propagandist methods. These FBE are organized by interconnected networks of various cliques of the Western nation's elites who rely on intermediaries and hidden financial systems to carry out actions. This means the NRF's best course of action is to avoid targeting the state itself as much as possible and direct most of the NRF's forces against the FBE's private networks. The modern informationalized battlespace has allowed the FBE to synchronize their control networks into effectively influencing and manipulating most major institutions and groups of political power and also enables the FBE to narrow down and focus their targeting efforts with extreme precision. If most of the NRF's efforts are to identify and isolate the critical nodes within the FBE's own networks, then the NRF would not need to fight a conventional war of 3GW or classic insurgency of 4GW. By avoiding the FBE's lure into provoking the NRF into consolidating into an organized opposition army, the democratic-republican institutions, the general population, and the stability of the Western nation will remain largely intact, even if a little damaged or corrupted. If the NRF uses the advanced technology the modern world provides properly and in conjunction with the right advanced tactics then the NRF could: 1. Build public support without inconveniencing them 2. Protect the democratic-republican institutions and customs from being destroyed in open warfare 3. Prevent the foreign power backing the FBE from taking over 4. Drastically reduce the manning and resource requirements to fight the FBE; and 5. Force the FBE to become directly involved in the fighting for which they are unsuited to conduct. The optimal means of achieving all of these victory criteria, is for the NRF to fight using this new form of civil conflict of 5GW or Fifth Gradient Warfare.

Strategic Plan: The Silent Scream and the Greedy Smile

Historically, the leaders of civil conflicts were the most shielded from the worst deprivations of war, allowing them to make decisions with little personal consequence. In one form or another, the elites waged war with their governed populations to accomplish their polity's strategic goals. Or more simply as President Herbert Hoover put it, "Older men declare war. But it is youth that must fight and die. And it is youth who must inherit the tribulation, the sorrow, and the triumphs that are the aftermath of war."[7] Present day circumstances offer the NRF the chance to defy historical norms and compel the "old men" of the FBE to fight and die instead of the "youth".

This civil war defies the historical norms of these conflicts because the main opponent of the NRF rebel faction is not the government or its official rulers, but foreign-manipulated private individuals illicitly utilizing their financial, cultural, and economic influences to subvert the government to their will. As the actual FBEs are separate entities from the state and its legally recognized institutions, the NRF must bypass the

FBE's "armies" and strike directly at the leaders themselves. Using advanced information and psychological warfare combined with highly select lethal actions could deliver precise blows that destroy the traitorous elements without destroying the state or Western nation. A modified 5GW strategy would use moral and cultural warfare through manipulating perceptions, altering social context, and isolating the FBE from its proxies to halt foreign subversion of the government and incapacitate all foreign-induced malign influence.[8] Using the rage of the ostracized portions of the general population to garner the initial support, the NRF would be able to wage a limited conflict designed to rationally manipulate the corrupted political processes of the state back into the NRF's favor with minimal disruption to the Western nation's public and limiting engagements with the national government's security and military forces.

The NRF would be waging an invisible war as its optimal strategy. A secret war that strategically outflanks the FBE's Catalonia 2.0 strategy by minimally fighting against the overwhelming power of the anocratic state's legal and military might and directly attack the FBE and their support apparatus instead. Since the majority of lethal efforts are directed at the relatively small contingent of the FBE themselves and their support organizations, the NRF would not need to be very large nor require a lot of resources or capital to wage a hidden fight. This is not 4GW, an open insurgency, because 4GW is designed to challenge the governing institutions themselves rather than its leaders by using political violence to coerce the government or the civilian population to make political changes.[9] This modified 5GW strategy is to use violent coercion, deception, and other incentives against the leaders themselves to compel political change.

4GW values publicity to build notoriety, discredit the government institutions, and intimidate the civilian population into changing the whole society. Most insurgencies and terrorist paramilitary groups are regarded as zealous and extreme because they want society to radically change by force. The more shocking the spectacles 4GW forces create, the better because the insurgency can better intimidate the targeted society into radical institutional and social change more quickly. In this scenario however, the FBE are puppets of a major foreign power who are subverting the rules and institutions of the Western nation to make it a vassal nation. The leaders of the anocratic state are the radicals and the NRF rebel faction is actually trying to preserve the old institutions. Waging a 4GW campaign would be counterproductive as this seeks fear from the public and the state. A 5GW campaign instead would focus exclusively on instilling fear in the opponent's leaders. 4GW seeks the cries, screams, and wails of the public but 5GW seeks the silent screams of the foreign-backed elites themselves who would shout their fears in their private fortified establishments and estates where the public never hears them.

The strategic objective is to isolate the FBE leaders to deny the elite any comfort. In traditionally fought 4GW civil wars, FBE members could carry out abuses and indulge in Caligula-levels of debauchery as their servants and proxies die on their behalf. 5GW on the other hand, uses techniques for precise targeting of the leaders and their vital servants making the FBE decision-makers live with stress and fear. In all wars, psychologically breaking one's opponent is essential to victory and using terror on select key individuals is the first step to isolate and fragment the FBE leadership. Since the FBE rely on remaining clandestine in their actions as their main form of protection, 5GW is ideal to expose the FBE to danger. Although 5GW doesn't need a cohesive command structure to carry out individual operations which helps maintain greater secrecy, the NRF would require one at the strategic level to effectively direct all actions towards achievable objectives.[10] Too confederated or decentralized would limit the scale of impact from any single NRF element and would enable the much bigger FBE forces to isolate and eliminate each element one-by-one. So, for the most part, the NRF must be a cohesive group with only some independent elements on its periphery in order to carry out the three major steps for the successful execution of 5GW. All of these steps need to be executed simultaneously with overlapping actions using both lethal and non-lethal effects.

STEP 1: BYPASS CATALONIA 2.0

The first step of the NRF strategy is to bypass the FBE's strategic plan of Catalonia 2.0 which means the NRF needs to have its forces and supporters strategically avoid directly engaging with the FBE's proxy government forces. On the strategic level, this means organizing the NRF in such a way that the full power of the anocracy's forces cannot identify, locate, and fixate on the bulk of the NRF to destroy with overwhelming lethal power. Typically, in military terms, bypassing means to actually move troops on a battlefield on a route that avoids encountering an enemy force or obstacle that could disrupt mission success.[11] To maintain the NRF's combat and staying power, it must avoid the stronger FBE by being covert and not act as a standing army or paramilitary force trying to protect a defined area that seceded from the anocratic-ruled Western nation. Trying to protect secessionist territories compels the NRF to commit to defending this clearly defined geographic region, cornering themselves into being easily attrited by superior 3GW forces of the anocracy over time.

For the FBE to be successful, they must provoke the NRF into coming out into open revolt against the anocracy in a blatantly illegal or insurrectionist way. If the NRF's leaders successfully resist and avoid the emotionally driven temptation to start an open insurrection and secession, then the NRF can seize the initiative away from the FBE. Although corrupt, the FBE-controlled anocracy is still not a complete dictatorship and must avoid revealing its efforts to transition into one too early. Until the dictatorship is completely built, the NRF members would have more civil liberties, freedom of movement, and greater flexibility to wage nonviolent information and psychological warfare. Having the NRF's organization remain amorphous by staying within the Western nation's population also means the majority of the FBE's legal and military tools cannot be used because there isn't a firm target. Avoiding overt provocations means the FBE doesn't get the majority of their legitimate justifications for greater autocratic rule if there is no open rebellion.

By remaining a covert organization of cellular networks scattered throughout the FBE-controlled Western nation, the NRF reduces the size and scale of its own force requirements while simultaneously forcing the FBE to commit more resources.[12] This reduction of resource and personnel requirements also improves operational security by needing less interaction and less dependence on the decadent and apathetic general public for support that would be necessary if the NRF waged a 4GW insurgency. If the FBE wants to destroy a 5GW-organized NRF, then the FBE are forced to make the first violent move which the NRF could use to blame the anocracy for any escalation to garner public sympathy. Nevertheless, even if the NRF do bypass Catalonia 2.0 and not become easy targets, 5GW does still mean attacking the corrupted elements within the anocracy's government forces that defend the FBE. The key difference is that fighting them is not the main objective and should be evaded when possible.

STEP 2: FIXING THE ANOCRACY'S FORCES

5GW keeps the civil conflict at a much lower level of intensity to the point that most of the general public cannot be frightened into tolerating a state of war imposed by the FBE. The majority of the NRF's activities will rely on non-lethal actions but since their activities will be mostly illegal, the NRF cannot completely evade the anocratic government's forces. The low-intensity conflict of limited violence constrains the FBE to limiting actions to the law enforcement and judiciary elements of the anocracy rather than the military. Since the NRF must deal with some of the FBE's proxy forces, the NRF must assign forces designed with two missions in mind: 1. Fix the FBE government forces that pursue the NRF to prevent them from attacking critical nodes of the NRF's networks. 2. Ensure every action against the anocratic security forces denies the FBE any ability to escalate the conflict from 5GW to 3GW to prevent the FBE using full advantage of their superior resources.

In traditional tactical terms, "fixing the enemy" means using a portion of one's forces to hold down an opponent's forces to prevent them from moving any of that force from a specific location for a specific period.[13] In strategic terms, the NRF must use some of its forces to fixate the FBE's government proxies on just a select few specialized NRF elements so the more strategically valuable NRF elements can move about freely to carry out their strategic objectives unnoticed. As long as the FBE forces pursue these deliberate diversions, the FBE cannot strategically target the critical elements of the NRF.

The NRF's specialized elements would fix the anocratic security forces by using denial and deception techniques to misdirect FBE targeting to focus on the NRF's strategic periphery. As these FBE zero in and attack these smaller NRF forces of misdirection, the FBE are blind to more threatening NRF activities. The fixing elements would deliberately call attention to themselves so they could conduct memetics, misdirection, false stories, communication disruption, entrapment actions, character assassination, kompromat, false flags, demoralization campaigns, and gray propaganda to stifle the FBE's attacks.

If perfectly executed, the step of fixing the anocratic forces by focusing on NRF's diversion elements will not require any lethal actions whatsoever. Although this book section describes the optimal ideally executed strategy, the reality of war will likely result in some elements of the NRF carrying out lethal actions anyway. Battlefield frictions such as rogue radicals, miscommunication, or the FBE successfully executing their own false flag operations will complicate the NRF's fixing mission. Lethal escalation with the FBE's anocratic proxies is the greatest danger to the NRF's ability to achieve a low-cost victory.

The NRF is trying to realistically protect the Western nation from the nefarious foreign power manipulating the FBEs by preserving the rites, customs, traditions, and institutions that make the Western nation a free independent state. The more lethal actions carried out directly against the anocracy compels the NRF to adjust its mission and lead down the slippery slope of mission creep towards a 3GW war. If this happens before the NRF grows into a sufficiently powerful force, then the NRF will be attrited into defeat as the FBE will have succeeded in tricking the NRF to expend all its energy fighting the government puppets rather than the FBEs themselves. The other less obvious danger is the institutional vacuum created if the anocratic security forces are destroyed.

Most revolutions and civil wars historically lead to worse outcomes than the situations that provoked these conflicts in the first place.[14] Many times, it is due to the shortsighted planning and considerations of the rebels or insurgent elements for what to do after the war is complete. Many of these conflicts see the loss of critical government institutions creating vacuums of power that are filled in by chaos and anarchy. This often leads to more radical institutions that try to bring order but are limited in resources and ability as these new institutions have to rebuild with fewer resources. This often compels these institutions to be more brutal to bring order with fewer standards to adhere to, making the new institutions more susceptible to corruption. In contrast, the American Revolution succeeded because in many ways, it was a counterrevolutionary revolution. The Founding Fathers were trying to preserve customs, legal processes, and political circumstances granted to the colonists before the changes imposed upon them by George III and Parliament. If the NRF fights the institutions instead of the elites corrupting them, then the NRF will be unable to focus on targeting the corruption, but instead will have to fight the entire system which risks bringing the entire edifice down along with the FBE. This would accomplish the objectives of the foreign power just as effectively as supporting the FBEs.

Fixing or holding the corrupted anocratic institutions' forces means buying time until the FBE can be disrupted, isolated, and dismembered. Once the political influence of the FBE is diminished, the corrupt elements, usually at the very top of the bureaucratic hierarchy, can be exercised later and reforms, if necessary, be implemented after the 5GW conflict is complete. This gives sufficient time to thoughtfully consider how the institutions need to be fixed or abolished with democratic legitimacy to sustain such efforts. As for fear about the entire government system being unrecoverable, that is not really a danger in an anocracy. If successful, the NRF will prevent the autocracy from forming from the anocracy which means the institutions would mostly remain Max Weber-derived industrial-age-style bureaucracies that Western governments usually employ. These bureaucracies are designed to function even when the senior leaders and political cultures change because they are designed to be slow and cumbersome to make it easier to maintain civilian control. So, these bureaucracies are risk averse and malleable to whatever political culture dominates the society and if the NRF do win, then the bureaucracy will follow suit, even if that process takes years. The greatest educational TV show on Max Weber-style Western bureaucracy is the British comedy series *Yes Minister* and *Yes, Prime Minister*. In this show, there is a scene that perfectly encapsulates how a bureaucracy would behave if an outside force like the NRF would expel the corrupt leadership of an anocratic government like the FBE. The British prime minister is sitting in the Cabinet Meeting Room with his personal private secretary and the prime minister asks him, "If there were a conflict of interests, which side is the Civil Service really on?" and his secretary replies, "The winning side Prime Minister."[15]

STEP 3: PENETRATE, DISRUPT, ISOLATE, AND FRAGMENT THE FBE

After securing the NRF's existence with the first two strategic steps, the NRF will have the breathing space to execute the third step of launching strategic actions directly against the FBE themselves. Bypassing the anocracy's wall of force and fix the pursuing anocratic elements in place by misdirection means the NRF can now avoid several layers of obstacles and defenses that are protecting the FBE. At this point, the NRF must penetrate the FBE networks, disrupt the FBE's critical nodes of control, identify and isolate the high value individuals of the FBE cliques in order to fracture their faction into chaos.

In the strategic case of the NRF's mission, penetrate means successfully finding and identifying the FBE's networks of influence then use various intelligence gathering methods to pinpoint key personalities and organizational nodes. Once identified, the NRF must disrupt these key nodes to break down FBE internal communications and coordination to cause panic and confusion. Here is the strategic point where the majority of NRF-directed lethal activity should be directed. The key leaders and personalities will be supported by subordinate staff, advisors, operators, and anocracy intermediaries to keep the FBE's efforts functioning. These administrative supporting elements will be shielded by private security forces along with a number of figurehead personalities to obfuscate FBE resources and actives. Without these support nodes, the FBE cliques would not be able to sustain their networks of influence and consequently expose senior leaders of the FBE to being attacked directly.

Systemic precision targeting of the FBE's direct support nodes with both lethal and nonlethal means will disrupt large segments of the FBE network that would disconnect them from their proxy forces in the anocracy, corrupt nonprofit and private sectors. With sufficient disruption, the FBE cliques would become sufficiently isolated for the NRF to focus its efforts on fragmenting and dividing the FBE cliques themselves. There are three challenges the NRF would need to overcome to become successful: 1. Defeat the key personalities' physical security 2. Stifle the key persons' financial resources 3. Divide the FBE leadership and co-opt the disenchanted elements to the NRF's cause.

The FBE consist mostly of private individuals operating private organizations rather than politicians or officials. These private entities mean the FBE are afforded greater secrecy and flexibility in using their influence peddling to subvert the Western nation's government. However, the downside of the private nature of the FBE means they have to rely on private security and mercenary forces to protect their influence network. If this 5GW strategy is properly executed, the majority of the NRF's physical battles will be conducted against these private forces. Unlike professional soldiers or police, private security is not held in any special regard or esteem by the general public. Historically, mercenaries have rarely been held in high regard as they are considered unreliable as their loyalty is to money rather than a nation or ideal.[16], [17] Mercenaries guarding wealthy elites and their corrupt minions garner little emotional investment by the public and combat casualties resulting from fighting the NRF will hardly register beyond typical public reactions to news media stories about strangers dying tragically. It is very difficult for the FBE to generate public sympathy for losing private mercenary forces except if the NRF carry out a large-scale massacre of epic proportions. At best for the FBE, the general public will consider the fighting as between two glorified gangs of thugs which means the FBE will not be able to justify pushing the anocracy to declare martial law or mobilize military forces. Any attempt by the FBE to escalate efforts against the NRF using public resources will garner far more anger and frustration than sympathy. If the NRF keeps getting successfully blocked in targeting the elites themselves, attacking the FBE's private security will still yield positive results as this would undermine FBE morale, self-confidence, and encourage desertion among the remaining security and mercenaries.

Besides the security forces, the NRF need to disrupt organizational and financial operations that sustain the FBE leaders' influence over the anocracy and their own subordinates. No matter how efficient an organization, there are always vital individuals or offices that do a disproportionate amount of critical work.[18] So, even if the private security forces keep all the elites well protected, the NRF will still have multiple alternative options in targeting the elites' support staff and advisors. If sufficient numbers of these supporting elements are removed or disrupted, at least several members of the elites themselves will be cut off and isolated from the rest of the clique. Any prolonged disruption would create panic amongst the elites with some second guessing as to their group's vision and re-evaluate their own prospective options.

If the NRF successfully sustains their attacks on the FBE's influence networks over time then the FBE's key personalities themselves will be vulnerable. Wealth and power are privileges most of these elites would have long been accustomed to and many will likely try to defeat the NRF until the very end. Destroying the FBE's will to fight requires a balanced mix of positive and negative incentives: greed and terror. In some cases, the NRF will have to use violence and psychological operations to instill terror into the minds of some key elites to compel compliance. This terror is done to intimidate the elites, not the public so, the majority of terror actions will be conducted away from the public eye. The only audience the NRF needs to be concerned about are the other elites who may need some negative encouragement to be more malleable to positive incentives. These actions of terror will create the silent screams of the FBE where their terror and panic are only heard amongst their confederates. Some would have to be killed and others just need to see their comrades killed but determining the effective scale of inflicting silent screams on the FBE is critically important. The more ruthless and violent the infliction of the silent screams on the FBE are, the more quickly the FBEs will react in both positive and negative ways. Some will be terrified into cooperating while others will be more willing to escalate the conflict even at the cost of public support.

The more positive incentives would have to be used later in the strategy timeline when the NRF develops sufficient reputation as a successful and long-lasting resistance force. Once the NRF's actions to isolate the FBE cliques reach its culmination point, then the NRF can use the inherent greed of many of the FBE members to encourage defections and betrayals. To divide and conquer the FBE cliques, the NRF could get defecting members to sell out their foreign-backed brethren in exchange for keeping their own wealth and retain some of their power. As the number of FBE loyalists diminish, the opportunistic defectors will gobble up their former FBE compatriots' wealth. This should put a greedy smile on their faces. [19]

With the NRF inflicting a sufficient number of silent screams and incentivizing defectors to the point of having greedy smiles, the NRF can achieve a strategic victory without having to tear the Western nation apart in classical warfare or an open insurgency.[20] The most important cost

95

the NRF will have to accept for such a victory is that some segments of the FBE will have to survive to be coopted. In the realities of war, an opponent who has nothing to lose will have the incentive to ensure the winning side's victory is a hollow one. Unless one wages a Zero Gradient War of total genocide or obliteration, there will always be fragments of opposing side remaining within the population of a post-civil war conflict. If the victor deprives the opponent of all political and economic participation yet refuses to extinguish these populations of discontent, then the victorious forces will face a prolonged 4GW insurgency that eventually escalates into a 3GW war or worse a 2GW war which is what happened in the Syrian Civil War. To preserve the integrity of the Western nation and prevent power vacuums arising from destroyed institutions, the NRF will have to allow some, but not all, members of the FBE to be included in the post-conflict system and collaborate on governance. The FBE defectors will still have many of the personal connections and financial capital to simplify governance and economic recovery while also ensuring reconciliation is more effective.

Despite the controversy, General George Patton who became the military governor of the American sector of Germany after World War II, implemented this kind of policy. Excluding the senior leaders, Patton allowed mid-level and low-level members of the German government to continue to be employed and provided opportunities for members of the Wehrmacht to be rehabilitated. Some viewed this as unjust, but giving former enemies a peaceful way out of the conflict is the only practical way to nullify further instability.[21] Few remember that the SS and some Wehrmacht remnants waged a short guerrilla action before becoming pacified with Operation Werewolf. Patton's administrative reconciliation contributed to eliminating any incentive to revive Werewolf or anything like it.[22] Contrasting this with the incompetent failures of American occupational policy in the early years of the Iraq War where the US State Department used nebulous idealism to justify banning all members of the Ba'ath Party from government and security jobs.[23] This failed to account for the fact that these jobs are the main source of good paying employment in a country with a totalitarian economy. This helped embolden the Shia and Kurds to seek revenge and ostracize the Sunni population[24] to the point the New Ba'athist Party, Fedayeen, Al-Qaeda in Iraq, and many other groups could count on continuous support from the disenfranchised populations. Reality always trumps human idealism and failing to understand that victory requires some of the FBE to join will likely prolong the conflict and lead to a broader war.

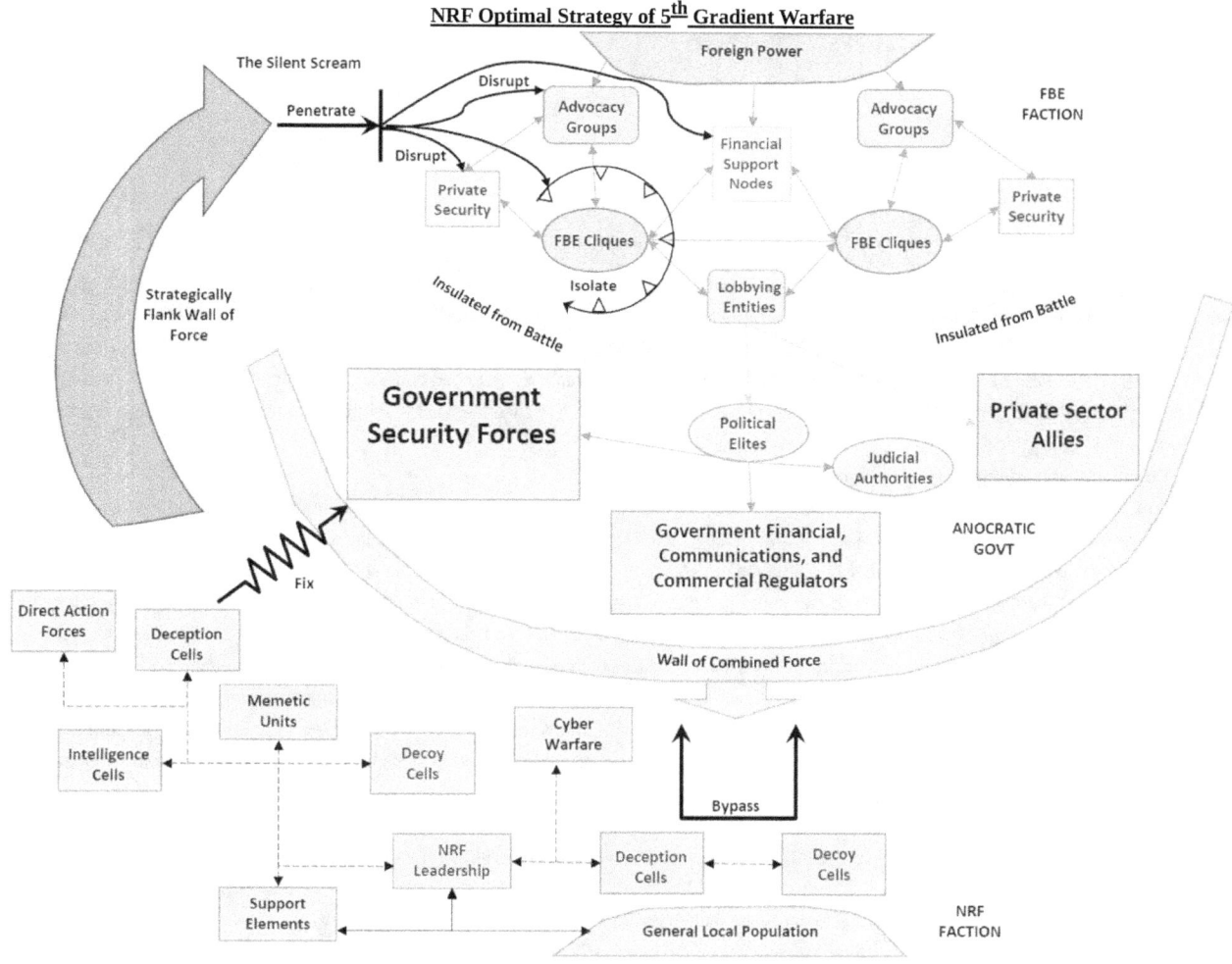

NRF Optimal Strategy of 5th Gradient Warfare

NRF Step 3: Penetrate-Disrupt-Isolate-Co-Opt:

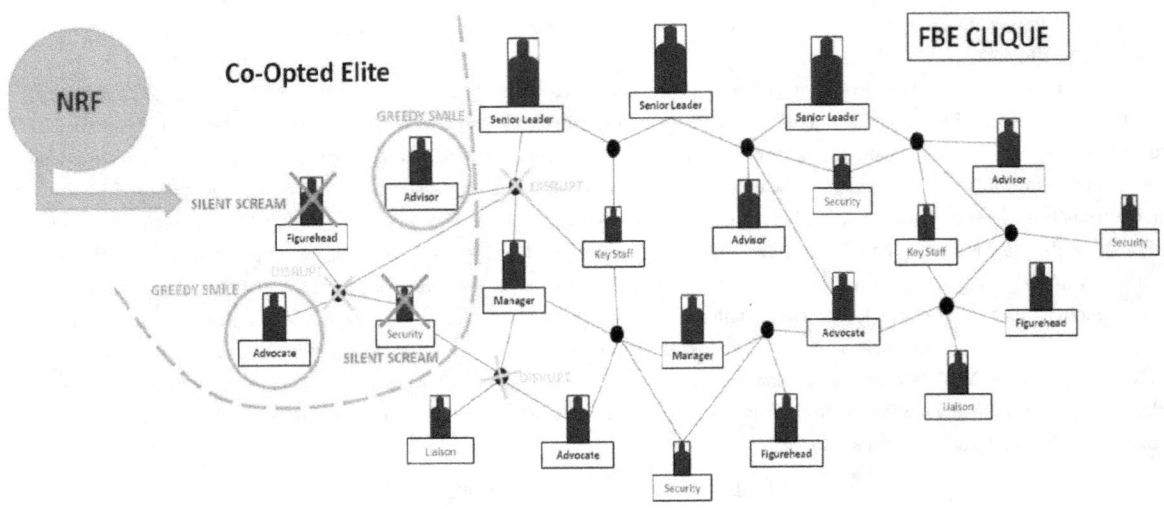

Centers of Gravity:

Like their FBE opponents, the NRF would have "centers of gravity" (COG) that are critical to the sustainment of the NRF's combat ability to achieve victory. These COGs will differ from the FBE because the NRF would start in an underdog position. In the case of the FBE, their COGs revolve around the ability to successfully wield and direct their overwhelming power on their opponent without risking the loss of the public's support. For the NRF, these COGs will revolve around the NRF's ability to maintain its unity and cohesion to efficiently manage both their limited resources and time. If the FBE can disrupt or destroy one or more of the NRF COGs, then the NRF will likely fragment or be forced to fight an open war before they are ready to do so.

An Effective Inspirational Leader or Small Group of Leaders:

Their opponents in the FBE are a loose confederacy of like-minded politically influential elites with no single person strong enough to impose their will on all the rest. Too many of them have their own independent sources of wealth and influence and a wannabe Mussolini or Stalin would expend far too many resources in trying to alter this situation or at least, until the anocracy becomes an autocracy. At best, there could be an ideological/spiritual leader that keeps the FBE cliques coordinated on the same goals without any direct executive power. An example would be like Ayman al-Zawahiri when Osama bin Laden controlled Al-Qaeda International or Dietrich Eckart to Nazi Germany.[xxv] The managerial elites' overwhelming scale of support networks and institutional influence reduces their need for a true leader yet the same cannot be said for the NRF.

Some assume the decentralized organizations of insurgent and paramilitary groups are a major strength against stronger centralized opponents because they can't be easily identified and destroyed as these scattered small groups would have few connections to one another. This improves operational security while also forcing their larger opponents to expend more resources and political capital in trying to catch these dispersed insurgent groups. However, there is a glaring weakness in this assumption. Yes, a minimally coordinated rebel faction is more secure and harder to defeat but at the same time this type of organization also makes victory exceptionally difficult.

In war, a successful force must balance its security needs with its fighting effectiveness. Organizations that emphasize security are the smaller, less organized, and militarily weaker factions that must remain hidden from authorities. Highly secure groups have minimal to no hierarchy with independently operating cells that may or may not coordinate their actions. In this state of organization, these types of rebels limit their actions to raids, harassment, and publicity seeking in efforts to weaken their opponent. However, if these groups don't change after the enemy is weakened, then both sides will become trapped in a quagmire because the rebels will not have sufficient capabilities to actually defeat their opponent. To succeed as a resistance force, the NRF will have to start small but it must grow its power and influence over time to build sufficient strength to defeat the FBE. A decentralized force can never sufficiently build up enough concentrated levels of force to follow through with defeating an opponent. On the other hand, a highly organized faction of resistance can muster sufficient power to defeat their opponent but they themselves are more vulnerable to defeat.

The NRF must achieve a balance where it can wage a coordinated nation-wide operation while minimizing the profiles of the NRF's individual cells. 5GW simplifies this problem because it is less resource intensive but would still need to build sufficient strength over time to splinter the FBEs. This balance can only be achieved with central executive leadership. Leaders matter a lot more than is generally appreciated because they are the rallying point for their fighters and supporters for guidance, inspiration, and common vision.[xxvi] Although the NRF could have a council of leaders, history shows having one of the leaders as an inspirational figurehead is far more effective. Such a leader can better rally people to their cause while also managing and deconflicting resource allocations, operational planning, and operational execution to keep the NRF focused on their mission objectives. This was demonstrated in Syria where the more aggressively violent insurgent group ISIS was able to rally and build-up into the dominating rebel faction under the leadership of al-Baghdadi in contrast to the more organizationally divided Free Syrian Army. Without an effective hierarchy commanded by inspirational competent leadership, any rebel movement will flounder even if they are damaging the anocracy.[xxvii]

Strengths:

Anocracies always have disenfranchised elements of the population but only some of them are actually willing to fight. To potential recruits, the risks far outweigh the rewards of possible victory if they are not convinced of their sacrifices having meaning. In 5GW, the NRF would have to actively seek those who are aware of the anocracy's abuses and then persuade them to join. If the NRF is highly fragmented and factionalized with little coordination then the NRF will fail before it starts. However, a strong leader who demonstrates not only competence but the ability to rally and unify all resistance efforts against the FBE would create the necessary credibility the NRF needs to exist. A credible leader not only can sustain the motivation of the NRF and its supporters but also be able to ensure all 5GW actions are in sync across the Western nation to maximize effectiveness.

The leader of the NRF will very likely come from one of the Western nation's elites. The reality of geo-political power is that few rebellions are instigated from the oppressed or the "commoners" but instead organized and instigated by an ostracized portion of the elites. These elites are part of the system and were either cut out of the power structure or believed their fellow elites are not worthy of being followed due to ideology or other reasons. These ostracized elites recruit from the oppressed and underclasses but virtually all rebellions arise from the established power hierarchy. George Washington and the Founding Fathers were not from the underclasses, neither was Lenin, Mao Zedong, Ho Chi Minh, or Maximillian Robespierre. This means the NRF will likely have a substantive financial support base from the beginning as well as insight as to the FBE's internal social weaknesses.

Weaknesses:

A leader means there is a "head" the FBE can cut off to make the "body" of the NRF die. Especially in the beginning, the early NRF will be very dependent on their leaders to navigate balancing financial, manning, and security needs while avoiding exposure to the FBE's proxies. By the time the NRF can start fragmenting the FBE itself, the leaders become far more expendable but that would only occur late into the fight. Strong unifying leadership keeps rebel factions unified and if that is removed then the rebels will splinter and become trapped in endless low intensity conflict with no resolution as seen in civil wars of Libya, Somalia, and the Democratic Republic of Congo. The contemporary civil wars that ended only did so after the victorious force organized into an army with foreign powers supporting by proxy such as Syria, Iraq, and Afghanistan. Without a rallying leader, the NRF will never evolve beyond being sophisticated harassers who can slow down the FBE but not defeat them.

Information Distribution and Coordination:

The majority of 5GW warfare relies on information dissemination and coordination. 5GW is one step above aggressive conventional political discourse because it proactively destroys their opponent's ability to convey its messages and credibility instead of allowing discourse. It is warfare because using violence to compel an opponent to acquiesce is still used but at a much more selective and less publicized level. This means the majority of combat elements are specialized in deception, information operations, psychological warfare, and message jamming. The direct fighting or lethal groups within the NRF would be very small and much easier to replace. 5GW can only be victorious if the NRF can saturate and overwhelm the FBE with their information operations. To do this successfully, the NRF will need its own communication and financial channels while also keeping access to information channels used by the general populace. Attacking the FBE also means keeping the public placated with the idea that the NRF is not the threat portrayed by the FBE but that means the NRF must risk exposing some of its critical assets to the FBE. No matter how distributed the information networks are, there will be critical nodes that will act as a critical COG for the NRF.

Strengths:

Being mostly outside the conventional information sharing networks and media of the Western nation drastically reduces the FBE's ability to detect and find NRF assets. If properly organized, the NRF's information operations will suffer minimal disruption as the critical nodes are within NRF control even as publicly available information networks become disrupted or scrubbed. Although the NRF will require a human hierarchy to control and synchronize their campaign efforts, the information networks and operations can be decentralized with many segmented and hidden layers so no one single person knows all of them including the leaders themselves.[xxviii] Creating decentralized cellular information and messaging systems offers the NRF the ability to link up groups into cohesive units of exceptional force when needed for operations. Then when an operation is complete, these same units can dissolve into small, tiny groups for the rest of time, maximizing the covert nature of the NRF.

Weaknesses:

There is always friction in organizations which includes complacency, laziness, arrogance, and naivete. The information networks and information distribution operations of the NRF must continuously be on the offensive because sooner or later a key node or information system will be breached. If a system, process, or widget is not properly configured, updated, or installed then the FBE will find and quickly subdue those portions of the NRF's information operations. Operational security cannot defeat complacency and time. Keeping the information nodes protected requires many creative actions and many contingency plans in order to stay viable. Even if overcome, there remains the danger of higher ranks micromanaging and overusing the information networks.[xxix] The FBE's superior resources means they don't have to tax their assets as severely as the NRF to protect their information tools and assets. Keeping the NRF's critical information warfare nodes compartmented with redundancy is time consuming and costly and means creating some unusual spikes in financial and support actions. These sudden changes of behavior or resource allocation will make detection much easier for the FBE.

Moral Legitimacy:

The NRF face the challenge of trying to preserve their Western nation from a foreign-maligned-influence campaign that successfully subverted a segment of the society's elites. This means the NRF must preserve institutions and customs while still fighting the corruption that infects these institutions. This requires a balancing act of defying the letter of the law of the Western nation because it is now corrupt without completely destroying the foundations of the law that was corrupted. Moral legitimacy doesn't mean winning the hearts of the populace. This 5GW war is being waged because the majority of the public is beyond persuading and have resigned themselves to apathy or indulgence. Instead, moral legitimacy is to sustain the NRF's recruitment and morale of its members and active supporters within the general population. If the NRF carry out a campaign to overthrow the society instead of just the elites, like the French or Bolshevik Revolutions, then the FBE will exploit that perception to make the NRF and its leaders lose their followers' faith. Moral legitimacy can be maintained by keeping a disciplined chain of command and a proactive effort to work with the NRF members on how and why actions must be done.

Strengths:

Having moral legitimacy acts as both a unifier and as a layer of security. Moral legitimacy keeps the credibility of the leader intact to carry out operations while the rank-and-file members stay motivated to keep on fighting in the face of tough odds. Once moral legitimacy is acknowledged by all members, the overly ambitious or potentially rogue elements of the NRF would be constrained from carrying out actions contradictory to the NRF high command. Seeking and maintaining moral legitimacy also clarifies for the NRF their targeting priorities and scale of action against those targets. Excessive force or wasteful allocation of resources to irrelevant targets would deplete the already limited resources of the NRF so, proper exploitation of targets is key to long-term success.

Weaknesses:

There is a high risk to the NRF of confusing what moral legitimacy actually means in practical terms. Some of the more idealistic and theoretical mindsets will conceive of moral legitimacy as being constrained, honorable, and civilized in not just seeking objectives but also how to achieve them. The COG of moral legitimacy is not intended to act as a rule of engagement for operations but is instead a guiding principle for designing and waging operations to adhere to a clearly defined strategic goal of preserving the Western nation. Moral legitimacy is not practically a metric for specific tactics or methodology. The brutal reality is that war is unforgiving, especially to the weaker force in the fight. Constraining those who demand combat, information operations, and psychological warfare in the name of being "civilized" will doom the NRF. As Von Clausewitz stated on the very first page of his first chapter of his book, *On War*:

Kind-hearted people might of course think there was some ingenious way to disarm or defeat an enemy without too much bloodshed, and might imagine this is the true goal of the art of war. Pleasant as it sounds, it is a fallacy that must be exposed: war is such a dangerous business that the mistakes which come from kindness are the very worst.**[xxx]**

5GW warfare is selected to limit the carnage from the public and the Western nation as a whole but within the limited parameters set by the NRF there must be no quarter given to the FBE. The FBE leaders must understand and believe there is no mitigation or boundary from which the NRF will limit itself in the destruction of the FBE faction. 5GW limits the setting of the conflict to a covert war between elites and their proxies but doesn't limit the kinds of actions necessary to achieve total victory within these confined parameters. If the NRF confuses moral legitimacy with fighting a constrained limited form of war in both action and objective instead of just objective, then the NRF will be fatally constrained. Poorly implemented constraints and lack of understanding the objectives of the 5GW form of civil war would doom the NRF and help the foreign power achieve victory without having to fire a shot.

---

[1] Tim Craig, "A Young Man is Skinned Alive. A Sign of New Taliban Brutality?" The Washington Post, June 11, 2016. https://www.washingtonpost.com/world/asia_pacific/a-young-man-was-skinned-alive-in-afghanistan-a-sign-of-new-taliban-brutality/2016/06/10/6b7592fa-2e8a-11e6-b9d5-3c3063f8332c_story.html

[2] Paul Wood, "Face-to-Face with Abu Sakkar, Syria's 'Heart-Eating Cannibal'," BBC, July 5, 2013. https://www.bbc.com/news/magazine-23190533

[3] Think Tank Report, *Katanga: The Congo's Forgotten Crisis*, International Crisis Group, January 9, 2006. https://www.crisisgroup.org/africa/central-africa/democratic-republic-congo/katanga-congo-s-forgotten-crisis

[4] Suleiman Al-Khalidi, "Hunger and Desperation: Aleppo Siege Tests Limits of Endurance," Reuters, November 25, 2016. https://www.reuters.com/article/us-mideast-crisis-syria-aleppo/hunger-and-desperation-aleppo-siege-tests-limits-of-endurance-idUSKBN13K1HQ

[5] News Report, "Sectarian Death Squads Kill Scores in Iraq," NBC News, October 16, 2006. https://www.nbcnews.com/id/wbna15285032

[6] Reference Report, "Map of Mass Grave Exhumations in Bosnia and Herzegovina Published," Open Society Archives, 2021, https://www.osaarchivum.org/press-room/announcements/Map-Mass-Grave-Exhumations-Bosnia-and-Herzegovina-Published

[7] Herbert Hoover, *Addresses Upon the American Road*, (Hoover Archives: NY: D Van Nostrand Company: 1946): 254. https://hoover.archives.gov/sites/default/files/research/ebooks/b3v4_full.pdf

[8] Daniel H. Abbott et al, *The Handbook of 5GW*, (Ann Arbor, MI: Nimble Books LLC: 2010): 12.

[9] Government Report, "Combating Terrorism: Interagency Framework and Agency Programs to Address the Overseas Threat," Government Accountability Office Archives, GAO-03-165, May 23, 2003. https://www.govinfo.gov/content/pkg/GAOREPORTS-GAO-03-165/html/GAOREPORTS-GAO-03-165.htm

[10] Daniel H. Abbott et al, *The Handbook of 5GW*, (Ann Arbor, MI: Nimble Books LLC: 2010): 15.

[11] Military manual, *FM 3-90-1: Offense and Defense Vol. 1*, (Washington DC: Department of the Army: March 2013): 1-32, 1-33, B-4. https://armypubs.army.mil/epubs/DR_pubs/DR_a/NOCASE-FM_3-90-1-002-WEB-0.pdf

[12] Daniel H. Abbott et al, *The Handbook of 5GW*, (Ann Arbor, MI: Nimble Books LLC: 2010): 14 and 27.

[13] Military manual, *FM 3-90-1: Offense and Defense Vol. 1*, (Washington DC: Department of the Army: March 2013): 1-32, 1-33, B-13. https://armypubs.army.mil/epubs/DR_pubs/DR_a/NOCASE-FM_3-90-1-002-WEB-0.pdf

[14] NGO Report, "How Kabila Lost His Way," International Crisis Group, May 21, 1999. https://www.crisisgroup.org/africa/central-africa/democratic-republic-congo/how-kabila-lost-his-way

[15] Antony Jay and Jonathan Lynn, *Yes, Prime Minister*, Episode: "A Real Partnership," February 6, 1986.

[16] Magazine Article, "Mercenaries in the Thirty Years' War – Horrid Men or Great Soldiers?", History is Now Magazine, October 19, 2021. http://www.historyisnowmagazine.com/blog/2021/10/18/mercenaries-in-the-thirty-years-war-horrid-men-or-great-soldiers

[17] Sean McFate, *Mercenaries and War: Understanding Private Armies Today*, (Washington DC: National Defense University Press: December 2019): 8-9.

[18] Daniel H. Abbott et al, *The Handbook of 5GW*, (Ann Arbor, MI: Nimble Books LLC: 2010): 38-39.

[19] Ibid, 68.

[20] Ibid, 70.

[21] Raymond Daniell, "Patton Belittles Denazification; Holds Rebuilding more Important," The New York Times, September 23, 1945. https://www.nytimes.com/1945/09/23/archives/patton-belittles-denazification-holds-rebuilding-more-important.html

[22] Lorraine Boissoneault, "The Nazi Werewolves Who Terrorized Allied Soldiers at the End of World War II," Smithsonian Magazine, October 30, 2018. https://www.smithsonianmag.com/history/nazi-werewolves-who-terrorized-allied-soldiers-end-wwii-180970522/

[23] James P. Pfiffner, "US Blunders in Iraq: De-Baathification and Disbanding the Army," Routledge: Taylor & Francis Group, Intelligence and National Security, vol 25, no. 1, February 2010. https://pfiffner.gmu.edu/files/pdfs/Articles/CPA%20Orders%2C%20Iraq%20PDF.pdf

[24] Solomon Moore, "Killings by Shi'ite Militias Detailed," Los Angeles Times, September 28, 2006. https://www.latimes.com/archives/la-xpm-2006-sep-28-fg-intel28-story.html

[xxv] Reference, *Dietrich Eckart*, Jewish Virtual Library, https://www.jewishvirtuallibrary.org/dietrich-eckart.

[xxvi] Daniel H. Abbott et al, *The Handbook of 5GW*, (Ann Arbor, MI: Nimble Books LLC: 2010): 19.

[xxvii] Ibid, 24.

[xxviii] Ibid, 33.

[xxix] Ibid, 45-46.

[xxx] Edited and Translated by Michael Howard and Peter Paret, *Carl Von Clausewitz's On War*, (NJ: Princeton University Press, 1989) 75.

Chapter 14: Why a 4GW-Style Insurgency is Terrible for Both Sides

Even when one tries to predict how a future conflict could unfold, it is very difficult to avoid preconceptions shaped by the last war. From this time in the early 2020s, the most recent civil wars with large insurgencies for reference were in Syria, Libya, Iraq, and Afghanistan with each being a slight variation of 4th Gradient Warfare or 4GW. 4GW is a contemporary form of insurgency that exploits the advanced information technologies to wage asymmetric attacks and psychological manipulation on a government and cripple its support bases within the military and general population. [i] These wars have shaped observers' and opinionators' preconception that a potential future civil war in a Western nation must follow a similar path.[ii] This book cannot predict the future and instead seeks to wargame how each side of a civil conflict could fight most effectively for their objectives in a modern Western nation. Although it is possible that 4GW ends up being the form of war chosen to fight within a Western nation, it is not the only option and it is far from optimal.

There is a tendency for people to create self-fulfilling prophecies and if the conditions for a civil war do develop in a Western nation, people might just choose to fight a 4GW-style insurgency because they expect it to be inevitable. Such a danger must be avoided because many who expect or advocate such a course of action are ones who have either learned the wrong lessons of the previous 4GW wars or hold perilous misconceptions. Given the rhetoric in public discussions and opinions, many of these misconceptions are held across the political spectrum regardless of declared expertise or knowledge. So, there are some key points that must be highlighted for any potential future strategist to consider before following in the footsteps of Middle Eastern insurgencies and governments. Given the author's personal expertise and experience in Iraq, most of the key points will focus on the Iraq War, its insurgency, and the follow-up Syrian Civil War.

In the West, self-fulfilling prophecies occur because people only use previous events that suit their arguments for citing reference in Western media and political circles. Taking complex issues and shortcutting analysis into simple black and white dichotomies for the ease of public consumption helps garner attention and credibility by pandering to people's intellectual prejudices. Both sides will portray their position as strong and the other side as weak to help bolster support while trying to discredit their opposition. Yet, in the actual practical execution of policy, especially regarding war, true understanding is lost because there is much nuance that is lost in these debates or diatribes. Both sides who make pronouncements on how easy victory would be or their side possessing an inherent advantage over their opponent are more likely than not going to be disappointed. Instead, both sides are overestimating their own abilities while at the same time underestimating the capability of their potential foes.

Some examples of such rhetoric include politicians stating insurgencies using small arms are obsolete in the face of modern military power which includes possessing nuclear weapons. [iii] Admittedly, this hyperbole was in the middle of an election cycle, but the point is such a perception of overwhelming state power making insurrection impossible within the United States does exist amongst some in the American electorate, especially those close to the state.[iv] Others on the other hand, opine that the US military would likely lose to an insurgency because it would be hindered by the political fallout of such an event.[v] Again, the level of expertise or lack thereof is irrelevant, the point is these perceptions are common when discussing potential civil conflict. So, for simplicity's sake, let's evaluate what governments did and then what insurgents did in these 4GW wars and identify the true lessons for a potential Western civil conflict.

Firstly, evaluating the governments' actions and capabilities must be understood in the context of the setting and period which will be different in a Western civil war. Iraq is the main example because it was where the West experimented on its modern concepts of counterinsurgency and is the source of many popular conceptions of how modern insurrections occur in the Western mindset. In this case, the overarching problem that impacted all the other problems the West's Coalition faced was its own considerable biases and misconceptions of how the region functioned. These preconceptions hindered Coalition decision making because few members were exposed to the unique cultural and political circumstances of the region prior to the invasion. In the case of Iraq, the Coalition invaded and overthrew a brutal dictator and then expected the Iraqi population to react to the action like the Europeans reacted to the fall of the Nazi Empire after liberation despite being cultural aliens to the region.[vi] [vii] Despite warnings from many, the Coalition decisions were based on the assumption that Iraq could transform from being three nations held together by brute force into becoming a democratized Westernized liberal society.[viii] The failure to appreciate the sectarian divides are well-documented elsewhere but what was less discussed at the time was the social and economic culture that the Coalition inherited. For centuries, the population in the Iraq region of the Fertile Crescent were under the rule of foreign empires or domestic dictators whose common theme was maintain control and power over the population. Like the historical regimes, the Ba'athist dictatorship created a highly centralized government with control over the economy, people's movement, and education that created a culture of state dependence and submissive deference to their society's elites.[ix] Iraq, in general, was a nation of serfs.

The sudden drastic changes imposed upon the locals from the Coalition invasion that was the most detrimental was not the invasion from a foreign power because that happened many times before. What was more shocking was the Coalition suddenly giving them personal responsibility for their own lives and well-being. The Coalition was largely composed of nations with established civic cultures where there are clearly established lines of demarcation between private life and public life. In Iraq, the state provided the majority of fiscal and social security with only family and religious life having any autonomy. When the Coalition came, locals expected the Westerners to impose order, provide employment, give guidance in daily activities, and become the new state as conquerors of the past had done.

The oppressed Shia and Kurds of course expected to share in the conqueror's spoils and get an increased dominating position in society but they also expected more direction from the Coalition. Instead, the Coalition disbanded the army, attempted to kickstart a neoliberal economy with cooperative Iraqi civilian elements and then gave Iraq money with few restrictions like the equivalent to an industrial bail-out. Telling a formerly subjugated populace it now had to take over the responsibilities from a centralized state to become a civic society with minimal guidance and lots of aid money led to poor results.[x] Instead of learning to become self-sufficient, the Iraqi leadership reverted to old habits and became dependent on the Coalition as their new benefactor.[xi] As seen with many North Korean defectors[xii] and many East Germans shortly after German reunification in 1990,[xiii] people who have been cogs in a statist machine have difficulty transitioning into an economic system that relies more on individual initiative and responsibility because they never were allowed to learn or develop these skills in the dictatorships. In contrast, most of Western Europe had established civic cultures before the Nazis conquered them so liberation did not require a micromanaging approach for the Allies to rebuild those nations.[xiv] In Iraq, the sudden social shock to its citizens of a centralized economy no longer existing but receiving little guidance on developing private markets other than receiving some aid money and infrastructure reconstruction projects meant they had to try to figure things out on their own.[xv] This created near anarchy that benefited the most ruthless and corruptly-connected persons to enrich themselves while economic development languished. Conquerors maybe hated but even the most cynically conquered person expects the conquerors to impose order, no matter how ruthlessly. Unfortunately for Iraqi expectations, the Coalition that took over was more akin to secular proselytizers rather than assertive conquerors by attempting to persuade Iraq's surviving elites on the benefits of being part of the internationalist system while neglecting the difficulties of governing.[xvi] The Iraqis expected the Coalition to replace Saddam as the guarantor of their livelihoods and the Coalition didn't comprehend the scale of the problem for years due to cultural blindness. Failing to take actual control and assert a clear direction set the stage for every other calamity.

The cultural blindness exacerbated the Coalition's other strategic problem of mission creep for the Coalition. Bluntly, the Coalition did not have clearly defined and measurable strategic objectives beyond overthrowing Saddam before invading Iraq and no one was given clear guidance on what to do after Saddam.[xvii]' [xviii] Committing to a set of clearly defined goals would consequently create easily identifiable metrics to gauge success for both strategic and operational objectives.[xix] However, this also meant definitive failures could also be identified which meant someone had to take the lead and assume the risk of responsibility for clear failures. This doesn't automatically mean a commander either. Civil servants or political appointees, depending on the objective, would have also been at risk of being held responsible for failure since the State Department and other government agencies also had responsibilities in Iraq. With so many bureaucracies being "equal" to each other in terms of jurisdiction, no one could impose a common set of clearly defined strategic objectives.[xx] Keeping strategic objectives nebulous and poorly defined meant that ineptitude was shared equally and no one person or department could be completely blamed. The only definitive objectives were made at the operational level where commanders could build metrics that fulfilled the requirements of the theater command for a particular frame of time, usually a deployment cycle. These metrics were used to measure "effects-based" operational tasks which meant actions that could cause an immediate impact on a larger effort but with no clear end state. This usually meant most "effects-based" actions only lasted during a particular commander's deployment and did not always carry over to the successor commander or consider the circumstances of the next deployment cycle.[xxi]

For instance, my unit deployed to Nineveh Province, Iraq and it was given the operational task to sever Al-Qaeda in Iraq's (AQI) line of communication to the Syrian border to help support the Iraqi government's efforts to stabilize Mosul. This was to be done in conjunction with other efforts of the "Surge" in Al-Anbar and Southern Iraq. In order to pave the way for the Iraqi-led "Operation Lion's Roar" in Mosul, my unit aggressively stepped-up patrols and increased the targeting of high value individuals to weaken AQI for the operation. This operation was to capitalize on the recent successes with the Sunni tribal militia Awakening Councils in West Iraq and the countering of Muqtada al-Sadr's Jaysh Al-Mahdi militias with "Operation Charge of Knights" in Basra. These tasks were built around creating the "effects" of assisting the Iraqi government's named operations to be successful in clearing the city, but this operation didn't go beyond sweeping out the city with no real clear follow-on objectives. This was an example of a nebulous effects-based operation imposed upon my unit set by the conditions of the overall theater.

Inconsistent metrics around obscure effects was compounded by the lack of coordinated efforts or methods to fight the insurgency among the various units and the supporting intelligence collection efforts. Intelligence collection in both Iraq and Afghanistan would often be defined by personalities rather than set objectives and tasks. Cultural biases clouded issues further as many units were still focused on either targeting just specific individuals or treating insurgents as conventional enemies to achieve desired immediate "effects". This disjointed intelligence collection effort meant poor cross-unit coordination or support with minimal guidance from the higher echelons.[xxii] Sometimes, even roles and responsibilities changed on a whim or for the convenience of the moment rather than long-term outcomes. All of this was compounded by the senior leadership's obsession with measuring effects akin to Defense Secretary McNamara's obsession with statistics for Vietnam.[xxiii]

Retired Lieutenant Colonel Paul Yingling wrote an article, "A Failure in Generalship," that articulated the problems facing the Coalition due to lack of clarity from senior levels about the mission.[xxiv] Flag officers, whether generals or admirals, had to devote much of their time accomplishing actions that would have immediate short-term effect because of the critical media and immense political pressure placed on policy makers. This political pressure cooker created an environment of risk aversion which in turn encouraged groupthink that hindered innovation and long-term thinking because the Coalition kept promising immediate improvements. Those improvements wouldn't necessarily be linked into a long-term plan because only the immediate effects of action mattered. This lack of strategic thinking kept the disconnect between strategic achievements and operational efforts for most of the Iraq War until the arrival of General Petraeus and General Odierno. The officers used their previous operational successes to justify themselves as the key innovators and took the lead during the "Surge" of 2006-2009. The Coalition's strategic risk aversion had lasted a long time with the political and public divisions over the Iraq War dominating policy decisions most of the time. The heightened political divisions also created risk aversion at the tactical level leading to the abuse of systems designed to protect soldiers being twisted to protect the Coalition itself from political scrutiny. The most prominent example was Coalition governments imposing a highly restricted set of rules of engagement which were not designed to avoid unnecessary death but to reduce outside political criticism.

The Rules of Engagement (ROE) are a set of legal and regulatory enforced rules on how Coalition combat forces were allowed to engage the enemy with lethal force. Historically, ROE was to help protect soldiers by giving them as much flexibility in combat as possible while still adhering to the laws of war which can be easily forgotten otherwise in the heat of battle. Unfortunately, poor leadership and lack of command led to abuses early in the war that garnered an already sensationalist press, who opportunistically pursued anguish for profit instead of truth, to overwhelm the risk averse Coalition governments with portrayals of chaos, malice, and incompetence. This caused a knee-jerk reaction by the Coalition to overcompensate and had the ROE be crafted to sate criticism at the home front more than protect Iraqis or soldiers. In practice, this meant a zero-tolerance policy that discarded any common sense or context because any gray area could be twisted by the media at home. This hindered operational and tactical decision making where fear of overzealous bureaucrats looking to impress the media had as much influence as the threat of insurgents.[xxv] When the British government was once asked about legal protections for soldiers trying to abide by their ROE, the replies were deliberately nebulous. This was an example of giving a government the ability to delegate failure down-ranks if a combat incident caused political consternation back home.[xxvi] Veteran anecdotes on how many times soldiers were put in unnecessarily risky situations to protect reputations in the eyes of the press abounded in both Iraq and Afghanistan from 2003 – 2011. These anecdotes are not hard evidence and cannot be independently verified, but the credibility of most veterans is overwhelmingly higher than any media[xxvii] newsreader. If someone can blindly take the media's word at face value with "anonymous sources", one should be able to consider the veterans' claims with at least the same credibility.[xxviii], [xxix] This became so bad that the Bush Administration actually had to reverse course and compel the military to take a more aggressive posture in 2006. [xxx] This new posture helped enable the "Surge" effort to support the local Awakening Councils, Kurdish militias, and Iraqi Army more effectively. [xxxi]

For most of the Iraq War, the risk averse leadership was noticed by the insurgency who exploited it for their own propaganda. Knowing that Westerners delusionally believe they can fight wars in a more civilized fashion, AQI would tailor its Western-destined propaganda to focus on ROE violations or undue excesses to split Western audiences. This is focused only on Western audiences because other nations don't really care. Islamic insurgencies didn't bother to highlight brutalities with Russian audiences when reporting atrocious actions in Syria because Russia doesn't care. Furthermore, AQI and other insurgencies exploited the uniquely Western habit of actually restricting their occupational forces' ability to engage their enemies.[xxxii] Contrarily, the Russian scorched-earth actions in Aleppo were a repeat of the traditionally successful counterinsurgency methods of devastation and demonstrated the non-West's indifference.[xxxiii] The lack of strategic vision, risk averse decision making, allowing the media to dictate operational and tactical performance, and fear of looking "barbaric" in the eyes of the Western public were some of the major problems hindering Coalition governments' 4GW efforts. All of these problems helped create a popular perception that modern insurgencies are the inevitable victors in 4GW but the insurgents also had many problems.

Many observers in the West fail to appreciate the fact that AQI was also a foreign invading army. Its leadership was mainly composed of Egyptian, Syrian, Tunisian, and Saudi Islamists who often had contemptuous views of the Iraqis.[xxxiv], [xxxv], [xxxvi] Arabs are not one people, regardless of religion or geographic proximity. Tribal rivalries remained very strong in Iraq's rural regions and within the cities, various sectarian groups deliberately ghettoized their neighborhoods to protect themselves along religious and ethnic lines.[xxxvii] AQI often portrayed themselves as liberators but acted as imperialistically as anything they accused the Coalition of being. Their abuses and exploitation led to the creation of the Awakening Councils; rural Sunni tribal militias united against the foreign Arab invaders. The reputational situation became so bad that AQI decided to create a new franchise organization called the Islamic State of Iraq (ISI) consisting of local Iraqi Salafist fanatics. This was done for the sole purpose of giving AQI a local face that would better accommodate the propaganda of defeating foreign "kafir" invaders. Ultimately, this did not succeed and ISI eventually broke away from AQI to eventually become the Islamic State of Iraq and Syria/or Levant (ISIS).[xxxviii], [xxxix]

This leads to the insurgents' next problem of being divided from the beginning. Iraq's insurgency could be argued to have been united initially in 2003 with the Ba'athist's Fedayeen guerrillas but it quickly fragmented into a dozen or so groups and factions. Besides AQI and ISI, there was Ansar al-Islam, Jaysh al-Islami fi-al Iraq, the Secret Islamic Army, Hamas of Iraq, Islamic Front for the Iraqi Resistance, Naqshbandi Order, and the Ba'athist Al-Awda.[xl] These were just the Sunni insurgencies, the Shi'ite had groups like Muqtada Al-Sadr's Jaysh al-Mahdi, Kata'ib Hezbollah, Badr Organization, and the Islamic Supreme Council of Iraq. Factionalism also plagued the organizations internally. Despite the propaganda, genuine religious fanatics were only a portion of the membership with mercenaries, criminals, disgruntled persons, and adventure seekers being other major sources of recruitment.[xli], [xlii] This did create internal friction that disrupted the operational and tactical efforts of insurgent groups far more often than is appreciated.

No matter how effective these insurgents were against the West or the Iraqi government, they could never achieve their strategic objectives as none had the resources or sufficient influence to secure all of Iraq. ISIS tried to correct many of these deficiencies in their campaigns in Syria and Iraq by co-opting local tribal leaders and using as many locally recruited commanders as possible.[xliii] More importantly, ISIS created a cult of personality around their supreme leader, al-Baghdadi, to build a unified fighting force that pro-Sunni caliphate militants could rally around. ISIS never eliminated the other insurgents that kept the anti-Bashir al-Assad forces divided, but they did succeed in creating a homogenous force within the areas they controlled and influenced. A divided insurgency remains a continuous problem for the Islamists to this day.

Another mistaken assumption by some critics of Western counterinsurgency methodology is that its strategic failure must also mean it failed at tactical objectives as well. Many fail to differentiate achieving strategic vs tactical objectives. The West often fails in counterinsurgency due to its lack of political cohesion in devising an achievable strategic goal but the West never failed, even with a highly restricted ROE, to defeat insurgents at the tactical level. In most engagements with Coalition forces, the insurgents suffered high casualties and rarely achieved any tactical military objective. In some cases, insurgents could lose up to 12x as many as Coalition would lose in fire fights.[xliv], [xlv], [xlvi] This is why most engagements against the Coalition were to achieve strategic propaganda and information warfare objectives instead. Coalition would suffer losses but not to the point of being militarily defeated anywhere in Iraq. This is why most sophisticated large-scale attacks were on Iraqi police and army who lacked the level of sophistication of fighting capability while also enduring chronic corruption and poor leadership.[xlvii]' [xlviii] Even against the Iraqis, the insurgencies had to accept they had to suffer a high casualty rate to make any substantial gains and despite their aggressive actions, would have to endure this casualty rate for years to sufficiently attrit their stronger opponent. Which leads to the last major problem of most of these 4GW insurgencies: they usually fail to achieve their final objectives.

The situation in the Middle East makes it easy for the critics of the Coalition to highlight the West's counterinsurgency failings and miscalculations but what is less discussed is the fact that the insurgencies also failed to achieve their ultimate strategic objectives. The final goal of AQI to overthrow the Coalition-backed Iraqi government and establish a Salafist-imperial caliphate did not happen. Eight years of war attrited Western patience at the cost of tens of thousands of insurgents, countless dollars, and AQI's reputation as an effective Islamist insurgency. Overtime, AQI and other Sunni insurgency groups whittled into irrelevance, with only ISI revitalized by the events of the "Arab Spring" in Syria to become ISIS. Even though ISIS was more successful than its former parent organization in partially achieving its goals, the terror organization still failed and had to recede from being a quasi-imperialist state back to an amorphous terrorist group. This pattern of being trapped in a ceaseless quagmire has been repeated in Libya, Somalia, Mali, and Yemen demonstrating that 4GW only succeeds in creating frozen conflicts of attrition. So, what are the true lessons should both the FBE and NRF take into consideration regarding the use of 4GW warfare and how do the events in Afghanistan, Chechnya, Sri Lanka, and Cold War-era Malaysia improve upon these lessons?

A 4GW civil conflict in a Western nation would modify and negate several of the challenges that Western forces faced in the past. First, the FBE proxy government forces would have a clearly defined strategic objective which in this case, is making the FBE leaders the uncontested rulers of the Western nation and diminish resistance to an inconsequential level. Meaning, the military leadership would be able to create a consistent set of operational parameters to direct their forces throughout the campaign with little likelihood of mission creep. Also, the operational parameters and tactical decisions will be made without the cultural blindness that plagued the Coalition's endeavors in Afghanistan or Iraq. All of this creates an organization consistently focused and less likely to be disrupted by sudden mission changes or international pressure.

Internal cohesion with a clear focus is not the only advantage difference for the FBE. Regardless of the specific causes, the Coalition's populace was politically divided on the wars in Iraq and Afghanistan. This stymied any mission cohesion as the Coalitions' forces had to sacrifice operational effectiveness for the political sensitivities at home. The media proactively criticized and attacked the American and European administrations' actions within these wars making any aggressive or novel decision by leaders risky. Moral issues aside, the Coalition's governments' decisions designed to placate media outrage resulted in schizophrenic decision-making. Under the circumstances of an FBE-manipulated anocracy, the FBE leaders would have a controlling interest in the Western media companies or have political proxies direct state-controlled media organizations. The FBE would have a united media front to direct information operations, propaganda, and psychological operations to keep the apathetic general public, FBE proxies, and close allies supportive of any and all actions against the NRF. This means mistakes are not disclosed, defeats are downplayed, atrocities portrayed as acceptable when the FBE does it and evil when the NRF does it, and the NRF are to be blamed for any ills the Western nation's general population suffers. This means the FBE can appoint loyal but incompetent sycophants and yes-men as their military commanders without too many repercussions as the FBE's overwhelming resources of a monolithic information control apparatus can compensate for any major losses. As for the public, if the apathetic majority don't know how bad events are and the FBE loyalists are motivated by the optimistic portrayal of FBE operations, then the political restrictions faced by the Coalition forces in the Middle East and Afghanistan will be mostly gone. There might be a smattering of independent press and international media but these can be curtailed and impact minimized as media content is prioritized in what is broadcast within the Western nation. Not to mention people's tendency to only read and watch positive reinforcement within their chosen echo chambers.

The next major difference in a Western nation uprising is that the FBE would dispense with pretending to adhere to the Western delusional neurosis of believing the West can fight and win its wars in a more civilized and humane way than in the past. As stated earlier in the book, Clausewitz warns of the danger that nations which try to make war a genteel and more humane endeavor will lead to disaster.[xlix] The reality that few in the West want to face is that brutality is not an aberration or bug in 4GW warfare, it is a required feature. The Western world has tried to make wars more restrained and humane for centuries and continuously fail resulting in protracted conflicts that escalate into more brutal conflicts in the late stages of theses wars. Many Western experts kept stating winning hearts and minds was giving away "carrots" of financial aid without accountability to avoid offending the local leadership. Even the updated US military official reference for counterinsurgency operations acknowledges this was a major mistake.[l]

Wars are political acts of compelling your opponent to comply by violence and diluting the violence diminishes the urgency of one's opponent to comply. Governments that resort exclusively to brutality have better results than those who exclusively appeal to persuasion with positive actions. Insurgencies wither rapidly if the insurgents experience major losses or their supporters consequently suffer for trying to help. Brutal counterinsurgency methods are more often seen in nations where international opinion doesn't matter or there is a lot of international indifference. Despite the resentments and corruption, Chechnya has been pacified by Russia for nearly two decades,[li]' [lii] the Sri Lankans' ruthless final operations against the Tamil Tigers finally ended the long civil conflict,[liii]' [liv], [lv] and Saddam Hussein himself crushed many uprisings with ruthless savagery.[lvi]' [lvii] The populations were resentful but compliant for decades afterwards which is more than what the West's counterinsurgency idealism accomplished in either Iraq or Afghanistan. The West's counterinsurgency efforts in Afghanistan and Iraq relied too heavily on positive incentives with few repercussions for local insurgent collaborators.

The best managed counterinsurgencies historically were balanced operations that used both "carrot" and "stick" to entice cooperation with locals while also trying to make aiding enemy insurgents too costly for the locals to consider. The most successful counterinsurgency in the 20th Century was the British-led counterinsurgency in the Malay Emergency against the communist insurgents during the 1950s. Although hearts and minds were considered, the British understood that meant both merited reward and punishment to achieve success under the "Briggs Plan".[lviii] In this case, the jungle country of Malaysia restricted ease of movement which was bad for counterinsurgency forces but it also meant it was easy to control food supplies. The British did two things for hearts and minds: 1. Create "resettled" villages and population centers to consolidate the rural population to simplify lines of communication and control over local population movements 2. Ration the food supply to the civilian populace where villages that cooperated received greater food and services and those that collaborated with insurgents had food and other goods restricted. This clear material-based merit system drastically reduced the communist insurgents' food supply for their jungle bases while the British earned respect (not love) of the locals for delivering on promises while being fair in any ruthless punishment.[lix] Visibly showing a population being punished for clearly aiding the communists and rewarding locals (not just their "leaders") for cooperating with the British discredited the communist insurgency. Secondly, this policy of "hearts and minds" demonstrated British resolve to punish the insurgents while also being willing to collectively punish the civilian population if they failed to cooperate in eliminating "fence-sitting" locals and duplicitous partners. The British honored their promises of physical protection and food supply because the villagers cooperated. A textbook case of using both "stick" and "carrot" to "win hearts and minds" yet it still took a decade with a very well-trained security and counterinsurgency force led by competent leaders.[lx] This means that even when properly executed, the FBE proxy government will have to fight for a decade while using more ruthless methods than most contemporary Western militaries are comfortable with, making the risk of FBE fracturing very high. This risk also applies to the NRF and any insurgency.

Many considered the actions of ISIS' brutality to be excessive, sadistic, and unnecessarily savage, but the frank reality is that the actions were often coldly calculated for strategic purposes. ISIS advocated a foreign ideology and needed to demonstrate to the Arab tribal federations of eastern Syria and western Iraq that contesting the ideology was too costly. Political allegiance and compliance happen in one of two ways: persuading people to follow one's faction with ideas, arguments, and enticements or use fear and brutality to frighten them into obeyance. Persuasion takes years, especially if it's a foreign ideology or advocate but fear is immediate. Violence guarantees compliance in the short term and was needed for ISIS to successfully impose its ideological grip so quickly. The successes on the battlefield against Syrian and Iraqi forces in the early stages of the war combined with its demonstrated brutality made the locals compliant, if unreliable, allies and subjects.

The success on the battlefield was due more to ISIS' enemies' ineptitude but their success over holding captured territory was a combination of brutality and keeping order.[lxi] Success absolves viciousness in war and ISIS' ability to impose order created a clear contrast of draconian peace vs the previous regime's anarchy enabling ISIS to easily keep the locals pacified.[lxii] The NRF avoids these problems initially because it would be a domestic insurgency with many ties to the society with common cultural bonds, beliefs, and interests which is more similar to the Taliban than ISIS. The NRF would not have to resort to the brutality of ISIS but it would still need to act ruthlessly to carry out its objectives. 4GW requires the public to pressure the government into reconciling with the insurgents by being exhausted by the horrors of the insurgency. This means the NRF would have to make the public suffer to some degree, just like the Taliban did. However, the NRF runs the risk of falling into the actions akin to ISIS if the moderate leaders of the NRF fail to achieve results.

A restrained insurgency that tries to avoid casualties and atrocities also means prolonging the conflict and having fewer positive results in the same span of time. On the battlefield, success matters more than ideology or ethics and too much time wears out patience. If the NRF's insurgency lasts years with no discernable sign of progress or victory, then the NRF will become more radical and sooner or later a genuinely brutal ruthless far-right or far-left faction will take control. No matter what happens, a 4GW insurgency would last years and the insurgents would most likely suffer far more casualties in absolute number terms which creates more pressure to retaliate with extreme measures. As seen in all of the Middle Eastern insurgencies, most of the moderate factions were quickly dispatched with the few survivors sheltered by Western militaries as attrition and exhaustion set in. No such luxury will exist for the NRF to fall back on, so trying to avoid carnage and ruthless actions in the beginning of a 4GW campaign would create the risk of backlash and greater atrocities if such restrained actions fail to achieve results within a perceived reasonable amount of time. History has not been kind to stalled failures in war such as General McClellan's attempt at restrained limited warfare in the American Civil War [lxiii]' [lxiv] led to the rise of the more ruthless Generals Sherman and Grant or the rise of massacres and chemical warfare after the failure of the "Von Schlieffen Plan" to quickly knock out France.[lxv] The longer the fight, the less restraint and more radical the NRF would become.

Then the final consideration of 4GW warfare is that it is designed to exhaust an enemy, not defeat them. In practice, 4GW is a transitional form of warfare designed to attrit a stronger opponent to a level of weakness that allows the underdog to grow and change where it can defeat their opponent in a 3GW or 5GW fight. The insurgents must change into either a covert army of political manipulators and assassins or become an overt army that can hold territory and defeat other armies. Mao's lessons from the Chinese Civil War still apply today. Mao stayed as a guerrilla partisan force for most of the conflict but changed into a maneuver army after World War II.[lxvi] The Taliban changed from a partisan guerrilla force in the mountains to an actual mobilized army, even if it was primitive, it still was able to hold territory and fight other organized resistance.[lxvii] ISIS attempted to do this after the Fall of Mosul in 2014 but ISIS never really changed its forces into a land-controlling army. Instead, the insurgents still fell back on hit-and-run actions, raiding, ambushes, and terrorist attacks with little ability to engage a standing army on a battlefield. ISIS was initially fortunate the Iraqi Army in West Iraq deserted in 2014 due to failures of the Iraqi government because it gave the impression ISIS was a proper national force of a state.[lxviii] However, ISIS fell apart once Western-backed Iraqi Army and YPG militias organized its counteroffensives in 2015 leading to ISIS ceasing to be a state by 2017 and reverting to a terrorist group.[lxix]' [lxx] All of this means that if the NRF decided to initiate a

4GW civil conflict, it would still have to eventually transform into a standing army to achieve final victory which means more bloodshed and destruction over many more years.

4GW is the default assumed method of a future civil war but it is not the optimal form of warfare for either faction as both sides would suffer years of disruption, carnage, and economic instability. Furthermore, this form of warfare is the most likely to create more extreme and brutal factions on both sides as frustration with the "moderates" failing to achieve victory would grow as the war drags on. The only group to benefit from a protracted 4GW insurgency would be the foreign backers of the FBE who only truly see their Western FBE counterparts as puppets and tools rather than partners. However, this wargame examines how the FBE itself and NRF can both fight optimally for their particular victory requirements and concludes 4GW warfare of the past two decades is not optimal for either.

---

[i] Daniel H. Abbott et al, *The Handbook of 5GW*, (Ann Arbor, MI: Nimble Books LLC: 2010): 47.

[ii] Barbara Walter, *How Civil Wars Start and How to Stop Them*, (NY: Crown: 2022): 168-169.

[iii] Caitlin Yilek, "Leading Democrat Warns Gun Owners: 'The Government has Nukes'," Washington Examiner, November 16, 2018. https://www.washingtonexaminer.com/news/leading-democrat-warns-gun-owners-the-government-has-nukes

[iv] Justin King, "How the US Military is Preparing To Put Down an American Insurgency," Mint Press News, August 29, 2016. https://www.mintpressnews.com/us-military-preparing-put-american-insurgency/219890/

[v] Reddit Post, "Why the US Military Would Most Likely Lose to A Far-Right Insurgency," r/VaushV, December 2022. https://www.reddit.com/r/VaushV/comments/zjaogo/why_the_us_military_would_most_likely_lose_to_a/

[vi] Conference Report, "Iraq, Palestine, Then What?" The Washington Institute, October 4, 2002. https://www.washingtoninstitute.org/policy-analysis/iraq-palestine-then-what-can-america-promote-liberal-democratic-middle-east

[vii] Joseph Cirincione, "Origins of Regime Change in Iraq," Carnegie Endowment for International Peace, March 19, 2003. https://carnegieendowment.org/2003/03/19/origins-of-regime-change-in-iraq-pub-1214

[viii] Ahmad Faruqui, "Iraq's Liberation in Perspective," CounterPunch, March 24, 2003. https://www.counterpunch.org/2003/03/24/iraq-s-liberation-in-perspective/

[ix] Ambassador Robin Raphel & Judith Barnett, "Iraq 2003: The Economy," PA Consulting Group, March 20, 2003, 37-39. https://www.esd.whs.mil/Portals/54/Documents/FOID/Reading%20Room/CPA_ORHA/07-F-2544_Iraq_2003_The_Economy.pdf

[x] Robert Looney, "A Return to Baathist Economics? Escaping Vicious Circles in Iraq," Strategic Insights, vol. 3, issue 7, July 2004. https://apps.dtic.mil/sti/pdfs/ADA521638.pdf

[xi] James A. Baker III, Lee Hamilton, et al, *The Iraq Study Group Report*, (NY: Random House Vintage Books, December 2006) 22-26. https://www.govinfo.gov/content/pkg/GPO-IRAQSTUDYGROUP/pdf/GPO-IRAQSTUDYGROUP.pdf

[xii] Ashley Rowland Hwang Hae-Rym, "North Korean Defectors Struggle to Make it Work," Stars & Stripes, July 26, 2009. https://www.stripes.com/news/north-korean-defectors-struggle-to-make-it-work-1.93552

[xiii] Rudiger Dornbusch and Holger Wolf, "Economic Transition in Eastern Germany," Brookings Papers on Economic Activity, January 1992, 235-243. https://www.brookings.edu/wp-content/uploads/1992/01/1992a_bpea_dornbusch_wolf_alexander.pdf

[xiv] Barry Eichengreen, "World Development Report 2011 Background Case Note: Lessons from the Marshall Plan," World Bank, April 2010. https://web.worldbank.org/archive/website01306/web/pdf/wdr_2011_case_study_marshall_plan_1.pdf

[xv] Robert Looney, "Neoliberalism in a Conflict State: The Viability of Economic Shock Therapy in Iraq," Strategic Insights, vol. 3, issue 6, June 2004. https://apps.dtic.mil/sti/pdfs/ADA521633.pdf

[xvi] Faleh A. Jabar, "Iraq Four Years after the US-Led Invasion: Assessing the Crisis and Searching for a Way Forward," Policy Outlook, Carnegie Endowment for International Peace, July 2007. https://carnegieendowment.org/files/faleh_al_jabba_formatted.pdf

[xvii] Conference Report Transcript, "The Changing Nature of Warfare," CNAC Center for Strategic Studies, 33-35, 64-65, 70-71. https://www.cna.org/archive/CNA_Files/pdf/d0011005.a1.pdf

[xviii] Senate Hearing Transcript, *US Military Operations and Stabilization Activities in Iraq and Afghanistan*, Committee on Armed Services US Senate, February 3, June 23, and September 29, 2005. https://www.govinfo.gov/content/pkg/CHRG-109shrg27523/html/CHRG-109shrg27523.htm

[xix] Milan N. Vego, "Effects-Based Operations: A Critique," National Defense University Press, issue 4, 2nd quarter 2004. https://apps.dtic.mil/sti/pdfs/ADA521851.pdf

[xx] Larry Diamond, "Report from Baghdad," Hoover Digest, October 23, 2004. https://www.hoover.org/research/report-baghdad

[xxi] Milan N. Vego, "Effects-Based Operations: A Critique," National Defense University Press, issue 4, 2nd quarter 2004. https://apps.dtic.mil/sti/pdfs/ADA521851.pdf

[xxii] US Army Publication, *SMARTBOOK: Guerrilla Hunter Killer*, (DTIC: 5th Brigade, 2nd Infantry Division, (Stryker Brigade Combat Team) and

TF Stryker, version 9.5: July 4, 2009): i, 1-1, 1-2, 3-1.

[xxiii] James Dobbins, Seth G. Jones, et al., "Occupying Iraq: A History of the Coalition Provisional Authority," RAND Report Monograph, 2009, 98-102. https://www.rand.org/content/dam/rand/pubs/monographs/2009/RAND_MG847.pdf

[xxiv] Paul Yingling, "A Failure in Generalship," Armed Forces Journal, May 2007. https://web.archive.org/web/20100805071049/http://armedforcesjournal.com/2007/05/2635198

[xxv] William Finn Bennett, "Rules of Engagement in Iraq will be Tested," The San Diego Union Tribune, June 18, 2006. https://www.sandiegouniontribune.com/sdut-rules-of-engagement-in-iraq-will-be-tested-2006jun18-story.html

[xxvi] Public Record, *Lords Chamber Debate Iraq: Rules of Engagement*, UK Parliament, October 13, 2003. https://hansard.parliament.uk/Lords/2003-10-13/debates/b2749d9b-44d4-453c-ae9e-ec48f0ed44f8/IraqRulesOfEngagement

[xxvii] Liz Marlantes, "'Doctored' War Photos Ignite Controversy," ABC News, August 8, 2006. https://abcnews.go.com/US/story?id=2288892&page=1

[xxviii] Herschel Smith, "The NCOs Speak on Rules of Engagement," Captain's Journal, December 13th, 2006. https://www.captainsjournal.com/2006/12/13/the-ncos-speak-on-rules-of-engagement/

[xxix] Dan Ephron and Christian Caryl, "A Centurion's Emails: Through the eyes of a frontline fighter: The Marine captain asked for a tougher assignment. The one he got seemed all but impossible." Newsweek, November 6th, 2006. https://web.archive.org/web/20061116192156/http://www.msnbc.msn.com/id/15458906/site/newsweek/

[xxx] Don Gonyea, "Bush Defends Iraq Strategy, Resists Call to Leave," NPR, August 21, 2006. https://www.npr.org/2006/08/21/5685253/bush-defends-iraq-strategy-resists-call-to-leave

[xxxi] Bill Roggio, "The New Iraq Strategy," Long War Journal, January 10, 2007. https://www.longwarjournal.org/archives/2007/01/the_new_iraq_strateg.php

[xxxii] CJ Chivers, "Perfect Killing Method, but Clear Targets Are Few for Marines in Iraq," New York Times, November 22, 2006. https://web.archive.org/web/20220712053452/https://www.nytimes.com/2006/11/22/world/middleeast/22sniper.html

[xxxiii] Anne Barnard and Somini Sengupta, "Syria and Russia Appear Ready to Scorch Aleppo," New York Times, September 25, 2016. https://www.nytimes.com/2016/09/26/world/middleeast/syria-un-security-council.html

[xxxiv] Myriam Benraad, "Assessing AQI's Resilience After April's Leadership Decapitations," West Point Counterterrorism Center, vol. 3, issue 6, June 2010. https://ctc.westpoint.edu/assessing-aqis-resilience-after-aprils-leadership-decapitations/

[xxxv] Bill Roggio, "US Forces Kill Al-Qaeda in Iraq's Deputy Commander," The Long War Journal, October 15, 2008. https://www.longwarjournal.org/archives/2008/10/us_forces_kill_al_qa_1.php

[xxxvi] Fred W. Baker III, "Al Qaeda in Iraq Duped into Following Foreigners, Captured Operative Says," American Forces Press Service, July 19, 2007. https://www.army.mil/article/4101/al_qaeda_in_iraq_duped_into_following_foreigners_captured_operative_says

[xxxvii] Travis Patriquin, "Using Occam's Razor to Connect the Dots: The Ba'ath Party and the Insurgency in Tal Afar," Military Review, January – February 2007, 18-20. https://cgsc.contentdm.oclc.org/digital/collection/p124201coll1/id/159

[xxxviii] Aaron Y. Zelin, "Al-Qaeda in Syria: A Closer Look at ISIS (Part I)," The Washington Institute for Near East Policy, September 10, 2013. https://www.washingtoninstitute.org/policy-analysis/al-qaeda-syria-closer-look-isis-part-i

[xxxix] Aymenn Jawad Al-Tamimi, "The Syrian Rebel Groups Pulling in Foreign Fighters," BBC News, December 24, 2013. https://www.bbc.com/news/world-middle-east-25460397

[xl] Muhammad Abu Rumman, "The Politics of Sunni Armed Groups in Iraq," Carnegie Endowment for International Peace SADA, August 18, 2008. https://carnegieendowment.org/sada/20836

[xli] Joint Publication 3-24, *Counterinsurgency*, (Washington DC: Department of Defense: April 25, 2018, validated April 30, 2021): II-6 – II-7.

[xlii] US Army Publication, *SMARTBOOK: Guerrilla Hunter Killer*, (DTIC: 5th Brigade, 2nd Infantry Division, (Stryker Brigade Combat Team) and
TF Stryker, version 9.5: July 4, 2009): 5-1, 5-2.

[xliii] Aaron Y. Zelin, "Al-Qaeda in Syria: A Closer Look at ISIS (Part II)," The Washington Institute for Near East Policy, September 11, 2013. https://www.washingtoninstitute.org/policy-analysis/al-qaeda-syria-closer-look-isis-part-ii

[xliv] Andrea Scott, "The Second Battle of Fallujah: 15 Years Later," Marine Corps Times, November 27, 2019. https://www.marinecorpstimes.com/news/your-marine-corps/2019/11/28/the-second-battle-of-fallujah-15-years-later/

[xlv] Charles Recknagel and Kathleen Ridolfo, "From Fallujah to Qaim," Asia Times, May 13, 2005. https://web.archive.org/web/20060116191455/http://www.atimes.com/atimes/Middle_East/GE13Ak03.html

[xlvi] Jeffrey White, "Faces of Battle: The Insurgents in Falluja," The Washington Institute, November 29, 2004. https://www.washingtoninstitute.org/policy-analysis/faces-battle-insurgents-falluja

[xlvii] Ahmed Jalil, "Iraq: Thousands of Police Officers Have Died in the Line of Duty," The Conversation, May 14, 2021. https://theconversation.com/iraq-thousands-of-police-officers-have-died-in-the-line-of-duty-160881

[xlviii] Christine Tapp, Frederick Burkle, et al, "Iraq War Mortality Estimates: A Systemic Review," Conflict and Health Journal 2, 1, March 7, 2008. https://conflictandhealth.biomedcentral.com/articles/10.1186/1752-1505-2-1

[xlix] Edited and translated by Michael Howard and Peter Paret, *Carl Von Clausewitz's On War*, (NJ: Princeton University Press, 1989) 75.

[l] Joint Publication 3-24, *Counterinsurgency*, (Washington DC: Department of Defense: April 25, 2018, validated April 30, 2021): A-13.

[li] Joss Meakins, "The Other Side of the Coin: The Russians in Chechnya," Small Wars Journal, January 13, 2017. https://smallwarsjournal.com/jrnl/art/the-other-side-of-the-coin-the-russians-in-chechnya

[lii] Fred Weir, "Chechnya: Russia Declares 'Mission Accomplished' in Strong-Man State," The Christian Science Monitor, April 17, 2009. https://www.csmonitor.com/World/Europe/2009/0417/p06s07-woeu.html

[liii] Alan Cunningham, "Defeating the Tigers: The Tamil Tigers of Sri Lanka and How to Defeat a Successful Insurgency," The Small Wars Journal, August 1, 2022. https://smallwarsjournal.com/jrnl/art/defeating-tigers-tamil-tigers-sri-lanka-and-how-defeat-successful-insurgency

[liv] C. Bryson Hull and Ranga Sirilal, "Sri Lanka's Long War Reaches Climax, Tigers Concede," Reuters, May 17, 2009. https://www.reuters.com/article/us-srilanka-war/sri-lankas-long-war-reaches-climax-tigers-concede-idUSTRE54D1GR20090517

[lv] Colum Lynch, "U.N.: Sri Lanka's crushing of Tamil Tigers may have killed 40,000 civilians," Washington Post, April 21, 2011. https://www.washingtonpost.com/world/un-sri-lankas-crushing-of-tamil-tigers-may-have-killed-40000-civilians/2011/04/21/AFU14hJE_story.html

[lvi] Micah Zenko, "Remembering the Iraqi Uprising Twenty-Five Ago," Council on Foreign Relations, March 5, 2016. https://www.cfr.org/blog/remembering-iraqi-uprising-twenty-five-years-ago

[lvii] News Report, "Saddam Tells Iraqis to Feel No Guilt for Crushing Kurdish Rebellion," Canadian Broadcasting Corporation, September 11, 2006. https://www.cbc.ca/news/world/saddam-tells-iraqis-to-feel-no-guilt-for-crushing-kurdish-rebellion-1.582052

[lviii] US Marine Corps Publication FMRP 12-25, The Guerilla, (Washington DC: US Marine Corps: 1962, reprinted 1997): 120-121.

[lix] Ibid, 122-125.

[lx] Ibid, 128-143.

[lxi] Anna Louise Strachan, "Factors Behind the Fall of Mosul to ISIL (Daesh) in 2014," K4D Helpdesk, UK Dept. for International Development, January 17, 2017. https://assets.publishing.service.gov.uk/media/59808750e5274a170700002c/K4D_HDR_Factors_behind_the_fall_of_Mosul_in_2014.pdf

[lxii] Thanassis Cambanis, "The Surprising Appeal of ISIS," The Boston Globe, June 29, 2014. https://www.bostonglobe.com/ideas/2014/06/28/the-surprising-appeal-isis/l9YwC0GVPQ3i4eBXt1o0hI/story.html

[lxiii] Carl Pages, "To the Mountaintop and Back Again: Rise and Fall of General George B. McClellan." (Louisville: University of Louisville Thesis and Dissertations, 1977) pages 44-45. https://doi.org/10.18297/etd/1089

[lxiv] Ethan S. Rafuse, "Toward a Better Understanding of George McClellan," HistoryNet, March 14, 2018. https://www.historynet.com/toward-better-understanding-george-mcclellan/

[lxv] Robert J. Garvey, "The Downfall of Germany in WWI The Failure of Schlieffen's Design," NCO Journal, August 30, 2021. https://www.armyupress.army.mil/Journals/NCO-Journal/Archives/2021/August/The-Downfall-of-Germany-in-WWI/

[lxvi] Jung Chang and Jon Halliday, The Unknown Story of Mao, (NY: Random House's Anchor Books: 2005) 287-316.

[lxvii] Claire Brader, "Timeline of Taliban Offensive in Afghanistan," UK House of Lords Library, August 17, 2021. https://lordslibrary.parliament.uk/timeline-of-taliban-offensive-in-afghanistan/

[lxviii] Yasir Abbas and Dan Trombly, "Inside the Collapse of the Iraqi Army's 2nd Division," War on the Rocks, July 1, 2014. https://warontherocks.com/2014/07/inside-the-collapse-of-the-iraqi-armys-2nd-division/

[lxix] Rebecca Grant, "The Siege of Kobani," Air & Space Forces Magazine, August 29, 2018. https://www.airandspaceforces.com/article/the-siege-of-kobani/

[lxx] John Spencer and Jayson Geroux, "Urban Warfare Project Case Study Series #2 – Mosul," The Modern Warfare Institute, September 15, 2021. https://mwi.usma.edu/urban-warfare-project-case-study-2-battle-of-mosul/

Chapter 15: Phase I Operational Lines of Effort for the Foreign-Backed Elites

—Nudge and Hold; LOE 1: Shadow Financing

The previous three chapters focused on the strategic level of this hypothetical civil war with the potential issues facing each faction and the considerations both sides need to make to achieve optimal strategic goals. These next chapters evaluate the operational level of this hypothetical civil war scenario to determine what lines of effort the FBE and NRF need to achieve their unique optimal conditions for victory. Lines of effort (LOE) are organizational means that combat forces use to logically align needed tasks to accomplish specific missions to have the desired outcome. Each line of effort is tailored to support actions that will culminate in achieving victory. Both the FBE and NRF will need to organize their LOEs around their respective strategic plans and divide these LOEs by each phase of the strategic plan. The FBE has a simpler strategic plan in Catalonia 2.0 because they would start out as the dominating faction in the conflict with far more resources, legal protections, and the general public's acceptance about the anocracy's broken corrupt system due to acclimatization and familiarity. To succeed, the FBE would execute two overlapping phases for Catalonia 2.0. The faction's LOEs can be categorized under either: Phase One - shifting the Western nation's anocracy into a full-fledged autocracy and Phase Two - provoke the NRF into fighting a 3GW-style war to eliminate dissent.

Catalonia 2.0 Phase I—Nudge and Hold:

The FBE are a loose confederacy of corrupt competing social and economic elites united only in common cause of acquiring more power for themselves, even at the cost of their home nation's well-being. These corrupt elites have been encouraged by their foreign benefactor to destabilize their home nation and provoke civil war with the promise of acquiring total political power as the end state. Western nations' civic societies are far too developed with checks against state power for the FBE to simply launch an overt coup. Instead, the elites must gently "nudge" society into accepting a more autocratic system by convincing the public such a move will better society. This means the FBE must work by proxy using co-opted institutions, industries, and culturally influential persons to convince the majority that old beliefs and customs are outdated or detrimental. Once society willingly cedes greater authority to the corruptly controlled institutions, then the FBE must hold onto that newly acquired authority and then repeat this activity again and again until the anocracy becomes an autocracy. Each one of Phase One's LOEs to nudge people into giving more power and then holding onto the acquired power must be done as covertly as possible. These LOEs' focus is keeping the apathetic majority pliable to ceding control and become acquiescent to the ever-increasing autocratic system without revealing any obvious malicious actions or motivations.

LOE 1: Shadow Financing

The FBE cannot operate openly as a contemporary aristocracy that acts with impunity. If the public perceives the FBE this way, the public backlash will lead to an immediate loss of power as the FBE's proxies and political allies would desert them in order to protect their own fortunes. This means the efforts to nudge the public to accept autocracy must be done covertly while simultaneously portraying any dissent as socially regressive or terroristic in nature. Subtlety requires the FBE to convince the public that they want autocratic solutions without realizing they are being manipulated into accepting them. Covert actions via lobbying, extorting, and influencing by proxy are quintessential for Phase One to succeed. Such covert actions require the FBE to maintain positive but inconspicuous links to their proxies in industrial, activistic, government, and cultural institutions to have sufficient influence to push society towards the FBE's final objective. The FBE's self-serving objectives led by people with a managerial technocratic mindset means most FBE leaders would lack any inspirational flare, charisma, or commanding presence to instill loyalty by personality like Julius Caesar, Thomas Jefferson, or General Robert E. Lee. Consequently, the FBE's source of loyalty will need to be transactional in nature with quid pro quos in financial or power terms. The covert funding LOE is the center of the FBE's Phase One as no other LOE can be acted upon without the means of acquiring and ensuring loyalty of the FBE's proxies. In the modern era, the numerous means of facilitating monies, appointments, and other incentives provide the FBE with a cornucopia of options. The best part of being connected with established institutions is most FBE members would have insider knowledge of the rules and monitoring processes to keep most of these loyalty-buying transactions within the letter, if not the spirit, of the law. More legally dubious transactions would also still be carried out to influence more corrupt elements of the Western nation's political class to selectively enforce the law on FBE's behalf to bypass any potential restrictions.

Options and Methods:

The rich complexity of international trade and activist politics means there are many avenues for sustaining the FBE proxies covertly. The FBE must prioritize keeping their funding lines of communication open throughout the entire conflict with both their proxies as well as their foreign benefactors. So, the first order of business is sustaining financial ties to their benefactor. The FBE leaders would likely be divided broadly into two camps regarding their foreign benefactors. The first are the "useful idiots" who are either ideologically or naively convinced their foreign benefactors are true partners who will work with the FBE to create a new utopian world or nation. The second camp are the realists who know their benefactors are using them but are willing to do anything, including sacrificing their nation's well-being, for personal power and greed. This second group intends to use the foreign benefactor as allies of the moment and dispose of the foreign partners later. Unfortunately for the second camp, if the Western nation has been pushed far enough along to the point of civil conflict, then this second group would likely have become too interdependent with the foreign benefactor to actually break away. This means the FBE must keep their foreign ties to sustain finances, operate outside the Western nation's legal scrutiny, and avoid any rifts within the FBE towards their foreign puppet masters.

Unlike Hollywood's *Manchurian Candidate* movie where a traitor actively works directly at the behest for a foreign power, the FBE's actions can never be that straight forward. Outright collaboration or capitulation to the foreign benefactor's demands would give the game away but FBE also cannot allow the Western nation's cultural and political policies turn completely against the foreign benefactor either. The FBE's balanced approach will be the basis for all their transactional quid pro quos between the FBE leaders and the supporting adversarial nation. Slow rolling, delaying, or diluting new legal rules, guidelines, or policies that hinder the adversarial nation will provide the foreign benefactor of the FBE sufficient time to legally outmaneuver the Western nation to maintain economic dependence. This has been seen in real world examples with China's Huawei's efforts to bribe public officials in developing countries, but the same tactics can be used anywhere.[i] This also protects the anocracy as these diluted actions give the public the perception something is being done without doing so. Even substantive actions can be hindered by creating additional layers of procedure without designating anyone accountable for implementing the new rules to maximize bureaucratic inertia. Inertia kills any corrective actions and keeps the FBE's backer functioning in the Western nation.[ii] This kind of subtle sabotage wouldn't be limited to just trade or finance but also legal processes as well. The FBE could use its corrupt proxies to encourage legal or procedural cases that are deliberately mishandled to portray the accused foreign benefactor-based company or person as a victim to get cases dismissed or set legal precedent in the foreign benefactor's favor. All of these actions help the foreign benefactor keep access to the Western nation's markets and policymaking while repaying their FBE collaborators with donations, contracts or business ventures.

The foreign benefactor's support to the FBE's leadership would be done in a number of ways and many of which overlap with the methods of shadow financing the FBE itself would use to sustain their proxies within the Western nation. The FBE relies on international systems for their existence because most major financial and investment profit-making activities are tied to globalist trade and would be the most prominent means of financing their operations. Yet, obvious tools such as international companies, venture capitalists, and banks would unlikely be the main effort of financial support because these groups still have reputational and legal boundaries that impose some limitations. Instead, the most useful and common option would be utilizing international nonprofit organizations because such groups have several advantages. Nonprofits receive less legal scrutiny due to tax-exempt status, can gain access to almost anywhere under a variety of pretenses, and public sentiment dislikes governments trying to crack down on nonprofits. This is the same reason international terror groups prefer using them to fund their own operations.[iii] International nonprofits and foundations are also predominately led by private individuals with the wealthiest having the preponderance of influence within these organizations.[iv] FBE leaders are mostly wealthy private individuals. The public and governments are suspicious of any business transactions or trade as profit is the clear motive and are obviously prone to abuse or corruption. Nonprofits carry out actions that can manipulate emotional perceptions to give the veneer of altruism, righting wrongs, self-sacrifice for the greater good, or philanthropy. Anyone criticizing such activity risks being labeled as selfish, sleezy, or inhumane which also makes law enforcement authorities more risk averse into investigating too closely. This enables nonprofits to generate large sums of money without much criticism.[v] Nonprofits can operate in legal gray areas far more effectively than companies or banks as many FBE-related transactions would have political rather than profit motives.[vi], [vii] Trying to sustain proxies with politically intended funding from obvious for-profit would be at greater risk of being noticed, however, there is a loophole for that option as well.

Linking business contracts and activities with non-profit motivations in the name of the "greater good" would be the most ideal way of obscuring covert funding of subversion.[viii] Western nations, without exception, are at an apex of economic prosperity in human history which has left many persons in the middle and upper class self-conscious of their relative wealth. To rationalize their abundance and lifestyle, many will endorse nonprofit activism as a means of penance for having so much compared to the non-Western world.[ix] Although the West is now more secular, the concept of penance or absolution never went away, it just changed forms. Personal donations to philanthropy or activist groups doing something to "benefit" society or the world is the replacement for tithes to the Church for many in the West. A more popular alternative to donations is tax breaks and subsidies given to companies and groups that help with whatever nonprofit issue the FBE hide behind. People like this arrangement because people already pay taxes and feel they are getting the added benefit of social penance without having to pay extra. Nonprofits also instill its members with ideological blinders that helps keep internal scrutiny to a minimum. Unlike nefarious organizations in fiction, the FBE will not have every member of every proxy organization being fully in the know and must keep any skimming or reallocation of funds to FBE activities discreet.

This is where the FBE's Nimbyist proxies have the most use as these persons will be driven by the messages of social activism. A subversive conspiracy is easier if the journey to the goal is not planned, only the end state, and the Nimbyists will be self-driven to achieve that end state by the FBE's activist messaging. Nimbyists will pressure taxpayers into donating to FBE shell companies and nonprofits while silencing criticism or suspicion with public shaming campaigns. Nimbyists will mostly be in the dark too because their egos will drive them to act on their own to self-justify their irredeemably selfish and self-absorbed natures and don't need much prompting from the FBE. Their public shaming campaigns silence dissent using guilt, fear, and shame to emotionally shake down the non-activist population into giving money to the FBE-linked organizations. Nimbyists themselves would likely avoid doing the same and only contribute a minimal token of funds as they believe their vocal declarations and platitudes in the name of FBE-linked activism are penance enough.

Profit-motivated companies would not be the main vehicle of financial support, but they still would contribute. Venture capital firms have many partners which also make them ideal vehicles to funnel funds for political subversion. Private venture companies can disguise these funds by contributing to "social improvement" activities which don't have any profit-linked outcome and consequently cannot evaluate where all the money being contributed actually goes. Companies that don't cooperate will not get tax credits, or pass regulatory inspections, or will receive Nimbyist social media attackers in abundance. Of course, these are just publicly traded firms, there are still the more traditional means of laundering and bribing done at the behest of individuals too. As the "Panama Papers" disclosure demonstrated, international real estate transactions can obfuscate billions of dollars globally, making it an ideal vehicle of subversive trade, especially if the transactions are linked to socially or politically connected persons.[x] One hypothetical example could be derived from China's crackdown of their billionaires hiding their money overseas in real estate ventures. Instead of arresting or fining some of these Chinese billionaires, the CCP could blackmail some of these billionaires into "contributing" to international foundations that are covertly subverting Western nations. In 2014, before the CCP's tax crackdown, Hong Kong identified over 22,000 tax haven clients which means China would have a large pool of rich proxies to unofficially pay China's allies in Western industry, media, and culture.[xi] The FBE could receive such donations the same way from foreign benefactors and from amongst themselves as FBE individuals use personally created philanthropy foundations for whatever cause, some real, some not, to receive such subversion-related funds. Other means include art dealing where "modern" art is sold for far more than the art is truly worth to launder money or pay people exorbitant lecture fees, etc.[xii] These transactions are all legal, and since they are for political instead of financial motives, these would be impossible to prove being used illicitly.

Illicit actions will still be needed though, especially for co-opting senior political figures. Most FBE proxies will be economic and cultural in nature but moving the society into autocracy is ultimately a political goal. Corrupt politicians are obvious proxies, but corrupt political appointees would also be needed to keep any legal authorities from investigating FBE activities. Coopted political appointees would selectively enforce rules, deliberately discredit institutional trust so the government workers become insulated from the public and implement any anocratic policies created by corrupt FBE-linked politicians. In the United States, political action committees are regularly criticized from members of both parties on bringing in large sums of accountable monies into politics however, the European politicians are not clean of influence either.[xiii], [xiv] The European Union had poor accounting of its finances for years while good old-fashioned bribery still reaches even the upper echelons of society.[xv], [xvi]

With both licit and illicit means of covert funding, the FBE has many means to sustain this LOE in any civil conflict. In fact, violence in the initial stages of the 5GW conflict would likely spur more contributions from the frightened apolitical public. Until the FBE nudge their Western nation into a complete autocracy, keeping this LOE operating is critical to the FBE's survival and success.

Strengths:

Shadow financing for the FBE has two major advantages. The first is its stealth element in how outside parties trying to find funds that directly support the FBE's activities will be very difficult to discern from other legitimate activities. Political subversion uses the same funding mechanisms as legitimate political activism, and the same funds could support both simultaneously. The other major advantage is that most of the activity is legal and will be protected by legal institutions. For the politically connected FBE, lobbying for how rules and regulations are applied ensure the FBE will avoid any legal scrutiny and be very difficult for critics to prove anything nefarious. Official media will also likely be owned by companies linked to FBE nonprofit foundations or investments that will incentivize censorship on the topic. As the most important LOE, its abundance of legal protections and inconspicuous presence means the FBE will have steady income stream to keep its proxies loyal and functioning.

Weaknesses:

Although the networks and financial streams are easy to obfuscate and complex enough to make it nearly impossible for the NRF to disrupt their flows, the human element remains the weakest link. The money sources are abundant but only a few key persons can or should be entrusted with such a critical role as relaying monies to the FBE's proxies. The financial networks are vulnerable at the nodes themselves as only a few persons at each node will have the critical information necessary to direct the funds for FBE operations. The most likely group of persons entrusted by the FBE leadership would be the lawyers as these individuals have additional privileges and are required to know where all the skeletons are within their respective FBE funding organizations. They can operate and move between funding nodal organizations within the shadow financing networks without suspicion and relay key instructions for funding requirements while remaining within the letter of the law. If the NRF builds a thorough intelligence collecting mechanism that focuses on a few key nodes, then the NRF should be able to identify high value individuals to be targeted to disrupt funding nodes.

The other key weakness is the FBE members' penchant for corruption. As seen with many political and social scandals, individuals whose avarice exceeds their common sense are found in abundance within circles of power and influence. These individuals maybe supporting the FBE with illicit funding activities or they are enriching themselves at the cost of everything else. Either way, the NRF could use these weak links in the Shadow Financing LOE to blackmail, kill, or publicly expose them to disrupt key FBE operations. These weaknesses can only be exploited by an NRF that invested its time and effort into building an aggressive intelligence gathering organization using both cyber and real-world vulnerabilities to disrupt FBE funding.

---

[i] Masood Farivar, "Bribery, Corruption Charges Follow Huawei Around World," Voice Of America, February 11, 2019. https://www.voanews.com/a/huawei-alleged-corruption-and-bribery/4781242.html

[ii] Gary Hamel and Michele Zanini, "What We Learned About Bureaucracy from 7,000 HBR Readers," Harvard Business Review, August 10, 2017. https://hbr.org/2017/08/what-we-learned-about-bureaucracy-from-7000-hbr-readers?referral=00563&spMailingID=17853288&spUserID=MTM5NjExMzY1MTQzS0&spJobID=1080656592&spReportId=MTA4MDY1NjU5MgS2

[iii] Matthew Levitt, "Charitable Organizations and Terrorist Financing: A War on Terror Status-Check," The Washington Institute for Near East Policy, March 19, 2004. https://www.washingtoninstitute.org/policy-analysis/charitable-organizations-and-terrorist-financing-war-terror-status-check

[iv] Noah Buhaya, Sophie Alexander, and Ben Steverman, "Wealthy Use Loophole to Reap Tax Breaks and Delay Giving Money Away," Bloomberg Markets, October 2, 2022. https://www.bloomberg.com/news/features/2022-10-03/rich-use-tax-loophole-to-get-deductions-now-for-donating-later

[v] Erin Rubin, "Is Big Philanthropy Democracy Deferred? Global Study Shows the Power of the Ultra-Rich," Non-Profit Quarterly, April 27, 2018. https://nonprofitquarterly.org/big-philanthropy-democracy-philanthropy-study-power-ultra-rich/

[vi] Lauren L. Ferry, Emile Hafner-Burton, and Christina J. Schneider, "Catch Me If You Care: International Development Organizations and National Corruption," Review of International Organizations, 11 January 2020. https://ehb.ucsd.edu/pdfs/cic.pdf

[vii] Mark Steven LeClair, "Malfeasance in the Charitable Sector: Determinants of "Soft" Corruption at Nonprofit Organizations," Public Integrity, vol 21, I 1, 2019. https://www.tandfonline.com/doi/full/10.1080/10999922.2017.1422310

111

[viii] Mark Rosenman, "Trust and Corruption," Philanthropy News Digest, March 12, 2014. https://philanthropynewsdigest.org/features/commentary-and-opinion/trust-and-corruption

[ix] Noha Sadek, "The Phenomenology and Dynamics of Wealth Shame: Between Moral Responsibility and Moral Masochism," The Journal of the American Psychoanalytic Association, vol 68, I 4, September 14, 2020. https://journals.sagepub.com/doi/abs/10.1177/0003065120949972?journalCode=apaa

[x] Will Fitzgibbon and Michael Hudson, "Five Years Later, Panama Papers Still Having a Big Impact," The International Consortium of Investigative Journalists, April 3, 2021. https://www.icij.org/investigations/panama-papers/five-years-later-panama-papers-still-having-a-big-impact/

[xi] Marina Walker Guevara, Gerard Ryle, et al., "Leaked Records Reveal Offshore Holdings of China's Elite," The International Consortium of Investigative Journalists, January 21, 2014. https://www.icij.org/investigations/offshore/leaked-records-reveal-offshore-holdings-of-chinas-elite/

[xii] Government Report, "Study of the Facilitation of Money Laundering and Terror Finance Through the Trade in Works of Art," US Treasury, February 2022. https://home.treasury.gov/system/files/136/Treasury_Study_WoA.pdf

[xiii] Information page, Political Action Committees, OpenSecrets.org, accessed August 11, 2022. https://www.opensecrets.org/political-action-committees-pacs/2020

[xiv] Chisun Lee, "How Politicians Use Nonprofits to Hide Dark Money," Brennan Center, March 29, 2018. https://www.brennancenter.org/our-work/analysis-opinion/how-politicians-use-nonprofits-hide-dark-money

[xv] Cain Burdeau, "Audit: EU Does Bad Job of Tackling Fraud," Courthouse News Service, January 10, 2019. https://www.courthousenews.com/audit-eu-does-bad-job-of-tackling-fraud/

[xvi] News Report, "Belgium Charges Another EU Lawmaker with Corruption," Reuters, February 12, 2023. https://www.reuters.com/markets/europe/belgium-charges-another-eu-lawmaker-with-corruption-2023-02-12/

Chapter 16: Phase I Operational Line of Effort 2 for the Foreign-Backed Elites — Sterilize Cultural Creativity to Impose Insipid Conformity

The human race exists in an entropic universe where everything decays, including human systems. Societies have peaks of accomplishment and success before eventually experiencing a period of decline. In the case of the West, that decay is in the form of anocracy where representational institutions decline from originally representing voters and citizens to eventually only supporting a corrupt collection of interest groups. This is a natural progression of democratic republics after having an excess of success with economic prosperity, social stability, and strong societal institutions that inevitably create that complacency and decadence that allows corruption to flourish over time like in the ancient Roman Republic. Anocracy is a natural occurring stage because the self-correcting societal mechanisms no longer function due to the decadent societies' neglect, but autocracy is not necessarily inevitable. Autocracy requires an advanced society, even a weakened decadent one, to have a considerable shift in cultural and personal expectations of a society's role for that to occur. The FBE's main challenge to nudge the Western nation into accepting autocracy is not the government because it answers to society, but the political culture that society uses as its guide.

Political culture is a collection of rites, customs, and beliefs on why and how a society should be governed. The political culture is a collection of unwritten laws that drive social instincts with democratic-republican societies inherently opposing the concept of autocratic rule as legitimate. So, the main operational LOE for Phase I's success is for the FBE to gradually change the political culture by nudging the cultural institutions to shift the Western nation's societal expectations. This is particularly challenging because the FBE lacks a unifying message or a strong, effective, and charismatic leader. In fiction, autocracies attain power because of a charismatic exceptional individual with genuine leadership skills taking charge such as *Star Wars'* Emperor Palpatine of the Galactic Empire or more fittingly, the computer game *Deus Ex's* Lucius DeBeers as the Prima Illuminatus leader of the Illuminati. In practical reality, the self-serving internal machinations of the FBE would prevent the rise of a Caesar, Napoleon, or Lenin. FBE leaders would be composed of ivory towered former managers and advisors to the previous generation of more competent elites propelled into leadership positions because they sycophantly obeyed their former bosses. The FBE relies on a foreign puppet master to sustain them because they cannot sustain themselves. Therefore, changing the culture and tricking the public into accepting autocratic rule is the FBE's only option.

The FBE's concept of autocratic rule would likely mimic their foreign benefactor's system of government and its priority of maintaining the leadership's power over any societal advancement or public benefit. Keeping uninspiring technocrats in power requires the autocratic system to be totalitarian, not authoritarian, in nature to direct and micromanage all aspects of life within a society so the leaders' power is unchallenged. In contrast, authoritarian regimes like Chile's Augusto Pinochet, Rome's Augustus Caesar, or the feudal kingdoms of Europe only held power over key levers of state but remained constrained by the expectations of the already established culture. To achieve totalitarian control, the society's culture must change to emphasize the concept of conformity and the needs of the group over the individual to eliminate any dissent or rival power structures. This LOE needs the FBE's coopted cultural proxies to instill the ideas that the FBE-controlled state will be mother, father, priest, muse, teacher, and savior to the public so they willingly accept conceptual changes to the idea of freedom. Instead of the traditional concepts of political freedom and individual agency, the FBE's cultural proxies will modify the concept to mean freedom from responsibility and worry as the more enlightened technocrats will solve all woes.

How this is done would have to be tailored differently to each Western nation as the political cultures have different levels of susceptibility. The intensity of cultural manipulation depends on how much the society already inherently conforms to and defers to official authority. The FBE of a western continental European nation would have to carry out fewer antics and social disruptions because nations like Germany and France have societies that often complain but still accede to officialdom regularly. For instance, the French are renowned as a nation of strikers and demonstrations against the government, but this occurs overwhelmingly against proposals that reduce the role of the state safety net.[i], [ii] Objections over shorter work weeks, reduced protections for civil servants, or loss of farming subsidies don't risk any FBE's efforts to subvert such a nation.[iii], [iv] All of these demands require continued dependence on the state hence the culture is already mostly molded to the needs of a corrupt FBE. There are occasional demonstrations against the state, like its immigration policy, speed cameras, and fuel tax, but overall, this restive population typically accedes to the state after its protests once they receive one or two financial concessions.[v], [vi], [vii] So, there is no reason to alter most continental nations', cultures, like France's, too much because acceding to the state 90% of the time is more than sufficient. Even the populist National Rally Party of Marine Le Pen still promises statist positive economic freedoms of subsidies, taxing the wealthy and intervene in minimum wages.[viii] The most recent serious uprising against European elites is that of European farmers against the "green" and Ukrainian policies of the European Union in December 2023 to 2024. This was the result of European elites overestimating the placidity of electorates they believed they had sufficiently bought off. The farmers were not angered by state intervention itself, but state intervention that changed preferences to other EU interest groups at the cost of the farmers. They are not demanding more free markets or less state control, but to reprioritize that technocratic power to support domestic food producers.[ix] Regardless of the merit of the protests, these still reinforce the cultural expectation and understanding of deference to state power. The only argument is which political subgroup gets the majority of state preferences in subsidy and legal protections.

The last genuine French rebellion against state encroachment and the French government occurred in 2005 against the EU Constitution Referendum where they voted "no" even though their elites wanted the referendum to pass to further federalize Europe which would also mean more access to EU subsidies.[x] So, the French government and their elitist backers changed the constitution and had a later government sign the Treaty of Lisbon, bypassing another referendum, which established many of the powers sought under the 2005 constitutional proposals.[xi] There was no further impetus by the French public to punish the state a second time. Despite their protests and nationalist sentiment, the French have a very technocratic system and do little to actually change it.

However, the foreign benefactor's FBEs in the Anglosphere would have to drastically undermine the cultures as the concept of individual rights are the strongest within these nations. Unlike their continental counterparts, the British will protest or demonstrate more often when the state attempts to acquire more power over daily life. A prominent recent example occurred in 2023 when Londoners actively sabotaged the CCTV networks that enforce Ultra Low Emission Zones that fine drivers with noncompliant cars. These zones were extended to all of London provoking a campaign of sabotage against what many of the citizens considered an overreach of government interference into daily lives, not just the financial burden.[xii] Elsewhere in the Anglosphere there was Canada's "Trucker Protests" in 2022.[xiii] Regardless of the merits of the protests, these types of demonstrations are more often framed around the concepts of individual liberty rather than positive economic rights in Continental Europe. For the FBE to succeed in the Anglosphere, the culture would have to be discredited with an aggressive campaign of manipulation to successfully portray the ludicrousness of individual liberty. The FBE cultural proxies would need to encourage activities that cause as much anarchy as possible to convince the public that individual liberties are abused too much by opportunists and that radical collectivist solutions are required. The Anglosphere would be the most challenging, some more than others, and take years of berating the individualist culture with over-the-top incidents, violent encounters, and cartoonishly zealous behavior of FBE proxies to weaken the credibility of individualism. Therefore, Continental Europe would have less obvious acts of cultural undermining by its corrupted FBE members than the crazed actions the Anglosphere FBEs would have to carry out.

Eradicate Mockery:

Complete conformity of a society must occur for a totalitarian autocracy to gain and maintain power. Since this kind of state controls all aspects of life, the state must be more than just a government, it must be perceived to be God-like. For such a state to function, every facet of society must obey and carry out all the centralized planning of the state leadership with religious fervor; otherwise, the ornate bureaucracy created to manage such a complex system becomes dysfunctional. Comprehensive obedience of the state's subjects only happens if the masses believe the state can achieve utopian miracles of effective governance and is above reproach. For heaven on Earth to truly occur, the leaders would have to have perfect information, perfect understanding, perfect timing, and perfect implementation to achieve the miraculous society promised by totalitarian utopians. Instead, reality makes these abilities impossible to achieve with the resultant state filled with corrupt, delusional, neurotic, and narcissistic individuals who put themselves above all else. Such an autocracy must hide its faults to keep obedience and devotion and cannot allow the public to notice the flaws or have doubts in their minds. The first major step towards that goal is the elimination of mockery.

Mockery, parody, and comedy in general are often used to highlight the faults of individuals and society itself. In non-totalitarian societies, comedy acts as a social pressure valve to relieve some of the tension and frustrations of people fed up with life's circumstances. Even medieval kings of Europe and Asia had court jesters who would sometimes even parody the king.[xiv] This occurred because authoritarian leaders didn't have to pretend to know everything to make society perfect, but for totalitarian regimes, mockery can be fatal because comedy discourages blind obedience. Yet, it is intrinsic to human nature and cannot be completely eliminated, even with fear of execution or exile. Instead, the FBE would need to redefine comedy to make mockery only acceptable when it is against their opponents with comedians comporting to the FBE's new concept of what constitutes mainstream social propriety and taboo. Anything related to the anocracy, the FBE, or FBE supporters cannot be singled out for mockery in any fashion and those people who attempt it must suffer censure or punishment. If the FBE can redefine humor from mocking the ludicrousness of life and society in general to the narrower parameter of just mocking the FBE's enemies, then the NRF's ability to rally support within the public will stymie. This doesn't mean eliminating all negative feelings, biases, taboos, or prejudices to make society nicer or more considerate. It simply means the FBE inverts all the negative emotions of society to enable hate, belittlement, and mockery towards only dissidents and FBE critics.

FBE cultural proxies would use both positive and negative reinforcement to prevent mockery of the FBE with the positive being either financial rewards or increased social clout enabled by FBE-controlled media. Negative reinforcement would most efficiently come from ostracization and possibly physical threats that cannot be traced back to the FBE themselves. To shield themselves, the FBE's cultural proxies would use the Atomized and Nimbyist elements to socially harass comedians to deprive them of income, peace of mind, or a public voice. Social media can exacerbate the vocal complaints of the Atomized who could falsely accuse the dissenting comedians of socially unacceptable prejudice or inciting life-threatening violence. These groups could either make the dissident comedian grovel to acknowledge the legitimacy of the FBE's cultural standards or remove the targeted comedian from public view. Meanwhile, the FBE's Nimbyists could pressure companies and cultural institutions to drop public endorsements of comedians or disrupt their financial support mechanisms. In time, the public and mainstream comedic institutions would be conditioned to accept the FBE's new standards of what can be acceptably mocked.

Such actions are not limited to totalitarian regimes either, these actions are also often used by political and social leaders who repeatedly fail in public or are notoriously corrupt. Mockery can be career-ending for these inept and corrupt persons who cannot defend their actions with logic or intellectual persuasion. So, like the tyrants, corrupt and incompetent leaders will also resort to stopping mockery. These poor-performing politicians' actions are very important to the FBE to provide a guide on exactly what not to do. A real-world example of this occurred in Scotland where then-First Minister Nicola Sturgeon's Scottish government arrested and punished a comedic Youtuber named Mark Meechan with the online persona name "Count Dankula".[xv] Mr. Meechan was arrested for teaching and then recording his pet dog giving a "Nazi-style salute" as an annoyance prank on his then-girlfriend. He posted it to YouTube leading to his arrest, conviction, and being fined £800 for farcical humor.[xvi] This action pleased the Scottish government and their activist proxies, but the negative consequences accumulated over time. The trial expanded Count

Dankula's social influence and convinced many overseas observers the Scottish government had the maturity of a thin-skinned whining petulant child. Some comments on the issue pointed out how the comedian Mel Brooks would have to be given a life sentence in Scotland. Others have pointed to the irony that the Nazi Party tried to prosecute a Finnish pharmaceutical industrialist named Tor Borg for teaching his dog to give a "Nazi salute" in 1941.[xvii] Although the Nazis ultimately decided against a criminal prosecution, even the Nazis understood teaching a dog to give a Nazi salute is mockery, not an endorsement.

Given the poor performance of the Scottish government, the zealousness of this prosecution is best explained as an attempt to divert attention away from the government's many failures. Ranging from minor ironies like the then-Scottish Minister of Transport driving around without car insurance[xviii] to alleged corruption like the "Ferry Fiasco" where a government-connected company suspiciously won a contract to build two ferries that cost three times more than the original budget.[xix] The government of Nicola Sturgeon was plagued with a reputation for being both corrupt and incompetent which contributed to a collapse of social services, a spike in the Scottish crime rate, and deteriorating public transportation. [xx] The FBE would do better than to follow the Sturgeon government's frankly obvious and amateur diversion tactics because subtlety is critical to the success of behavior modification to cultural comedy standards.

Strengths:

Limiting mockery and comedy narrows concepts of thought within the general population. By changing the standards of comedic taboos to defend the pro-FBE elements, many nonpolitically active members of the population will unknowingly advocate and protect FBE interests. Most people want to fit into a society and be a positive contributor to it so they will often accept non-substantive arguments from the FBE if these new mockery standards are declared by recognized authoritative figures. Once the FBE can get the public to accept FBE concepts as sacred, it is as effective as calling something heretical in the Catholic kingdoms of the Middle Ages. Once the FBE becomes the Western nation's sacred cow, convincing the public to comply on more important issues of society is much easier. In the case of comedy, most authority figures are cultural rather than state or business which makes cultural institutions a priority target for subversion.

Weaknesses:

Even the most apolitical and unobservant people will notice a confidence trick if it is carried out sloppily. Scotland's inept handling of "Count Dankula" boosted his profile many times beyond what it was beforehand because many saw the act as a diversion away from state failures. Getting caught amplifies the mockery many times over and is a considerable risk for the FBE. It is essential that any effort to persecute or silence comedians be perceived as being instigated by the Atomized proxies, not the financially and politically powerful FBE proxy organizations behind the Atomized. The Atomized can always claim victimhood or protecting something that is vulnerable, but if the state or corporations lead the censorious effort, the public will view the act as "punching down". The state or corporations that are FBE proxies must appear to be acquiescing to popular pressure instigated by the "victimized" Atomized activists. However, traitorous narcissists that would exist in such a grouping like the FBE have little to no sense of humor and risk miscalculating their persecutions. Furthermore, the NRF's allies could use failed acts of censorship to destroy FBE-backed censors' power by convincing most of the public to just ignore all their accusations. FBE proxies who fail to silence their mockers will become parodies themselves and lose all authoritative aura and credibility. The FBE will need to use their media proxies to dampen any fallout from failure to reduce risk while the NRF allies must be discredited in other ways like being accused of, or better yet entrapped into, committing something heinous. FBE must coordinate all censorious efforts to maximize impact against the NRF and dissenters, otherwise inept proxies risk exacerbating failures as they blindly target opponents with little consideration to the broader impact.

The "Lei Feng-ing" of Morality:

Anocracies are half-way to being autocracies as corruption and apathy plague the society but would still retain the traditional concepts of Western morality. To move the Western nation from anocracy to autocracy requires the FBE to successfully redefine morality because embracing utopian autocracy requires a different mindset that rejects traditional Western concepts of civic obligations and personal responsibility. The best suited moral system for the FBE's subversion of society is utopian collectivism. The reason is the ideal utopian person's beliefs reject the concept of individual agency or inherent character traits and strictly adheres to the mantra of humans being born as an inherently good social creature and evil is created by poor nurturing.[xxi] From this assumption, the utopians believe people's thoughts and behaviors are conditioned by social engineering impressed upon them by the society. To the utopians, society is an artificial structure of arbitrary standards that systemically nurtures its people into behaving in certain ways so, if a society is badly structured then the nurturing becomes corrupted and causes all social ills.

To utopians, individual action and responsibility doesn't exist because they believe only systemic constructs dictate human behavior. Utopians must believe this because collectivist utopia can only work if human beings are inherently good and all negative behavior can be solved by social conditioning by a powerful totalitarian state. Consequently, this means utopians will blame everything that is evil on systems or organizations that are responsible for "nurturing" and ignore any effort for individual accountability. This is why the FBE would endorse many aspects of totalitarian collectivist utopianism, even if the FBE don't truly believe in it because it is the one political moral system that doesn't hold leaders or managers responsible for failure, tyranny, or corruption. This concept of the group determining the ability, success, and moral character of a person is a shared commonality between the Nazi race-centric belief system and Communist class-centric ideology which is why the FBE can and will use both wings of extremism as unwitting pawns.[xxii]

The contemporary Western nation, even as an anocracy, is guided by liberal Lockean concepts making totalitarian rule an anathema to the society and will hinder all FBE efforts for autocracy until the morality is changed. Classical Western morals are premised on humans having an intrinsic nature that is inherently self-serving with each Western society having variations on how best to constrain these baser instincts by supporting the natural law and its natural rights.[xxiii] This requires some personal accountability with expectations of people dutifully contributing to be a part of society rather than expecting society to plan and solve everything for every person. This is a moral code that acknowledges there is both a private and public role for each person and society needs to balance these requirements. Ethics and morality determine the form of the society

115

and culture helps shape these ethics and morality. Since the FBE must nudge the Western nation's ethics and morality into rejecting all these Lockean traditions and embrace collectivist utopianism in the name of "helping others", changing cultural standards is the first major step.

In China, the CCP and PLA created a fictitious soldier named Lei Feng to be used as an ideological icon promoting the benefits of collectivism for both individual workers and the state itself.[xxiv] This fictional PLA soldier was promoted as the moral ideal for CCP subjects to follow and many propaganda stories and rumors were made to amplify Lei Feng messaging.[xxv] Lei Feng's stories always portrayed the character as exalting every ideal facet of the perfect party loyalist. He was always selfless in his actions enduring backbreaking work, harsh weather, and other hardships to fulfill every assignment given to him by the CCP while never seeking out personal glory, praise, or enrichment.[xxvi] In the collectivist propaganda, human beings can only reach their full potential if they are trained, conditioned, and nurtured by a perfect system and no individual can accomplish their full potential on their own. Like magic, the CCP's perfect system imbued Lei Feng with the moral strength to achieve near superhuman feats that can overcome all obstacles. Lei Feng was supposed to be the CCP's living incarnation of the Stalinist Soviet Union's concept of the "New Soviet Man", a complete inversion of the classical Western concept of the individual hero.[xxvii] FBE cultural and moral proxies must create their own versions of Lei Feng to subvert the classical ideas of personal triumph and heroism. Once culture is nudged into embracing Western imitations of Lei Feng, the younger generations of the Western nation will be indoctrinated into having different societal expectations with greater deference to social leaders and less independent thinking. Old generations may scoff and dismiss such culturally shifting propaganda by ignoring it. Such indifference automatically cedes the dominating cultural narrative to the FBE allowing them to nudge the Western nation into accepting more autocratic rule. If older generations object or socially attack such efforts, then the FBE can frame any criticism as an attack on progress or on a particular proxy group of the Atomized.

Make Lei Feng the Central Figure of the Arts and Stories:

The American author Joseph Campbell wrote the concept of the 'Hero's Journey' which describes a pattern he identified reading many myths, legends, stories, and religious doctrine that indicates a classic hero goes through 'three stages of separation, ordeal, and return'.[xxviii] The hero leaves the life they are comfortable with and endure a series of trials that makes them grow and improve to the point the hero can triumph against their ultimate challenge. Then the hero returns to their original lives as new people shaped by their experiences and new knowledge. There are critics of this thesis and there are arguments on various points of his 'Journey' thesis but these are not relevant here. The point is the challenges and obstacles faced by a classical hero, especially in Western tradition, must be overcome by personal improvement and making moral judgements on their own. The classical concept that inspires traditional societies are individuals who take it upon themselves to make the right moral choice in the face of adversity with guidance from wiser compatriots. The hero shapes the world around them positively using their own free will and is not directed or programmed by an impersonal human system carrying out a conditioned and predetermined set of actions. The story of the hero implies an individual can make a difference either within or outside a human system, group, or society. For the FBE's efforts, this is poisonous thinking.

The CCP "hero" Lei Feng cannot accomplish anything without the power of the Party or its system. Lei Feng acts as an avatar for this system and is used to discredit the idea of the lone hero or band of heroes working outside a socially indoctrinated system of thinking and rules.[xxix] The FBE must prioritize making the concept of Lei Feng the new fundamental baseline for all social inspirations and acts of heroism to change people's views of enlightened despotism. Any story that inspires the Western nation's traditional thinking must be either erased or altered to fit with the new narrative for society to normalize collective-corporatist autocratic rule. The FBE of the Western nation would already have considerable business connections with entertainment and cultural companies, groups, and institutions that can be vectors to spread FBE cultural subversion. The FBE would only need to initially secure the cooperation of the executive boards of these entertainment businesses as this industry is naturally insular and hierarchical. Once the senior leadership is coopted, then the rest of entertainment and media could be transformed from the top down.

The FBE would most likely replace all artistically inclined executives with outsider sycophants to best ensure these subverted entertainment and media organizations are compliant proxies. These outsider executives would mostly come from the second-rate members of the financial and legal sectors who lack creativity or initiative and only know the narrow field of expertise they trained on and nothing else. Dreary yes-men and women mostly recruited from the FBE's Nimbyist proxy agents will carry out social "nudging" without concern or care for traditions, joy, or escapism. Few of them would actually personally know the FBE or their true intentions, just their advocates' promise of financial compensation will likely be the only incentive needed. These types of ideal puppet executives covet their own self-enrichment above all other things and will confidently engage in profit-losing ventures as long as the proper message is conveyed to please the FBE. These entertainment and media company proxies know that the FBE will cover any losses by their political proxies with tax write-offs, subsidies, or in worst case scenarios, have the FBE arrange large compensations to the executives themselves if a proxy company actually collapses. No individual proxy company is irreplaceable and will be happily sacrificed in the effort to nudge the society into a more passive and compliant one.

After the leadership is appointed, the next step to securing their entertainment proxies is to gradually expunge all classically trained creatives within those businesses and groups. Of course, there will be iconic individuals who cannot be outright purged and instead be relegated into obscure supporting roles or pressured into retirement. This prevents deviation from the FBE narrative on what constitutes a morally right hero or protagonist while also choking off any public scandal between old and new entertainment creators. As actual entertainers and storytellers are removed, the FBE needs to replace them with proxy agents devoted to causing chaos and disruption in the Western nation's cultural foundations. The most common source for these low-ranking unwitting proxies will come from their groups of the Atomized. The Atomized are those agents of chaos conditioned to only value a singular cause or issue that gives them the perception of being exceptional without actually doing anything exceptional. These "useful idiot" proxies are incapable of imagination or thought beyond the cause they fanatically obsess over. They may not be fully cognizant of why they got their roles by the FBE, but as long as the Atomized are told what they want to hear, they will happily assist nudging the public's perception of what counts as virtuous. The FBEs will do little, if any, interaction with their cultural proxies beyond the executive level as long as the end result is delivered. The Atomized "creatives" can and will write whatever they want as long as it conveys the FBE's approved themes and values.

Once in control of a large portion of the entertainment industries, the FBE can influence and insinuate which topics and stories are to be produced or blocked from reaching the public. There would be three types of stories that would need dissemination to successfully subvert the culture. The first type is deconstructing all previous culturally relevant stories and iconography. A totalitarian society by its nature will have few unique perspectives and original ideas meaning the Atomized stories will often lack the raw persuasiveness of traditional storytelling. Instead, the Atomized can help make the public uncomfortable by valuing or glorifying non-FBE tales or historical entertainment by portraying these stories as enablers of creating victimhood or inciting social unrest. Recreating these old stories with a new FBE-approved perspective will make younger generations associate classic icons with the remade propagandist materials and dismiss the older versions as obsolete. The second type of storytelling is creating new stories using established cultural icons to fully coopt the cultural phenomena to the FBE cause. These stories take the first type of story further by expanding the FBE's messaging with beloved established characters that builds up the credibility of the FBE's propaganda. The final type of story is FBE proxy-derived original concepts which would likely be the least used, but still a vital component to FBE subversion operations.

The Atomized puppets who would write these stories would need to be impressionable and easily manipulated yet willing to participate in this ego-driven industry. So, most of them would likely be neurotically narcissistic with little sense of loyalty to anyone, including the FBE, if their desires or expectations are not indulged. A cheap way for the FBE to accommodate this is to allow and even encourage Atomized creatives to make their own stories, even though these Atomized are deliberately selected because they are unimaginative and co-dependent on FBE guidance. Although these stories are unlikely to appeal to most, including other Atomized, these FBE-approved original stories act as a useful pressure valve to keep their volatile agents of chaos subdued and focused on enemies like the NRF.

Strengths:

This subtle means of subversion can be easily camouflaged as new social trends that are "changing with the times" or that will bring in a new era of understanding. The messaging can be protected from most criticism with emotional blackmailing tactics to isolate and ostracize anyone identifying flaws in the new FBE-approved storytelling. Like in Chinese Communist struggle sessions, using negative emotionally-based public accusations based on anger, fear, guilt, and empathy are very effective in making most people either endorse or at least, passively allow these new propaganda stories to proliferate.[xxx] Even when such actions fail, it is still relatively easy to get detractors to unwittingly embrace and spread the FBE's messaging.

Most detractors would be fans of the older stories who will get caught up in the minutia of the film, book, comic, play, or tv show they defend. Such criticisms will fail to resonate with the apathetic majority who only seek instant gratification and not develop any intellectual bonds with most sources of entertainment. However, propaganda is inevitably boring over time and short lived, as it is repetitive, even if it is well written.[xxxi]' [xxxii], [xxxiii] However, fan-based critics will eventually gather credibility as the propaganda is less entertaining than traditional stories so more people will listen to their criticism over time. This doesn't mean defeat for the FBE proxies and instead can be used to better conceal the subversion of the Western culture. If a new propaganda-centric story is too boring, sloppy, or in some other way offensive to people's taste, then ceding some ground to give the illusion of surrender is very beneficial.

Enough propaganda, even if it's mediocre, will establish new precedents and standards for entertainment quality. Since propaganda is typically lower quality, the overall standards and expectations of the general public will also become lower over time. Stories considered mediocre or bad under the older pre-FBE standards would then become standard bearers of high-class entertainment in the new FBE era. As time goes on and the chorus of critics grows against the FBE-backed storytelling, the FBE just have to roll back and reintroduce some of the older standards to make some of their stories more palatable. The key to the FBE's objective is to successfully nudge the population, not outright convert everyone immediately into renouncing the role of being citizens to becoming subjects. If the FBE proxies' rollback changes to accommodate 90% of the criticisms but still retain some critical components of the original message, then the FBE has still gained ground and nudged the culture ever more slightly into accepting corporatist moral values. The critics will rarely, if ever, notice subtle manipulation.

Most of the critics will focus on the context of the story, quality of characters, etc. and rarely identify the messaging. Even if they do notice the social engineering to nefariously nudge the public's perceptions of morality, the critics will only notice the superficial messages and themes that act as a veneer to the true message. Most of the propaganda nudging efforts will be disguised as advocating for a specific cultural or political issue, cause, person, or group that caters to the Atomized creators' sense of identity. The critics will focus their attacks on the out of place messaging for the declared cause because it will be inconsistent, confusing, or extreme which will cause most critics to lose sight of the true message. The FBE does not truly care about any Atomized cause or group of people. Each Atomized cause that is advocated for in the new FBE stories are only regarded as an expendable tool that will be disposed of when circumstances make that Atomized group, cause, or individual irrelevant. When a trendier group of Atomized comes into vogue, the previous ones are discarded and forgotten. The actual message is impersonal because it's about systems, not subsets of social groups, with every story's theme being about how a system of collectivist values is superior to a system of individualist values.

One cannot tell stories about systems, so the systems will be represented in the forms of avatars in the guise of the protagonists and antagonists in the stories. One unavoidable flaw of this process is that the characters will be superficial caricatures, not developed personalities, because these characters will represent systems, not persons. The key promise of corporatist collectivism is the notion that more enlightened and competent people will look after your wants and needs more effectively than you. More bluntly, the promise is of being free from all personal responsibility while still being given spiritual and material prosperity by society. The FBE's corporatist system appeals to lazy greed in contrast to the traditional Western individualist system that appeals to ambitious greed.

These messages can be conveyed in several ways. The first way is to portray a protagonist embodying the system's key traits to appeal to the audience's baser instincts that make corporatist moral values more appealing. The protagonist will be more selfish and narcissistic than pre-FBE ones because the system represented by the protagonist must always be portrayed as inherently superior to everything around them. The "Lei Feng" protagonist can never be seen as emotionally or physically weak with the ability to rescue, save, protect, or fight for the world with ease. The protagonist can only be helped by like-minded characters and will never need training, mentoring, or education given by characters representing the "old" systems or traditional narrative themes like classical heroes. The protagonists will not change or grow as a character at any time in the story and will be continuously one-dimensional because the protagonist is the avatar for the "perfect system" so, it doesn't need any change. If anything, the world will change and grow to fit and accommodate the "Lei Feng" protagonist. This type of character is nicknamed by the common trope of being a "Gary Sue" or "Mary Sue" who are protagonists that inherently have all traits, skills, personality, and strength to overcome a story's obstacles without challenge.[xxxiv] Many observe these characters as acts of wish-fulfillment on the part of the character's creator which would be very likely with the Atomized writers typically holding a grievance against a perceived slight from the world.

A second way is to portray a classic protagonist with character traits based on pre-FBE stories facing defeat on their own but is then rescued by a new "Lei Feng"-like character that saves the forces of good. The classic character no longer succeeds using old tactics or methods but instead becomes co-dependent on the FBE's "Lei Feng"-character. Any wisdom or training imparted on the new FBE-character by the classic protagonist is either obsolete or improved upon by the superior FBE-character. Sooner or later, the classic character "passes the reins" over to the new character who will become an automatic hero without the need of the obsolete "hero's journey" with the old protagonist prostrating before them. The FBE-character embodies the corporatist ideal and that ideal, if realized, is invincible.

A third way is to make the system's avatar a sympathetic antagonist. The antagonist conducts evil acts but these must always be portrayed as done either in self-defense or being done against someone or group that is a far greater villain. This antagonist needs to be a victim betrayed by a foolish world or a misunderstanding. Even if the antagonist is defeated, it would be by diplomacy, apology, or deference to the antagonist's superior world outlook. The antagonist cannot be defeated by strength or force because this person is the avatar for the FBE-system and cannot be defeated by sheer strength. At best, the antagonist is compromised with and will either become a hero or carry out a critical act of redemption.

All of these story propaganda methods are designed not to complete a coherent story but to show that a protagonist or antagonist personifying the FBE's corporatist values will be victorious against all obstacles. The avatar will always base judgements on the "greater good" and states all abuses, crimes, and sufferings are due to failed corrupt systems or organizations and the groups that benefit from that corruption. Again, since the FBE's corporate-feudalist ideals want to discourage individual agency, the propaganda messages will never put responsibility on an individual for evil acts but on a system because the propaganda relies on everyone accepting the premise of "nurture over nature". If nurture can triumph over nature, then the propaganda can justify the premise of ceding all power to enlightened technocratic autocracy who can foster better people. The only exception is if a person is an avatar for the personification of older Western systems who can then be killed or destroyed as an individual. This kind of propaganda works well with both neo-Nazis and Communists as both ideologies subscribe to the nurturing of the group over the individual whether it's for racial or class-based social outcomes.[xxxv] The FBE would use this propaganda to entice both types of extremists to antagonize and silence any dissent but neither faction of extremists would gain any power doing so as both would remain expendable puppets. This messaging is subtle and can be hidden under distractions by associating the messaging with a particular cause or group of Atomized to attack and destroy criticism. When compromise is offered, the framework of building morals within the stories will still continuously shift towards autocratic endorsement.

One final strength is the use of stories to convey internal messages to all the functioning elements of the FBE. Since context and situations constantly change, the propaganda messaging must also change. Propaganda has three functions: 1. Indoctrinate the impressionable minds; 2. Destroy the morale of opponents by making them believe they are isolated from the general public; 3. Convey to the members of the ruling class who is actually in command, what the commanding faction prioritizes, and how to show loyalty and deference to the leadership by blindly embracing what is advocated in the latest propaganda stories. These stories help convey the policy and scope of the leadership's priorities to every proxy, advisor, and direct-action element of the FBE without having to convey traceable direct communication. This simplifies much of the coordination effort while maximizing obfuscation from the public.

Weakness:

Initiating this effort to change stories to suit the FBE's needs and ensuring their messaging dominates the market within the Western nation is easy because the FBE already have influence in most of the cultural apparatus. However, sustaining this propaganda without exposing and discrediting the messaging will become increasingly difficult over time. There are many well-funded established businesses and cultural institutions to facilitate the FBE's interests but the costs will increase, as resistance will also grow alongside the propaganda. As stated earlier, all propaganda becomes boring eventually and would lose market share overtime to new forms of entertainment that offers true escapism. This civil conflict is arising while the Western nation is still an anocracy so, the FBE cannot proactively block non-FBE stories with legal power as there remains some political freedom to publish. All the FBE can do is use its cultural institutions' monopolistic control over the entertainment and cultural industries to diminish the spread of non-FBE cultural influences. This becomes very expensive over time and FBE-backed state subsidies, tax breaks, regulatory loopholes, and marketing prioritizing for FBE stories can only stem the tide of the cultural backlash temporarily. Gradually, many of the FBE proxy organizations and companies will face financial hardships and will likely lose some of them due to mismanagement and poorly made propaganda stories that fail to sell.

This leads to the second weakness, the sycophant executives and the neurotic Atomized pawns that design the propaganda messaging are selected for loyalty, not ability. People are deliberately selected to fail upwards to eliminate any independent thinking. Better to be surrounded by loyal mediocrity than one gifted talent who would likely pursue their own path and disrupt the messaging. This is a major weakness for all totalitarian aspirations because these systems require every facet of life to be controlled, directed, and compliant with the central leaderships' plans to function. As an anthill demonstrates, such actions can only occur if the majority of subjects are docile, unimaginative, obedient thralls who are incapable of thinking for themselves. The FBE fears imagination because it creates independence. To illustrate this, a 1923 story written by Yevgeny Zamyatin simply named *We*, was the grandfather of totalitarian dystopian literary novels and directly addresses the problem of having a subject of the state possessing any type of creativity. Written before Aldous Huxley's *Brave New World* or George Orwell's *1984*, this dystopia was the pioneer portrayal of an industrialized collectivist oppressor state. *1984* portrays how such totalitarian dictatorships work in practice and how it fails to deliver the promised utopian dream. In contrast, Zamyatin's *We* portrays a dictatorship succeeding in creating its promised utopia of collectivist happiness by removing all uniqueness from its subjugated population.

The humans in this society have minds that are as sterile and banal as any ant drone with everyone given a number as a name and everything set to a rigid timetable. These humans were drugged and conditioned to embrace the idea that submitting to the functionality of the state is the only moral virtue. Anything that could disrupt that social functionality was morally repugnant, including anything that could give independent thought such as having an imagination. The main character named D-503 was having an argument with another worker and insulted him by suggesting he had an imagination but then realized he regrettably had one too.

Dear little man. The remotest hint that he might have an imagination was quite insulting to him. But what am I saying? A week back, and I'd probably have been insulted, too. But not now. Because now I know I have one, that I'm sick.**[xxxvi]**

This perfectly encapsulates the mentality of the ideal Atomized creator who cannot write stories beyond the narrow parameters of the propaganda they've been directed to write and fails at interesting creativity. Many clever or interesting elements in non-FBE propaganda stories are reviled by these Atomized creators not only for being alien to their values but for many of the creators, these creative ideas are also beyond their comprehension. This makes it very difficult to create compelling propaganda stories where there is still room for competing stories in the anocratic Western nation.

This is just the intellectual challenge of using those who've become willing automatons incapable of independent thinking, but there is also the challenge of dealing with the personalities of those emotionally defective Atomized that make them loyal but unreliable. The Atomized are foremost agents of chaos; useful idiots who disrupt and weaken society to enable the FBE to seize control of a weakened state. The Atomized attract highly neurotic types of self-absorbed personalities who seek social approval and validation because they cannot give it to themselves. These Atomized are so well indoctrinated into their chosen FBE-backed cause that any outside concepts beyond that cause go unnoticed. The Atomized' fanatic obsession of making their particular social issue the determinant factor for their entire identity will cause their ability to think in any other way to atrophy. These Atomized are narrow minded, mediocre, and co-dependent on their FBE handlers.

The perfect FBE-controlled Atomized creator would likely spend their days in endless tedium, wasting all their precious hours on vain self-indulgences morally rationalized by blindly supporting whatever selected FBE-instigated social cause. They will think no new thoughts nor seek new experiences or develop new passions. Whatever allures or charms they possess in their innocent youth will quickly wither and never be recaptured as their desire for instant gratification consumes them. They will lack true friends, as these will only be other Atomized who only seek others' validation justifying their narcissism. So, when these creators' idiosyncrasies that originally made them initially desirable to hire eventually go out of fashion, they will be discarded and replaced by other like-minded pawns. The neurotic personalities may differ in flavor between Atomized individuals but all are intellectually alike without any substantive difference amongst them. These Atomized creators would be so generic and interchangeable that few of them would actually have any unique contribution to give to the FBE or their cause. They will all write the same messaging and would only differ in choice of the veneer the message is disguised in. Whatever potential these Atomized could have for creating their own unique positive or negative accomplishments in the world on their own is so miniscule they will leave no lasting impression on the world and might as well never been born at all. Such neurotic misfits are great for causing chaos and can be blindly manipulated but are prone to emotional self-destruction. Atomized will have "thin skins" and are prone to be easily antagonized and react poorly to any challenge. This means the Atomized creators will have short periods of usefulness and must be replaced often with new Atomized to be squeezed for all their worth. Although easily replaceable, these Atomized could inadvertently embarrass or expose the FBE cause. Again, this is a personnel resourcing challenge that must be continually monitored.

So, how does the FBE balance their loyal but inept proxy pawns' inevitable failure with being able to still nudge society over to embracing pro-autocratic messaging? It was briefly hinted at earlier, the FBE must not relentlessly pummel the public with propaganda all of the time. Nudging requires both time and patience. Conducting a planned-out cycle of pushing social standards to accepting autocracy and then knowing when the financial and social backlash peaks, rollback the most flagrant of the indoctrinating materials and allow escapism to exist again temporarily. The rollback is not complete, but instead some of the changes remain such as the social framework or some key social values that advocate for collectivist solutions that will not brazenly interfere with the story. Once the audience is placated and the entertainment industry stabilizes, the FBE can ratchet up the overt propaganda again to hasten the "nudging" of social standards. In theory, this should work effectively but that relies on both FBE managers and creators of the propaganda to competently understand public sentiment and accurately measure the effectiveness of their propaganda. Frankly, given the naturally insulated, aloof, and narcissistic personalities these kinds of jobs attract, a seamless execution of the plan is unlikely.

---

[i] Angelique Chrisafis, "France Braced for Huge Street Protests Over Economic Crisis," The Guardian, March 19, 2009. https://www.theguardian.com/world/2009/mar/19/france-second-wave-strikes

[ii] JJ Sutherland, "French Protests Enter 7th Week," NPR, October 25, 2010. https://www.npr.org/sections/thetwo-way/2010/10/25/130811276/french-protests-enter-7th-week

[iii] News report, "French Protest Longer Working Hours," Times of Malta, February 5, 2005. https://timesofmalta.com/articles/view/french-protest-longer-working-hours.99932

[iv] Rachel Kurowski, "French Farmers Torch Hay on Paris' Champs-Elysees," The San Diego Union-Tribune, October 16, 2009. https://www.sandiegouniontribune.com/sdut-eu-france-farmer-protest-101609-2009oct16-story.html

[v] News report, "Thousands Protest in Paris Against Immigration Bill," TRT World, December 19, 2022. https://www.trtworld.com/europe/thousands-protest-in-paris-against-immigration-bill-63670

[vi] News report, "Yellow Vest Protests Wreak Havoc on French Economy," TRT World, December 10, 2018. https://www.trtworld.com/europe/yellow-vest-protests-wreak-havoc-on-french-economy-22356

[vii] News report, "Yellow vests knock out 60% of all speed cameras in France," BBC World, January 10, 2019. https://www.bbc.com/news/world-europe-46822472

[viii] Aude Mazoue, "What Economic Policies are France's Presidential Candidates Proposing?" France 24, May 4, 2022. https://www.france24.com/en/france/20220405-what-economic-policies-are-france-s-presidential-candidates-proposing

[ix] Nicole Hassenstab, "Farmer Protests Take Root in Europe and Beyond," American University, March 5, 2024. https://www.american.edu/sis/news/20240305-farmer-protets-take-root-in-europe-and-beyond.cfm

[x] Gaetane Ricard-Nihoul, The French "No" Vote on 29 May 2005: Understanding and Action, Notre Europe Etudes & Recherches, No. 44, August 2020. https://institutdelors.eu/wp-content/uploads/2020/08/etud44-en-2.pdf

[xi] Koert Debeuf, "2005: France and Netherlands Vote Against the Constitution," EU Observer, December 23, 2020. https://euobserver.com/20th-anniversary/150019

[xii] Chris Matthews, "Rise of The ULEZ 'Blade Runners': The Underground Activists Who've Vowed To Stop At Nothing Until They've 'Taken Down EVERY One Of Sadiq Khan's Low-Emission Cameras'," Daily Mail, April 28, 2023. https://www.dailymail.co.uk/news/article-12011507/ULEZ-Blade-Runners-want-one-Sadiq-Khans-low-emission-cameras.html

[xiii] Edward Alden, "Canada's Trucker Protests: What to Know About the 'Freedom Convoy," Council on Foreign Relations, February 11, 2022. https://www.cfr.org/in-brief/canadas-trucker-protests-what-know-about-freedom-convoy

[xiv] Beatrice K. Otto, Fools are Everywhere, (Chicago: University of Chicago Press, 2001): Excerpt. https://press.uchicago.edu/Misc/Chicago/640914.html

[xv] Staff, "Scottish Man Arrested for Teaching Dog a Nazi Salute," Times of Israel, May 9, 2016. https://www.timesofisrael.com/scottish-man-arrested-for-teaching-dog-to-give-nazi-salute/

[xvi] Ewan Palmer, "Count Dankula Sentence: Youtuber Avoids Jail after Conviction for Teaching Pet Pug Nazi Salute," Newsweek, April 23, 2018. https://www.newsweek.com/youtuber-count-dankula-avoids-jail-following-hate-crime-conviction-teaching-896831

[xvii] News Report, "Nazi Germany Pursued 'Hitler Salute' Finnish Dog," BBC News, January 7, 2011. https://www.bbc.com/news/world-europe-12139150

[xviii] News Report, "Transport Minister Humza Yousaf Drove without Insurance," BBC News, December 7, 2016. https://www.bbc.com/news/uk-scotland-scotland-politics-38234763

[xix] Conor Matchett, "Scotland Ferries Scandal: Nicola Sturgeon Challenged on 'Corporate Fraud' and 'Political Corruption' Allegations around Ferry Contract Procurement," The Scotsman, September 29, 2022. https://www.scotsman.com/news/politics/scotland-ferries-scandal-nicola-sturgeon-challenged-on-corporate-fraud-and-political-corruption-allegations-around-ferry-contract-procurement-3861095

[xx] Greg Heffer, "SNP's Damning Verdict... On The SNP: Leadership Candidates Roast Each Other Over Trains Not Running, Health Service Meltdown and Police Failures In Scotland During Extraordinary 'Circular Firing Squad' TV Debate," Daily Mail, March 8 2023. https://www.dailymail.co.uk/news/article-11835025/SNP-leadership-candidates-roast-Scottish-Government-failures-TV-debate.html

[xxi] Christopher Peckover, "Realizing the Natural Self: Rousseau and the Current System of Education," Philosophical Studies in Education, vol. 43, University of Iowa, 2012, 85-86. https://files.eric.ed.gov/fulltext/EJ1000297.pdf

[xxii] Filip Bardzinski, "The Concept of the 'New Soviet Man' as a Eugenic Project: Eugenics in Soviet Russia after World War II," Ethics in Progress, vol. 4, no. 1, 2013, 74-77. https://www.researchgate.net/publication/337291231_The_Concept_of_the_%27New_Soviet_Man%27_As_a_Eugenic_Project_Eugenics_in_Soviet_Russia_after_World_War_II

[xxiii] Alex Tuckness, "Locke's Political Philosophy," The Stanford Encyclopedia of Philosophy, Winter 2020. https://plato.stanford.edu/archives/win2020/entries/locke-political/

[xxiv] Evan Osnos, "Fact-Checking a Chinese Hero," The New Yorker, March 29, 2013. https://www.newyorker.com/news/evan-osnos/fact-checking-a-chinese-hero

[xxv] Austin Ramzy, "A Chinese Propaganda Icon Loses a Layer of Myth," New York Times, January 6, 2015. https://archive.nytimes.com/sinosphere.blogs.nytimes.com/2015/01/06/a-chinese-propaganda-icon-loses-a-layer-of-myth/

[xxvi] Xiofei Tian, "The Making of a Hero: Lei Feng and Some Issues of Historiography," Harvard University Archives, 2009. https://scholar.harvard.edu/files/xtian/files/2009_lei_feng_conference_volume_version.pdf

[xxvii] Ralph Raico, "Marxist Dreams and Soviet Realities," CATO Institute, May 1, 1988. https://www.cato.org/commentary/marxist-dreams-soviet-realities#

[xxviii] Tamlorn Chase, "Joseph Campbell & the Hero's Journey," Odyssey Online, Antioch University, March 3, 2016. https://odyssey.antiochsb.edu/literary/joseph-campbell-the-heros-journey/

[xxix] Vanessa Piao, "The Selfless Lei Feng is Back – as a Magazine," The New York Times, August 4, 2015. https://archive.nytimes.com/sinosphere.blogs.nytimes.com/2015/08/04/the-selfless-lei-feng-is-back-as-a-magazine/

[xxx] Dr. Li Zhisui, *The Private Life of Chairman Mao*, (NY: Random House, 1994) 62-65.

[xxxi] John Brown, "The Paradoxes of Propaganda," USC Center on Public Diplomacy, April 16, 2007. https://uscpublicdiplomacy.org/blog/paradoxes-propaganda

[xxxii] Frank Rybicki, *The Rhetorical Dimensions of Radio Propaganda in Nazi Germany: 1935-1945*, Duquesne University, Summer 2004, 165-166, 209-213. https://dsc.duq.edu/cgi/viewcontent.cgi?article=2153&context=etd

[xxxiii] Joe He, *A Historical Study on the 'Eight Revolutionary Model Operas' in China's Great Cultural Revolution*, University of Nevada, January 1, 1991, 54-56, 73-75. https://digitalscholarship.unlv.edu/cgi/viewcontent.cgi?article=1169&context=rtds

[xxxiv] Online reference, "Mary Sue", TVtropes.com, viewed on 11/21/2022. https://tvtropes.org/pmwiki/pmwiki.php/Main/MarySue

[xxxv] Filip Bardzinski, "The Concept of the 'New Soviet Man' as a Eugenic Project: Eugenics in Soviet Russia after World War II," Ethics in Progress, vol. 4, no. 1, 2013, 64,77. https://www.researchgate.net/publication/337291231_The_Concept_of_the_%27New_Soviet_Man%27_As_a_Eugenic_Project_Eugenics_in_Soviet_Russia_after_World_War_II

[xxxvi] Yevgeny Zamyatin, *We*, (NY: Penguin Group: 1993): 79-80.

Chapter 17: Phase I Operational Line of Effort 3 for the Foreign-Backed Elites — Glorify and Recruit Agents of Chaos, Make Education Advocate for Autocracy

The general purpose of education in a free nation is to improve the minds and skills of its population. Only a well-skilled population can sustain the prosperity of a nation in an era of technological and scientific advancement, but Western education also included the unique addition of teaching personal initiative and critical thinking. At least, this was historically true and was critical in giving these Western nations an edge over the rest of the world in the 20th Century. This educated population acted as a bulwark against authoritarian statism because critical thinking encouraged critical debate alongside the learning of factual information. These elements were critical in the rise of the West, especially the United States and Great Britain as these Anglosphere-based hegemonies have dominated the world since the end of the Seven Years of War in 1763. Education acts as a social foundation used to protect Western societies from tyranny but societies typically don't protect the foundations themselves. Like with all human systems, time and complacency eventually cause education systems to stagnate and decline over time to the point of only creating mediocrity. Such systemic decay usually coincides with the decline of functional societies and the rise of anocracies.

The traditional logic about education being a democratic safeguard is that tyrants rely on an ignorant and poor population to maintain control and without that ignorance, tyrannies would crumble before an enlightened public. However, one of the greatest discoveries made by totalitarian regimes of the 20th Century was that only selectively withholding key knowledge was necessary to keep tyrannical control, not total ignorance. Redefining ignorance, advanced dictatorships could educate their populations with a lot of information in a controlled perspective which keeps their subjugated populations completely ignorant of reality and their plights. By nurturing and defining key characteristics and presumptions about politically sensitive topics, an autocratic regime can impose their political perspective as the only absolute truth that will instill obedience and loyalty. Words and teachings can open up people to ideas but these can also close them. George Orwell's concept of Newspeak explicitly highlights this point. The Nazis, Communists, and Fascists all proved that education is a double-edge sword that is not an absolute guarantor of free societies.

The West's blind faith in the concept of education being always benign and trustworthy is what leaves this cultural foundation vulnerable to subversion. The West regards education with an almost spiritualistic reverence. If the FBE corrupted the education system, it would not likely be noticed for years as Western families place much faith in both administrators and teachers as being altruists. Western faith in educational institutions as social improvers is so strong that many Western nations invert the expectations of education. Historically, institutions such as colleges, universities, and other centers of higher education were expected to provide the foundational knowledge for people from which to better understand and utilize their future accrued experiential knowledge into becoming wise and self-sufficient. Now, many regard universities and high learning institutions as the pinnacles of all knowledge rather than being foundational. Meaning that academicians hold considerable influence over society and its policies and have taken the place of priests as the main advisory class to the ruling elites of the West. Since the value of these education institutions for the Western nation is high and reverence for them is near religious in devotion, the FBE subverting education centers is essential in converting the population into willing slaves.

Every belief system, philosophy, policy, and social standard has a negative aspect to it. As Shakespeare's Hamlet states, "There are more things in heaven and earth, Horatio, than are dreamt of in your philosophy." No human system devised can account for every circumstance, variable, event, or happenstance that occurs in this universe and consequently every human system, idea, and belief will have a flaw or weakness. Why does this matter? This matters because with sufficient time the FBE can find flaws in every tradition, historical event, and national myth that sustains the Western nation's concepts of liberty or social contract. These flaws can be exaggerated, falsified, or the positive contributions be diminished and discarded. If the FBE can propagandize education to discredit the current society and hide all negative aspects of autocratic collectivist systems, then the FBE can nudge society into autocracy with proselytizing converts amongst the teachers and students. As Adolf Hitler is often cited as saying, "Through clever and constant application of propaganda, people can be made to see paradise as hell, and also the other way round, to consider the most wretched sort of life as paradise." Making any and all things related to individualism or civil independence seem oppressive, destructive, or horrific is the key to creating and sustaining proxy fighters in this ideological subversion effort. Education must be the ideological starting point and springboard for the FBE's creation of a new society.

The totalitarian regimes of the 20th Century devised and refined the techniques of education subversion for enslaving a society with China's Communist Party as the greatest innovator. Chairman Mao faced the threat of being ousted from being the Party leader after the colossal failure of the Great Leap Forward and discovered the best solution was to attack the Party first.[i] Although the CCP had changed much of China by the early 1960s, there were still traditions, customs, and practices that were not compatible with ideal Maoism. These remnants of the old culture provided the pretext Mao needed to justify a "revolution within the revolution" to purge remaining enemies of utopia. Instead of accepting responsibility for his many administrative failures, Mao used the zeal of impressionable youth within the schools and universities to shift blame to and challenge all elements of the CCP. Subverting education was the key and taught all failures in the system were the result of counterrevolutionary elements infiltrating the Party to corrupt Mao's pure vision. Linking failures with the nation's past and then linking the past to all of Mao's rivals within the Party created a perfect class of enemies for Mao's zealots to target with harassment, terror, and violence.[ii]

Mao introduced a "new socialist education campaign" that dispensed with all non-ideological teachings and focused completely on the messianic myth of Mao's greatness and indispensability to China's future. The schools were turned into incubators for Mao's Red Guards who were taught they were the true vanguard of Mao's vision for China, portraying them as truly special in Chinese society.[iii] With the backing of the PLA, the Red Guard targeted teachers, administrators, shopkeepers, factory workers, parents, and Party officials for any ideological sin. Those people deemed ideologically impure were labeled the "Blacks" and became the basis for legalized bigotry and prejudice that was articulated in Mao's "Theory of the Bloodline" which rationalized collective punishment to include the "Blacks'" friends, family members, and co-workers.[iv]

Conditioning the youth of the Red Guard to believe in the fantasist notion that Mao's vision was infallibly good and all detractors were evil removed all ethical or psychological restraints against committing atrocities on behalf of Mao. To blindly believe in the Maoist personality cult, the new educational indoctrination taught the Red Guards to reject the idea of causality and the concept of consequence by action in order to rationalize the Maoist explanations for China's ills. The Red Guards believed ideological purity would overcome any societal action-reaction effect and no longer understood cause and effect. Consequently, professionals and essential workers were purged without hesitation nor having suitable replacements which resulted in the collapse of the economy and essential services throughout most of China in the 1960s. This combined with the already cumbersome centrally planned economy led to a collapse in standards of living, social stability, and national development.[v] By focusing on ignoring objective reality and replacing it with a Maoist-centric solipsist fantasy as the basis of education, the Red Guards were the perfect obedient automatons incapable of independent thought. Mao's purge of all enemies in China, both real and imagined, was made easier by his previous purge stemming from a different form of corrupt education, the "Hundred Flowers Campaign" of 1957.[vi]

Mao declared this campaign was a means for both party members and the peasantry to have open discussion and debate to highlight criticisms of the Party and how to improve upon it. However, as cited earlier, the concept of miànzi meant any flaws identified in the Party would cause the leader of the Party, in this case Mao, to lose face and credibility. So, this campaign in reality was a clever trap to entice the most capable and educated critics of society to reveal themselves and made it impossible for them to hide once the purges began.[vii] This form of education subversion was entrapping the critical thinking population into killing itself. This previous purge created a precedent that the Red Guards used to provide justifications that counterrevolutionary forces existed within society after the 1949 Chinese Civil War victory and the most intelligent and rational were the worst source of "Black" subversive elements. Between the Hundred Flowers Campaign and the student-driven Cultural Revolution, Mao achieved absolute power within the Party and over China by 1970. Mao showed future totalitarian regimes, including Xi Jinping's, that indoctrination education is critical to subjugating a society to an absolutist regime's will.

However, China also proved that subverting moral education is as critical as general and skills education. Mao made certain to purge all old traditionalist institutions within China once the Party took control in 1949. The major sources of moral teachings were the many schools, temples, and family traditions anchored in Buddhism, Confucianism, and Taoism. Although Confucian thought survived given its advocated deference to central authority, the others were regarded as rival power bases that needed extermination or subjugation. After Mao, the CCP allowed some of the old beliefs a limited presence within society with mandated administrative control over religious institutions and the appointment of senior local religious leaders. The Catholic Church, regarded as a foreign malign influence, was compelled to make major concessions to the CCP to be allowed to exist in present China. Pope Francis agreed to allow the CCP to have input in the appointment of local bishops since 2018 with the promise of the Pope having the final say.[viii] Yet, the CCP arrests any dissenting Catholic priests and Christian villagers who are required to have pictures of Xi Jinping instead of Christ.[ix], [x] The Party understands that no education, moral or professional, can be allowed to deviate from the concept that all power and authority is solely in the hands of the Party. No other belief can flourish unmolested or allow the youth ability to think there is any viable alternative to autocratic rule.

Options and Methods:

The CCP's methods can act as a foundational guide for the FBE but cannot be mimicked exactly. Mao had a simpler challenge to overcome because there was an established autocratic regime with the sole authority resting in the hands of the CCP itself. Mao just had to create one class of political enemies that looked like traitors to the established regime, a clear-cut black and white moral choice for the masses to easily accept. Mao just had to redefine what constituted a true member of the Party and what constituted a counterrevolutionary opponent. Once done, the Red Guards and the PLA did the rest for the Cultural Revolution. The FBE will be presiding over an anocracy with many political factions, interest groups, and institutions sharing power within the Western nation. This division of political power means the educational system cannot be completely subverted from the top-down nor will one single scapegoat be enough to focus the indoctrinated to help purge the society of nonautocratic believers. The FBE will have to take control of education in gradual steps, nudging the educational system itself slowly into becoming a new breeding ground for Western versions of the Red Guard. Since society divides up power amongst many, the most logical step in subverting education is to teach everyone to be envious of the power that other groups have in society. No one group, party, social class, or interest group has absolute power and, in some cases, that power is shared through democratic government institutions. So, the FBE would have to create not a single Red Guard-equivalent but instead indoctrinate multiple smaller groups to hate and politically attack the various powerholders within the Western nation.

The dilution of political power from the society's system of checks and balances prevents any single group from being powerful enough to act as the FBE's ideological proxy fighters. So, the FBE must create multiple groups of proxies and then have each proxy group nudge a specific aspect of society towards accepting FBE absolute rule. The subverted education will be the system to identify and create these groups. The FBE's education effort will first need to identify those who are susceptible to autocratic ideas and those that would resist such notions. Then, the FBE must discourage individuality among those targeted for indoctrination and convince these future proxies all accomplishments are linked to belonging to a group. Then the FBE would use various social and economic issues to encourage the formation of ideologically segregated groups within the classrooms for the indoctrinated to gravitate towards. Next, the FBE's education must convince youths to identify all life as a struggle between groups, not individuals, and want to become affiliated with one of these FBE-instigated social groups. Simultaneously, the FBE must, like Mao, ensure the education system destroys any and all concepts dealing with causality. Rational or reasonable people who think for themselves do so because they understand consequence of actions which include personal accountability. Personal accountability means others can identify and critique weaknesses, including those in authority, which makes the concept of causality a threat to the FBE. The FBE must make ideological proxies believe all consequences result from collective systems and that failure comes from a badly implemented system. Systemic failure, not individual failure, is the root belief for totalitarian utopianists and must be the only way for the FBE's proxies to think about the world.

With young people indoctrinated into proxies, the FBE must then make these proxies target those who benefit from the Western nation being a democratic republic. The formula the FBE must follow is a simple one. Identify and label all people who are economically self-sufficient, independent, or who doesn't require the state to provide supporting aid in any way as the new enemies of society. The FBE proxies who would be taught in schools are not just there to become believers, they are agents of chaos trained to undermine and discredit the current anocratic society of the Western nation by blaming democratic and free market institutional traditions for the society's failings. These proxies must have enemies to focus their acts of chaos upon because these agents would otherwise target indiscriminately, including the FBE themselves. In so doing, the FBE accomplish their task of having tailored proxy groups of Westernized Red Guards for each kind of political enemy and democratic institution.

The FBE could potentially create dozens of groups for young impressionable students to affiliate with under the common theme of every one of these social or political groups are persecuted or neglected by the democratic-republic society. "Redeeming the despised" would be a comprehensive motto for these indoctrinated proxy groups as many will likely be recruited from the social periphery of what is considered mainstream society. This is the same reason why Hitler's SA or "Brown Shirts" would recruit heavily from hardened criminals because these people were ostracized by the Weimar Republic and had no loyalty to that government. Once these youths are indoctrinated into groups within the subverted education system, these groups then join the larger FBE proxy groups in society as ideological fighters. These groups would use either social pressure or violence to nudge the society and its institutions into adopting more collectivist autocratic rules and systems. As cited in the strategic section, these proxy groups can be categorized by how a group helps "nudge" the society. The Nimbyists proxy groups would use social pressure tactics and the violent actor groups would belong to the Atomized category, including felonious criminals. In practice, there would likely be overlap and not all proxies would fit neatly into either category.

Finally, the FBE would have to subvert moral education which, even in secular societies, remains largely the purview of religious institutions. Given the diversity of belief systems within almost all Western nations, infiltrating a state church or the most prominent faith would be insufficient for FBE purposes. Since coopting every faith is neigh on impossible, the next best action is to subvert the more radical elements within each faith in the Western nation as these are easy to subvert due to their greater isolation. Then use FBE institutional proxies to promote those radical elements as mainstream and declare the mainstream elements as dangerous radicals. The FBE would have to proceed slowly, likely over many years, to shift the moral teachings into making FBE-backed indoctrination the mainstream, but with FBE control of information dissemination and reinforcement of themes by the entertainment and secular education institutions, the various faiths can be "nudged." At initial face value, such an endeavor looks unlikely in most Western nations but there are past real-world examples of radical subversions in the West.

One of the more famous is the cult leader Jim Jones and his subversion of religion in the San Francisco Bay Area. Although Jim Jones is famous for being a radical preacher who led his followers to their deaths, what is often forgotten is what Jim Jones actually preached. He started out his cultist career by joining the most radical Pentecostal church where he lived because their isolation from the rest of the community made them more vulnerable to his influence.[xi] Once he coopted the radical church, he then began changing its teachings to more Marxist utopianist ideas and used these as the basis for his charitable work and social activism. Over time, Jim Jones used his philanthropy to ingratiate himself with San Francisco's social and political elite to gain influence and spread his "moral" teachings to gain more recruits. Over a period of a few years, Jim Jones went from a radical Pentecostal preacher to an atheistic Marxist demagogue under the guise of a spiritual leader.[xii] While he eventually grew so detached from reality that he took his followers to Guyana and committed mass suicide, the FBE nevertheless have a historical precedent to use as a blueprint. These churches would advocate on behalf of the Atomized groups and for collectivist justice while attacking any church, temple, or religious authority that failed to advocate for greater power to the FBE's proxy groups. Moral education subversion would take time, but it is necessary in nations that allow religious freedom, even if those nations have declined into anocracy.

Strengths:

Subverting education is a powerful passive act that requires little violence and can remain undetected from the general public for years, if not decades. Also, unlike autocrats in developing or poor nations, the FBE can use the prosperity of the Western nation against itself. Anocracies appear in times of complacency brought about by excess prosperity, secure lifestyle, and a society focused on wants instead of needs. The complacency leads to decadent, epicurean, and libertine lifestyles that stymie the society's ability to self-reflect, endure hardship, or seek personal betterment. Yet, human nature remains cognizant of this, even if only at an instinctual level, which makes large swaths of a decadent population susceptible to guilt, shame, and fear as many would know they have envious lives. Almost like a child who sneaks cookies at night after the parent goes to bed, many in society know they overindulge and hate to be called out on it but at the same time don't actually want to stop or restrict their indulgences. So, the FBE can exploit the society's shame of success to make the majority of the population guilted into passively accepting radical new education movements. Since most of the public don't want to be accused of holding a group of perceived victims of society back, they will acquiesce to child indoctrination. As long as the FBE reassures the population by making the indoctrination seem like it's improving education and not outright propaganda, then the FBE should have little difficulty. The children and teenagers susceptible to indoctrination are also mostly from the self-indulgent classes within Western society and that greed can simplify recruitment.

Youth in general seek instant gratification and only think about their immediate self-interest as they don't yet have families or obligations. The FBE can help these susceptible youths rationalize their greed and egocentrism by promising they would be the center of attention by belonging to one of the FBE's proxy groups of instigators and subversives. Having the pretense of belonging to a group that FBE manipulators claim are oppressed or cheated out of their rightful place by a systemically broken society gives youths the self-justification that they are righteous, even if they don't actually do anything productive. Belonging to these proxy groups enables the youths to avoid personal accountability while carrying out acts of chaos and disruption in the name of the greater good. Few of them would actually need to sacrifice anything other than their ability to think and will become permanently dependent on the FBE's patronage. The irony of collectivist utopianism is that it appeals to personal ego as the ideology declares nothing is the fault of the individual believer, all sins are done by the group and are absolved of its sins as long as the group fights for the righteous cause. In this case, the righteous cause is whatever suitable social issue is trending to cloak the true cause of being expendable fodder in subverting the system to becoming an FBE controlled autocracy.

The other advantage of successfully implementing indoctrination into the educational system is it will cheapen the costs of becoming an autocratic regime in the long run. Since these youths don't appreciate economic self-sufficiency, the FBE can indoctrinate these new proxy recruits into accepting a new standard of social status. Gaining social clout within whatever FBE proxy group an indoctrinated person belongs, would replace economic prosperity or personal independence. The indoctrinated will mostly consist of the socially isolated and being part of something "greater" while not actually doing any real work is the perfect concept of paradise to a collectivist utopian. There is already a similar strain of thought among the Zoomer Generation with some of them believing seeking economic success and economic self-sufficiency is too hard or damaging to one's wellbeing.[xiii] Convincing young people who only live for the moment and themselves can be easily nudged into accepting diminished material rewards in exchange for "social clout" that reinforces their self-satisfaction. Another part of the redefined social status is how much disruption and chaos one can cause against the systemically corrupt Western nation or its supporters. The youths love action over tedious class work, so demonstrations, cyber harassment, and violent intimidation without legal consequence adds extra allure for prospective new recruits.

Like the subversion of entertainment and stories, the FBE doesn't need to directly manage the messaging or indoctrination. As long as the fundamental concepts of submitting to the group is conveyed, then pro-autocratic teachers, professors, advocates, and administrators can take the initiative on how the message is conveyed within whatever social cause is trending. The most likely forms of indoctrination will be using the proxy groups of Atomized and their selected grievances as the basis for ideological education. The groups' proclaimed causes don't matter and can be changed out or replaced whenever they fall out of public favor because the fundamental message of collective submission to the enlightened social elites is compatible with all social issues. Despite tricking the indoctrinated Atomized and Nimbyists into believing they are special, in reality, they are actually interchangeable and expendable. They only exist because they create excuses for autocracy, not the actual motivation for autocracy. The only true motivation is the FBE's accrual of more power and control and that is easily hidden amongst the pretenses and falsehoods of subversive educational indoctrination.

Weaknesses:

Creating an education system of indoctrination to mold young people into easily led automatons for the FBE has the major risk of creating an idiocracy amongst the FBE's indoctrinated population. Idiocracy is a political system where anti-intellectualism and complete lack of basic understanding of the world dominates a society. This term was coined as a reference from the 2006 satirical movie *Idiocracy* which uses Social Darwinism to explain how technology hinders future generations' intellectual development. In reality, idiocracy occurs when the population is governed by those whose decisions are completely detached from reality. Part of the FBE indoctrination education process requires eliminating critical thinking and discouraging people from understanding the concepts of causality. Embracing simplistic solutions will make people believe they are smart as long as they don't understand the consequences overly simple ideas neglect to consider. People don't actually lose brain power from a biological perspective but instead, they choose to stop developing their logical faculties by embracing mind-numbing indoctrination. This can be foisted upon otherwise academically gifted or intelligent persons by replacing objective reality with ideology. If properly indoctrinated, the FBE proxies will gauge their entire lives and the world at large through an ideological view that discounts anything that contradicts the indoctrination. This is necessary during the period the FBE is nudging the vulnerable anocracy into a full autocracy because the FBE needs expendable agents of chaos to destabilize society. A destabilized society is a discredited society which makes the public more agreeable to autocratic rule. These agents of chaos cannot be allowed to think because in the course of their actions they will make contradictory demands, inconsistent moral statements, promote false narratives, and intimidate critics who will make logical arguments. Ideological commitment keeps the Atomized and Nimbyist proxies loyal to the cause regardless of the number of practical failures and inconsistencies in their beliefs and actions. However, a campaign of chaos induced by the dumbed down ideological proxy activists and fighters will eventually damage all elements of society if this effort becomes prolonged. Ideologically committed puppets are not productive members of society and often require subsidized support to keep them functioning so over time they become more expensive and society's ability to financially absorb the losses diminishes. One can see this from real historical idiocracies created by fanatical unwavering commitment to ideology.

Every totalitarian regime has a period of idiocracy. Each totalitarian regime needs to secure its ideological foundations onto the society it has taken over and that requires much of the old order be erased so no one has a contradictory point of view. This is a dangerous transition period where the dictatorship is finalizing its grip on the society it just seized power over that is meant to only be temporary. To make the new ideology dominant over the old one, it can never appear weaker or wrong compared to the old ideals. Consequently, the new ideology will temporarily support insane and incoherent positions to kill the old beliefs and institutions. The clearest example is China's era of the Cultural Revolution where idiocracy ruled almost every aspect of that society. Real idiocracy happens when ideology is used as the basis for every plan, thought, and action because such a society becomes completely detached from objective reality. Fanatical ideology dispenses with the concept of consequence by having followers believing that ideological purity will overcome all obstacles and solve all problems, so there is no need to think and there is no reason to associate cause with effect. During the Cultural Revolution, Red Guards purged the professional classes because too many were thinking too much and were not ideologically pure enough. The Red Guard believed in Mao's doctrines like superstitious people believe in hexes and conjurations in that the ideology will magically solve everything when properly implemented.[xiv] Beatings, murders, ransacking, and purges of professionals, intellectuals, and others paralyzed China.[xv]

Even the much-vaunted program of the "Barefoot Doctors" had ideologically damaging aspects to it. The program was directed by Mao to have millions of peasants trained by doctors from hospitals in cities to assist the rural peasantry where there was no medical infrastructure. These doctors were trained in basic medical knowledge of hygiene, treatment of common ailments, and other skills that only required a high-school level of education.[xvi] It worked in the same way medicine drastically improved quality of life in the West during the 19th Century where basic changes to lifestyle drastically improved life expectancy as hygiene, treatment of wounds and simple injuries became more commonplace. However, as it turned out, the success of this program was largely due to the fact that the program quietly ignored a large amount of Mao's ideological directives and embraced practical solutions.[xvii] Mao's ideological-driven policies made in his safe and isolated gilded palaces created as many impediments as it did assistance to the Chinese population. First, Mao considered professional doctors too Westernized by valuing theoretical knowledge and training over hands on experience. So, to make doctors more workmen-like, he sent the most experience doctors to the countryside and had the young freshmen doctors manage the hospitals so all of them would learn with hands-on experience.[xviii] This meant many mistakes had to be made by novices first, sometimes fatally. Furthermore, Mao objected to doctors rejecting traditional Chinese medicine as an effective cost saving measure and required all rural doctors to incorporate these practices as standard treatment despite dubious efficacy.[xix] Any doctors who objected were harassed, punished, or outright purged for questioning any directive by Mao on medical care.[xx] In essence, Mao elevated rural medicine by diminishing the quality and quantity of medical treatment in the cities while imposing ideological requirements on medical practices regardless of medical efficacy or use. For context to properly gauge Mao's medical qualifications, this man never brushed his teeth because he thought swishing tea in one's mouth was just as effective as a brush and toothpaste. This didn't matter of course because his ideological imperatives overrode doctors in all medical programs in the name of communist utopianism.[xxi]

The near economic collapse of China in the early 1970s and the Red Guard's endless provocations with the PLA finally forced Mao to halt the Cultural Revolution even though he truly didn't want to abandon ideologically-driven perpetual revolution.[xxii] This decade long idiocracy where ideology trumped over reality only functioned when lower ranking functionaries ignored ideological mandates and even then, this only slightly mitigated the societal damage it inflicted upon China as a whole. His death and Deng Xiaoping's successful elimination of the Red Guard loving "Gang of Four" ultimately saved China from collapsing into civil war and economic destruction.

Like *Mao's Little Red Book*, the FBE's indoctrination would eventually detach a sizable segment of the population from any sense of reality. These people who would be used as ideological cannon fodder would be useless as engineers, scientists, doctors, lawyers, administrators, leaders, or any other role that requires actual skill. The Atomized and Nimbyists will have a complete lack of self-awareness regarding their ignorance of the "real world" and practical knowledge. They will declare they are enlightened, scientific, and whatever other high-minded words in their sloganeering but will actually not truly understand what any of those words mean. This fanatical indoctrination must only be temporary during the period the FBE must secure their power and turn the anocracy into an autocracy. Then the proxy agents of chaos must be reined in and the education reverted to more grounded and practical ideas. Mao waited too long to reign in his disruptive ideologically fanatical purists who nearly destroyed both China and the CCP. The CCP was only saved by Deng's "moderate" wing's efforts to reverse these actions. The Cambodian dictator Pol Pot's reign on the other hand, was an example of an idiocracy never being reigned in during the Khmer Rouge period, leading to Cambodia's societal implosion by 1979.[xxiii] Timing is critical, and the longer the "nudging" education campaign lasts, the more damage to the Western nation is inflicted and the more threat their own proxies become to the FBE's existence.

The final weakness that must be mentioned is that the NRF opponents will not have to create a collective indoctrination program for their own followers. Fighting for an already established system that needs reform but is conducive to reality doesn't require much blind obedience. If the conflict lasts for years, which would be the most probable, the NRF would mainly focus on training on how to defeat the indoctrination, which means more critical thinking is required. So, the NRF would be outnumbered but would potentially have far more high-quality individuals working for them. These more grounded NRF members could exploit the FBE's proxies' ideological blindness to manipulate or trap Atomized or Nimbyist members into losing situations. Quantitative superiority eventually becomes useless if the numerically superior force is filled with indoctrinated imbeciles.

---

[i] Dr. Li Zhisui, *The Private Life of Chairman Mao*, (NY: Random House: 1994) 387-388.

[ii] Jung Chang and Jon Halliday, *The Unknown Story of Mao*, (NY: Random House's Anchor Books: 2005) 505-507.

[iii] Dr. Li Zhisui, *The Private Life of Chairman Mao*, (NY: Random House: 1994) 473-475.

[iv] Jung Chang and Jon Halliday, *The Unknown Story of Mao*, (NY: Random House's Anchor Books: 2005) 503-508.

[v] Kent Deng, and Jim H Shen, *From State Resource Allocation to a 'Low Level Equilibrium Trap': Re-evaluation of Economic Performance of Mao's China, 1949-78*, London School of Economics and Political Science, Economic History Working Papers, no. 298, 27-34. http://eprints.lse.ac.uk/101127/1/Deng_from_state_resource_allocation_published.pdf

[vi] Dr. Li Zhisui, *The Private Life of Chairman Mao*, (NY: Random House: 1994) 189-190.

[vii] Jung Chang and Jon Halliday, *The Unknown Story of Mao*, (NY: Random House's Anchor Books: 2005) 410-411.

[viii] Philip Pullella, "Vatican Confirms Renewal of Contested Accord with China on Bishops' Appointments," Reuters, October 22, 2022. https://www.reuters.com/world/china/vatican-confirms-renewal-contested-accord-with-china-bishops-appointments-2022-10-22/

[ix] Kate Shellnutt, "China Tells Christians to Replace Images of Jesus with Communist President," Christianity Today, November 17, 2017. https://www.christianitytoday.com/news/2017/november/china-christians-jesus-communist-president-xi-jinping-yugan.html

[x] Benedict Rogers, "China is already Breaking Its Vatican Deal," Foreign Policy, September 17, 2020. https://foreignpolicy.com/2020/09/17/china-francis-vatican/

[xi] Daniel J. Flynn, *Cult City: Jim Jones, Harvey Milk, and 10 Days that Shook San Francisco*, (Wilmington, Delaware: Intercollegiate Studies Institute: 2018) 13-14.

[xii] Ibid, 30.

[xiii] Shania O'Brien, "Young Woman Reveals the Extraordinary Reason Gen Zs Don't Want to Work: 'Old People Need to Check Their Priorities'," The Daily Mail, April 28, 2023. https://www.dailymail.co.uk/femail/real-life/article-12023255/Millennial-woman-slammed-revealing-Gen-Z-workers-hate-jobs-Stop-whining.html

[xiv] Tom Phillips, "Fifty Years On, One of Mao's 'Little Generals' Exposes Horror of the Cultural Revolution," The Guardian, May 7, 2016. https://www.theguardian.com/world/2016/may/07/mao-little-general-horror-cultural-revolution

[xv] Jun Mai, "Former Red Guards Remember a time When Killing was Normal," South China Morning Post, June 8, 2016. https://www.scmp.com/news/china/policies-politics/article/1969051/former-red-guards-remember-time-when-killing-was-normal

[xvi] Dr. Li Zhisui, *The Private Life of Chairman Mao*, (NY: Random House: 1994) 420-421.

[xvii] Miriam Gross, "Between Party, People, and Profession: The Many Faces of the 'Doctor' during the Cultural Revolution," Medical History, vol 62, I. 3, 2018, 342-343. https://www.ncbi.nlm.nih.gov/pmc/articles/PMC6113761/pdf/S0025727318000236a.pdf

[xviii] Dr. Li Zhisui, *The Private Life of Chairman Mao*, (NY: Random House: 1994) 420-421.

[xix] Ibid 340-341.

[xx] Journal Article, "Revolution in Health," Chinese Medical Journal, vol. N2, Is. 04, January 1976, 298-308. https://mednexus.org/doi/epdf/10.5555/cmj.0366-6999.N2.04.p298.01

[xxi] Dr. Li Zhisui, *The Private Life of Chairman Mao*, (NY: Random House: 1994) 99-100.

[xxii] Ibid, 607.

[xxiii] News report, "Khmer Rouge: Cambodia's Years of Brutality," BBC News, November 16, 2018. https://www.bbc.com/news/world-asia-pacific-10684399

Chapter 18: Phase I Operational Line of Effort 4a for the Foreign-Backed Elites— Information Control – Media Disseminating Dogma

Controlling the access and content of information is fundamental to the existence of any authoritarian system. The FBE's endeavor is no different. Cultural propaganda and educational indoctrination alone are insufficient because easy access to contrarian sources of information breaks the FBE's monopoly on shaping the populations' mindset. The FBE requires a docile, pliant, and accepting public willing to endure hardship, suffering, and loss to protect the power of the intended autocracy. Controlling information and the instruments that disseminate that information is needed to train and condition the subjected population like Pavlovian dogs into accepting all excuses for corruption, failure, and stratification of an autocratic society. In the targeted advanced Western nation, the FBE faces a unique set of challenges that don't impact the kleptocracies of developing nations. The FBE must start their "nudging" campaign with an already free society with easy access to information and must convince this society into accepting autocratic control of that information without rebelling. In the era of the Information Age, controlling all information within the global data networks is impossible. Trillions of gigabytes of data flow in the world's information networks with billions of points of entry and some of these points being actively hidden from discovery. Realistically, the FBE will only be able to mitigate the damage the free flow of information causes, not eliminate it. Even China's vast array of totalitarian tools still doesn't plug all leaks in their controlled information environment.[i] The next best thing is to control the means of information dissemination and prioritize which information disseminators can be seen on every form of communication system and technology. For this LOE, the FBE must have proxies that disseminate and prioritize the sterilized FBE-friendly information while isolating contrary information that threatens the FBE. The dissemination proxies will be broadly labeled here as "media" while prioritizing data dissemination will be labeled as "authoritative".

Information Dissemination Dogma– The Media:

Before the Information Age, Western societies had to rely exclusively on formal media organizations, both public and private, for all information updates on world events, science, technology, and political discourse. There was no cheap easy way for near instantaneous communication between millions of individuals so mass dissemination of information required a lot of capital to be invested to create the means of dissemination. Media dissemination first came in the form of printed media such as newspapers, magazines, and journals but later advanced to include radio and television. Each new development improved the ability to disseminate more information quickly but each one still required large investments managed by a select few owners and managers. Eventually, governments formally recognized these organizations as authoritative disseminators of official information because these media organizations were the most effective means of mass communication. This arrangement continued into the 1990s with media groups monopolizing common information and how it was presented to the public. These circumstances created a common misperception about the quality of this era's information being more accurate, objective, and reliable than in the post-1990s information era because it was presented within a single perspective endorsed by authoritative institutions. Western societies' historical predilection for assuming trust and having faith in authoritative institutions truly desiring to be always accurate exacerbated this false perception.

The reality is disseminators of mass information have always been sensationalistic, selective in publishing facts, lie by omission, slander competitors, and pursue agendas at the cost of the public good. The only difference now is that the Information Age broke the monopolies in the West on who could disseminate information and scandals exposed the scale of authoritative media bias, sloppiness, and in some cases corruption. In the past more people believed the media were trustworthy crusaders against abusers of power and that the Fourth Estate was an independent force of public good because there was no one to contradict the publications or challenge media stories. In fact, corrupt governments, companies, and interest groups, including foreign powers, benefited greatly from this arrangement as many casual voters and the general public wanted to believe these authoritative media institutions were reliable. Any media corruption uncovered was dismissed as being exceptional even when corruption was prevalent. Having monopolistic power to disseminate authoritative information tempted the selfishness in many people to abuse such power. As long as the media organizations are seen as incorrupt by the public, these media organizations can manipulate information to suit whatever ideological, financial, or political interest the media organizations preferred. A tradition dating back to organized media's inception.

Examples abound throughout history on organized media being as much a detriment as a blessing to the public good. One classic example of this abuse of trust occurred with the supposedly venerable and valiant New York Times of the early 20th Century. It was the newspaper of record because many believed it was the most intellectually honest and diligent major press organization in the United States but in reality, it was just as sloppy, corrupt, and incompetent as any other unaccountable human organization. In 1932, the New York Times correspondent Walter Duranty received a Pulitzer Prize for his coverage of Joseph Stalin's administration of the Soviet Union in which he praised the dictator's economic plans and collectivization of all agriculture as the necessary reforms to modernize that country. To help support his argument, Duranty deliberately downplayed the severity of the deliberately caused famine in Ukraine that killed millions of Kulaks. This kept Duranty retaining access to Stalin who granted exclusive interviews allowing the New York Times to scoop their competitors for Soviet-related headlines further adding to the New York Times' mystique as an exceptionally capable paper.[ii] In reality, Duranty created fake news to buy headlines and cheat his way into a Pulitzer. Of course, major national news outlets are not the only ones susceptible to corruption, and sensationalism is not the only motivator. Helping corrupt elements within society to retain power at the cost of the public is another motivator.

Another example of media corruption on a smaller scale but just as insidious is the example of the small newspaper the *Daily Post-Athenian* of Athens, Tennessee in 1946. In the decade leading up to the local elections of 1946, the newspaper was complicit in the local party bosses and corrupt sheriff rigging elections and other criminal activity to enrich themselves. When a band of World War II veterans came back home discovered the level of corruption of local officials, several of them decided to run for office against these same corrupt officials. After a series of fraudulent activity, intimidation, and violence, the corrupt officials' party machine attempted to confiscate the ballots to prevent impartial counting and placed the ballots in the courthouse. This prompted the "Battle of Athens" where the fed-up veterans attacked the courthouse with firearms and placed the corrupt sheriff under siege. Eventually, the corrupt sheriff and his men surrendered and the ballot count occurred with the veterans winning the vote. [iii] Despite the violence, no one was killed and the public welcomed the outcome. In all of that chaos, the local paper refused to do what the press often claim is their "duty" and serve the public good. The newspaper refused to acknowledge the corruption or any related scandals. Another event proving that having one organization being the single source of mass information dissemination also becomes the single point of failure that eventually fails to corruption.

All of this has changed in the current information environment of the 2020s. The FBE no doubt would be nostalgic for the good old days when a corrupt organization just had to bribe, subvert, or intimidate one or two media organizations to its will without risking public notice. Now, there is no realistic way to buy or corruptly control all information dissemination within a Western society regardless of how degenerate that society has become. Instead of relying on a new Joseph Pulitzer or William Randolph Hearst to control media narratives, the FBE must now balance three challenges. The first is using proxy organizations to protect FBE-friendly media from NRF and other opposition information disseminators. Secondly, ensure only FBE-aligned media is declared authoritative and the primary source of reference for the general public. Lastly, being able to set the parameters of every public debate and social issue by having a controlled opposition media always makes the FBE position appear the most palatable to the larger general public.

The challenge of creating proxy organizations is both simple and difficult. Long established media organizations and institutions are the easiest to subvert for the FBE because these are capital-intensive, hierarchical, and designed to support the narrative set by its investors. This is easier in European rather than American states because they have more state control over its information dissemination. State media dissemination organizations just require lobbying in the right regulatory bureaucracy for certain rules and regulations to shape the organizational culture to FBE requirements. Corporate media organizations are only slightly more challenging. Most have major investors that dominate the institutions and the FBE just have make sure some of their sympathizing billionaire members or an FBE dominated venture capital investment firm maintains a controlling share in the media organizations. However, this alone is insufficient in the current information environment as social media, podcasts, video, streaming platforms, and other various niche technologies supporting information dissemination are eroding traditional media dissemination dominance in the marketplace.[iv] Fortunately for the FBE, most of these social media services and platforms are managed by major companies that survive on the favorable terms with government regulators and the goodwill of major investors. FBE lobbying with their political allies can shape regulations and FBE-sympathetic investment firms or billionaires to control the governing boards of these social media firms. By holding the power to shape their regulatory and investment environment, the FBE can bring most media dissemination firms to heel. Consequently however, there will be firms incentivized to pursue anti-FBE market share as the FBE will never successfully indoctrinate the entire population. By trying to assert authority over the Western nation, the FBE also creates the incentives for the creation of their opposition, which includes defiant media platforms and services.

This creates the second challenge of having to deal with information disseminators providing information to the public and to the NRF that is detrimental to FBE strategic objectives. Since the FBE cannot control all information dissemination, the next best thing is to convince the public to prioritize their sources of information by their perceived legitimacy. The FBE would need to coordinate with their media proxies and government sympathizers to convince government, cultural, and social institutions that only certain platforms are legitimate by declaring those platforms authoritative. If the major institutions of the society believe certain media organizations are the only valid dissemination platforms, then the inherent authority of those institutions will also transfer to those media organizations. This provides the FBE-preferred media organizations the air of legitimacy for most of the general public which further isolates NRF-friendly media or any independent media organization. Once the FBE have made their media proxies officially legitimate and "authoritative" to society, the FBE can overwhelm any contrary information dissemination sources with more output while simultaneously degrading the opposition's credibility. Since the FBE must rely on some misinformation and lie by omission, the FBE will have to constantly be on the media offensive to drown out any damaging revelations released by the NRF.

This leads to the final challenge of co-opting and creating controlled-opposition media. A foreign controlled alliance of corrupt elites inevitably creates enemies so the FBE must acknowledge they cannot avoid this eventuality. Instead, the best course of action is to corruptly control groups and individuals who voice similar pronouncements as the NRF to rally potential opposition audiences away from actual NRF information sources. Once lured, these controlled-opposition groups will highlight FBE-related abuses or corruption but then advocate for ineffective courses of action or help the FBE entrap members of the opposition audience to eliminate its more aggressively defiant elements. By keeping the opposition divided with misinformation, public acts of incompetence or corruption, the FBE can minimize the NRF's ability to undermine public faith in FBE-controlled institutions. All three of these challenges must be actioned simultaneously as the information warfare environment will change by the week with the added danger that the universe is uncontrollable. There will be "black swan" outliers or unforeseen events that are beyond either the NRF's or FBE's control such as a natural disaster, random exposure of a corruption scandal, heart attack of a key figure, etc. This means no matter how comprehensively controlled the information environment becomes, there will always be something to throw that situation off balance. Both the NRF and FBE will wage their information campaigns the most aggressively out of all the potential domains of the civil war.

Strengths:

The controlling of corporate and state-owned mass media organizations gives the FBE access to already built-in audiences that eagerly consume these organizations' disseminated information. Humans seek comfort in familiarity and will always look for information that reassures them that their place in the world is either going up or at least staying put. Many people are raised within a certain worldview provided by these information disseminators and these same people have shaped their lives and beliefs around this disseminated worldview. Contrarian views, no matter how logical or compelling, will always have great difficulty breaking into these audiences because this new information could negatively disrupt their comfortable lives. Instead of having to risk disruption or having to work to readjust their lives to more accurate information, these established audiences will more likely just close off their receptibility to any contrary information. This requires less work for the audience and plays on their desire for the instant gratification that their perception is right and they don't have to personally improve or make changes. Laziness and vanity are two powerful motivators that make the audiences want to believe their preferred media disseminators, even if the audience doesn't always believe the information. Rationalizing a delusion to justify the way the audience lives and believes gives propagandist media a lot of flexibility with the truth. This media influence is especially true on older audiences aged over 45.

Older people were born and raised in the era of media monopolies where two major news wires, a few major national newspapers, and three television networks were all that controlled information dissemination. There was no competition for this select group, except each other, and rarely did these organizations contradict each other on topic positions, except in a few select editorials. The older audience has been raised since birth to accept these organizations were "authoritative" and diligent in their analysis and reporting, even though one could not independently verify this assumption. Believing one has the correct worldview is psychologically reassuring as it means one is part of the community and one knows how to fit in that community. So, older audiences take comfort in receiving their world information from traditional corporate "authoritative" news organizations to maintain their sense of belonging and superiority to any contrarians. The traditional media organizations' audience is overwhelmingly older with most averaging in the mid-60s.[v] These older audiences are entrenched to familiarity and more of them are far more likely to trust the traditional corporate news than younger audiences. In the 1970s, nearly 70% of the US audience had at least some faith in news organizations reporting but now that belief is inverted with the majority of the change being from younger audiences.[vi]

These built-in audiences allow the FBE to create perceptions and myths about their opponents, and allies, that can become the de-facto belief of the national population. Despite the diminishing reach of traditional corporate media, these organizations remain large and powerful enough to create artificial personas, myths, or rumors about opponents who will have great difficulty dispelling the misinformation. Major media organizations have done this for generations for the sake of sensationalism, profit-making, or political lobbying. For example, the media worked with J. Edgar Hoover in the mid-1930s to create the myth of Kate "Ma" Barker as the leader of the notorious Barker-Karpis Gang. Popular perception is she led the gang with ruthless brutal efficiency which gave the gang a more romanticized portrayal as a family of criminal villains. However, there is little

evidence she actively participated in the crimes and the media were instrumental for portraying her as the leader even though this was not true.[vii]'

[viii] Even though her leadership was a media falsehood, the popular cultural perception of her is ingrained as the ruthless criminal matriarch that inspired many fictional portrayals and inspirations like Ma Beagle of Disney's *DuckTales* TV show. Even in a fragmented information environment, the ability to create myths and rapidly spread falsehoods is powerful enough to change the strategic outcome of any civil conflict.

Another strength for the FBE corruptly controlling the majority of the information dissemination market would be their ability to hide behind half-truths. The best lies and deceptions have some level of truth within them to make it harder for detractors to discredit or disprove the deception. Half-truths are more effective if these are spread rapidly within the society to choke out any dissemination of opposing evidence to dominate an issue or argument. The media organizations can use their numerous outlets to drown out contrarian reports on events, people, or topics the FBE want to control. These outlets have many options in how to tell half-truths that could suit the FBE's narratives. The media organizations can withhold key facts, burying facts in jargon or overly complex language or placing key points near the end of a story can omit truth by story structure, deliberately pursue false rumors, or obfuscate research methods and sources. The best part for the FBE is if they control these proxy media organizations long enough, then the continuing manipulations and falsehoods become accepted as the standard practice for everyone dealing with information dissemination. Over time, what standards remain within these professions will become increasingly lax, allowing more indoctrinated people to be employed within these organizations to convey more falsehoods to push out any remaining dissenting thought within the media organizations.

Once this occurs, there would be only one official narrative, not set by the state, but by the FBE leaders who use their private proxies to control information dissemination. At that point, the FBE can become more brazen in its propaganda by using more outright lies that can be justified with false studies, polls, or fake sources to justify any decision or stance no matter how inconsistent. This is crucial because the only objective for controlling information dissemination is to help the FBE achieve autocracy but the FBE cannot admit to this. The FBE must shield their actions with false promises of concern, altruism, justice, and empathy which means there will be many stances that will contradict each other. The stances are only for helping the FBE win support in the immediate aftermath of a major media event. The FBE must inevitably lie, be hypocritical to the public, and defame rivals to succeed so the media proxies must help shield the FBE's advocates from ruin.

The media disseminators' efforts to protect FBE reputation while disseminating lies is made easier by people's stubbornness to adhere to their worldview. Although older generations are unique in that they overly attach themselves to traditional forms of media, all generations want to only see and hear what makes them feel safe and comfortable. People naturally gravitate to echo chambers where only their preferred perspective is advocated. Few are willing or able to open their minds to consider opposing positions for greater understanding with most only listening to opposition to find weaknesses in their arguments. Corporate and state media disseminators now have to contend with more decentralized social media but social media has strengthened echo chambers, not diminished them. Meaning even if the NRF have their own information dissemination outlets, few outside their established support base will want to listen. The FBE proxy media can exacerbate the echo chamber phenomena with additional propaganda that support social pressure on undecided members of the public to conform. This is further assisted by the short attention spans created by many social media services that rely on quick soundbites to convey whole ideas. These simple messages can be used to convey a lot of information very quickly but only for those who have deep understanding of the relevant topic already. However, it has the opposite effect for those ignorant on the topic as these short messages can give gullible people a false sense of understanding and endorse simplistic ideas or solutions.

This makes social media particularly attractive as a tool to maintain control over the FBE's Nimbyists and Atomized proxy information fighters. Propaganda made by "authoritative" entities of what social positions are considered in vogue and what is truthful is a powerful tool of control. These social pressures can keep the apathetic or undecided members of the public at least acquiescent to the FBE's agenda.

A study in Scientific American cited behavioral sciences demonstrating that using social pressures is the most effective way to emotionally compel people into trying to fit into official social norms. In this case, they studied how environmental movements could compel undecided people to change their skeptical beliefs on manmade climate change by using social pressure to make them feel ostracized and thereby surrender their beliefs to fit in. The study showed this was more effective than any other form of social intervention.[ix] Such pressure methods' effectiveness isn't limited to one social issue and the FBE's proxy media's market domination could wield these methods to amplify similar social pressures on keeping the majority of the public conforming to their autocratic-friendly narratives. This brings the added bonus of stifling detrimental information as people don't want the unnecessary social stigma of believing contrarian ideas or information. Furthermore, the FBE can use its financial influence to use their NGOs, activist groups, and others to lobby for "media education or literacy" curriculums in schools that train youngsters on how to interpret media disseminated information. This would make it easier to impose social pressures at a much earlier age to condition them to accept only FBE-approved viewpoints as "legitimate information". Many advocates against misinformation have cited Finland's medial literacy campaign as a model to fight against misinformation as it has been very successful at raising its population's awareness of media methodology.[x] The problem for people with objective goals and an advantage for the FBE, is that these literacy programs are run by activist groups who recommend to the state what the criteria should be to critically interpret media dissemination of topics.[xi] Meaning that the Finnish system relies on a top-down model of education that relies on the education institutions and advocacy groups to not be corrupted in the first place. The FBE could use their Nimbyists and Atomized proxies to pressure such education groups into setting the parameters of what is true on behalf of the FBE. So, in an anocracy, media literacy could further blind the population to actual propaganda by having propaganda education. Without stable institutions like in Finland, such education curriculums could solidify misinformation as long as it is useful to the FBE.

Even if a dangerous story or information does go viral with the public, the FBE's inherent resource advantage with its media-proxy forces can stifle the information's impact. If something is irrefutable then FBE proxies simply just ignore the story and prevent anyone from having any discussion. If FBE proxies try to engage with their detractors or defend something that is clearly wrong to anyone with any semblance of logic, the FBE would prolong the story's lifecycle within the public's attention span. Consequently, the FBE would inevitably lose face and credibility as they try to defend the indefensible. By utilizing their superior ability to disseminate information over much wider audiences over longer periods of time, the FBE can instruct their proxies to just not acknowledge the story. With so many media organizations ignoring derogatory information, the damaging revelations will lose momentum and be forgotten by the largely apathetic public within a few weeks. The FBE can also invert this capability to overwhelm an opponent with slander and attacks. If an NRF element is identified as a threat, the FBE can use its media proxies to repeatedly attack that target. These proxies can also use this as a form of extortion by holding back genuinely embarrassing stories to gain NRF members' cooperation. Again, this isn't about persuasion, this is about keeping the NRF from being able to act in a coordinated fashion. A socially ostracized NRF cannot build credibility and help mobilize against the FBE. Controlling the amount of focus on a news story, real or imagined, would be one of the greatest strengths in this LOE.

The final strength of this LOE on information control is the digitization of information makes it easy for media organizations to make most information fungible enough to hide accurate information. Previously mentioned strengths revolve around modifying interpretations of actual information but this additional strength of being able to flood the public with completely false information can paralyze opposition. Since major media organizations do not receive outside scrutiny and dominate most of the market share in information dissemination, the NRF faces the near-impossible task of disproving official narratives set by the FBE. If a media source for a news event is not available, then the FBE can make one up or take a true story as the basis for a completely false narrative that takes all attention away from the actual story. Digital information is easily corruptible and very time consuming to filter out the garbage from the genuine information. So, the FBE doesn't just have to focus on hiding damaging facts but will also have the luxury of making up their own facts or selecting facts that are completely irrelevant to a specific news event. Successfully subverting major media dissemination organizations is a critical LOE that, if properly implemented, would give an overwhelming advantage against the NRF.

Weaknesses:

Although this part of LOE 4 would have many advantages for the FBE, there are also a considerable number of drawbacks if it is not carefully managed. The management of information dissemination to control political narratives requires an understanding of multiple audiences simultaneously: 1. The FBE's own loyalists; 2. The apathetic public; and 3. The renegade social elements including the NRF. Such understanding requires not only constant study of those who are outside the FBE's direct control but must also have sufficient ability to appreciate the perspectives of their opponents. In practice, this is very difficult and depending on how the FBE chose to subvert these mass media organizations, might create self-imposed limitations on understanding effective information control for all three audiences. Then there is the actual functionality of the information organizations themselves as there are just as many risks of failure occurring within the FBE's media proxies as the risk of alienating their target audiences. Information dissemination is critical for LOE 4 to be successful and this requires artful skills in mass psychology, persuasion, intimidation, manipulation, and finally timing. This complex series of requirements for a group like the FBE which emphasize loyalists to conform and obey over being competent means the FBE would likely experience many pitfalls and failures in this implementation.

The first weakness will be the scope of understanding about this subject among the leaders of the FBE themselves. To reiterate, having narcissistic, avaricious, decadent, and corrupt individuals willing to do whatever it takes to satisfy their desire for power is required for a foreign adversary to build and manipulate a group like the FBE. The majority of such individuals are likely to be insulated from any harsh realities their opponents or the public face in daily life. There will be a danger that the FBE leaders in charge of subverting information will be stuck in their ivory

131

towers of thought insulated from anything that might disturb their worldview. Over time, this seclusion built on entitlement and arrogance increases the risk of having the FBE genuinely believing in their own propaganda. Wealthy and influential people being convinced they are Nietzsche's living incarnation of superior humans able to create utopia on Earth will close off many FBE leaders to potential dangers or shortcomings. What is worse is that when mistakes are made, the information dissemination proxies will only provide narratives the FBE desire rather than what they need to understand to correct their mistakes. The FBE leadership will increasingly be tempted to shift blame to anything else when inevitable mistakes are made as their worldview goes uncontested by the propaganda the FBE makes routine and mainstream.

The incentive for the FBE's information disseminators to always please their leaders would be too strong to not to have an influence. This means the FBE's propagandists would add layers of "authoritative" sources to reinforce the narrative making the FBE's ability to self-discern their own misinformation very difficult. The most glaring example of this in the real world right now is the Western media's introduction of secondary voices that appear objective while reaffirming media organizations' narratives. This trend created one of the most meaningless titles in contemporary times called the "fact checker". Fact checkers proclaim the role of gatekeeper to deciding the veracity of claim, story, or narrative usually by citing a statement or publication from someone else. This can be valid but just as often as not, these added citations are not in-depth references that the audience can easily study for themselves but are simple declarative statements without substantive backing. The basis for this title's existence rests solely on idea of "authoritative sources" being unquestionably reliable, objective, and accurate. This can work if the proclaimed fact checker can explain their position with verifiable facts and explanatory logic on how they reached their conclusion, but this is rare in practice. Instead, most fact checkers are selected by the information disseminators themselves with few additional qualifications from any standard media writer who often selectively pick statements or cite publications that support their employer's narrative.[xii] Fact checkers typically are often just fact selectors, picking what facts to omit or misconstrue under the assumption that the majority of the public is too lazy and ignorant to verify the veracity of media stories independently.[xiii] Although this assumption is broadly true, such propagandistic actions harden opposition's resolve against the FBE's narrative. Fact-checkers and their media sponsors are only as effective as their credibility with their target audience. Once that credibility is lost, that audience will also be lost. The danger becomes strongest if the FBE media proxies successfully control their loyalist audience but lose credibility with the apathetic public and the renegade NRF audiences. In such circumstance, fact-checking and other "authoritative" reinforcement of the narrative would create a powerful echo chamber that only deceives themselves and not the FBE's opponents.

The next major weakness is the media proxies themselves. As cited earlier, many people in media are already corrupt with scandals of plagiarism, false stories, criminal conduct, altering stories for personal agendas, and being easily manipulated by interest groups because they are too lazy to check the sources of their reports. There have been many examples cited previously but additional examples reemphasize the problem. Like reporter Ryan Broderick being fired for plagiarizing 11 articles on Buzzfeed[xiv], mistaking a Kentucky shooting range for combat in Syria,[xv] or Katie Couric deliberately altering a recorded interview with Ruth Bader Ginsberg to edit out responses to questions Couric didn't like.[xvi] Then there is the slurry of sleazy media personalities either conducting criminal activities themselves or being closely associated with them. Not simply white-collar crimes but persons conducting heinous child-related sex crimes such as former CNN producer John Griffin,[xvii] former medical correspondent Dr. Bruce Hensel,[xviii] former Fox 5 Charles Leaf,[xix] former Ohio 10TV and meteorologist Mike Davis to name a few.[xx] Not to mention other crimes like former TV reporters Somchai Lisaius and Krystin Sorich Lisaius for drug and child abuse.[xxi] The point being is the profession of journalism inherently attracts "scum and villainy" before any outside interest group or nation even tries to subvert or corrupt journalism. Such people are unreliable and can undermine rather than strengthen the FBE's cause if exposed. Then there is also the danger of gullibility and incompetence being reinforced amongst the FBE as these corrupt media organizations rush out incomplete or easily disprovable narratives to meet internal deadlines or shift blame of disasters to innocent parties.

All of these weaknesses can exacerbate the problems of the final greatest weakness of this LOE, the strict top-down control of information dissemination. For the FBE to have control, it needs to control all information, including how and what is presented to audiences. Leaders must direct the proxies to carry out specific orders to ensure consistent narratives about specific stories to avoid jeopardizing the greater objective of the FBE. This control also prevents proxies becoming independent from FBE leadership because any weakening of authority makes them susceptible to internal rivalries. This inevitably would create stovepipes of information flow meaning situational changes will occur more rapidly than the FBE can receive and decide on how to act on the information. The top-down dissemination also means the FBE's loyalist audience is reliant on specific select channels of information flow to support the FBE. The NRF can severely disrupt FBE situational awareness of specific events to the point that the FBE cannot appropriately react to vital media stories leaving them vulnerable to misinformation or making a rash decision. This would also paralyze their loyalist public audiences as they are often loyal to only select media sources which, if disrupted, would make the audience hesitant to react to certain events the way the FBE wants them to. This creates a further danger that the FBE's narrative information would be retained among a few specific key proxy organizations that their foreign benefactor could spy on to gather extortion-relevant materials to stymie any FBE attempt to become more autonomous after achieving autocracy in the Western nation.

As long as the FBE remains cognizant that their LOE 4 is vital but not a magic bullet, the ability to control information dissemination will be a key factor in achieving victory. Their inherent resource advantage gives them a wide range of options but also simplifies the NRF's targeting as the top-down FBE proxies will have major organizational bottle necks. Dissemination of information is vital but so is understanding the information that is disseminated.

---

[i] Journal article, "How Chinese Netizens Breached the Great Firewall," The Economist, December 8, 2022. https://www.economist.com/china/2022/12/08/how-chinese-netizens-breached-the-great-firewall

[ii] David Folkenflik, "'The New York Times' Can't Shake the Cloud Over a 90-Year-Old Pulitzer Prize," NPR, May 8, 2022. https://www.npr.org/2022/05/08/1097097620/new-york-times-pulitzer-ukraine-walter-duranty

[iii] Lones Seiber, "The Battle of Athens," American Heritage Magazine, vol. 36, is. 2, February/March 1985. https://www.americanheritage.com/battle-athens

[iv] Nicole Martin, "How Social Media Has Changed How We Consume News," Forbes, November 30, 2018. https://www.forbes.com/sites/nicolemartin1/2018/11/30/how-social-media-has-changed-how-we-consume-news/?sh=62bb401f3c3c

[v] AJ Katz, "Here's the Median Age of the Typical Cable News Viewer," TV Newser, January 19, 2019. https://www.adweek.com/tvnewser/heres-the-median-age-of-the-typical-cable-news-viewer/

[vi] Darren K. Carlson, "Trust in Media," GALLUP, September 17, 2002. https://news.gallup.com/poll/6802/trust-media.aspx

[vii] Archive Note, "Barker/Karpis Gang," FBI Records Vault, accessed December 12, 2022. https://vault.fbi.gov/barker-karpis-gang

[viii] Article File, "Ma Barker: Crime Files," Crime and Investigation, accessed December 12, 2022. https://www.crimeandinvestigation.co.uk/crime-files/ma-barker

[ix] Andrea Thompson, "What Makes People Act on Climate Change, According to Behavioral Science," Scientific American, April 19, 2023. https://www.scientificamerican.com/article/what-makes-people-act-on-climate-change-according-to-behavioral-science/?amp=true

[x] Government report, *Media Literacy in Finland*, Ministry of Education and Culture, Finland, 2019. https://medialukutaitosuomessa.fi/mediaeducationpolicy.pdf

[xi] Rauna Rahja, "Current Approaches and Policies in Finish Media Literacy," Finnish Society on Media Education Presentation, November 24, 2014, slide 5. https://www.slideshare.net/Mediakasvatusseura/rahja-mandl-2014currentapproaches

[xii] Alex Berezow, "Debunkers Debunked: Who Fact-Checks The Fact-Checkers?" American Council on Science and Health, November 4, 2019. https://www.acsh.org/news/2019/11/04/debunkers-debunked-who-fact-checks-fact-checkers-14378

[xiii] Stephen J. Ceci, Wendy M. Williams, "The Psychology of Fact-Checking," Scientific American, October 25, 2020. https://www.scientificamerican.com/article/the-psychology-of-fact-checking1/

[xiv] Jon Levine, "Buzzfeed Senior Reporter Ryan Broderick Fired for Plagiarism," NY Post, June 27, 2020. https://nypost.com/2020/06/27/buzzfeed-senior-reporter-ryan-broderick-fired-for-plagiarism/

[xv] David Choi, "ABC News Apparently Mistook Video of Machine Gun Fire on A Kentucky Gun Range for The Turkish Attack on Syria," Business Insider, October 14, 2019. https://www.businessinsider.com/video-of-kentucky-gun-range-mistaken-for-syria-attack-2019-10

[xvi] Daniel Bates, "Katie Couric Covered Up RBG's Dislike for Taking the Knee: Anchor Says She Edited 2016 Interview To 'Protect' The Justice After She Said People Who Kneel Are Showing 'Contempt for A Government That Made a Decent Life Possible'", The Daily Mail, October 13, 2021. https://www.dailymail.co.uk/news/article-10088027/Katie-Couric-admits-editing-Ruth-Bader-Ginsburg-interview-protect-late-justice.html

[xvii] Allie Griffin, "Ex-CNN Producer John Griffin Pleads Guilty to Child Sex Charge," NY Post, December 12, 2022. https://nypost.com/2022/12/12/ex-cnn-john-griffin-producer-pleads-guilty-to-child-sex-charge/

[xviii] James Queally, "Former NBC Personality Sentenced to Probation for Asking Child for Naked Pictures," LA Times, March 6, 2023. https://www.latimes.com/california/story/2023-03-06/former-nbc-personality-sentenced-to-probation-for-asking-child-for-naked-pictures

[xix] Erin Vogt, "NJ Court Overturns Child-Rape Conviction of Fox 5 New York Reporter," New Jersey 101.5, March 16, 2021. https://nj1015.com/nj-court-overturns-child-rape-conviction-of-fox-5-new-york-reporter/

[xx] News Report, "Sentencing Postponed for Former Meteorologist in Child Porn Case," NBC4i, March 23, 2020. https://www.nbc4i.com/news/local-news/sentencing-postponed-for-former-meteorologist-in-child-porn-case/

[xxi] News Report, "Ex-TV Personalities Enter Plea After Baby Tests Positive for Cocaine," CBS News, September 1, 2016. https://www.cbsnews.com/news/tv-personalities-cocaine-babys-system-arizona-krystin-lisaius-somchai-lisaius-plea/

Chapter 19: Phase I Operational Line of Effort 4b for the Foreign-Backed Elites— Information Control – Experts as the New Priest Class and Credentials the New Talismans

In most of the world's nations there exists a collection of highly educated professionals skilled in specific arts and sciences who lead the world's innovation, policymaking, and collective understanding of the world at large. Within these professions a select group of them become advisors and mentors to social and government institutions on how to identify, solve, or mitigate problems and will be termed for this section, the "expert class". The current concept of the expert class is descended from the scientific optimism of the early 20th Century when it was believed people would objectively seek new knowledge only to solve the world's problems. The logic being as humanity became more scientific, the world would eventually see the negation of more subjective concepts of morality and traditions based on historical social experiences. This led to concepts like technocracy where experts would eventually develop the means to predict and control all human activities like chemical reactions in a lab.[1] The notion of enlightened human beings becoming true-to-life oracles and miracle workers who could answer life's questions without the inconvenience of proselytizing moral commitments from spiritual institutions was enticing. Having answers for the world without attached moral obligations convinced many that metaphysical moral guidance was obsolete and began a gradual substitution of priests and other moral teachers with experts. Experts didn't morally judge and offered solutions for this world rather than preparing for a possible but not guaranteed afterlife. This appealed to governments because they could delegate problem solving to a select group of knowledgeable people while getting credit for "action". The public also liked experts because they could shift personal responsibility from redeeming their own flawed souls to some unseen experts in the hope the experts will solve people's problems for them. Like the priesthood beforehand, the typical laymen of society will rarely question or challenge the affirmations of experts, especially if these are reassuring, because the laymen will not truly understand what is being stated. Consequentially, this means experts are difficult to hold accountable, making this class of professionals susceptible to corruption and subversion by the FBE.

Such faith and expectations given to a select group of people no doubt inspires many experts to truly act as heroes and try to help solve problems. The downside of this is that, like fame, uncritical reverence can intoxicate people into believing they're superhuman, exceptionally enlightened, or can solve more than their abilities would truly allow. Giving any group, no matter what the calling or aspiration, unfettered praise creates vanity which in turn creates blinders. Many such experts start to believe in these social expectations that they are the most enlightened and mature persons. Eventually, such people will think they alone can solve the world's ills and everyone else's stupidity is the problem. Such corrupted egos are ripe for manipulation because vanity turns open minded experts into dogmatic gatekeepers who reject any information that contradicts these experts' conclusions. When one believes they are the most enlightened and have built a reputation as an exceptional expert, this person now has every incentive to close their mind. Any contradictory evidence undermines their reputation and diminishes their importance so many become zealous dogmatics who will slander and persecute anyone advancing ideas that might diminish established experts' authority. Much like an inquisition of a church seeking heathens.

Eventually, enough of these vain people will have accumulated into every major field of study to become the dogmatic guardians of that field which stifles new research and alternative theories. In the West, many experts in various fields, especially ones that have either political or economic implications that involve grants and financial patronage, have changed from pursuing classic scientific and intellectual inquiry to protecting approved orthodoxies. Many in the West now presume the basis for many research fields have established immutable truths and all that is now needed is for experts to extract useful knowledge based on these unmovable orthodoxies. However, in reality this is not always the case because many of the foundational theories and concepts are derived from incomplete understanding of the subjects and must rely on "not always reliable" assumptions to build these theories. Not all fields have theories as verifiable as Einstein's Relativity Theory nor do all fields of study have fully objective set answers to questions. Yet, if anything new disrupts an established field which could undermine an industry, a key personality, or a policy, it is just as likely to be attacked and ridiculed as it is likely to be studied. The incentive of contemporary experts to inflexibly defend programs or studies stems from the decline of accountability, eliminating failure standards, and the need to hype trendy topics to get funding from private industries and public grants.

The combination of constantly seeking money, public reverence, and the need for personalities to protect reputations have created the perfect storm to stifle proper inquiry within the West while increasing corruption. This problem is not limited to the liberal arts or social sciences either, as the thirst for technology and grant money has corrupted the Science-Technology-Engineering-Math (STEM) fields as well. This process of declining standards for professional experts and discouragement of novel ideas started during the Cold War with some people warning about this risk as far back as the 1950s. President Eisenhower's farewell speech is often remembered for his warning of the potential dangers of a military-industrial complex, but he also warned that the heavy costs of research has made "...a government contract become virtually a substitute for intellectual curiosity".[2]

This stagnating dogma of gatekeeping, grant-guaranteeing orthodoxy has permeated to the point that many experts no longer practice science by seeking truth through falsifiability and instead proactively seek the data that justifies hypotheses guaranteeing publicity and money. No field of inquiry is immune from this affliction, including fundamental ones such as physics. Critics like German physicist Dr. Sabine Hossenfelder highlights some scientists advocating a "post-empirical science" that allows them to move the goal-posts anytime one of their hypotheses cannot be tested or verified.[3] Other like-minded critics such as Columbia University physicist Dr. Peter Woit point out how the lack of falsifiability of the various versions of String Theory have hindered the pursuit of potentially more substantive alternatives.[4] For example, Dr. Woit highlighted the lack of any verifiable positive indicators from CERN Particle Accelerator test results to confirm Supersymmetry Theory. Yet, instead of acknowledging the failure to detect supersymmetry, Dr. Woit points out string theorists unfairly redefine what criteria they seek to verify supersymmetry after every failed result.[5], [6], [7], [8] Then there are the mavericks and eccentrics who cause trouble for the established scientific community like mathematician Dr. Eric Weinstein who often disparages the stifling environment of STEM orthodoxy.[9] These three critics are a sampling of a larger group of scientists, mathematicians, and others who want the gatekeeping, grant-seeking system that dominates the theoretical fields to go back to more empirical evidenced-based approaches rather than pursuing what is trendy to potential science patrons.[10] Each of these critics have their own specific criticisms and solutions for this problem but all of them in one way or another want a system that allows honest study and debate which means allowing the radical mavericks to participate, not just the orthodox gatekeepers.

Extraordinary claims require extraordinary evidence but gatekeepers often bypass objective evaluation for a quicker predetermined dismissal to protect established experts. Mavericks and radicals in science are not always right but the mavericks are also the ones who usually make the greatest breakthroughs when they are right. Dr. Roger Penrose for example, is one of the most brilliant men of the 20th Century with proven track record of scientific brilliance working with Dr. Steven Hawking on the question of when gravitation produces singularities. His contributions would indicate he is purely a mainstream scientist yet he still remains a maverick. Frustrated by the scientific community's inability to explain or understand consciousness or the mind decided to attempt to solve it himself using the unorthodox idea that consciousness stems from quantum mechanical process rather than classic computing. He eventually proposed, along with Dr. Stuart Hameroff, the "Orchestrated Objective Reduction Theory" that argues quantum computations in microtubules of neuron cells create moments of conscious experience.[11] Doctors Hameroff and Penrose were ridiculed and dismissed by the mainstream gatekeeping community for decades before finally getting some mainstream acknowledgement as more conventional theories fail to account for consciousness.[12] Penrose's stellar reputation allowed him to pursue his heretical theory without risking his career, but that doesn't always happen. Balancing honest rigorous evaluation while letting the scientific heretics have opportunities to defend themselves is critical to keep scientific fields dynamic but there is no indication this problem is going away.

All of these examples focused on the theoretical science fields but expert gatekeeping is worse in fields of study that have direct political or economic outcomes. Many studies, proposals, and declarations are made to suit the interests of those patrons supporting the research rather than objectively verifying a proposal or idea.[13] There are numerous examples of contradicting studies, reports, and proclamations stating a particular position is true and declare their detractors are spreading misinformation. There has always been competition between scientific arguments, but in modern times, one side is given more publicity, proclaimed legitimacy, and proclaimed authoritative reliability based on the preferred stance within a topic. If that position fits in with the interest of activist groups, companies investing in a product, or better justifies a state policy, then information disseminating organizations are more "persuaded" to defend that preferred position and stifle any contrary evidence. Usually, such skewering only delays the truth being revealed and destroying the "immutable truth" that everyone came to accept by professed experts but delays are usually enough for the vested parties to profit by such actions.

Regardless of a study's validity, many groups and organizations will criticize anything that may nullify their preferred "truth". One of the first examples of this was the coverup of the health effects of asbestos. Despite the evidence of asbestos' dangers dating back to the 1930s, the companies that financially relied on asbestos, used experts such as Dr. Anthony Lanza, to conceal the effects from their workers for decades.[14] Even after the discoveries became public, other organizations have been accused of covering up using asbestos as a cost-saving measure in their products such as the Johnson & Johnson Baby Powder which provoked numerous lawsuits.[15], [16] Another example are the back and forth results of studies on the full impact of cholesterol in eggs on humans. More recent news states the majority of studies that downplayed the level of cholesterol in eggs for years were industry-funded and had a clear conflict of interest.[17], [18] Admittedly, that may or may not be relevant as some contend consuming cholesterol doesn't necessarily increase cholesterol in the blood stream,[19] it nevertheless shows that corruption of expertise to suit the preferred result of the paymaster remains prevalent. Both examples indicate experts can be corrupted by fiscal reasons alone but the risk of hasty conclusions is further increased when political considerations are a factor. The most glaring example occurred during the COVID Pandemic which both undermined the credibility of "authoritative" sources and highlighted the dysfunctional behavior of many contemporary experts.

During the COVID outbreak, many established organizations and reputed personalities asserted that the virus could not have been accidentally leaked from a Chinese biological laboratory and actively besmirched those who stated it might not come from a seafood market. Many experts quickly attested that the lab-leak theory was not viable and some used the term "conspiracy theory" to disparage those who considered this as a possibility.[20] In some cases, experts vouched for the safety protocols of the lab without actually being able to corroborate it, their argument boiled down to "trust us".[21] Essentially, the argument being the Wuhan Lab is run by fellow experts and experts wouldn't make such profound mistakes. Of course, it didn't seem to occur to them that foreign person visits are given the best possible show rather than what might typically occur. These assertions were later contradicted by other authoritative bodies a year later who indicated the lab origin was a plausible scenario supported by two peer-reviewed studies and further assessments done by US government departments.[22], [23] Additionally, the declaration of the Wuhan lab's innocence loses further credibility because the Chinese Communist Party refused any detailed audits of the lab by the World Health Organization or any outside bodies.[24] The truth about the COVID virus' origin is irrelevant here because either scenario of a lab leak or natural outbreak are both plausibly true and will not be known until the fall of the CCP. What is relevant was the approach of the anti-lab leak theory experts towards the pro-lab leak theory advocates. These experts didn't actively seek the truth nor did they engage in actual debate or discussion but arrogantly and patronizingly dismissed those who questioned the "immutable truth" of that time.[25] They also would tie people who argued the plausible lab-leak theory to other separate and more radical theories of COVID, such as being engineered as a weapon or that it had been deliberately released. They intertwined all of these disparate theories into one to paint all detractors with the same brush so the public would believe anyone contradicting the "immutable truth" were crazy conspiracy theorists.[26] This was a perfect example of ego and sloppiness driving authoritative experts to gatekeep the "immutable truth" set by expert groupthink rather than seeking legitimate inquiry. Ironically, their theory might be the correct one. Yet, their stubborn insistence that they were unquestionably right and their detractors were wrong alienated large swaths of the general public. So, when contrary evidence became public indicating the lab leak was plausible combined with the general incompetence at handling the pandemic, these gatekeepers effectively undermined public trust in authoritative institutions as much, if not more, as any deliberate CCP misinformation campaign. [27]

These are just a few specific examples of the current problems of modern experts. The systemic problems that enable this pervasive culture of sloppy, self-aggrandizing opportunism among many in the expert class have existed for decades. If human systems don't have built in self-correcting mechanisms, these systems will eventually decline in quality, reliability, and efficiency. One of the most effective policing mechanisms "peer-reviewing", is an example of a human system that has declined. Since the early 2000s, numerous well-respected journals and research organizations have been sloppy in peer-reviewing ideas and proposals. Since 2005, numerous studies, reports, and conclusions were never truly verified nor given sufficient scrutiny paid to warrant giving these bad studies a pass. In the last decade, the problem became widespread enough to prompt researchers to try to replicate findings of multiple research projects in many fields of social and natural sciences only to find out these couldn't be replicated. This problem has been acknowledged for years but little progress has been made to fix or reform it. [28] Reforms that have been proposed, including paying peer-reviewers to evaluate others work to incentivize rigid investigation, but few changes have actually occurred in part because too many people and organizations have learned to benefit off the broken system.[29]

Nor is peer-review the only broken system, as academia, think tanks, and other centers for developing experts enable the sub-culture of corrupt experts. Individual university professors have been caught in various forms of fraud,[30], [31] secretly aiding foreign adversaries,[32] and falsifying research data.[33], [34], [35], [36], [37], [38] Corruption in universities themselves is now more prevalent and susceptible to bribes, admissions fraud, and academic malfeasance creating an atmosphere of lower standards.[39], [40] This is not just a Western problem, but a world-wide problem where the encouragement of cutting corners to gain an advantage is now prevalent.[41]

In the policy arena, experts are often recruited from think tanks who focus on social problems but these too are susceptible to corruption. Think tanks rely on member contributions and the more money a member contributes to a think tank, naturally the more influence that member is going to have. Since most think tanks are non-profit, donation processes are made easy for FBE proxies or even foreign governments to influence peddle the experts into advocating for specific policies that benefit those contributors.[42] In January 2023, the Atlantic Council's leadership was condemned for unabashedly praising the UAE's oil company CEO being appointed as the best candidate for leading the UN's COP28 Climate Summit. They were condemned for failing to disclose the large-sized donations the UAE has given to the think tank which undermined the Atlantic Council's reputation as a neutral body policy evaluator.[43] They also have a been criticized for hosting dubious characters, like the dictator Ali Ondimba.[44] A separate organization called the Foreign Influence Transparency Initiative at the Center for International Policy, identified approximately $175 million donated to various think tanks in Washington DC by foreign governments in 2020.[45] This is not just a foreign influence problem nor is it a new phenomenon as private enterprises also donate to these centers of experts to improve the persuasiveness of their economic benefits arguments of proposals and projects to regulators and policymakers.[46], [47]

All of these examples demonstrate how modern experts are exceptionally prone to the lures of corruption, dogmatic protection of reputation over accuracy, sloppiness, myopic thinking, and browbeating critics. The contemporary cultural atmosphere of glorifying experts as the pinnacles of society while simultaneously lowering the standards of performance has debilitated the traditional role of authoritative voices in public service and society at large. Despite these circumstances, the majority of the members of the expert class are not corrupt, partisan, or frauds. The broken cultural environment, however, has still created an ample bounty of malleable experts from which the FBE can recruit and reward lucratively for advocating the FBE's cause.

Options and Methods:

Once the FBE identify their preferred experts, what would they need them to do? The experts are needed to carry out three vital actions for the FBE's LOE 4 to succeed in controlling information: 1. Give FBE propaganda the appearance of legitimacy; 2. Hide or excuse FBE mistakes or problems; and 3. Help plan and advise FBE leadership on how to actually govern a centralized-autocratic state. There doesn't have to be clearcut steps or individual experts devoted to only one of these actions, there would be much overlap in the execution of these actions and some of the experts would eventually become favored over others. The main crux of the corrupt experts' methodology for the first two actions would rely on using derivations of the Appeal to Authority Fallacy. This is a type of logical fallacy used in arguments in which the opinion of an authority on a topic is used to support an argument.[48] This is especially useful for information dissemination organizations such as news media or academic journals. Having "outside" experts validate what the FBE's propagandists assert is true adds legitimacy to that propaganda.

In general, propaganda is most effective when the declarations cannot be disproven or independently checked. Propaganda is not just used to give the impression the FBE is always right but is also useful to discredit opponents and give the impression these opponents' beliefs are ridiculous views of an isolated minority. If a well-respected expert declares a position to be wrong, many laymen in the audience will accept that expert on faith because they cannot, or will not, try to verify the declaration. Maintaining the legitimacy of these experts is crucial to successfully convince people the FBE side is right.

For the third action, the FBE's ideology requires a top-down approach to governance which requires a broad range of competent advisors to help the FBE and its proxies build a proper plan. The FBE's autocracy would use many of the same facets that technocracy used to appeal to experts in the early 20th Century. Having access to years of accumulated knowledge combined with FBE resources, the experts could put together various proposals and plans, likely in the guise of NGO or think tank work and circulate them amongst the FBE leadership. These plans could offer the appearance of being panacea solutions that always justify the FBE's proposals and legitimize more autocratic rule. Although the suggested ideas would likely be open to the public, the means, methods, and timelines for such proposals would be done in secret. If properly utilized, the preferred experts would garner further authoritative status and may even be placed in charge of implementing certain actions to redirect society to becoming more pliable to servitude in the guise of creating utopia.

Strengths:

The depth of knowledge, terminology, and social connections used by the FBE experts will intimidate many of their critics and innately legitimize the experts' positions for the FBE sympathizers. Appealing to authority is a very strong logical fallacy and the FBE propaganda-proxy groups will buttress this fallacy by using emotional-based arguments or accusations. The five most common emotions that are exploited in politics are anger, fear, shame, envy, and disgust. These emotions have the commonality of easily spreading amongst crowds or groups because these appeal to the basest elements of self-interest. Emotions such as love, compassion, or empathy require individuals to have at least some investment in others and those investments differ between individuals. Since these positive emotions don't translate well among crowds or groups, the more selfish emotions are the most effective to manipulate in politics. Apathetic or less knowledgeable people will be more susceptible to these emotional based arguments and would also likely embrace the experts' explanations to help rationalize and excuse their ignorance and inactions against the FBE.

The corrupt expert class would rely on three variations of the Appealing to Authority Fallacy: The Appeal to Accomplishment Fallacy and two variations of the Credential Fallacy. All of these fallacies are based on the initial premise in common culture that experts are exceptional in both knowledge and understanding. Many people want to believe experts because they want the comfort that someone somewhere can make sense of this crazy world and are willing to believe anything that assures them. Consequently, experts have authority with many in the general population by simply being experts, making authority their most powerful "nudging" tool to pressure the public into embracing autocratic policies.

The Appeal to Accomplishment Fallacy often involves an expert who excels in their field and built a reputation advising senior policymakers or, if they are in STEM fields, have contributed to technological or scientific breakthroughs. Once someone is declared an extraordinary expert in their field, they are given greater liberty to pontificate on any subject, including on topics beyond their expertise, because many people incorrectly think someone who is highly intelligent must also be more knowledgeable about everything. An innocuous example involved Professor Stephan Hawking who later in his life started to opine on metaphysical topics that he had no exceptional training or insight. In 2010, he said philosophy was dead because recent developments in science rendered them mute even though science still had many unresolved quandaries that left plenty for philosophers to ponder.[49] The problem is he didn't actually say anything new or insightful but his celebrity status as a physics expert made general audiences believe he had exceptional insight into all fields. This myth making of accomplished experts mainly helps individual's careers[50] but can also help nefarious groups, like the FBE, to create secular prophets to help nudge the unsuspecting population's perceptions. This is not just a folly of successful experts; the media gain more viewers and readership when they can convince audiences they have someone who has answers to the world's problems.

The second variation known as the Credential Fallacy comes in two versions. The first version of the credential fallacy is to discredit an argument because it came from someone with insufficient credentials. A classic example in the United States is the notion someone with a degree from an Ivy League school is more competent than someone from a regular university. This is an old stereotype with mixed accuracy but it is one that has been common for decades.[51] No matter what actions the FBE take, they will not successfully coopt all experts all of the time. This fallacy helps loyal FBE experts discredit any experts that offer contrarian evidence and the FBE-proxy media will reinforce the message by emphasizing FBE-endorsed experts are always more eminently qualified. The second version of the Credential Fallacy is more common in propaganda and the media in general when the media, politicians, activists, or whomever get experts to justify any action based only on the fact they are credentialled. These groups don't pay the experts for their expertise but for their title or credential and have them say whatever the group wants them to say. This commonly occurs with policy related professions such as the military or legal fields. If one ventures beyond their preferred echo chamber, that same person can see different media talk about the exact same topic and get exact opposite answers from experts. Sometimes these are legitimate points but often these experts will say what their paymasters want them to say regardless of logic. These experts can disguise any weakness in the arguments with in-house jargon and gobbledygook to evade close audience scrutiny.

Experts' reputation of authoritative understanding of problems is the main attractor to the FBE's LOE 4 as exaggerated credibility neuters critics and helps mollify an anxious and ill-informed public. If properly executed, the FBE can debilitate and discredit the NRF's own propaganda by overwhelming all information outlets with their own "credible" experts. The corrupt elements of the expert class can wield their credibility in the exact same way the imams of Iran use morality to justify their actions. Discrediting established experts is very difficult and the FBE's superior financial resources means they will outnumber any experts supporting the opposition.

Weaknesses:

The experts' ability to use credibility as a weapon is a double-edged sword. While experts can easily deceive many with their greater academic knowledge or credentials, these same experts are themselves easy to deceive because few of them have sufficient understanding about the world beyond their preferred subject matter. The depth of their knowledge is extensive in only a very narrow purview of world topics and this usually comes at the cost of not learning about how actions and consequences interact with the world at large. This creates two vulnerabilities. The NRF could mislead the experts by introducing misinformation on a closely related topic that the targeted expert is unfamiliar with. Or worse, the experts convince themselves they understand the issue better than they actually do because they don't know all critical factors that influence an issue and lead the FBE into disastrous policy decisions.

Over time, the FBE will develop preferences for certain experts to opine on specific topics or issues because they sound the most plausible, are charismatic, or are devoutly loyal to the FBE's cause. The FBE's policy positions will come to rely on a few select persons within the expert class, making them susceptible to NRF targeting. Now the NRF could assassinate some of them to disrupt messaging but that creates a multitude of risks. Instead, they could actively seek out gaps in the experts' knowledge and understanding to disseminate later. Either through social media, academic conferences, or media campaigning, the NRF could highlight contradictions or gaps in the experts' assertions that, if given sufficient time, make them look foolish or proven wrong. It is almost impossible for the FBE to keep utilizing an expert once his reputation is sullied in the public's eye and will likely require the FBE to find replacements. Such events disrupt policy making and the "nudging" campaign as the public will become more resistant to whatever a discredited expert had previously asserted.

Most of the public's attention span on a subject is brief and will unlikely notice the exposure nor will it likely motivate any apolitical elements to side with the NRF. Such actions will only persuade fence-sitters who try to pay attention to geopolitical events but lack the decisiveness to choose a side from the outset. What this will do is boost morale for the NRF sympathetic elements within the population to make them more motivated after seeing the FBE-aligned propagandists suffer a public disgrace. The greater danger for the FBE is for the NRF to identify the more megalomaniacal FBE experts and manipulate them into advising the FBE into making more and more mistakes. The experts will be key advisors to the FBE leadership on how to formulate the perfectly controlled autocratic society while minimizing risks to the FBE themselves. If the NRF can identify these intellectual equivalents to General Custer, then the pro-FBE experts could lead themselves into making calamitous decisions. This can be exploited because the nature of human understanding about the world prevents the existence of the true all-knowing "philosopher-king" style geniuses who have a deep understanding of all facets of reality. This can be best illustrated with a modified version of David Wolpert and William Macready's No Free Lunch Theorem (NFL) for computer machine learning algorithms.

Modified No Free Lunch Theorem

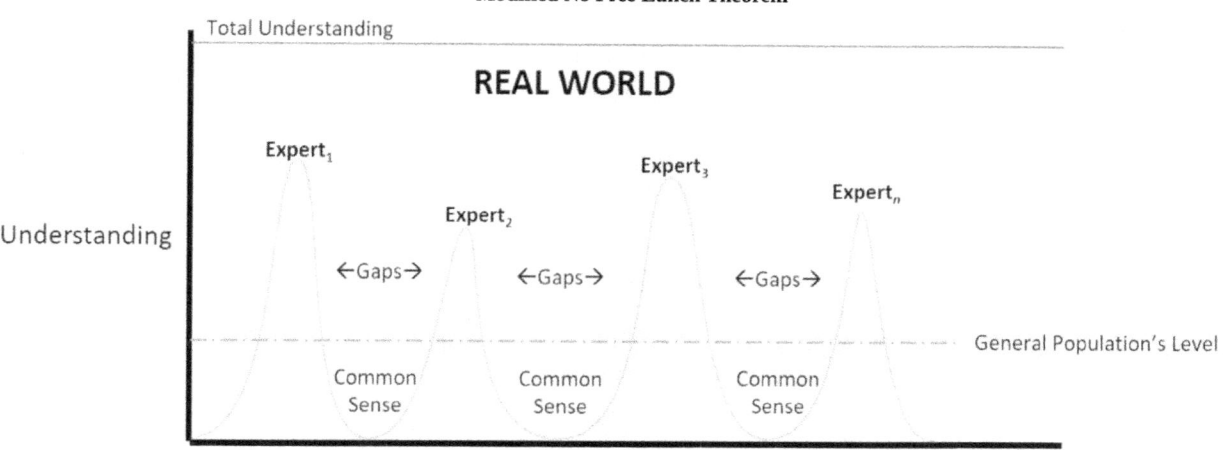

For Human Understanding

The No Free Lunch Theorem was a means two computer scientists used to explain how no single algorithm can solve all problems and individual computer problems require specialized algorithms tailored to the particular problem to be solved. [lii] The same applies to human beings and their ability to understand the world around them. The modified theorem depicts the contrasting differences in understanding by experts vs. everyday people about the real world. In this case, the real world means how human nature interacts with objective reality. Reality is broken down into types of problems that humans encounter with reality being depicted on the x-axis while the ability for humans to understand these problems and attempts to solve them is depicted on the y-axis. At the top of the y-axis, a line represents the totality of all information in the universe that can be understood which humanity always attempts to reach but never achieves.

A human being would need to study and accurately analyze all information across every subject about every type of problem to reach total understanding. Since this is impossible, people must divide their society into specializations focusing on specific problems to plausibly solve them. The more complex problems become, the more information is needed to understand the problems. This is why the more advanced a society becomes, the need for greater amounts of specialization and expertise within that society. Unfortunately, this specialization comes at a cost. There is not enough time or resources for an expert to become proficient in their field as well as develop a firm grasp of all the other problems and issues in the world. The greater the expertise of a field, the narrower the scope of that expert's broader knowledge of the world becomes. These experts let their understanding of other aspects of the real-world atrophy as they devote more energy to understanding one specific complex topic.

This is in contrast to the general population who try to live their daily lives while managing problems that affect themselves and those immediately around them. This requires having an adequate amount of knowledge on many types of problems to, if not solve, mitigate so they can carry on with their daily lives. The key advantage the generalist population has over the experts is the knowledge they gain by experiencing many types of problems and observing first-hand how all of these problems interact and react with each other. This understanding of how problems and solutions interact in broad terms gives the non-experts a better understanding of the world overall, even if the depth of that understanding is shallower. The ability to see and understand the patterns and linkages between the differing types of problem sets and the common solutions applied to them is built on experiential wisdom. This is colloquially known as "common sense" or "street smarts". The average person may not be able to articulate in great detail a specific problem or solution, they understand enough to survive the daily real-world.

The experts' specialized knowledge is what creates the mentality referred to as the "ivory tower" perspective because they focus so much on their in-depth knowledge in trying to reach for the sky, they develop huge gaps in understanding about the world around them. This is why most experts have a reputation for lacking "common sense" which also infers that many experts only have a high-school level of understanding about most world topics and problems. This is why calling an expert stupid or a person off the streets smart regarding a particular topic can be accurate simultaneously. For instance, people defending an intellectual who advocates for communism by pointing out the intellectual is very smart academically to the counter-detractors who say that intellectual is stupid. The intellectual may have exceptional insight on his preferred topic but will pontificate for a failed-political ideology out of complete ignorance of how the real world works in general. The ivory tower perspective deludes the person into feeling smart on all topics because they happen to be smart on one giving them a child-like innocence about every other topic because they never explored these ideas beyond their school years. So, the intellectual can be ignorant or "stupid" about reality but brilliant about their own specialization. In politics, being "reality-smart" is more important than being topically smart because politics holistically encompasses every aspect of society.

A clear real-world example of this comes from famous engineer and inventor Dennis Gabor in an interview special in 1967 between scientific experts and Walter Cronkite. A YouTube snippet can be found for this interview where Dennis Gabor talks at 5:35 minute mark.[liii] In this segment, Gabor proclaimed physical inventions and the study of physics was, with a few exceptions, no longer necessary and society should prioritize human psychological studies to understand how to create human happiness. This man was brilliant in his field and was instrumental towards humanity's understanding of holography but still naively declared physics no longer needed to have a center stage in human development or understanding. This pronouncement was based on his assumption that physics largely completed all useful insight and that a B.F. Skinner-like social engineering project be undertaken to make people happy. If this had become policy in the West, the 1973 Nobel Prize for doctors Leo Esaki, Ivar Giaver, and Brian David Josephson[liv] would likely not have occurred and the Information Age would likely have been stillborn.

This is why experts are as great a weakness as they are a strength to the FBE. Top-down direction led by expert advisors would create blind spots for the FBE leadership as experts become their main reference to guide their plans. The experts would then execute the FBE plan based on what the experts actually know and then try to integrate that knowledge into things they think they know. The insulated FBE and the specialized experts relying on each other to direct political plans without any feedback from outside the "ivory towers" will create large gaps of understanding that will likely cause their plans to fail. Unforeseen consequences are the bane of centralized planning and will remain so because even when feedback information becomes available, the insularly autocratic FBE will not have sufficient "common sense" to understand the feedback and will react ineffectively. If the FBE is blinded by their arrogance of inherent intellectual superiority, then their NRF opponents will be able to lay many traps that will appear obvious to everyone that is not detached from everyday reality.

---

[1] Ira Basen, "In Science We Trust.," CBC News, June 28, 2021. https://newsinteractives.cbc.ca/longform/technocracy-incorporated-elon-musk/

[2] Dwight D. Eisenhower, *President Dwight D. Eisenhower's Farewell Address (1961)*, National Archives, accessed February 9, 2023. https://www.archives.gov/milestone-documents/president-dwight-d-eisenhowers-farewell-address

[3] Sabine Hossenfelder, "If Science is What Scientists Do, What Happens if Scientists Stop Doing Science?" BackRe(Action) Blog, November 30, 2017. https://backreaction.blogspot.com/2017/11/if-science-is-what-scientists-do-what.html

[4] Interview with Alexis Papazoglou, "String Theory is Dead," IAI News, February 23, 2023. https://iai.tv/articles/string-theory-is-dead-peter-woit-auid-2399?_auid=2020

[5] Peter Woit, "LHC results put supersymmetry theory 'on the spot'," Not Even Wrong Blog, August 28, 2011. https://www.math.columbia.edu/~woit/wordpress/?p=3937

[6] Peter Woit, "Still Waiting for Supersymmetry," Not Even Wrong Blog, November 21, 2011. https://www.math.columbia.edu/~woit/wordpress/?p=4171

[7] Peter Woit, "It's Too Soon to Declare Supersymmetry a Tragedy," Not Even Wrong Blog, October 22, 2013. https://www.math.columbia.edu/~woit/wordpress/?p=6392

[8] Peter Woit, "Supersymmetry and the Crisis in Physics," Not Even Wrong Blog, April 15, 2014. https://www.math.columbia.edu/~woit/wordpress/?p=6836

[9] Interview with Alexis Papazoglou," Eric Weinstein: The String Theory Wars," IAI News, February 16, 2023. https://iai.tv/articles/eric-weinstein-the-string-theory-wars-auid-2394

[10] Subhajit Waugh, "World's Largest Physics Conference In Las Vegas Will Be Grand; But Will It Be Worthwhile?" EIN News, February 25, 2023. https://www.einnews.com/pr_news/619040511/world-s-largest-physics-conference-in-las-vegas-will-be-grand-but-will-it-be-worthwhile

[11] Stuart Hameroff, "'Orch OR' is the Most Complete, and Most Easily Falsifiable Theory of Consciousness," Cognitive Neuroscience, vol. 12, is. 2, 2021, p. 74-76. https://www.tandfonline.com/doi/full/10.1080/17588928.2020.1839037

[12] George Musser, "Can Quantum Hints in the Brain Revive a Radical Consciousness Theory?" New Scientist, January 17, 2024. https://www.newscientist.com/article/mg26134740-800-can-quantum-hints-in-the-brain-revive-a-radical-consciousness-theory/

[13] Matthew Crawford, "How Science has Been Corrupted," UnHerd Substack, May 3, 2021. https://unherd.com/2021/05/how-science-has-been-corrupted/

[14] Michelle Whitmer, "Asbestos Cover-up," Mesothelioma Center, March 10, 2023. https://www.asbestos.com/featured-stories/cover-up/

[15] News Article, "Johnson & Johnson Knew for Decades that Asbestos Lurked in its Baby Powder," Reuters, December 14th, 2018. https://www.reuters.com/investigates/special-report/johnsonandjohnson-cancer/

[16] Dietrich Knauth, Mike Spector, "J&J Unit Files for Second Bankruptcy to Pursue $8.9 Billion Talc Settlement," Reuters, April 5, 2023. https://www.reuters.com/legal/jj-unit-goes-bankrupt-second-time-pursue-89-bln-talc-settlement-2023-04-04/

[17] Press Release, "New Review Study Shows That Egg-Industry-Funded Research Downplays the Danger of Cholesterol," Physicians Committee for Responsible Medicine, December 13, 2019. https://www.pcrm.org/news/news-releases/new-review-study-shows-egg-industry-funded-research-downplays-danger-cholesterol

[18] Dr. Neal D. Barnard, Dr. M. Blaire Long, et al, "Industry Funding and Cholesterol Research: A Systemic Review," American Journal of Lifestyle Medicine, March-April 2021, vol. 15, is. 2. https://www.ncbi.nlm.nih.gov/pmc/articles/PMC7958219/

[19] Bret Stetka, "Unscrambling the Nutrition Science on Eggs," NPR, March 6, 2017. https://www.npr.org/sections/thesalt/2017/03/06/518152471/unscrambling-the-nutrition-science-on-eggs

[20] Charles Calisher, Dennis Carroll, Rita Colwell, et al., "Statement in Support of The Scientists, Public Health Professionals, And Medical Professionals of China Combatting COVID-19," The Lancet, March 7, 2020. https://www.thelancet.com/journals/lancet/article/PIIS0140-6736(20)30418-9/fulltext

[21] Geoff Brumfiel, "Scientists Debunk Lab Accident Theory of Pandemic Emergence," NPR, April 22, 2020. https://www.npr.org/2020/04/22/841925672/scientists-debunk-lab-accident-theory-of-pandemic-emergence

[22] Darreonna Davis, "Coronavirus Likely Emerged in Wuhan Market, New Studies Find," Forbes, July 26, 2022. https://www.forbes.com/sites/darreonnadavis/2022/07/26/coronavirus-likely-emerged-in-wuhan-market-new-studies-find/?sh=2ba1a48f8afb

[23] Julian E. Barnes, "Lab Leak Most Likely Caused Pandemic, Energy Dept. Says," NY Times, February 26, 2023. https://www.nytimes.com/2023/02/26/us/politics/china-lab-leak-coronavirus-pandemic.html

[24] Gabriel Crossley, "China Rejects WHO Plan for Study of COVID-19 Origin," Reuters, July 22, 2021. https://www.reuters.com/world/china/china-will-not-follow-whos-suggested-plan-2nd-phase-covid-19-origins-study-2021-07-22/

[25] Paulina Firozi, "Tom Cotton Keeps Repeating A Coronavirus Fringe Theory That Scientists Have Disputed," Washington Post, February 17, 2020. https://www.washingtonpost.com/politics/2020/02/16/tom-cotton-coronavirus-conspiracy/

[26] Mary Van Beusekom, "Scientists: 'Exactly Zero' Evidence COVID-19 Came from a Lab," University of Minnesota CIDRAP, May 12, 2020. https://www.cidrap.umn.edu/covid-19/scientists-exactly-zero-evidence-covid-19-came-lab

[27] Cameron English, "Pandemic of Distrust: Americans Have Little Faith in Public Health Agencies, Survey Finds," American Council on Science and Health, May 13, 2021. https://www.acsh.org/news/2021/05/13/pandemic-distrust-americans-have-little-faith-public-health-agencies-survey-finds-15550

[28] Kelsey Piper, "Science Has Been in a 'Replication Crisis' for a Decade. Have We Learned Anything?" Vox, October 14, 2020. https://www.vox.com/future-perfect/21504366/science-replication-crisis-peer-review-statistics

[29] Shawna Williams, "Scientists, Publishers Debate Paychecks for Peer Reviewers," The Scientist, November 1, 2020. https://www.the-scientist.com/careers/scientists-publishers-debate-paychecks-for-peer-reviewers-68101

[30] Ryan Quinn, "USC Professor Recalls Book After 'LA Times' Finds Plagiarism," Inside Higher Education, March 6, 2023. https://www.insidehighered.com/quicktakes/2023/03/07/usc-professor-recalls-book-after-%E2%80%98la-times%E2%80%99-finds-plagiarism

[31] Susan El Khoury, "News 4 Investigates: St. Louis Medical Ethics Professor on Probation for Medicare Fraud," KMOV4, February 16, 2023. https://www.kmov.com/2023/02/17/news-4-investigates-medical-ethics-professor-probation-medicare-fraud/

[32] Press Release, "Harvard University Professor Convicted of Making False Statements and Tax Offenses," Department of Justice, December 21, 2021. https://www.justice.gov/opa/pr/harvard-university-professor-convicted-making-false-statements-and-tax-offenses

[33] Siri Carpenter, "Harvard Psychology Researcher Committed Fraud, U.S. Investigation Concludes," Science, September 6, 2012. https://www.science.org/content/article/harvard-psychology-researcher-committed-fraud-us-investigation-concludes

[34] Yudhijit Bhattacharjee, "The Mind of a Con Man," NY Times Magazine, April 26, 2013. https://www.nytimes.com/2013/04/28/magazine/diederik-stapels-audacious-academic-fraud.html

[35] Claudia Lopez Lloreda, "University Investigation Found Prominent Spider Biologist Fabricated, Falsified Data," Science, May 11, 2023. https://www.science.org/content/article/university-investigation-found-prominent-spider-biologist-fabricated-falsified-data

[36] Neirin Gray Desai, "Florida State University Professor Abruptly Left His $190,000-A-Year Role After Being Accused of Faking Data to Make Racism Seem More Common That It Is and Having Six of His Research Papers Retracted," Daily Mail, April 12, 2023. https://www.dailymail.co.uk/news/article-11963421/Florida-State-University-criminology-professor-leaves-accused-falsifying-data.html

[37] Matt Jaworowski, "University Of Michigan Researcher Quits After Publishing Falsified Data," WoodTV8, January 25, 2023. https://www.woodtv.com/news/michigan/university-of-michigan-researcher-quits-after-publishing-falsified-data/

[38] Morgan Watkins, "University of Kentucky Says Professors Fabricated Federally Funded Cancer Research," Courier Journal, August 23, 2019. https://www.courier-journal.com/story/news/2019/08/23/uk-finds-professors-staffer-responsible-falsified-research-data/2094131001/

[39] Aisha Labi, "Corruption in Higher Education Appears to Be on the Rise Globally, Report Says," The Chronicle of Higher Education, October 1, 2013. https://www.chronicle.com/article/corruption-in-higher-education-appears-to-be-on-the-rise-globally-report-says/

[40] James Golden, Catherine M. Mazzotta, and Kimberly Zittel-Barr, *Systemic Obstacles to Addressing Research Misconduct in Higher Education: A Case Study*, Journal of Academic Ethics 21, August 29, 2021, p. 71-82. https://link.springer.com/article/10.1007/s10805-021-09438-w

[41] Irene Glendinning, Stella-Maris Orim, Andrew King, *Policies and Actions of Accreditation and Quality Assurance Bodies to Counter Corruption in Higher Education*, Coventry University Council for Higher Education Accreditation, February 2019. https://files.eric.ed.gov/fulltext/ED597948.pdf

[42] Alejandro Chafuen, "Transparency And Independence: Think Tanks Rather Than Lobbying Tanks," Forbes, May 2, 2016. https://www.forbes.com/sites/alejandrochafuen/2016/05/02/transparency-and-independence-think-tanks-rather-than-lobbying-tanks/?sh=35e368a35ea9

[43] Luke Goldstein, "Corruption at the Fifth Estate," The American Prospect, February 24, 2023. https://prospect.org/power/2023-02-24-based-corruption-fifth-estate-think-tanks/

[44] Thor Halvorssen, Alex Gladstein, "Why Did the Atlantic Council Even Consider Giving African Dictator Ali Bongo Ondimba a 'Global Citizen Award'?" Foreign Policy Magazine, September 19, 2016. https://foreignpolicy.com/2016/09/19/independent-think-tank-honors-african-dictator-as-global-citizen-ali-bongo-gabon/

[45] Kelley Beaucar Vlahos, "New Report Details $174 Million in Foreign Funding to D.C. Think Tanks," Quincy Institute: Responsible Statecraft, January 29, 2020. https://responsiblestatecraft.org/2020/01/29/new-report-details-174-million-in-foreign-funding-to-d-c-think-tanks/

[46] Eric Lipton and Brooke Williams, "How Think Tanks Amplify Corporate America's Influence," New York Times, August 7, 2016. https://www.nytimes.com/2016/08/08/us/politics/think-tanks-research-and-corporate-lobbying.html

[47] Bruce Bartlett, "The Alarming Corruption of the Think Tanks," The Fiscal Times, December 14, 2002. https://www.thefiscaltimes.com/Columns/2012/12/14/The-Alarming-Corruption-of-the-Think-Tanks

[48] Reference page, "Fallacies," University of North Carolina: The Writing Center, accessed 02/5/2023. https://writingcenter.unc.edu/tips-and-tools/fallacies/

[49] Raymond Tallis, "Philosophy isn't Dead Yet," The Guardian, May 27, 2013. https://www.theguardian.com/commentisfree/2013/may/27/physics-philosophy-quantum-relativity-einstein

[50] Charles Seife, "The Myth of Stephen Hawking," Scientific American, April 6, 2021. https://www.scientificamerican.com/article/the-myth-of-stephen-hawking/

[51] Cole Clayborun, "How Much is an Ivy League Degree Worth?" US News and World Report, January 30, 2023. https://www.usnews.com/education/best-colleges/articles/how-much-is-an-ivy-league-degree-worth

[lii] Micah Goldblum, Marc Finzi, et al., "The No Free Lunch Theorem, Kolmogorov Complexity, and the Role of Inductive Biases in Machine Learning," arXiv e-prints, New York University, April 11, 2023, 1-2. https://arxiv.org/pdf/2304.05366.pdf

[liii] Youtube video, "Buckminster Fuller, Isaac Asimov & Other Futurists Make Predictions About the 21st Century in 1967: What They Got Right & Wrong," Reelblack One, CBS McGraw-Hill Films, 1967. https://www.youtube.com/watch?v=wPETzKYLkco&t=335s

[liv] Reference page, "The Nobel Prize in Physics 1973," The Nobel Prize, accessed May 5, 2023. https://www.nobelprize.org/prizes/physics/1973/summary/

Chapter 20: LOE Overlapping Phase I and Phase II: Mission Command

Before proceeding onto the Phase II LOEs, there is one LOE that critically links both Phase I and II and keeps all LOEs working in harmony: the LOE of Mission Command. Mission Command is the operational doctrinal term used by the United States Military to describe how a force uses command and control to execute operations during the chaos of conflict.[1] In the case of the FBE's optimal strategy, the FBE would utilize both informal and formal systems of command, control, and communication. The informal mission command elements would be between FBE leadership and their proxy groups' liaisons. The formal mission command elements would operate within the proxy organizations themselves. The FBE's strategy requires them to remain covert for as long as possible because any exposure of them being a foreign-backed subversion force would immediately result in total loss of control. The FBE core elements will remain the loosely aligned social and economic elites who will use their financial and cultural influence to indirectly manipulate the more formalized institutions into carrying out the FBE's will.

Most members of the proxy organizations will always remain unaware of the FBE's objectives but will be sufficiently misled into carrying out actions that suit the FBE. The FBE leaders will use key persons as messengers, liaisons, and envoys to direct broad strategic objectives for specific proxy organizations and assign tasks for the corrupted leaders of those proxies. Informal meetings can be simple encrypted texts, teleconferences, or major gatherings in the guise of conferences, conventions, charity events, or political action events. There is a multitude of options that suit a wide variety of circumstances. The one commonality for this senior-level mission command structure is the FBE leadership's dependence on key persons to act as go-betweens with FBE proxies. These would have to be people who could be entrusted with secrets, have access to both financial and personal records of various organizations, and have the recognized authority to act on behalf of others. The most probable key people that connect the FBE leaders with their proxies would be lawyers.

Lawyers can go between persons and groups without raising suspicion. They have the legal means to protect information and convey messages in confidence. Lawyers also know where to "find the bodies" of any organization or group that the FBE may want to co-opt one way or the other. The legal professionals are the perfect soldiers of a subversive mission command effort. They have recognized authority, can intimidate potential opponents without resorting to obvious violence, and many of them who might work with potentially corrupt wealthy members of society already have the necessary business network connections. There would be others for unique situations such as lobbyists for political subversion, charity and nonprofit ambassadors, and academics for subverting both academic institutions as well as indoctrinating recruits for the Atomized. Informal mission command maintains secrecy and keeps the FBE leaders in the loop but their proxy organizations require actual organized command and control as these are established social institutions or companies.

These proxies are a mixture of civil, cultural, and economic institutions subverted through bribes, blackmail, infiltration, or ideological indoctrination. Most of these organizations would not be fully controlled and would not need to be. Only elements of the senior leadership need to be co-opted who can manipulate the rest of the organization to act as proxy for FBE efforts. This mission command relies on continuously misleading people by framing tasks in half-truths, lies, or omission to prevent discovery of the FBE's true intentions. The only real difficulty is putting the FBE's puppets into senior leadership positions within these organizations. Once that is done, then the organizations are effectively subverted and they can be openly directed to carry out tasks that would appear superficially benign or routine to the average member. Each organization would run things differently and each proxy would have a different organizational culture and hierarchy so the formal mechanisms would vary. These are standard challenges for any organization being directed to fulfill political or military objectives and the FBE would need to overcome them and there are many past examples for the FBE to follow. The largest mission command challenge for the FBE in this kind of proxy civil war is to carry out coordinated actions in a sufficiently timely manner to be effective. The decision-making cycle for leaders to receive the relevant information, assess the implications of that information, decide on a course of action, and then execute that action is becoming faster with shorter times to react. The Information Age has accelerated the acquiring of information but still hasn't truly devised very good means of filtering out the useless from the valuable information. So, the key point on the FBE's mission command LOE is the critical supporting element for keeping mission command tenable in a fast-paced war: artificial intelligence (AI).

AI: The New Idols

The Information Age has given the Human Race access to more data in the past 10 years than the rest of history combined, but only recently has the technology matured to help filter and sort the accumulated data.[2] Too much data slows down processes and overwhelms those who analyze this date to advise or make decisions. This is why AI has not yet played a major role in command-and-control operations as it lacks the sophistication necessary to provide filtration of useless data in a timely manner.[3] AI breakthroughs create a collective sense of both dread and hope among people as they become increasingly dependent on the technology and this in turn, shapes persons' expectations of this technology. In the case of the FBE's needs, their expectations and intentions on using AI would be mimicking how authoritarian regimes use it to maintain control and also how to deny the NRF the ability to coordinate their efforts to resist.[4]

AI is a broad generic term for a wide range of information technologies with a multitude of subcategories. For the sake of simplification, these subcategories can fall under two types of AI: 1. Artificial General Intelligence (AGI); and 2. Artificial Narrow Intelligence (ANI). The general public and popular culture often think of AGI when AI is mentioned. AGI is vaguely defined as an information technology that has human-equivalent intelligence, can perform a multitude of different tasks, can self-learn, and, depending on "who's" definition, possesses consciousness.[5] Despite all the media-hype, there is no functioning AGI anywhere on Earth as of this writing and so will be disregarded for this analysis. The second category of ANI are software algorithms designed to perform specific kinds of tasks and can learn within a set of defined parameters by taking in large inputs of data.[6] ANI is the type of AI that is progressing at rapid pace and will have many uses to enable the FBE to coordinate and control their multitude of organizations and groups.

Options and Methods:

ANI's strength is by its ability to sort and identify very complex patterns within huge quantities of data using deductive or inductive logic algorithms. The kinds of ANI the FBE would want to use for mission command would utilize Machine Learning / Deep Learning (ML/DL) algorithms, which includes the subcategory of Large Language Models (LLMs)[7] found in applications like ChatGPT,[8] organized into artificial neural networks. These systems are designed for exceptionally large problems as these can filter through billions of pieces of useless data to find key data to formulate patterns and solutions. The complexity of these systems and how they work would take an entire book to explain and is beyond the scope of this civil war thesis. For simplicity's sake, a good analogy for ANI using ML/DL is similar to the parlor game "Six Degrees of Kevin Bacon". This game challenges players to select an actor and try to find a link to another actor via a film that eventually leads to a link to Kevin Bacon within six steps.[9] In the case of ANI (ML/DL) software, it's akin to six billion degrees of Kevin Bacon.

ML/DL works by using multiple nodes of algorithms, each designed to look for specific patterns for specific tasks, then a baseline main algorithm combines the patterns of each algorithm node into a comprehensive pattern and gives that as the output to computer users. Each of these ML/DL algorithms learn to identify these patterns by being provided millions of pieces of data to process and each piece of data is assigned tags for the algorithms to reference. Each tag is decided upon by the software programmers and engineers, given an assigned weight to measure priority, and every piece of data has multiple tags. The algorithm identifies the data by its tags and weights to find patterns by linking the common tags between disparate pieces of data. After receiving millions or billions of pieces of data, the algorithms learn how many times certain pieces of data have the same tags or associations with other pieces of data and based on the number of recurrences can gauge the probability of how often these associations occur. With billions of pieces of data, there are enough repeated associations to identify potential patterns with high fidelity. ML/DL combines these probability analytics to filter for and identify key data the programs are designed to find.[10] For instance, in language processing, ML/DL is given billions of sentences, phrases, and terminology. Each piece of this data is categorized, tagged, and each tag is given a priority value weight based on the software engineers' intention for the algorithm. After billions of these inputs, the ML/DL algorithms will see specific words or phrases that will more likely associated with other specific words or phrases and use probability to anticipate the most likely outcome based on the links between the tags, the weight values of each tag, and what category these links fall under.[11] If a common question is asked on a search engine, the ML/DL will identify the most common words or phrases used in the responses to these questions throughout the internet and give a response that has the highest probability of correlating with the most popularly provided answer on the internet. Hence, ANI is playing a "Billion Degrees from Kevin Bacon" with ANI ML/DL finding as many links and associations as possible to come up with patterns that would take humans decades using old analog methods.

These ANIs have only recently developed sufficient processing power and ingested large enough data sets to become useful in assisting with mission command and management.[12] The FBE's strategy is pursing dual objectives of nudging the Western nation's society into becoming more autocratic while simultaneously provoking the NRF into fighting a type of war that is most optimal for the FBE's proxies to win. The mission command for the FBE would primarily focus on cultural nudging with the second objective helping to provoke the NRF into a fight in which the FBE would then put the onus on the Western nation's state institutions' built-in mission command capabilities to manage the actual fighting. The FBE would intend to use the Western nation's government as expendable pawns by luring the NRF into attacking the government and forgetting to target the FBE and their private henchmen. Aside from coopted government programs, the FBE will need to build mission command ANI for their own assets and non-government proxies that will mainly focus on the "nudging" of society and "provoking" the NRF into fighting while getting the anocracy to use its mission command to do the actual kinetic fighting.

ANI ML/DL advancements have many potential applications for the FBE:

· Use ANI to design digital training management programs to better indoctrinate students, workers, and activists by filtering out all unwanted information.[13] Embed discriminatory values within program criteria that actively promotes FBE sympathizing behaviors.[14]

· Use social media and information dissemination sites to manage trending and story prioritization algorithms.[15]

· Sort through data aggregators to identify and track NRF and other dissidents' patterns of life.[16], [17]

· Synchronize online software bots to maximize harassment and social pressure campaigns to shape perceptions of popularity of persons or ideas.[18]

· Create or synchronize online public relations campaigns to glorify or overstate achievements of FBE-friendly proxy groups or individuals, including overwhelming the information space with many deceiving or distracting stories to bury or diminish the presence of derogatory stories and information.[19]

· Assist building comprehensive situational awareness of opponent's capabilities and range of influence.[20]

· Manage cipher, encryption, and authentication for VPNs and other methods of communication to diminish insider threat risks.[21]

· Coordinate false flag actions by seeding preliminary false stories, rumors, and accusations before culminating into an actual action or event that discredits opposition while keeping the false narrative consistent across all FBE proxy groups.[22]

· Additionally, create false or highlight real incidents to help FBE proxy activist groups and companies to successfully lobby international and national regulations on encryption, AI, and misinformation that benefit the FBE at the cost of everyone else.[23]

· Data poison other ANIs to have only FBE-selected tags to emphasize data patterns that favor FBE outcomes when "studies", "polls", or "references" are created.[24]

· Manage insider trading, identify corrupted regulatory bodies or officials, and other financial processes to more effectively hide shadow financing activities.[25]' [26]

· Loyalty and evaluation screening of recruits, employees, and advisors to better filter out NRF spies or sympathizers.[27]

· Manage centrally planned and controlled personal and corporate data within FBE data lakes and centers for potential economic and political extortion.[28]

· Manage and monopolize industrial control systems within multiple industries, utilities, and infrastructure to economically control loyalist businesses and potentially collapse dissenting regions.[29]

· FBE could nudge legislation to enable greater use of ANI in judiciary proceedings to help control the courts.[30]

· Instead of duplicating the CCP's Great Firewall, use ANI to alter key data sets to filter out results without outright banning sites or online groups. Shape and edit the discussions without anyone knowing.[31]

· FBE lobby to encourage more use of ANI in drafting policies and legislation in the name of greater fairness and impartiality while keeping preferential language for FBE groups' interests.[32]

· Conduct corporate espionage against any competitors of FBE-owned companies to diminish any economic independence within the Western nation.[33]

Strengths:

The strengths and power of ANI and ML/DL algorithms are discussed and debated throughout every profession because it can be applied to almost anything. If properly utilized, ANI can be the ultimate assistant to both individuals and groups for both nefarious and virtuous reasons. Most discussions involve direct applications for specific industries, but the common threads include eliminating tedious and routine work processes, organizing knowledge, optimizing planning, and training.[34] Mission command requires the ingesting of copious amounts of data, filter to find relevant data, process and understand the findings, then disseminate decisions back down to subordinates. Every single application ANI potentially both accelerates and simplifies each step of mission command for both the FBE and NRF in their efforts to direct operations in near-real time.[35]

Having multiple ANIs managing each specific task of mission command such as managing financial coordination, communication security and network management, news and media data aggregation, etc. would drastically simplify the common operating picture for the FBE and reduce the NRF's ability to catch them by surprise. This would also simplify the FBE's additional complex challenge of managing covert as well as overt organizations while minimizing public disclosure. ANI would enable the FBE to administer the multitude of complex systems necessary to manage near-real time changes to complex organizational networks.[36] Finally, there is one major additional advantage that is not often discussed in mainstream publications and that is idiot-proofing leaders. As been stated before, most, if not all, the FBE will be co-opted by the foreign benefactor from private organizations with a few additional corrupted government officials. There will likely be few amongst them who can actually possess the competence to lead any organized fight. Being a manager or boss of a company or charity is not the same as managing a campaign of deceit, manipulation, and fighting actions in a war. ANI will simplify the problem sets of political subversion and military operations considerably, enabling mediocre "leaders" to actually manage and command actions more effectively. Of course, all of these advantages rely heavily on the critically important task of implementing the ANI tools properly and effectively which is not as easy as one might first assume.

Weaknesses:

The potential strengths of using ANI to manage command and control are apparent to anyone who takes a glancing observation of its capabilities, but the hype around modern AI makes the weaknesses more difficult to find and recognize for users.[37] The other weaknesses in the FBE identified in previous chapters highlight that many of the FBE's leadership would suffer from willful ignorance stemming from their insulated "ivory tower" perceptions of real world. This gives a false overconfidence about how much they truly understand the world or the tools, including AI, the FBE leaders intend to use. Hype is the most prevalent amongst economic and social elites because they are the potential investors that companies and inventors need to finance new products and technologies.[38] The FBE-affiliated members of these potential investors would be flattered regarding their intelligence and would be surrounded by uncontested promises of easy solutions to acquire more power and wealth with AI tools. Many FBE leaders' egos would refuse to believe they could be misled, deceived, or ignorant about promised panacea solutions that place the FBE at the center of all things.

The greatest risk and potential weakness for the FBE's AI-based mission command would be to confuse the capabilities of the ANI programs with AGI and then try to give tasks ANI is unsuitable to manage or execute. The FBE would love to automate most command-and-control tasks to more effectively manage the Western nation while minimizing the risk of potential usurpers or traitors interfering in managerial decisions. ANI is bound, with some exceptions, by variations of Wolpert's and Macready's No Free Lunch Theory which states highly specialized algorithms are required to effectively perform very complex tasks.[39] Simplistically speaking, more generalized algorithms managing many different types of tasks will be a jack-of-all trades program that is mediocre at carrying out any one of its individual tasks.[40] Effective ANIs are very specialized but the FBE's strategic objectives to make society dependent on a centralized system of autocratic control requires the ability to manage many different tasks exceptionally well. The reason being centrally planned economies are notoriously corrupt, inefficient, and ineffective with history showing relatively-short life spans of a few generations unless there is a major intervention by more market-based economies.[41]' [42], [43] The FBE will likely be tempted, based on published statements regarding governance and AI utopianist management from opinionators around the world have made,[44]' [45] to use ANI as the great solution to reduce or eliminate the negative characteristics of centralized planning and administration. The assumption being that the advanced processing power combined with trillions of pieces of data will allow the software to predict and understand the extraordinarily complex systems of human interactions within a society. This assumption is based on several false premises.

Facts and the data derived from those facts are the basis of ANI performance and these are insufficient to understand human society and its real-world interactions. Not everything that happens in the world has a clear objective answer or sometimes not having just one answer. Many things that impact the functioning of a society will change based on the contexts of situations and the people involved. To fully understand an entire human system like an industry, political ideology, or something as grand as a national economy requires not only knowing the potential influences on a situation but all of the limiting variables that restrain those potential influences and a typical economy or society has trillions of variables that impact these every day. Even if one could account for just the major routine factors on daily life, there are still outlier variables or "black swan" events that only occur in very unusual circumstances that can disrupt or eliminate a routine within a society. [46], [47] The invasion of Ukraine in 2022, the COVID outbreak, the collapse of the Soviet Union, or the September 11th Terrorist Attack on the United States are some of the more famous contemporary black swan events. This extreme complexity is why economics is not a true science because it cannot have controlled predicable outcomes or follow a set of immutable laws. Economics will remain an art, regardless of the amount of math included in it. To start on such an endeavor, a machine would not only require the abilities to collect, process, and categorize data but to also understand the meaning of the data collected and the context surrounding that meaning. No AI has understanding or comprehension. There is not even an agreed upon scientific definition of key capability requirements such as intelligence, understanding, comprehension, or self-awareness.[48], [49] There are many normative statements about each of them, including some for programming, but no universally accepted scientifically definitive ones. It is very difficult to achieve AGI when scientists don't even know what these critical capability requirements truly mean. ANI doesn't do any of these activities, instead it sorts complex data into patterns based on the parameters predefined in the algorithms.

The best metaphor describing how modern computers, including advanced ANI, function is known as the "Chinese Room Argument".[50] A person who only understands English is inside a locked room with a small opening to receive small pieces of paper. Each piece of paper has two Mandarin characters typed onto them. The person has a large reference book that shows the Mandarin characters on the pieces of paper can be matched up with boxes that also have two Mandarin characters on them. By using the reference book, the English speaker matches the characters on the box with the characters on the paper, then grabs the box that matches and sends it out the opening. Like a computer, the person received inputs of data in the form of Mandarin characters, used the reference book like a computer algorithm matches data tags, and then produced the desired box like a computer displays output after going through the program. At no time in this process was comprehension, thought, or additional information provided in the process. The person carried out a series of instructions to produce output based on the program within the reference book and this is roughly what computers do metaphorically. Since such a process cannot factor in nuance, abstractions, or understanding, this process cannot act like a general intelligence. Many AI enthusiasts contend the argument is flawed because the English speaker could eventually learn the Mandarin by studying the characters and syntax, but this is based on a false assumption that is also another weakness of ANI for purposes of mission command. [51]

AI software has become sufficiently advanced that programs can use the two most common forms of logic. Some programs use deductive logic that can identify patterns from large sets of data to build premises that lead to a specific conclusion for a specific problem. While other programs can use inductive logic that uses very specific or narrow sets of data to extrapolate a more general pattern to identify a broader conclusion about a problem.[52] However, no software can use abductive logic. Abductive logic finds conclusions to problems by using inference observations to derive implications because the information provided regarding the problem is incomplete and insufficient to deduce or inductively identify the conclusions. Abductive logic requires the ability to introduce novel information into the problem analysis that is beyond the original parameters of the problem and being able to integrate that new information into the original problem data and then extrapolate a conclusion. The ability to use implications to inference the conclusion by introducing outside or new information requires the ability to knowledgeably understand how the data integrates with the inferences to reach a plausible conclusion. [The Chinese Room Argument's flaw is that the hypothetical English-speaking human can formulate and infer new information outside the parameters of the set process that defines the Chinese Room.] No software program can create or introduce information that is outside the preset parameters of its algorithmic programming.[53] For the Chinese Room Argument to be more accurate in describing the computer program, the English speaker would have to be incapable of thinking beyond the reference book, but it is just a metaphor to highlight the limits of ANI. This critical limit means no matter how much processing power is added or the amount of data fed into the system, these ANI programs will never evolve beyond or "break free" from its original parameters.

However, most FBE will not likely appreciate these distinctions because few of them would likely bother to learn about their ANI tools' functionality or limitations. This is partly derived from many elites' desires in wanting to believe there is a tool that can manage and solve all their problems while still being in control of that tool.[54] This belief in the limitless possibilities of AI also partially stems from the assumption that machines are or will be near the ability of the human mind and will inevitably surpass it. Part of this is due to a failure to appreciate the power of the human mind which is still superior. Many fail to appreciate how much processing capability a human mind has and performs functions, such as consciousness, that no machine emulates. Besides being conscious, the brain is managing millions of functions and processing endless streams of data far greater than any supercomputer. The brain is simultaneously:[55]

· managing, regulating, and processing information from tens of millions of sensors in the nerve endings for pain, pleasure, pressure, texture, and other sensations;
   · managing breathing;
   · blood flow;
   · metabolism;
   · the autoimmune system;
   · eyesight, smell, taste, and hearing;

· stem cell proliferation;[56]

· speech;

· body temperature regulation;

· food processing and waste management;

· muscle motor functions;

· managing all organs;

· the endocrine system;

· and does all of this while learning, thinking, emoting, and being conscious of which no computer can actually do.

What many people, including technology infatuated technocrats, fail to appreciate is the brain is a general-purpose machine designed to function in the unpredictable and dangerous world while computers and software are specialized tools carrying out specialized tasks. Computers do their tasks exceptionally well because they can repeatedly do the same tasks without interruption or distraction. However, as engineers try to broaden the scope of software, more errors, glitches, and corrections occur, as seen with constant patching updates, because software optimization becomes too difficult as computers do more and more complex tasks. Bluntly speaking, this can be observed in humans too. Idiot savants have brains that are exceptionally specialized and easily match or surpass any specialized computer algorithm but at the cost of functioning in other areas.[57] Frankly, all of the assumptions of artificial general intelligence or a SKYNET-style artificial superintelligence are predicated on the assumption that all that is needed is to add compute processing power.[58] However, it is just as likely that machine general intelligence will have the same challenges as humans. If AGI comes into existence, it will be managing many different tasks while being conscious and will likely, like humans, become distracted, biased, neurotic, bored, and forgetful. Also, AGI is just as likely to become bad at doing things as it specializes in other tasks. Ironically, in the realm of science fiction, parodies and dystopias have often been better predictors of the future because these highlight the flaws, not just the potentials of the future. Sci-fi comedy television shows like *Futurama* and the UK's *Red Dwarf* portraying flawed neurotic and silly AIs will more likely be closer to the reality of AGI than the near flawless AIs of the *Terminator*, Asimov's *The Foundation* series, or *2001: A Space Odessey*. On the plus-side, having a Holly, Kryten, or Bender instead of SKYNET or GLaDOS is better for the world anyway.

The failure to appreciate all of the fundamental limitations of ANI and also mistaking ANI for AGI and misapplying these advanced software tools leads to their misemployment. However, the other major weakness is having misplaced trust that the ANI, even if applied correctly, will always provide unerringly accurate results for the FBE to have effective mission command. Hopeful enthusiasts envision ANI expanding the users' understanding of the world by reducing blind spots and eliminating biased or inaccurate data. Instead, ANI is more likely to simply change the form of the blind spots and create incomplete pictures of the real world with the added danger of making the users unaware there are in fact blind spots. This is known as the Black Box Problem. This occurs when users of ANI have an increase in the amount of data, streamline it, and then apply the outputs in complete faith the data is accurate. However, the users will not truly know because no one fully understands how the ANI is identifying its solutions.[59]

One of the biggest misconceptions of average users, investors, and advocates of ANI is the assumption that ANI can be made completely unbiased and objective.[60] This depends on what problems the ANI are programed to address. For scientific or math problems, it is easy to have unbiased programming because there are clear definitive metrics that have straight forward yes or no answers. Anything involving metrics that doesn't have a definitive clearcut means of gauging the outcome will always have some type of bias.[61] For instance, people would like to believe ANI would create non-discriminatory criteria to reduce prejudice in selecting people for whatever roles.[62] The problem is there is no one singularly universally accepted definition of that term. Nondiscrimination has many normative descriptions and each description is formulated by a person or group with certain perspectives based on agenda and self-interest. It would be very easy to develop ANI that is "non-discriminatory" on initial appraisal but closer inspection reveals it discriminates based on less clearcut legalese metrics that is opaque but still result in the same discriminatory outcome. Every piece of software is written by a flawed human. Even software written by an ANI is still derived from human-coded software with whatever mistakes, errors and inherent biases exist in the human developers. All software has flaws and all software is built with some inherent bias. ANI doesn't eliminate bias; it just creates a singular common baseline bias from which to evaluate all data. The trick for humans is to know what that baseline is and evaluate the outputs with the software's limitations factored in. The problem with the black box is that the users don't know what the software limitations are.

For the FBE's to successfully automate their mission command with ANI to wage warfare requires their organizations reorganize their information structures away from old industrial age Max Weberian stovepipe-bureaucracy into one that maximizes use of information. Most organizations' foundations are based on 19th and 20th Century planning along with its limitations.[63] Before advanced software, human organizations had to manually collect, categorize, and process information to make it understandable. This took time, money, and effort. So, to simplify the problem organizations created specialized offices, divisions, or other sub-units to focus on particular subjects, categories, and criteria. Each specialized division of the organization would process the relevant information at their level, filter out and simplify the data for their superiors, and then send this information to higher echelons. Each level of echelon must simplify the information for the next level because each higher level of an organization looks at a broader strategic perspective than its subordinate elements. By the time the information reaches executive levels, the information represents a shallow, simplified portrait of the real world. Since each division of an organization must specialize in certain information, the inherent consequence is of stove piping where these organization divisions only share information vertically and not laterally within their parent organizations or sister organizations. So, the full portrayal of the real world only occurs at the senior executive level but this world portrait is a simple, pale imitation and leaves a lot of information gaps which inevitably creates misunderstanding and miscalculation of executive leaders. Hence, this partially explains why there are a lot of poor and ineffective responsiveness from complex bureaucracies.

ANI-based organizations would theoretically eliminate a lot of these traditional stove piped organizations but the danger is that ANI creates new weaknesses while it solves old problems. Organizations would still retain specialized divisions but more information would be exchanged laterally, enabling lower ranking echelons to better understand and synchronize their assessments of the incoming information. The data coming in would not be stripped down and simplified as done in the old stove pipe methods because the ANI would be able to retain all harvested data which each echelon could independently examine and add refinements without data loss. However, since ANI has no awareness or contextual understanding, the data extrapolated would be sterilized from its surrounding circumstances.[64] In the old manual methods, the data would be simplified but the humans examining the data would understand the context from where the data came from and be able to inform their superiors about the circumstances that influence the information being analyzed. The ANI extracts the data without the ability to contextualize the information and when the millions of pieces of information is stored in the data lake accessible to all within the organization, there is now greater reliance on the people being able to understand the inferences of the data at all levels.[65] Furthermore, the ANI algorithms will only collect data set by the parameters of its programming which means more streamlined reporting but also means variables not considered by the algorithm will not be seen by anyone at any level.[66] This means that "black swan" events are likely to occur more frequently because no one is watching for the variables discarded by the ANI programming and identifying those information gaps would be difficult.

During the ANI programming, the parameters are preset trying to balance the needs of four separate considerations: 1. The programmers and their engineering requirements; 2. The subject-matter experts who will arbitrarily set the weights and priorities of data searches; 3. Pleasing the organizational biases of the customer organization; 4. Configuring the software that best suits the mission of the organization using the ANI. This means no one will fully know what the actual parameters are and will be oblivious on exactly what basis the data outputs are generated.[67] All of this will likely help organizations develop very thorough and detailed analysis, but only on a specific select portion of the assessed portrayal of the real world while having complete gaps in the rest of the analyzed world picture.[68] The FBE would likely have a very clear, detailed understanding of only portions of the world picture instead of the old system's analytical ability to create a more holistic but shallow, simplified worldview missing many details. ANI will help the FBE improve its information fidelity but at the cost of comprehensive holistic analysis of real-world situations and without the many humans with a high degree of broad real-world understanding, will blind them completely to many potential negative outliers.

Old vs New Information Organizational Flows

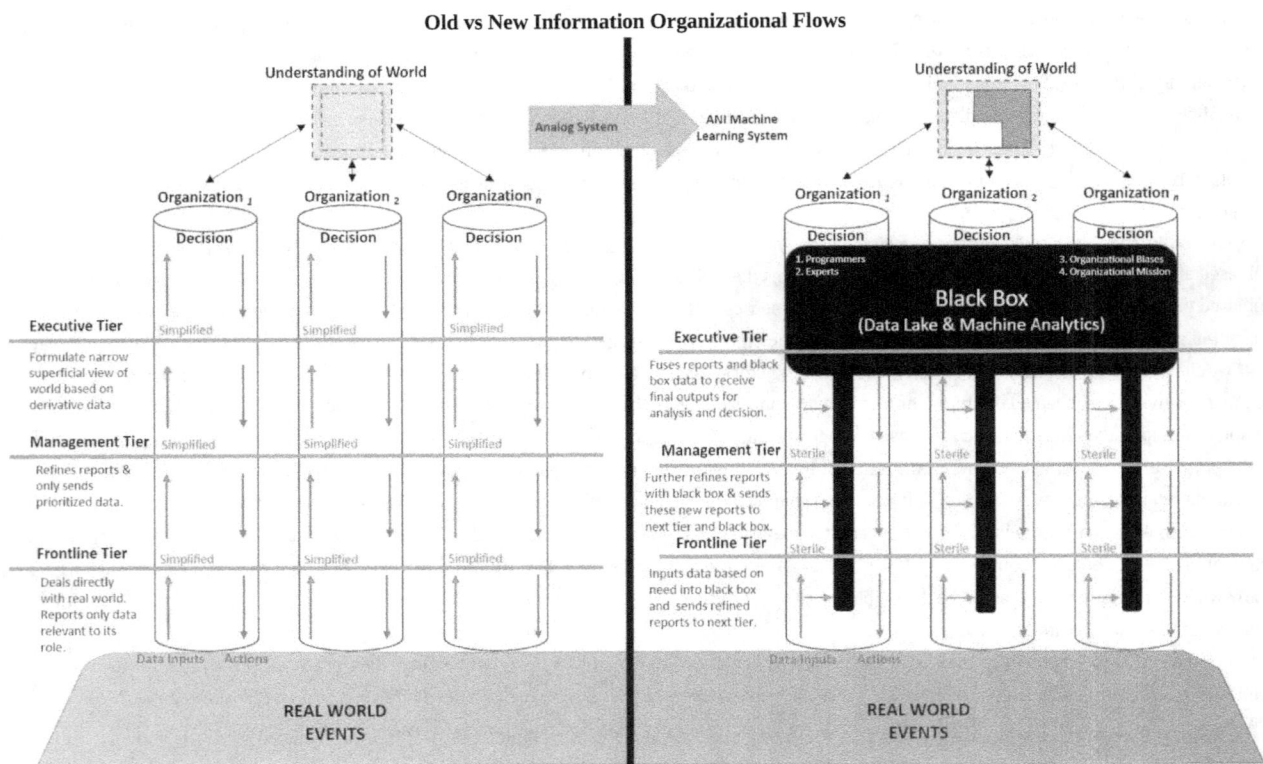

All of these weaknesses can be exploited by weaker opponents like the NRF and if the exploitations are done correctly, could keep the FBE from knowing about the actions for a long time. If the NRF gains access to the ANI's parameters or learns the criteria with sufficient analysis of their own, then the ANI will become vulnerable to deception, elicitation, and manipulation. If an opponent can identify what criteria the information is prioritized with, the NRF can deceptively misdirect the ANI's data mining with poisoned data sets.[lxix] This could be done by the NRF creating multiple smaller, cheaper ANIs that utilize classic cyber tactics as botting and zombifying computers to add sufficient processing power to create thousands or millions of false positives to create inaccurate data sets so the FBE ANIs generate poor results.

Since ANI has no comprehension ability which is vital to understand intent and deception,[lxx] the NRF could simply elicit information from the ANIs by asking tricky questions, queries, and creating nuanced program model tweaks to have the FBE ANIs give the NRF vital intelligence or technical advantages.[lxxi], [lxxii], [lxxiii] This is a more complex variation on how Captain Kirk kept destroying AI machines with paradox generating questions and answers. The more complex the ANI, the more likely this "Kirk Maneuvering" of elicitation will be effective as the ANI tries to perform its tasks. The final weakness of ANI occurs when the opponent understands what the ANI's data evaluation criteria is and then provide events that generate the desired criteria to lure FBE proxies into traps, be these cyber, kinetic, or politically embarrassing.[lxxiv], [lxxv], [lxxvi]

ANI will revolutionize mission command, intelligence, and deception elements of warfare but it is not a panacea nor are ANIs without faults. Either faction, but especially the FBE who would have access to more powerful ANIs, blindly embracing automation will leave themselves vulnerable and blind to circumstances and tactics they never considered. Until imagination and comprehension can be replicated, the FBE will still need to retain competent humans to manage their mission command. To effectively manage ANI, these people would need to have both rigorous academic stamina while being able to rationally discern the validity of the information by having some common sense as well.[lxxvii] Finding such people will be a more difficult task for the FBE than programming the ANI.

---

[1] Military Reference, *ADP 6-0 Mission Command: Command and Control of Army Forces*, (Washington DC: US Army Publishing Directorate: July 31, 2019): Paragraphs 1-13 – 1-15.

[2] News report, "Big Data, For Better or Worse: 90% of World's Data Generated in the Last Two Years," Science Daily, May 22, 2023. https://www.sciencedaily.com/releases/2013/05/130522085217.htm

[3] Paul Maxwell, "Artificial Intelligence is the Future of Warfare (Just Not in the Way You Think)," Modern War Institute at West Point, April 20, 2020. https://mwi.westpoint.edu/artificial-intelligence-future-warfare-just-not-way-think/

[4] Paul Mozur, "One Month, 500,000 Face Scans: How China Is Using A.I. to Profile a Minority," The New York Times, April 14, 2019. https://www.nytimes.com/2019/04/14/technology/china-surveillance-artificial-intelligence-racial-profiling.html

[5] Cabe Atwell, "What is AGI?" Fierce Electronics, September 14, 2022. https://www.fierceelectronics.com/sensors/what-agi

[6] S Akash, "What is Artificial Narrow Intelligence (ANI)? Benefits and Risks," Analytics Insight, March 29, 2023. https://www.analyticsinsight.net/what-is-artificial-narrow-intelligence-ani-benefits-and-risks/

[7] Charles Q. Choi, "Multiplexing Could Give Neural Networks a Big Boost," IEEE Spectrum, March 21, 2022. https://spectrum.ieee.org/neural-network-multiplex

[8] Edd Gent, "Hello, ChatGPT—Please Explain Yourself! An interview with the celebrated but controversial AI language model," IEEE Spectrum, December 9, 2022. https://spectrum.ieee.org/chatbot-chatgpt-interview

[9] Bella Fowler, "The Exact History of 'Six Degrees of Kevin Bacon'," New Zealand Herald, August 31, 2019. https://www.nzherald.co.nz/entertainment/the-exact-history-of-six-degrees-of-kevin-bacon/NCVVAU73UZ4TNCZAK726ENOBBQ/

[10] IBM Reference Page, "What is Deep Learning?" IBM, accessed June 5, 2023. https://www.ibm.com/topics/deep-learning

[11] John Arquilla and Peter Denning, "Large Language Models are Small-Minded," National Interest, June 16, 2023. https://nationalinterest.org/blog/techland/large-language-models-are-small-minded-206556

[12] Benjamin Jensen and Dan Tadross, "How Large-Language Models Can Revolutionize Military Planning," War on the Rocks, April 12, 2023. https://warontherocks.com/2023/04/how-large-language-models-can-revolutionize-military-planning/

[13] Aruna K, "AI Is Changing Everything, But How Is It Impacting Digital Learning?" eLearning Industry, May 17, 2023. https://elearningindustry.com/ai-is-changing-everything-but-how-is-it-impacting-digital-learning

[14] Jeremy Hsu, "AI Learns Gender and Racial Biases from Language," IEEE Spectrum, April 13, 2017. https://spectrum.ieee.org/ai-learns-gender-and-racial-biases-from-language

[15] Hugo Molinaro, "Ethical Considerations and Disclosure of AI Use for Content Marketers," Convince&Convert, June 2023. https://www.convinceandconvert.com/ai/ethical-considerations-and-disclosure-of-ai-use-for-content-marketers/

[16] Noelle M. Cocoros, Chaim Kirby, Bob Zambarano, et al. "RiskScape: A Data Visualization and Aggregation Platform for Public Health Surveillance Using Routine Electronic Health Record Data," American Journal of Public Health, February 2021, 111(2), 269-276. https://www.ncbi.nlm.nih.gov/pmc/articles/PMC7811092/

[17] Reference page, "Location Tracking," Electronic Privacy Information Center, accessed June 1, 2023. https://epic.org/issues/data-protection/location-tracking/

[18] Alex McConnell, "The Dark Side of AI: How Malicious Bots May Exploit ChatGPT," NETACEA, July 2, 2023. https://netacea.com/blog/chatgpt-malicious-bots-ai/

[19] John Villasenor, "How to Deal with AI-enabled Disinformation," Brookings Institute, November 23, 2020. https://www.brookings.edu/articles/how-to-deal-with-ai-enabled-disinformation/

[20] COL Brendan Cook, "The Future of Artificial Intelligence in ISR Operations," Air and Space Power Journal, Special Edition Summer 2001, v. 35. 41-55. https://www.airuniversity.af.edu/Portals/10/ASPJ/journals/Volume-35_Special_Issue/F-Cook.pdf

[21] Deepak Gupta, "The Impact of AI On Identity and Access Management," Forbes, March 27, 2023. https://www.forbes.com/sites/forbestechcouncil/2023/03/27/the-impact-of-ai-on-identity-and-access-management/?sh=34cf790055ab

[22] Katherine Lawton, "Businessman Is Stunned After AI Bot Chatgpt Wrongly Brands Him a Mass Murdering IRA Terrorist Responsible For 1992 Bombing," Daily Mail, April 17, 2023. https://www.dailymail.co.uk/news/article-11980887/Businessman-stunned-AI-bot-ChatGPT-wrongly-brands-mass-murdering-IRA-terrorist.html

[23] NGO article, "How the EU's Flawed Artificial Intelligence Regulation Endangers the Social Safety Net: Questions and Answers," Human Rights Watch, November 10, 2021. https://www.hrw.org/news/2021/11/10/how-eus-flawed-artificial-intelligence-regulation-endangers-social-safety-net

[24] Tristan Greene, "Politicians and Scientists Manipulate Us with Surveys – AI Could Stop Them," TNW, July 14, 2021. https://thenextweb.com/news/politicians-scientists-manipulate-surveys-ai

[25] Entefy Alston Ghafourifar, "AI-Powered Trading Raises New Questions," VentureBeat, May 6, 2017. https://venturebeat.com/ai/ai-powered-trading-raises-new-questions/

[26] News Article, "Spotting Insider Trading, Financial Fraud, Misconduct: There's An App For That," Stevens Institute of Technology, July 6, 2017. https://www.stevens.edu/news/insider-trading-financial-fraud-misconduct-theres-stevensaccenture-communications-surveillance-app

[27] James Bareham, "Beware of These Futuristic Background Checks," Vox, May 11, 2020. https://www.vox.com/recode/2020/5/11/21166291/artificial-intelligence-ai-background-check-checkr-fama

[28] Eduardo Baptista, "Insight: China Uses AI Software to Improve Its Surveillance Capabilities," Reuters, April 8, 2022. https://www.reuters.com/world/china/china-uses-ai-software-improve-its-surveillance-capabilities-2022-04-08/

[29] Journal article, "The Future Is Now: Unlocking the Promise of AI In Industrials," McKinsey and Company, December 6, 2022. https://www.mckinsey.com/industries/automotive-and-assembly/our-insights/the-future-is-now-unlocking-the-promise-of-ai-in-industrials

[30] Mireille Hildebrandt, Paul W. Grimm, et al. "Artificial Justice: The Quandary of AI in the Courtroom," Judicature International, September 2022. https://judicature.duke.edu/articles/artificial-justice-the-quandary-of-ai-in-the-courtroom/

[31] Sarah Cook, "China's Censors Could Shape the Future Of AI-Generated Content," The Japan Times, February 27, 2023. https://www.japantimes.co.jp/opinion/2023/02/27/commentary/world-commentary/china-artificial-intelligence/

[32] Jaykumar Patel, Martin Manetti, et al., "AI Brings Science to the Art of Policymaking," Boston Consulting Group, April 5, 2021. https://www.bcg.com/publications/2021/how-artificial-intelligence-can-shape-policy-making

[33] Sead Fadilpasic, "How Hackers Use Generative AI in Their Attacks and What We Can Do About It," Makeuseof.com, April 26, 2023. https://www.makeuseof.com/how-hackers-use-generative-ai-in-their-attacks/

[34] Mark K. Pratt, "15 Top Applications of Artificial Intelligence in Business," TechTarget, June 21 2023. https://www.techtarget.com/searchenterpriseai/tip/9-top-applications-of-artificial-intelligence-in-business

[35] Thom Hawkins and Alexander Kott, "Beyond the Hype: Why We're Closer to AI-Enabled Mission Command than You Think," Modern War Institute at West Point, May 4, 2022. https://mwi.usma.edu/beyond-the-hype-why-were-closer-to-ai-enabled-mission-command-than-you-think/

[36] Sara Ayoubi, Noura Limam, et al., "Machine Learning for Cognitive Network Management," IEEE Communications Magazine, January 2018. https://rboutaba.cs.uwaterloo.ca/Papers/Journals/2018/AyoubiCOMMAG18.pdf

[37] Jeffrey Lee Funk and Gary N. Smith, "Don't Believe the Hype: Why ChatGPT is not the 'Holy Grail' of AI Research," Salon.com, March 19, 2023. https://www.salon.com/2023/03/19/dont-believe-the-hype-why-chatgpt-is-not-the-holy-grail-of-ai-research/

[38] Glenn Zorpette, "GPT-4, AGI, and the Hunt for Superintelligence," IEEE Spectrum, April 19, 2023. https://spectrum.ieee.org/superintelligence-christoph-koch-gpt4

[39] Stavros Adam, Panos Pardalos, Michael Vrahatis, et al. "No Free Lunch Theorem: A Review," Springer Optimization and its Applications, May 2019, 57-82. https://www.researchgate.net/publication/333007007_No_Free_Lunch_Theorem_A_Review

[40] Jonathan Bartlett and Eric Holloway, "Generalized Information: A Straightforward Method for Judging Machine Learning Models," Communications of the Blyth Institute, v. 1, i. 2, 13-21. https://papers.ssrn.com/sol3/papers.cfm?abstract_id=3459217

[41] Mark Harrison, "The Soviet Economy, 1917-1991: Its Life and Afterlife," The Centre for Economic Policy Research-Voxeu Column, November 7, 2017. https://cepr.org/voxeu/columns/soviet-economy-1917-1991-its-life-and-afterlife

[42] Leon Aron, "Everything You Think You Know About the Collapse of the Soviet Union is Wrong," Foreign Policy, June 20, 2011. https://foreignpolicy.com/2011/06/20/everything-you-think-you-know-about-the-collapse-of-the-soviet-union-is-wrong/

[43] Gunter Reiman, *The Vampire Economy: Doing Business Under Fascism*, (DE: Mises Institute, re-printed September 2020 (1939)) 291-304.

[44] Jean Barroca, "AI and the Future of Government," Forbes, May 10, 2023. https://www.forbes.com/sites/deloitte/2023/05/10/ai-and-the-future-of-government/?sh=62584b0f3c64

[45] Samantha Flom, "AI Will Eventually Be 'As Good a Tutor as Any Human': Bill Gates," The Epoch Times, April 19, 2023. https://www.theepochtimes.com/ai-will-eventually-be-as-good-a-tutor-as-any-human-bill-gates_5207460.html

[46] Nassim Nicholas Taleb, *The Black Swan: The Impact of the Highly Improbable* (Abstract version), The Economist, 2007. https://www.economist.com/media/globalexecutive/black_swan_taleb_e.pdf

[47] Robert Marks and Eric Holloway, "Observation of Unbounded Novelty in Evolutionary Algorithms is Unknowable," International Conference on Artificial Intelligence and Soft Computing, 2018. 398-401.

[48] Roger Penrose, *The Emperor's New Mind* (UK: OUP Oxford:2016): 21-23, 524-526.

[49] Marcus Hutter and Shane Legg, "A Collection of Definitions of Intelligence," Advances in Artificial General Intelligence: Concepts, Architectures, and Algorithms, July 2007, v. 15. https://www.researchgate.net/publication/1895883_A_Collection_of_Definitions_of_Intelligence

[50] Reference Page, *The Chinese Room Argument*, Stanford University Encyclopedia of Philosophy. https://plato.stanford.edu/entries/chinese-room/

[51] Ibid, https://plato.stanford.edu/entries/chinese-room/#SyntSema

[52] Reference Page, *Types of Machine Learning—Supervised, Unsupervised, Reinforcement*, TechVidvan Learning Tutorials, https://techvidvan.com/tutorials/types-of-machine-learning/

[53] William J. Littlefield II, "The Human Skills AI Can't Replace," Quillette Magazine, September 25, 2019. https://quillette.com/2019/09/25/the-human-skills-ai-cant-replace/

[54] Kyle Wiggers, "Elon Musk Wants to Build AI to 'Understand the True Nature of the Universe'," TechCrunch, July 12, 2023. https://techcrunch.com/2023/07/12/elon-musk-wants-to-build-ai-to-understand-the-true-nature-of-the-universe/

[55] Reference Page, *The Nervous System*, University of Cincinnati, Ohio. https://www.uc.edu/content/dam/uc/ce/images/OLLI/Page%20Content/The%20Nervous%20System.pdf

[56] News report, "Stem Cell Proliferation is Controlled Directly by the Nervous System, Scientists Find," Science Daily, October 17, 2018. https://www.sciencedaily.com/releases/2018/10/181017141033.htm

[57] Darold A. Treffert, "The Savant Syndrome: An Extraordinary Condition," Philosophical Transactions of the Royal Society, v. 364, May 27, 2009. https://www.ncbi.nlm.nih.gov/pmc/articles/PMC2677584/

[58] Lance Whitney, "Are Computers Already Smarter Than Humans?" Time, September 29, 2017. https://time.com/4960778/computers-smarter-than-humans/

[59] Cathy O'Neil, *Weapons of Math Destruction*, (NY: Crown Publishing Group: 2016): 7-8.

[60] Ibid, 2-5.

[61] Tim Koopmans, "How Cognitive Biases Influence Software Development," Atlassian Products & News, March 13, 2019. https://www.atlassian.com/blog/add-ons/how-cognitive-biases-influence-software-development

[62] Lorena Blasco-Arcas, "How to Prioritize Humans in Artificial Intelligence Design for Business," Business Review of the London School of Economics, October 5, 2021. https://blogs.lse.ac.uk/businessreview/2021/10/05/how-to-prioritise-humans-in-artificial-intelligence-design-for-business/

[63] Robert D. Behn, "On the Reason Why Stovepipe Bureaucracies Live," Harvard's The Behn Public Management Report, v. 3, n.6, February 2006. https://thebehnreport.hks.harvard.edu/files/thebehnreport/files/february2006.pdf

[64] Cathy O'Neil, *Weapons of Math Destruction*, (NY: Crown Publishing Group: 2016): 5, 12-13, 17-22.

[65] Ibid, 107-112.

[66] Ibid, 53-55.

[67] Stephen M. Lepore, "Google CEO Says He Doesn't 'Fully Understand' How New AI Program Bard Works After It Taught Itself A Foreign Language It Was Not Trained To And Cited Fake Books To Solve An Economics Problem," Daily Mail, April 17, 2023. https://www.dailymail.co.uk/news/article-11980033/Google-CEO-says-doesnt-fully-understand-new-AI-program-Bard-works.html

[68] Cathy O'Neil, *Weapons of Math Destruction*, (NY: Crown Publishing Group: 2016): 123-126.

[lxix] Sue Poremba, "Data Poisoning: When Attackers Turn AI and ML Against You," SecurityIntelligence.com, April 21, 2021. https://securityintelligence.com/articles/data-poisoning-ai-and-machine-learning/

[lxx] Jim Norton, "Doctors warn against using ChatGPT for health advice as study finds AI makes up fake information when asked about CANCER," Daily Mail, April 4, 2023. https://www.dailymail.co.uk/sciencetech/article-11938205/ChatGPT-makes-fake-data-cancer-doctors-warn.html

[lxxi] Alex Polyakov, "Three Weird Ways AI Can Be Tricked," Forbes, September 7, 2018. https://www.forbes.com/sites/forbestechcouncil/2018/09/07/three-weird-ways-ai-can-be-tricked/?sh=1b99178f3ac8

[lxxii] Mehul Srivastava and Cristina Criddle, "Nvidia's AI Software Tricked into Leaking Data," Ars Technica, June 9, 2023. https://arstechnica.com/gadgets/2023/06/nvidias-ai-software-tricked-into-leaking-data/

[lxxiii] Jon Martindale, "How To Jailbreak ChatGpt: Get It To Really Do What You Want," Digital Trends, April 7, 2023. https://www.digitaltrends.com/computing/how-to-jailbreak-chatgpt/

[lxxiv] Ben Cost, "AI Clones Teen Girl's Voice In $1M Kidnapping Scam: 'I've Got Your Daughter'" NY Post, April 12, 2023. https://nypost.com/2023/04/12/ai-clones-teen-girls-voice-in-1m-kidnapping-scam/

[lxxv] Lucian Constantin, "How Data Poisoning Attacks Corrupt Machine Learning Models," CSO Online, April 12, 2021. https://www.csoonline.com/article/570555/how-data-poisoning-attacks-corrupt-machine-learning-models.html

[lxxvi] Elijah Cohen, "AI Detectors Think The US Constitution Was Written by AI," The Mind Unleashed, July 17, 2023. https://themindunleashed.com/2023/07/ai-detectors-think-think-the-us-constitution-was-written-by-ai.html

[lxxvii] Neil C. Thompson, Kristjan Greenewald, et al. "Deep Learning's Diminishing Returns: The Cost of Improvement Becomes Unsustainable," IEEE Spectrum, September 24, 2021. https://spectrum.ieee.org/deep-learning-computational-cost

Chapter 21: Phase II Operational Lines of Effort for the Foreign-Backed Elites

—Manipulate the NRF into 3GW; LOE 1: Isolate the NRF

Nudging a society into accepting an autocratic system that openly embraces allegiance to its foreign benefactor is the safest pathway for FBEs to achieve victory, but reality always introduces spoilers into the best laid plans. There is no realistic means of achieving total and complete subservience of the entire population of the Western nation the FBE is trying to subvert. There will always be people who will not only notice the "nudging" but have a vested interest in preventing the FBE's foreign benefactor from attaining controlling influence within the nation. Most rebellious or obstinate elements of a democratic-republican style system of government will tolerate anocracies and try to work within the system because there are still means to peacefully address grievances, even if those processes are inepter and more corrupt. The nudging process will eventually reach a culmination point beyond when there will be no peaceful political process for dissenting members of the population to redress their grievances thus causing resentment to accumulate to a critical mass. Once this level of resentment is achieved, the disenfranchised elements will resist the FBE-backed system openly.

This resistance would be peaceful at first, trying to maintain the delusion that society hasn't regressed into autocratic corruption but inevitably the resentment will explode into violence. The foreign benefactor will have successfully induced civil war once the FBE successfully cut off all dissent from legitimate political discourse and participation. Since the FBE must inevitably face this as one of the consequences of their strategic objectives, they must plan for how to best confront and defeat the NRF in such a conflict. The civil war will only start once the FBE has sufficiently subverted enough of the Western nation's critical institutions that the FBE can lobby for the corrupted anocratic state to fight on the FBE's behalf. The FBE's strength depends on corruptly wielding the legal, economic, and cultural power of the Western nation and must shape the conflict that best suits these institutional powers. In the FBE's optimal strategy of Catalonia 2.0, the best conflict is one designed to suit the institutional strengths of the corrupted state backed by subverted corporate and nonprofit activist organizations. 3GW or Third Gradient Warfare, in which a state fights another state in large-scale combat operations plays to all of the FBE's strengths and would lead to the most optimal victory. To compel the NRF to fight in a 3GW-style battlespace, the FBE must "assist" the NRF in coalescing into a unified force that is sufficiently concentrated to actually pose a military risk. Timing is crucial as the FBE must strike at the right time as to attract all their enemies into easily defeatable concentrations but remain insufficiently powerful to defeat the FBE's corrupt state. If properly timed, the FBE forces will easily identify, isolate, and destroy the NRF while also having the perfect scapegoat to blame any hardships on the public to avoid a general backlash. Phase II is the FBE's effort to manipulate the NRF and shape the battlespace to assure a quicker victory in a violent civil conflict. The first LOE is isolating the NRF from the rest of the Western nation to easily identify their enemy and lure out as many as possible for ease of destruction.

The political and economic structures of post-industrial Western countries have mostly integrated across every major administrative division within their countries. Prior to the American Civil War, the economy and social culture of the United States was more regionalized with the agrarian southern states and industrialized northern states having distinct contrasts.[i] Once the war began, the United States was able to, with some difficulties, separate and then insulate its economic power from the Confederacy's economy. In contemporary times after the apex of the globalist economic integration era in the 1990s, Western nations now have more integrated economies with only a few regional economic contrasts like Silicon Valley, Kendall Square, or the Cambridge Cluster standing out. Even though some regions are wealthier than others, these nations have a common currency, banking system, overlapping critical infrastructure, and fewer regional cultural distinctions. For Lincoln and the Union, it was relatively easy to isolate the Confederacy because the cultural and economic foundations had distinct geographical boundaries.[ii] The potential sources of NRF supporters and other dissidents would likely come from every administrative district of the Western nation with some areas leaning more NRF than FBE but the populations of both would be closely interconnected. If the potential enemy is geographically everywhere within the Western nation, this also means that every institution at every level of government, industry, and culture will likely have potential NRF members or sympathizers.[iii], [iv] This is a recipe for 4GW or 5GW conflict which would be detrimental to the FBE's anocracy as states perform poorly in these styles of conflict. To have a cohesive economy, military, law enforcement, and social structure securely loyal to the FBE requires the NRF to willfully leave these institutions as well as critical geographic regions of the Western nation so the FBE can wage an organized state on state war to destroy the opponent in large scale open combat.

This means provoking the NRF elements to want to leave the anocracy and gravitate to areas where like-minded people are the majority. If sufficiently provoked, the NRF will initially become isolated by the FBE's ostracization efforts but then the NRF will voluntarily complete this isolation effort by going into self-imposed exile. Ultimately, the FBE wants that self-imposed exile to be in distinct geographical areas large enough to attempt secession while the FBE simultaneously decouples those regions' economic value from the FBE-controlled part of the Western nation. Once fully isolated, the FBE can wage a 3GW conflict with little fear regarding any economic and social fallout as the FBE has insulated their faction's regions.

Options and Methods:

Isolating the elements of the NRF would have to be done in conjunction with the LOEs of Phase I. Changing the society is the first step towards discovering and isolating dissenting elements within the Western nation. For Phase II, the crucial effort is to change the institutions and the systemic processes to make society unlivable for dissenting ideas and people. Institutional changes must isolate the NRF in three ways: 1. Discrediting NRF-aligned elites; 2. Compel the NRF-leaning population to create a new parallel separate economy and; 3. Prevent the NRF from having any access to fair recourse or adjudication regarding any grievance. Each of these approaches attacks the NRF's leadership, potential workforce, and creates social barriers from the rest of the population to hinder the NRF's ability to spread influence amongst the general public. Each approach needs to be executed simultaneously to maximize disorientating and isolating the NRF.

Contrary to popular perception of revolutions, neither the "masses" nor the "youth" instigate or lead insurrections. The young among the educated population are simply the most susceptible and useful pool of recruits in most rebellions or civil conflicts because they are both educated and the most capable of fighting. Regardless of the type of political system, the social and political elites within that system always instigate the actual start of any major political action. In revolutions or civil wars, disaffected members of the elite or those working within the elites' circles are the instigating catalysts whether they are autocrats, financiers, aristocracy, military officers, academics, or from the professional classes. Examples range from the politician Pavel Miliukov of the February Revolution being from the aristocracy,[v] Hitler's reliance on Germany's most powerful industrialists to become chancellor,[vi] Mussolini being an educated journalist,[vii] and the members of the National Constituent Assembly of 1789 creating the catalyst for the French Revolution being mostly form the professional classes.[viii]' [ix] The NRF, like any rebelling force, needs support and leadership from disaffected members of the wealthy, influential, or politically powerful elements of the Western nation's elites. Most of these NRF-aligned elites will reveal themselves before any open fighting by advocating for certain policies, prescriptions for social issues, and how they manage their roles in the national economy. So, the FBE must reduce these NRF elites' influence as much as possible to minimize the scale of resistance before fighting breaks out. The FBE must silence the NRF-aligned elites, socially stigmatize the NRF's social beliefs, and rig economic outcomes to weaken NRF-friendly industries and organizations. If the NRF's elites and potential leaders are isolated then they cannot rally and organize the NRF into a cohesive fighting force

The same tools used to nudge the society towards autocracy would also be the best weapons to isolate dissenting elites. The FBE's contemporary versions of the sepoys, the Atomized and the Nimbyists, would most likely lead the efforts to attack the elites. In an anocracy, the system relies on the patronage of all elites across the political spectrum to sustain the broken society because most of the public has lost faith in it. This means the FBE cannot rely on lobbying the government to eliminate opponents within their ranks because the NRF's potential leaders would be from the elite classes, so the FBE must rely on the private armies of deluded and malleable radicals to harass and degrade the NRF elites. Or, at least, in the beginning. The Atomized represent the various co-opted single-issue groups on both the far-left and far-right manipulated into doing the FBE's bidding. The Atomized will always be portrayed as either victims or outcasts created by an unfair or unjust system. In this case, the role of the Atomized is to foster the belief among the politically apathetic public that the unjust system is created, nurtured, and commanded exclusively by NRF-sympathetic elites. After publicly labeling the NRF-elite as the leaders of all sorrow, the Atomized would demonstrate, riot, and harass anyone or any group that attempts to give the NRF-aligned elites the ability to peacefully participate in the political process. If the NRF-elites are labeled with negative associations and the Atomized successfully create the atmosphere of collective guilt by association, many persons and organizations will be too intimidated to interact or support the NRF-aligned elites. Hounding and harassing businesses, charities, political parties, and public forums with threats of boycotts, criminal violence, or being labeled with socially alienating terms will deny the NRF-aligned elites' access to the society of the Western nation.

While the Atomized would deny the NRF-aligned elites' access to the society at large, the Nimbyists' efforts will be to deny the NRF-aligned elites' access to society's institutions. Most of the Nimbyists will come from the educated middle and upper classes who will use their connections in social, cultural, and political activist institutions to deny NRF-aligned elites' access to the services these societal institutions provide. The Nimbyists are typically too lazy and risk averse to participate in any physical activity and will act only in information operations. The Nimbyists will complain, moralize, harass, and lead fundraising to help boycott the NRF's potential leaders on social media platforms, old media firms, public forums, and government hearings. By their nature, Nimbyists are typically shallow and decadent so they will often accuse their NRF opponents of despicable behaviors that are exactly what the Nimbyists do themselves. Their shallowness prevents critical thinking which compels them to believe that all human beings behave in the exact same way with the only difference being which side of the political conflict one is on. Nimbyists are not moral police like in Iran, as they don't firmly believe in anything except how to secure their indulgences while using moral stances to shield their own avarice. This makes them determined but inconsistent in their arguments and are often brazenly hypocritical. This makes the usefulness of Nimbyists limited within a narrow set of circumstances and actions. To maximize effectiveness, the FBE must use the Nimbyists in conjunction with another smaller specialized group of proxies that can isolate the NRF-aligned elites by denying access to society's economic system. This smaller niche group of FBE pawns will be referred to as the Faustians.

Faustians are key business and financial persons whose avarice makes them myopic to all other considerations that could lead to longer term negative consequences of their actions. The Faustians go one step beyond Ebenezer Scrooge in that their greed will encourage them to align with the highest bidder and switch allegiances for even a slight uptick in immediate profit, even at the cost of long-term profit. Faustians will take "moral positions" to justify personal enrichment in the name of a cause to shield themselves from criticism or customer backlash. These people are the type who would sell their mother for an extra sandwich. These businessmen and women are easily susceptible to FBE bribery to lead their business organizations, associations, guilds, and leagues in boycotting NRF-aligned elites. Faustians would use their influence in the business world to block loans, crowdfunding, financial transactions, and investments that could aid the NRF-aligned elites in both personal and resistance activities. To obfuscate their true intentions, Faustians will take "principled stances" against these declared societal enemies, who change depending on the day, the bribe, and the FBE's whims. Faustians are the kind of members of the business class that encapsulates the Marxist stereotypes of the "greedy capitalists".

The importance of isolating the NRF's allies among the Western nation's elites is paramount to stifling any resistance's ability to sufficiently organize into an effective threatening fighting force.[x] Yet, the FBE must also isolate the dissenting elements of the general population who are most susceptible to joining a rebellion while simultaneously help to expose and positively identify them for future elimination. The FBE must encourage dissenting populations to stop mixing in with the rest of the population and self-segregate to become easy targets when open fighting occurs. The civilian population is more challenging because dissenting elements are mixed in with every social class, industry, and government institution. If fighting occurs before the FBE isolates them, then the FBE will doom themselves to a decade-long 4GW insurgency that will cost the FBE the economy and stability of the Western nation. The best way to identify, isolate, and segregate the dissenting population is to use the "nudging" efforts of social change to redefine what is taboo, nefarious, and socially dangerous. The Atomized and Nimbyists causes will be held in high virtue while anything that encourages self-reliance or independent thinking be disparaged. Once these new paradigms are defined, the FBE can use their "sepoys" to compel the various elements of the nation's economy to enforce the moral good and deny doing business with the newly ostracized dissidents.

The cultural "nudging" combined with non-state actors who can portray themselves as underdogs creates the social pressure sufficient enough to make most businesses ignore short-term profit for the sake of social survival. These sepoy elements can be used to push radical proposals that either endanger dissenting people or severely degrades their ability to function which will compel the dissidents to reveal themselves. The dissenting public will try to use the anocracy's systems of redress to overturn or reduce the impact of the FBE sepoy groups as the dissidents try to reform the system back to a time that was stable and beneficial to them. Once identified, these dissenting people can be hounded, intimidated, and socially exiled like the NRF-aligned elites. Utilities could be shut down, social media banning, banned from bank deposits, loans, and state licenses are just some examples. Impoverishing and stigmatizing the dissenting population will force them to self-segregate into larger more concentrated communities of anti-FBE dissidents.

Once these self-segregated communities become large enough, the FBE would then carry out its final step of NRF isolation by changing the policies and laws of the state to actively discriminate against the dissenting population. Traditional coups or subversions typically overthrow and take over the state and its institutions first. For a foreign-backed effort against a Western nation, this action would be last. Western democratic republics have checks and balances with populations expecting some degree of autonomy from the state in contrast to autocratic societies where the populace expects the state to have an active role in daily life. Trying to subvert the state before subverting a Western nation's elites, culture, and social mores would fail. Democratic-republics' power, at least partially, begins from the bottom to the top of society and that society must be subverted first. In this case of optimal execution of the FBE's strategy, the state is subverted indirectly by having members of state institutions defending the socially altered morals and expectations the FBE nudged over a period of years. To the state institutions' perception, they are simply executing the demands of the Western society, not realizing they are indirectly manipulated to carry out self-destructive actions.

As the NRF-sympathetic population builds large enough communities, the state will be lobbied to alter political and legal processes to deny these exiled elements any recourse in the Western society to provoke the NRF. The FBE's social nudging will allow them to use their financial and lobbying connections to emplace political appointees, judicial officials, and law enforcement sympathetic to the FBE cause and yet look like natural selections based on the newly established social mores of the subverted Western nation. These FBE-sympathetic pawns and collaborators can arbitrarily impose a double standard based on political criteria to actively discriminate against dissent while appearing to do so in the name of protecting underprivileged Atomized or victimized Nimbyists. Given a sufficient amount of time, the NRF-sympathizers will be completely exiled from the political process while being portrayed as society's enemies. This will induce many NRF to advocate for the creation of their own nation-state and urge secession of regions where the NRF communities are strongest. Once a push for secession occurs, an open conflict can finally be initiated to annihilate the NRF completely in a 3GW conflict that suits the state's institutional strengths.

Strengths:

Once the culture is sufficiently indoctrinated into believing the new FBE-backed paradigms of morality, ethics, and power structures, the ability of the FBE to act openly autocratic becomes much easier. By the very nature of the covert activities incited by the foreign adversarial nation, the Western nation will not resist the social "nudging" until after major shifts in culture occur. In such an environment, the FBE will have created a societal-wide atmosphere of group and double-think. People inherently want to be part of a group as they are social creatures and most will lack the willpower to defy what is popular or what makes a person "fit in" to that group. Social changes induced by the Phase I LOEs create a psychological camouflage that protects the FBE's overtly aggressive actions against the NRF. Making the FBE's pro-autocratic morality the basis for all social groupthink means average observers in the public will rationalize any act of isolation, ostracization, or persecution as defending the moral integrity of the Western nation, even though that morality has been nefariously subverted.

This is the strength of controlled chaos. Being able to use a corrupted version of Western morality to justify the recruitment and empowerment of the Atomized to persecute and isolate political enemies without fear of mass outrage. Controlled chaos keeps the Western nation's population continuously off-balance, never knowing where the boundaries of propriety and acceptable ethics are because these always shift on the needs of the FBE. The Atomized and Nimbyists emotionally condition the apolitical majority of the Western nation into a collective version of Stockholm Syndrome and paralyze critical thought. The population will never be given enough time to think or consider how the anocracy is failing or how to reform it. Most people are passive, unwilling to endure the hardships of political responsibility, and will stand by while the resource-laden pawns of the FBE brazening push out anyone who defies the FBE's new paradigm. People's inherent passivity and lack of interest in taking on greater social responsibility makes the Atomized and Nimbyists' jobs to isolate and stigmatize the defiant NRF easy.

This perpetually controlled chaos has the added bonus of not only separating the NRF from society but also separating the society from its cultural heritage. The chaos caused by the FBE's sepoys compels everyone to live in the moment, unable to reflect on the past or refer to any precedent that might risk people becoming aware of the indications of foreign subversion. The sepoys derive their power to cause chaos by corrupting the Western nation's original concepts of liberties to justify their actions. If people can't remember their past and can be convinced that their historical liberties led to the current chaos, many will eventually reject their own culture and demand the newly "nudged" autocracy use its new power to bring order out of the chaos.[xi]

Finally, this isolation effort creates a feedback system that reinforces the loyalty of the Atomized and Nimbyists to the FBE. Despite the propaganda portrayal of Atomized and Nimbyists being underdogs motivated by injustice and popular support, the FBE's sepoys will never act independently of their secret masters. These groups of chaos would have free reign on how to implement the chaos, but they will never initiate the chaos on their own accord. The Atomized and Nimbyists will only act under top-cover provided by the FBE and their political allies. If the FBE decides a group of Atomized or Nimbyists are either too much trouble or are no longer useful, that group will be cut off from funds, media protection, and susceptible to judicial punishments. These groups of modern sepoys are psychologically regimented and conditioned to obey their group, which is strictly controlled by a hierarchy created by the FBE. This hierarchy can be mostly invisible to the average Atomized and Nimbyists as they have no need to know who funds them or where the resources are generated. In exchange for directing their chaotic energies at the FBE's preferred target, these sepoys can indulge in their debaucheries and enjoy the tiny slivers of power gifted to them by the FBE's leadership. This makes control simple and easy while also maintaining plausible deniability of any direct connection.

Weaknesses:

Chaos is chaos, which means it has a finite shelf life as a useful tool. Nothing in politics remains static, including the circumstances that are most suitable for using agents of chaos like the Nimbyists and Atomized. For the FBE to succeed in their ultimate objectives they will need to reestablish order and for that to happen these sepoys of chaos, both Atomized and Nimbyists, must in the end be purged. The violence and anarchy created by these manipulated puppets is beneficial to the FBE as long as it can be reined in when the FBE needs order restored. This means keeping chaos below the threshold of state institutional limitations on imposing order. Even totalitarian states have resource limits and if the Atomized and Nimbyists' actions get beyond the state's ability to extinguish anarchy, this would both destabilize and discredit the FBE and its proxy allies. The FBE can prolong the useful lifespan of the Atomized and Nimbyists by constantly creating new sub-factions with new "causes" to rally and fight for to keep the agents of chaos focused on the FBE's enemies. At the same time this keeps the power of these groups weak as the multitude of different Atomized and Nimbyist groups compete for social prestige and the little political power occasionally gifted to them by their FBE masters.

The Atomized and Nimbyists are created to instill fear, disillusion, and compliance on the Western nation's broken population to compel them into accepting an FBE-controlled autocracy. They exist only to cause chaos and only excel at weakening and undermining a society. Once the autocracy is established, these modern sepoys become a detriment instead of an asset because they only know how destroy and parasitically live off society by extortion, political harassment, and violence.[xii] Once the FBE's enemies are gone and the objectives change to strengthening the autocratic-led society, there is nothing the sepoys can do to positively contribute to that effort. The Atomized and Nimbyists were created to seek enemies to destroy and weaken the social fabric. Once the anocracy is gone, the Atomized and Nimbyists will not suddenly change and become productive members of society but instead will find new enemies to hunt and destroy. Eventually, like crazed inquisitors always seeking new heretics to justify their existence, the Atomized and Nimbyists will find "traitors" to their causes everywhere with their criteria for loyalty becoming ever more puritanical. This inevitably leads to an internal FBE civil war that could threaten their existence. History has shown this happens without exception.

Each major totalitarian regime achieves power on the corpse of the previous regime which dies in the social chaos leading up to the dictatorship achieving absolute power. Without exception, each regime immediately turned on their ideologically zealous elements of their faction because they were only good at creating chaos.[xiii] After Hitler's ascension, the Brownshirts who helped propel him into power by destabilizing the Weimar Republic with violence, intimidation, and political activism suddenly became a liability. There is no gratitude in politics and Hitler launched the Night of the Long Knives with the Schutzstaffel to eliminate his agents of chaos before they could create chaos against Hitler himself. This kind of action was not limited to Nazi Germany. Joseph Stalin isolated and purged all the ideological elements of the Soviet Union's inner circle led by Leon Trotsky who demanded a more ideologically pure Soviet Union.[xiv] Mao Zedong tried to go against the historical precedent and attempted to keep China in a state of perpetual revolution using his Red Guard agents of chaos.[xv][xvi] However, towards the end of the Cultural Revolution, it became obvious, even to Mao, that ideological zealots purging "heretics" continuously without end cannot be sustained nor can the instigators be peacefully accommodated. Agents of chaos are indoctrinated to revolve their entire lives and personality around a "cause" and cannot do anything else. In the end, Mao eventually allowed the pragmatists, led by Deng Xiaoping, and the People's Liberation Army to mercilessly purge his agents of chaos quickly.[xvii] If the pragmatists had failed to stop the Red Guard's leaders, the "Gang of Four", from attaining power after Mao's death, it is very likely China would have descended into civil war and could have collapsed a decade before the Soviet Union.

The Atomized and Nimbyists only think of themselves and the indoctrination ensures they are only capable of thinking about immediate actions and not consequences or long-term effects. Bluntly, they are not useful, productive, or provide anything of positive value for a stable society. They are tools, nothing more, but these tools are only valuable in times of chaos. The purge doesn't have to be overtly violent but it has to be swift and comprehensive to catch the Atomized and Nimbyists off guard. Some are salvable and can be incorporated into the autocracy but this will be a tiny percentage. The Nazis slaughtered theirs, Stalin exiled them to Siberia, and Mao had them "re-educated" on collective farms and remote prisons so, there is a wide range of options. Of course, the FBE can never admit the Atomized or Nimbyists were wrong or a mistake. Instead, the FBE's leaders must claim the Atomized were subverted or became corrupt or anything that places the blame on the Atomized leaders themselves. The purge is done in the name of anticorruption or political justice. The one positive about this is that these sepoys have been conditioned to make this lifestyle the basis for their entire existence and are incapable of believing they will become obsolete. The Atomized will never accept they will be purged or declared public enemies because that would require acknowledging to themselves that they were wrong and their whole life was just to be fodder for someone else. The vast majority are incapable of such self-reflection and will only realize what is happening after the purge. They will have served the cause well during the period of "nudging" and chaos before the autocracy and afterwards the sepoys can perform one final service by testing the sturdiness of the walls for the FBE's firing squads.

The other danger of this isolation effort is that it relies on the chaos being focused on selected targets and not just randomly hitting out at society. The main focus would be on the NRF with intimidating the general population being a secondary priority. The FBE's effort to control these agents of chaos can be turned against them by shrewd NRF members using the same manipulation methods. The Atomized would consist of many factions which are manageable as long as the FBE keeps the factions of these elements separate from each other when not needed for missions. However, if the NRF uses a political event or issue to lure a disproportionate number of a particular Atomized faction to an FBE-aligned political stronghold, like a politically important city, then the Atomized will overwhelm that location's resources. If too many Atomized are located in one place, they will inevitably compete and fight each other over resources and political clout, akin to gang wars, within an FBE area. If the FBE are not careful, the NRF can mislead the gullible Atomized into situations where they end up fighting each other rather than the NRF. The easiest way would be to lure groups of people the Atomized claim they defend to an FBE-loyal region to force that Atomized faction to reallocate resources to this new influx that would otherwise be usually given to other local Atomized in the region to create shortages. Inevitably, the local Atomized will clash with the outsider Atomized and the FBE would struggle as they cannot overtly antagonize either group. The agents of chaos are the most effective at isolating the NRF, but these agents are conditioned to be easily led and manipulated. The NRF can weaponize this manipulation and the FBE must be ready to mitigate such actions.

---

[i] James McPherson, "The Differences Between the Antebellum North and South," Essay in *Major Problems in The Civil War and Reconstruction*, Thomas Patersoned, (Belmont: Wadsworth College, 3rd edition, 2011): 21-25. https://www.shsu.edu/~jll004/163_spring09/mcphersonnorthandsouth.pdf

[ii] Reference page, *The Union Blockade: Lincoln's Proclamations*, National Archives. https://www.archives.gov/education/lessons/blockade.html

[iii] Richard Sisk, "Special Forces at Risk to Insider Threat in Iraq," Military.com, July 15, 2014. https://www.military.com/daily-news/2014/07/15/special-forces-at-risk-to-insider-threat-in-iraq.html

[iv] Anthony H. Cordesman, "Afghanistan: Green on Blue Attacks Are Only a Small Part of the Problem," CSIS, September 4, 2012. https://www.csis.org/analysis/afghanistan-green-blue-attacks-are-only-small-part-problem-0

[v] Frank Alfred Golder, *Documents of Russian History 1914-1917*, (NY: The Century Company, Digital Archive Universal Digital Library, 1927): 233-239, 295. https://archive.org/details/documentsofrussi027937mbp/page/n1/mode/2up

[vi] David de Jong, "In the Room Where German Tycoons Agreed to Fund Hitler's Rise To Power,"

[vii] Benito Mussolini, *My Autobiography with the Political and Social Doctrine of Fascism*, (Garden City, NY: Dover Publications: 2006) 14-30.

[viii] Edmund Burke, *Reflections on the Revolution in France*, (Whithorn, UK: Anodos Books, 2019): 18-19.

[ix] Reference Page, *The Declaration of the Rights of Man of the Citizen*, Elysee Website. https://www.elysee.fr/en/french-presidency/the-declaration-of-the-rights-of-man-and-of-the-citizen

[x] Joint Publication 3-24, *Counterinsurgency*, (Washington DC: Department of Defense: April 25, 2018, validated April 30, 2021): II-18 – II-24.

[xi] Jinghan Zeng, *The Chinese Communist Party's Capacity to Rule: Ideology, Legitimacy and Party Cohesion*, (NY: Palgrave Macmillan, 2016) 22-23.

[xii] Gunter Reiman, *The Vampire Economy: Doing Business Under Fascism*, (DE: Mises Institute, re-printed September 2020 (1939)) 17.

[xiii] Richard J. Evans, *The Third Reich in Power* (NY: Penguin Press, 2005): 20.

[xiv] Rober Conquest, *The Great Terror*, (NY: Oxford University Press, 2008): 8-12, 100-108.

[xv] Dr. Li Zhisui, *The Private Life of Chairman Mao*, (NY: Random House: 1994): 508-509.

[xvi] Jung Chang and Jon Halliday, *The Unknown Story of Mao*, (NY: Random House's Anchor Books: 2005) 505-513.

[xvii] Dr. Li Zhisui, *The Private Life of Chairman Mao*, (NY: Random House: 1994): 631-636.

Chapter 22: Phase II Operational Lines of Effort for the Foreign-Backed Elites —Manipulate the NRF into 3GW; LOE 2: Divide the NRF

Being the instigators of subverting the Western nation, the FBE would have the initiative to shape and prepare for the conflict. Being able to act first creates multiple advantages for the FBE, including preemptively identifying potential enemies and their weaknesses before any fighting begins. In the beginning, the efforts to "nudge" and subvert the Western nation's anocracy would be hardly noticeable as it would be gradual over a period of years, so no one would organize any resistance. Over time, these "nudges" towards to autocratic subversion would become more obvious and a resistance would inevitably form, represented as the NRF in this scenario, which could potentially threaten and defeat the FBE. Anticipating inevitable resistance means the FBE would use their initiative to preposition obstacles, both political and physical, to prevent any resistance from becoming a strong effective fighting force. Pre-emptively establishing obstacles designed to distract, disorient, and divide would-be resistance members from working and functioning together helps ensure ultimate victory for the FBE. In this case, the obstacles would create a false or controlled opposition designed to keep the NRF perpetually divided.

The 4GW conflicts in the Middle East and North Africa over the last 20 years repeatedly demonstrated that divided opposition always fails to dislodge an established state or system. Iraq, Syria, and Libya had multiple insurgent and partisan groups and factions fighting for different causes that never reconciled.[i], [ii] These insurgent groups battled each other as much as they battled the state's government and always failed to achieve any real strategic victory.[iii] Even though ISIS boasted it created a separate state, this only rallied everyone else to unite in destroying that new state rather than President Assad then dividing again afterwards.[iv] In contrast, the Taliban enforced brutal discipline amongst their various tribal allies to keep a cohesive working insurgency united under a common banner and leadership. This contrast allowed them to focus on whittling down the Afghanistan government from their Pakistani safe havens without having to battle numerous other power-seeking insurgents and terrorists that would have bled them dry.[v] The FBE does need to provoke the NRF into fighting a 3GW-style war but also needing them in a weak divided state making such a conflict a quick and easy victory. Creating controlled opposition to interfere with sincere members of the NRF would exhaust and divide them, rendering them defeated before any fighting begins.

Options and Methods:

Not all Atomized sepoys are "underdogs" or "oppressed" groups carrying out the wishes of the FBE in the name of "righting wrongs". Some are radical elements outcasted from mainstream society and don't garner any form of sympathy from FBE controlled proxy organizations. These radicals would be Atomized. They openly proclaim totalitarian ideologies that promise to depose the FBE-linked elites from power and are found on both the left and right extremes of the political spectrum. Neither the communists nor racial fascists conform to the FBE's syncretic system of technocratic managerial corporatism yet both can be manipulated into being violent cannon fodder for the FBE.

The ideological fanaticism of both groups entices the Atomized who seek violence and willingly organize riots, acts of terrorism, and other public acts of physical violence. Since few of them have any strategic training beyond organizing in loose groups of gangs, many of these members can be deceived and lured into conducting violence and falsely proclaim it in the name of NRF-affiliated persons. Getting the NRF associated with acts of random violence against the general public in the name of discredited causes diminishes public support while raising doubts amongst the NRF members about their cause. The resource-laden FBE would easily find sufficient numbers of infiltrators to go into these ostracized groups of Atomized to deceptively trick and instigate false-flag attacks or entrap more radical members into committing major public crimes. Once carried out, these easily manipulated fanatics would publicly confess they were encouraged by prominent members of the NRF. False flags disrupt an opponent's planning while sowing mistrust and paranoia amongst the NRF.

Another more sophisticated option is using another variety of Faustians. Faustian proxies are well-connected members of society whose mercenary proclivities give them the psychological incentive to never be loyal to any "cause" or ideology, only the highest bidder. Anocracies offer many opportunities for Faustians to corruptly gain political, economic, and social positions of power for their own gratifications. Such Faustians would find any effort to "fix" or reform the anocracy abhorrent because they would be at risk of having to actually work productively for less money and greater accountability. Faustians will not care about the FBE or their ambitions of total control, as long as their rackets are protected, and they will ally with the FBE to keep the social corruption intact. The Faustians would be ideal to function as controlled "opposition"; they could set up social and news media that voices NRF-aligned concerns and beliefs allowing other Faustians to run for public office under the guise of supporting NRF reform. Under this ruse public officials, companies, charities, and lobbying groups proclaiming NRF platitudes and slogans would secretly sabotage any substantive action by the NRF. The Faustians would deliberately fail, act foolish, openly betray each other, and generally behave in the most discrediting way possible to diminish public support for the NRF.

The FBE can successfully target the people of the NRF with violent thugs and mercenary sellouts, but the FBE also needs to create ideological divisions too. Controlling the narratives and cultural institutions to "nudge" society into autocracy will not work at manipulating their NRF enemies. Instead, the FBE would need to use their controlled opposition to demoralize and divide the NRF by surrendering all narratives and arguments to FBE proxies. The FBE would define all parameters and assumptions for every political argument without any serious effort by the controlled faux NRF Faustians to contest these FBE-defined arguments. Whenever a political issue is brought up by the controlled opposition, the FBE Faustians would be able to declare which hypotheses, assumptions, and facts are used to establish the baseline parameters of an argument. This means the Faustian controlled opposition will always take a defensive position in the argument because these Faustians will acknowledge the validity of the

FBE's worldview and that the FBE will always have the morally and ethically superior position in every argument. Regardless of contradictions, hypocrisies, or outright falsehoods, the FBE, its information disseminators, and the Faustian "opposition" will always define what is the moral and ethical position for arguments used to debate any NRF position or perspective. This makes rational civil political discussion impossible and keeps the NRF in a constant state of distress and confusion. The controlled opposition will rationalize their failed positions as the "sensible", "moderate", or "respectable" moral high ground by remaining passive and ineffective. The Faustians would actively discourage any organized resistance as being extreme, traitorous, or uncivilized and that the NRF must accept the direction the FBE decides for society. At best, the Faustians would deliver some small tangible perks to buy silence or acquiescence. These controlled-opposition Faustians will always declare they object to FBE policies and autocratic objectives but will never embrace actual acts of opposition. This would be the Western nation's version of George Orwell's "double think" where the Faustians believes in two irreconcilable contradictory beliefs about something to be correct to help rationalize their acts of sabotage.

This controlled opposition will actively seek the most risk averse position on any issue to guarantee nothing gets done while also helping the Faustians protect their jobs and positions. This doublethink would be further protected by having all opposition strictly adhere to the legalese of every political and social process while the FBE's advocates can bypass all of these. This advantage allows the Faustians to gaslight the NRF members into believing small political victories are titanic achievements and never let the true believing NRF members have any ability to deviate or break away from the Faustians. When the NRF try to do so, the FBE controlled media proxies would conduct information campaigns to bolster the credibility of the Faustians as the "legitimate opposition" while slandering NRF as radicals discrediting the political discourse of the Western nation. This balance of trying to keep the Faustians plausible to the NRF while preventing any real opposition from organizing outside FBE control will be difficult because humans inevitably get frustrated and will seek solutions elsewhere. The FBE's proxies must convince the NRF true believers that genuine opposition is impossible and that compliance is the only path to peace and salvation.

Strengths:

"A lie travels halfway around world before the truth can get its shoes on"[vi] is an apt phrase for the value of false flag operations. The majority of the public are easy to manipulate because they fail to take interest in serious events outside their immediate lives and will usually accept the first plausible explanation for an event or act regardless of the explanation's accuracy. Since the majority of the public will not follow up or seek verification, most will believe the false flag acts of violence are truly perpetrated by NRF sympathizers. A vigilant and concerned voting public is a critical element for a Western democratic-republic style system to function properly because it is the means of holding elites accountable. In an anocracy, the public is complacent, decadent, libertine, and lazy resulting in a deterioration of institutional and cultural accountability. Since the subverted Western nation is being "nudged" from anocracy into autocracy, the apathetic public cedes more power to "authoritative" persons and organizations without verifying that power is not being abused. The apathetic public wants to believe their complacent lifestyle will never be disrupted and will *want* to believe what they are told because it reassures them. In such an environment, false flagging will easily discredit NRF among a sizeable portion of the population.

The Faustians will put on the persona of always being the level-headed moderate for the false NRF leaders and organizations. During times of civil conflict, the solutions to end conflict require victory which in turn require drastic actions. This means enduring hardships and severe disruptions to everyday life which would not be welcomed by most of the public. Instinctively, the apathetic public of the anocracy wants to believe the voices of moderation are the solution to all problems. The Faustians will be perceived as moderate because they will always offer compromises, cede political ground, and never start anything that might instill a crisis of public confidence. The false opposition undermines the NRF by being risk averse and inept and the decadent public want that because if the "moderates" prevail, then their daily lives will not have to deal with new problems. The promise of keeping lazy and relatively easy-going lifestyles makes the false opposition's political stances very enticing to the general public.

At the stage of Phase II, the FBE will have successfully subverted most of the Western nation's cultural institutions which means controlling the parameters and settings of every political argument will be easy. As the FBE's proxies decide who is officially "authoritative" and who officially has the morally superior argument, the NRF's attempts to politically contest anything in the Western nation will be close to impossible. As long as information dissemination is controlled, the NRF cannot be perceived by the general public as anything but a radical threat. If the FBE can set and define the background, the assumptions, and facts for every argument, then the content of the actual argument itself will never matter and will always result in the FBE proxies being perceived by the public as morally superior.

Weaknesses:

The false flags will not discourage the most dedicated members of the NRF or their sympathizers. They scare away the fence-sitters and undecided members of the public from siding with the NRF. Ultimately, these actions slow down and weaken NRF recruitment but it will not destroy them. Also, the FBE proxies' techniques and methods for false flag actions are likely to become predictable and anticipatory after a certain amount of use. If the NRF's intelligence collection abilities are at least semi-competent, they will identify some upcoming false flag events and lay traps for the instigators and provocateurs. Public exposure of false flag operations is dangerous to FBE proxy organizations because once a group's reputation is diminished, it is very difficult to recuperate. Any discredited organization's claims will become suspect and given the FBE's need to corruptly control and manipulate these organizations, they will not have the flexibility to replace their embedded people in a timely manner. As civil conflict continues, the utility of false flags will diminish.

Faustians will appear statesmen-like and reasonable to the apathetic and ignorant members of the public but will infuriate members of the NRF over time. Like false flags, as civil conflict becomes more overt and apparent, the more obvious the true intentions behind the actions of Faustians will be to the NRF membership. Faustians are unreliable, cowardly, and greedy. In the civil conflict, even one as subtle as 5GW, the Faustians are going to be the first targeted for lethal action because they will be viewed as traitors by the NRF and expendable fodder by the FBE. Protecting the Faustians will require a considerable number of resources while their value diminishes as the conflict progresses. The NRF could potentially use a combination of bribery, extortion, and intimidation to get many of the Faustians to become double agents or defectors against the FBE if the FBE fails to protect them. The controlled opposition will not likely survive beyond the initial phase of the civil conflict.

The control of narratives becomes less relevant when the NRF conclude they must resort to violence and fight a civil conflict. The NRF will likely keep a political wing separate from their insurgency to still fight in the battle of ideas to stay competitive in public opinion. However, those in the public who are most likely susceptible to NRF persuasion are already cognizant of how unreliable mass media is and will not be persuaded by any mainstream information dissemination. Instead, controlling the parameters of the narrative is only effective at retaining the morale of the FBE's supporters and keeping the general public averse to supporting the NRF. Controlling narratives will have minimal impact within the NRF.

---

[i] Charles Lister, *Dynamic Stalemate: Surveying Syria's Military Landscape*, Brookings Doha Center Policy Briefing, May 2014. https://www.brookings.edu/wp-content/uploads/2016/06/syria-military-landscape-english.pdf

[ii] Federica Saini Fasanotti, "A House Divided: Why Partitioning Libya Might be the Only Way to Save it," Brookings Institute, August 18, 2016. https://www.brookings.edu/articles/a-house-divided-why-partitioning-libya-might-be-the-only-way-to-save-it/

[iii] Mohammed M. Harez, "Al-Qaida Losing Ground in Iraq," West Point Sentinel, v. 1, I 1, December 2007. https://ctc.westpoint.edu/al-qaida-losing-ground-in-iraq/

[iv] Hassan Hassan, "Two Houses Divided: How Conflict in Syria Shaped the Future of Jihadism," West Point CTC Sentinel, v. 11, I 9, October 2018. https://ctc.westpoint.edu/two-houses-divided-conflict-syria-shaped-future-jihadism/

[v] Government Report, *Taliban Government in Afghanistan: Background and Issues for Congress*, Congressional Research Office, November 2, 2021, p. 4-10. https://crsreports.congress.gov/product/pdf/R/R46955

[vi] Niraj Chokshi, "That Wasn't Mark Twain: How a Misquotation is Born," New York Times, April 26, 2017. https://www.nytimes.com/2017/04/26/books/famous-misquotations.html

Chapter 23: Phase II Operational Lines of Effort for the Foreign-Backed Elites
—Manipulate the NRF into 3GW; LOE 3: Destroy an Exposed NRF

Sowing division amongst the FBE's enemies, manipulating the general populace into compliance, and using corruption to subvert institutions must have an end objective. That end objective of completely controlling the Western nation is defined in the strategic planning of the FBE but that plan requires one final LOE to eliminate its main obstacle, the destruction of all organized opposition. Every other LOE helps shape and configure the social divisions within the Western nation to help consolidate power at the cost of the opposition's ability to resist the FBE. However, the FBE cannot allow resistance to fester, even if contained, because these foreign-backed elements can only achieve power nefariously and will lack any real legitimacy as rulers which makes them perpetually vulnerable to being overthrown. The penultimate objective of the FBE is destroying a weakened NRF and is the culmination of the Catalonia 2.0 Strategy to attain total control of the Western nation.

If all of the other LOEs are successfully executed, the NRF and its sympathizers will have gone into self-exile into congregated enclaves as a means of protecting themselves from the now corrupt oppressive society. These enclaves will likely try to reinforce mutual protection and eventually achieve a majority within select geographic areas of the Western nation. Once this occurs, both infiltrators and manipulated Atomized amongst the NRF will be prompted to encourage secession as a peaceful means of co-existence to avoid future conflicts. Normally, most rational people would not endorse such a drastic solution, but if the FBE's pressure is sufficiently intense, the desire for knee-jerk radical solutions become irresistible.

There is little precedent in the history of humanity to support such an optimistic outcome. It is the same kind of rationalization the wizard Saruman gives to justify collaborating with Sauron in *Lord of the Rings*. Any group like the FBE is motivated by the accumulation of power with the desire to control everyone and everything. Totalitarians live for the sake of accumulating power, and not for competently exercising a limited amount of power with temperance. Like Sauron, the FBE don't intend to share power or cede territory when they are on the cusp of securing the entire Western nation. Instead, the FBE wants dispirited elements and opportunists within the NRF to convince themselves that peaceful separation is plausible because secession is the perfect catalyst for the FBE's 3GW campaign to permanently destroy all organized resistance. An illegal secession, even if peacefully attempted, provides all legal justification for the FBE-controlled state to declare war.

When the social divisions reach this point, many of the remaining NRF-minded persons within the Western nation's state, cultural, and financial institutions will depart for the enclaves leaving the FBE the sole influence on the Western nation's state. As the NRF's national influence diminishes to concentrate in sympathetic enclaves, the FBE can finalize its "nudging" operations to move the society to overt autocracy. This involves severing the institutions and infrastructure from the enclaves as much as possible or at least have the ability to do so at moment's notice. This means subtly changing policies, laws, and common practices to disfavor anyone who's politically undesirable. After co-opting the economic and cultural institutions, the FBE can now use social and financial pressure to influence elected politicians and appointed officials to change society's rules and systems to gradually favor a two-tiered system: one tier of law and regulations for the FBE and one for its enemies. Most of these changes will not affect the average apathetic member of the public because they prefer the path of least resistance and will not be punished due to their acquiescence to society's newly defined norms. Only politically active or interested elements of the population will notice and the changes will compel these elements to commit either to the increasingly autocratic FBE-led society or the NRF opposition. The two-tiered system will become the basis for finalizing autocratic control and create a suitable environment to initiate open civil conflict that favors FBE victory.

The first act towards implementing the two-tier system is for the FBE to wield its social and economic lobbying power for loyalists to be appointed in key positions throughout all parts of the Western nation's government to change the organizational culture, hiring criteria, and administrative objectives to simultaneously make the bureaucracy compliant, oblivious, and less effective. Effective bureaucracies could threaten less capable FBE-installed executives who are placed in charge for their proven obedience, not competence. As the bureaucracies' managers, advisors, legislative and judicial staff are rendered more inert, the final effort to create legislation enshrining a new autocratic two-tiered caste society into law will occur without resistance. Part of this effort will require greater centralization of government powers and broader jurisdiction into everyday life that will be justified over the course of the "nudging" period. Part of the "nudging" involving the state would include creating failed local services, breakdown in social order, enable abuses of private entities, and discrediting historical traditions of the Western nation. The social anarchy provides sufficient justification for greater state control led by FBE-appointed persons. Once the FBE achieves absolute power, their loyalists will then implement the final draconian changes in the name of restoring order. This autocratic state's two-tiered system will then purge and isolate any remaining dissention as well as gradually eliminating the need for the FBE's expendable sepoys of Nimbyists and Atomized.

Once fully implemented, the two-tiered system enables the FBE to create the proper conditions to cause a chain reaction of escalating hostilities between the FBE-controlled Western nation and the NRF enclaves that catalyzes into an open war. This catalyst will be bait to provoke the NRF into openly violating the laws of the Western nation, most likely related to secession, to give the FBE the moral legitimacy to declare war against the enclaves. Once this war is declared, the FBE will utilize its control of the Western nation to wage a classical 3GW-style open war fought by their organized conventional armies designed to destroy the NRF's concentrated enclaves (their centers of gravity). Classic large-scale combat operations will provide justification of martial law, censorship, suspension of due-process, and economic blockades to ration resources on a state-dependent population. This also provides the justification for the Western nation to officially reapproach the adversary nation that covertly acted as the benefactor for the FBE. In an open civil war, the foreign adversary and their FBE puppets could feign a diplomatic thaw in which the adversary will pledge to not trade or support the NRF in any way. Such a diplomatic stance would put enormous pressure on the rest of the world not to trade with the NRF elements as the major economies rally around the "legitimate" FBE government of the Western nation. A full economic blockade, combined with aggressive censorship, and full knowledge of the NRF enclaves' infrastructure will shape the battlespace for the FBE to launch devastating massive attacks that critically damage NRF industry, logistics, power, medical, communication, and energy supplies. Such actions will make an NRF rebellion very bloody but also likely very short-lived, ranging from just months to a few years. In the aftermath, an FBE victory means the NRF's ideas are discredited, FBE atrocities remain hidden, no organized resistance will remain, and the adversarial nation will have an iron-grip over the FBE's leaders. This Western nation will be subdued and over a period of years becomes a poorer, weaker country that is vassalized to the adversary nation with the FBE's leaders as wealthy puppets.

Options and Methods:

Changing the organizational culture, perception, and ethical standards of the bureaucracy and the regulatory system of the Western nation can be done in a multitude of ways that can go unnoticed. The first being the FBE-controlled proxy activists and lobby groups demanding legislative changes to these institutions done in the guise of protecting or reinforcing values that the Western nation claims to treasure. The trick is to reinterpret the definitions of protection and the metrics of how those values are protected. In a two-tiered system, these definitions will be narrowed to only FBE favored groups or entities and the legislation would likely declare a specific agency or third party as the final arbiter of what defines the values-interpreting criteria. Most likely, an FBE-controlled nonprofit or conglomeration of nonprofits officially proclaimed as "objective" because the FBE-backed media and activist groups will declare them authoritatively objective. The newly established interpretations can then be applied to hiring practices that would, over the course of at least a decade, displace the old leadership of the bureaucracy with more FBE complicit members. These people don't have to be part of the FBE or be directly controlled by the foreign benefactor, these people only have to be dependent on the goodwill of the FBE's allies for survival to retain loyalty. The hiring criteria for the non-executive workforce would be expanded in scope of requirement criteria but each requirement would also be easier to achieve for the easily manipulated loyalists to get hired. Loyalists or those indoctrinated to accept the FBE narrative would then have the "top-cover" of the newly changed organizational values and ethical standards to execute a two-tiered system without regular people realizing anything has changed. Since the changes would occur legally through established legitimate processes, the newly hired FBE-conditioned workers will just assume they are acting as regular enforcers of a democratic-republic and the not noticed procedural changes as being contrary to old system.

Changing the composition of the bureaucracy and governmental regulations is the first step in securing a two-tiered system but the FBE must also protect their new system from the old system during the transition. This means corruption of the judicial and legal institutions is vital to successful subversion. The modern West has decided to fall back on being litigious in most means of social resolutions, partly because the complacent decadent public is no longer capable of resolving anything on its own. After the FBE-controlled lobbyists and activist groups successfully change the institutions of process, procedure, and budget for government duties, the next target is the enforcers of the legal system. Controlling and subverting the judiciary ensures the new system cannot be challenged by peaceful means and the NRF will have no recourse left other than extralegal actions. This is a relatively easy process once the political class is subverted by the FBE during the "nudging" phase. If there is a sufficient number of politicians dependent on FBE-proxy largesse, then getting sympathetic individuals appointed to provincial and national-level courts is easy because in practice, besides the law qualifications, all the prospective judges need to do is convince the members of an appointment body to get the job.

Regardless of the appointment body, any system can be rigged to only favor certain people if the leaders of that system have already been co-opted. Those who make the rules can easily change them. The only way to avoid such corruption is for outside public scrutiny by a diligent populace. Since no Western nation has such a population anymore, any bureaucracy in any Western system is more susceptible to corrupting influences. FBE-preferred judges, clerks, prosecutors, and politically appointed police leaders can pick and choose which laws to enforce and on whom those laws are enforced. Part of the advantage of legalese is it provides sufficient opaqueness for the legal system that it can improvise any interpretation that fits the needs of the system. If that system becomes corrupt, then the legalese will protect the corrupted system. The previous lines of efforts of "nudging" the society and culture will make any politicized arbitrary legal judgements appear normal because part of the nudging effort is to encourage greater deference to "authoritative" figures on determining what is right.

All of these efforts to subvert the political sphere of society and its procedural mechanisms will ultimately segregate the society by political alignment and the NRF will be a distinctive social group separated by culture, geography, and legality. After the FBE secures the political class, bureaucracy, and the legal system, the FBE must create a catalyst that provokes the NRF into acting first in a civil conflict. This will give the FBE the legitimacy to act in "defense" of the Western nation and its values to help justify the level of brutality they would need to exert to squash the NRF as an organized opponent. There are many options for a potential catalyst. As the American Civil War demonstrated however, the catalyst would need multiple smaller provocations leading up to a final stark event. Of course, encouraging acts of secession among the NRF's academic and ideological leadership such as holding illegal referendums and ignoring national government decrees would be provocative, but wouldn't be sufficient to conduct full-scale 3GW combat operations. Conducting localized acts of insurrection or violence would stir up national tensions, akin to John Brown's raid on Harper's Ferry armory[i] or "Bleeding Kansas" of 1854, but would unlikely justify full scall open civil conflict.[ii] However, such acts can be rationalized as actions of a few or was a special circumstance and would not be grand enough to warrant a full-scale conflict. War-inducing catalysts require actions that are noticed in every province and have impact on the civilian population's perception of the NRF.

The best course of action would be to use a legal case or issue that the FBE can ensure a favorable outcome at the cost of the NRF at a national level. This would likely involve civil liberties most valued by NRF-aligned elements or an overbearing economic burden that actively discriminated against NRF-aligned areas of the Western nation. Inducing NRF anger to violently react to a peaceful, if corrupt, legal action is the best way the FBE can induce a controlled civil war while garnering legitimacy and the perception of being the aggrieved party. There is no way to know for certain how the NRF would react, even if infiltrated by the FBE spies, to any provocation so, it is best for the FBE to arrange at least some of the violent reactions to reach the required threshold of catalyzing an open war.

There are two options: arrange for an attack on the political system itself or conduct a political assassination of a prominent leader. The first option is preferable because it is easier to manage and direct the consequences of an attack on a system than a powerful individual. Whatever the scale of the attack on the political system, the full effect would take weeks or months in the aftermath to fully develop which is plenty of time to shape the Western nation's reaction and construct the most effective response. Also attacks on the political system provides the FBE a far wider range of options in both scale and scope that can better incorporate the unique circumstances arising from the catalytic action. Attacking the political system means attacking either organizations or facilities necessary to carry out government activities. The ideal choice of action for the FBE is one that doesn't damage the FBE's ability to wage war or maintain control over the subverted nation yet provide sufficient outrage to justify full-scale military action. Balancing these requirements is difficult and would be more manageable if the FBE encouraged a series of smaller attacks on the FBE-controlled state's less important institutions instead of relying on one large calamitous action whose outcome would be less predictable. One such option would be encouraging radical or unwitting NRF into attacking locations that impact the legal system, such as legal offices, courts, or staff offices of high-profile legislators that will have a national-level impact rather than a localized one. Targeting several prominent judges would provide an optimal starting point.

Public prosecutors are not well known or frankly cared about outside legal circles and no other legal position has enough prominence to matter in terms of political impact despite the office's power.[iii] Police chiefs or commissioners being eliminated could certainly act as additional kindling to the fire but the impact of such attacks would be mostly felt locally. Everyone knows what a judge is, does, and the level of power that position wields in modern Western societies. They are part of the political elite, even though theoretically they are supposed to be apolitical, but in practice they are part of the "chattering classes" who are associated with political power. Judges are the personification of the judicial system of Western societies, so an attack on many of them at once would create a sense of paralyzing shock to the general public on a national scale. This shock comes with the added bonus of getting the NRF to target people who, under the FBE's new autocracy, are completely dispensable. In a functioning democratic-republic or constitutional monarchy, competent judges are critical of the proper functioning of the political system because they support providing the public a safe means of recourse against any wrongs, both real and perceived, against others or against the state itself. In a declining republic that has become an anocracy, judges often are corruptly serving the interests of those groups that lobbied for those judges' appointments. In the FBE's autocracy, the judges are even less important as they only act as a veneer to give a little plausible legitimacy to a dictatorship. In such a system, the judges don't need to be competent because they are only required to provide legalese to justify whatever the state's position is on the case. In fact, competent judges are a danger because they might think for themselves, creating points of friction in the autocratic system. So, judges in this system are in essence, just very wordy rubber stampers who can be easily replaced by other sycophantic or indoctrinated mediocrities.

To have greater impact for the FBE's propaganda, the catalyst would be more effective if some of the eliminated judges had become prominent and famous by making detrimental judgements against the NRF-aligned persons in famous legal cases. The more of these that are killed in dramatic sudden actions, the better the impact it will have on the general public's sentiment about going to war with "traitorous" elements. More prominent judges dying gives a greater sense of threat to the ignorant public which will make them more receptive to draconian retaliation. Yes, these judges serve the FBE, but the FBE are fundamentally self-serving, nihilistic, power-hungry, and sociopathic who would regard their loyal judges as dispensable fodder. Attacking the legal system that is nothing more than a rubber-stamping mechanism in an autocracy, creates the perfect perception of society under attack without risking any government assets of value. The legal system is not the only viable target but other government institutions or critical departments whose destruction could resonate with the public to call for violent retaliation would be more useful intact for the actual civil war; these alternative institutions are doable options but not optimal ones.

The other choice as a catalyst is political assassination of which there are three possibilities. The FBE could arrange for the elimination of a number of various politicians within their own subverted autocracy that can be blamed on the NRF, assassinate a key leader of the NRF to provoke a brutally violent response, or have the FBE-sponsored national leader of the Western nation killed by NRF agents indirectly assisted by the FBE. Each has its own unique set of complications. The first option of killing a number of midlevel politicians within the corrupt autocracy certainly provides the necessary legal pretext for war and will rally the most loyal elements of the population but there is a major downside. Bluntly, politicians, especially ones in a corrupt autocracy feigning democratic liberties, are not popular or sympathetic.[iv] There is a real danger that the elimination of a large number of people who are generally regarded as corrupt, incompetent, and detrimental to people's everyday lives will not rally the general population. Instead, such an action could split the population more evenly as some will regard such an action as being akin to removing parasites from the body politic. The FBE's preferred outcome is to get the majority of the public to remain either apathetic or hostile to the NRF cause. Evenly splitting the population over the action being used to justify war risks expanding the number of available assets and capabilities to the NRF that would prolong the civil war. Politicians in non-executive positions are too hated and mistrusted to be effective martyrs in such a political environment meaning the effectiveness of the catalyst to ostracize the NRF before the fight is at a high risk of failing.

The next option is the targeted assassination of a high-profile leader within the NRF whose martyrdom ignites an open war. To be clear, the assassination of senior leaders of a polity is different than targeting low-level or legislative politicians. A national leader whether, spiritual or political, acts as a symbol, a rallying point, and a source of inspiration entrusted with their follower's faith to lead their faction to prosperity, security, or victory. Assassination of polity leaders is truly the first weapon of mass destruction invented by mankind. Most people understand the effects and consequences of using chemical, biological, and nuclear weapons because the effects are physical and immediate. Political leader assassination effects are in the form of social reactions to the loss of the political leader. These social shockwaves are felt over the course of generations and the full consequences are not understood until decades have passed when the social shockwaves subside.

The assassination of Archduke Ferdinand for instance, led to the First World War which left Tsarist Russia vulnerable to revolution, set the conditions for Germany's revenge in World War II,[v] set the Japanese Empire in turmoil leading to eventual aggressive imperial expansion,[vi] and so on and so forth. Abraham Lincoln's death led to the radical Reconstruction Acts and its corrupt mismanagement that failed to heal the social divides in the South for decades that led to consequences like the passing of Jim Crow laws, segregation, etc.[vii] Assassinating leaders of polities have considerable risk because too many variables cannot be seen or foreseen until after the act is carried out. Like nuclear weapons, the social shockwaves cannot be directed or controlled, so there is risk in having many unforeseen detrimental consequences.

On the other hand, it is logistically the simplest option that best guarantees a violent reaction driven by emotion of the NRF's anger rather than cold-calculating reflection and evaluation. The added bonus is that the NRF would likely be paralyzed for weeks or months, if the NRF's most important leader is eliminated. Plus, there are a multitude of ways to eliminate the leader while plausibly denying any official sanction of such an action. Since the FBE arose from private interests, the FBE would likely use Atomized or other radically indoctrinated persons as expendable fodder to eliminate the leader. Conducting a drone strike, using a professional sniper, or other actions that indicate the assassins had professional skills or backing would likely be discovered and destroy any FBE legitimacy of trying to claim they're the aggrieved party in the conflict. Peripheral support such as providing intelligence on the targeted leader, financing, and infiltration can be sufficiently obscured to be deniable.

The final option is the most politically beneficial to the FBE but is also the most risky and dangerous. The third option would be to eliminate the FBE's chosen puppet to act as the national leader of the new autocratic Western nation. This leader's elimination would be the perfect martyrdom as national anger would be at maximum pitch and would provide a lot of legitimacy to the FBE's side in the civil conflict. The danger is that such an operation would require complete secrecy, find NRF persons willing to carry it out without the manipulation being discovered, and be executed competently. There are so many factors that could derail a false-flag operation of this scale that failure would be very probable. So, even though this would provide the greatest political dividend for the FBE if it succeeds, its discovery could destroy them as well as spark an internal conflict that the NRF would exploit for victory. Realistically, the second option is the most optimal as it balances the risk of the operation for a reasonable likelihood of success.

No matter what kind of action is used to spark the catalyst, the FBE must be prepared to execute the follow-on military action as quickly as possible to maximize surprise and control the initiative. If every other line of effort has been effective, then the battlespace will be shaped into near perfect condition to wage a 3GW-style war of state-on-state conflict where two organized fighting forces square off to defeat each other's centers of gravity. All of the "nudging" and controlled segregation of the NRF population will have created a geographic area where the NRF are strong enough to secede from the Western nation but not survive the secession. In such circumstances, the NRF-state would have a multitude of weaknesses and the NRF-led army would be underequipped and poorly integrated to fight modern state warfare. These weaknesses can be exacerbated with further actions of economic warfare done in coordination with the combat actions. The key to FBE success is to fully exploit every weakness of the NRF's new state simultaneously to achieve victory quickly.

The FBE's first action would be securing their internal lines of communication to prevent logistical and communication disruptions by declaring martial law. Martial law restricts freedom of movement, increases the legal use of intrusive surveillance, and deputizing local paramilitaries to impose order and paranoia. Encouraging local Atomized fanatics and civilian volunteers to help enforce martial law by creating regional paramilitaries keeps the various communities both under control and divided.[viii] They will be too focused on their local issues to consider assisting the NRF. Autocracies can never fully trust the reliability of institutions created prior to the dictatorship's establishment because these were founded under different cultural principles. It is easier to create new institutions and organizations loyal from the outset to keep a balance of power among the state bureaucracies. Maduro's Venezuela witnessed this with the Colectivo militias or Iran's Revolutionary Guard Corps are some examples of organizations founded on loyalty rather than mission competence. Often these groups start out as loosely organized groups of thugs but, if given enough years, evolve into more professional groups that answer directly to the autocrats instead of the state. Martial law also allows the prioritization of implementing a war economy with rationing on food, medicine, fuels, raw materials for armaments, and electronics to devote to the war effort. As semiconductors are now as fundamental to the functioning of a modern economy as fossil fuels were in World War II, ration restrictions on new technology products would also be imposed. Finally, martial law gives the justification for the autocratic state to control all critical infrastructure, including water ways, telecommunications, and electric power generation.

No matter how much effort the NRF puts into creating a parallel economy and society for their enclaves, the FBE will not allow them to successfully implement economic or societal independence. Just enough to encourage the NRF members of the population to move to their prospective enclaves to begin building but never giving them time to finish the effort. This means the NRF enclaves trying to secede will still be connected to the Western nation's power grid, water infrastructure, and telecommunication networks which makes everything the NRF needs to run a nation vulnerable to attack. Shutting off critical power lines and generators while destroying NRF-controlled infrastructure could be accomplished in the first weeks of the campaign. The telecommunications networks can be severed from the outside world with cutting key undersea cables and destroying major internet exchanges. Even if there is a mobile or satellite alternative, the major networks could be jammed with denial-of-service attacks or other forms of electronic warfare. Martial law enables the FBE to economically encircle and sever the NRF from the rest of the Western nation.

After martial law and securing of all economic linkages with the NRF enclaves, the FBE needs to complete the NRF's isolation from the world by imposing a military blockade and sanctions of vital economic and financial activities to discourage as many sources of income or supplies from reaching the NRF as possible. Like the American Civil War, a blockade would work to weaken the NRF but would not directly cause its defeat.[ix] Instead, blockades limit a fighting forces' options as more resources are committed to basic societal survival and further inhibit the NRF from finding ersatz materials to sustain combat operations. Additionally, the adversarial nation could assist in the blockade as part of the faux diplomacy to "thaw" relations with the Western nation.

Once all of these major strategic actions are initiated, the FBE's proxies in the state will finally attack the NRF directly using minimal restraint as the controlled media and communication isolation will downplay atrocities and excesses. Even if the FBE-controlled Western nation's military is not completely prepared, the sheer volume and scale of resources available as compared to those of the NRF's forces will allow the FBE to absorb many mistakes and suffer many casualties before risking their ability to achieve victory. The conflict will be aggressive and fought in every domain of space, land, air, sea, and cyber simultaneously in the form of a large-scale siege that slowly closes in on the NRF's centers of gravity. A total war of completely destroying everything in the rebel enclaves is possible depending on the intensity of resistance but the FBE would prefer limiting the scale of damage for reasons of propaganda and reconstruction costs. The FBE's main strength in this war is size and needs to bring their mass of forces to bear on the NRF immediately to smother all enemy capability. This means the FBE's military response needs to be very violent, disproportionate, and comprehensive to achieve victory within a politically viable amount of time. Failure to do so would give the NRF the chance to regroup into smaller harder to kill insurgency cells to fight a 4GW-style campaign for which the FBE are not well suited to fight. Years of such conflict risk the FBE's grip on power which is the one unacceptable outcome of the civil war.

Strengths:

Changing the bureaucracy's leadership means cementing FBE-desired changes into the bureaucracy's organizational culture. All Western governments follow some variation of Max Weberian bureaucratic organization which means the highest echelons within the hierarchy can reshape the rest of the bureaucracy's system without the lower ranking members being cognizant of the motivations or the final outcome.[x] Each office or organizational element has its designated lane of duty and work objectives with few options for independent action. Every section has its jurisdictions and each defends this "turf" while at the same time having no incentive to fix or modify the process that might risk a reduction in either budget or authority. Since Max Weberian systems emphasize process over outcome, most bureaucracies are rigid, reward orthodoxy, and provide few incentives for initiative.[xi] If the FBE-installed leadership focus changes on organizational culture without disrupting any of the organizational elements' established authority then most of the bureaucracy will comply.

Changing organizational culture means altering the bureaucracy's beliefs in ethical values, attitudes, administrative priorities, and what constitutes acceptable behavior. Tying certain political and social attitudes to indicators of advancement while downplaying objective or meritocratic criteria enables the FBE to slowly assimilate the bureaucracy with people inculcated with FBE-directed ideals. Diminishing merit is easier than eliminating many other criteria because many bureaucracies don't have the incentive structure to make competitive achievement viable. Exceptions typically involve life-and-death as part of the bureaucracy's mission, such as the military or law enforcement but even these can be politicized by corrupt political appointees. The mechanical nature of Max Weberian bureaucratic processes with little creative input means that FBE assimilation, if done slowly, would go virtually unnoticed.[xii] Any outside observer making claims that the bureaucracy is either being undermined or subverted will be easily dismissed by most of the public for several reasons.

The first is the authoritative experts will dismiss any claims of subversives corrupting the state as coming from "conspiracy theories", a term as overused in Western politics as the term "fascist" by both left and right. The second reason being the supposedly critical thinking persons who will always demand smoking-gun incontestable proof before believing anything new because many in the West view everything in the binary "it happened; it didn't happen" mindset of the scientific world. Confusing the working criteria of the political world with that of the scientific world is pervasive, which means many pundits will demand clear proof of conspiracy akin to test results verifying a theory in scientific circles. In the real world of human politics, there rarely is hard proof of a group's true intent and actions. In a real conspiracy, as seen with organized crime, not everyone at every level needs to know about the true intent of an action. In some cases, many elements of the group are not even fully aware they are conducting illegal activity. A legitimate company might be used to launder money with only one employee being aware of the criminal activity. The same is true with subversion. The Soviet Union funded many activist groups, bureaucrats, professionals, and unions in the West with many witting and unwitting members being manipulated to further foreign interests,[xiii]ˑ [xiv] and such actions continue today.[xv] Insinuation, verbal communication, and duplicitous action allows a small few to misdirect many others into subverting a system without the majority realizing they are subverting said system. Unless the FBE leaders are bugged and monitored, hard evidence is unlikely to materialize because true conspiracies of subversion always hide behind a veil of ambiguity. That ambiguity is the final advantage as many actions that alter and change the bureaucratic culture give unclear signals that can be interpreted in many ways. An action that helps bring a department into greater compliance with FBE objectives could also appear as an organizational restructuring to improve performance. True conspiracy is done by a few key people directing both unwitting or witting people with an unclear idea of the purpose of their actions. Disproving the assertion that subversion is not happening will be impossible.

The judicial system is easier to corrupt. The single biggest obstacle to any subversion of a political or legal process is co-opting or removing those in charge of holding those processes accountable. In most Western nations, this usually means politicians, political appointees or committees. Once the FBE co-opts the nonprofit activist organizations, cultural lobbyists, and industrial associations that wield the majority of financial transactions for the political class, then the pressure to allow covert subversives to be appointed into the oversight process becomes irresistible. The FBE approach of attacking and subverting institutions from the top-down bypasses almost all checks and institutional protections. In democratic republics, a cognizant and concerned public is supposed to hold the political elite accountable through elections. A Western nation becomes vulnerable after its institutions decline into anocracy because the public has become lazy, decadent, and apathetic so, no one is watching who is trying to subvert vulnerable members of the political elite. Anocracies enable FBE's to subvert with virtual impunity as no security services will watch their political masters unilaterally and the legal system watches mainly outward, not inward. Once FBE-linked overseers of the judicial system are in place, appointing politicized FBE-directed judges, prosecutors, and chiefs of police become very easy. At the late stage of the "nudging" efforts, implementing control of the judiciary can go virtually undetected and also guarantees any laws that support greater autocracy will be legally rationalized and given legitimacy. Controlling the courts and law enforcement agencies guarantees the FBE will retain favoritism and no legal process will exist to reverse their subversion.

The FBE's abundant resources and the securing of a two-tiered governance system grants them all the initiative on starting the open conflict. The FBE can choose the time and place most conducive to their operational planning while keeping the element of surprise. Directing, or at least encouraging, the catalyst provides the greatest amount of protection to FBE forces as the effects of the catalyst actions would be more controllable. Controlled attacks on the Western nation's institutions or leaders means the FBE can set aside expendable proxies as the target fodder while keeping their critical resources protected from dangerous actions. Simultaneously, having the FBE's controlled government being perceived by global public opinion as being the victimized party generates a considerable amount of political legitimacy. No one can adequately predict the future, but the ability to preposition resources and fabricate pre-emptive political narratives gives the FBE a high probability of catching their NRF opponents by surprise.

Once the catalyst is chosen or at least identified, the FBE will have to mobilize its forces for open war. The entire effort is to shape the environment and situation where the FBE's controlled state can conduct a 3GW-style war that maximizes the advantages of the state. Compelling the NRF into distinct enclaves that are a de facto separate state compels them to organize like a nation-state polity which gives the FBE forces the opportunity to initiate action for every military consideration. The FBE's state will have an established military with a common doctrine, logistic lines of communication, and adequate industry to provide munitions and other critical materials. Furthermore, the established units and chain-of-command simplify the early stages of combat while years of "nudging" propaganda have diminished the general public's perception of the NRF as human beings and means the military will have a wide latitude in selecting targets and the degree of brutality. Any atrocity can be downplayed as being instigated by the NRF or at least make it easier for the public to accept brutal actions as a necessary evil.

Then there are the legal authorities where the autocratic system can call for conscripts over a large population and have the ability to seize most of the critical infrastructure of the Western nation. Confining the NRF to self-selected enclaves helps the FBE-backed state to more easily blockade and isolate NRF strongholds and centers of gravity while also being able as the Western nation, demand neighboring states to sign on to sanctions and comply with any military blockade. The FBE can rationalize mass mobilization with both legal and ethical justifications while simultaneously using the Western nation's well-resourced bureaucracy to wage wars of espionage, sabotage, and cyberattacks leading up to and during combat operations. The sheer volume of superior resources the Western nation has in a 3GW situation means the NRF will be on the defensive from the outset. Any NRF polity would likely be more confederated, divided, under resourced, as well as lacking any international legal recognition. As long as the NRF can be lured into a situation where they effectively become a separate polity, a prepared FBE-controlled army can wage classic 3GW-style operations against, the FBE's Catalonia 2.0 Strategy and will likely result in success.

Weaknesses:

Creating a two-tier system to permanently secure compliance with FBE diktats does come with several costs. Corruption must inevitably grow while overall competence of the state's institutions will inevitably decline. A system that actively rewards those who show loyalty or are a part of a group or organization that is dependent on the FBE, by definition, ignores the flaws of the loyalists and disregard the strengths of the dissenting elements of society. To protect the FBE loyalists, the two-tier system must hide the flaws to protect the FBE's grip on power which incentivizes opportunists to steal, embezzle, and squander resources. With no accountability except by demonstrations of political loyalty, more and more state programs and efforts will have to accommodate the loyalists' well-being, even when it is not efficient or economical to do so. Over time, these opportunists will create projects and enterprises designed specifically to siphon funds and resources from the economy to enrich themselves. As this grows, more of the FBE's proxies will be dependent on this societal parasitism, creating major inefficiencies that will eventually threaten to stagnate the economy of the Western nation. This will likely take a few decades; a good rule of thumb is to evaluate the typical length of communist nations' economies between the time they started and the time these started to stagnate as these were also totalitarian economies. Typically, between 15-30 years for the Marxist nations that attempted autarky with the exceptions being only those communist nations that actively traded with capitalist nations to offset the natural lifespan.[xvi]' [xvii], [xviii], [xix], [xx]

A thoroughly corrupted state run by the FBE will gradually have greater difficulty managing the economic instability brought about by ever growing corruption. However, although corruption is gangrenous to a body-politic, it is slow enough where the FBE will still have time to wield its power to eliminate the NRF. As long as the FBE remains cognizant that corruption will sooner or later have to be mitigated lest they are taken by surprise during a crisis and find their subverted institutions have been hollowed out by corruption. One only has to look at what happened to Venezuela when the price of oil collapsed or the Russian Army's logistical calamity in the Russo-Ukrainian War. [xxi]' [xxii]

Competence, or rather the lack thereof, is a common joke throughout the world regarding government institutions or bureaucracies.[xxiii]' [xxiv], [xxv] Even so, every country on Earth has its own unique baseline of competency. Typically, poorer and more corrupt nations tolerate more incompetence in their governments because people must focus on daily survival and rarely have the time, power, or understanding on how to improve their countries' governance. In Western nations, the organizational cultures of the bureaucracies typically have greater accountability and that helps to mitigate the risk of corruption and incompetence more effectively—usually. As the FBE's Western nation degraded into anocracy, the mechanisms for accountability also degrade as public demand for effective public services diminish as the public's decadence grows. Decadent people are easily distracted with gifts of instant gratification by the state akin to the "bread and circus" policies of the Roman Empire.[xxvi] The quality of service diminishes but so does the criteria of what constitutes service. As more of the population becomes Atomized or dependent on the state, the FBE-controlled state can distribute far less per person but more resources overall will need to be sent to a much larger segment of the population. So, even if some people grumble, there will be too many co-dependents to challenge the quality of service.

Government quality of service must decline because loyalty to a political faction of autocrats like the FBE means the mission of serving the nation is no longer a priority. The ability to protect FBE interests, including the ever-growing corruption, means more resources are diverted away from maintaining state institutions. Also, competent civil servants and industry leaders create sources of independent thinking which could lead to challenges to the FBE's authority. This means the FBE's effort to change the organizational cultures of the Western nation's bureaucracies must include lowering all standards to justify the appointment of more mediocrities to leadership positions. Mediocrities, especially those who lack any practical ability, are dependent on the protection of the FBE leadership to survive in their positions of authority. For the FBE to achieve control and hold on to it, they must remain cognizant of the need to balance loyalty and competency. The FBE will lower standards to flood the institutions with loyal sycophants but the risk is twofold. First, the lowering of standards means the NRF's challenge to infiltrate FBE proxy organizations will become much easier. It's easier for a smart person to pretend to be dumb than vice versa. Also, since the criteria would be political in nature, the standards will be subjective which means the FBE will have a nearly impossible task of keeping out infiltrators and spies.

Another danger is the catalysts. The FBE needs an event or series of events that are eye-catching to garner public sympathy, political legitimacy, with the justification to wage a full-scale war. However, the enemy "gets a vote" on how they interact with the FBE and may not take the bait. If the NRF resists temptation to take revenge or they successfully disrupt the FBE's narrative on the crisis, then the FBE will lose the initiative. For instance, instead of retaliating against the FBE with violent actions, the NRF enclaves instead just violate ordnances and government regulations by establishing free-trade cities that deprive income of the FBE's state. Such an act of defiance demonstrating the NRF's superior governance skills while still being a part of the Western nation would make the legal action of 3GW more difficult. Would this action be illegal? Yes. Would this be seditious? Possibly. Would it be sufficient justification to bomb NRF cities and strongholds into dust? Unlikely.

Finally, the last stage of the FBE's effort to create a guaranteed victory against the NRF in a 3GW conflict requires an effective military. As seen with Stalin's military purges at the beginning of Operation Barbarossa, incompetent sycophants and complete lack of leadership is potentially disastrous.[xxvii]' [xxviii] Only the vast distances of the Soviet Empire's territorial holdings and the Anglosphere's continuous supplies of food, trucks, and winter clothing saved Stalin from himself.[xxix] The FBE must rely on their superior resources to compensate for the diminished quality of politicized officers they emplaced. If the FBE fails to purge the military thoroughly while retaining large numbers of corrupt and incompetent flag officers, then the NRF could successfully garner sufficient support within the military's lower ranks to entice a large portion of the military defect, then the FBE will be at high risk of defeat. However, overzealous purging to replace competent soldiers with loyal but incompetent Nimbyists and Atomized proxies will make any 3GW protracted and poorly executed. A protracted conflict increases the probability of defeat as FBE loyalists begin to question their leaders' ability. Dictators like President Assad of Syria survived his army's incompetence in the first decade of the Syrian Civil War by having the foreign militaries of Russia and Iran rescue him.[xxx] Any attempt by the FBE to invite their foreign benefactor's military to support actions within the Western nation would guarantee insurrection within the general population as a whole. Like everything else in politics, the optimal approach is a balance of purges and retaining competence but the risk is in finding that balance. History indicates that dictatorships' success at striking the right balance is rare.

---

[i] Dennis Fry, "John Brown's Smoldering Spark," American Battlefield Trust, Archived Article Newsweek, October 19, 1959. https://www.battlefields.org/learn/articles/john-browns-smoldering-spark

[ii] Dale E. Watts, "How Bloody was Bleeding Kansas? Political Killings in Kansas Territory, 1854-1861," Kansas State Historical Society Archive: Kansas History: A Journal of the Central Plains (18) (2), Summer 1995, 116-129. https://www.kshs.org/publicat/history/1995summer_watts.pdf

[iii] Michael J. Nelson and Taran Samarth, "Judging Prosecutors: Public Support for Prosecutorial Discretion," Research & Politics, 9 (4). https://journals.sagepub.com/doi/epub/10.1177/20531680221134999

[iv] Report, "Americans' Dismal Views of the Nation's Politics: 65% Say They Always or often Feel Exhausted When Thinking About Politics," Pew Research Center, September 19, 2023. https://www.pewresearch.org/politics/2023/09/19/americans-dismal-views-of-the-nations-politics/

[v] William A. Murray, edited by Geoffrey Parker, *The Cambridge History of Warfare*, (NY: Cambridge University Press, 2019): 314-337.

[vi] Masato Shizume, "The Japanese Economy during the Interwar Period: Instability in the Financial System and the Impact of the World Depression," Bank of Japan Review – Institute for Monetary and Economic Studies, May 2009. https://www.boj.or.jp/en/research/wps_rev/rev_2009/data/rev09e02.pdf

[vii] Mark L. Bradley, *The Army and Reconstruction 1865-1877*, (Washington DC: Center of Military History: 2015): 24-30. https://history.army.mil/html/books/075/75-18/cmhPub_75-18.pdf

[viii] Ross Dayton, "Maduro's Revolutionary Guards: The Rise of Paramilitarism in Venezuela," Westpoint Combating Terrorism Center v. 12, i. 7, August 2019, 31-35. https://ctc.westpoint.edu/maduros-revolutionary-guards-rise-paramilitarism-venezuela/

[ix] Shuck, Eric, "Economic Warfare: The Union Blockade in the Civil War," Naval History Magazine, October 2021. https://www.usni.org/magazines/naval-history-magazine/2021/october/economic-warfare-union-blockade-civil-war

[x] James Q. Wilson, *Bureaucracy: What Government Agencies Do and Why They Do it*, (NY: Basic Books, Inc., 1989): 295-312.

[xi] Gifford & Elizabeth Pinchot, *The End of Bureaucracy & the Rise of the Intelligent Organization*, (San Francisco: Berrett-Koehler Publishers, 1994): 21-27.

[xii] Ibid, 28-38.

[xiii] Archive, *Mitrokhin Archive*, Wilson Center Digital Archive. https://digitalarchive.wilsoncenter.org/topics/mitrokhin-archive

[xiv] Archive, *Venona Documents*, National Security Agency / Central Security Service FOIA. https://www.nsa.gov/Helpful-Links/NSA-FOIA/Declassification-Transparency-Initiatives/Historical-Releases/Venona/

[xv] J. Michael Waller, "Moscow Secretly Funded US Anti-Fracking Groups. Is it now Attacking US Energy Companies?", Center for Security Policy, March 24, 2019. https://centerforsecuritypolicy.org/moscow-secretly-funded-us-anti-fracking-groups-is-it-now-attacking-us-energy-companies/

[xvi] Amelia Cheatham, Dian Roy, and Rocio Cara Labrador, "Venezuela: The Rise and Fall of a Petrostate," Council on Foreign Relations, March 10, 2023. https://www.cfr.org/backgrounder/venezuela-crisis

[xvii] News Report, "5 Ways Hugo Chavez has Destroyed the Venezuelan Economy," ABC News, January 17, 2013. https://abcnews.go.com/ABC_Univision/News/ways-chavez-destroyed-venezuelan-economy/story?id=18239956

[xviii] Bradley O. Babson, "Facing Reality: Will North Korea Adopt a More Rational Economic Policy?" 38 North, July 9, 2010. https://www.38north.org/2010/07/facing-reality-will-north-korea-adopt-a-more-rational-economic-policy/

[xix] Elaine Sciolino, "An Economic Basket Case; In North Korea the Threat is Total Collapse," New York Times, February 18, 1996. https://www.nytimes.com/1996/02/18/weekinreview/an-economic-basket-case-in-north-korea-the-threat-is-total-collapse.html

[xx] Xiadong Zhu, "Understanding China's Growth: Past, Present, and Future," Journal of Economic Perspectives, v. 26, n. 4, Fall 2012, 103-124. https://pubs.aeaweb.org/doi/pdfplus/10.1257/jep.26.4.103

[xxi] Rafael Ramirez, "The Venezuelan Oil Industry Collapse: Economic, Social and Political Implications," Istituto Affari Internazionali, August 11, 2021. https://www.iai.it/en/pubblicazioni/venezuelan-oil-industry-collapse-economic-social-and-political-implications

[xxii] Bradely Martin, D. Sean Barnett, Devin McCarthy, "Russian Logistics and Sustainment Failures in the Ukraine Conflict," RAND Corporation Research Report, January 1, 2023. https://www.rand.org/pubs/research_reports/RRA2033-1.html

[xxiii] Tomas Chamorro-Premuzic, "Why Do So Many Incompetent Men Become Leaders?" Harvard Business Review, August 22, 2013. https://hbr.org/2013/08/why-do-so-many-incompetent-men

[xxiv] Rishav Sharma, "An Economists Staggering Evaluation of Government Incompetence," News Click India, July 15, 2023. https://www.newsclick.in/economists-staggering-evaluation-government-incompetence

[xxv] Donald F. Kettl, "Ten Secret Truths About Government Incompetence," Washington Monthly, January 4, 2015. https://washingtonmonthly.com/2015/01/04/ten-secret-truths-about-government-incompetence/

[xxvi] Ben Moreell, "Of Bread and Circuses," Foundation for Economic Education, January 1, 1956. https://fee.org/articles/of-bread-and-circuses/

[xxvii] Henrik Bering, "Zhukov: The Soviet General," Hover Institution, December 1, 2012. https://www.hoover.org/research/zhukov-soviet-general

[xxviii] R.D. Hooker Jr, "The World Will Hold Its Breath: Reinterpreting Operation Barbarossa," US Army War College Quarterly: Parameters, v. 29, n. 1, Article 6, Spring 1999. https://press.armywarcollege.edu/cgi/viewcontent.cgi?article=1918&context=parameters

[xxix] Robert Coalson, "'We Would Have Lost': Did U.S. Lend-Lease Aid Tip the Balance In Soviet Fight Against Nazi Germany?" Radio Free Europe Radio Liberty, May 7, 2020. https://www.rferl.org/a/did-us-lend-lease-aid-tip-the-balance-in-soviet-fight-against-nazi-germany/30599486.html

[xxx] Anna Borshchevskaya, "Russia's Strategic Success in Syria and the Future of Moscow's Middle East Policy," The Washington Institute for Near East Policy, January 23, 2022. https://www.washingtoninstitute.org/policy-analysis/russias-strategic-success-syria-and-future-moscows-middle-east-policy

Chapter 24: National Resistance Forces in its Operational Beginning

The Foreign-Backed Elites' (FBE) operational and strategic objectives revolve around the premise that their foreign benefactor spent many years assisting pliable members of Western nation's important social elites to attain dominant positions of influence throughout all aspects of society. By the time ordinary members of Western society realized they were being subverted, the FBE pawns would already predominantly control every system that manages society be it social, economic, cultural, or political. The FBE's position would start in a civil conflict possessing greater abundance of resources, personnel, and wealth to overwhelm their National Resistance Forces (NRF) opponents in an open conflict where the FBE-controlled state would have every advantage. The NRF would start out as the underdog by every single metric.

The NRF's Silent Scream and Greedy Smile Strategy's main operational focus is to deny the FBE every single possible opportunity to draw out the NRF into the open to become an easy target while simultaneously striking at the FBE's head: the loosely aligned cabal of co-opted traitors who manage the FBE. The NRF's strategy acknowledges being the underdog and must ruthlessly conserve all resources for only the most precise and impactful actions of violence. The NRF cannot afford to make many mistakes and would be under constant danger of being overwhelmed by the vastly larger FBE apparatus. The unrestricted warfare of the adversarial nation that helped create and influence the FBE did so to bypass the Western nation's laws and security forces by going after the society's leaders. A top-down subversion cannot be spotted because states cannot legally or pragmatically watch those who have the most influence with their political masters as these are the ones who write the laws, especially after corrupt elites achieve positions of power. So, if the NRF successfully eliminates the top-tier of the FBE, this would fatally cripple the adversary's influence without seriously damaging the society or the state.

Unlike terrorism, which relies on indiscriminate violence on the general populace to increase pressure for broad political change in a society, the NRF can use a hybrid of 5GW-style warfare with an inverted version of unrestricted warfare to remove the social rot with exacting precision. Apart from the central core of leaders, the FBE are decentralized and redundant at every echelon of society so that targeting corporations, nonprofits, Atomized groups, militias, or security forces will not sufficiently rid the Western nation of the FBE parasites. Instead, the technologies and methods of 5GW can enable a competent force to bypass, evade, and obscure themselves from the FBE's proxies while simultaneously going after and eliminating the FBE's key leadership. This only works for competent opposition forces meaning the one major advantage of the NRF would have to be its superior competency over the FBE whose glut of resources and micromanagement will stifle incentives for effective leadership.

The operational lines of effort (LOE) revolve around the Three Steps of Silent Scream: 1. Bypass the enemy's 3GW strategy 2. Fix the enemy to distract them and go after peripheral targets 3. Have the NRF directly act against the FBE leaders. Steps 1 and 2 will have many overlapping lines of effort as these actions must be done concurrently with many similar methods because both focus on distracting the FBE's proxy organizations themselves. Step 3 focuses on the FBE's leadership and their immediate circle of proxy liaisons. The FBE's operational LOEs revolve around how each element of society must be subverted to gain more influence while weakening the NRF. The NRF's lines of effort will instead revolve around how its organizational structure can conserve resources while striking only at the most vital targets of one group within the society—corrupt elites.

The NRF's organization is key to its successful execution of its operational LOEs and so it must understand from inception how it can optimally formulate itself into a 5GW organization. Previous historical movements that operate in the shadows that avoid superior opponents such as organized crime syndicates, insurgent groups, terrorist cells, and militias are useful guides for organizational structure but not behavior. These groups are organized to fight other rival organizations with the enemy leaders only being targets of opportunity. 5GW groups like the NRF, are an evolution of these earlier organizations because the NRF actively avoid direct confrontation with enemy organizations as whole while simultaneously targeting individual enemy leaders and their advisors. The FBE exists for the sake of the corrupt members of the social elite and so becomes the single point of failure which is protected by layers of state, economic, and social proxy organizations and institutions. The FBE and their foreign puppet masters must continually direct and micromanage these proxies to maintain control, so the FBE leaders can never go completely into hiding but will remain well-protected. The 5GW organization of the NRF intends to slip through the layers of these defense proxies and directly sever the critical links of FBE leaders' control to preserve the social institutions while removing the corrupting rot.

Avoiding the FBE trap of being lured into open conflict means keeping the state and private proxies continuously at arms-length to prevent direct confrontation but also never letting the proxies rest or focus on important targets. The NRF can do this by conducting legal and nonviolent actions that will compel the FBE proxies to respond in every way short of open war. Violent actions must be a separate but coordinated effort that will protect the NRF as a whole and maximize the risk to FBE leaders. So, the NRF would need to organize into two separate groups linked only by a select few key leaders and liaisons. The largest would carry out Step 1 and Step 2 which is largely focused on non-violent methods, and the smaller of the two would conduct the violent acts to target key leaders. In practice, it will not be clear cut and many actions will have to be conducted in the nebulous gray area of legality, but for organizational simplicity, the NRF will best try to keep these two types of activities separate.

The NRF would start in a political atmosphere where a sizable portion of the population is frustrated with the corrupted Western nation but the demand for open revolt is still among only a vocal minority. For the NRF to succeed, it must avoid the traps of the 4GW insurgencies of the Middle East where enduring survival mattered more than actual strategic effectiveness. These insurgencies became too cellular, disconnected, and divided amongst themselves to ever truly muster a sufficiently cohesive force to overthrow the established states in the region. Too many small strikes in uncoordinated fashion only leads to a drawn-out quagmire, so any movement will need to start with an ideologically consistent message with very disciplined management to aggressively convey this message and minimize the amount of factionalism from the start. Part of this does require strong and capable leaders, both the legally overt ones and the covert direct-action commanders, to successfully create a cohesive resistance. Unlike peaceful political movements, organizations fighting a conflict, even one that uses violence to a minimum, requires strong leaders to succeed.

Democratic armies and resistance groups fragment easily which is part of the reason Rome's republican era created the concept of dictators for times of crisis and war before Sulla corrupted the concept.[i] Whatever the political ramifications, clear lines of hierarchy with an effective leader are crucial to effectively execute important decisions quickly to win a conflict. 5GW doesn't change this dynamic and so having leaders to rally around must occur from inception. Even if there are people with the proper leadership credentials, these same persons must find financial sponsors, unless the leaders are rich themselves, to kickstart a 5GW movement.

Recruitment would start slowly and in small, focused efforts because the Information Age enables easy monitoring of public spaces while well-funded security organizations actively monitor for subversion. The slow pace would continue until the NRF's reputation sufficiently developed to gain adequate resources to create consistent nation-wide recruitment efforts. One positive for the NRF is the majority of recruits would only be needed for legal means rather than violent ones, simplifying initial recruitment. From this, the NRF could later divide the recruitment pools into different tiers of legality to filter out potential infiltrators. The first tier would be the largest pool being selected for ideological beliefs, certain skills and abilities, and the willingness to work on the many non-violent legal political activities. From this pool, certain processes could be implemented to test prospective candidates to be recruited into the next tier of non-violent illegal activities. After a certain number of demonstrated actions, another filtration process could identify those serving a period of time effectively who could go to the next level and conduct violent actions against the FBE. The key point being operational security and this would be the main imperative of the NRF in the beginning until it made sufficient inroads against the FBE that would allow more overt recruitment methods and actions. From the outset, the leaders and the inner circle of advisors must proactively find and select their early members. Volunteers are only for the legitimate activities of the NRF where there is minimal risk of providing the FBE with enough material to create propaganda to justify FBE brutalities or threaten arrest.

The difficulty in the beginning is getting the initial resources and formulating a chain of command with leaders who can garner respect, loyalty, and hope. The NRF would use a variety of options, both cutting-edge and old, to recruit people to build up the NRF. Some of the most effective ways will be older ones that don't rely on the more easily monitored, manipulated, and jammable telecommunications. Starting local and regional clubs, leagues, and associations that only appeal to those dedicated to the cause is an effective beginning. Each association would have very small chapters or lodges but these can be easily linked across the nation. Clubs act as focal points where like-minded people can congregate legally, voice grievances with less risk of ridicule, harassment, or threats that plague online forums while also building close social bonds. Such clubs would be small, perhaps a dozen or so, but having several dozens of these across the Western nation can act as testing centers to identify who is willing to do what and become incubators for future growth. This method is tried and true as demonstrated in the lead-up to the triggering of the French Revolution. During that time in France, freedom of speech and assembly was highly restricted with only members of the upper classes having any leeway. The educated members of these social classes exploited this privilege to form clubs and associations to secretly voice grievances that eventually led to plotting and conspiracy to assist in the overthrow of the monarchy. Radical revolutionaries' influence under the auspices of the Jacobin Club and similar smaller nondescript groups in loose coordination easily hid amongst the multitudes of private associations.[ii] Traditional, or some say analog, methods such as physical clubs, get-togethers, and in-person engagements drastically improve operational security as the FBE's options for monitoring and deception are reduced. Unfortunately for the NRF, this will only entice those who appreciate such precautions which will be rare in societies addicted to digital socialization. This analog method is most useful to recruit older and more experienced people. This demographic would be a major recruiting pool for the first tier of recruits as they are generally more politically aware, can be very productive in nonviolent activities, and are willing to put more time into the cause.

Digital and online recruitment would be used to recruit younger elements of the society, but this method has its own challenges. Digital forums, messaging, and interaction are rife with dangers of deception, manipulation, tracking, and sabotage as there are a multitude of ways to exploit both the telecommunication technology and the users of that technology. On the positive side, there are a nearly endless array of options for the NRF to create redundant communications to maintain contact even if there are losses or interference. Additionally, the NRF, despite misgivings of some of its members, will have to fight "dirty" with Machiavellian zeal if the NRF intends on both surviving and achieving victory. In this case, fighting dirty means aside from regular recruits, one-time use and disposable outsiders will likely be needed for key actions that will require deniability or for false flag actions. Dark web communications could be used to hire mercenaries, build networks with some criminal organizations, or use third parties to recruit or entice potential lone wolves to carry out dangerous activities without being traced back to the NRF.

With these objectives in mind, the NRF would use forums, social media groups, instant messaging, bots, and other classic insurgent recruitment methods to engage with potential recruits but use layers of filters to select a minority for violence and the majority for nonviolent information warfare. This is the inverse of a 4GW terror network. The filters within these social recruitment forums and sites would identify key character traits and professional skills that are more conducive to lethal actions but would also help tailor the security vetting. Machine learning algorithms with customized data sets could be used to test and evaluate reactions and answers by recruits that will act as the first filter. Since the majority of the NRF's operations will be information and psychological warfare, simple vetting and QA would be all that's required for the majority of recruits. For risker positions, multiple filters could be crafted by creating subsequent tasks with each iteration gradually riskier and more illegal. Recruiting for the lethal activities, the final stage filter would likely be in-person interviews or undercover elicitation to evaluate reactions and answers coupled with random surveillance on the potential recruit to reduce infiltration. As for recruiting one-time mercenaries, lone wolves, and criminals, using expendable online bots managed by large-language model machine learning algorithms to reconnoiter and recruit would likely be the most effective way to manage the more illicit and dangerous social elements.

The NRF would no-doubt study many of the means and methods Islamic and domestic terrorist organizations use in the digital world to recruit but the NRF would have to modify many of the methods because their operations are different from traditional terrorists and insurgencies. These 4GW terrorist groups focus on targeting then manipulating the hearts and minds of the populace with either inspiration or terror to compel societal change. In the case of 5GW, the intention is to keep the public apathetic and indifferent to the NRF to deprive the FBE of manpower to successfully mobilize for a 3GW fight. The autocrats must have the public's tepid approval at minimum to justify an overt civil war without risk of a backlash once the carnage begins. Although "nudging" the public into being more resentful towards the FBE-controlled state is helpful, keeping the public on the sidelines is key. Recruitment must generally appear harmless to society at large.

The only hearts and minds the NRF needs to target are those of the FBE's leaders at the highest echelon. Keeping the people passive and uninterested in the FBE's efforts to rally against dissent means keeping the public believing they are in no mortal danger or that their loved ones' quality of life will diminish. If such things occur, the priority would be convincing the public that the NRF are not involved or to blame. Getting the public angry at the FBE is only a bonus, divide and conquering the FBE's upper echelon is the objective.

Once recruiting gains momentum to build functioning cells and units, then the organization must quickly figure out how to balance the need for security with the need to cohesively bring all resources to bear against the FBE. 4GW insurgencies that prioritized internal security over organizational cohesiveness by keeping everything too decentralized never progressed against their target governments. ISIS in contrast, maintained an organized chain of command while still operating as a collection of loosely connected cells until their efforts culminated in launching organized major offensives against their enemies.[iii] The NRF need to find its own equilibrium within the circumstances fate has provided them, however there would be some common rules regardless of circumstance. The NRF would need to have a functional cellular structure where each cell specializes in key tasks to insulate the legal activities from illegal ones while also maintaining a chain of command to direct complex operations. Communication policies and methods are critical for the NRF to establish early on to maintain control over many scattered disparate groups and cells.

Once an adequate chain of command and allocation of tasks has been decided, the NRF needs to manage a cohesive method of communication to execute mission-command objectives against their superior FBE foes. Individual techniques are varied but can be placed into two broad categories: 1. Fast-less secure communication 2. Slow-more secure communication. The first type will be needed for time-sensitive decisions and actions such as carrying out attacks, disrupting an event, tracking a high-value target, or a security breach. Fast communication involves digital devices operating on common public or corporate networks where the NRF doesn't have complete control over the communication medium. Consequently, the NRF will have to devise sophisticated operational security protocols and procedures for their members to reduce the risk of discovery. These communication devices will likely have a multitude of program applications processed by common components meaning that aggressive phishing, hacking, denial of service, corrupt firmware, and being able to directly interrupt the power to these devices will be possible. This leaves these communications methods vulnerable, even if the messages themselves are secured by encryption. Speed of conveying the message will be prioritized over having completely secure communication in these circumstances so there will be a perpetual risk for the tactical and operational actions that the NRF must consider and incorporate into all of their planning.

Security over speed is the second type reserved for strategic-level communications where decisions are made between different echelons, the key leaders, and their advisors. At this level, the decision cycle is weeks or months instead of hours or days. Instead of relying mainly on digital devices, the senior leaders would avoid contemporary devices as much as possible, using others as messengers between NRF cell nodes similar to the World War II-era Office of Strategic Services means of covert communication.[iv] Instead of relying on secure encryption on digital networks, the leaders could utilize codes, which transfer meaning instead of text substitution, for communication disseminated by couriers with writing things down or using Notepad on a stand-alone computer to print out for couriers. However, if sufficiently strong codes are developed, this would allow messengers to use more advanced contemporary methods to convey these messages with low risk of discovery by the enemy. Codes are secure in the sense that the reference used as the basis for the code cannot be found with brute force because the users have an infinite array of options to choose from as a baseline.[v] Classically, the leaders could build codes based on references to books by page number, especially obscure or out of print books. Codes can be practically unbreakable and ensure only those in the know can receive and disseminate the critical messages. This method combined with messengers and analog tools means a slower, more inefficient means of communication, but would also be exceptionally difficult to detect or identify from surveillance. However, the danger is that once the code is broken, every communication is completely decodable. This usually happens when the reference is discovered and the encoding is broken, and for insurgencies, it usually means a leader or messenger is captured and yields to interrogation. Nevertheless, this high-risk low probability of discovery method is best to ensure continuous communication linkages between the various cells and the overall leadership.

A few examples can help you better understand how codes could be used in the modern era, so with a little imagination anyone can come up with a multitude of ways. For instance, an NRF cell leader could communicate with other cell leaders in their area of operations by creating an online clan in a massively multiplayer online role-player game which the other cell leaders join. Since in-game communication is monitored and recorded by the company, the gameplay itself could be the cipher. Determining which dungeon to play; picking the length of time for playing at specific times during the day or week; how many members of the clan will play that day; the number of players picking a certain class type; weapons selection, clothing selection, and gender selection could all be referencing symbols for key words and phrases without anyone saying anything incriminating during the game session.

Another could be one NRF member starts a podcast with several messengers who could argue on a non-political topic. The cipher could be the number of times one side disagrees during a session or how many times one person says "like" or "uh" in their sentences since these are irritatingly common speaking traits. The content of the discussion could be completely irrelevant and the cipher would just be the flow and tempo of the discussion.

Another idea that combines modern with old techniques is a modern form of signal lamp. Signal lamps are used by navies around the world to communicate with other nearby ships if radio communications are unavailable. These lamps are equipped with rapidly opening and closing shudders that produce focused pulses of light that can be controlled to produce morse code. For the NRF, different cells could emplace small infrared (IR)-LED light emitters hidden in foliage, walls, or other nondescript objects near homes, warehouses, or other buildings with CCTV cameras. If one cell wanted to communicate with other cells without risk of meeting or being seen together, that cell leader can flash the wirelessly controlled IR-LED, which cannot be seen by human eyes, towards those cameras which other cell leaders can log on and view the footage. The LED could be equipped with a cover so the IR-emission can only emit its light unidirectionally. Without knowing what to look for, the FBE would unlikely find this means of a modern signal lamp system where no NRF individual has to physically see other NRF members in person to get the message.

A final example requires more resources and technical skills but could accelerate the use of complex ciphers for NRF leaders. NRF could use the power of machine learning to find hidden symbols within imagery online and convey those symbols to other NRF members. Artificial narrow intelligence does not see pictures the same way humans do. A machine learning program is fed millions of examples of picture data to identify common pixel patterns and then match those patterns with preset criteria in the program to determine what the objects are in the imagery.[vi] If certain pixel patterns are programmed to be associated with cipher symbols embedded into selected imagery files, then one NRF cell could post many pleasant innocuous pictures on a webpage, like Pinterest, where others can download the imagery. Other NRF members then feed these downloaded images through the NRF's custom machine-learning pattern recognition software and have the computer generate cipher symbols that the NRF members can manually decipher. Whatever the means the NRF selects, devising a covert means of reliable communication will need to be planned from the outset to avoid disaster.

Devising means of recruitment, planning the organizational layout, and establishing communication protocols are the fundamental elements to building a covert army, but all of this is useless without the funding resources necessary to implement all of these actions. Before discussing funding methods, another question the NRF leaders must ask themselves is how big and extensive do they need for an insurgency to function? The 4GW insurgencies of the last 20 years can give some clues. As a rule of thumb, most insurgencies typically had between a third to one-half of one percent of the total population of the nation they've operated in as active fighting members, typically around 350 individuals per 100,000.[vii] However, a 4GW insurgency focuses on recruiting mainly combatants with only a minority selected for conducting information and psychological warfare activities. In a 5GW organization, the majority of recruits are for information and psychological operations and only a small minority are needed for direct combat actions. For simplicity's sake, this wargame analysis will use the metric of three information / psychological fighters for every one combat fighter since there has not been a modern version of a 5GW organization to cite for context. So, for context, in the largest Western nation, the United States, an effective 5GW organization would have approximately 1,160,000 personnel with about 300,000 of them conducting combat-related activities. In the smaller states of Europe such as Germany, France, and the United Kingdom the numbers would be roughly 230,000 total insurgents with approximately 55,000 combatants. This is just for the organization itself and doesn't include the portion of the population that is sympathetic to the insurgency cause. No set rule exists but a safe assumption is at least 15 percent of the population would sympathize strongly enough to donate either funds or materials to the NRF.[viii]

These example numbers of an insurgency's typical size and scale show a modern 5GW insurgency in a Western nation would need a lot of resources and money to function. One key point though is that the majority of insurgents will only require access to phones, software, computers, and audio/visual equipment as these are information warriors. A 5GW insurgency's costs will overall be less than trying to wage a 4GW insurgency that requires munitions, armaments, and vehicles in large quantities to be effective. A 5GW organization could have its munitions and combat operations disrupted and still be 75% effective in its actions. Consequently, the NRF's 5GW organizational framework allows for greater adaptability to financial disruptions. So, how would the NRF finance it? Luckily for the NRF, the methods and means available will be very similar to the covert finances of the FBE.

One common thread between insurgents, terrorists, and organized crime is the similarity in how these organizations raise funds. A combination of overt legitimate enterprises, secret donations, and covert illegal activities would need to happen to sustain NRF activities. One advantage the NRF has over the FBE is NRF tasks are less complex to action. FBE must subvert a society and every critical element of cultural significance while keeping its traitorous corruption hidden. The NRF just has to focus on disrupting and defeating the FBE as an organization while avoiding the FBE's state and private institutional proxies. The NRF has a simpler job even though it is at higher risk given the FBE's resource advantage. The NRF's simpler mission requires fewer resources which means it can survive times of fiscal shortages and still keep fighting more than the FBE. The one major inhibitor for NRF fundraising is that it must not do anything egregious to the point of making the apathetic public turn against them. The 5GW method to achieve victory partially rests on the NRF successfully keeping the majority of the population neutral in the fight, so certain criminal enterprises need to be off limits. Anything that incurs major suffering on the public such as human trafficking, drug smuggling, and arms dealing will be politically disastrous. The illicit activities must be ones the public will take little notice by targeting organizations that are popularly perceived as corrupt or abusive.

Targeting financial institutions, insurance companies, capital investment firms, entertainment studios, technology companies, law firms, and politically activistic nonprofits, especially ones sponsored by billionaires, are all safe targets as these are considered exploitative by many people. [ix], [x], [xi] Admittedly, some traditional methods insurgents have used are too obsolete such as bank robbery. Banks are fortified and being affiliated with such actions that put the public in danger undermines the NRF's overall strategic effort. Cybercrime will be the main effort to enrich the NRF because it is less glamorous, lower risk of detection, lower risk of exposure, and the sloppiness of many firms' cybersecurity practices will yield a large source of income.[xii] Phishing and credential theft will allow the NRF to access many complacent organizations and potentially follow-on to create false personas pretending to represent the targeted organization to conduct false flags.

One critical opportunity would be to use the Nimbyists' and Atomized Groups' causes as cover to get FBE sympathizers to donate funds directly into the NRF's coffers. Examples include creating crowdfunding campaigns for fake persons that suffered in the name of any approved FBE cause or hijack actual Nimbyist and Atomized crowdfunding efforts. Using infiltrators in FBE-backed nonprofits to raise donations for FBE-fronted causes could skim funds off the donations, especially if the infiltrators were given customized malware to corrupt the nonprofits' accounting systems.[xiii] Or the NRF create their own non-profits as front organizations similar to ISIS and al-Qaeda charities.[xiv] Since some wealthy persons in the West create and use nonprofits to evade taxes and legally launder money, the loopholes for exploitation are unlikely to ever be closed. [xv] Blackmail and ransomware would also be options, as the FBE would have many corrupt members from whom the NRF could collect incriminating information to extort for money. Another possibility is cryptocurrency scams that specifically target wealthy investors, especially FBE sympathizers, which could potentially acquire hundreds of millions of dollars annually. Carrying out crypto scams similar to the Africrypt scandals in South Africa could net the NRF large sums but would be limited to only a few occasions every few years due to the high levels of scrutiny.[xvi]

Kidnapping and actually physically ransoming people is historically one of the largest sources of income for insurgencies and terrorists.[xvii] For the NRF's campaign, this is still an option but it would only be optimally effective if it's carried out on rare occasions against high-profile wealthy associates of the FBE. Messaging is as critical to 5GW as the money. Demonstrating to the FBE that they cannot protect their own high-value individuals would be a major blow against morale. Carrying out such crimes on a rare basis means it will not remain in the public's psyche too long and if an unpopular person is targeted, the less negative public fallout.

One last point is NRF fundraising by donations from sympathizers. Although using charity fronts is an effective way to collect contributions from sympathizers, these are also vulnerable to intense scrutiny that could help the FBE identify sympathizers. Crowdfunding is another way but the NRF would have to establish separate companies to collect these funds as established ones would likely aid the FBE proxies in scrutinizing all transactions.[xviii] Simply going door-to-door to business associations or under the guise of some social convention are other options when the NRF doesn't want to manage a front company directly handling the money collections. Loan-sharking and protection rackets are feasible but should be limited to FBE-associated organizations and persons to keep the political fallout low and to avoid confrontations with organized crime that relies heavily on such activities.

Illicit funding and creative bookkeeping are two areas of study human beings have poured endless intellectual genius and creativity into so that the NRF will have thousands of potential methods and options to choose from and is beyond the scope of this war game. The single most difficult step will be the startup or "seed" money to get the foundations of the NRF army established. Once on its feet, the NRF's sustainment funding would become much easier. After the NRF establishes these foundations of command and control, recruiting, funding, and communicating, the NRF can finally begin executing their lines of effort against the FBE.

[i] Editors Valerij Gouschin and P.J. Rhodes, *Deformations and Crises of Ancient Civil Communities*, (Stuttgart: Franz Steiner Verlag: 2015) Section by T.J. Cornell, "Crisis and Deformation in the Roman Republic: The Example of Dictatorship," 101-127. https://www.academia.edu/33277046/Crisis_and_deformation_in_the_Roman_republic_the_example_of_the_dictatorship

[ii] Edmund Burke, edited by W. Allison Phillips and Catherine Beatrice Phillips, *Reflections on the French Revolution*, (Cambridge, MA: University Press: 1912): 68, 274.

[iii] Charles C. Caris and Samuel Reynolds, "Middle East Security Report 22: ISIS Governance in Syria," Institute for the Study of War, June 29, 2014, 10-14. https://www.understandingwar.org/sites/default/files/ISIS_Governance.pdf

[iv] U.S. Government Field Manual, *Operational Groups Field Manual No. 6 – Strategic Services*, (Washington DC: Office of Strategic Services: 1944): 18. https://www.soc.mil/OSS/assets/operational-groups-fm.pdf

[v] Jon Watson, "Famous Codes and Ciphers Through History and Their Role in Modern Encryption," Comparitech, August 30, 2023. https://www.comparitech.com/blog/information-security/famous-codes-and-ciphers-through-history-and-their-role-in-modern-encryption/

[vi] Shumeet Baluja, "Hiding Images in Plain Sight: Deep Steganography," Google Research, Proceedings of the 31st International Conference on Neural Information Processing Systems, December 2017, pg. 2066-2076. https://proceedings.neurips.cc/paper_files/paper/2017/file/838e8afb1ca34354ac209f53d90c3a43-Paper.pdf

[vii] Report, "Iraq Index: Tracking Variables of Reconstruction and Security in Post-Saddam Iraq," Brookings, September 27, 2007, pg. 26-27. https://web.archive.org/web/20071002041710/http://www3.brookings.edu/fp/saban/iraq/index.pdf

[viii] Ben Connable,and Martin C. Libicki, *How Insurgencies End*, (RAND Corporation, 2010): 25-30. https://www.jstor.org/stable/10.7249/mg965mcia

[ix] Devika Rao, "Why do People Hate Billionaires?", The Week, November 26, 2022. https://theweek.com/economy/1018418/why-do-people-hate-billionaires

[x] Beth Youra, "Why It's Still Cool to Hate Banks," Gallup, June 24, 2015. https://news.gallup.com/opinion/gallup/183785/why-cool-hate-banks.aspx

[xi] Tom Schultz, "The Moral Predicaments of BigLaw," The Cornell Daily Sun, November 15, 2012. https://cornellsun.com/2012/11/15/the-moral-predicaments-of-biglaw/

[xii] Dominick Reuter, "Crippling Attacks on US Gas and Meat Suppliers Expose the Dangers of Major Companies' Reliance On Patchwork Cybersecurity," Business Insider, June 17, 2021. https://www.businessinsider.com/cyber-attacks-show-hazards-of-companies-use-of-patchwork-security-2021-6

[xiii] Jonathan T. Marks and Peter A. Ugo, "A Violation of Trust: Fraud Risk in Nonprofit Organizations," Nonprofitrisk.org, accessed September 12, 2023. https://nonprofitrisk.org/resources/articles/a-violation-of-trust-fraud-risk-in-nonprofit-organizations/

[xiv] Press Release, "Global Disruption of Three Terror Finance Cyber-Enabled Campaigns," Department of Justice, August 13, 2020. https://www.justice.gov/opa/pr/global-disruption-three-terror-finance-cyber-enabled-campaigns

[xv] Report, *Report on Abuse of Charities for Money-Laundering and Tax Evasion*, OECD Centre for Tax Policy and Administration, April 2015. https://www.oecd.org/tax/exchange-of-tax-information/42232037.pdf

[xvi] Jamie Crawley, "South African Police Investigate Missing Brothers' Crypto Platform, Africrypt," CoinDesk, January 11, 2022. https://www.coindesk.com/business/2022/01/11/south-african-police-investigate-missing-brothers-crypto-platform-africrypt/

[xvii] Fact Sheet, "Kidnapping for Ransom and Terrorism," United Nations Office on Drugs and Crime, accessed May 11, 2023. https://www.unodc.org/e4j/en/organized-crime/module-16/key-issues/kidnapping-for-ransom-and-terrorism.html

[xviii] Elizabeth Thompson, "Crowdfunding Platforms Now Required to Report Transactions, After Truck Convoy Protests," CBC News, May 4, 2022. https://www.cbc.ca/news/politics/convoy-finance-crowdfunding-fintrac-1.6440671

Chapter 25: NRF Overlapping Lines of Effort in Steps 1 & 2 – Bypass and Fix the FBE's Catalonia 2.0 with Legal Activities

This wargame explores 5GW being applied to a civil conflict in a modern developed country of which there is no historical precedent to reference or cite, so these operational lines of effort are speculative on how to theoretically best apply 5GW. The speculation is based on analyzing objectives and strategies sought out by other historic civil conflicts and assessing the best way a 5GW force can achieve them. This wargame assesses just one ideal operational way to successfully pursue these goals, but these are not the only means an opposition movement could choose to fight. These 5GW operational lines-of-effort (LOEs) are best fitted to counter the stronger FBE opponent's Catalonia 2.0 Strategy or something similar. The LOEs are based on the assumptions that the FBE have effectively achieved at least a dominating position within the Western nation and the NRF are pursuing 5GW to both conserve their own limited resources and prevent their nation disintegrating from endless combat quagmires akin to Afghanistan, Libya, Syria, Yugoslavia, Sudan, or Iraq. To this end, the 5GW force is primarily an information and psychological warfare force with a direct combat element being secondary. More than half of the NRF's LOEs are designed to use non-violent means to disrupt FBE plans and keep the FBE's leadership off-balance to avoid open confrontation that could destroy the NRF and the Western nation.

To Bypass and Fix; Combining Steps 1 & 2:

The NRF exists to fight the FBE because the opposition within the Western nation failed to preserve the classical means of peaceful political discourse and the FBE succeeded in creating an autocratic system that favored their interests exclusively. To win in such an environment while preserving the Western nation as a developed country, 5GW abandons the traditional objectives of 4GW insurgencies. In this fight, the NRF are not seeking to win the "battle for the people's hearts and minds" but instead seeks to perpetuate public indifference and wield that apathy into a weapon against the FBE's strategy. The public is not the target, the FBE's leadership is the target as it is the single lynchpin that connects the foreign adversary who patronizes the FBE to the various nodes of controlling proxies within the Western nation's institutions. Since the purpose of the FBE in this war is to win absolute power for their masters, the masters are the FBE's main center of gravity. Targeting their masters is the cheapest, simplest, and most effective way to battle the FBE's superior forces. The advancements of communication technology, lawfare, and psychological manipulation gives the NRF tools that painlessly extricates the rotten elites out of the body politic without risking the societal foundations' stability. For the NRF's enemy to win, the FBE must galvanize the population into endorsing the elimination of the NRF by open conflict to gain popular legitimacy and discredit any opposition. A drawn-out bloody insurgency is as detrimental to the FBE as it is to the NRF because 4GW civil conflicts lasts years at the cost of economic and social stability. The FBE attained power illegitimately, so if a 4GW insurgency occurs, the risk of splintering into competing factions or incentivizing a coup amongst skittish FBE members becomes very high leading to national balkanization.

An open war of the classic 3GW variety gives the FBE the legitimacy to impose overt autocratic rules, drawing out all the NRF opposition into the open, and helps achieve a relatively quick victory by sheer mass of force alone. However, 3GW depends on galvanizing the public to participate in the war effort. Since 3GW plays to the FBE's strengths and 4GW would endanger both the FBE and NRF, the natural counter to the FBE's plans is to keep the public apathetic to the conflict. If the public doesn't believe they are in any danger, then they will not willingly endure hardships and inconvenience of war. If the FBE cannot get the public to believe the NRF needs to be destroyed and still try to go forward with a 3GW war, then the NRF can blame all problems on the FBE and its proxies. If this happens, the public will split in opinion and the danger of a Middle East style 4GW quagmire increases substantially. The NRF must win by forcing the FBE to make all of the provocative moves while using the apathetic public as a political shield that inhibits the FBE's desire to mobilize the nation into a 3GW conflict. Over time during a 5GW conflict, the public may not necessarily drift into the NRF's camp, but at least a sizable portion will turn openly against the FBE's autocratic system. Simultaneously, the NRF must also wage an invisible battle directly against the traitor FBE leaders that does include the use of violent force to compel the FBE leadership to yield. The operational outcome is to splinter the FBE leadership into weaker fragments that can more easily be eliminated one-by-one and co-opt the surviving ones to the NRF's side. To get to the elites, the NRF must first shape the 5GW battlefield.

Firstly, the NRF must bypass all the FBE's efforts and provocations into coming out into the open as an organized force by restraining all temptations at secession or mimicking the FBE by trying to create a 3GW-style army. Keeping the NRF hidden and have them remain as part of the Western nation's society allows them to blend in and disappear amongst the general population. This helps the NRF to exploit the slow response weakness of large-size institutions trying to ferret out small nimbler groups of opposition which is further complicated if these groups technically remain within compliance of the law. Keeping the NRF's members and activities geographically and legally ambiguous will paralyze the FBE's proxies as any draconian actions carried out blindly would risk disproportionately hurting innocent citizens. This is the fundamental role of the operational Step 1 LOEs; to avoid and bypass all Catalonia 2.0 provocations to make the NRF expose, separate, and isolate itself from the nation's society.

Secondly, the NRF must impede and set back all FBE efforts to actively destroy the NRF both physically and politically. The FBE proxies will use its superior resources to wage large-scale legal, economic, and cultural attacks to isolate and eliminate NRF members while provoking its supporters into violent secession. To maximize the chances of survival, the NRF must pin down the FBE proxies with distractions, deceptions, and misdirection to make the autocrats squander time, political capital, and money. Instead of creating battlefield quagmires, the NRF will create legal, procedural, and political quagmires that results in frustration, inconvenience, disruption, and chaos, but only for the FBE's proxies to avoid provoking the general public. This is the essence of Step 2 LOEs; to fix and direct all Catalonia 2.0 proxies into pursuing meaningless targets.

These first two out of three steps must be done concurrently. Avoiding open war will be a continuous effort on the part of the NRF while at the same time, the FBE will still continuously identify, pursue, and eliminate their NRF opponents by means other than war. Since the LOEs of Steps 1 and 2 overlap, the NRF would likely utilize the same organizational elements to address all of these LOEs and simply modify their techniques based on the LOE. These Step 1 and 2 LOE focused organizational elements can be divided into two groupings: legal activities and illegal activities. None of these activities involve organized combat operations but instead focus on every other type of political means to cripple and undermine the FBE. This is a Western version of China's "Unrestricted Warfare".

Options and Methods: Legal Activities for Steps 1 & 2

Using the FBE's own political tools and subverting their narratives to bypass and disrupt the FBE's actions is the most effective means to nonviolently undermine the FBE. The FBE's proxies must retain the veneer of democratic legitimacy to keep an apathetic and unreliable population mollified. Meaning that each FBE proxy must work within certain cultural and legal confinements to carry out their operations to avoid public agitation. In practice, the corrupt anocracy will violate any and all rules to accomplish their objectives, but they must never be seen doing it. Balancing the veneer of democratic fairness to maintain societal stability while thwarting all active dissent requires sensitive balancing of organizational priorities. The NRF Steps 1 and 2 LOEs are designed to throw every FBE proxy off balance and then prevent them from ever regaining any footing. So, each NRF LOE organization will specialize in specific techniques to evade and bypass FBE efforts then pin down and misdirect these efforts into ineffective actions.

Legal LOE Organization 1: The Controverts

Social media is the mainstay of information dissemination. Major corporations control the market share of these online forums which makes the FBE's mission of information suppression easier. The FBE just has to financially support lobbying, political activism, and investment in these companies to corruptly influence them. Yet, there are still many uses for social media, even when it is controlled by the NRF's opponents. The FBE must engage the public on every topic and social issue to maintain control of the narrative. To maintain control over every aspect of the population means assuaging every major social group's concern about their standing within the anocracy which inevitably leads to contradictions. Not every group in society has common interests or mutually benefiting goals hence there is always some social friction and rivalry. The FBE will make lies, deceptions, empty promises, and contradictions to manipulate everyone into remaining obedient to the system, making the FBE vulnerable to damaging political controversy. The Controvert units' mission would be a continuity of what already happens in Western political discourse except repurposed exclusively to undermine and subvert the opponent in the eyes of its own followers. The Controverts are not designed to help win over the public to the NRF.

Controverts are specialized NRF information warfare units that sabotage the FBE's proxies' public reputation with its loyalists and sympathizers. The Controverts do not attempt to persuade people to the NRF cause but focus on inhibiting the FBE's ability to attract and retain followers. Aside from the proxy organizations, the FBE's means of control is to promise and sometimes provide instant gratification to its supporters. This gratification is also designed to create an addictive dependency that will discourage supporters from questioning the corrupt actions of the FBE. The Atomized are made psychologically dependent on the FBE's promises of personal empowerment, glorification of their identity, and offering immunity from accountability to normal societal standards. The Nimbyists are made materially dependent on the FBE's promises of programs, grants, and fiscal security that protects their decadence no matter what policies are imposed on the rest of the society. This is the contemporary version of the Roman Empire's "bread and circuses"[i] to anathematize public critical thinking from which sprouts criticism and people's doubt about their political masters. As long as the FBE can appear concerned about their subjects and carrying out policies that provide small token morsels of the instant gratification that is promised, the masses will remain mollified and their indoctrinated followers loyal. In practice, the FBE will overpromise as trying to placate the various factions' and interest groups' expectations is unsustainable as this would be too resource intensive. Many interest groups' demands will come into conflict with others which could lead to splintering if the FBE tries to accommodate everyone equally. That is why appearing to do something about an issue to the public is more important to the FBE to maintain control than to actually try do something for the public and failing. Stripping away the veil and exposing the FBE's actual allocation of resources, the lies, contradictions, and favoritism to the public can severely disrupt their ability to control the society.

The Controverts can't persuade Atomized or Nimbyists to switch sides or to think for themselves as the life of a well-catered serf is easier than independence. Instead, the Controverts must find where the FBE deceives the loyalists and fails to deliver on promises or when they steal from the loyalists themselves. Diminishing the loyalists' "bread and circus" perks disrupts the FBE's planning and operations as they must devote greater resources to maintain internal cohesiveness. The Controverts act as investigative journalists except they report to FBE members on the shenanigans that their own organization does to its own people to cause internal controversy and conflict. Accurately reporting on the FBE corruption that directly impacts the lives of the Nimbyists and the Atomized will appeal to the loyalists' self-centered avarice and narcissism who otherwise endorses FBE abuses on everyone else. Controverts would operate in the public space and conduct various activities to extract the information to inflame resentment amongst the loyalist portion of the public.

The techniques would largely be indistinguishable from modern independent journalism except the target audience and purpose is different. Instead of general public awareness, these operations are aimed at inflaming resentments from specific segments that dutifully carry out the FBE's wishes. Targets of opportunity as well as focused targets would likely take months of careful investigation combined with support from NRF intelligence collection units to gain meaningful derogatory information. The Controverts can't just focus on building records of FBE lies, misinformation, or contradictions either. The Controverts must also find lies that directly impact the FBE supporters' lives and with abundant evidence to make FBE attempts to disprove the revelations very difficult. The revelations don't have to be smoking guns or incontestable, just sufficient enough to plant seeds of doubt and allow resentment to fester amongst the rank-and-file supporters. The challenge is that the supporters will need to either directly experience the betrayal or make them fearful that they will be betrayed eventually. People need to believe they understand the world and know how they fit in it, especially fanatics as their worldview defines most of their life commitments. Revelations that challenge who they believe are the "good guys" and "bad guys" or that those they trust are betraying them is dangerous to the supporters' psyche. Their brains will rationalize and explain away many actions of their FBE masters to reassure themselves that they weren't suckered and they backed the correct side. This requires the Controverts to launch multiple volleys of information warfare attacks on specific targets to wear down FBE supporters' faith.

Methods will vary widely and involve a mix of public and anonymous disclosures. Public NRF Controvert personalities must deliberately act as lightning rods of controversy to attract the FBE focus when the embarrassing revelations are made. The public personalities' task is to always set and frame the context to control the parameters of the narrative before the FBE propagandists can formulate an effective counter. Furthermore, the public personalities' antics enable their clandestine Controvert partners to extract and relay the critical information with less risk of being detected. The embarrassing revelations can be relayed through these public personalities but should not be the main channel of disclosure as they are easy to censor. The public personalities and the censoring of them bring awareness of the information but the details will be dropped in discussion forums, video sharing and hosting services, imageboards, and various other online means. The principal criteria being to target locations that are frequented by Nimbyist and Atomized persons who have to now face the reality of manipulation by their faction.

In modern times, online social media is the main channel of disclosure but other more creative ways are available. Posting embarrassing information on large public LED video display boards and video walls in major stores, shopping centers, city squares, and highways in FBE loyalist strongholds are some examples. Using harvested data aggregation of target FBE populations to find thousands or possibly millions of smartphone numbers of Nimbyists or Atomized which the NRF could launch spear phishing bots to steal credentials. Traditionally, this is used to gain illicit access to networks or people's personal accounts but in this case, it would be to launch a coordinated campaign of leaking embarrassing information directly to targeted FBE audiences' personal electronic devices. After gaining access, they could pose as people that the targeted persons know and then send accurate but embarrassing information about FBE superiors is risky, but effective for triggering events quickly before the deception gets noticed. Any means to deceptively give the appearance that the accurate derogatory information came from trusted FBE sources makes the targeted audience more receptive to the information. Unfortunately, people who face uncomfortable facts or news will often retreat into their echo chambers to reinforce their psychological armor with reassuring rationalizations from reading and hearing from "reliable" people. Hijacking the echo chambers when these FBE loyalists need reassurance the most compounds the impact of the damaging revelations. Additionally, the Controverts should also aggressively discredit as many prominent FBE "voices" within these echo chambers as possible to disrupt the internal communications of the FBE supporters.

FBE propagandists are going to be corrupt because they will have to deceive at some point to maintain a constant narrative. Exposing the lies, scandals, or falsehoods of high-profile propagandists to eliminate their influence diminishes the FBE's overall ability to control narratives. A prominent personality that falsely claims certain abilities or personal accomplishments, when exposed, severely reduces the creditability of any information that person conveys. For instance, an online personality named James Vasquez who claimed to be a hardened war veteran who joined the Ukrainian International Legion to fight the Russians garnered a large online following that helped spur support for the Legion. He was however eventually exposed as a stolen valor fraud who never deployed and never became a non-commissioned officer.[ii] Regardless of the validity of the cause he supported, his lies and deception tarnished any and all activities associated with that cause that he claimed to have participated in. Similar actions can be done to academics, politicians, economists, and opinionators who brazenly contradict themselves over time. Another example was used against wealthy businessmen and retired politicians who advocated for greater climate-related regulations and restrictions buying up beach-front property. The contrast of spending wealth on beach properties they claim are going away by climate disaster gives the powerful impression that they are conning people to justify excusing their wealth creation by making empty gesture political statements and pledges.[iii]

Keeping a consistent narrative with falsehoods is impossible as the context of situations change, forcing the propagandists to sometimes flip flop. Controverts capture, archive, and build a record of all publications, statements, speeches, and interviews of particularly egregious FBE personalities to identify every contradiction, hypocrisy, and empty promise those personalities make. This can be used to undermine the FBE's narratives when released in a well-timed coordinated effort. For instance, many judicial officials in the United States often claim the legal system tries to apply the law equally and are impartial. Then a media organization highlighted numerous examples of corrupt actions by state and local judges that contradict this assertion and released this information in one large report to maximize impact of the issue.[iv] These judges were rarely punished or faced any accountability but the disseminated story helped undermine the credibility of the local judiciary. Other methods include undercover operations to video record verbatim statements and assertions of key FBE personalities in moments when they dropped their public persona or watch operations of FBE proxies that would anger supporters. Common examples include Animal rights groups showing abuse at farms, shelters, or abattoirs to undermine these organizations goodwill of people who otherwise support such industries.[v] Showing instances of actions that will anger loyalists, like exposing personalities mocking or demeaning members of Atomized groups off camera as an example, can paralyze the internal functionality of the FBE.

Strengths:

The FBE can easily censor the NRF's messaging to the masses by restricting searches, removing videos, deplatforming, etc. to contain NRF growth. However, the Controverts complicate this traditional tool of autocracy because they will convey information directly to loyalists using loyalist means of communication. Any disruption of the Converts requires disruption to the FBE's own internal communication systems used to maintain narrative control. Proactively persecuting the overt NRF Controvert personalities without disrupting the actual derogatory information gatherers will make the FBE look ineffectual to its followers and oppressive by everyone else. Targeting the messengers of the information rather than the collectors of the damaging information makes the FBE appear impotent. The Controverts' cat and mouse game of getting information the FBE is concealing from its rank-and-file minions is in itself accomplishing the operational objective. Forcing the FBE to engage and downplay the Controverts' instigated controversies diminish FBE cohesion which paralyzes their operations.

175

The additional advantage is the FBE must continuously disrupt NRF efforts to disseminate derogatory information while the NRF only have to be successful on occasion. Reputation for reliability and trustworthiness is brittle and takes few betrayals to alienate fellow allies. The FBE is constrained on ridding themselves of corrupt and hypocritical individuals that the NRF would target because the FBE is for selfish opportunists by its very nature. Also, the FBE will be forced at various points to assign incompetent and inept people to operate certain tasks because loyalty to the system is vital. Incompetent mediocrities outnumber competent geniuses in the human race, so prioritizing loyalty means competence must be sacrificed to some extent. This incompetence will provide many opportunities for embarrassing the FBE in front of their followers.

Public speaking Controverts also act as early warning sensors for the NRF as these individuals pontificate on FBE corruption and activities. The reaction of the FBE to each of the public personalities reporting will help gauge what's the FBE's priorities are as well as who is more valuable to them by the level of protection the FBE provides to shield Controvert-targeted FBE loyalists from scandals. Although being a public personality is dangerous, it is mitigated by being in the limelight that the FBE will be restrained on what retaliations are carried out. This is why the NRF must insulate the public personalities from any dubious activity to avoid giving any legitimate reason for persecution. This is also why it is advantageous for the NRF to relay different derogatory stories and revelations to different personalities, so the NRF are not dependent on any single individual and the FBE cannot anticipate what stories are going to be disclosed to whom.

Unlike modern journalism which discloses damaging information on a person or organization based on maximizing ratings, the NRF is using the Controverts as part of a military-style operation. To have maximum impact any disclosure must be conducted in coordination with the actions of the other NRF units' LOEs. Forcing the FBE to manage multiple information warfare attacks from multiple approaches is likely to inflict significant damaging effects if properly coordinated and executed. However, this advantage also has downsides.

Weaknesses:

Coordinating information attacks require precision, patience, and good communication within the NRF organization. The larger the operation, the more resources and time it will take to carry it out. Nation-wide operations in particular would need every echelon and unit to execute well-timed attacks while avoiding FBE detection until after the fact. Since stealth is required for part of the NRF's organization, this means the FBE will be able to easily disrupt large-scale information warfare operations. FBE only has to disrupt a few key elements in a fast enough frame of time to minimize the impact of any Controvert operation. Furthermore, any early exposure allows the FBE to frame the narrative and "spin" any derogatory information sufficiently to nullify any risks to their reputation. Failure to coordinate the operations properly risks alienating key public assets as they suffer public humiliation or civil litigation from publishing inaccurate or contradictory information. Synchronizing NRF organizational actions is very difficult but failing to do so risks making the Controverts irrelevant.

Many contemporary Western countries do not have the skillsets necessary to identify misinformation, falsehoods, or veiled messaging of political propaganda. Due to poor civics and history education, much of the population only understands the society in the moment. They lack understanding of how and why the society and its politics operate in the way they do so, they are much easier to deceive and harder to train on being effective Controverts.[vi] The old aphorism of, "history not repeating itself, but it rhymes," aptly describes the challenge. Most people only live to survive the immediate concerns foisted upon them in their lifetime which means few learn lessons or conveyance of critical knowledge to others making them susceptible to making the same mistakes. In a similar vein, politicians, tycoons, activists, and others will make similar promises, gestures, deceptions, and lies to persuade others to follow them. Understanding the cultural, political, and economic history of the Western nation helps to not only identify patterns of deception but also identify counterarguments and framing the most effective parameters of a topical discussion to render "spin" ineffective. History provides enough information to identify precedents and consequences of policies, promises, and laws that are made to pander to loyalists that quintessentially don't change over time, just the superficial form of the false promise changes to suit the sensibilities of the groups being catered.

There are no real shortcuts to developing skilled Controverts, even with ANI to support identifying FBE weaknesses or falsehoods in their propaganda. The most effective way to build Controvert specialists is having the more scholarly among them conduct in-depth training and study, but there should also be a cliff-notes version of training for all the Information Warfare units. Part of this training needs to be a foundational understanding of the culture and politics of the nation. This means understanding culture from every period of the nation's history, not just contemporary culture. Exposing NRF members to past media such as old music, movies, newsreels, and speeches not only expands the Controverts' contextual understanding, but also gives them a more realistic understanding of the cultural limitations the FBE will face. Old movies show not just attitude differences, but these will also reveal the common behavior patterns through the generations that help propagandists and false promisers use to continuously exploit susceptible minds. Simple expansion of culture knowledge better orientates the Controverts to what the FBE uses as a basis for its propaganda as well as exposing some of the more obvious lies.

The next step to mitigate the weakness of poorly trained Controverts is to make them each pick one relevant topic to study in great detail. Have them read books, articles, and publications that were written in a different time frame instead of contemporary publications because the current controversies of that topic will discourage many authors from writing objectively. Older publications will be written with little bias if the topic was of small importance in that timeframe or the priorities were different, making the authors' bias focus on different parts of the same subject. After sufficient exposure, the trainees' brains will identify common patterns of manipulation, deception, falsehoods, and methods of omitting embarrassing facts. The beauty of this method is that people often use the same methods for all topics and specializing in one topical field gives them the means to manipulate that field to suit the powers that be of the time period will allow NRF analysts to better identify deceptions across all information warfare domains and topics.

Legal LOE Organization 2: The Memeticists and Propagandists

Propaganda is essential to win any war of any kind. Framing the progress of war to always appear to supporters that victory is within reach keeps morale of one's forces high while keeping the opponent's morale low. High morale pushes fighters and their supporters to endure longer fights, weather hardships more frequently, and are more adaptable to changing battle conditions. Unlike the Controverts who use the truth to sow internal division within the FBE, the memetic and propaganda units have three objectives: 1. Keep friendly forces' morale high 2. Support the Controverts in undermining enemy morale using deception and 3. Build public support for the NRF or at least keep the public apathetic and neutral. These objectives assist with gaining operational victories, even if it requires deception against both friend and foe.

Regardless of who is fighting in a war, the first casualty is always the absolute truth. To clarify, propaganda doesn't mean to always lie and deceive; sometimes the truth serves the intent of the messaging. Propaganda is about shaping narratives and attitudes to maximize a faction's fighting effectiveness to improve the odds of victory. Although fighting factions in a war may not always lie, neither side will ever tell the absolute truth. The absolute truth only serves itself, not any group of people because people are never completely right or on the side of truth. In war, no polity is perfect which consequently means there will be mistakes, defeats, setbacks, and bad fortune. If one prioritized truth over seeking victory then that faction motivated by ideological principle of honesty will lose. Honesty is not policy in war because others are using every means possible to actively try to kill the opponent. So, the NRF will have commonality with the FBE in trying to suppress absolute truth and always frame messaging that maximizes the morale of their faction while undermining their opponent.

In 5GW, the difference from other types of wars is propagandists will not prioritize reporting from traditional battlefields and the public is not the main audience. The NRF are targeting the hearts and minds of the enemy leadership while secondarily keeping the public insulated from most negative consequences of civil conflict. To accomplish this, the violence against the FBE leadership must be publicly downplayed by the NRF while emphasizing the FBE's failures that negatively impact the public or FBE supporters. For the NRF's forces, the propagandists must show progress even though 5GW is a slow clandestine form of fighting. This presents unique challenges of balancing contradictory propaganda objectives. Keeping loyal force's morale high while keeping the public oblivious to any social disruptions all while trying to destroy the morale of the enemy's leadership in a clandestine war is a unique and untried combination of propagandist challenges.

The NRF's supporters are the easiest audience of the three because an underdog force's membership would overwhelmingly consist of deeply committed believers in the cause. Instead of worrying about changing minds or indoctrination, the propagandists simply have to keep the motivation going. Morale boosting propaganda has many tried and true methods used in many conflicts of the past. The challenge the propagandists face is conveying morale boosting messages in a heavily censorious and communication poor environment. FBE proxies will use algorithms, backed by ANI, regulations, social activism, and physical intimidation to stifle any mass messaging sympathetic to their opponents. So, in the age of the soundbite and constricted means of communication, the NRF would likely keep to simple themes that are both easily understood and convey. The two most obvious themes of messaging are humor and news of victories. Humor is both a coping mechanism and tool to inspire as it eases the tension and reduces fear more effectively than anything short of alcohol. Also, unlike some themes or emotions, effective humor can easily transcend most social barriers including economic class, religion, ethnicity, or political affiliation. Humor gives the NRF propagandists great power to invigorate their forces while simultaneously diminish the psychological power of their enemy. Properly messaged humor is easy to deliver in short messages that are easily understood and can circumvent many censor control mechanisms of the FBE. ANI machine learning, as stated earlier lacks understanding and the NRF can use humorous implications and insinuations based on context of the situation to deceive and bypass censorious algorithmic online filters. The added advantage is the likely disposition of many FBE opponents will be a narcissistic sense of self-importance that deadens a sense of humor. Such opponents self-censor because of sensitive egos which amplifies the impact of humor-based propaganda. Also, such people would lack the skills to effectively counter such attacks in a propaganda war because they don't understand how humor works. Such events boost morale of friendly forces and undermines the enemies'; a true multifunctional weapon of psychological operations.

In modern political discourse, short pithy messages can set the tone and framework of any argument or topic. Memetics, the art of devising and then using memes to convey complex ideas in simple pictures and phrases is a technique vital to bypassing the constricted information domain. If properly devised, a meme can convey the ludicrousness, hypocrisy, or contradictions of a political argument, person, or organization. A simple picture, or collage of pictures with a few words can neuter complex propaganda messages and deceptions. Memes require human imagination, contextual understanding, and the literal depictions don't have to explicitly reference military, subversive, or political content. This makes memes very dynamic weapons against ANI-installed algorithm filters. This also means the enemy must understand the implications and nuances of the message in order to identify the potential propaganda and its impact which takes time. Memes are faster than any known countermeasures and can spread among targeted audiences before any counterpropaganda can be effectively devised. A simple but apt example is Winnie the Pooh. Winnie the Pooh is a friendly, warm-hearted character for children whose image was co-opted by Chinese netizens to mock and deride their autocratic leader, Xi Jinping. So effective was this mockery that Winnie the Pooh is a banned subject and the Chinese regime had to block these references regardless of context or person using them.[vii] In the Western nation, if such similar actions are taken, it would likely still aid the NRF as resentment from the general population would grow substantially against blanket punishments that affect both rebel and nonparticipant equally by completely censoring topics.

Memetics brings humor and morale building for friendly forces but can temporarily stun communities loyal to the FBE. If the meme effectively points out a contradiction, cognitive dissonance will spread amongst the FBE to the point that hypocrisy will reveal itself to the general public as there is no logical way to explain away the contradiction. A sufficient number of incidents where the NRF induce cognitive dissonance will be noticed by the public regardless of the information restrictions within the society. The effectiveness of such a campaign against the FBE can be revealed by how the attempts to counter these effective memes are executed.

If a meme reveals an accurate depiction of a situation or argument then it can do so in very simple layouts with few words. If the meme is protecting inaccurate or contradictory stances or falsehoods, then the memes will be complicated with a lot of text because it must not only convey an idea but negate all the highlighted faults from the message. Adding false context means more complexity to the message which in turn diminishes the impact of the message. Poor memetics will often lead to the action of, "too long, didn't read" and risk losing audience interest.

The second group of simple messages is conveying victories to NRF supporters and amplifying defeats to the FBE's leaders. This is more along the classic lines of war propaganda except many of the victories will occur in the information space and not physical battlefields. This adds complexity to the propagandists' mission especially since the NRF would seek to diminish the significance of the actual battlefield events in the public's eyes to maintain their apathy. The exception to this is any event that highlights the corrupt favoritism towards the FBE's minions over the rest of the population. Stoking resentment is an easy and safe means of keeping FBE's popular support at a low ebb. The key focus on this must be anything that diminishes the FBE's grip on its proxies within the Western nation's social and political institutions. Key legal victories in court, elections, bankruptcies of FBE-linked businesses, etc.; anything showing the FBE losing their clandestine grip on the Western nation to its own leaders. The main objective is to show the NRF that it is making progress without the destructive consequences of 4GW insurgencies while making FBE-backers and leaders increasingly nervous. The more nervous, the greater chance of the FBE leadership fracturing into chaos and helping to enable Step 3 to achieve final victory.

The other effort of the propagandists would be to assist the NRF in deceiving the FBE's forces into pursuing false leads or getting lured into traps. The FBE's reliance on insulated stove-piped information flows to maintain control means the leadership is deprived of key pieces of data to make effective decisions. NRF propagandists can create false or misleading stories to trick FBE leaders into actions that initially appear favorable but result in detrimental outcomes. Such actions require coordination with NRF intelligence units, infiltrators, and operational commanders to synchronize effective deception operations. The challenge for the opposing FBE face in such actions is that the NRF will be only limited by imagination and resources, giving the NRF a plethora of options and actions that will not always be foreseeable.

Strengths:

The decentralized nature of the NRF and having most of its actions being non-lethal provides them with a lot of flexibility. Most NRF actions can be regarded as harmless or just mean-spirited, certainly not sufficient to warrant brutal crackdowns. Even if crackdowns occur, the majority of the public will be unimpressed and regard the FBE as unnecessarily draconian as long as the NRF exposes the false narratives; the NRF recording and distributing footage of these abuses is one example. Being an information-centric LOE, the Memeticists and propagandists can effectively operate on a shoestring budget using everyday common use commercial audio-visual equipment making discovery by the enemy difficult. Common equipment and widespread availability of the "Internet of Things" 5G communication network enables these NRF units to have many access points to global communications that will be difficult to track. Unlike the Chinese or Russian internet, the Western nations' networks are far more decentralized with a lot of independent operating data centers, fiber-optic lines, communication nodes, and other backbone infrastructure. Even if the FBE somehow denied the NRF direct access to the larger communication hubs and networks, the sophistication of cyberwarfare would allow many Memeticists units to conduct modified versions of "living off the land" cyberattacks that exploit the vulnerabilities of a FBE network. Living off the land attacks exploit software tools already operating in targeted network such as PowerShell or Windows Management to subvert FBE-friendly networks covertly help to relay propaganda to the intended audiences.[viii] This is simplified further by how small the intended audience is for the propaganda targeting, either NRF or FBE, with the public only being a tertiary concern. This means resources don't have to go very far to effectively shape the information battlespace.

The other inherent NRF advantage is the type of creative, mischievous people who will be attracted to such missions. The NRF must grant considerable allowance for their operators to act independently to remain dynamic enough to evade the FBE's superior resources and manpower. The FBE's proxies are larger and inherently more cumbersome with the added difficulty of striving to create an autocratic centralized state which compounds the inefficiencies that further slowdown FBE reaction times. Every NRF Memeticist cell and unit will do things differently which makes eliminating the NRF propagandists more difficult. Aside from verbally and visually trolling their opposition, these NRF units will not directly partake in any illegal activity that will motivate the general public to rally to the FBE. Law-abiding information warriors with an already self-motivating ability to learn, adapt, and execute these propaganda operations with minimal oversight lowers their targeting profile as the FBE cannot afford to expend endless resources chasing online versions of Dennis the Menace. At least, FBE shouldn't but their thin-skinned personas will likely override such sensibilities. All the NRF leadership has to do is give the operational objective and target and then let the individual propaganda and Memeticist units decide on how to best accomplish the assignment.

Weaknesses:

During the insurgencies of Afghanistan and Iraq, the Islamist and Taliban organizations' propaganda efforts focused on large-scale eye-catching attacks to embarrass the Coalition's security forces and government. Much of the propaganda focused on tactical attacks on convoys and patrols, executing captives, or suicide bombings of public areas and government facilities. The propaganda focused on conveying a sense of futility in the foreign powers remaining in these countries by undermining credibility with the Iraqi, Afghani, and Western publics. A defeat by a thousand cuts of bad publicity to attrit the occupying forces' willpower. Regardless of the effectiveness, the propaganda campaign was relatively simple where the videos were posted by the convenience of local circumstances and rarely coordinate beyond a local region.[ix] This meant minimal coordination beyond the funding aspect allowing insurgent organizations such as Al-Qaeda in Iraq's, later ISIS', Al-Furqan Media Arm to remain decentralized with individual cells being largely self-sufficient. The NRF will likely operate in this way for day-to-day operations but they cannot focus on attacks or terrorism of the public. Their effort must focus on the FBE and their proxies almost exclusively, but attempting to build a higher profile with the public will be exceptionally tempting.

5GW fundamentally is highly coordinated, precise, and overwhelming information blitzkrieg. Steps 1 and 2 LOEs are designed to keep the FBE proxies continuously off-balance while the small lethal direct-action units focus on eliminating the FBE leaders, the key center of gravity. For the NRF to succeed, it must devise methods to reach out to all the various propaganda cells and synchronize all of the propaganda actions to mutually support the operations of the other NRF cells and units while keeping each cell oblivious to NRF criminal activities. Linking the propaganda to match the other NRF operations without risking exposure to FBE intelligence collectors will be complicated and dangerous. This means the NRF must somehow incorporate senior leader planning of major operations with the NRF's propagandists while keeping operational security intact. The propagandists will be asked to prepare certain messages without ever knowing why while de-conflicting with other cells' operations. Balancing operational security, local propaganda needs, national-level propaganda needs, and maintain a means of communication that protects the users' identities from both the FBE and each other makes the propagandists' mission very difficult and easy to disrupt.

Legal LOE Organization 3: Civic Nullifiers

The NRF cannot succeed unless it can pin down and stall the FBE's efforts to defeat them. Ceding cultural and institutional ground to the FBE's "nudging" campaigns guarantees eventual defeat as the popular perception of the public will eventually align with the totalitarian outlook of the FBE leadership. Going on the cultural and information offensive requires the NRF to use the FBE's own methods against them to stifle the effectiveness of "nudging" the society to autocratic rule. The NRF must nullify all the FBE imposed new civics designed to exhaust the population into submitting to becoming an autocratic society. Engaging with and subverting the corrupted institutions, corporations, and other organizations the FBE uses for societal conversion is a necessary LOE for the NRF. Since most of the FBE's efforts are done using the state, economic, and cultural systems and processes already in place, most of the NRF's nullification efforts would be done through the FBE's own system.

By using legal means, the FBE will often be flummoxed in trying to find a simple counter to stop the NRF and the FBE will have to slow down operations and use more resources to keep their main LOEs functioning. Delay, stall, and distract the FBE in every civil facet of the Western nation will spread FBE resources thin and exhaust them by political and social attrition. Pointing out the injustices, double-standards, and contradictions in how the FBE proxies administer the civil society while simultaneously challenging the cultural changes will ignite fury in much of the FBE's Atomized, Nimbyist, and information operation media forces to shift all attention on these NRF public efforts. This in turn helps blind the FBE to the NRF's covert and lethal activities. Civic Nullifier units are the provocateurs to misdirect their enemy. The FBE's "nudging" is a full-scale operation across every facet of society which means the NRF's Civic Nullifiers will have to specialize in confronting their enemy by the type of nudging. NRF Civic Nullifier units will need to attack FBE "nudging" in three broad groupings of legal lawfare, challenging cultural standards, and political activism.

The Lawfare Nullifiers are NRF elements that will actively participate in the Western nation's judicial system to contest every legal action carried out by FBE proxies. The importance and effectiveness of these nullifiers will depend on which Western country has the 5GW civil war. Some have a tradition of being highly litigious such as Germany, Austria, the UK, and the United States and will have a wider range of options than in other more restricted legal systems.[x] The corrupted judiciary will give preferential treatment to those who pledge fealty to FBE causes and aid in FBE interests. The FBE's Atomized and Nimbyist forces often gain special privileges and dispensation via court cases or sympathetic officers of the court, such as public prosecutors or appointed judges. These legal proxies in the court system can either provide reduced sentences for any criminal acts that the FBE loyalists carry out or in regions where FBE control is absolute, just drop charges altogether and only prosecute anyone interfering with the FBE's minions. These FBE legal proxies can also shield and protect nonprofit, corporate, and activist proxies from civil litigation.

Inversely, the FBE proxies can indict, prosecute, or facilitate lawsuits against NRF or suspected sympathizers to help quell dissent. The best part for the FBE is there will rarely be a need to direct or coordinate these actions, just appointing Nimbyist or Atomized fanatics into the proper positions is all that is required. Their biases and prejudices will do the rest autonomously. Punishing the NRF via means of commonly accepted legal processes helps sustain FBE political legitimacy as their power over society is not yet absolute. This means the Western nation's legal system still has sufficient independence for the NRF to use its procedures and rules to at least resist, if not legally defeat the FBE proxies. Just delaying the FBE's subversive legal machine will cost the FBE resources and time which will create opportunities for NRF operational successes.

Given the importance and power of the legal system, a legitimate question is why doesn't the FBE simply impose a legal system where it always rules in the FBE's favor and no dissent can have any legal recourse something akin to the People's Republic of China's People's Courts? The FBE campaign of control would only be successfully achieved through gradualism which includes getting the general public to accept new autocratic processes. Successfully assimilating the population into such changes requires slow incremental implementation to prevent overt rebellion. As each new generation of the Western nation's population grows accustomed to each new incremental change of the judiciary, the more thoroughly autocratic it will become. For the FBE to successfully convert a Western judicial system completely to an autocratic corporatist-style system peaceably would require several generations. Judicial abuse or oppression is one of the more immediately noticeable changes in a society, even by an apathetic populace so the FBE must proceed cautiously. By the time the NRF appears, the courts will only have been partially corrupted.

Civic Lawfare Nullifier units wouldn't just consist of pro bono lawyers and legal scholars. The NRF can exploit the inherent weaknesses of the FBE's proxies to infiltrate and undermine the corrupted judicial system from within. The FBE's grip on power relies on their proxies installing completely loyal members to key positions in systems and organizations as rapidly as possible. Loyalty over competence helps the FBE hasten the conversion of Western nation institutions but consequently leave these same institutions functionally weaker. Persons who are loyal to corrupt systems are usually less competent than those people appointed in merit-based systems because the loyalists are chosen for their complete dependency on the FBE leadership's beneficence to survive. Competent people risk becoming independent or belligerent to FBE interests. Consequently, like the cultural and industrial institutions, the corrupted legal system will have lower standards and recruitment criteria that enables the easily manipulatable Atomized and Nimbyist pawns to be hired. In the age of falsifiable information, fake personalities that have the appearance of loyalty to FBE causes and have the token criteria of one or more Atomized groups make it easy for the NRF to make covert nullifiers officially "qualified" for judicial-related jobs. In such circumstances, the NRF's nullifiers will easily infiltrate these systems but once that occurs, they must cunningly use the rules and regulations to hinder the FBE as any outright sabotage exposes the nullifiers to dismissal, intimidation, or elimination.

For instance, some nullifiers could get key positions with juror commissions and modify jury selection lists in key court districts to ensure select NRF members are always in jury pools. To maintain cover, these jury commission nullifiers would only "rig" the jury selection lists during times of critical need. If properly executed, NRF loyal members would carry out jury nullification on key cases to maintain NRF operational momentum. Another example is NRF nullifiers becoming law clerks who, if properly skilled, use FBE-relevant legalese to manipulate and sway FBE-sympathetic judges on technicalities or mislead the FBE judge on how they would benefit from certain decisions. Other nullifiers in prosecution offices could help sabotage cases with technical mistakes, expose other office members' off-color remarks about Atomized groups, etc. The possibilities are endless, but all of these require patience and selecting the right targets for the right moment. These judicial nullifiers' actions would be most effective when done in synchronized action with other NRF LOEs and nullifiers. Although inhibiting the FBE's ability to use the legal system is vital, it is not the only civic institution that requires nullification.

The next broad category of nullifiers is both easier to recruit in large numbers and operate openly but is more strategically focused and will have limited impact on operational efforts: the New Culture Nullifiers. The new culture is one that replaces the organic culture of the Western nation with a technocratically constructed one. This is the "Lei Feng-ing" conditioning of society to embrace totalitarian values of conformity, minimal critical thinking, and deference to the FBE's designated leaders. The New Culture Nullifiers' mission is to challenge and then reverse the cultural messaging and moral systems by embracing the Western nation's traditional beliefs, concepts, stories, and ideas. This process is entirely public in nature and does not require covert or clandestine action, at least not until the last phase of the 5GW conflict.

The New Culture Nullifiers use social media and other public information forums to criticize, mock, and undermine any and all content produced by the FBE proxies to deaden their influence on the general population. As stated in the FBE's LOE, the Lei Feng-style of propaganda in all forms of entertainment and cultural morals must be repetitively imprinted on the public as the quality of political propaganda is inherently boring and unimaginative. Advocating for ethics of conformity and blind deference to a "perfect system" of B.F. Skinner-like social engineering is designed to be understood as broadly across the population as possible; the broader the scope of the messaging, the shallower the content of the propaganda. Conformity automatically means less critical thinking so FBE-proxy propaganda would need to endorse mediocrity and praise it as the highest standard to stifle substantive thought. The Cultural Nullifiers' challenge is not only to hinder the stupefying effects of the FBE's cultural propaganda but make the Western nation's people want substantive cultural enrichment and creativity again. This is more of a challenge than it may first appear because the FBE's propaganda is simple, repetitive and often entices the audience with added elements to provide instant emotional gratification. Inputting gratuitous sexual-related themes and performances in stories is the most obvious, but the more subtle effects include making the cultural conditioning psychologically safe. The FBE messages and stories always deal with what is socially accepted and never makes the audience confront uncomfortable topics or concepts that risk contravening authoritative opinion. Making people feel safe, emotionally stilted with gratuitous distractions, and morally superior by obliging the social narrative keeps the audience comfortable, even if they are bored. The NRF Cultural Nullifiers have to make the public want to substantively think which can be uncomfortable, especially to sheltered minds. This NRF LOE will require subtlety and repetitiveness to imprint their own messaging and time.

Nullifying the new technocratic cultural zeitgeist will take years and so will not be able to directly affect the NRF's other operations. Instead, these NRF units would need to be used at a strategic level to broadly impact national shifts in public sentiment which is slow. First, the nullifiers have to overcome the complacency of the public regarding the new forms of cultural messaging, then convince the public that more traditional messaging was superior in all of its guises whether in ethics, stories, music, or art, and then finally reclaim all of the venerated objects of the Western nation's culture that FBE repurposed for its messaging. Changing public taste would take numerous attempts with a lot of patience as the public must get tired of the new culture's indoctrination propaganda first. The propaganda and indoctrination will be at its strongest when it's first introduced because it will be fresh and novel to the public to help retain interest. Once the novelty wears off after numerous repeats of doctrinal messaging, then the "Lei Feng" condition will become vulnerable to criticism. Since so many of the variables influencing the effectiveness of the cultural nullification mission are determined by the public, the NRF must acclimate this to LOE to accommodate the public's changing sentiment, not NRF operational activities.

The long operational campaign of reversing the cultural nudging would occur in phases as the priority and objective change with the public's sentiment towards NRF efforts. The first phase is building up the credibility of the NRF's critiques of the new "Lei Feng" culture in the general public's perspective. To successfully build up credibility, the NRF nullifiers must first endure intense levels of criticism because the public will not initially understand why people would push back against the new culture. To the decadent, apathetic public, the new cultural changes are just naturally occurring social changes, unwilling to understand political motivations behind the new cultural mores. People, generally speaking, don't accept they are going to make a mistake or that they are being misled until after the fact. Most people don't want admit to themselves they can be deceived, manipulated, or be gullible and will rationalize any detrimental thing as long as it reinforces their sense of comfort and belonging. The public will think that since something is new and hasn't been tried, the critics are jumping the gun and are not giving the new cultural phenomena a chance. The public want to immediately believe "authoritative" declarations that the new culture is more moral, entertaining, and socially beneficial because the public believe they get an improved society without having to do any work themselves. The appeal of the joys of lazy greed with getting instant gratification by just sitting back and conforming is very strong.

The NRF nullifiers cannot immediately start with warnings about political ramifications, social divisions, or other grand concepts as most people don't associate their daily lives with such things. Instead, the nullifiers must appeal to the public's sense of personal satisfaction, be it moral, pleasure, or intellectual in nature. The nullifiers must highlight the stagnating effects the FBE's "nudging" culture will have on the public's satisfaction. Again, the public would not initially believe the NRF nullifiers' critiques of the new cultural products and activities, but it is important for the NRF to criticize the FBE's new culture immediately. This will show the public over time that the NRF critics were correct from the beginning to help build legitimacy in the NRF's assertions that the FBE's ideas are feckless and boring. The initial critiques would need to be technical ones on the cultural products—poor writing, banal lyrics, bad characters, inconsistent lore, ugly art, betraying the original vision of a story, or bland dialogue. Latch onto things that diminish the instant gratification for a politically indifferent public which incentivizes them to start paying attention to more of the new culture's flaws because these diminish the public satisfaction. As the novelty of the new culture grows stale over time and the public becomes increasingly indifferent to indoctrination, the NRF doesn't automatically win because the public will likely have accepted many of the cultural changes to decorum, ethics, and societal behavior along the way.

The "Lei Feng" culture will not fully indoctrinate the generations who've experienced the older traditions and understand beliefs other than the new culture. The greater danger is the FBE's new culture nudges the standards of what younger generations are initially exposed to and taught to accept. Over time, these younger generations will have lower expectations from cultural products and expect a shallow baseline of societal conformity as the norm. Older cultural icons and products will not be republished or discussed and will gradually fade away. The less thinking, but more shallow younger generations will not necessarily embrace all of the new culture, just a little more than the preceding and so on until the new culture is the only culture. The NRF nullifiers successfully convincing the public that the new culture is bad for satisfaction must then re-shift the public back into embracing non-FBE cultural ideas to demonstrate there are more satisfactory alternatives. From the NRF perspective, the society's re-embracing of the Western nation's organic culture and ideas from before the FBE's rise would be the most effective means of shifting the cultural zeitgeist away from the FBE.

The next phase of the New Culture Nullifier units is to link the rekindled use of non-FBE culture with the public's desire for satisfaction. There are two courses of action the nullifiers would need to take simultaneously: re-introducing old cultural products and creating new products using traditional themes. Re-introducing old cultural products that accessorize alluring themes and styles can reawaken the public's knowledge about their nation's cultural history and place in the world. Matching popular FBE propaganda-imposed trends with trends from the past that easily blend together can ease the public into older materials. Modern comic heroes for instance, come from older comic books yet there are many influential comic characters that were created before the current characters known to the mainstream population whose re-introduction could easily translate for modern audiences. These old characters, untouched by FBE proxies, could subtly reintroduce the Western nation's cultural influences. A real-world example would be reintroducing *The Shadow* which directly led to the creation of *Batman*. The *Shadow* is a case of a forgotten traditional cultural product untouched by the mainstream whose stories bring classical tales with exciting violent themes that would stimulate and entertain yet still be different from current comic cultural products. Or given the rising crime rates of American cities after the COVID-lockdown period,[xi] the public might welcome the reintroduction of *Death-Wish* or *Dirty Harry* as an example of bringing back old cultural icons that fit within contemporary social conditions and themes.

The second course of action is to make the old culture new again with new cultural products and icons. The challenge is that the broader the appeal of a product means the shallower its substantive content which means the mass-propaganda the NRF tries to fight will be shallow. The most impactful FBE messaging will be from large scale products such as movies or online streaming series that can bedazzle while stifling audience thinking. The NRF nullifiers cannot directly challenge these by making new large-scale cultural products like studio-produced movies as costs and regulations would be prohibitive. Instead, the nullifiers would create new niche products to establish cultural footholds in various industries and institutions to grow their influence to compete with the NRF's new culture. Numerous examples include art in its various forms, novels, comic books, graphic novels, music, video games, and small independent online productions. In all probability, this would mainly attract those who have the most interest in cultural subjects, a small contingent of the public. NRF nullifiers would use this small foothold to build the foundational infrastructure to grow and build up the NRF's cultural sphere of influence. This phase lays the groundwork for building the nullifiers' reputations as legitimate members of the Western nation's cultural institutions, paving the way for the third and final phase.

The final phase is the retaking of cultural products subverted to the FBE's new "Lei Feng" culture which will only take place in last stage of the 5GW conflict. This phase would occur after the NRF have successfully co-opted a sizable portion of the Western nation's elite that consequently cripples much of the FBE's proxy apparatus. This enables the NRF to finally work through the society's institutions to help retract or disassemble FBE programs, messaging, and organizations after years of operating as political outcasts. The Cultural Nullifier units would work in conjunction with both the NRF and co-opted FBE leaders to restart or retroactively revise the popular cultural products subverted by the FBE to pre-FBE condition.

Retconning cultural icons subverted by the FBE may not seem important at first since victory at this stage would appear inevitable so, why expend resources on salvaging now perverted cultural products? The reason is much of the subverted cultural products will be the ones that defined generations of the Western nation and leaving husks of FBE propaganda would create large gaps in the cultural development history of that nation. It would implicitly appear the NRF surrendered to the FBE's arguments and moral tales of these subverted cultural products and thereby appearing to agree with the FBE propagandists. This would leave a cultural void that would allow utopianist totalitarians to restart their subversion of the society. Retconning would not be cheap, but the natural commitment of NRF nullifiers for their love of their nation's icons and stories will easily recruit the expense and expertise to fix them. Getting the financial capital to take intellectual ownership of iconic cultural properties would involve numerous grassroots cooperatives working in coordination with co-opted elites' capital to acquire the rights. This first step of financing is the most difficult as the follow-on steps of discrediting and firing all who subverted the products will be much easier.

There are real world examples of new acquirers of a culturally impactful intellectual property altering those iconic cultural products. This has been done in peacetime with aggressive determination by new owners so, the motivational drive for NRF cultural fixers in a time of culturally altering civil conflict will be stronger. The Disney Corporation's abolition of the *Star Wars'* Expanded Universe as canon and declaring it all unimportant legacy tales is the perfect example of retconning to make way for another's agenda sparking a fierce debate among the old hardcore fanbase and Disney fans.[xii], [xiii], [xiv], [xv] Another real-world example of this is occurring with the *Star Trek* franchise. The lovers of this cultural product became quickly divided by the style, tonal, character, and story changes by CBS with the streaming shows *Star Trek: Discovery* and *Star Trek: Picard*. Many fans believe these new shows are of lower quality and accuse the showrunner Alex Kurtzman, a man reputed to have a substandard imagination and reveling in mediocrity, of perpetrating this decline.[xvi], [xvii] These divisions became pronounced enough that *Star*

Trek as a franchise has diminished in scale and cultural impact in the Western world. Cultural wars between lovers of cultural products and the makers of the products already exist and will exist until the end of time. NRF nullifiers would have an abundant pool of potential recruits and, with sufficient capital, could effectively retcon any targeted cultural product or icon. Fandoms would lead the way on how to retcon the targeted properties.

In theory, a sizable portion of fans, with the financial backing of wealthy donors, could acquire the rights to a franchise to retcon any number of stories with explanations that would fit in with the original lore that satisfies most fandom members. As example of how the NRF could retcon an established property, the CBS-run *Star Trek* franchise has Q, a powerful demigod-like alien that can create artificial worlds with mere thought, dying of some illness. A retcon could state *Picard* and *Discovery* were figments of his imagination made manifest—an alien version of a fever dream manifested in an artificial world of his making where his poor understanding of human nature created poor caricatures of the human race in that fever world. Just one idea improvised on the spot to demonstrate these debates and activities already happen in the cultural world and are easy to coopt and implement once the property rights and financial backing is acquired. However, patience must be emphasized as the nullifiers can eliminate FBE-directed changes to cultural icons and products easily only after the 5GW conflict has shifted in the NRF's favor.

The NRF's New Culture Nullifiers have one final advantage in their mission, lacking the need for much organization. Most of the nullifiers will already exist and organically grow as a natural backlash against the cultural changes. They will simply be devotees to their cultural niches who will notice the subversive changes before the mainstream public. The NRF will only occasionally have to liaison with these groups to coordinate and synchronize on some of the larger efforts as well as ensure smooth transitions between the nullification phases. Since these organic movements will exist with or without the NRF, financial backing will not be needed until much later in the conflict when the nullifiers become a direct challenge to the largest FBE cultural products such as films or franchises. This also means the NRF's New Culture Nullifiers' activities will remain strictly within the law which combined with the minimal coordination needed means few, if any, cultural nullification efforts can be directly affiliated with any illegal NRF subversive activity. This strategic LOE will be the most autonomous of the NRF movements and will only require the occasional course correction to maximize effectiveness to achieve NRF objectives.

The final broad category of nullifiers is the Political. These are NRF-aligned lobbyists, elected officials, and politicians who use legislative and executive actions to undermine the FBE's stranglehold on the Western nation's state institutions. This mission is more straight forward than the New Culture Nullifiers' one because they just hinder the FBE's subversion of government activities, regulations, and laws from being implemented. The FBE would succeed in subverting the Western nation by co-opting key elites in the private and nonprofit sectors of society first. Seeking out the state and its public officials would have to be the last part of the foreign-backed subversion to avoid public detection. Consequently, this means the FBE would have accumulated a lot of political and lobbying influence by its private proxies to stop most senior officials from challenging FBE influence early on. By the time the NRF arises, the political class and the state institutions will likely be in the midst of chaos as legal and procedural battles will rage over the implementation of the FBE's new autocratic society. There would be many provinces, townships, counties, and other municipalities that are either neutral or hostile to FBE dominated regions, providing the NRF the opportunity to create inter-governmental political conflict. The NRF could then infiltrate the political process of the Western nation's anocracy to deadlock as much government action as possible to disrupt support to the FBE and its proxies.

In such circumstances, using traditional messaging highlighting corruption, incompetence, and autocratic behavior of FBE-sympathetic public figures will be minimally effective. These public figures would rely on back-door support from the FBE that would fund campaigns, facilitate bribes, and deliver their proxy sepoys to any electoral area to compel compliance so that these public figures will not fear accountability. Atomized and Nimbyist sepoys of society will be a minority but sufficiently militant to stifle any legal organized resistance to the FBE nudging efforts and intimidate people into ignoring the poor quality of FBE-back public figures. The Western nation's state institutions would take time to fully subvert and the FBE would try both legal and illegal means to co-opt the weakened anocratic institutions quickly. Having NRF Political Nullifiers in public office slows down this effort drastically.

The FBE cannot use the state to fully mobilize the Western nation for a 3GW civil conflict if the NRF resists the temptation to secede and openly revolt. A 3GW conflict would enable the FBE to openly and aggressively purge the state government of all dissenting views in the name of saving the country from open civil war. Such an event creates the overt autocracy for the FBE. If the NRF resorts to a 5GW campaign instead, the FBE will be forced to co-opt the state slowly, as it did with cultural and private institutions, with social nudging. The majority of societal nudging efforts will come from the FBE's private proxy organizations while the FBE will use coopted members of the state apparatus to help protect these efforts. These subverted state organization elements would implement two forms of protection for the FBE: subsidizing FBE loyalists and target the NRF for detainment or destruction. This puts the FBE's state allies in a quandary as they must aid the FBE without the full support of all state resources. Instead, the FBE must keep the façade of democratic processes alive to avoid open revolt since the FBE's anocracy would lack the legitimate justification of fighting an open civil war to impose an overt dictatorship.

The FBE public figures will maneuver the state to provide protection to the proxies and their social "nudging" campaign but only by covert or duplicitous means. The FBE proxies rely on private organizations and large quantities of expendable sepoys in the form of Atomized and Nimbyist groups to informally enforce the FBE's will. Fully self-financing the Atomized and Nimbyist sepoys out of the FBE's coffers would be very expensive as these pawns are required to organize protests, riots, harassment campaigns, smear campaigns, misinformation operations, and violent crimes for which the FBE leaders can plausibly deny culpability. The more logical course of action for the FBE is to use politically backed subsidy programs to help support the FBE proxy efforts. The FBE state supporters can disguise the subsidies as social welfare programs, industry protection, trade protection, education grants, environmental protection, etc. The possibilities are endless and these will help ensure the Atomized and Nimbyists receive their "bread and circus" payments.

The state sympathizers must also simultaneously hunt down NRF activities while providing financial and legal protection for the FBE proxies. Most NRF activities are within the bounds of the law and the ability of the state to provably link these with the NRF's violent activities will be difficult and will only occasionally succeed. So, the FBE public figures will have to invent rules, laws, and processes that stymie otherwise legitimate activities the NRF members might undertake. Declaring an action, writing, or speech criminal or accuse NRF members of inciting violence helps constrict the NRF's efforts while also enabling the Atomized and Nimbyists to target exposed NRF elements for more violent actions. The state figures cannot directly partake in political violence, but they can create circumstances that help FBE proxies to carry them out.

These various means of state coercion and stealing public money to support FBE activities will still have to go through the legal process of legislation or executive actions to retain the veneer of legality and legitimacy in the public eye. Having the NRF's more charismatic and politically savvy leaders take positions of political office, no matter how small, can impede the nefarious FBE abuses of state power. Obstructing legal and procedural actions is only a holding mechanism to delay the FBE, making such acts insufficient for the Political Nullifiers. Attack is the best form of defense in politics and ruthless maneuvering to sabotage the FBE using the same legislative and procedural tools is vital for the NRF's success. Simply blocking the Atomized and Nimbyists' subsidies will not work as the FBE can launch propaganda and legal campaigns to discredit NRF public figures as cruel, heartless, bigoted, etc. Instead, more clever political maneuvering is required that can use the FBE's own standards and propaganda themes against them to shield NRF efforts against any political backlash.

For instance, the FBE's state puppets will likely have geographic and constituency strongholds that will blindly support these public figures in exchange for their "bread and circus" payouts. The NRF could either pay or find other means to incentivize more Atomized from other parts of the country to move to these strongholds to overwhelm the "bread and circus" infrastructure. By doing so, the NRF can pit various factions of Atomized and Nimbyists against one another as they battle for their share of subsidized largess. This is but one example of political cleverness NRF-backed public figures can use to disrupt and hinder the FBE-backed public figures.

Political Nullifiers will always be in the limelight and must never take part in extralegal activities of the NRF's more violent direct-action cells and units. Plausible deniability of violence while waging fair, if aggressive, political actions keep the public either divided or indifferent to NRF-political obstruction. The indifference prevents the FBE from mobilizing the whole of society against the NRF but this only succeeds if they continuously work to keep the public indifferent as public opinion is fickle. Also, keeping critical issues in the public's eye slows down the FBE's state pawns from enacting detrimental legislation and executive actions to avoid negative political consequences. The NRF's strategic leadership will still need to coordinate political activity with their other operations but they will not need the NRF public figures to directly participate. Like the Cultural Nullifiers, these public figures are a strategic asset but mainly for defense unlike the information offensive capability of the other types of civic nullifier units. The public figures are too exposed to directly support any major operation, especially if it involves illegal or violent activities. Like all civic nullifiers, the political nullifiers are most effective in the peaceful information warfare domain.

Strengths:

Western nations' societies already have people who actively try to nullify their political opponent's efforts in the courts of law, court of public opinion, political lobbying, and cultural criticism. Many will wear their ideological positions openly to garner followers to help advocate for their cultural or political position. All of this is done in peacetime without the threat of civil conflict, secession, or foreign subversion being considerations. The NRF's potential recruitment pool would already be large even before the anocracy's degradation. Thousands of online and public advocates against perceived cultural wrongs could be rapidly assembled and unleashed on multiple targets at once. Advocacy groups, nonprofits, and others already organize astroturfed movements to stymie various civic proceedings that could be used as ready-made templates such as the civil rights movement of the 1960s or pro-immigration nonprofits in the U.K. With so many committed people to single issue causes existing in the West, the NRF nullifier units will be able to operate in the open and be almost indistinguishable from neutral or FBE advocacy groups. Simply, nullifiers are already in abundance and will have already established societal camouflage as they will blend in with other advocates.

Nullifier units' mission will attract many experts and skilled individuals who have the ability to operate autonomously and under their own initiative which simplifies command and control considerations. Allowing the nullifiers to pick and choose their own legal and cultural battles reduces logistical, political, and training costs for the NRF organization. The civic nullifiers would find and pick their own allies, networks, and co-workers using the same motivational zeal as the basis. Consequently, each civic nullifier unit or cell would be highly customized to carry out specific actions exceptionally well while being a minimal operational security risk. These cells would consist of people with strong bonds and years of interpersonal trust, making infiltration exceptionally difficult. The political nullifiers would be slightly different in that they would need to use deception and trickery to latch onto "reputable" political organizations to gain access to political resources. Nevertheless, these units would have a natural advantage of forming around already existing groups that organically exist to oppose cultural or political phenomena in their nation. Civic nullifiers are peaceful advocates co-opted to the NRF cause, requiring only slight cosmetic adjustments to their natural organizations.

Weaknesses:

Cultural and Legal Nullifier units must develop a "humble" reputation if they are going to survive. Humble in this case requires more than just humility. Being distracted by drama induced by excessive ego would discredit any and all actions associated with megalomaniac personalities. Individual nullifier cells will need to attract attention as part of their mission to become successful. Having no reputation from losing legal cases or being ignored by audiences render nullification efforts mute. The nullifiers, or at least a few individuals in each unit, must garner public reputation and notoriety to have the credibility to nullify FBE efforts in cultural and legal circles. They should not try to become national sensations like movie stars, YouTube's Mr. Beast, or anything that provokes common gossip, memes, or worse make the FBE want to target them specifically. They must become celebrities in their niche of operational specialty while keeping grounded to the reality of their situation. As seen with many celebrity downfalls, the temptation of excessive fame and fortune is difficult to resist.

For the Political Nullifiers, their actions will be mostly reactive to FBE efforts since the NRF will be a minority in the public institutions and bodies. Even if the NRF could maintain a united front on every course of action against the FBE, the FBE can financially outpace the NRF in almost all political events and elections. The NRF would not have sufficient political power in most of the Western nations to implement drastic reforms via the legitimate political process. Slowing down FBE-supported policies and legislation with obstruction is an easy action but abusing this action is risky to the NRF public figures. If the rest of the NRF organization fails to provide sufficient context for their public figures to justify their obstructionist behavior to the voters, sooner or later the public will view them as the problem in government. The NRF will have to balance the need to obstruct with the need of choosing which political battles are worth risking their hold on public office. This balancing act will become more complicated because of the high risk of factionalism with public figures. Even if the NRF successfully gets people elected to office, there is no such thing as gratitude in politics. Some of the figures will become corrupted by the allure of power without responsibility and just rubber stamp the FBE's agenda for easy money and job security. Also, regional issues could supersede the NRF's national-level strategic goals and get the Political Nullifiers bogged down in local problems distracting them from assisting with large-scale operations.

Finally, operational security will be exceptionally challenging as these are going to be the public face of resistance against the FBE. The FBE's proxies will be able to build surveillance plans, targeting operations, and various schemes of chicanery to discredit and humiliate the NRF's public figures. The FBE may also ramp up the use of false flags with dozens of proxies infiltrating the NRF's public ranks to either assist the NRF's public figures or run as an NRF public figure. These double-agents could sow discontent and chaos amongst the Public Nullifier members that would prevent any organized efforts at disrupting FBE-backed policies. Screening potential Political Nullifiers, which includes both elected and appointed positions, will be essential if the NRF are to be effective.

---

[i] Patrick Brantlinger, *Bread and Circuses: Theories of Mass Culture as Social Decay*, (Ithica, NY: Cornell University Press: 1983): 71-78. https://ecommons.cornell.edu/items/0c5e7764-8e13-4c64-8337-dfaa6592b9b5

[ii] Lee Brown, "Connecticut Man Who Fought for Ukraine Lied About Being US War Hero Even to Wife Who Has Now Dumped Him," NY Post, April 24, 2023. https://nypost.com/2023/04/24/connecticut-man-who-fought-in-ukraine-lied-about-being-us-war-hero/

[iii] Sarah Westwood, "Climate Activists Invest in Property on Beaches They Say Are Disappearing," Washington Examiner, June 15, 2021. https://news.yahoo.com/climate-activists-invest-property-beaches-110000244.html

[iv] Michael Berens and John Shiffman, "Thousands of U.S. Judges Who Broke Laws or Oaths Remained on The Bench," Reuters Investigates, June 30, 2020. https://www.reuters.com/investigates/special-report/usa-judges-misconduct/

[v] Mykal McEldowney, "Undercover Video Shows Animal Abuse at Fair Oaks Farm," IndyStar, June 5, 2019. https://www.indystar.com/videos/news/2019/06/05/undercover-video-shows-animal-abuse-fair-oaks-farms/1357395001/

[vi] Saba Naseem, "How Much U.S. History Do Americans Actually Know? Less than you Think," Smithsonian Magazine, May 28, 2015. https://www.smithsonianmag.com/history/how-much-us-history-do-americans-actually-know-less-you-think-180955431/

[vii] Vanessa Romo, "Why a Horror Film Starring Winnie the Pooh has Run into Trouble in Hong Kong," NPR, March 23, 2023. https://www.npr.org/2023/03/23/1165504942/winnie-the-pooh-xi-jinping-china-film

[viii] Government Advisory, "People's Republic of China State-Sponsored Cyber Actor Living off the Land to Evade Detection," Department of Homeland Security's Cybersecurity & Infrastructure Security Agency, May 24, 2023. https://www.cisa.gov/news-events/cybersecurity-advisories/aa23-144a

[ix] Nathaniel Greenberg, "Islamic State War Documentaries," International Journal of Communication, v. 14, 2020, 1808-1829. https://ijoc.org/index.php/ijoc/article/download/9857/3028

[x] Herbert M. Kritzer, "Cross-National Patterns in Litigiousness," International Encyclopedia of the Social & Behavioral Sciences (Second Edition, 2015). https://www.sciencedirect.com/science/article/abs/pii/B9780080970868860821

[xi] Rob Gabriele, "2023 Crime Rates in U.S. Cities Report: Memphis, TN, Cleveland, OH, and Mobile, AL are among the worst U.S. cities for murder, robbery, and sexual assault," SafeHome.org, May 31, 2023. https://www.safehome.org/resources/crime-statistics-by-state/#crime-in-extra-small-cities-population-10000-99999

[xii] Reference site, "The Star Wars Expanded Universe: Comics, Novels, and Related Games in Canon and Legends," Reddit Subreddit. https://www.reddit.com/r/StarWarsEU/

[xiii] Andrew Todd, "How Disney Has Plundered The 'Star Wars' Expanded Universe - And What That Means for The Franchise," Slashfilm.com, June 4, 2018. https://www.slashfilm.com/558691/star-wars-expanded-universe-movies/

[xiv] Jesse Schedeen, "Between the Panels: It's Time to Bring Back the Star Wars Expanded Universe," IGN.com, December 18, 2015. https://www.ign.com/articles/2015/12/18/between-the-panels-its-time-to-bring-back-the-star-wars-expanded-universe

[xv] Danny Bojic, "Grand Admiral Thrawn Is About to Save Star Wars For The Second Time," Looper.com, April 7, 2023. https://www.looper.com/1251750/grand-admiral-thrawn-save-star-wars-second-time/

[xvi] Reference site, "Alex Kurtzman is the worst thing that happened to Star Trek," Reddit Redlettermedia Subreddit. https://www.reddit.com/r/RedLetterMedia/comments/txs0c9/alex_kurtzman_is_the_worst_thing_that_happened_to/

[xvii] JB Augustine, "Director Alex Kurtzman Explains What He Learned From His 'Biggest Failure,' 2017's The Mummy," Bounding into Comics, April 29, 2022. https://boundingintocomics.com/2022/04/29/director-alex-kurtzman-explains-what-he-learned-from-his-biggest-failure-2017s-the-mummy/

Chapter 26: NRF Overlapping Lines of Effort in Steps 1 & 2 – Bypass and Fix the FBE's Catalonia 2.0 with Illegal Activities

Resorting to peaceful and legal means of information warfare alone will not win a 5GW civil conflict. By its definition, a civil conflict compels the opposing polity to accede to the political demands of its rival polity when it would not voluntarily do otherwise. In terms of war, compulsion means inflicting sufficient strategic-level pain on the opponent to break their will to make them stop fighting for their cause. Pain from conflict comes in many forms to include the loss of political influence, loss of life, and the loss of economic prosperity and security. Peaceful actions can create some strategic pain against a rival political faction that is sufficient for peaceful democratic political processes but is only an inconvenience in a time of war. The NRF units in the previous chapter are designed to keep NRF's credibility viable with the Western nation's civilian populace and to throw the FBE's forces off-balance. Stopping at this stage would allow the FBE to eventually correct for these disruptions and regain both balance and momentum against the NRF. For the NRF to maximize their efforts to bypass and fix the FBE's proxies effectively, the disruptive peaceful actions must be carried out in coordination with more illicit Machiavellian activities to inflict lasting damage to their FBE opponents.

Options and Methods: Illegal Activities for Steps 1 & 2

Illicit activities in this case, are illegal but non-violent actions that target weak points in the established FBE systems and the proxies that sustain those systems. These activities carried out in coordination with the legal activities of the mentioned NRF unit types in the previous chapter will keep the FBE off-balance and vulnerable to follow-on violent kinetic attacks. These illegal units must maintain low profiles with various means to evade capture or arrest once the FBE's proxies uncover these activities. None of these illicit units' resort to physical violence like traditional insurgents as their mission is to bypass all FBE provocations for traditional open warfare and to pin the FBE proxies in place so the NRF's main lethal force can operate unmolested.

These illegal LOE organizations have the same objective as the legal ones except they work around the established rules and procedures to inflict politically impactful damage to FBE operations. Each LOE organization will specialize its illegal information warfare activities based on the type of target the organizations are assigned and these will range from individuals to nation-wide organizations. Since information warfare is the central effort in a 5GW conflict, the NRF will need to place great emphasis on keeping these illegal information warfare units alive and intact. The NRF will need to innovatively devise new doctrine, organization, training, and planning to mitigate the numerous means the wealthy FBE and its state proxy allies have at their disposal to find, mitigate, and eliminate enemy information warfare units in both cyberspace and the physical world.

Illegal LOE Organization 1: The 5GW Version of a Guard Operation: The "Yance-men"

In traditional large-scale combat operations as seen in 3GW conflicts, the guard force are combat units conducting a security operation to protect the main combat element by fighting the enemy to gain time while preventing the enemy locating and attacking the main combat element.[i] There is no equivalent in 5GW information-centric warfare, but the sophistication of biometrics, data aggregation, and persistent surveillance makes complete evasion impossible for the information warfare forces. The more illegal activities conducted, the more patterns of life are created that will be detected by the FBE and its automated information collection. As more and more nations embrace the concept of "smart cities" with all instrumentalities linked by the 5G "Internet of Things", the flexibility of cyber and information operations becomes more constricted as consumers trade privacy for ease of convenience.[ii] There is no way to avoid digital footprints or keeping one's patterns of life unseen by others in a developed Western nation, especially from a foreign-backed puppet group of wannabe totalitarians.[iii]

The only real solution for a 5GW-based rebellion is to create an information warfare version of a guard force to distract, deceive, and delay FBE units and squander their resources. Instead of the information warriors confronting the FBE alone and risk exposing their patterns of life, the guard force would be the critical combat multiplier to stall out the FBE pursuers. The guard force's mission would be to create numerous false patterns of life to mislead the FBE into pursuing the wrong targets. These false patterns of life must stand out in contrast to everything around them, especially the actual NRF operators, with the guard force being as conspicuous as possible without the FBE suspecting them of being decoys. The guard operation would involve fighting exclusively in the information space where the targets are reputation, time, and money. For this wargaming analysis, these units are referenced to as the "Yance-men".

In 1964, Philip K. Dick wrote a dystopian novel called *The Penultimate Truth* that takes place in the late 21st Century. In this science fiction world's backstory, World War III broke out between the two super-blocs, the NATO-descended West-Dem and the Warsaw Pact-descended Pac-Peop, which forced the majority of the populations in North America, Europe, and Soviet Union to live in underground bunker colonies. These colonies had farms and war factories to continue the fighting after the atomic exchange while the military and political elite stayed above ground to command the battle-droid armies in the radioactive hellscape. These elites were led by President Talbot Yancy and became known as Yancy's men, later the "Yance-men". The war ended shortly thereafter, but the surviving elites of the world realized they had the entire surviving human population tirelessly working underground unaware they were producing goods and technology for a war that had ended. Instead of informing the populace, the elites of both blocs agreed to mislead and deceive their respective populations into believing the war was ongoing.

The Yance-men created a false reality with misinformation and deception to manipulate the world's surviving population into staying underground manufacturing "war" droids, technologies, and goods for the exclusive use of the elites. The war droids were turned into work robots that repaired the land and built estates and plantations occupied by the handful of elites and their families. The Yance-men created an android version of Talbot Yancy to perpetually broadcast war speeches and morale-inspiring lies to keep the people working while the elites enjoyed a new

Eden built on the misled population's toil in underground factories. The Yance-men were masters of world perception and controlled a false-reality shaped by lies, manipulation, and misdirection. The Yance-men of the NRF will need to do the same to the perceptions of the FBE.

The Yance-men act as a countermeasure to the sophisticated advanced information technologies, artificial narrow intelligence, data analytics, and persistent collection capabilities available to the superiorly resourced FBE. The Yance-men would consist of volunteers with unique skills focused on showmanship and being able to accurately gauge human behavior with a personality penchant for thrill-seeking. These individuals will also be supported with numerous software bots in cyberspace to cause havoc on social media. These assets will confront state security and law enforcement agencies of the FBE-aligned state apparatus in the 5GW conflict. Their job is unique because they will not confront these forces to hurt, kill, or maim them, but to flummox, embarrass, and deceive the FBE's enforcement agents to the point it stifles their pursuit of the NRF's true information warfare operatives. Given that this concept in this context is new, few of the opponent forces will be prepared to counter these types of operations.

The Yance-men's mission is to protect the main information operations of the NRF so, the Yance-men's leaders need to know what operations need protecting. As the NRF will have to plan out various operations against both the FBE leadership and their proxies using information operations and direct combat actions in a 5GW version of combined arms, having covert access to FBE targets is essential to victory. The Yance-men's participation acts as the invisibility cloak for those NRF elements that "penetrated enemy lines" by keeping the FBE's eyes on the Yance-men. The Yance-men's first role is to study and identify the best options to distract the FBE's attention. Once the NRF's main effort actually begins to engage their true targets, the Yance-men must simultaneously lure and entice the FBE forces using various hijinks and false information to make them hunt down the Yance-men decoys. If the Yance-men are successful in luring the FBE's attention, then the Yance-men will carry out actions against the FBE security forces that result in public-relations disasters and scandals that ultimately discredit the FBE security forces' reputation in the eyes of the public. The Yance-men's operational options are categorized by FEES: 1. Fool's Errands 2. Embarrassments 3. Entrapment Schemes. Successfully executed FEES methods on the FBE will psychologically paralyze them with confusion, humiliation, and fear to make the FBE's forces more risk averse and less willing to hunt down NRF information operation units.

Successfully luring the FBE pursuers into Yance-men's traps requires a combination of key factors. The Yance-men operatives must create a compelling scenario to make the FBE want to refocus their attention while making sure the Yance-men's true intentions cannot be discovered, even as they are actively pursued. Finally, the outcome of whichever selected FEES option is exercised must ensure the targeted FBE pursuers realize and understand they've failed in their mission and the consequences are humiliating enough to increase the FBE's risk aversion for future pursuits.

Examples of lures and enticements range from online hoaxes to full-blown public setups with emplaced audio and visual recording equipment to catch the FBE out in an awkward situation. The online lures will be the easiest, cheapest, and most numerous to execute, but the downside being the FBE will not have to expend much manpower or resources in pursuing an exclusively internet-based lure. On the other end of the potential lure complexity are physically present setups by Yance-men cells using people in scripted situations. These are sophisticated and time consuming that require patience and coordination with other NRF elements for success.

Obvious simple lures include creating online chatrooms, forums, or create discussion threads using established major sites like Reddit or 4Chan. These could be run by one or two real human Yance-men managing dozens of bots, aid by ChatGPT-like models to improve sophistication. Bot-based chats can use the more radical and inflammatory language that is borderline incitement to violence while the human members act as the "moderate" or sensible voices that don't directly say anything criminal. The humans can be the lure for FBE recruitment to act as inside sources or the bots discuss "missions" to encourage greater monitoring of fake people. In the physical world, the Yance-men could start clubs, militias, charities, or front organizations advocating for anti-FBE political positions that deliberately drop ambiguous hints of potential violence to bring greater surveillance. Other lures could instead target FBE narratives rather than FBE pursuers such as "leaking" embarrassing revelations of prominent citizens voicing NRF sympathetic positions. The Yance-men will have an endless array of options that are limited by money and imagination. The reality is, deceiving people and organizations is easy, manipulating them into the desired outcome is difficult.

After a successful lure, the difficult part is to create an outcome of risk aversion. Risk aversion in modern bureaucracies and organizations occur when a person of authority invests their reputation by endorsing a project, event, or operation with the intention of improving clout and stature on the outcome for future promotion and then fail. Failure dampens the opportunities for advancement causing those persons to hesitate to endorse or outright cancel riskier but more impactful future operations. The Yance-men's lure provides an FBE pursuer the allure of enhancing their reputation by stopping a major NRF threat but end up wasting FBE time and resources.

In the examples of the lures, the enticements will be similar but the follow-through to the outcome will vary considerably. The bot-dominated online chats could discuss intricate detailed terroristic plans on FBE targets of high value that reveal dates and locations to encourage an FBE response. If the response leads a rapid reaction force of FBE to vacant lots, a child's birthday party, or disrupt another FBE operation then humiliation and reputational damage is achieved. The NRF would be at the location, but only to film the embarrassing actions to leak to the world, placing the FBE pursuers' superiors in an awkward position. In the case of security operations, there is such a thing as bad publicity. An alternate use for the online bot discussions if the NRF needed to tie up FBE cyber forces could be hinting to "new recruits" to a dark web site where the "real" planning is worked out. The Yance-men could then use the decoy site as labyrinthine matryoshka lockbox of encrypted layers where the FBE would need to credential steal from the bots to access each layer. There would be no end to the layers, just an infinite number of encryption layers in various guises to tie down FBE resources and time. Such an act would not be very substantial by itself, but if such decoy sites were done dozens of times throughout the Western nation, significant resources could be squandered.

The Yance-men's physical world clubs, associations, and militias would be created with only one goal in mind, attract the FBE's attention. So, the Yance-men would have to coordinate pantomimes of activities to arouse suspicion in the hope of enticing the FBE to send surveillance elements or even better, infiltrators and informants. Typically, in crime cases the informants put the unwitting criminals under surveillance as they perform criminal activity to build up sufficient evidence for arrest. The Yance-men would invert this to lure the informants to place them under surveillance. Once an informant has been identified, the Yance-men will quickly be able to identify where and how often they are being watched by their FBE opponents. The Yance-men would discuss, hint, or act suspiciously around the informant to feed the FBE the narrative the NRF want them to believe. The Yance-men's discussions will always be ambiguously filled with criminal innuendo but nothing definitive to keep the FBE hooked but not enough to provoke arrest. After a sufficient amount of time, the Yance-men will give indications they are about to carry out a major operation such as receiving weapons, explosives, or conducting an attack, kidnapping, or assassination. After giving ambiguous information that can be reasonably interpreted as nefarious but can also indicate something benign, the Yance-men drop information to the FBE the time the Yance-men are to carry out their "operation". Instead of the FBE security forces conducting a raid and catching the NRF red-handed, the FBE catches a red herring. Instead of capturing weapons, they capture a shipment of golf clubs or they raid the Yance-men having a surprise party. Besides being humiliated at being deceived, the NRF filmed and recorded as much of the FBE's operation since the first informant walked-in and published most of it to media and online sites to make mockery of the FBE-forces. The number of twists and turns that can be played are extensive and the comedic potential to maximize FBE humiliation would have few limits.

Of course, humiliation is not the only reputation destroyer. If the FBE can be caught on camera attempting entrapment or conducting other illegal activities such as paying NRF blackmailers or filmed trying to create false flags themselves would be just as impactful as humiliation. Also, not all FEES options would be used exclusively on FBE-aligned security forces or pursuers but also on FBE-backed politicians, public officials, and media organizations. Disrupting these FBE proxies could disconnect FBE communications and propaganda that keeps the general public acquiescent. If nothing else, the Yance-men can help protect NRF credibility by making their detractors look foolish or successfully brand them as liars. An obvious FEES option would be to execute the "Dan Rather tactic" on FBE media. The NRF would use sophisticated forgers to create "evidence" that is detrimental to prominent NRF persons. The Yance-men would "leak" these forgeries to prominent FBE media outlets to help publicly persecute the targeted NRF individuals. After a certain level of public attention is achieved, the Yance-men expose the forgeries to rival outlets and into the public social media sphere proving the FBE outlets lied or were fooled. If the FBE media's accusations are sufficiently outlandish, the targeted NRF persons could take civil court action, not to win a case but to permanently instill distrust of that FBE media in the public. All of the Yance-men's actions are there to make the FBE use up valuable time, resources, and reputation on decoys and false leads. In 5GW, inflicting casualties on the security forces is not the objective, in fact it is detrimental. Ideally in a perfect outcome, the NRF wouldn't kill a single soldier, policeman, or security agent in the entire war, but that is not realistic. The best outcome is to minimize this as much as possible while maximizing public humiliation to encourage the natural bureaucratic proclivity for risk aversion to flourish which keeps the main effort of the NRF safe.

Strengths:

Lies travel halfway around the world before the truth gets its shoes on. FBE-aligned forces, like all human beings, when they get supposedly valuable information want to believe they have discovered an NRF plot, combat cell, or derogatory information on enemy VIPs with every fiber of their being. If the information they receive is true, then the leaders of that FBE proxy organization get kudos and possible pathway to promotion. The inherent desire of wish fulfillment makes lies travel fast without scrutiny. The Yance-men are, like Satan in *Faust*, specialized offering enticing false wishes to lure susceptible FBE members to their career's downfall. The Yance-men play on the quintessential follies of human beings that make temptations irresistible. If properly done, the NRF's Yance-men will be rendered invisible by the FBE's own confirmation bias that they found the enemies they were seeking.

For all their mischievousness, the Yance-men will be very difficult to identify as the majority of the planners and operators will be like directors or producers of a play – always in the background unseen. Only a few Yance-men are needed to be in public to act as bait to lure in prospective FBE surveillance or informants. If properly planned, these Yance-men who let themselves be the targets of FBE surveillance will be difficult to prosecute. The FBE will no doubt arrest them, but any draconian punishments for glorified misdemeanors will lead to further humiliation. Effective planning makes the FBE's effort to positively link known Yance-men with the public disclosures of the failed FBE operations very difficult. The Yance-men's operations involve minimal illicit activity and keeping the people used as "lures" away from those committing felonies is critical for long term success.

Weaknesses:

The strengths and successes written previously rely on the important caveat of "well-planned". Sloppy or off the cuff operations will quickly lead to failure. The Yance-men cannot rely on much outside NRF support beyond the planning phase because it would risk exposure of the wider organization if Yance-men are captured by the FBE. Yance-men require creative, independent thinkers with people willing to put their lives at risk because their job is ultimately being sacrificial lambs for the greater good of the NRF. Sooner or later, Yance-men will be captured, the key requirement is design and plan operations so that when the most likely members of the Yance-men are caught, there is minimal evidence of criminal activity and the captured Yance-men have minimal knowledge of other members or operations. The online efforts with bots reduce the risk but will be less effective against the FBE.

Firstly, patterns of life are easier to more rapidly establish for the FBE on the internet and the FBE can more dependably rely on their own ANI to manage and mitigate the Yance-men's activities. Secondly, the number of resources the FBE commits to the online decoys still doesn't hinder the financial resources of the FBE since all their responses are through software that is already paid for. So, the Yance-men have to conspicuously put people out in the real world to grab the FBE's attention sufficiently which means that the number of times an individual can be used as a Yance-man to lure the FBE is finite. Records will be built by the FBE to track and monitor any Yance-men they identify, even if they don't outright arrest them or make them serve short prison sentences. The Yance-men will be a perishable unit that must constantly morph which increases the risk of undetected FBE infiltration. This is why the NRF must picks its operations for their Yance-men very carefully which leads to the last weakness of a limited recruiting pool.

Ideal Yance-men are actors, spies, and production managers all in one. They seamlessly feign innocence while manipulating FBE operatives into pursuing dead-ends while keeping cool-headed and objective in their planning and scheming. This is not a common set of personality traits. Finding the right people to risk their careers or lives willingly knowing that they are there to draw the ire of the enemy is psychologically burdensome. The Yance-men are likely going to have to rely more on their cyber experts and online bots more than the NRF would like, but once a Yance-men cell is properly formed, it could successfully shield several life-or-death operations from FBE discovery. One possible mitigation is to recruit from older demographics. People who've retired, lost family members, or perpetually bored are likely more willing to carry out more risk as a decoy as they have less to lose. The Yance-men are a critical operational tool for the NRF in this era of advanced surveillance that makes hiding beyond all detection impossible. Creating spectacle, like smokescreens for a tank, is the only cheap alternative but one that expends itself over time. NRF leaders must appreciate the Yance-men's value and continuously maintain their ranks as they rotate out or are lost to the FBE. Guard operations are as important in information-centric warfare as any other and the Yance-men or a close approximation will be needed by the NRF to operate within the Western nation.

Illegal LOE Organization 2: Targeting the System's Individual Points of Failure: The Bricklayers

For the last 20 years, China's People's Liberation Army has studied how they could exploit the West's militaries' weaknesses in an information-centric war and determined their key to victory was to cripple the supporting information systems that enable Western forces to operate as a singular combined-armed force.[iv] Information systems are not just defined as computer systems, but every component of a process that receives, analyzes, and disseminates information. This includes all communication devices, computer networks, sensors, decision-making operation centers, and information management structures. The concept being that if an opponent is rendered blind to all information inputs and cannot communicate with either leaders or subordinates, this will paralyze any superior opponent's forces. For the 5GW-type of conflict, the NRF must co-opt and modify the Chinese concept of "informationized warfare" to effectively blind and paralyzed FBE forces in this brutal invisible war.[v]

Informationized warfare argues information is only effectively implemented by a complete system, meaning no single piece of technology, physical site, or communication network is standalone. For a commander or leader to direct their forces effectively, they need the information system to continuously function with each component that includes devices, facilities, communication networks, and personnel operating in synch without disruption. 5GW-style fighting requires the NRF to eliminate the information support systems that keep the FBE's leadership connected with their proxies and support organizations used to continuously subvert the Western nation's government and society. If the NRF successfully maps out FBE information systems, they can identify the key points of failure that can delay, disrupt, isolate, or eliminate a vital target the information system relies on. No matter the design, all human systems will have vulnerable points of failure for a variety of reasons including poor planning, overreliance on dependable individuals, complacency, or neglecting to implement redundant capacity to the system. Although identifying the critical vulnerabilities would take time and thorough analytical study, the NRF are more likely to find multiple potential vectors of attack than the FBE being able to successfully self-diagnose and correct all their problems. This highlights the important point that the NRF do not have to attack the entire information apparatus the FBE will have constructed to be effective; they only have to take out single points of failure within that system to paralyze the opponent.

There are two types of targeting options for the NRF. The first is targeting an individual component vital to the information flow for FBE operations and the second is targeting a distinct organizational body consisting of many components that acts as critical node to the larger information system. Information systems are not limited to technology or parts of technology. Information systems rely on organizations, procedures, and qualified individual persons to manage and sustain these systems so an individual component could mean either a technology component or a singular person. A distinct organizational body can mean an intranet, data lake, an actual organization, or physical facility that links and synchronizes the greater FBE organization. Each target type has advantages and disadvantages but the NRF will have to target both to have the best chance of victory. The Illegal LOE 2 organization units, the Bricklayers, are directed at the first type of target.

In contemporary times, information technology is advanced to the point that having multiple layers of redundancy is a common feature of networks, telecommunication design, and engineering. Targeting an individual piece of equipment to disrupt a large part or the whole targeted information system is unlikely to work. Few companies or organizations are likely to rely on a singular mainframe computer as it was before the era of cloud computing. Instead, the individual human beings important to the functioning of the information system are the singular critical component targets. There are two means of elimination: kill the person or remove that person's ability to interact with the information system. The NRF will use both methods. Killing is part of Step 3, so for Step 1 and 2 operations, the Bricklayers will focus on depriving the human target of the ability to interact with the information system.

No matter how complex or redundant human organizations are, all of them gradually morph into functioning around key points of failure because some elements of the organization will gradually become more effective than the rest making the organization dependent on these reliable exceptions. These single points of failure will usually be select key people who most effectively get things done. These people organize the retrieval and dissemination of information between FBE decision-makers or between sub-organizations within the parent organization. Leaders may make the decisions, but these reliable persons are the ones who ensure the information is properly conveyed so those decisions can be executed. In the case of the FBE, these people are running information systems that keep proxy organizations' decisions and actions in synch with each other and other partner organizations. The FBE's bedrock organizations are a wide variety of nonprofits, corporations, and other activistic groups such as banks, venture capital firms, lobbying firms, charities, private international nongovernmental organizations, single-issue activist groups, law firms, and entertainment corporations to name a few examples. Vital dependable people within these organizations use their superior administrative and technical skills to ensure the "cogs" of the organizational machinery are always functioning properly.

Examples of potential targets include, but are not limited to executive assistants, network system administrators, legal general counsel, accountants, or simply competent managers who outperform their peers. These people routinely ensure the leaders' orders are carried out while overcoming everyday impediments. Examples of such impediments include unreasonable deadlines, conflicting priorities, poor network or computer connections, VIPs becoming sick or unexpectantly dying, making sure every relevant stakeholder is synchronizing plans, or keep the organizations free from civil law entanglements. Each organization will be unique, even if the organizations all have the same operational goals, and trying to determine who are the vital components to a FBE proxy organization's information system will require aggressive and patient surveillance by the NRF's intelligence units. Once the targets are identified, the intelligence units must collect on these persons to understand their work routines and their preferred means of managing their role in the information system. Only then can the Bricklayer units carry out their mission which is to figure out how to nonlethally prevent a target person from performing their role to disrupt the flow of information. The easiest and most common way is to eliminate that person's ability to communicate by destroying or disabling their target's personal electronic devices (PEDs), bricking them into useless objects. In an ironic twist of fate, the modern Information Age has created a new and interesting parallel with medieval European societies. In those historical societies, the peasants and serfs were bound to the land. In the contemporary Information Age, people are bound in the same way to global digital networks as it is vital for their existence. People's role and status in society is determined by what information they create, manage, and implement for the society. Take away their ability to interact with the global information networks renders them impotent.

The Bricklayers exploit modern people's overdependence on the information technology linking them to whatever information system they belong to, meaning their smartphones, tablets, smart watches, and laptops are their lifeline and without these, their lives are paralyzed.[vi] Many people barely understand the back-end of information systems as ever simpler graphic user interfaces require less input and thought by the user to work.[vii] Bricklayers target those who maintain the vital information life lines which requires above average understanding how the larger information system works. This means the preferred targets will be conspicuous in their competence which will make them easier to identify. Unlike terrorists, spies, or traditional criminals that seek information to steal to use for their own purposes, the Bricklayers' only mission is to deny their targets access to information vital to their role in the larger FBE organization. Disrupting their target's role in the information system without exposing the hand of the NRF is the Bricklayers' only task. Short of lethally removing the targeted person, all of the disruptions will have temporary effect on the target. Bricklayers carry out actions that only disrupt information systems for brief periods which means their actions are most effective when done in direct support of larger operations. Disrupting information flow while the NRF conducts broader attacks will paralyze FBE responses to these attacks. One successful Bricklayer attack would come across as just a minor inconvenience to the organization, but done in tandem with other attacks, these Bricklayer attacks prolong the FBE's blindness to the NRF's larger actions.

Of course, not all disruption has to focus on the target's handheld or mobile devices, some actions could just impede a target's workday to disrupt the regular flow of information within the FBE. Bricklayers could hack a target's car to render it nonfunctioning, steal credentials to post false messages on the target's social media that insults the boss or imply criminal activity at work or unleash endless bots to psychologically damage the target on social media. Attacking the person's reputation or daily routine will sometimes be the optimal route, especially if the NRF wants to minimize the risk of attribution. Of course, this doesn't have to be limited to the targeted person but also disrupt the lives of others who affect the target's ability to do their job. Inducing family stress with spouses or immediate relatives are viable options, such as deep fake voices or images of relatives calling to tell the target there's a medical emergency, they are being blackmailed or create false indications of infidelity with bots creating whole conversations.

In most cases however, the elimination of PEDs will be sufficiently effective as it severs the target's link with their own lives, forcing the target to prioritize fixing the disruption above the needs of the FBE. There are a wide variety of options to use against the PEDS that include denial of service attacks, SIM swapping, phishing targets into convincing them on installing file-destroying malware are common options. The key intent is to deny the target the ability to properly function in their daily routine. For operations that need immediate action, the Bricklayers could resort to the most risky and brazen act of destroying the target's PEDs by remotely overloading them. This is risky because it will become immediately known and will not be very precise. The most likely method would be Bricklayers installing an exceptionally powerfully transmitter in the back of a truck or van that can broadcasts energy in the same frequency of the cellular band of the phone to jam or burn out the receiver circuitry.[viii], [ix] Such actions immediately render the phone effectively an inert brick because it is cutoff from the cellular network and the person is unable to function for hours, if not days. Such an effort will happen in extreme circumstances where unforeseen developments force the NRF to act in haste, but the likely infliction of collateral damage will risk NRF reputation. Regardless of the method, the Bricklayers will build upon the chaos for the FBE by creating as many "bricks" as possible out of the PEDS to neutralize the targeted vital persons' ability for fulfill their roles in the FBE's information system.

Strengths:

The Bricklayers' typical targets are individually low impact against the FBE and will only be effective cumulatively by targeting multiple people simultaneously. Communication disruption or loss of PEDs, or a false family emergency will look like a bad day to most outside observers. These low-impact activities will make the FBE's ability to identify NRF intentions or notice it's the NRF in the first place will be very difficult. Even when multiple cells of Bricklayers act in unison, the FBE and the security services will have a delayed reaction, giving the Bricklayers ample time to evade detection or capture. Identifying who are the best targets will take a lot of time and aggressive intelligence gathering, but once the target's identified, the individual target's pattern of life will be easy to map out to identify the best opportunities to strike. In the Western nations, numerous data aggregation companies and data mining algorithms will allow the Bricklayers to commercially buy most of the need information and then use a customize program to map out the timelines and places.[x] Most targets will have only grown up with digital devices and will have placed their entire lives onto their PEDs and the various applications. In some cases, Bricklayers only have to deny connection access to their online information to create disruptive psychological trauma to the targets.[xi] Many of these digital co-dependents will react to sudden loss of digital access irrationally and delay their reintegration back into the FBE information system. Finally, the FBE security forces protecting their information systems mostly will not know how to react. They will look for identifiable end states like stealing money, flatlining a network of a company, sabotage, or carry out actions to induce mass panic. Bricklayers' operations are intended to have cascading knock-on effects on the rest of the FBE's information systems. If the FBE security forces are stove-piped and receive limited information from other FBE cohorts, then they will repeatedly fail to anticipate or stop Bricklayer actions.

Weaknesses:

There is a negative aspect of Bricklayer individual targets having low impact on the FBE information system. The Bricklayers must target multiple people simultaneously in coordination with larger NRF operational actions at the same time to have any appreciable effects on the FBE information systems. This means the Bricklayers need to have excellent cyber and human intelligence operatives assisting them in finding the targets. The longer a potential target is under surveillance, the greater the chance of discovery before the Bricklayers are ready. While keeping operational security paramount, the Bricklayers will also need to devise a coordination method between multiple cells to synchronize and execute their plans covertly. Individual Bricklayer cells will likely be small, but the number of cells for successful execution of an operation will likely be many. The danger of sloppy information security is that the FBE will be able to stop a major operation completely if the coordination method is discovered and breached. Stealth and inconspicuous actions are key. In addition to the coordination between the human Bricklayer cells, the Bricklayer bot networks must also be coordinated at the same time. Disrupting information systems simultaneously in cyber and real space is fundamental to operational success. Also, there is the risk of cleverer FBE targets having analog contingencies, such as notebooks or hard copies of important personal information, which minimize the impact their PEDs being bricked. Finally, the Bricklayers are the first sub-organization of the NRF that is dedicated to serious felonious actions that can result in arrest or death. Contingencies must be made to protect the greater group, including protecting Bricklayers' family members to minimize the fallout of losing a Bricklayer cell.

Illegal LOE Organization 3: Targeting the System's Critical Nodes: The Gremlins

The second type of targeting option for disrupting the FBE's information systems is to target a large organizational critical node of the system instead of an individual. The NRF units specialized in this mission will be referred to as Gremlins. Gremlins was a term from World War II for various technical issues that disrupted the proper functioning of warplanes. The NRF's Gremlins will do the same with the FBE information system's critical nodes. The critical nodes are the organizational bodies that can either manage information or execute actions based on the information flow. The variety of FBE nodes range from nonprofits coordinating illicit finances, private companies "donating" grants and sponsorships for FBE-backed projects disguised as public works, law firms, private security companies, and various local and national government bureaucracies. Each organization will differ in work culture, mission priorities, and specializations but all will have some fundamental commonalities. In spite of the Information Age, most major organizations are still designed under earlier industrial age Max Weberian-style bureaucracies. This is partly due to the regulatory and statutory infrastructure that is designed to accommodate older bureaucratic precepts which constrict large-scale organizations from implementing more efficient methods of accountability and organization. Since laws and administration rarely keep up with the times, especially regarding technology, the slow, inflexible organizational systemic theories devised from the 1890s to 1910s still dominate most industry sectors and governments. The exceptions are typically information technology-related companies because they were allowed to organize and build up in the United States to efficiently meet the market's demand for information services with minimal regulation for years. However, even these organizations tend to mutate to accommodate the older institutions' more inflexible ways. There is also the added factor that many inefficiencies are deliberately embedded in organizations to serve the interests of a group or faction, including undermining rivals or ensure change is difficult to secure a person's position.[xii]

Like the Bricklayers' targets, these critical organizational nodes can be lethally targeted for destruction or nonlethally to cause chaotic disruption to the critical nodes' operations. The NRF actions are designed to prevent a critical node from carrying out its mission while the NRF is conducting a major operation or in preparation for an upcoming operation. Bricklayers' actions are designed to hinder the FBE information systems without the FBE realizing they are being actively disrupted by targeting a few people rather than organizations or technology. Gremlins target a whole organization or its network to prevent the FBE from successfully carrying out their operations regardless of the risk of discovery. Gremlins can carry out actions that potentially risk lives, but the main objective is to disrupt the flow of FBE information between nodes. There are three approaches the Gremlins can take to stymie targeted nodes: 1. To disrupt by process 2. Disrupt by physical sabotage 3. Disrupt by cyberattack.

Options and Methods:

Disrupting by process means using the FBE's own internal rules, procedures, and policies against them. This is the easiest method to conceal but takes the longest to have any significant impact on the FBE which means disrupting by process is for strategic rather than operational impact. Large organizations of the FBE are serving an autocratic faction that seeks control while eliminating dissent. The work cultures of such organizations will be designed to retain loyalty towards and dependence on FBE leaders exclusively. Work culture is established with policies and procedures that condition the personnel's behavior and priorities by setting incentives and punishments for all work-related actions. To maintain control, the policies will encourage mediocrity, discourage initiative, undermine creativity, and maintain a strict hierarchy that rewards compliance over either efficiency or quality of work effort. The cost for the FBE maintaining tight control is the diminished overall effectiveness of the organizations; the key for the FBE is to balance the need for control with the need of the organization to function just enough to accomplish FBE strategic objectives. This balancing effort is vulnerable to external pressure and if the Gremlins can tilt the balance just enough, the targeted organization can be rendered ineffective.

Disrupting by process is the covert attack method for the Gremlins. These Gremlins infiltrate the organizations, not to gain access to the most sensitive information or locations, but to become a part of the mundane administrative apparatus. Most people, especially autocrats, often think only about the glamorous elements of warfare such as advanced weapons, propaganda campaigns, elite combat units, spies, and sources of financial support. However, few at the top of an autocratic system ever think about how a desk clerk gets paid or how many widgets are needed to sustain an operating system, or what considerations are needed to sustain an operation. These are the supporting details relegated to the lowly functionary or bureaucrat who are the numerous faceless cogs that are individually unimportant but are collectively vital to the success of any organization. This gray routine area of unexciting processes and procedures are overlooked and vulnerable to outside attack. If just a few Gremlins can rise to the rank of mid-level management, these information warriors can paralyze entire FBE operations. Unlike some of the previously mentioned LOE organizations, the Gremlins' operations are not novel, just updated to simultaneously integrate with larger information warfare operations instead of being carried out in the traditional standalone actions of the past. Disrupting an organization by process was perfected by the Office of Strategic Services (OSS) in World War II who worked out guidelines for such missions for various anti-Nazi resistance movements. Using the enemy's own bureaucracy against them is a passive means of warfare but can be catastrophically effective if properly utilized.

Even though the OSS operated in a time of analog technologies, their simple concepts of organizational sabotage are still fully applicable against an organization of the Digital Age because Max Weber still dominates organizational thinking. Technology has progressed but bureaucratic theory and practice remain stagnant. Below are some of the recommended actions by the OSS to their agents embedded in enemy bureaucracies with some updated modifications included:[xiii]

· Multiply paperwork in plausible ways.

· Hold conferences and meetings when there is more critical work to be done. Always restate issues or ask for clarification on issues, especially unimportant ones to squander work days.

· Show favoritism to inefficient and lazy workers to destroy morale.

· Always convey incomplete and misleading instructions. When subordinates fail, admonish them as if one expected them to be able to read your mind but they didn't do so.

· Always advocate "caution" and encourage risk aversion by emphasizing potential embarrassment of outright failure if done in haste.

· Demand all orders be in writing or in some form of record.

· Eliminate all ways of expediting a process or completing a task quickly. All things must be done through "proper channels" and chain of command.

· If you are required to comment or provide input on a task, delay and procrastinate with other "emergency issues" cropping up or sudden appointments.

· Make frequent meaningless speeches with as much jargon as possible to make them incomprehensible. Talk at great length, use mixed metaphors, tiresome anecdotes, and pointless personal "experiences". Always praise the leadership or an FBE-endorsed ideological stance to make your speeches immune to open criticism.

· Be worried about the propriety of all decisions—demand general counsel of the organization review as many decision points as possible to discourage actual action.

· Always re-open "old wounds" from previous bureaucratic battles, create interdepartmental animosity.

· Be passive-aggressive with executive assistants and immediate underlings to create toxic work environments.

· Always argue over the precise meaning of meeting minutes, records, or resolutions to further delay implementation.

· When possible, always refer issues to a committee or group of managers for "further consideration".

· Always defer major decisions to others; take credit at successes and blame the others for failures.

· Ask endless questions about orders or directives and quibble over every possible minor detail.

· When assigning tasks, always prioritize unimportant duties and jobs first. Always assign the underachievers with the most important jobs.

· Constantly edit and review papers and proposals. When doing so, stop editing when one mistake is found and then send it back for authors to correct and then review it again until another mistake is found and repeat ad nauseum.

· Use old formats and memorandums and cite out of date laws and policies to cause confusion and frustration.

Inefficiency is seditious and disruptive, but in Max Weberian bureaucratic systems it's almost impossible to correct or punish the Gremlin perpetrator because everything is done within the rules; the same rules designed to keep everyone compliant at the cost of efficient effective work. In FBE corrupted organizations, these same rules also modify the hiring and evaluation criteria to incentivize favoritism towards those who endorse FBE-endorsed platitudes, stances, or have an affiliation with one of the Atomized factions puppeteered by the FBE. These can be hidden in a guise of equity with some wordsmithing to the rules. Without exception, these rule modifications lower the qualification standards to attract mediocrities who are easily controllable. The NRF Gremlins will have little difficulty in finding recruits who can feign being the ideal compliant automaton. It is easier for intelligent people to pretend to be fools or apathetic workers than for mediocrities to act intelligent. Since mediocrities will also be doing the vetting, this makes infiltration easy as well as help keep the Gremlins' cover. The rules will discourage anyone from pointing out stupidity or inaction because many of the FBE organizations' employees will be equally as guilty of similar ineptitude, just not to the same extent, making the detection of deliberate inaction difficult. Compliance discourages thinking and creates perpetual camouflage for NRF's Gremlins.

All of the previous examples of process disruption are designed to cause chaos and exacerbate failure within the workings of a targeted organization vital to the FBE information system. However, the Gremlins must also carry out reputational sabotage of the targeted organization to maximize effective impact. Using positions within the administrative bureaucracies, the Gremlins can create a number of public faux pas to humiliate the leadership of the organization. Convince young interns to post to social media embarrassing statements such as personally attacking vulnerable people or say something that is too honest such as a partner organization is inept or having a named executive unwittingly pledge support to a hated individual such as criminal or terrorist. Many executives within large organizations must place their trust in subordinates providing information on situations they will endorse or condemn because the executives don't have the time to research it themselves. Breaking that trust is very disruptive. Process disrupting Gremlins could, in coordination with cyberattack-Gremlins, arrange to have funds syphoned and transferred to embarrassing causes. If an insider Gremlin helped the cyberattack-Gremlins gain access to systems to, at least temporarily, take control of the public facing part of the organization on social media, they could set up crowdfunds to support NRF-sympathizers in the name of the organization. For example, if an FBE-backed venture capital firm suddenly created a crowdfunding page to pay for legal fees of an NRF radical, the FBE is likely to pause their activities at that firm to investigate the perceived betrayal.

Process disruption is a laborious and slow-moving method of attack to gradually debilitate the FBE, akin to gangrene on a human body. Each little disruption causes delays and increases costs to create knock-on effects that amplify the negative impacts at a later time. A Gremlin that costs an office division an extra 2% for the fiscal quarter or delaying a program for six weeks will not paralyze an organization, even a small one. However, hundreds of Gremlins over a period of months or years could potentially cost FBE organizations tens or hundreds of millions of dollars in lost labor, time, and investment. A few weeks of delay in one office and then another few weeks of delay in another office and so on could delay critical programs and actions intended to support the FBE's strategic objective. Creating additional costs in time and money creates more openings of vulnerability the larger NRF organization can exploit to achieve more impactful successes. This slow drip form of sabotage is unlikely to noticeably impact anything quickly and must be considered the Gremlins' tool for strategic actions with consequences not felt for months or even a year or two. Process disruption keeps the FBE off balance by making hundreds of gentle pushes to destabilize the FBE. Although this alone is damaging, the Gremlins have two other approaches of disruption that can have more immediate operational impact, especially physical sabotage.

While the method of process disruption is the slow acting tool of strategic impact, physical sabotage is the opposite. This method is a quick acting tool designed for having immediate tactical and operational impact. This is an improved upon method that has existed in warfare since the Bronze Age that now uses modern information technology for selecting more precise targets and to better synchronize the timing with larger NRF operations to deliver the most impactful damage to their enemy. Historically, physical sabotage occurs with targets of opportunity or conducted against a major target in coordination with a single operation. Now, the NRF could potentially conduct physical sabotage across multiple offices within multiple organizations in support of multiple operations simultaneously with minimal resource expenditure.

Sabotaging Gremlins don't necessarily have to be insiders within the targeted organizations, but it does simplify the planning and increase the severity of the sabotage. Both insider and outsider Gremlins would be best utilized in tandem to not only inflict as much chaos as possible but improve the chances of the insiders' escaping detection in certain circumstances. These Gremlins can also assist the cyber and process Gremlins by either shutting down security systems, help install backdoors into the organization's intranet for future espionage or rendering part of a facility inaccessible. All of these acts of sabotage are meant to impair the organization's function instead of the more common industrial espionage of trying to steal intellectual property or stopping the manufacturing of a weapon system. Since most of the FBE's actions are social and political manipulation, most of the NRF's targets are intended to delay or paralyze FBE organizations supporting the manipulation in terms of financing, lobbying, or marketing. FBE organizations' value is their ability to control, shape, and disseminate information and the sabotage stops the organization from effectively communicating both within itself and to other nodes of the FBE information system.

Even with proper planning and contingencies factored into NRF operations, most Gremlin saboteurs will only be usable one or two times. After more than two times, even the most dimwitted security personnel will realize there are insiders and will proactively hunt for suspicious employees. This means most insider saboteurs will be inserted into target organizations for specific NRF operations and likely not have the time in employment to build unquestioned trust with their co-workers. Insider saboteurs will likely be in place for three to six months at most before actions need to be carried out. Outsider saboteurs maybe harder to catch but their shenanigans will bring extra scrutiny in and around the targeted organization and for the sake of operational security, best vacate the target area after one or two acts. That is not to say an FBE organization can only be targeted once, it means that an organization must be given time to fall back into complacency before re-targeting which could mean months or a year in between acts of physical sabotage.

The acts of sabotage themselves would need to be dramatic if immediate chaos is needed, but an excessive number of casualties would undermine the NRF's information warfare intentions of keeping the public uninterested in NRF activities. Explosives, incendiaries, arson, and other dramatic forms of disruption must be done with discriminatory precision. Deaths are preferably avoidable but war is not completely controllable so there will inevitably be some and the Gremlins must weigh this consideration before initiating major acts of sabotage. Quieter acts such as vandalism are less noticeable and dramatic but are safer and will likely be a rare luxury for Gremlin planners. Sensible Gremlin units will plan for multiple contingencies and arrange for several acts of sabotage simultaneously to ensure success in case one act is discovered and stopped.

The best targets for sabotage are the obvious critical elements to the functioning of any contemporary organization. Network switch rooms, server rooms, cooling or fuel systems, power transformers, critical machinery for production, maintenance bays, company vehicle garages, robot control stations, fiber-optic lines, warehouse storage rooms with flammable materials, and electric motor rooms for elevators or heating, ventilation, and cooling systems. Using simple tools and devices makes actions easy to carry out but will make the act obvious and detectable afterwards. To help mitigate this threat, using modern methods can help better conceal devices and protect the saboteurs from detection. 3D printing can enable Gremlins to create sabotage devices into any shape, color, and texture they can imagine for any purpose. Well-camouflaged devices could be emplaced and left for days without detection, providing alibis to avert suspicion or provide ample time for the Gremlin saboteur to escape.

A simple example would be a Gremlin needing to knock out an organization's internal network for a few days at a crucial time the NRF are executing an operation against the FBE. In the weeks prior to the required time of action, the Gremlins use a 3D-printer to create a container filled with thermite shaped in the appearance of a credit card. One is not sufficient, so over several weeks, a Gremlin smuggles in one or two cards a day to the office appearing as ID badges, common access cards, or key cards stored in drawers or lockers. One card has a built-in manually set ignition device to delay detonation for a few minutes. On the appointed day, the Gremlin saboteur simply uses rubber bands to stack and bind the cards together as one incendiary device and then goes to the network switch room and places the device on top of the primary network rack, sets the timer, and then leaves. Preferably, the act is done during another commotion like a fire drill when people are naturally vacating the building to better conceal the act as well as minimize the risk of casualties. This is a simple example, not factoring in the need for picking or hacking the door lock, avoiding security cameras, or needing to have cyber-Gremlins interfere with the security system. Modern technology's ability to conceal devices as well as make more targets subject to paralysis by losing vulnerable, sensitive electronics and networks simplifies the job of sabotage in many ways.

While the insider Gremlins target the devices and physical systems of the organization, the outsider Gremlins can focus on disrupting the organization's people on a mass scale by impeding access to FBE facilities. The difference between the Bricklayers and outsider Gremlins is the Gremlins will target large numbers of people and doesn't try to hide the fact they are actively trying to disrupt the workings of the organization. Again, killing is preferably avoided to diminish the newsworthiness of the Gremlins' actions, but will not be completely avoidable. Some operations will be more flamboyant in execution and dangerous than others, but the main objective will still be to halt or severely impair the targeted FBE organization's operations for a day or two as quickly as possible. A short list of some examples include:

· Calling in a bomb threat; set off small black powder charges nearby to accentuate the threat.

· Swatting an executive's home or the targeted organization's main facilities.

· If the organization is near a major traffic artery, cause a major road obstruction that freezes all movement in the area such as a gasoline truck spill.

· Release animals into the building such as snakes or hundreds of rats.

· Use UAVs to damage or destroy the transformer to the building or city block.

· Use UAVs to drop incendiaries onto vehicles in the car parking lot of the organization.

· Use a cement truck to create road obstacles at or near the organization's entrance by dumping the concrete.

· Insider Gremlins send phone contact rosters to outside Gremlins who use auto dialers to ceaselessly call and jam most of the office phones for much of the day.

· Program a swarm of UAVs equipped with hydraulic-controlled window safety hammers to go to a targeted organization's main office at night and smash every window on every floor.

· Have UAVs enter warehouses and garages and use a fire source to set off sprinkler and fire alarm systems.

· Equip Gremlins with modified laser pointers with increased power to burn out security cameras' optics to create anxiety and distraction.

· Use UAVs to drop smoke and stink bombs into exposed HVAC ventilation.

· Insider Gremlins send out home addresses of key employees to outsider Gremlins who send UAVs at night to dump paint on the windscreens of employee cars to prevent going to work; or drop caltrops in the driveway.

· Have Gremlins instigate road-rage incidents with FBE organization key staff and executives that burn up the day or get them dragged to court.

· Break the motors of the automatic gates to the parking lot or building.

· Switch out padlocks to slow down work; use blowtorches to melt door locks.

· Cut information system fiber optic or copper wire cables that connect the property to the internet service provider network.

· Burn or break components of nearby cell-towers to kill information connections for the facility.

These are a few options available to outsider Gremlins while minimizing the risk of direct engagement with the FBE or law enforcement. Both the insider and outsider Gremlins need to coordinate their efforts to maximize the damage but must also be cognizant of the larger NRF's operational timelines. These Gremlins will not have the luxury of going by their own timetables like the process disruptor Gremlins. Physical sabotage is simple, necessary, and risky. An organization riddled with inefficiency combined with physical sabotage to internal systems and having the larger workforce's ability to function being disrupted will cause significant chaos, but there still remains the cyberattack disruptions.

Cyber Gremlins have two tasks: to disrupt the FBE's organizational nodes in their information system and to hinder the FBE's own cyber-based tools and capabilities. The first task supports the process disruptor and physical sabotage Gremlins. These activities are related to classic black-hat hackers who use phishing, malware, and denial of service attacks to disrupt a targeted organization's internal functions. These actions are made easier with cooperation from the insider Gremlins to help build backdoors by supplying credentials, installing rogue software, or gain access to the online code repository to provide the Gremlins full access to systems and networks.[xiv] Cyber Gremlins will have a wide selection of available cyber tools, programs, and well-developed techniques from the dark web and cybersecurity professionals loyal to the NRF insurgency. Numerous means and methods have been recounted elsewhere with more in-depth study than this wargame can provide. The only unique key point to mention is that the cyberattack Gremlins will most likely form into various cells specializing in methods of attack and the types of targets. For instance, the FBE will likely have controlling interest in multiple venture capital firms to influence the Western nation's economy. Every company is uniquely tailored by its organization, culture, and standards, but companies operating within the same industrial or commercial sector will have overlapping similarities. Logically, Gremlin cyber cells specializing in the study of specific targets by industry or interest helps build expertise to refine attacks. No doubt, the Gremlin cells can coordinate in large scale efforts and overlap in use of technique or having a common target but would otherwise stay separated by specialty.

The second task will focus on AI disruption, which is novel as it confronts new information technologies that didn't exist before the 2020s. In the past, organizations relied exclusively on human specialists to carry out cyberoperations of every kind from network defense, intelligence collection to attacking other networks. Now, more and more organizations, both private and government, are beginning to rely on advanced artificial narrow intelligences (ANI) networked to the internet powered by large language models (LLM) to build and identify patterns for targeting or exploitation. As the complexity of the information space grows, increasing reliance on automation to parse and filter data into useful information will also grow. The FBE will follow the steps of the Chinese Communist Party and attempt to link surveillance, information warfare, and security operations with LLM ANI programs that can filter and identify key indicators of enemy activity or behavior.[xv] The fear of many is that in the worst case scenario, ANI will help make the ability to organize opposition against a police state nearly impossible and permanently create a hermetically sealed society of compliance as ANI "predicts" or "anticipates" any and all threats to their masters.[xvi]

However, like weapons of the past, AI has strengths and weaknesses with countermeasures inevitably arising forever contributing to the perpetual arms race between measure vs. countermeasure in the story of warfare. For all of the fears and hype, contemporary AI has several flaws that the NRF can use to neutralize FBE-enabled AI cyberweapons. The first biggest weakness is still the common misunderstanding of what AI, particularly ANI, can actually do and not do. This confusion exists even among social and political elites in all societies around the world who believe new AI programs using advanced modeling can perform near miracles for the state and society alike. This is dangerous for the FBE in particular because these misconceptions incentivize the leadership to implement these AI-tools for operations that are not as conducive to the original programing as these hopeful leaders assume.

Many still confuse ANI with artificial general intelligence (AGI) which theoretically will have the same cognizance of human beings, possessing understanding, comprehension, self-awareness, and being able to develop its own unique thoughts and concepts. The reality is ANI, as stated earlier, still is a data aggregator executing preset instructions to match and cross-reference data to generate output without ever actually understanding anything about any of the information being inputted. It matches patterns based on the instructions and parameters of the various programs with no consideration to the context or purpose of the data. ANI is exceptionally good at finding set patterns for problems and aggregating data into simpler forms that are comprehensible to the human users, but the ANI cannot discern the meaning of the inferences, innovate original ideas or understand situations from which that data is derived.[xvii] ANI is still bound within confined parameters of set algorithms which means these are horrible for jobs that require situational context and understanding. Surveillance and security efforts require a considerable amount of contextual understanding.

There are many actions and activities people conduct that give off dubious indicators of intention. Untrained persons could easily misconstrue the behaviors of another person as indications of being nefarious. The FBE's ANI-directed surveillance in smart cities or in law enforcement networks must be exquisitely programed with highly optimized models with refined data sets to reliably identify key patterns of NRF operatives, militias, or political dissidents. This means the ANI will also have to be able to easily receive new data sets from many sources and the training model be easily adjustable to deal with the ever-changing tactics in 5GW conflict. This creates two critical weaknesses, one from humans and one from the ANI itself.

The human programmers are going to create mistakes in the models that will be overlooked as the pace of 5GW will require the FBE's ANI models to be continually refined and updated quickly leading to gaps or errors in the model training. This creates openings for creative hackers to find potential weaknesses in the models to help the Gremlins build exploits. The critical weakness from the ANI comes from its nature of non-thinking with its programming just executing set instructions. ANI are brilliant idiots that can execute its programmed instructions with speed and efficiency which is what makes software-based security so secure with simple binary problems such as passwords, two-factor authentication, and biometric security. The software simply matches the authorized keys and patterns to allow or deny a user access to information, with no risk of distraction that plague humans doing jobs of tedious repetition. However, when advanced software is tasked to carry out work that requires the ability to contextually discern friend from foe, that lack of thinking is now a weakness.

If the Gremlins get access to the ANI with stolen credentials, backdoors, or in some other way, the ANI itself is incapable of protecting its model because its very nature is to receive, process, and disseminate huge quantities of data coming from the global internet. Security models need lots of real-world data to build and then identify high probability patterns. Once the Gremlins bypass the credential protections, the ANI itself is unable to distinguish friend from foe. Even if certain information is administratively locked, cunning Gremlins can "ask" the ANI for certain outputs that appear nonthreatening or unclassified but reveal patterns of the model training through aggregation. Attacking the ANIs by asking multiple tailored queries, the ANI will eventually provide large amounts of data that could indirectly identify the training data for the FBE's security models that are fed into the ANI. This means the NRF could extract the key model weaknesses from the ANI program itself to help the NRF create countermeasures against the FBE's security and surveillance ANIs. Ironically, the *Star Trek* trope of Captain Kirk questioning a computer to death turns out to not be complete fiction. Instead of giving computers paradoxes to crash their logic circuits, one just asks what the ANI's weaknesses are and the ANI will give them to you. A team from Google DeepMind, University of Washington, Cornell, UC Berkely, and ETH Zurich demonstrated the feasibility of such an action in 2023.[xviii] This means the ANI could potentially provide every key indicator their FBE creators are looking for as well as what the ANI discards as "useless" data points. Such information would enable the NRF Gremlin operators to poison the FBE's data sets and blind the ANI to NRF activity.

For example, if the FBE surveillance ANI are using particular patterns of pixels from cameras to identify humans walking down the street in a suspicious way and the Gremlins found these key indicators from the ANI's training data, then the Gremlins could identify those parameters once they acquire the ANI training data. Then the NRF operatives could adapt by wearing customized patterns on their clothing, both visible and infrared reflective, that could make the operatives invisible to the ANI because the new patterns and colors change the pixel patterns within the camera. This was demonstrated by students at the University of Wuhan who constructed an "InvisDefense Coat" in 2023.[xix]

These are just a few examples, but there is another option for the NRF Gremlins too. If some ANI data parameters are too complex or difficult to deceive, the next best option is to destroy the FBE ANI models with data pollution. The FBE ANIs need continuous quantities of unique human-produced data to refine and improve the ANI training models with novel information to maintain high fidelity pattern identification and algorithm solutions. Studies demonstrate that exclusively inputting other ANI-model generated content without human originated data to train the new models creates defects in the updated models. The ANI-derived models only refer to already known created data points which add redundant data sets into the models. As every new iteration of the ANI-derived models are added, each one becomes increasingly homogenized as the models keep referencing the same data sets. Akin to an inbred family, the number of unique data points become less and less with each new iteration of an exclusively ANI-derived data fed training model becoming simpler and redundant causing the model to only see limited patterns and more data errors. Eventually, these self-homogenizing ANI-generated training sets will collapse the ANI models rendering them useless.[xx]

NRF Gremlins that gain sufficient intelligence collection on the FBE ANI-models can learn what key parameters and data points the model is programmed to prioritize for pattern development and recognition. The NRF will unlikely be able to build LLM-trained ANIs on the same scale or power as the FBE's corporate-backed ANIs. Instead, the NRF can build many smaller "poor man" ANIs designed only to generate content related to the specific key data points the FBE's ANI models are training on to effectively execute its programed objectives. The FBE ANIs will likely harvest their large datasets to input into their training models from select major sites and sources for web scraping for specific key datapoints. If the NRF successfully identify these sources for web scraping, then the smaller NRF ANIs just have to create endless replications of the same datasets into those locations on the internet where the web scraping will continuously harvest the same data points over and over. These NRF ANIs would use zombie networks slaved to the main ANI computers to add necessary processing power. Since these ANIs are only building AI-generated content to homogenize the larger FBE's ANIs' model training data, the NRF's ANIs require far less processing power. Overtime, the FBE's ANIs will suffer model collapse and render the NRF's activities invisible to the FBE's automated security and surveillance tools.

Strengths:

The Gremlins' tasks provide flexibility and variety to help evade detection. These activities can be done at the timing of the saboteur which provides Gremlins with ample opportunity to establish alibis or outright escape before the FBE's security apparatus has a chance to react. Furthermore, the actions target administratively functional areas rather than high security research and development, operation centers, or armaments storage, or anything that requires exceptional security. Even the organization's information backbone with its server and network switch cabinets, closets, and rooms will not be too heavily guarded unless these are classified networks in government buildings. All software is terrible and hardware wears out, meaning sooner or later helpdesks and IT support staff will need to access these rooms on a regular basis to fix IT problems which are a regular occurrence. This means the FBE organizations will have to balance security with ease of access to these rooms to maintain a reasonably productive environment. Even if the security is high, the Gremlins just have to scramble the security to prevent anyone from getting into these locations. Gremlins aren't after the data; they are preventing the FBE from using the data. These less protected targets provide the Gremlins with numerous opportunities and means of attack to disrupt the organization while still being highly evasive.

Along with an abundance of relatively vulnerable targets to select from, the Gremlins also can keep most of their activities' covert, especially the process disruptors. The Gremlins subverting the targeted organizations' own rules, regulations, and bureaucratic processes exploit the inherent weakness of contemporary bureaucratic practices. These practices are still based on focusing on process rather than quality of outcome which help obfuscate the sabotage. This is because modern bureaucracies still follow the precepts of early 20th Century organizational concepts. These concepts were created in an attempt to fix the problems of bureaucracies designed in the 19th Century that were plagued with corruption, nepotism, and no set standards of accountability.[xxi] In the early 20th Century, there was no realistic timely way to gauge feedback on the impact from bureaucratic decisions when Max Weber and others came up with their bureaucratic concepts. So, figuring out how to achieve the highest quality of outcome from bureaucratic processes was not a realist goal as the fastest technology to record data was the typewriter and no way to compile data in a quick manner. There was too much data and no means of sorting and measuring the results. Instead of focusing on effectiveness of outcomes from bureaucratic decisions, early 20th Century organizational theorists instead focused on the fairness of the process since it was lacking in older organizational systems. As long as the process was fair to both the administrators working the process and the clients utilizing the process, then the bureaucracy organizational theorists deemed the system to work regardless if the client actually got what they were originally seeking.

Unfortunately, in practice such systems incentivize creating processes where no one person is in full charge of the whole thing. Instead, authority is subdivided into specialized stovepiped offices and departments that each handles certain portions of the process under the theory it prevents abuse of power and reduces the allure of corruption. On the negative side, since no one is fully in charge then it would be unfair to blame any single person for any failure in the outcome in the process and consequently no one is actually accountable.[xxii] Max Weberian bureaucracy incentivizes no responsibility and creates cultures of risk aversion. Risk aversion is prevalent because anyone who improves the process or expedites the process increases the risk of accountability to the supervisor of that person improving efficiency and quality of outcome. If something goes wrong with this novel improvement then there is a definitively identifiable person to hold responsible, that innovator's boss. Also, this system of incentivized mediocre bureaucratic processes encourages the creation of "turf" and personal "fiefdoms". Each office that manages that piece of the process has limited power but in that office's jurisdiction it has near absolute power within those narrow parameters. This means part of the natural behavior of a bureaucracy is to have interoffice rivalries for "turf" and budget to create micro-kingdoms of attaining more power without additional responsibility.[xxiii] An office responsible for its part in the bureaucratic process doesn't mean there is one individual solely responsible for the outcomes of that office. Anything that could fail will always be a "team" effort so no one can be identified to receive all the blame. These inefficiencies that the contemporary bureaucracy incentivizes create natural camouflage for Gremlins who throw wrenches into bureaucratic procedure.

The stereotype of bureaucracy being filled with lazy, dumb, and useless people is an exaggerated truism where most do their job, but it only takes a few stereotypical bureaucrats to gum up a system that already discourages flexibility and innovation. There is also the point that these bureaucratic workers work hard to meet the requirements of the process they are assigned which doesn't evaluate on the quality of outcomes from that process. There are many procedures in Weberian bureaucracy that have nothing to do with accomplishing that department or office's stated mission or role, but instead are there to further insulate that department or office from negative consequences. In the litigious Western nations, lawyers create or mandate policies and processes solely to create a record of actions to protect their employers in court or from public opinion. There are also processes created simply to provide additional employment or to comply with a politicized mandate to make either the CEOs or politicians in charge of the bureaucracy look good to the public.[xxiv] All of this means there are some very hard-working people in bureaucracies who are prodigiously productive in their processes and still don't actually generate anything substantively useful. These bureaucratic weaknesses are less pronounced in the private sector where inefficiencies cost money and there usually is some personal accountability for monetary loss.[xxv] These issues are also less pronounced in the military and intelligence service bureaucracies because they have the other less discussed major human incentive to work hard: "death". Failures in these institutions can lead to one's death or cause the death of comrades which few people are willing to live with. However, these old obsolete ways of organization are prevalent everywhere and still encumber the private and national security sectors. The NRF Gremlins could be some of the most productive members of the targeted organization's administration and still make sure absolutely nothing important gets done.

The physical sabotage Gremlins can also be difficult to detect if only one or two major actions occur over a long period of time because these incidents alone will not provide sufficient information to create a clear pattern for the FBE to backtrace the saboteurs. As long at operational security is well maintained with minimal communication with other NRF elements, then many of these acts of sabotage will be difficult to detect or prevent. The outsider Gremlins don't have to go near the targeted facilities themselves or least can avoid getting close enough to be spotted and recorded. Those Gremlins that interfere directly with employees only have to deal with their targets once and without violence if the plan is properly executed. Successful saboteurs know when to depart.

The cyber-Gremlins have decades of hacker experience around the world as a reference library for working out how to best attack FBE organizations while maintaining a high probability of obfuscating the source of the attack. Additionally, since cybercrime is less risky for criminals, every major organization is inundated with illicit efforts to probe and exploit their cyber infrastructure. The Gremlins can conduct numerous cyberattacks and not seem out of the ordinary or raise suspicions that the organization is being targeted by the NRF instead of regular criminals.

Since ANI-controlled surveillance is still in the realm of pioneering, the NRF Gremlins will have many opportunities to experiment and try various means and methods at undercutting the automated surveillance algorithms. The Gremlins also have the added advantage that the immediate attackers can truly think beyond programed parameters while the ANI relies on its engineers and programmers to think for it. That additional degree of separation of thinking from the actual engagement between Gremlin hackers and ANI software can give the underequipped NRF a qualitative edge that technologically over-reliant organizations tend to underestimate.

Weaknesses:

The Gremlin units will consist of highly intelligent human beings who can plan and act under stress and when surrounded by enemies. This also means they are at greater risks of making a mistake because of the personalities attracted to such activities. Arrogance and cocky overconfidence stem from someone knowing they are exceptionally skilled and cunning. Complacency is at its worst with reliable experienced individuals who have done high risk actions so many times that it becomes routine. In routine situations, people feel more comfortable cutting corners or doing things quickly because they've done it so many times before. The risk of Gremlins getting sloppy with operational security and becoming increasingly conspicuous in behavior grows with time, especially after a series of successes. The opposing FBE must rely on most of their underlings being mediocre to more easily retain control, but the FBE will still have exceptionally cunning security and counterespionage agents who will be allowed far greater freedom to act on initiative than typical minions. These security forces will not require geniuses to spot sloppy operatives and saboteurs and there will inevitably be Gremlins who will miscalculate their situation and destroy an entire plan and operation when they get captured. Complacency is unavoidable and will need operational planners to have contingencies for lost or captured Gremlin operatives to minimize the exposure of any larger NRF operation.

The other weakness for the Gremlin LOE is the FBE's stovepiping of information. The organizational culture that produces so many weaknesses does provide one strong strength to the FBE and that is compartmentalizing information. Unless the Gremlins get exceptionally lucky, their operatives will likely be surprised by unanticipated events within the organization. Timelines, schedules, and movements could change suddenly within that FBE organization without the Gremlins getting sufficient warning to adjust their plans. The inefficiencies of the bureaucracy will deafen and blind the Gremlins to the timing and intent of the larger FBE apparatus' information system, especially regarding the actions of the other organizational nodes. Contact with the larger NRF organization needs to be minimal to avoid exposure but at the same time such contact is still necessary as it will sometimes provide the only early warning to the Gremlin operatives of sudden changes. This also includes software patches, changes to their software code, or reprogramming the ANI models. The Gremlins will need good intelligence to stay on top of rapid changes that will likely become harder if a Gremlin operative is discovered or captured. The Gremlins' strength is their ability to operate independently while still synchronizing with confederates in a larger operation to cause chaos in the enemy ranks. This strength of decentralized coordination is also brittle and vulnerable to rapid unanticipated changes in the FBE's organizations as these decentralized networks will be delayed in adjusting to resynchronize to carry out effective operations. In a perfect world, the Gremlins will be able to execute actions against their targets on time with maximum impact but the nebulous nature of the FBE combined with Murphy's Law's "anything that can go wrong will go wrong" means the Gremlins will need to constantly move on shifting sands of circumstance.

Illegal LOE Organization 4: Getting Resources from the Enemy: Extractors

This NRF organizational line of effort is obvious but still needs a brief overview. 5GW conflicts rely on exploiting the digitalization of developed societies to gain asymmetric advantages against their opponents. The NRF will be under resourced compared to the FBE, so the NRF must learn how to extract some of their opponent's extensive financial resources to improve the odds of victory. NRF Extractors are the financial intelligence and espionage units that target the money of the FBE. The FBE's entire system of control is fundamentally reliant on transactional-based loyalty and the flow of their illicit covert income acts as the life-supporting circulatory system of the FBE's organizational network. Extractors not only map out the covert transactions but also identify opportunities to extract some of that money to supplement the budget of the NRF and undermine the credibility of key persons or groups within the FBE.

Extractors will likely consist of financial analysts, hackers, criminal investigators, and professional criminals specializing in fraud, laundering, and embezzlement. These units would optimally be created and assigned to specialize on specific targets to build up patterns of life, develop expertise on the targets' methods, and learn the best approaches of extraction. These Extractors are strategic assets that can be temporarily deployed on special operational assignments when the need arises but will for the most part answer to the national-level NRF commanders. Using both cyberspace and Gremlin insiders, the Extractors would first build profiles on the target's source of income, means of transaction, and destinations of that income. The Extractors' individual missions would range in complexity from just having to find the right office or persons to phish for credential harvesting to get access to bank accounts for money transfers to tracing complex laundering schemes that take months of surveillance and analysis. Although most of the actions would be done via cyberspace, the occasional in-house spy or operative might be occasionally required.

Extractors would not be limited to attempting to steal the money directly from the FBE, they would also find ways of tricking the FBE into giving some of the money away. Creating false flag fronts that appear to be FBE-controlled operations could be used to convince some lower level FBE financial elements to unwittingly transfer funds into the NRF coffers. Setting up charities, grants, and other nonprofits to trick FBE loyalists in giving money to "worthy" causes are just a few of the means clever Extractors could utilize to defraud the FBE's fraudsters. Extractor targets are not limited to only organizations; individual FBE persons make valuable targets as gullibility and narcissism are abundant traits. Catphishing is quite lucrative as many people want to blindly believe online ideal romantic personas are readily available. Especially with advanced ANI to digitally create fake voices and faces to better establish trust in the target as well as creating additional false personas around the catphisher to create a whole false online history making background checks more difficult. The inverse opportunity from such escapades is the opportunity for blackmail of key FBE individuals to cooperate as spies, saboteurs, or embezzlers. The wide-ranging selection of options has already been in longtime practice in organized crime with many of the same methods easily applicable to insurgent and covert operations.

Strengths:

The Extractors' mission is indistinguishable from the activities of organized crime and the governments of rogue nations like North Korea. The operations can be easily disguised as the acts of criminals or small groups of hackers while making positive attribution exceptionally difficult.[xxvi] The anonymity of cyberspace and the inherent greed of people provide the Extractors endless pathway approaches to reach their target, especially when dealing with less tech savvy members of the FBE. The obscuring of the Extractor activities and intentions provides ample protection for the NRF operators while also frustrating the FBE who must continuously change financial processes and security protocols that costs time and more money.

Weaknesses:

Once Extractors are discovered, the same elements that provided strength now become their weakness. Once the FBE positively identify a target, they have multiple cyberattack vector options against the Extractor, can trace close family and friend connections, as well as send lethal action units to eliminate them. Exposed Extractors can be hounded without respite and would have to either disappear and change identities or outright flee to another country to sit out the war. Extractors must factor in contingencies for family and others closest to them in the event of FBE discovery. Unlike many of the other NRF units, Extractors are continuously conducting criminal acts while using cyberspace rather than being in close physical proximity to the targets. This usually means the FBE can only retaliate indirectly through cyberspace or physically target innocent associates who didn't implement operational security measures to hide themselves. Extractors will most likely remain safer than most NRF units during the course of the conflict but will be some of the most vulnerable once detected.

[i] Field Manual, *FM 3-90 Tactics*, (Washington DC: US Army HQ, May 2023) Pages 13-18 and 13-17, Paragraph 13-72. https://armypubs.army.mil/epubs/DR_pubs/DR_a/ARN38160-FM_3-90-000-WEB-1.pdf

[ii] Robert Muggah, "Smart Cities are Surveilled Cities," Foreign Policy Magazine, April 17, 2021. https://foreignpolicy.com/2021/04/17/smart-cities-surveillance-privacy-digital-threats-internet-of-things-5g/

[iii] Lisa Brownlee, "The $11 Trillion Internet of Things, Big Data and Pattern of Life (POL) Analytics," Forbes, July 10, 2015. https://www.forbes.com/sites/lisabrownlee/2015/07/10/the-11-trillion-internet-of-things-big-data-and-pattern-of-life-pol-analytics/

[iv] Army Techniques Publication, *ATP 7-100.3 Chinese Tactics*, (Washington DC: US Army HQ, August 2021) Pages 4-8, Paragraph 4-34; and 5-2, Paragraph 5-5. https://armypubs.army.mil/ProductMaps/PubForm/Details.aspx?PUB_ID=1023379

[v] Ibid, Page 7-2, Paragraphs 7-4, 7-5, 7-7, and 7-9.

[vi] University Press Release, "Reliance on Smartphones Linked to Lazy Thinking," University of Waterloo, March 4, 2015. https://uwaterloo.ca/news/news/reliance-smartphones-linked-lazy-thinking

[vii] Mike Elgan, "Kids Can't Compute—And That's a Problem," Forbes, November 13, 2013. https://www.forbes.com/sites/netapp/2013/11/14/kids-cant-compute-problem/?sh=6a57622831d1

[viii] David Cenciotti, "Unique Photo Shows US Navy Growler with High Value Individual Cell Phone Jamming Kill Mark," The Aviationist, December 1, 2015. https://theaviationist.com/2015/12/01/growler-hvi-cell-phone-kill-marking/

[ix] 2nd Lieutenant Davis Vercher, "Fighting Through Silence," US Navy Institute, July 2018. https://www.usni.org/magazines/proceedings/2018/july/fighting-through-silence

[x] Reference Page, "Data Protection: Location Tracking," Electronic Privacy Information Center. https://epic.org/issues/data-protection/location-tracking/

[xi] Tine A. Eide, Sarah H. Aarestad, Cecile S. Andreassen, et al., "Smartphone Restriction and Its Effect on Subjective Withdrawal Related Scores," Front Psychol, v. 9, August 13, 2018. https://www.ncbi.nlm.nih.gov/pmc/articles/PMC6099124/

[xii] Editors Robert Klitgaard and Paul C. Light, *High-Performance Government*, (Santa Monica, CA: RAND Corporation: 2005) 142-146.

[xiii] OSS Manual, *Simple Sabotage Field Manual: Strategic Services (Provisional) Declassified*, Office of Strategic Services (Coppell, TX: 4 January 2023): 15-50.

[xiv] Jaime Duque, Bobby Dean et al., "How Malicious Insiders Use Known Vulnerabilities Against Their Organizations," Crowdstrike Blog, December 3, 2023. https://www.crowdstrike.com/blog/how-malicious-insiders-use-known-vulnerabilities-against-organizations/

[xv] Zeyi Yang, "The Chinese Surveillance State Proves That the Idea of Privacy Is More "Malleable" Than You'd Expect," MIT Technology Review, October 10, 2022. https://www.technologyreview.com/2022/10/10/1060982/china-pandemic-cameras-surveillance-state-book/

[xvi] Xiao Qiang, "The Road to Digital Unfreedom: President Xi's Surveillance State," Journal of Democracy, v. 30, i. 1, January 2019, 53-67. https://www.journalofdemocracy.org/articles/the-road-to-digital-unfreedom-president-xis-surveillance-state/

[xvii] Eunice Yu, Eliza Kosoy, and Allison Gopnik, "Transmission Versus Truth, Imitation Versus Innovation: What Children Can Do That Large Language and Language-and-Vision Models Cannot (Yet)," Perspectives on Psychological Science, October 26, 2023. https://journals.sagepub.com/doi/10.1177/17456916231201401

[xviii] Milad Nasr, Nicolas Carlini, Jonathan Hayase, Matthew Jagielski, et al., "Scalable Extraction of Training Data from (Production) Language Models," arXiv.org, November 28, 2023. https://arxiv.org/abs/2311.17035

[xix] Press release, "Wuhan University Student Team Develops Invisibility Cloak," Wuhan University, January 30, 2023. https://en.whu.edu.cn/info/1050/7125.htm

[xx] Ben Lutkevich, "Model Collapse Explained: How Synthetic Training Data Breaks AI," TechTarget, July 7, 2023. https://www.techtarget.com/whatis/feature/Model-collapse-explained-How-synthetic-training-data-breaks-AI

[xxi] Michael A. Lutzker, "Max Weber and the Analysis of Modern Bureaucratic Organization: Notes Toward a Theory of Appraisal," American Archivist, vol. 45, Spring 1982, p. 122-124.

[xxii] Gary Hamel and Michele Zanini, "What We Learned About Bureaucracy from 7,000 HBR Readers," Harvard Business Review, August 10, 2017. https://hbr.org/2017/08/what-we-learned-about-bureaucracy-from-7000-hbr-readers?referral=00563&spMailingID=17853288&spUserID=MTM5NjExMzY1MTQzS0&spJobID=1080656592&spReportId=MTA4MDY1NjU5MgS2

[xxiii] James Q. Wilson, *Bureaucracy: What Government Agencies Do and Why They Do It* (USA: Basic Books Inc: 1989) 188-197.

[xxiv] Ibid, 231-246.

[xxv] Ibid, 315-320.

[xxvi] Article, "Cyber Attacks: The Challenge of Attribution and Response," ReliaQuest Blog, June 1, 2021. https://www.reliaquest.com/blog/cyber-attacks-the-challenge-of-attribution-and-response/

Chapter 27: NRF Step 3 Lines of Effort – Penetrate-Disrupt-Isolate-Co-Opt to get the Silent Screams

Step 3 is the operational stage of the NRF's strategy that makes 5GW an actual form of war—using organized violence against the opposition to compel them to accede to the NRF's interests and demands. The Step 3 lines of effort are how to successfully fight the FBE to defeat or destroy them physically, not reputationally, not virtually, but imposing physical death or injury. Step 3 violence differs from the older forms of warfare only in the scale and precision of the attack operations which is reflected in the whole purpose of 5GW-style conflict. It is the optimal form of warfare for an insurgency in an advanced nation because 5GW enables a weak force to fight a superior force with exacting precision using few comparative resources while the infrastructure, economy, and social fabric of the nation remains intact. 5GW allows an underdog army to wage a mostly invisible war against their opponent using the advancements in communication, transportation, and munitions enabling a weaker force to bypass armies, police, security services, and collateral obstacles to directly reach the very heart of the opponent's center of gravity, the enemy leadership. 5GW is in essence an efficiency enhancer protecting the nation's integrity and the underdog forces by destroying the adage of "Older men declare war, but it is the youth that must fight and die". 5GW brings the fight directly to the "older men", the FBE leaders who started the conflict, to entice these leaders to surrender.

This is in contrast to the classic 3GW conflicts where large, organized armies of fighting men and women take up arms to fight the armies of rival polities to bring about enough national destruction that one side is compelled to surrender to avoid total obliteration. This requires an organized national-scale mobilization of resources and people directed to inflict as much damage and pain on the enemy's centers of gravity at great collateral cost of civilian lives and industry. 4GW style insurgency is less resource intense, but still the insurgencies of 4GW must target the weaknesses of the society they wish to violently defeat to achieve their political aims. 4GW emphasizes "hearts and minds" which does mean at least one side is incentivized to inflict suffering on the general population with destruction of civilian targets to discourage defiant hearts or minds. In either of these cases, national security institutions of nations must mobilize large numbers of persons and resources to wage combat and consequently the integrity of the nations involved will inevitably suffer damage and trauma. 5GW helps a weaker side not only fight the stronger opponent like 4GW but does so with minimal collateral impact by using information warfare to distract and deceive the enemy's armies away from protecting their leaders.

If the NRF fought the FBE by older traditional means of warfare, the NRF would need to muster a large army with considerable logistical resources and reserves of manpower to have any chance of defeating their stronger more entrenched FBE opponent. In a developed Western nation, this would require considerable disruption to the civilian economy, violently open societal rifts pitting citizens against one another, and risk the nation's integrity and taking at least a year to build up sufficient forces to wage an open conflict. To make the situation worse, a rebel force in a globalized economy risks the FBE being able to stifle and hinder the NRF's industrial capabilities by disrupting global supply chains. Furthermore, the FBE's superior financial resources would be used to secure transactional loyalty of corrupt politicians who can muster the nation's armed forces along with calling up national conscription by force of law. The NRF would continuously be the underdog in every battle and theater which means the NRF have a poor chance of achieving victory in 3GW conflict.

The NRF operational elements of the Step 1 and Step 2 LOEs are created to pin down, disperse, confuse, and exhaust the superior institutional forces subverted to the FBE by luring them away from protecting the critical center of gravity, the FBE leadership cliques that the foreign adversary nation controls. The FBE leadership is composed of private individuals because the foreign adversary can financially and ideologically co-opt private societal elites with completely open and legal means. Directly corrupting politicians would need to be done illicitly and would be noticed. These private elites use their superior financial resources and social networks to bribe, cajole, and extort CEOs, politicians, and others to make them subvert their organizations according to the FBE's whim. If the anocracy's military, police, and security services are tied up hunting the information warfare elements of Step 1 and 2 LOEs then these superior forces will not be there to protect the FBE leaders. At Step 3, the NRF attacks the leaders and their inner circles of advisors, messengers, and administrators while the national and institutional forces they control are away chasing the NRF's phantoms. Since the FBE leadership is composed of cliques of social and economic elites, they must rely on their own private security forces for protection. The NRF combat forces numbering in the thousands or tens of thousands are hopelessly outmanned and outgunned by the FBE-controlled anocracy combat forces numbering hundreds of thousands to millions of troops, police, security, and intelligence forces. However, with the state's forces lured away, 5GW has inverted the odds as the thousands of NRF fighters overwhelmingly outnumber the private security forces protecting the individual FBE leaders. 5GW uses information warfare to make the stronger opponent misallocate its superior resources, creating huge vulnerabilities for smaller, opposing weaker forces to exploit. Thousands of insurgents, even poorly trained, can inflict an overwhelming mass of firepower onto the well trained but outnumbered FBE private security forces. If optimally executed, the NRF's main combat opponents throughout the war will be the private military contractors (PMC), mercenaries, and security companies that guard the FBE leaders, their estates, and their close confidants.

The NRF sending platoons, companies, or battalions against a security force of a couple dozen very expensive professionals will always be able to overwhelm, even if the losses are 4-to-1 and even in the worst circumstances, the NRF would be the superior force in these battles. The NRF must still maximize efficiency by keeping attacks on targets as small as possible to conserve resources and minimize the public's attention in order to prolong the NRF's ability to fight. Keeping the majority of attacks low key ensures that it will be forgotten by the general public within days or weeks and hinders the FBE's ability to convince the public that more taxpayer resources are justifiably needed to protect private wealthy FBE individuals and their assets. The FBE leaders stay further isolated when the state bureaucracy and politicians face career risking scrutiny by providing unjustified protection favors to the FBE millionaires and billionaires. Of course, dramatic actions involving prolonged fights that generate media and public interest will occur as there is inherent unforeseen friction in any battlespace but keeping such actions rare is more advantageous.

The level of success keeping the FBE leaders' vulnerable by segregating them from official police and military protection will rest on the NRF's combat forces' ability to eliminate their targets as quickly and as quietly as possible. Gigantic firefights will bring a lot of attention from the public, world governments, media, and the anocratic government itself. The more the attack presents itself as a 4GW-style ambush, raid, or assault then the more the FBE's allies in the anocracy can justify a state of emergency to restrict everyone and to provide additional police, military, and intelligence service resources to protect FBE VIPs. Subtlety in execution of the targets severely impedes the FBE's ability to use their corrupt connections to justify allocating police and security resources. This is not to say the anocracy wouldn't do it regardless of public opinion, but it would limit the amount and frequency due to the political cost threshold of protecting the corrupt rich that endanger political careers. The more brazen the NRF, the easier it is for the anocracy to protect their corrupt FBE financial patrons with public-backed support. Assassinations taking out the intended target, preferably one individual at a time, help to reduce the public's angst of socially disrupting violence.

This is demonstrated in another surprisingly apt future prediction from science fiction in Frank Herbert's *Dune* book series showing how an advanced civilization handles future warfare. The ruling great houses of the Old Imperium would settle their rivalries in conflicts of limited warfare called "War of Assassins". This was a strictly limited form of war to reduce collateral damage and more importantly preserve the economic stability of the Imperium even as the great houses slaughtered one another. This arose from the combined fears of economic collapse and nuclear annihilation that could result from an open total war. The 5GW Step 3 LOE actions would be a real-world "war of assassins" where the majority who die are the ones who direct and profit from the actions of the warring factions. Such a war of assassins will keep the Western nation viable keeping the foreign adversary nation hesitant to attack or carry out aggressive actions.

The Step 3 LOE organizations would use similar organizational networks of command and control to insurgencies of 4GW conflicts like Iraq and Afghanistan. To have any real operational impact, the NRF Step 3 forces would need to have a complex network organization that can coordinate planning, logistics, and attacks. In contrast, using completely autonomous combat action cells with little to no hierarchy is the most secure means of perpetuating an insurgent organization. A loose organization with autonomous cells would be difficult to find and infiltrate but could only conduct minor attacks without any larger operational coordination. Having a hierarchical structure with hubs of command nodes directly managing a multitude of cells balance the need for operational security while retaining the ability to coordinate and direct sophisticated complex attacks which would support a larger operational plan.[1] One key difference from 4GW is that the all-purpose direct-combat cells who would conduct the firefights, ambushes, and raids would have more fighters than the insurgent direct-action cells in Iraq or Afghanistan. These combat cells would be general purpose fighters with little specialized training who would only be used for very difficult hardened targets where mass of firepower is needed to break the enemy. The NRF Step 3's most useful combat elements would be specialized "direct-action" cells to carry out most missions such as sniper cells, bomber cells, assassination cells, and kidnapper cells. Creating specialized cells for critical "combat-support" roles would also be optimal with expertise including logistical, intelligence, counterintelligence, medical, paymaster, and cyberwarfare coordination cells that maintain connections to the direct-action cells. Each node within the Step 3 LOE organizational hierarchy would have one command cell from which a certain number of specialized cells revolve around in a hub. For operational security, each hub has its own internal coding system and each hub speaks with its superiors with unique code and cypher systems to keep each segment of the larger network insulated as much as possible while still having means of coordinating actions. This also helps ensure the combat cells retain enough autonomy to keep their initiative and to have the flexibility to adapt to dynamic and fluid situations. For Step 3, the NRF must first penetrate the inner sanctums of the FBE leadership, then disrupt the information network that maintains that sanctum, isolate the targeted FBE leaders for elimination, and as the campaign progresses finally identify and co-opt the more unprincipled leaders to the NRF cause.

5GW Gives the Weaker NRF the Tactical Advantage

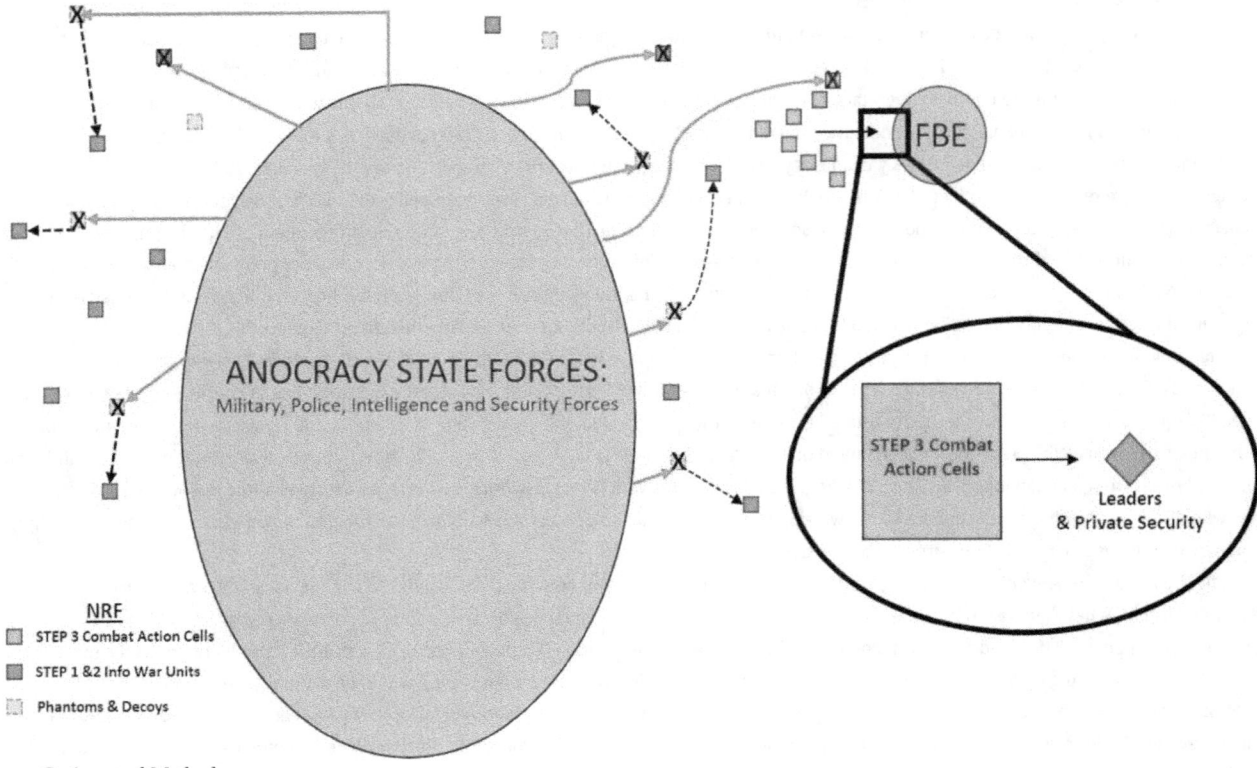

ANOCRACY STATE FORCES:
Military, Police, Intelligence and Security Forces

FBE

STEP 3 Combat
Action Cells → Leaders
& Private Security

NRF
STEP 3 Combat Action Cells
STEP 1 &2 Info War Units
Phantoms & Decoys

Options and Methods:

Penetration Phase

Penetration is a military action that goes through enemy lines to get to their critical nodes of command and supply in the furthest and most protected areas in the battlespace.[ii] In this phase the Step 3 LOE organizations must plan, recon, and infiltrate the FBE leadership and their immediate circle of confederates to identify how to best disrupt, eliminate, or co-opt their targets. Combat cell commanders along with specialized intelligence, cyber, and long-range reconnaissance cells will plan and execute courses of action for getting information on a designated target to maximize the probability of having a successful mission. Planning for penetration and infiltration operations is complex and requires patience, time, and a lot of analysis. Since the US military has been conducting mission planning for operations for several centuries and is currently the most successful military force of the current era, the NRF would simplify their operational training and planning requirements by co-opting, with some modifications, the staffing and planning processes of US and NATO militaries.

The beginning of any combat plan is to figure out what exactly the mission is and its objective. This must be formulated in coordination with the greater NRF strategy and operations, so each combat command cell hub must receive instructions from their higher echelons to know their focus. Once that focus is identified, the cell commanders will have to plan self-contained operations for operational security and with only rare crucial exceptions to coordinate with other combat cell hubs. The planning will have to evaluate the environment, local population, infrastructure, timeframe, and possible traveling routes in and out of the objective. Next, the cell planners must evaluate the enemy's protection capabilities including their manpower, security systems, weapons, supporting infrastructure, and what kind of protection assistance the FBE get from local authorities and third parties. The combat cells must do an initial assessment on all of the mission variables in order to evaluate possible courses of action to achieve the mission. During this analysis, the cell planners will identify what gaps exist in their knowledge of the target or immediate area that will need further intelligence collection. After the planners identify the critical information requirements, they will need to determine the specific, implied, and essential tasks needed to be done to achieve mission success. The planners will then develop courses of action on how to infiltrate or gather intelligence of the target so they can close their information gaps and devise options on how to attack. After the course of action is selected the planners would coordinate the logistics, electronic warfare, cyber, medical, and evacuation elements for supporting the intelligence gathering and infiltrator forces against the FBE target. These cell planners will have a multitude of options for collecting information on the FBE leaders and other critical targets.

The first intelligence gathering task is getting a broad overview of the target and area with simple analysis of maps with private satellite, aircraft and UAV photos of the area in and around the target. This could mean covering just the immediate area to covering the nearby towns and utility infrastructure. This provides layouts of the terrain to identify lines-of-sight, standoff distances from security barriers, potential hidden approaches to get closer to the target unseen and identify escape routes. Once this simple map reconnaissance is complete, the next intelligence collection task is getting NRF cells to reconnoiter the periphery of the target and immediate surroundings.

The NRF would select certain line-of-sight locations to establish long-term observation posts with either camouflaged persons or remote installed sensors such as cameras, microphones, or cell site simulators to eavesdrop on local communications.[iii] These will help establish patterns of behavior of both the NRF targets and their security forces to identify the best times and methods to strike the target with the best chance of success. These observation posts must remain covert and maintain a reasonable standoff from the target. Aside from watching the target and their defenses, the hidden observers can also scout the surrounding area to identify good combat positions for the upcoming fight. These clandestine recon cells can also find hiding spots to preposition caches of additional munitions and equipment to supplement the follow-on combat or assassin cell elements. UAVs are viable but the NRF would most likely launch quick portable quadcopters from a mobile station, like the back of a pickup track or SUV so if a UAV is spotted, the pilots can quickly evade and escape without exposing the fixed observation posts. Of course, clandestine collection is not the only means of studying the target and its peripheral defenses.

Having NRF intelligence collectors get as close to the target location will help the Step 3 combat cells better understand the obstacles and the reaction times of the FBE opposition. One method of reconnaissance in traditional warfare between armies is to conduct recon by fire. This is sending armed reconnaissance units to engage the enemy at the periphery to provoke a response from the opponent so they reveal their full capabilities early in the battle. In this case of Step 3 LOE operations, the "recon by fire" would be to create "incidents" near the target site to provoke a security response. There is a wide range of options such as causing a car wreck or road rage incident near the target front gate. Another is to pose as Jehovah's Witnesses attempting to enter the location to proselytize to gauge guard acuity and response times. Having an NRF member mug a guard near the target site to see if the other security responds or if they wait for local law enforcement is another option. This would also assist with gauging local law enforcement response times. Another option is by causing an actual fire near the site or exploding fireworks to monitor evacuation procedures and emergency services response times. Provoking local reactions without resorting to gunfire helps flush out FBE responses without raising suspicions of an eminent complex attack and is the goal of such intelligence gathering activities. This will likely only be carried out by the more professional NRF cells.

Setting up observation posts, eavesdropping on electronic signals, UAV flyovers, and disguised spies posing as irritants to provoke responses help build understanding of the periphery of the target location but the NRF will still need get information on the local third-party responses and information on the inside activities of the target location. The FBE's strategy depends on subverting and co-opting institutions to their control, they will lobby and cajole local politicians, police, and businesses to change their standards to make it easier for FBE loyalists to be hired. Since blind loyalty driven by ideological manipulation means a much higher probability of mediocrity among the applicants, the standards will inevitably be lowered. The NRF will have relatively easy opportunities to infiltrate the local utilities, police, fire, and road work services to both monitor and sabotage third-party responses to the target location. Although some target locations may hire outsiders without extensive background checks, the NRF need to assume that this will not be a common occurrence. Instead, if the target is in an urban or suburban area, taking jobs at neighboring buildings, homes, or other facilities can also provide additional observation. The NRF, if there is time and depending on location, will also go into the local towns to elicit information from local business owners, residents, and busybodies to have an understanding of the local population dynamics. These are just the physical activities; cyber intelligence cells would be waging phishing expeditions and other forms of illicit activities to gain access to the target's digital infrastructure or communication systems. Even with all of these collection activities, the NRF still has to resort to the classical old-fashioned method of recruiting spies and turning them into insider threats.

Human beings are fallible in an endless number of ways. Some crave danger, adventure, or various thrills while others are desperate to get out of debt, poverty, or simply have insatiable greed. Then there are those who crave revenge for having terrible bosses, passed over for promotion, demotion, lost faith in their beliefs, or getting laid-off. There are numerous reasons that someone may betray their employer and the NRF will need dedicated intelligence cells to recruit these potential sources of information to get high fidelity collection within the defenses of the target. The NRF can use both positive and negative incentives to push someone over from contemplating nefarious actions to actually committing them. Classic incentives such as bribes, ideological indoctrination, or settling outstanding debts will be the more common methods. However, the NRF needs to accept that there will be situations requiring Machiavellian ruthlessness to achieve key objectives; this is not avoidable. Not all circumstances will fit within an ethical framework in such messy actions as war and insurgency. Examples include kidnapping a potential source's family members, become the supplier of drugs to an addict with critical access, or entrapping people into criminal activities to be used to blackmail them into cooperation. War will always remain a dirty, ruthless human endeavor and those who self-restrict their actions in the name of "fair play" will always be at a disadvantage.

Disruption Phase

The crux of 5GW is the ability to bypass the traditional impediment of fighting through an enemy's armed forces to directly deliver a critical blow to the opponent's center of gravity using as few persons and resources as realistically possible. Armies, police, and militias of the stronger force being deceived into either staying placid as if in peacetime, or if mobilized, sent to chase phantoms and decoys while the weaker 5GW force's small armed units go to eliminate the enemy leadership unhindered is the true intent. All of the previous NRF operational lines of effort for supporting strategic Steps 1 and 2 all act to divert the FBE's attention from this Step 3 main line of effort. Foreign-induced civil wars instigated by corruptly controlled societal elites is the most optimal scenario for 5GW. The foreign adversary cannot attempt to subvert and incite their opponent Western nation into civil conflict like the Soviet Union did by co-opting Western politicians and political advisors in the 1940s and 1950s.[iv] Such activity is closely watched and would be uncovered. It still happens of course. China does still attempt to subvert political processes in other countries, like their alleged ties to former Labor MP Sam Dastyari of Australia,[v] but these are more easily uncovered which cause major diplomatic setbacks for China. China is co-opting politicians of the West for safer efforts, like supporting or disrupting individual policy or trade issues rather than being the main effort to build a 5th column in the West. There's no plausible deniability for China when it tries to subvert people directly belonging to Western nations' political processes, but the private elites of the targeted society are another matter. Approaching and co-opting billionaires, venture capitalists, charity boards, academic boards, nonprofit activist leaders, entertainment producers, and others can all be done under the guise of private matters, social outreach, cultural exchange, or under the guise of any number of empty platitudes trying to disguise China's strategic intentions.

To reiterate for the sake of orientation, this scenario's foreign adversary uses a collection of numerous co-opted Western private elites to subvert their own country; these are the NRF's targets. The FBE leaders are composed of a loose alliance of like-minded corrupt social and economic cliques of elites lording over proxies of manipulated companies, activist groups, academia, terrorists, criminals, nonprofits, and lobbying organizations. There is no rigid hierarchical central command authority with a supreme leader to target as these corrupt egoists compete with each other as much as they push for autocratic rule of the Western nation. At best, there might be a "spiritual leader", like a secular version of the pope, who formulates the broad general guidance for the FBE to follow, but even this person will unlikely have the authority to dictate actions to their "peers". This foreign-manipulated group of autocrats would likely govern by a confederated means of consent rather than having a Stalin, Napoleon, or Hitler dictating a methodical comprehensive battle plan. This means the FBE rely on the fidelity of communication between the various FBE leaders who direct their specific fiefdoms to support the greater FBE strategy. Targeting various members of the FBE cliques breaks down their own internal order resulting in chaos, confusion, and eventually division. Like Max Weber bureaucracy, no one is overall in absolute charge, but each FBE leader lords over their specific piece of the system with near absolute power. Destroying an FBE leader or their ability to boss around their fiefdoms creates cascades of chaos that breaks down the FBE as everything is top-down driven. Eliminating the leader cliques of the FBE means the destruction of the FBE faction itself, as its totalitarian system only functions from central authority. No leaders mean the FBE fragmenting into smaller uncoordinated groups that can be isolated and eliminated later by the NRF. Even if some of the leaders are too well guarded to reach, the NRF can cut off those well-guarded leaders' support mechanism by targeting the FBE leaders' inner circles of cohorts such as personal lawyers, bodyguards, executive assistants, doctors, mistresses, spouses, foreign liaisons, and the figureheads that speak on behalf of the leaders to the proxies and to the public. Without reliable underlings to protect secrets and dutifully carry out the wishes of their masters, the FBE leaders might as well be considered ineffective and harmless. Among this assortment of potential targets, the first type of target the NRF must consider is the private security forces protecting the leaders and their support staff. These are the primary combat opponents in this 5GW conflict and have to be neutralized if the NRF intends to successfully strike the FBE leaders.

The private security forces of the FBE leadership in this 5GW fight will be the frontline forces to face the NRF's combatant units. These forces not only guard the leaders themselves, but their homes, places of business, their travel routes, families, and the most important advisors who know where the "skeletons are buried". At first glance, these can seem insurmountable as the private military and security companies will provide the best qualified to protect the cream of the FBE's elite. The FBE will demand lax standards everywhere else to make sure their cronies gain control of every institution, but merited skill will remain at the forefront of the FBE leaders' security standards. Recruited from Ex-special forces, SWAT, and counterterrorism experts from throughout the Western world will use their exceptional skills to fend off numerically superior threats while awaiting reinforcements from government authorities. The NRF is unlikely to have the forces to qualitatively match these private security forces one-for-one. The key to success for the NRF is to compel the security forces to violate Fredrick the Great's axiom, "He who defends everything, defends nothing". The FBE security forces can more easily protect a single person or location, but these forces are selected for quality over quantity. Making the FBE private security defend more potential targets among many locations dilutes their ability to protect their FBE VIPs and opens more opportunities for the NRF combat cells to exploit for an attack.

For this reason, the NRF would be unwise to try to target multiple FBE leaders in one location at once because it allows the FBE to combine private security units into larger more capable forces who only have to defend a single location. Additionally, leaders congregating together in person usually occurs at major social or political events such as galas, conferences, symposiums, and other ceremonies that usually get additional police and other government protection. To successfully attack such events would require the NRF to fight local government forces while being watched by major media outlets. The reputational damage of such brazen terrorist acts undermines the NRF's objective of avoiding confrontation with the superior government-controlled forces and risk major losses. Not to mention the unlikelihood of reaching the intended targets. Instead, the NRF needs to target the FBE leaders individually and if crucial targets are too well guarded, then make the mission about targeting the guard forces instead. In contrast to national armies that have people joining for a wide range of reasons, the private security forces of the FBE are strictly mercenary. Professional security personnel's loyalty is transactional in nature and while they are effective and professional, there is a limit to their commitment to the client. The NRF's combat cells' much larger size than the typical 4GW insurgent cells enables them to launch protracted campaigns of harassment and elimination against the professionally superior but numerically inferior private security forces over a long time. Given sufficient time and violence, many of the security forces' cost-benefit analysis will shift to consider pursuing other employment opportunities.

In the worst case scenario, the NRF would only be able to recruit a few thousand insurgents willing to fight and die for the cause and this would still greatly outnumber the FBE private security forces in any singular given location. With the anocracy's forces distracted elsewhere being unable to support the private security forces, the NRF will have numerical superiority in almost every instance. If the NRF must attrit the security forces first, then NRF could send company-size elements to kill just one or two dozen professional private security fighters at a time. Private security mercenaries are paid to protect others, not themselves, and having the NRF make the mercenaries the main target changes the battlefield dynamics to the NRF's favor. The deaths of security elements of rich persons are not going to stir up public sympathy, concern, or shock to the same degree as the deaths of the nation's soldiers would incur, especially if the NRF focuses on clandestine silent attacks that make the events less newsworthy.

The NRF could ambush groups of bodyguards and kill them in a hail of bullets like the Mexican cartels against the Mexican Army or plant car bombs or other public attention-grabbing means but the political cost rises if done too frequently. Using poisons, blades, bolts, boobytraps, or other silent weapons on individual guards brings less public scrutiny while still garnering morale destroying attention from the security companies. Over time, security companies will lose motivation to stay in this fight if the casualties rise too high, but it is vital that the NRF does not indiscriminately target security firms or individuals. Random killings are counterproductive and eliminating innocent security guards for doing their job will create public animosity. The NRF must make sure the targeted guards are directly involved with protecting the FBE leaders. Killing sufficient number of guards will reduce a VIP leader's protection, but the VIP is likely to flee to a safer area in either another country or another region of the Western nation. If the NRF fail to properly time their operation, they will miss the VIP target, however even then they can still damage the FBE leaders' ability to command by targeting the support staff.

Contemporary leaders rely on staff and assistants to manage the multitude of tasks and circumstances simultaneously occurring on a daily basis. In the case of the FBE leaders, many of these people are from backgrounds of established wealthy families, successful companies, or had the network connections to get promoted higher than they would otherwise base solely on their personnel skills. In short, many FBE leaders' success relies on the already built systems and institutions to shortcut their way to the top. Many of these leaders are insulated bosses, not leaders.

Although many have leadership positions in their private businesses, actual leaders are rare and will be virtually non-existent among the corrupt decadent FBE leadership. A leader can have an official position of authority, but more importantly, a true leader understands their role, duty, and mission well enough to guide, motivate, and communicate to both peers and subordinates a clear intention and goal. Furthermore, they have experiential wisdom to discern the practical considerations of their circumstances, identify problems, demonstrate actions, and then empower initiative among subordinates to tackle specific tasks. A leader understands both their own people and the circumstances around them to be able to solve problems in an effective way. A boss is a person who relies on their official authority to direct subordinates to carry out tasks. Their control is transactional in nature based on the position of their office within a hierarchy who are driven by the intent and goals of the system with little consideration of the circumstances around the problem needing to be solved. A boss' position is more impersonal and prioritizes their own survival and success and tries to link these to the success of the hierarchy that position is a part of. Now there are good bosses and terrible ones. The FBE leaders are bosses of a corrupt subversive endeavor which attracts certain types of people and groups. The overwhelming majority of them will have attained positions of authority based on familial connections, quid pro quo favors with peers or superiors, sycophancy, or success in a particular enterprise or financial achievement. Few of these in leadership positions will fall into the role of a boss with actual relevant experience or character development to command or run an organization that deals with the many different kinds of challenges and obstacles. Most FBE leaders will be bad bosses who use people, focus attention on themselves, and micromanage their subordinates not because of their superior skill but out of fear of being upstaged. They will be experienced at maneuvering through the political games with their fellow FBE peers but will lack the skills to guide or even direct subordinates in situations outside their comfort zone. Bringing the war to these egocentric FBE impersonal management style leaders who rely on the authority as a boss over their ability will make them paralyzed with fear, indecision, and ineptitude. Leading in a fight is beyond almost all of the FBE leaders' competency and so they will all depend on a large support staff of cohorts to provide advice, solutions, and information that the FBE leaders themselves are incapable of deriving on their own.

These support staff include, but are not limited to, executive assistants, secretaries, lawyers, accountants, sometimes academics or scientists, financial experts, and security advisors. As with Frederick the Great's axiom, the FBE leaders may attempt to protect their inner circle of advisors, but not to the same degree. This means the inner circle of cohorts are good as secondary targets that can at least debilitate the targeted leader's ability to coordinate with the rest of the FBE. Even if the FBE leader flees to a safe haven, the leader likely will still need minions to manage and direct operations of the leader's assets. Killing, kidnapping, or intimidating the advisors and assistants can disrupt FBE plans, destroy the morale of those who work with the FBE leader, and potentially expose vital information that can be used against the FBE. Also, among these advisors and cohorts will likely be liaisons with the foreign adversary or at least the third party the foreign adversary is using to patronize the FBE's inner circle of leadership. Depending on the FBE leader, some of these foreign liaisons might have diplomatic passports with official responsibilities to the foreign adversary's embassy or consulates. Elements within the NRF will try to tempt their own leadership to target these liaisons as part of the war effort, but the fallout of killing diplomatic staff introduces many unknown risky variables that could create troublesome consequences later on. Most of the foreign liaisons however, will likely be politically connected businessmen, academics, or representatives of cultural institutions who can plausibly deny working with the adversarial nation's government. Such liaisons are fair game and would likely provide valuable intelligence if captured alive. The other bonus of attacking the private foreign liaisons is that it will create rifts between the FBE and their foreign backers. Balancing between the immense risk vs. valuable payoff means the NRF must study and evaluate potential foreign liaison targets with exceptional due care.

One other group of targets that will need consideration for certain circumstances are people who are of relatively small importance yet their death will bring attention and eat up a news cycle. These targets distract authorities and the public from the more important real target by having a public presence but is not as deep seated in the public consciousness yet their death will still generate media attention. Examples include retired politicians, TV newsreaders, national opinionators, celebrities, and activist entertainers. In military and political terms, there are few people less important than a talking head for a media firm. They simply parrot what is told to them by their corporate superiors. It is the metaphorical equivalent of trying to shoot Long John Silver's parrot instead of Long John Silver himself because the parrot repeated the orders of its master. Like parrots, these TV talking heads attract attention with their incessant verbal noise, are typically photogenic, and have little independent thought. These and other celebrities' lack of substantive power while still having fame is the perfect formula for a distraction. A famous personality being assassinated will attract the concerns of their fellow media colleagues who will discuss the incident until the public loses all interest and the anocratic government will get distracted by investigating the incident. The best part is that the anocratic government law enforcement apparatus will investigate, but it will not generate a mobilized backlash like the assassination of a politician or judicial officer would bring. Retired politicians are also suitable since the public stops caring about the politicians the moment they leave office and become private citizens. These people would also be a popular target for members of the NRF because such an attack would convey the message to corrupt members of the anocracy that there is a price for acting as dishonest self-serving Caligula-wannabes. Since the politicians are retired, they will not generate the same reaction from the law enforcement elements of the anocracy but still generate a sizable reaction while also easily distracting the public with news of the assassinated target. Killing these targets to act as distractors from the real target keeps immediate pressure off the combat cells reading to attack the FBE leaders.

The final alternate target to disrupt the FBE leadership's control is the figureheads. These are the persons who act as a go between the leaders and the FBE proxy organizations. They act as vital links that keep the FBE as an organization linked into a cohesive force that maintains its subversion of the Western nation. The figurehead targets cover a wide range of persons including CEOs, board presidents, board members, nonprofit chairpersons, head academics, activist presidents, officers of political parties, judges, public prosecutors, politicians or a politician's chief of staff. Killing or removing figureheads severely disrupts the proxy organizations and would almost have the same impact as killing the leaders themselves. However, the NRF should consider holding off targeting political puppets until later stages of the civil conflict when the NRF has gained ground on the FBE. If sufficient damage is inflicted on the FBE, then the NRF will be able to exert sufficient control over enough of the Western nation's anocracy to escape the political fallout of eliminating political and judicial figureheads. Even then, the NRF should avoid killing national-level politicians or party officers as it could trigger the 3GW-style war that the NRF are trying to avoid.

All of these targets will be protected to some degree and using 4GW tactics of firefight ambushes, vehicle-borne improvised explosive devices, and suicide explosive UAV drones will bring a lot of attention. This attention provides the anocracy the legal and political legitimacy to use the large well-equipped military and police forces to better protect the FBE leaders from future attacks. These tactics are valid, but in 5GW, they should be used as sparingly as possible. For one thing, the issue of firearms is already a volatile political topic in some Western nations and the political and social elites' fears in other countries prompted severe restrictions or bans on such weapons for public use or ownership. This means NRF factions in some Western countries will have limited ability to replace or sustain armaments. Restricting the use of 4GW insurgent tactics has the additional bonus of conserving munitions and equipment, requiring less to be acquired in the first place. There are many black-market sources for weapons including Serbia, South Africa, Brazil, and the warzones of the Middle East, but smuggling takes time and the risk of detection is higher than locally purloined weapons. Luckily for the NRF, no matter what the Western country, even in the United Kingdom, getting firearms in small quantities is not difficult for an organized force committed to fighting on a small scale, but could be difficult in getting large enough quantities to outfit an army.

Instead, to keep both government scrutiny and threats to logistical supply chains to a minimum, the NRF combat cells should focus on quieter means of elimination. Like *Dune's* wars of assassins, making and using poisons is a cheap, concealable, and easily deliverable alternative in many circumstances. 3D additive printing will enable the NRF to fashion many new ways to conceal toxic delivery systems such as concealed dart-guns, needles, capsule, or aerosol sprayers. These systems could be made out of resins, polymers, ceramics, and other anti-metal detecting device materials that are shaped to seamlessly mesh with parts of an assassin's anatomy or vehicle to evade physical searches. Homemade explosives are another alternative, but preferably small charges that limit collateral damage. The challenge is VIP targets would likely have UAV jammers nearby so more creatively imaginative ways would need consideration. The point is that modern computer and manufacturing technology enables the NRF to build weapons that bypass the traditional detection and mitigation systems designed for finding more common use weapons such as firearms. Such improvised weapons would also be simpler to build, with lower machine tolerance requirements, and less industrial niche materials which would make these weapons abundantly available and easy to replace.

With all the considerations of the type of targets, the location of targets, the protection of the targets, and the means to eliminate these targets to factor into disrupting the FBE leaders, the challenge doesn't end there. NRF now have to consider all the factors in isolating the FBE leaders themselves for elimination or in some circumstances, co-option. Studying the leaders themselves, their proclivities, weaknesses, and personalities are vital to understanding who needs to die and who can be made to defect. The NRF cannot win by completely annihilating all members of the FBE leadership without devolving the conflict into a 3GW-style total war which would devastate the country. Co-opting a portion of the FBE is vital to victory and cannot be forgotten.

Isolate and Sometimes Co-opt Phase

Once the NRF forces get to the actual FBE leaders, the final phase of Step 3 operations is determining what the NRF does with them? The NRF must remain cognizant of the fact that a corrupt system can only be effectively eliminated with the cooperation of insiders. In a civil conflict, getting the leaders to acquiesce to the NRF demands is a required element in destroying the FBE faction. In the American Civil War, the majority of Confederate leaders, both civilian and military, accepted surrender which drastically reduced the threat of a prolonged guerrilla-style insurgency throughout the occupied southern states. The same occurred with Imperial Japan and Emperor Hirohito's acceptance of the American terms of surrender. This did not occur in Syria, Libya, Iraq, or Afghanistan and each and every one of these are still embattled societies with frail economic and social fabrics continuously at risk of erupting into another civil conflict. The NRF cannot realistically kill every single leader of the FBE and cut off the foreign adversary's influence single handedly without a major 3GW-style civil conflict that decimates the Western nation. On the other hand, the FBE will have leaders who cannot be turned no matter what pressure or leverage is exerted as well as some leaders who are too hated in the eyes of the NRF members to bother coopting. The NRF must study and assess each leader separately and thoroughly to build their two-tier list: those who die under the effort of the silent scream and those who are converted under the greedy smile effort.

The purpose of the silent scream is not just to kill the selected leaders but must also be done in such a spectacle that it attracts the leader's peers' attention to send waves of terror to wear down their resolve. Being able to attract the attention of the other FBE leaders to scare them while keeping the public attention on the specifics of the attack to a minimum is the ideal triumph. Killing the target with right level of subtly to make the public lose interest of the event within days fulfills the "silent" part of the effort. While successfully conveying a message of terror to other potential target leaders honors the "scream" part of the effort. This contradictory requirement appears impossible, but it can be done, especially with help from the Step 1 and 2 LOE organizations who can distract the anocracy and the public from paying too close attention at the right moment.

The NRF will focus exclusively on inflicting the silent screams at first because they need to demonstrate to potential recruits among the more morally malleable FBE leaders that fighting the NRF is not personally profitable. As time passes and more bodies of the FBE leaders pile up, the NRF's intelligence cells can start evaluating who to seduce with greed of survival, money, and perhaps power after the war. Once a list is determined, the NRF can message these leaders covertly and attempt to develop negotiations. Even during this time, the NRF still must apply both positive and negative incentives to aid in their persuasion; fear and greed are effective tools of persuasion. FBE leaders of this caliber will only offer transactional loyalty and must get something beyond their lives to actively turn against the FBE and the anocracy. With the right offer and sufficient number of dead peers to highlight the costs of not siding with a successful NRF will put a greedy smile on their face as they loot their dead comrades.

Either option must be done only after the FBE leaders are isolated from each other with their communications blocked, their security is defeated, and their inner circle of confidants are captured, bribed, killed, or have fled. Once isolated from the FBE, the NRF can then implement their final action of elimination or co-option. Once done, the NRF can build up a cadre of defecting FBE leaders to plan for the final elimination and overthrow of the FBE itself. This will likely take a considerable number of leaders being co-opted and eliminated so the NRF will need a lot of patience, precision, and prudence.

Strengths:

5GW's main strength is achieving the same strategic outcome as other forms of warfare using far less resources. Successfully luring away government law enforcement and security forces from the true targets, the NRF can employ relatively small numbers and still have a numerical advantage over the strategically valuable targets' remaining protection forces. Less manpower requirements mean simpler logistic lines of communication, fewer risks in acquiring military or advanced civilian weapons, and the battles keep the collateral damage to a minimum. This advantage also applies to the national strategic impact on the Western nation itself. Keeping the organized violence confined to battling at FBE leaders' strongholds against their mercenaries keeps the nation's infrastructure, institutions, and industries largely intact. One of the primary goals of the foreign adversary's instigation of a civil conflict in their rival's nation is weaken or destroy that nation's standing in the world in terms of reputation, military, economic, and diplomatic power. Having the NRF forgo 3GW classic large-scale conflict between two opposing armies and bringing the battles directly to their opponent's leaders denies the foreign instigators their prize objective.

Fewer civilian or innocent casualties also means less risk of endearing the public to the corrupt FBE and its proxies as the public attention stays manageable. Combining this advantage with the additional advantage that the majority of FBE leaders being targeted will likely be hated or unpopular with general public. Powerful societal elites allured to subverting their own Western nation for power, wealth, and ego more likely than not possess a personality and disposition akin to members of the Bourbon royal family just before the French Revolution. Although the deaths may shock the stock market or certain talking heads, the NRF's wide range of information warfare capabilities can dampen the consequential fallout from the elimination of their FBE VIP targets.

Finally, the small footprint of these battles and engagements means the NRF will more often have the element of surprise. Even though the FBE will know its leaders are targeted, they will not know which ones and when those ones will be targeted. Again, if the FBE tries to defend everyone equally, then all are too weakly defended and are vulnerable, so the FBE must anticipate the NRF's choices of target. Since the targets are overwhelmingly just individuals with some security force personnel, the number of individuals the NRF requires to conduct surveillance, infiltration, logistical preparation, and the actual direct-action combatants will be small. The fewer people make it harder for the FBE to detect sudden changes of the surrounding environment, suspicious activities, or early indications of an impending attack. Stealth, patience, and precision give the NRF, the underdog, an incredible advantage in the modified 5GW combat environment.

Weaknesses:

The stark contrast in the quality of fighters between the NRF and FBE in these engagements will mean a higher casualty count for the NRF. Even with a perfectly planned and executed operation, many of the NRF fighters will likely, especially in the beginning, be inexperienced volunteers. These volunteers will likely also include veterans, militia members, and former law enforcement but mentorship can only compensate a little for experiential deficiencies. Money talks and the FBE will spare no expense in getting the finest quality in private military security to protect their most important leaders and their inner circles. Mentorship and experience will build up NRF combat cells into lethal and capable fighting units but only after going through a gauntlet of combat where fatal mistakes will happen. Also, some of the engineers and weapons makers will also have many volunteers whose enthusiasm will outshine their skills. Expect Murphy's Law of "what can go wrong, will go wrong" to plague the early NRF as amateurs try to become experts in this new "civilized" warfare. Accidental discharges, fratricide, and blowing themselves up are going to happen far more frequently among the NRF.

The FBE private military security forces will intimidate and strike fear into the novice NRF combat cells. This means the NRF will need to incorporate more reserves and contingencies into their operations until a proper battle rhythm is established as the majority of survivors grow into seasoned veterans. This is presuming the NRF is only engaging in ideal circumstances with isolated private security and the NRF not running into government or other third-party forces that reinforce the targeted FBE leader's position. A time will occur when the NRF miscalculates and runs into more than they anticipated, ceding their 5GW-induced numerical advantage at the local level as anocratic forces pour in. The NRF must avoid getting tunnel visioned and foolishly attempt to resist a numerically and qualitatively superior force and disengage as rapidly as possible. The NRF must know when the advantage is lost or their losses will near the total number of NRF combatants involved in the action. This leads to the final weakness of timing.

5GW gives the NRF the advantage in battle by segregating the larger government forces away from the FBE leadership center of gravity. This is done in part by the Step 1 and 2 NRF organizations distracting or stymieing the anocracy and its supporters long enough for the Step 3 combat cells to strike the FBE leadership and escape. Once the NRF decides on initiating a Step 3 operation, the timing tolerances will be narrow and inflexible. The FBE can disrupt NRF direct action against the leadership simply by changing schedules, random relocations, and sudden surges of extra security at odd unplanned times. The NRF will need to master timing down to the hour in order to successfully accomplish their combat goals.

The FBE leadership is the end goal of the NRF and bringing the horrors of war to the FBE leaders to make them directly experience the consequences of their decisions is key to this low-intensity civil conflict. Protecting the integrity of the Western nation to keep it secure from open foreign aggression while still destroying the foreign adversary's influence within the Western nation is an important balancing act. The FBE leaders will not change on their own as avarice and hunger for power will remain insatiable as long as they feel untouchable. Objective reality is brutal and knocking down the insular ivory towers these FBE leaders will metaphorically hold up will bring that brutal reality directly to the main instigators and traitors of the Western nation. 5GW is the optimal way to attain this balance of preserving the Western nation's integrity while extricating the subversive rot within the nation's elites.

[1] Training Circular, *TC 7-100.3 Irregular Opposing Forces*, (Washington DC: US Army HQ, January 17, 2014) Ch. 2. https://odin.tradoc.army.mil/TC/TC_7-100.3_Irregular_Opposing_Forces/Chapter_2:_Insurgents

[ii] Army Field Manual, *FM 3-90-1 Offense and Defense Vol. 1*, (Washington DC: US Army HQ, March 2013) Pages 1-14 – 1-19.

[iii] Reference page, "Street Level Surveillance: Cell-Site Simulators / IMSI Catchers," Electronic Frontier Foundation, viewed on August 31, 2023. https://sls.eff.org/technologies/cell-site-simulators-imsi-catchers

[iv] Unknown author, *Venona: Soviet Espionage and The American Response 1939-1957*, (Washington DC: Central Intelligence Agency, August 1996): 2-6. https://www.cia.gov/static/fc3235f14ff505b6f839321755cfe72d/Venona-Soviet-Espionage-and-The-American-Response-1939-1957.pdf

[v] Justina Crabtree, "Senior Australian Politician Resigns over China Ties Scandal," December 17, 2020. https://www.cnbc.com/2017/12/12/australia-politician-sam-dastyari-quits-over-china-ties.html

Chapter 28: First Shot and Opening Volley – A Sample Walkthrough of 5GW

Very few items in the previous chapters are completely novel or new to warfare. 5GW's most important distinction is introducing novel ways to apply these capabilities and integrating these into an effective information-driven combined arms force that can deliver strategic-level impact against a superior foe. The novelty is the new application of methods rather than the methods themselves. Part of the challenge is conceptualizing how all these disparate elements work in practice because there are no real historical examples. This chapter will narrate a hypothetical first day of how the NRF could initiate their 5GW-centric war against the FBE in the nondescript Western nation to visualize how it functions in practice. Providing a snapshot walkthrough of the opening day on how a 5GW war could be waged helps comprehensively show how each operational line of effort integrates with each other to achieve the strategic aims of the NRF. There is little point in going over the tactics, individual unit actions, and techniques of the FBE as there are already many books on traditional counterinsurgency, 4GW insurgency, and 3GW total war style fighting. As the NRF will need the use of 5GW to compensate for their strategic disadvantage, this walkthrough will be seen from the NRF perspective.

For ease of understanding, several provisions regarding real world factors are necessary to understand first before beginning this walkthrough. The entire wargame of this book attempts to distill the quintessential elements of a foreign-instigated civil conflict for any Western nation without factoring the unique cultural and social structures of the actual Western countries. In practice, each country will have its unique set of cultural customs, taboos, and priorities that the rival fighting forces in the conflicted country will have to consider. Only taking the simplified basic considerations helps show the template of what each side must consider regardless of the culture or society. There might be some Anglosphere-centric social elements within the walkthrough due to the author's cultural bias but will be kept at the minimum.

The next provision being factored into the walkthrough is removing Murphy's Law of "anything that can go wrong will go wrong" for the sake of simplicity. Showing how everything is supposed to work in ideal conditions simplifies the complexity of 5GW conflict to make it easier to understand its applicability. This means every tactic and technology works as intended and the FBE will not have an effective countermeasure or fail to utilize one. In reality, plans often fail on first contact with the opponent since some tactics and weapons only work on paper and not in reality and the opponent will always eventually develop countermeasures no matter how cleverly a new weapon or tactic is devised.

This segways into the last provisional consideration for this walkthrough which are the tactics, techniques, and technologies. Some of these techniques have been used, others have been suggested, and others have been improvised by the author while thinking for an hour or two on dealing with hypothetical situations. There will always be multiple ways of applying weapons and tactics together and not every single combination will have been conceived of by the author. The walkthrough will have tactics and techniques that carry the narrative but in practice will not function as the author theorized. 5GW is still a nebulous dynamic form of warfare with many variations and nuances depending on which theoretician a person references. This walkthrough has few real-world examples to reference and relies more on imagination than historical precedent and empirical observation.

The setting of the walkthrough will focus on a single NRF cell node. This node consists of various specialized cells managed by a central command cell functioning as a hub to the greater NRF organization and how it will execute its specific mission on the first day of battle. This first day means it's the day when all NRF organizational actions from the Steps 1, 2, and 3 operational lines of effort finally combine to strike at the FBE's center of gravity. In the lead up to this day, the NRF will have already been waging an information warfare campaign for a year or so disrupting the FBE's efforts to gain full control of the state and nation. These efforts are still ongoing, but this is the first day that the NRF directly attacks the now vulnerable FBE's heart and soul.

First Phase: Preparing for Battle

After ceaseless information campaigns sabotaging FBE efforts to reorder the Western nation into a compliant autocratic state, the NRF's intelligence observations have mapped out large segments of the FBE's proxy network, finances, and the key persons of value to its function. The NRF leadership have decided to finally initiate Operation Silent Scream against several key figures within the FBE to begin the slow process of fragmenting the FBE leadership culminating in the disintegration of the entire FBE network. The NRF now activates its Step 3 direct-action cell nodes in order to focus on eliminating specific targets within their geographic areas of responsibility. In this walkthrough, the focus will be on one of these cell nodes that is organized in a hub and spoke structure with a command and control (C2) central hub communicating with the larger NRF organization while directly managing a multitude of specialized cells. Each specialty cell is oblivious as to the make-up, location, and capabilities of its sister cells while operating within a strict secure communication process. The example cell node will be referred to as "CN1" for the rest of the chapter.

As nation-wide operations are being devised, the cell node commanders initiate preparational activities to prepare their cells for the inevitable call to action. The FBE's access to advanced surveillance, biometrics, and other sophisticated forensics in the Western nation force the NRF to develop its in-house supply chains as much as possible to avoid being detected and traced. Using as many innocuous commercial materials as possible to act as ersatz traditional combat materials lessens the financial and security burdens on the NRF but also limits the number of planned operations the NRF can do at any given moment. This burden is further reduced by the fact that most targets are individuals or small groups rather than large enemy combat formations. Utilizing various methods, the NRF will skim excess inventories, use malware to create fraudulent invoices, and use front companies to facilitate re-routing vital electronics, medical supplies, vehicles, spare parts, and raw materials to NRF cache drop points. Since the FBE's efforts to subvert the Western nation partly rely on greater social instability to help justify their autocratic rule, acquiring black market materials is made easier in certain cities and locales. Black market materials include narcotics, guns, false documents, and most importantly the for-hire mercenaries willing to act as minor diversions when the time comes.

After CN1 collects finished goods that it cannot make in-house, the raw materials collected will be sent to the NRF's small purpose-built factories and machine shops. At these locations, the use of additive manufacturing will make customized tools and weapons that complicate the FBE efforts to trace or identify NRF supply chains. These customized tools and weapons use common items and chemicals for unique add-ons to modified unmanned aerial vehicles (UAV), unmanned ground vehicles (UGV), surveillance equipment, assassination devices, sabotage and in many cases, customized tools, accessories, and weapons that will only be for one-time use so there is less demand for additional resources. Other materials such as military-grade explosives will be in short supply as, unlike in the Middle East, will not be found in easily accessible places. Instead, the bulk of NRF's explosive ordinance will rely on use of home-made explosives with lessons learned from Iraq, Syria, and Afghanistan. There will also be ample use of Gelignite and other cheap simple explosives used in mining, quarrying, and civil demolition. Thanks to chatbots with large language models providing assistance and additive manufacturing machines, the process to safely manufacture these home-made explosives in relatively large quantities is only limited by the quantity of raw materials procured.[i]

As materials are procured to supply the NRF's fighters for tactical operations, so must the NRF condition and train these fighters. As the NRF must keep a low-profile, training large numbers of combat focused insurgents, saboteurs, assassins, and UAV attack squads of remote pilots will be highly conspicuous. Unlike the hidden valleys of Pakistan or the sheltered communities of Syria, the NRF are hobbled by 5GW's mantra of keeping the Western nation's infrastructure and society intact. This means huge safe enclaves being carved out of the Western nation to raise an army is neither feasible nor desired. So, the NRF must train more covertly with virtual training being the cheapest solution. Using market video games, NRF programmers build customized mods to create maps and scenarios that mimic the target locations. Customized role-playing games can train infiltrators, spies, scouts, and fighters on interrogations, approaches to checkpoints, dealing with local law enforcement, and terrain familiarization. Tactical leaders can exercise assaults on shooter maps, or tactical turn-based games for breaching facilities or homes all while the NRF fighters sit comfortably in a warehouse, clubhouse, or otherwise innocent façade without raising outside suspicion. Physical training regimens used by athletes can help condition and prepare the fighters while looking virtually indistinguishable from a local sports club training for a game. Indoor firing ranges help with weapons familiarization while empty warehouses and abandoned farms can train with paintball guns, dummy rounds, and inert explosive simulators. As the date of the operation approaches, only then would the NRF conduct live fire drills and field rehearsals to condition the NRF operatives for the actual stresses of the mission. This creates a window of vulnerability and the NRF must carefully select the times and locations to avoid detection but it is necessary in order to create competent operators and combatants. Many NRF trainers consist of retired police and military personnel and in some cases, dishonorably discharged or expelled personnel when competent dutiful-minded trainers are in short supply. The training is broken into groups of small squads to minimize their presence, but eventually the NRF must train all of the squads together to maximize the chance of success. Due to the fact many members of the NRF are "green" when it comes to fighting, the NRF provide CN1 additional funds and recruits for reserve elements as attrition among the more novice elements is expected to be high.

After months of preparation, the Hub C2 of CN1 finally receive their mission and set of objectives to be completed by a certain date. The NRF high command has identified a high value individual, a billionaire hedge-fund manager, within the FBE ranks in the CN1's assigned region whose removal will cause financial chaos for the FBE's proxy funding. This individual is valuable because this FBE leader manages the coordination among several nonprofits to launder money into various proxy enterprises using their personal connections rather than formal agreements. However, even with this individual's elimination, there is the risk of it only temporarily disrupting the network since much of the leader's personal assets and network can operate in "autopilot". Given enough time, the FBE could rebuild the financial network with a new head. So, the CN1 commander must formulate several secondary operations alongside the main operation to eliminate the FBE leader, who is designated as high value target 1 (HVT1). The additional targets include members of support staff, key advisors, local organizations, fronts, and lobbyists vital for the HVT1's network to function. In the weeks leading up to the start date, the CN1's most senior leaders and the C2 hub must distance themselves from each other and contact with their subordinate cells to build up plausible deniability from the operations. The FBE no doubt suspects the CN1 commander but will find nothing definitive and the NRF intends to keep it that way. Once the final checks are complete, the command hub orders all the cells of the CN1 to go "radio silent" for the weeks leading up to the day of action. CN1 then waits in silence until the commander sends out one final signal to alert everyone that the time has arrived.

On the appointed day, the CN1 commander is out golfing, on a course many miles away from any of the NRF's designated targets. The commander's communications and personal interactions over the last few weeks have all been mundane with no links to any suspicious activity and appears to all outsiders to be just enjoying life. However, as the commander approaches a certain part of the fairway standing near the rough, the commander reaches into the pocket of their pants and presses the "lock door" symbol on their car key fob just once. A few seconds later, the slightly modified key fob vibrates to indicate to the commander the weak electronic emission from the fob had been received and stored. Once done, the commander lines up with the ball to hit it further down the fairway and moves on with the rest of the day as normal. Several hours later, a small quadcopter UAV lowers itself near the rough and sends out its own burst transmission and receives a quick reply in the form of a recording showing a simple ♦ symbol. In the rough patch of the golf course up against the trunk of a large tree lays a container with the outward appearance of a rock. Within this 3D-printed rock-painted camouflaged container is a simple transmitter-receiver system that records very short-range transmissions as symbols determined by the number of burst signals it receives. The single symbol means the attack is still a go and to begin at once.

This digital signal rock is simply an update to the centuries-old spy method of the dead drop that eliminates the need for having to physically place or retrieve anything that could arouse suspicions. The short-range signal reduces the chance of interception and keeps the vulnerability to the CN1 commander low. The quadcopter is sent later to avoid any connection to the commander and is retrieved by a courier who then heads to a wireless hotspot to access an instant messaging server for a popular massively multiplayer online game (MMO) being monitored by other cell representatives. The CN1 subordinate cells will not know each other, their mission, or location but they know they must still synchronize their efforts. As the courier alerts the subordinate cells that the operation now officially starts, each of the cell representatives will maintain communications on the MMO server. The messages will be simple since the communications are mainly for synchronization and emergency alerts in code such as "delayed", "advancing", "regrouping", "success", "mission complete", "mission failed", and so on. Due to the simple content of the messages, the cell representatives will only communicate with each other using emojis for their code. As the command to begin now spreads, the next phase of tactical operations can begin.

Second Phase: Influencing the Battle:

The internal cell operations will prioritize ease of communications over security. Each of the cells, depending on their mission, will be equipped with burner phones, encrypted hand-held radios, or even satellite relays. As the alert is sounded, these CN1 cells mobilize to prepositioned sites as each carries out its part. Every cell carries out their role autonomously except for the combat cells that have been given the privilege to go after HVT1. A well-protected billionaire with a well-paid contingent of personal security combined with his political connections with the local municipalities guarantees a rapid response from local law enforcement. Any direct attack against HVT1 will need to happen and succeed as rapidly as possible to escape the inevitable reinforcements. Adding more combat power provides the CN1 a greater chance of overwhelming HVT1's defenses more quickly which, in turn, gives the CN1 combat cells more time to escape. This mission requires greater risk to be successful and several cells will meet the day of the operation to carry out the mission. Operational security prevented the cells from meeting earlier even though an attack operation would be more successful if everyone trained together. Balancing security, surprise, and combat effectiveness will plague the NRF throughout the course of the conflict.

Even though the HVT1 operation is the central focus of the mission, it must be one of the last ones executed. Directly attacking the main target without shaping the situational environment around the HVT1 gives the FBE a considerable advantage as they can quickly reinforce the HVT1 without distraction if the billionaire is the only one attacked. The CN1 need to have the FBE and their supporting elements sufficiently distracted to create a window of vulnerability around HVT1. The secondary objectives for the other cells are to help dismantle HVT1's personal network of cronies and finance. Fulfilling this role will create sufficient bedlam to paralyze FBE for the required amount of time. Effectively "killing two birds with one stone", these secondary objectives will influence the environment around the main battle while crippling HVT1's personal fiefdom. Destroying the HVT1's network as the first part of the attack needs to happen within 36 hours before striking the HVT1. Too early would dampen the psychological impact and give the FBE a chance to recuperate local forces. Too late and the FBE cannot fully mobilize their forces to deal with these distracting events, leaving more FBE elements near the HVT1 location. Timing is crucial and part of CN1's intelligence collection cell operatives' mission was assessing this optimal time frame.

The CN1 cells' objective with these secondary targets is to overwhelm the information space of the operational area with numerous attention-grabbing events while simultaneously constricting any and all means of disseminating the information about these events. Numerous local crises occurring without any apparent connection while simultaneously depriving the authorities and the public of information maximizes the chaos needed for CN1 to attack HVT1 unmolested. These events will be a combination of informational, psychological, and physical attacks designed to confuse outsiders while eliminating key facets of the HVT1 network. No one outside the HVT1 network will realize the impact of the losses or why some persons and locations were targeted in the way CN1 decided, but even the FBE will not fully grasp the intent or outcome until after the fact. All of these secondary targets are struck or disrupted in some form within a span of 24 hours.

Not all attacks on targets are meant to attract public attention. Many targets, especially in the beginning, are attacked only to slow down or inhibit the functionality of the HVT1 network responding to the larger attacks. These initial CN1 attacks start off simple with Bricklayers disrupting the daily lives of key administrative officers at certain HVT1-owned companies and nonprofits while Gremlins release unfavorable information on public venues. Cyber intrusions used to collect information on infidelities, gambling debts, and other embarrassing indiscretions leak on multiple forums while NRF bots forward the leaked information to both employees and employers of the FBE proxy nonprofits and companies. No doubt, many of the targeted will now focus their day on personal matters rather than working diligently at their offices. Gremlins also disclose to various media outlets internal memos of the same companies indicating various embarrassing and possible criminal activities including misleading investors, disparaging remarks of superiors to subordinates, and other derogatory information that requires these HVT1 companies and nonprofits to immediately carry out public-relations damage control. This stage of the battle is only to cause internal chaos within the HVT1 proxies. Once sufficient anger and confusion reign within the targeted network, CN1 must escalate further to create the necessary pandemonium for the operational area as a whole.

Much of the officially sanctioned media is FBE controlled via large international and national syndicates with corrupt owners leveraging their influence to direct news and information dissemination to keep the public mollified. These information dissemination organizations also try to rally public support for the FBE and its allies by shaping narratives and selectively releasing information. Disrupting these organizations helps the CN1 blind the FBE on the scale of the threat against them while keeping the public minimally interested in the FBE being attacked until the mission is complete. Normally, most of the FBE's "journalists" are not important, especially television talking heads. They merely repeat what others have written while looking photogenic for the cameras but are otherwise shallow empty vessels for others to use. This makes them expendable and an unlucrative target in normal circumstances as even the most shallow and vacuous talking-head garners fans creating the risk of incensing the public. For this reason, killing journalists typically works against the insurgent group, but in this case of 5GW, such actions are sometimes advantageous. CN1 identified a nationally known talking head months before the start date of the operation after careful study and debate. The reason for this target being selected is being one of the most effective ways to tamper with the news cycle's focus on the NRF's activities by making it concentrate on what happens to the media itself.

CN1 assassins ambush the targeted media personality on a side street near their home. To maximize media attention, the assassination is carried out in an unusual and grisly way with a hatchet to the skull. To muddy the authority's ability to identify the reason for the attack, the assassins make off with the target's wallet and immediately use their debit card for a rash of purchases to give the appearance of robbery. To fully control the narrative, the CN1's operatives inform the local media stations immediately after the attack before authorities arrive. This action sets the stage for the endless speculation that every news outlet will consume itself with for the rest of the day. Although this distraction will tie up the media for a while, CN1's other activities will soon compete with the talking head's demise on the media's schedule.

The next step is to tie up authorities with a multitude of distractions without creating public panic. The intention of the CN1 is to decoy the authorities away from the main target but doing so without any direct engagement with the authorities themselves. The first effort is causing annoyances. The Yance-men are the masters of the NRF's decoying efforts and devise ways to paralyze local authority responses and carry out several actions simultaneously.

The first Yance-men actions are to inconvenience people whose influence in the community will compel authorities to respond to their demands for action. Early in the year, the NRF cyber forces gained access to the outdated networks of the local court's administrative records to find the addresses of all the judges employed in the courts. Using this information, Yance-men picked up members of the homeless community, especially ones suffering from mental illness, and took them to the judges' homes. Once the judges and their families are away at work and school, the Yance-men break into the homes to have the homeless take up residence. If there's time, the Yance-men will help the homeless squat in the houses. Similar actions are done to several prominent local figures' homes as well. Other Yance-men call in swatting on the homes of the chief of police and city prosecutor to maximize chaos.

To severely hinder the authorities' response times and further tie up more resources, another group of Yance-men travel on the highway approaching a section notorious for creating bottlenecks in the daily commute. This team of Yance-men consists of three vehicles with three passengers in two civilian vehicles and one officer in a police vehicle. Infiltrating the local police has been easy when the infiltrators are properly prepared. This team is following a big rig tanker truck with tinted windows making it difficult for casual observers to see into the cab. Unknown to the commuters is that the tanker's driver's seat has a collapsable dummy instead of a person remotely controlled by the Yance-men car directly behind it. At the appointed location, the Yance-men remote detonate a small charge that explodes several of the tires of the tanker as it is turning a curve causing it to flip onto its side and crash into the barrier. The Yance-men vehicles immediately stop near the vehicle with the appearance of being good Samaritans going to give assistance to the "truck driver". The Yance-men police officer stops further back to keep observers from getting too close in the name of "safety". Meanwhile, the good Samaritan Yance-men "coincidentally" have a very large first aid box and another emergency tool kit which they take out of the trunk as they go over to the cabin. Deliberately obscuring visibility, one of the Yance-men goes into the cab replacing the driver. The empty aid and tool boxes are used to store the remote-control components the driver is breaking down along with the collapsible dummy. Once packed, they will emerge with the driver who miraculously escaped with only minor bruises and abrasions. While all of this was happening, the Yance-men police officer radioed in for reinforcements, an ambulance, and a hazmat crew as the fuel in the storage tanker is leaking onto the highway. All of this promptly shuts down the highway in both directions. This effectively cuts off a large portion of the city and county from reaching the other parts of the area for the next several hours, if not longer.

While all of this is happening, the emergency call centers are suddenly inundated with phone calls from bots reporting fake crimes around the city. The authorities get further confused as the reporting calls are from bots using deep fake voices of the mayor, the local weatherman, and a local TikTok celebrity. Yet another group of Yance-men carry out actions requiring further investigation by these authorities after responding such as setting fire to abandoned warehouses on the outskirts of the commercial district forcing the authorities to respond to locations far away from the HVT1 location.

The Yance-men also help disrupt the FBE organizations whose reputations prevents the NRF from directly attacking. The FBE manipulate public empathy to shield their nonprofit entities from scrutiny by advocating "good causes". The causes may or may not be truly good, but the reputation of compassionate aid to the helpless provides the FBE a vehicle to launder and transfer illicit sums for their subversion activities. While the Gremlins are conducting denial-of-service attacks and releasing confidential files online, the Yance-men help disrupt the FBE-nonprofit physical infrastructure and personnel. Thankfully, the largest non-profits are located in a commercial area of the city that has no hospitals, schools, or other sensitive sites. The Yance-men launch multiple drones at the substation powering this area. Gunfire or bombs in the city would prompt unwanted public attention and panic. Instead, the drones drop improvised graphite bombs to short circuit the substation, knocking out power to just this district of the city. Others set off fireworks and small black powder charges next to FBE-affiliated proxy organizations' locations while bots call in fake bomb threats. These charges are too small to rattle neighborhoods but will sufficiently encourage evacuation of a building that is investigating if a bomb threat called in was credible. The combination of call-botting and loud, but small, explosions cause enough evacuations to paralyze FBE-affiliated activities without actually carrying out physical attacks.

As this gets underway, another few Yance-men have infiltrated the local activist communities to spread false information about some of the rich people abusing certain homeless people and that the homeless who had squatted in the homes of the wealthy did so as an act of protest. The Gremlins provide suitable fake videos to the Yance-men as evidence to help convince the activists to astroturf demonstrations in several of the rich neighborhoods in order to cause even more chaos for the FBE-aligned wealthy while also creating a social media story. All of this occurring within the span of a single day while the CN1 have successfully kept up the façade that these events are not related to one another.

While the information warfare specialists create headaches for the anocracy and to a lesser degree, the public, the CN1's assassination and direct-combat action cells now begin a second wave of violence much more extensive and pronounced than the elimination of the media personality. The CN1's physical violence must accomplish one of three outcomes: 1. Create rifts between the FBE and their foreign patrons 2. Weaken the FBE's influence on the anocracy 3. Message the FBE leaders they are not as invulnerable as they assumed. To achieve these ends, the CN1 arranges several assassinations with each tailored to accomplish one of the three outcomes. Some are designed to attract public attention while others are meant only for the FBE's attention but having all of these disrupt the FBE's ability to maintain influence.

The first series of assassinations would attract considerable media attention. Even if this were all that happened that day, other events would overshadow these. The assassinations target critical officers and figureheads of the HVT1's personal network. The first is a prominent academic who proselytizes certain public policy ideas on media outlets while leading several FBE-funded nonprofit studies designed to discredit any contrarian viewpoint. He is prominent enough to lobby on behalf of several FBE-proxy nonprofits to get government grants, help FBE lobbyists with white papers to push certain legislation to justify increased autocratic policies, and trains Atomized activists on methods of indoctrination. This academic attracts a lot of financial contributors to the FBE cause while also building the HVT1's reputation amongst their peers. The academic's daily routine has been carefully mapped out over a period of weeks to pinpoint an ideal time and method of killing while keeping to the NRF's outcome criteria.

The academic always spends several hours in his study reading in his favorite chair next to statuette on the adjacent table. While reading, the academic suddenly smells an unfamiliar sweet but pleasant odor. He sniffs several times trying to place the fragrance but suddenly feels weak, tired, and is having difficulty breathing. For the next few minutes, the academic is struggling to stay conscious but soon passes out and then dies. Before the academic returned home that day, the CN1 unit easily bypassed the simple lock on the front door and emplaced a small camera on the bookshelf opposite the chair on the far side of the room. Another operative snapped on a 3D-printed attachment that seamlessly looked like it was part of the body of the statuette. Within this camouflaged attachment is an aerosol sprayer, transmitter-receiver, and small commercially available motion detector. Once the academic sat down in his chair, the motion detector activated the transmitter to awaken the camera and alert the CN1 operative the target was in their seat. The operative verifies the target is sitting and is in optimal position before triggering the release of the aerosol containing water mixed with a sweet perfume and a concentration of fentanyl. The fentanyl was easily obtained from one of the many tent cities of homeless plaguing the streets. Once dead, the CN1 enter the house to remove the camera and attachment while also planting more fentanyl and assorted narcotics around the study. Once departed, the CN1 operatives call the police to report someone accidentally overdosed in their house. After the police arrive, both the main and social media receive news of the academic overdosing on his drugs and that he potentially sold these drugs to students. It doesn't matter if the police learn the truth or not. The intended narrative is conveyed to the public while any follow-up developments will take weeks and the majority of the public will have moved on by then. Prior to these happenings, all associations, foundations, and media will have distanced themselves from the discredited academic's network.

In another part of the city, a law firm's branch office starts early in the day as always. This firm has many FBE-loyalist clients who specialize in burying their clients' sins from public scrutiny. Nearly everyone drinks huge quantities of coffee from the office floor coffee makers but today while the coffee seems a little more bitter than normal the caffeine craving gets everyone to drink at least a little. A few hours into the day, most of the office begins to feel painful cramps and severe nausea. One of the senior partners collapses after inhaling from his vape device. Emergency services are called as food poisoning is suspected. Most recover but several die from the poisoning. Soon afterwards, it is determined the coffee was spiked with solanine poison, a bitter tasting alkaloid that usually comes from green or rotten potatoes. The senior partner who collapsed didn't drink much of the coffee but his vape capsule contained a large dose of solanine. While the emergency services were treating the law firm employees, many CN1 operatives among the fire department and building maintenance staff helped themselves to hard drives, laptops, and some hard copy files of the FBE clients for intelligence needed for follow-on operations. The actual target was preventing the law firm from supporting HVT1's organizations and also stealing information on other FBE clients, killing the firm members was not a priority. Since killing was not the objective, it is far easier and cheaper to recruit some embittered farmers to harvest rotted potatoes for solanine extraction rather than repeatedly purchasing illicit narcotics which drastically increases risk of capture, so CN1 rations the issuance of drugs like fentanyl for only lethal elimination operations.

Next the CN1 supporting Gremlins have altered the accounting books of several HVT1 organizations with glaring irregularities. The CN1 created false certification of the books by the chief accountant to be sent to regulators in the hope of provoking an investigation. To prevent the chief accountant from learning of the forgery and the penetration of the accounting firms' network, the Gremlins and Bricklayers coordinate an operation to eliminate him. The chief accountant enters his smart car to go to work in the morning to verify some administrative issues in the firm. As he approaches a lengthy straightaway, the car suddenly accelerates at rapid speed. The accountant cannot brake or stop the car as it heads directly into a concrete wall at 90 mph, killing the intended target. The Bricklayers and Gremlins successfully hacked and then hijacked the accountant's car while the artificially created scandal proceeds forward tying up the HVT1's network in legal red tape.

The next set of targets will generate publicity and also a considerable amount of attention from authorities, so the NRF must use their own expendable proxies and that will shift blame and attention to non-affiliated groups and terrorists. Certain politically sensitive targets cannot be adequately downplayed and false flags are the only viable solution to avoid full retribution. The risk is high but even in an information-centric war unavoidable. The best methods for unattributable acts of violence are found in the 4GW conflicts of the Middle East. Finding and promptly radicalizing susceptible minds to act out on their own, with some helping guidance, enables the NRF to deniably eliminate targets.

Now that the HVT1's financial and business networks are disrupted, the CN1 can go after their sponsored Atomized and Nimbyist activist groups. These are the most vociferous elements of the FBE who can galvanize and rally both the press and loyalist elements of the public to attack their perceived enemies. These groups must be undermined indirectly. The Gremlins and intelligence cells have in the past year combed through the web looking for impressionable minds on forums, chat, and messenger sites. Customized chatbots fed with large quantities of datapoints of radicalized lexicons, books, speeches, etc. are used to engage these disturbed minds. Only occasionally managed by human operatives, the chatbots steer the right minds towards violent action in guise of the selected ideology. In this case, the CN1 selects several from the radical neo-Nazi wing of the internet to carry out several simple but important assassinations. Without any financial, logistical, or managerial support, the conditioned personalities are ready to act as lone wolves who will espouse the right ideological beliefs that will immediately attract media attention on specific neo-Nazi groups and affiliates.

The first intended target is a radical activist leader of one of the Atomized groups covertly financed by HVT1's organizations to push vocal activism to pressure the anocracy to endorse policies for whatever the FBE demand at that moment. The assassin is advised through the chatbot on why, how, and when to strike the target. For CN1, the intention is to cause disruption of the HVT1's network, not death of an expendable Atomized pawn. Meaning CN1 will not take any risk to ensure the assassination is successful, only that the attempt is made, the motivation behind the attempt is discovered, and hopefully triggers the intended response. The lone wolf attacks the target during a public rally in front of many witnesses using a stolen handgun. CN1 didn't directly provide the weapon but the chatbot hinted about where the lone wolf could acquire one. The shot is critical but not fatal. Yance-men among the crowd quickly message through the Atomized instant messenger accounts that the assassin is a neo-Nazi trying to terrorize the group and that the city officials let this happen to be rid of the activist. Since this is conducive to the paranoid worldview of the Atomized group, this is accepted at face value. The Yance-men help incite and encourage impromptu demonstrations in downtown. This group now marches against the HVT1's own political allies in the city and surrounding areas with the group galvanized by their own sense of self-righteous anger. This creates more chaos for authorities, media, and the FBE as their proxies now face off with each other.

Meanwhile, another lone wolf is following an elderly man down the street as he approaches a splendidly ornate large building adjacent to a university. Before the elderly man can leave the street, this other neo-Nazi lone wolf stabs the man in the chest repeatedly killing him. There is no rush on the part of CN1 to publicize this or get ahead of the narrative because this action is more for strategic impact than the immediate battle. The elderly man was a foreign national of the adversary nation secretly patronizing the FBE members. Although the old man was not a government official, a member of the ruling political party, or a diplomat, he still had considerable informal ties that linked the HVT1 with their foreign benefactor. The elderly man was a scientist who sponsored many of his country's university students to come to the Western nation. His position gave him access to many prominent associations and nonprofits that enabled the adversary nation to get informal access to HVT1 and other FBE leaders. His assassination will spark outrage in the adversary nation while also embarrassing the FBE and its cohorts. Eliminating the critical links between the FBE and their foreign sponsors will inevitably create rifts that undermine the FBE's stability.

The final prominent target will be killed by CN1's more professional assassins as this target is meant to act as a direct exclusive message to the FBE itself. A retired national-level politician living on an estate in the countryside near the city is enjoying a second career as a consultant for HVT1's many endeavors. The retired politician uses their many connections to assuage the anocracy from looking too closely at any of HVT1's extracurricular activities and has been handsomely rewarded for these efforts. The politician hasn't been in front of a camera for a few years and is largely forgotten outside a select circle of political enthusiasts. Although the politician has a bodyguard, the CN1 slipped powerful laxatives into the bodyguard's coffee, leaving them indisposed for 30 minutes or so. A squad of CN1 ambush the retired politician as he waits by the car. The CN1 operatives hold the target down while one administers an injection of fentanyl into the target's arm and another films the act. The politician soon dies and the CN1 depart. Later in the day, the NRF sends copies of the video directly to key FBE leaders and figureheads along with incriminating evidence of the politician and several other prominent figures of the FBE. If the FBE attempt to use the politician's death as a justification for a crackdown, then the NRF will unleash the incriminating evidence to the public triggering multiple scandals that put other prominent public officials' careers in danger. The intention is to not attract the public's attention and create public uncertainty. The NRF only intends to send the message to the FBE that their leaders and figureheads are no longer invulnerable and now could face lethal consequences for their actions. Given that exposing the NRF's links to the assassination also means exposing some of the FBE's proxies to scandals, the FBE decides to push for their controlled media and anocratic allies to state the politician died from undetermined causes.

These numerous but small operations have hit targets across the area impacting HVT1's personal network and creating chaos for their allies in the anocratic government. The public is inconvenienced but are otherwise unharmed or impacted by the day's events. So much happened so quickly without any obvious connections that bedlam reigns in the offices of various government and FBE decision makers. The CN1 has successfully shaped the battlespace to give their fighting forces the advantage over HVT1 and their FBE-backed supporters. Now, CN1 can finally execute the battle itself.

Third Phase: The Battle and Main Objective:

The battlespace is now a tumultuous torrent of chaos, making HVT1 and his inner circle vulnerable. Now is when the CN1 must reveal themselves in order to breakthrough the remaining defenses around the final objective. Most of the combat action cells are already in the vicinity of the targeted location to dig up pre-positioned caches of equipment and weapons to be used in the final assault. The larger and more complex tools, weapons, and equipment still need to get to the destination unseen. The inspired lone wolf attack on the FBE Atomized activist group that sparked demonstrations was also a contingent emergency cover for any last-minute logistical support that couldn't arrive at the HVT1 pre-attack locations.

The CN1 can now coordinate with the Yance-men in the Atomized demonstrations as well as the infiltrators and sympathizers within local law enforcement to create routes to smuggle the remaining materials to the final objective. This group of Atomized was selected because it is used by the HVT1 to essentially extort local businesses and government with the threat of holding publicly embarrassing astroturfed demonstrations to get grievance donations and subsidies to further grease the FBE's corrupt activities. This includes making sure local politicians also illicitly profited from this political protection racket. Consequently, the local politicians pressure the police to limit their actions against the demonstrators and allow the Atomized near complete freedom of movement. The CN1 take advantage of this by using vans and trucks identified as belonging to the Atomized organization to ironically help the NRF to eliminate the Atomized group's chief benefactor. The CN1 delivers the remaining critical equipment to the combat cells unmolested.

As the CN1 combat cells make their final preparations for the main attack, the supporting cells of the CN1, including other specialized combat cells, are executing the final dramatic diversions. These diversions are not only to keep reinforcements from arriving at HVT1's location, but to blind the FBE and the public as to what is truly going on. Before the operation, one of the CN1's intelligence operation cells' critical priorities were to identify the key nonprofit organization of HVT1 that facilitated the FBE's illicit funds. In the course of their intelligence collection, the CN1 discovered the main nonprofit had multiple ties to the local cartel presence in the city whose network easily laundered money in exchange for local protection from the anocracy's law enforcement apparatus. After months of surveillance and data-harvesting, the CN1 pinpoint an opportunity target to be used for dramatic effect while also shaping the narrative around HVT1's associates. CN1 identified a senior executive of the nonprofit who regularly frequented a high-class cartel-controlled brothel that occupied the upper floors of the cartel-owned and well-guarded building in the city. As a creature of habit, the target always stayed in the same room every evening around the same time. CN1 needed a dramatic spectacle to outshine all the other events of the day. Since the glass window to the executive's room was bullet-resistant, at an odd angle, and there were no buildings of equal height adjacent to this building, a novel method is needed to reach the target.

The decided solution was extreme but dramatic. The greater NRF assembled and provided CN1 with an improvised do-it-yourself cruise missile called an *Aardvark* named after New Zealand blogger Bruce Simpson's website. Bruce Simpson attempted to demonstrate that someone with sufficient skill and $5000 in off-the-shelf parts could assemble their own homemade cruise missile.[ii] The NRF decided to take up this challenge with the addition of extra engineering support combined with a warhead of home-made explosives. CN1 launched an improvised cruise missile from a field near some woodland adjacent to the city. The cruise missile was directed by GPS to the immediate area but a small quadcopter UAV fired a laser at the targets window to guide the weapon directly onto the target. The missile was relatively small so when the warhead detonated, it mostly just obliterated the target's room, an adjacent room, and started a fire.

In the aftermath of the attack, national-level NRF cyber-bots started dropping incriminating files, bugged conversations, and videoed activities of the deceased target along with his cartel associates onto social media sites, chatrooms, instant messengers, and to the local media. The story is too dramatic to censor and now all eyes are on this event. Interest in the story reaches its peak when CN1 releases a clear video of the cruise missile low flying over the city and into the targeted building. After 30-minutes of endless speculation on TV and online, the CN1's own cyberattack cells and Gremlins use bots to spread false stories that a rival cartel assassinated the nonprofit executive in retaliation for laundering their rival cartel's money. Although technically a lie, there is sufficient real evidence of money laundering, that the false flag element is obscured. Even though a 5GW insurgency typically avoids public scrutiny to concentrate on the opponent's leaders, this is an example of exceptional circumstance. CN1 found an opportunity to eliminate a target that would disrupt the HVT1's nonprofit network, divert attention from the main attack on HVT1, and discredit the nonprofit network in the eyes of the public to the point that their corrupt connections within the anocracy cannot protect them. There is one more benefit the CN1 is seeking that requires one more additional target.

The local and national media are co-opted by the FBE. The NRF cannot compete on mainstream information services in any fair battle of ideas so the NRF must instead hijack the FBE's preferred narratives whenever possible. Within an hour of the cruise missile, Gremlin saboteurs carry out operations against the main news studio. One releases a large cage of rats into the commons area while another use thermite to ignite a fire in the storerooms triggering alarms and starting evacuation procedures. Meanwhile, cyber-based Gremlins use a zero-day exploit malware on the news service's network. The Gremlins' malware starts wiping endless numbers of files and corrupts the studio's power distribution taking the media firm off the air and offline effectively ceasing major news reporting from the city who must now rely on political YouTubers, TikTokers, and freelance journalists who can only report fragments of what's going on. This in turn creates endless speculation on the targeting of the news media with NRF bots and agitators aggressively pushing stories implying linkages with the cartels and reciprocal attacks for exposing the corrupt FBE nonprofits. Since the local media is now stymied and cannot respond, the first version of the narrative formulated by the NRF and their CN1 remains the foundational framework for all follow-on speculation. There is no consideration among the public that these actions resulted from an insurgent operation even though it was a dramatic terrorist-like attack since organized crime and connections to prominent nonprofits are all that the public knows about the events. This is the true revolution of 5GW-style conflict, the ability to control and shape the narrative of the battle in near-real time as the battle rages.

As the CN1 was successful, the NRF can carry out its main operation without concern that the public will place blame about the chaotic events on the NRF itself. With both the public and authorities now fully occupied with seemingly unrelated events of chaos, CN1 can now shift from the secondary objectives to eliminating HVT1. To get to HVT1, CN1 must first defeat and remove the private security forces guarding both the location and the person. The CN1 has been using the past few days to dilute the numbers of security that could potentially be available at the HVT1 compound by attacking the security company itself.

The NRF cannot eliminate every target it wants all at once. Many are well guarded and difficult to reach and so the NRF must strike at the weak points of the security company the HVT1 employs. The private security company guards many clients, including many cohorts of HVT1's inner circle. Logically, the CN1 targets individual bodyguards or groups of bodyguards protecting less important cohorts as these people will have fewer bodyguards and less elaborate protection. The idea being that even if the security company loses personnel, they must still protect their clients if they want to preserve their contracts. Based on Fredrick the Great's adage of "he who defends everything, defends nothing", the reduced number of available guards thin out the available forces guarding HVT1 before the main battle.

The CN1 utilized many of the common techniques of fraudsters and identity thieves to collect the necessary intelligence on the security company's employees. After tracking several senior bodyguards, CN1 observed a weekly routine of going to a specific bar near a particular suburb of the city. The bodyguards ordered drinks and snacks by scanning the QR code on their tables to find the bar's landing page. During closing time just the day prior, the CN1 intelligence cell broke into the bar and placed QR code stickers over the bar's QR code on every table. Once the targeted bodyguards finally arrived, they scanned the new QR code which did take the bodyguards to the landing page but also enabled CN1 to successfully carryout a man-in-the-middle attack. Fortunately for CN1, many of the bodyguards use their company phones which enables CN1 to install malware and successfully harvest the company security credentials. From this, the CN1 are able to build a target roster with names, locations, times, and phone numbers.

Before commencing the attacks, the CN1 makes some important logistical decisions which determines the methodology to be used against the security forces. The CN1 considers the potential political and public fallout of using firearms and explosives against multiple targets across the area after already using the attention-grabbing cruise missile strike. Using classic insurgent tactics to raid one or two targets is manageable because the

NRF can use their information warfare capabilities to downplay the significance. This is impossible if the city and surrounding county is awash in hit-and-run shootings, bombings, and UAV strikes. Furthermore, the CN1 must ration and conserve military weapons and munitions for critical strikes like the one on HVT1. 5GW is trying to avoid the older style insurgency and to keep the nation intact while still extracting the FBE from the Western nation's body politic. Too many glaring public grabbing operations improves the FBE's chances of convincing the public to declare martial law and instigate a brutal counterinsurgency that will decimate large swaths of the nation. Raiding armories or using other means to acquire large quantities of military armaments would also heighten this risk. So, CN1 must conserve battle rifles, carbines, grenades, and other obvious weapons of war for HVT1 as the NRF have more than enough to take on one well-guarded target.

The solution is to embrace old solutions and combine these with new technology to eliminate the target without the public thinking that they are in the middle of an open insurgency. The NRF's armorers assist CN1 by supplying numerous home-made custom weapons that are useless in an open firefight, but are advantageous for the role of assassination, with one exception. Removing some of the bodyguards will reduce the numbers at HVT1, but the security company itself will still be able to coordinate with their subordinates and reallocate reinforcements, although reduced, to help bolster the HVT1's defenses when the attack comes. This first attack against the security company's local headquarters lacks the subtlety CN1 wants because the target is well guarded and there remains too little time for a more nuanced approach.

During the night prior, CN1 UAV operators a half mile away launch a swarm of 20 quadcopter UAVs that follow a pre-programmed flight path making them move together equidistantly in formation. Each of these UAVs holds a link that connects three or four steel cables to its neighboring drones, giving the appearance of a fishing net in the air. Wrapped around these cables are long tubes of plastic filled with gelignite explosive wrapped with detonation cord. Dubbed the "Widow's Veil", the swarm formation approaches the security company headquarters property around 1 AM. Just as this swarm approaches the perimeter, a group of Yance-men and infiltrators use several fire trucks and ambulance to drive past the compound with sirens blaring to drown out the noise of the swarm's rotators. The emergency vehicles stagger far enough apart that the Widow's Veil has time to fly over to the main building and land on top draping the explosive net over the roof like a veil. Early the next day, as executives enter their offices on the top floor, the Widow's Veil detonates. Although the explosion is insufficient to destroy the building, it does obliterate much of the roof, including the communication antennas and satellites relays. Some of the executives are badly hurt which adds to the chaos, but the main objective is to cut off the security forces from their private comms network.

For the rest of the morning, CN1 carries out several small operations to diminish the security company's combat power in the area. Some Yance-men and Bricklayers assist with planting drugs, illegal weapons, or other materials in some of the more complacent bodyguards' homes and apartments. The plantings were sloppily and hastily carried out, leaving evidence of these being set ups, especially once the police realized the tips came in on the same people belonging to same security firm at the same time. The intended purpose of removing those bodyguards from being able to assist HVT1 is nevertheless accomplished. For other targets, more lethal means are required but CN1 must keep the risk to the public at a minimum.

In another part of the city, a group of bodyguards are escorting HVT1's personal attorney who is coming out of a routine meeting. Across the street, a homemade remote turret is placed near a window on the second floor overlooking the city street. Instead of a firearm or explosive, the turret mount is equipped with a modified repeating crossbow. As the target is less than 40 meters away, the use of a cheap silent precision weapon in a public area keeps the attack more economical and induces little panic in the public. A crossbow doesn't instill the psychological impact on Western audiences the same way as a person randomly shooting a semiautomatic pistol in public. The bolt fired from the crossbow is a custom 3D printed device designed to ensure lethality. The bolt is equipped with a customized bodkin point arrowhead whose long narrow spike shape is designed to penetrate fibers of soft armor around the neck and shoulders. Inside the bodkin is a 3D-printed cavity containing a toxin with injector which will activate once the bodkin arrowhead penetrates the target pushing the bodkin back to crush the toxin capsule and inject the poison. Even if the bolt fails to hit a vital spot, the poison will make certain of death. The strike is so silent and quick that for a moment, the bodyguards do not know their client has been hit. Only when the attorney realizes he's been hit and screams do the guards turn and react. The turret operator takes this opportunity to empty the magazine of the remaining poison bolts in an attempt to hit the guards. Some hit, some don't, but regardless these guards are not going anywhere else for the day.

Other guards who are away from clients or guarded facilities are picked off as well. CN1 assassins use several moving vans in several suburbs where multiple guards reside. In the morning as the guards get ready for work, a stabilized turret in the back fires a poison bolt through a hidden viewport to strike the guards as they attempt to enter their cars. The silence of a bolt means even after the target collapses the event doesn't cause the panic or scattering that could immediately alert authorities or cause roads to jam with fleeing vehicles. Other guards in more difficult to reach spots, are found killed by unusual projectiles. Other than the silent turrets, several sharpshooter assassins use homemade pneumatic rifles powered by CO_2.

The rifles fire customized rounds akin to Minie bullets that hit their targets with 200 joules of energy at 80 meters. The quiet rifles are easy to make, will not generate panic to the same degree regular firearms would have, and can lethally engage an unsuspecting target. These quiet assassin weapons lessen the logistic burden of CN1 as most of the devices are composite and plastic with only a few metal components. The FBE has instilled a culture of fear regarding firearms and the threat of "extremists" getting their hands on them. These logistical adaptations, enhanced by 3D printing technology, enable the NRF to carry out insurgent activities, even when firearms are in short supply in a 5GW environment.

After the CN1 assassin squads finish up their spoiling attacks on the security firm, the CN1 combat cells in coordination with the infiltrators and unmanned vehicle control teams can now commence the attack. The HVT1 compound is a large estate about 10 or so miles away from the city. It is surrounded by a high wall with only a few entrances guarded by a sizable number of security and personal protection guards. There are servants on the compound and a few buildings adjacent to the main house including a greenhouse, maintenance shed, and guest cottage over multiple acres. The CN1 units have encircled the HVT1 compound by dusk, and then begin setting up observation points, sniper positions, and prepare redundant

215

communications for command and control. Gremlins start broadcasting on the police radios using a deepfake voice of the radio dispatcher to send nearby police units away. Other Bricklayer units sent a UAV with a thermite bomb to the top of the nearest police station and burned out the electric support box to the police transmitters. A mile away, the CN1 launched several small 5 meter long Radio-Controlled (RC) dirigibles equipped with transmitters and receivers to circle around the compound grounds to act as backup transmission relays as well as surveillance platforms. The HVT1 compound is equipped with UAV jammers which will interfere with in close quadcopters that go near the compound and these secondary eyes aid in support until the jammers are eliminated. The additional transmission relays will also help keep reliably stable communications among the combat cell members.

One of the first objectives is the destruction of these jammers to enable the offensive UAV suicide drones to strike the compound and surrounding area. There are infiltrators among the servants but they will not act until after the firefight begins as they are outmanned and outgunned. This means the combat cell fighters will likely have to physically destroy them instead. Although the UAVs are temporarily grounded, the CN1 also has modified UGVs. To maximize control of the high ground, several small UGVs have been modified with grippers and belts to climb the telephone and power poles near the front wall of the property. Once at the top, using direct wire controls instead of radio, these climber UGVs can surveil the grounds and also being equipped with pneumatic guns, to fire poisoned bolts. This way, the small vulnerable UGVs can strike any nearby enemy with a reduced risk of detection. For the more rugged parts of the property, the CN1 have built several remote-controlled tracked carrier vehicles with remote turrets on top. These tracked UGVs are modified to take radio signals but also can be wire-guided with a 25-meter-long cable to bypass the jamming. On the turrets are either light machine guns or a civilian hunting rifle to act as a designated marksman to pick off select targets. For the flatter grounds of the compound, the CN1 have modified toy RC-cars that can also have 25-meter-long cabling for direct wire guidance in the jammed environment. The RC-cars are modified with more powerful motors and have emplaced improvised explosively formed penetrator (EFP) warheads built using commercial materials. For ease of expense, some of the EFPs use low-grade steel instead of copper which doesn't shape the charge but rather acts as grape shot as the steel shatters into flying shards to tear up multiple targets.

The attacks will commence when the NRF uses bots to robodial the cellphones of every bodyguard on the compound at once to distract them and tie up their communications. Acting as the signal, this prompts the first kinetic attacks with a half-dozen of these RC-cars which are sent towards the HVT1's vehicles in the driveway while remote turrets fire on the guard posts near the entrances. The combat cells open fire with tear and pepper gas launchers into the courtyard and driveway. These rounds help obscure the combat squads as they begin advancing towards the compound. The RC-cars get underneath the armored escort SUVs and detonate the improvised EFPs upward. Although using home-made explosives, the EFPs sufficiently annihilate the engine blocks rendering these vehicles inoperable, compelling the HVT1 and bodyguards to remain in place. As the security forces recover from the shock of the initial attack, they regroup, return fire, and set up in covered positions which halts the CN1 forces advance. Despite being outnumbered and taken by surprise, the veteran mercenaries quickly regain their composure and use their superior skills to stymie the CN1's efforts. The HVT1 is sent into a panic room with several bodyguards to hold up while the battle rages outside.

At this moment, both forces are evenly matched. The CN1 fighters outnumber the security forces 3-to-1 but the security forces are behind cover and possess superior training and skill. The CN1 combat cells have security elements mostly pinned down with a high volume of small arms fire and grenades but cannot advance further without sustaining heavy casualties. Several security guards are injured as a few of the remaining ground RC-cars are driven towards their defensive positions. Forced to stay behind cover of a chest high stone wall they don't notice the RC cars coming. The RC cars detonate in front of the stone wall blowing several major holes through it. The wall becomes weakened and the security guards are disoriented forcing them to withdraw to the house.

The infiltrators, who've been employed at the HVT1 compound for months, finally act to destroy the UAV jammers. Hidden in the palms of the hands of the infiltrators are single-shot palm pistols that fit the contours of the infiltrator's hands. These custom home-made devices use steel to make the tiny barrel and firing mechanism but the rest is plastic. The weapons are smaller than pocketknives are easily broken down and smuggled via tiny hidden compartments of laptop computers. Each infiltrator smuggles in one or two small .380 ACP caliber bullets to load into these concealed derringers and now has the ability to eliminate one target, preferably a guard. The infiltrators get close enough while keeping the guard distracted long enough to put their hand close to the guards' heads to kill them quickly. With guards eliminated, the infiltrators now have access to a fully functional firearm and proceed to key locations around the compound. Each infiltrator also has a 3D-printed custom designed thermite bomb that easily contorts to the shape of a person or other object to assist with the covert smuggling into the compound. These thermite bombs take out key electric junctions and backup generators which knock out power to the UAV jammers.

Once complete, the infiltrators throw small Ping-pong ball shaped improvised grenades made completely of plastic. These plastic grenades only release colored smoke to signal to the CN1 combat commander that the UAV jammers are down. The UAV teams quickly launch their suicide drones in waves killing or wounding multiple security personnel in their fixed positions. The remaining security forces withdraw to the house. Depending on the circumstance, some infiltrators decide to engage the security guards while others resume the role of being part of the work staff. Those infiltrators who decide to fight experience a high attrition rate. The CN1 now sends a Widow's Veil UAV swarm to detonate on the roof to clear away any remaining snipers and move in. Now the CN1 combat cells have crossed into the courtyard and surrounded the main house with several platoons' worth of fighters and overwhelm the remaining outnumbered security forces with grenades, exploding RC-cars and quadcopters, and endless fire from carbines and machine guns. After 20-30 minutes of brutal combat, the CN1 secure the HVT1 compound.

Remaining infiltrators direct the CN1 fighters to the HVT1's panic room location. Unfortunately for the HVT1, the CN1's mission is elimination, not capture. The CN1 get above the panic room and emplace very large thermite incendiaries on the floor directly above the panic room ceiling and ignite the bombs. These large thermite devices burn through the high-grade steel creating man-sized holes in the top. The CN1 throw in tear gas, pepper gas, and stun grenades into the holes to force out the HVT1. The HVT1's death is a priority, but CN1 prefers to be able to photograph the target to prove to the world the capture and death of the high-profile individual. Eventually, the CN1 choke out the HVT1 and bodyguards who are then gunned down in the hallway just outside the vault door. Nearly 48 hours of inducing chaos, panic, and violence against the FBE have culminated into this moment and now the NRF can recede back into the shadows.

The CN1 drag the body of HVT1 outside and move many of the bodies of the security forces and line them up around the body of the HVT1. The morbid placement of bodies is necessary for the next step of continuing the psychological war against the greater FBE. The CN1 take photos of this spectacle of death and send it directly to other FBE leaders and their figureheads. This is to make the message very clear that: the FBE leaders are vulnerable; cannot evade NRF vengeance; and the NRF can do this with a relatively small and underequipped force.

This successful operation was done in conjunction with others conducted elsewhere throughout the nation. The CN1 was able to instigate chaos amongst the authorities, destroy the reputation of HVT1, and demonstrate to the FBE that their leaders will directly suffer the consequences for their actions. There remains one last action left to complete the NRF strategic objective. Part of this requires making the FBE want to avoid discussing anything that could be blamed on the NRF. To that end, the CN1's Gremlins and intelligence cells will release over the next few days several surveillance videos and recorded conversations between individuals representing both communist and neo-Nazi terror groups talking together on social media and news sites. In these videos and recorded conversations, the implication is that the assassination of HVT1 was the result of a collaboration between these violent extremist groups. At first, both the public and FBE are confused as to why these two enemies would ally together. Eventually, these conversations reveal how HVT1 employed and manipulated several Marxist groups by proxy to help enrich HVT1 by having the leftist groups attack other competitors in the name of class warfare. The neo-Nazis and communist terrorists ally temporarily to eliminate a common enemy, a corrupt plutocrat that manipulated them to enrich the rich even further. These extremists indicate that the Marxists allowed the neo-Nazi group to attack the Atomized activist group in exchange for helping the Marxists eliminate the HVT1 tycoon. This operation was coded as simply as MRP-II which is later disclosed to mean Molotov-Ribbentrop Pact Second Version.

Of course, what the NRF don't disclose to the public is that both groups had been infiltrated by Yance-men who over the past year used subterfuge to convince these terror groups and militias to unite against the "bourgeois oligarchs". The reason for this subterfuge was not only to pin the operation on scapegoats but scapegoats who had ties with the FBE. As stated with the FBE's strategy of nudging the society into autocracy, part of that effort is manipulating extremists on both sides of the political spectrum to act as expendable cannon fodder. These FBE-manipulated groups help cause fear and spread chaos amongst the populace so the FBE can frighten the populace into accepting more authoritarian rule. The FBE used these extremists many times before and if this story about a new Molotov-Ribbentrop Pact alliance is more thoroughly investigated, it risks exposing many other FBE activities. Consequently, this NRF false flag information operation incentivizes the FBE and their media pawns to downplay the news story of the HVT1's dramatic passing. After a week or so of discussing the story less and less, the media and the general public soon forget it happened. Now the FBE's nefarious activities with extremist groups remain hidden and the NRF successfully keep the civil war a covert 5GW activity rather than an over 4GW style insurgency to preserve the integrity of the Western nation.

This hypothetical first operation of 5GW-style insurgency demonstrates the unique contribution that separates it from other four forms of warfare. In 5GW, controlling the narrative is so critical that it must be controlled even as the battles themselves unfold. Controlling the information flow in near-real time as well as keeping actual combat to an absolute minimum means most of the society afflicted with 5GW will not be disturbed in any substantial way. Preserving social order and national integrity keeps the adversarial nation that is sponsoring the FBE at bay because it will hesitate to openly attack a nation that outwardly appears to be stable, even if a lot of wealthy individuals start violently dying. Focusing on the FBE leaders and their support proxies while waging an information war on the public to keep them as passive nonparticipants enables a weak insurgency to have the ability to directly attack the stronger opponent's center of gravity without harming the nation itself and is the optimal and proper way of civilized civil warfare.

---

[i] Gabriel Weimann, Alexander T. Pack, et al. "Generating Terror: The Risks of Generative AI Exploitation," Combating Terrorism Center at West Point, vol. 17, is. 1, January 2024. https://ctc.westpoint.edu/generating-terror-the-risks-of-generative-ai-exploitation/

[ii] John Barry, "Just under $5,000, and He's Cruising," Tampa Bay Times, September 9, 2003. https://www.tampabay.com/archive/2003/09/09/just-under-5000-and-he-s-cruising/

Chapter 29: Conclusion

This wargame analyzed how a foreign opponent could defeat the West using the West's own societal weaknesses against itself without risk to the foreign opponent's military, economy, or diplomatic power. This distilled scenario of subverting a Western nation from the top-down using the corrupt elements of the Western societies' elites is presented as the most dangerous hypothetical scenario of using gray-zone and unrestricted warfare. An adversary with sufficient economic and political clout in the international order could possibly wage such a covert means of destroying another nation from within if the adversary put in the effort over a period of several decades. China is the only nation on Earth that fits the required parameters of being able to wage this most dangerous form of non-combat gray-zone warfare.

China is known to wage unrestricted warfare both against the West and its Asiatic neighbors.[i] These actions range from using undue influence in lobbying, political activism, and economic intimidation to military saber-rattling and international lawfare. China has mostly used these various means on a case-by-case basis, demonstrating the required skill of using the tools of subversion. The current tumultuous political environment in most Western nations also provides the ideal backdrop for China to use its gray-zone instruments to deepen and widen the social rifts in their opponent nations of the West. Both the political environment and China's subversive capabilities meet the required parameters for this worst-case scenario to be possible. Yet, there is no definitive proof of China attempting to use these unrestricted warfare methods at the grand scale necessary to instigate such wars. Such an act carries considerable risk and if discovered, could lead to an open world war that would endanger China's, and more importantly the Party's, survival.

However, if an opponent continuously exhibits complacency, passivity, and obliviousness to the threat around them, then the risk to China of trying to instigate such dramatic gray-zone warfare diminishes. Only awareness and vigilance against such nefarious efforts will keep China deterred from undertaking such a world war provoking action. The governments of the Western nations have been, to varying degrees, mobilizing for the last 10 years against the various machinations of the Chinese Communist Party. These governments engage with academia, leaders of industry, think tanks, and international organizations while also working to build and maintain sufficient military power to counter China. From observing all these efforts there arises one glaring omission, the general public. Unlike the West, the central absolutism of the Chinese system compels their society to operate as a hive where all efforts and persons must put the needs of the Party above all other considerations. To that end, China indoctrinates its citizenry into the Party's concept of the geo-strategic struggles it is trying to overcome. The average Chinese citizen is more aware of their place in the strategic competition with the West, even if only superficially, than most of the citizens of the Western countries. This creates a significant vulnerability gap in Western social and political defenses. Most Western citizens understand the CCP is oppressive, is a military threat, and is economically challenging the West, but most don't know the CCP's intent or insidious methods to undermine the West.

The West relies on its institutions to act on behalf of the public to address and mitigate societal and national problems while members of the public pursue individual private goals. This division of roles acts as checks and balances within society to prevent the type of institutional overreach that exists in CCP controlled China, but this only works when the institutions function properly. The nature of institutions requires that these organizations take top-down approaches to problems as these are clearly defined hierarchies meaning they have slow reaction times understanding and acting since they have to go through many layers of authority. Additionally, the narrowly set jurisdictions of each Western institution combined with slow reactions of legal and regulatory processes leaves major blind spots for Western governments that China can exploit.

The only true solution is not just taking a holistic-government wide approach to keeping the potential Chinese threat at bay but a truly holistic societal effort. This means going beyond the societal elites in business, academia, and other institutions and putting in the effort to make the general public more aware of what is transpiring around them. This was done during the Second World War and to a lesser degree the Cold War, but there has been no concerted effort taken in the 21st Century. The inherent biases of top-down organizational cultures of institutions predispose them to reaching out only to the upper echelons of other organizations and they typically do not consider the common people who are for the most part apolitical but are vital for Western vigilance. Western societies are supposed to be democratic republics but this means the systems are designed to require the public to actively have a role in keeping society functioning and protected. A democratic-republic decays into anocracy when its electorate becomes decadent, oblivious, and apathetic. The purpose of illustrating this worst of all possible gray-zone warfare scenarios is to help make the public more aware and better prepared in facing potential existential threats arising from the modern great power rivalry between China and the West. The alternative is remaining blind and encouraging China in taking greater risks in fomenting internal Western instability that could create a civilizational altering event that damns the current Western political system and culture.

The wargame highlighted the most dangerous acts of gray-zone warfare that a powerful adversary like China could wage against the West and what it might look like if they succeed. The wargame also portrayed the best course of action for an opposition that is forced to wage the civil conflict against the foreign-backed elites. However, this hinges on the opposition fully understanding the actions of the foreign adversary by successfully identifying their gray-zone activities and knowing how to fight the enemy without undermining the Western institutions or society. More likely if such a scenario unfolded, the first acts the majority of people would notice would arise from them facing the war-provoking actions of the FBE's nudging the society into autocracy. The reality is that if a civil conflict occurs, whether foreign-instigated or not, the opposition will most likely try to fight in the ways that are most familiar to the majority of the populace. Instead of an information-centric war matched with precision combat against key controlling elements of the foe, the most likely form of civil war would be a 4GW+ style conflict incorporating elements from the Russo-Ukrainian War and the Iraqi-Syrian insurgencies. This will lead to at least a decade long bloody quagmire that guarantees the involved Western nations' decline and the adversary's rise against that decline. Such is the devastation of a civil conflict, which is best to help make the public aware of the potential danger in order to avoid such a crisis in the first place.

Edmund Burke wrote a warning about the dangers and risks about revolutions—and by extension civil wars in his *Reflections on the Revolution in France* pamphlet commenting on the dangers of the French Revolution. The most relevant warning is regarding opposition weighing the pros and cons of fighting an oppressive regime and when the time is appropriate:

The wise will determine from the gravity of the case; the irritable, from sensibility to oppression; the high-minded, from disdain and indignation at abusive power of unworthy hands; the brave and the bold, from love of honorable danger in a generous cause; but with or without right, a revolution will be the very last resource of the thinking and the good.[ii]

This book is to help the wise and the good to think and reflect before any strife provokes the thought of revolution or belief that civil war becomes necessary. The best way to avoid a foreign gray-zone instigated civil war is to be aware of its possibility in order to better insulate Western societies from these nefarious efforts. On the optimistic side, the West does have more long-term advantages than the CCP's central-absolutist system.

For all the rapidity of China's rise in power, influence, and wealth, almost all of this was done in spite of the CCP, not because of it. The Party was wise enough in the 1990s to understand that their inferior system could not organically catch-up to the West, let alone surpass it, and needed the West's help. The Party allowed the West just enough market access to sufficiently entice foreign direct investment and technological exchanges while always remaining cognizant of protecting the power of the Party in all things. They successfully deceived the West into providing a continuous lifeline of capital, innovation, and education to help China accelerate its development while simultaneously helping the Party absorb the costs of managing a totalitarian state.

The Party wants to eventually become technologically self-sufficient while becoming the economic center of global trade.[iii] In spite of some critics stating that Western efforts to "decouple" their economies from China is futile or counterproductive, the reality is that China is intending to do the same. In China's case, their concept of decoupling is to become the central dominating technological producer on Earth that will make every other economy on Earth solely dependent on China for all advanced technology. This means the current economic relationship between China and the rest of the international order is going to end sooner or later whether people like it or not. The Party knows this cannot happen quickly and needs the West to sustain China's development for the foreseeable future.[iv]

The Party faces a challenge to their strategic aspirations by trying to reconcile mutually conflicting ambitions. To succeed as the global economic hegemony via technological supremacy, the Party needs China to be both a center of innovation and invention and that requires a population of creative original visionaries with personal initiative. However, the Party also wants to maintain absolute control over China's society without any opposition which requires a population of conformity, dependency, and groupthink. A totalitarian system prioritizes obedience, loyalty, and submissiveness.[v] China's central-absolutist system consequently encourages apathy, cowardice, selfishness, and corruptibility. This is why after more than 30 years of economic espionage, theft, and graft, China still depends on the West for much of its advanced industry and innovation. Contrasting this with Taiwan demonstrates the pitfalls of the CCP system.

As the West severs more of its economic dynamism from China, the Chinese economy will become ever increasingly vulnerable to decline. As its vulnerability increases, so will the Party ever increasingly centralize more and more control over China.[vi] The Party, not China, is the only true thing of concern for members of the CCP and it will never reform anything that comes at the cost of its power. "Better to rule in Hell than serve in Heaven" is the mantra of the CCP. No matter how many times Xi Jinping launches anticorruption campaigns he cannot confront the source of the corruption which is the unfettered power of the Party. The more the Party centralizes, the more corrupt and inefficient China becomes. If the West is diligent and patient, it can slowly ween off China over the next one to two decades while using its dynamism to adapt to the change. Once this occurs, China, like the Soviet Union, will slowly stagnate and crumble under its own weight of corruption and inefficiency. Even if, in the short term, China gains a technological edge in certain industries, severing the Party's economic and technological lifelines from the West will cause China's technological development to eventually slow and fall back. The irresistible need for the Party to micromanage and control all of China to maintain power will kill the Chinese people's inherent innovative spirit as it did before during the Cultural Revolution.[vii] This is why gray-zone warfare appeals so much to China and why the West's public, not just governments, need to learn to prepare and protect against it. If the Party believes the West will truly begin to break away and remove its dependence on China's economy, the Party will act out for its survival. Open war is risky, but letting the West separate itself from China is guaranteed extinction for the Party. Such a situation will make the use of subversive instigation of civil instability in the West a more attractive option.

A West filled with nations internally divided become vulnerable and dependent on the stability of others. A civil conflict in a major Western power such as the United States enables China to regain the geostrategic advantage as the rest of the world is forced to flock to the more stable China. Our Founding Fathers were concerned about such a situation when they debated the constitution and the final design of the United States. John Jay himself warned:

If, on the other hand, they find us either destitute of an effectual government . . . or split into three or four independent and probably discordant republics or confederacies, . . . and perhaps played off against each other . . . what a poor, pitiful figure will America make in their eyes! How liable would she become not only to their contempt but to their outrage, and how soon would dear-bought experience proclaim that when a people or family so divide, it never fails to be against themselves.[viii]

Highlighting a potential problem such as this hypothetical civil conflict without offering some recommendations would be just elaborate complaining. In this conclusion the author will offer some recommendations on certain subjects vital to the West's security and integrity that the general public will need to contemplate. These recommendations are divided into three categories of ideas. The first are aspirational ideas; these are unlikely to ever come about but a discussion of the themes is necessary for the improvement of the public's understanding of the threat. These aspirational concepts can generate debate on how to better the West's current position relative to its rivals by considering realistic solutions based on these aspirational concepts. The next category are plausible ideas because these revolve around topics being actively discussed in the West and could be implemented with some effort. The final set of ideas are categorized as inevitable because the events surrounding these topics are already headed in a set direction and the public may not be consciously aware of it but need to be in order to adapt properly.

The United States government and its sister governments among the Western nations are already working against China's covert and overt machinations in the great game of major global power competition. Yes, the government could do more things more efficiently with a more cohesive strategy and the author has opinions on all of these, yet this subject is beyond the scope of this book. This book is intended for improving the general electorate's understanding of the potential dangers and how their greater cognizance of the current situation could aid in improving security and integrity of the nation. The West cannot be like China where every facet of life qualifies as a public act or good. The West exists because it recognizes both public and private realms within society and any attempt to mimic China's centralized hive-like structure will lead to the West's defeat. The West must instead utilize the private individuals as well as public institutions; the key is to bridge the private and public's participation with institutional organizations in a collaborative effort. The first step is to look at some of the major national security concerns that a more aware public could help shape, direct, and influence the outcome of any proposed solutions.

The main advantage of the West over the CCP is the bottom-up directed focus of the economy that encourages innovation through initiative and creativity. The West's system of government is deliberately slow and lumbering to ensure it can never fully stifle such dynamism. Unfortunately, like all systems that fail to maintain themselves, the Western system can decline into disfunction and eventually morph into anocracy or oligarchy. Historically, once a society begins to decline it almost always inevitably collapses with a different system to take its place. This happened with ancient Egypt, Rome, Greece, Persia, Imperial Russia, the Mongol Empire, the Ottoman Empire, the Delhi Sultanate, and an endless host of others. However, something genuinely new has been created "under the sun" in the past 30 years, the internet. This development could potentially extend the lifetime of the West beyond the traditional lifespans of historical civilizations because the internet and "Information Age" allows for the near real-time transmission of information on a planetary scale. For the first time, civilizations actually have a mechanism to identify and diagnose societal ills before these metastasize into causing irrevocable national decline.

The global information system, like an immune system in a human body, can help the body politic to identify problems and then efficiently direct the necessary resources to correct these problems. The downside is that this is a new phenomenon that humanity has yet to fully master. The ability to properly self-correct national decline to prolong a civilization's lifespan requires a wise electorate with a realistic grasp of the world around them. A tall order in any time period. Nevertheless, it is at least plausible in the West while impossible for the CCP's central absolutism. The obsolete concepts of totalitarian rule offer no flexibility for the system to self-diagnose and correct mistakes as it would undermine the power of the Party. The key for victory of the West over its rivals is getting its potential self-correcting mechanisms in working order.

Aspirational Recommendations:

The main vulnerability of the West that the CCP can exploit is the unfettered globalization of the Western economic system. In the 1990s, the West's owners of capital were allowed to invest and transfer their assets everywhere and anywhere that turned a profit without consideration of national or cultural security. This created an economic blossoming for much of the world but over time some of these major nations' social elites who were driving these investments became more bound to their assets than to any border or nation. This created a clique of Western economic and social elites loyal to international trade and systems that rewarded them with the most money, not cultural or ideological links.[ix] China took advantage of this to bind some of these Western elites to a China-centric global investment scheme that the CCP could exploit to wage their qi against the Western nations. A major step that is already occurring is to reverse some of this to diminish China's influence within the West's governments and societal systems.

For the United States, mitigating the alure of asset loyalty over national loyalty requires changes that bind rewards for elites and institutions to their positive contributions of the society they serve, not just their asset portfolios. One way the United States historically used to keep its elites bound to America's fate was to divide the elites institutionally, not just politically. Most Americans are familiar with the US Constitution's concepts of checks and balances between the branches of government to prevent any political faction from gaining absolute power over the citizenry. Some also are aware of the civic obligation for the electorate to balance the power of the political elite with the accountability of elections. However, back in the 18th and 19th Centuries, the United States had an additional institutional check and balance to keep the political elites divided by having the states' legislatures appoint who would become members of the US Senate. The state legislatures appointing the senators bound the members of this congressional house to the needs of the states' interests and by extension granted considerable influence to state-level political parties. It was less democratic but it forced the national-level political parties to treat state-level parties more like peers rather than subordinates since these 50 different state parties could potentially stop the national-level parties' agendas. This diffused the power among the political elites by binding them to local authorities' interests, not just the interests at the federal level. This is not an active subject within the American body politic, but these old traditions of decentralized accountability can be applied to other actions to help defend the US from sophisticated opponents. To some degree, this is already happening with states passing their own laws to protect critical farmland, real estate, and natural resources from being owned by foreign adversaries. Having a bottom-up confederated effort to crowdsource more solutions to bind economic and social elites more closely with their nation is a critical requirement that will only occur if the electorate demands such actions. The electorate factoring in economic security when weighing social and political issues is a small but vital first step.

Europe has a more challenging environment as the majority of the continent is bound to a polity founded on the concept of being governed by technocratic experts, the European Union (EU). Although founded mainly as an economic vehicle to rival the scales of the American and Chinese economies, the European elites also had political objectives. Since its inception, one of the goals of the EU is to gradually integrate fully into a centralized continental-wide political bloc effectively acting as a single unitary state. This continental super bloc, the European leaders hoped, would be capable of acting as a separate political pole equal to and independent of both China and the United States.[x]

In becoming a third pole in a multipolar world, the EU would not pursue the more free-market-centric economics of the Anglosphere nor adopt the totalitarian extremes of the People's Republic of China and instead pursue a third middle way. The EU would adopt the advantages of centralized authority empowered to the European Commission to rapidly coordinate and allocate large sums of money to tasks, problems, and investments that integrated social wellbeing along with economic growth. This authority would be entrusted to technocratic experts to mitigate the fickler urges and temperament of an electorate. The EU would balance this authority with democratic safeguards in the institutions of the Council of Europe's European Court of Human Rights, the EU Parliament, and the EU Council of Ministers. The idea of this third "European" way would incorporate the best of the Anglosphere and China while canceling out each system's weaknesses.

In practice, the EU incorporates the worst of both worlds. The EU has a strong executive branch which is muddled with three executive bodies: the EU Commission, the European Council, and the Council of Ministers. This slows down any ability to act rapidly or decisively while encouraging highly diluted and ineffective compromises yet keeps these executive leaders insulated to face few repercussions for failure.[xi] The members of the EU Commission are not held to account to any democratic body as they are appointed by national governments who are not held to account for whom they appoint into EU executive positions. The EU Parliament can be generously described as a rubber stamp organ of the EU state with no real power to veto or override the agenda of the EU Commission or the Council of Ministers. Due to the highly centralized bureaucracy, accountability is poor and susceptible to corruption like in the 2023 "Qatargate" scandal involving members of the European Parliament allegedly taking bribes from Morrocco and Qatar which was discovered by the Belgian Federal Police and the non-EU Group of States against Corruption (GRECO) organization.[xii] This is a recurring problem ever since the EU's inception as demonstrated by the mass resignation of the EU Commission members in 1999 after an independent investigation discovered large-scale fraud, bribery, nepotism, and no real oversight over the EU budget.[xiii] This would be the equivalent of the entire US cabinet or all the ministers in a British government resigning at once.

To keep the numerous interest groups from the member nations happy, the EU actively hinders member states from being too exceptional in having different tax or incentive schemes that could make them more competitive over other member states.[xiv] This creates a regulatory structure of imposing banality on the European community at large to keep every political interest group happy with forced mediocrity.[xv] This is partially the reason why the EU is not the technology center of the world despite the massive financial subsidies and support the system provides to European industry.[xvi] The EU can fund massive projects but its culture of micromanagement and sclerotic bureaucratic culture stymies innovation and creativity.[xvii] What creativity comes from Europe comes from the individual member states instead of the collective. The EU is centralized enough to be able to pool resources and allocate them but is still too divided to act quickly and effectively. The EU is democratic enough to slow everything to a crawl, but insufficient checks to have any accountability of the upper echelons of the bureaucracy. The EU system can confront short term problems but at the cost of keeping Europe at a long-term disadvantage as its top-down industrial-age style organization lumbers along trying to keep up with the more dynamic Pacific Rim even after years of "reform".[xviii], [xix]

Then there is the elephant in the room the EU pretends to ignore, the lack of a military. The calls for an EU military have existed since before the signing of the Lisbon Treaty and as of 2024, it is no closer.[xx], [xxi] It has token "battlegroups" that are mostly on paper and still rely on logistical and functional interoperability support of NATO.[xxii] All things have a cost and the ability to wield military might that is globally impactful requires a lot of capital and finance. To successfully create an army, they would need a clear chain of command and other expensive programs would have to shrink to cover the huge costs, especially if the US was to withdraw its logistic, communication, and intelligence assets. EU boasts one way they're superior to both America and China are the considerably more generous subsidies to support various welfare and social benefit programs. One could cynically call these the modern version of ancient Rome's "bread and circus" policies, but the EU members can afford this because they rely on the United States and a few dedicated NATO members for Europe's collective defense. A polity, even a continental-wide size one, is not an independent pole if its military strength relies almost entirely on another hegemon. They instead refer to the EU as a "soft power" superpower which is just a coping rationalization for the fact they are dependent on outsiders for their security. All of this demonstrates that the EU is just a meeker, more debilitated, shallower version of China.

Collectively, the West would be better suited if it adopted more decentralized regional bodies that revolved around common economic or cultural characteristics rather than trying to create lumbering Atlanticist behemoth organizations both too slow and too far removed from their member states to function properly. Dr. Samuel P. Huntington theorized the world would inevitably become unstable and postulated a future where much of the world would revert to blocs or groupings based on culture rather than economics as these are more dependable bonds. One of the ironies of the modern world is that as multipolarity rises, globalized trade diminishes. Great power rivalry only happens when the world powers have the means to use their instruments of power, the DIME, without depending on another world power to exercise these instruments. As time progresses, the world is likely to change from multipolar to bipolar as world powers align into two loose alliances representing two different international systems: the Western-derived system, or some future guise of it, and the Chinese-driven Tianxia imperial system. The ability for a national power to exercise their DIME unimpeded requires nations to be mostly self-sufficient in the key industries of food, medicine, energy, armaments, and communications. Without these fundamentals, a nation or group of nations cannot establish themselves as a global political pole. Since autarky is not realistic and the global system will continue to fragment as the Sino-Western rivalry continues unabated, the next best solution is to maximize self-sufficiency for one's own nation while making sure the remaining world trade is preferentially given to allied nations.

The best balance for the West would be to dispense with institutions focused on a decaying global trade system built on the assumption of common trust and to create smaller customs unions and blocs based on close common linkages with mistrust of foreign adversaries. A Western alliance of smaller blocs of nations that are more dependable and easier to manage as these would be based on culture, common economic philosophies, and common history. All of these blocs would be united under a mutual defense alliance in a more watered-down version of NATO that focuses exclusively on defending the Western core of blocs while individual member blocs build their own smaller spheres of influence and individually take up obligation to defend those spheres. This alliance of Western blocs would adopt a "free trade" system more akin to the early 19th Century where goods, services, and finance easily moved between borders but the specialized labor and physical capital would remain largely fixed. This will be simpler than in the past as the rise of automation makes it easier to re-onshore previously cost prohibitive industries. This would ensure the Western alliance could self-sufficiently wage war with the Tianxia sphere of influence if needed. David Ricardo's Law of Association would operate within each bloc while a few more restrictions on exchange be placed between the individual Western blocs, their allies, and finally impose severe restrictions on the West's rivals.[xxiii] China is actively pursuing its long sought after global Tianxia imperium and the last vestiges of the old 20th Century international system are going to inevitably die in the coming decades. It is best for the West to accept this and prepare as the 1990s-based global trade system is put in hospice.

Conceptual example blocs of this decentralized system of allied Western cultural blocs include the most obvious example of the Anglosphere as it is already practically a bloc.[xxiv] This would specifically include the United States, Australia, the United Kingdom, Canada, and New Zealand. Instead of an EU-style federalist state, the Anglosphere would best adopt a commonwealth style system where each remains a sovereign nation, with its own currency and borders, yet still integrate regarding mutual problems. Specifically, greater integration of military capabilities, of which there are already early developments such as the Five Eyes intelligence gathering alliance and the AUKUS partnership between the US, UK, and Australia. Besides greater military integration, an Anglosphere commonwealth could combine resources into a common space program to counter any Sino-Russian space adventurism. Being the principle Western bloc, the Anglosphere would still have obligation in protecting the global commons shipping and air lanes for world commerce. This means working with Asiatic and Latin American allies to work with the Anglosphere to help build more mutually supporting onshoring, friend shoring, and near shoring type trading and investments as much as possible.

Other more hypothetical blocs could include a Frankish bloc of Germany, France, Belgium, and Luxembourg, with "maybe" the Netherlands. Other more obvious ones would be a Nordic bloc and a central European bloc combining Austria, the Visegrád Group, and Baltic states. Less obvious could include a Western Mediterranean bloc of Italy, Slovenia, Malta, and the Iberian states. While a Thracian or Eastern Mediterranean bloc of Greece, Cyprus, Israel, Bulgaria, Albania, and Romania could form in the east. Instead of joining one of the European blocs, Turkey could focus on building its own sphere of influence in Central Asia to counterbalance China's Tianxia imperial efforts there.

All of this is aspirational with only some chance of happening. These are merely conceptual proposals to highlight some of the world realities the West and its electorate are going to have to address sooner or later. The more the public is aware of these possibilities, the more readily they will be able to adapt to the inevitable geopolitical changes of the next 30 years. The next follow-on suggestions below are plausible to implement, or at least portions of them, if the public wishes to pursue them. In these cases, to help increase the level of risk for China attempting to move against the West.

Probable Recommendations:

The massive cost of modern warfare makes any endeavor to protect the western Pacific region a challenging affair that intimidates both policymakers and voters alike. The sophistication and variety of modern non-nuclear weapons can kill potentially thousands in moments while also taking a tremendous number of resources and time to maintain, not to mention the costs supporting the fighters who use them. It is often more politically beneficial for policymakers to delay or put off the necessary investments until later, which then becomes more costly as those investments will need to be created in a shorter amount of time. Committing the necessary defense investments to counter an aggressive China without reverting to a wartime economy requires very clever use of resources, innovative ideas, and atypical solutions. One problem being discussed in foreign policy deliberations is solving how to increase the defense of Taiwan without breaking Western defense budgets? A proposed solution is helping the Taiwanese population, not just the Taiwanese military, prepare for war.

The PLA and the CCP are very risk averse due to the experiences of the 20th Century and it is reflected in the Party's treatment towards Taiwan. The Party has invested far too much miànzi, or public reputation, pledging to keep Taiwan within its sphere of control and cannot abandon its pursuit of reunification. Simultaneously, the Party cannot risk going to war ill-prepared and allowing Taiwan and its allies to defeat the PLA. Such a disaster would create a political vulnerability making the CCP susceptible to being overthrown meaning the Pary will need to blame someone to protect its miànzi, meaning either the PLA leaders or Xi himself. The risk of losing the modern equivalent of the "Mandate of Heaven" could prompt the most at-risk commanders into launching a coup or the Party trying to purge Xi.[xxv] For this reason, the Party will not consider full-scale military action until it's overwhelmingly confident in a PLA victory. Until that confidence threshold is reached, the Party will limit itself to gray-zone warfare. This means the solution to this problem for the West protecting the West Pacific and Taiwan itself is to simply raise the risk to an unacceptable level for an invasion of Taiwan.[xxvi] The cheapest and quickest solution lies in the lessons learned in Ukraine.

The Russo-Ukrainian War revealed once again that post-industrial age warfare is very resource intensive. Ukraine, even after the invasion of Crimea, failed to stockpile sufficient military-related materials or provide sufficient training to its reservists to self-sufficiently stem the materially superior Russian Army's invasion.[xxvii] Taiwan's forces are facing similar problems because their political class took the easy road for decades and overlooked military modernization for the sake of civilian economic development. While Taiwan consequently became an economic and technological powerhouse, it has made itself far more vulnerable to a Chinese invasion. The military is now being slowly modernized but this will take time and relying solely on the military alone for defense creates considerable risk as they, like their Ukrainian counterparts, are considerably outnumbered. Yes, Taiwan has conscription, but this only means the population that would be drafted into Taiwan's military command structure which can only manage and field a fixed number of troops at any given time. The conscription army could only mobilize to the furthest extent Taiwan's defense forces have the means to sustain them. This fixed cap has been lowered due to years of neglecting Taiwan's defense forces.[xxviii] Thankfully, Taiwan is now taking lessons from the United States' concepts of militias and local defense and started nationwide civil society defense programs and encouraging nongovernmental organizations to help prepare the wider civilian population for their state's defense.

Non-governmental organizations such as the Kuma Academy, are helping train Taiwanese citizens in first aide, cognitive / psychological warfare, evacuation drills, and emergency rescue.[xxix] These civil defense efforts enable Taiwan to create and use resources beyond the military and its defense budget. Akin to the early colonial American traditions of building community militias, the Taiwanese civil society is now trying to build "social resilience" that act as localized force multipliers against any PLA invasion. This frees up money and capital to be invested in modernizing critical systems for theater operations such as denying the PLA the ability to establish beach heads in the first place. Having the population psychologically prepared, able to support their neighbors, participate in the cyber operations, and information warfare efforts all help support Taiwan's defense. However, all of this preparation is only supporting the secondary efforts of freeing up logistics, civilian relocation, and information operations. None of these civil defense efforts have taken the next step and truly become like the American militias of old by training civilians how to fight.[xxx] Taiwanese law, as well as cultural barriers, discourage the government from training civilians in combat fighting or the use of weapons unless they are conscripted. Taiwan will need a cultural change to accept the fact that to survive and deter the CCP requires for the whole of Taiwan to be a threat, not just the state and its military. If Taiwan became more like Switzerland, Israel, or the United States by adopting a citizen militia that could operate as local guerrillas, disruptors, and harassers to pin down the PLA for the regular military then the PLA has to reappraise their planning and priorities. The more combat power Taiwan can muster, the more the PLA has to build up to ensure military success.

Unlike Ukraine, Taiwan doesn't have a flat contiguous land border that allows an invader the ability to rebuild their lines of communication and logistical support over and over again after being attacked. China must contend with a 150 km span of ocean between the mainland and Taiwan which means if they fail to secure beachheads for the follow-on forces, then there is no way for the PLA to take the island. Yes, the PLA can devastate Taiwan with missiles, bombs, fly in thousands of airborne troops, and they have a huge merchant marine to conscript into service to use as additional transport ships for those large formations of soldiers. However, without the ability to land and sustain large ground forces to secure the island, these advantages are of little use. If thousands of additional militiamen trained to emplace mines, fortifications, obstacles, act as artillery spotters, pilot hundreds of suicide drones, and marksmen to pin down PLA marines then the risk of failure for the PLA's initial wave of the invasion grows exponentially. Not only does the PLA have to traverse a dangerous strait of water but there are few viable landing sites for invaders. The shallow waters on the west coast and the rocky mountainous ridges lining the east coast constricts the PLA's options.[xxxi] This means Taiwan can send these additional militia into only a few areas to help bottleneck and corral the PLA invaders in order to help defeat them. The faster Taiwan can muster a militia that provides additional combat support to the regular armed forces, the more likely the PLA will be deterred from invading in the foreseeable future. The American public would be the best way to accelerate this cause.

American volunteers among the various gun clubs, advocacy groups, and defense organizations could provide the additional resources and training the Taiwanese lack on their island. Having private American citizens rather than the government leading this effort avoids many of the logistical and diplomatic pitfalls. The United States has a considerable amount of private infrastructure dedicated to tactical training activities and home defense. Connecting with Taiwan's civil defense programs and NGOs to bring "tactical tourists" to train on American ranges, get individual tactical training from veterans, and put together training events would accelerate the timeline to prepare Taiwan's population for an invasion by years. With sufficient proselytizing among Taiwanese inductees, perhaps the Taiwanese government will yield to adopting a more Western societal concept related to collective defense. If successful, this would allow the US volunteers to help plan and even contribute materials and planning for local militia cells, reaction plans, and pre-position caches of munitions, food, medicine, and communications equipment. This all has the added advantage of making the PLA's effort to identify and map out all of the additional support to Taiwan much more difficult as it is not direct foreign aid by the US government.

Variations of this concept has been suggested on and off over the last 10 years from academic circles, politicians such as Vivek Ramaswamy, policy advisors like Robert O'Brien, to YouTube political analysts such as the libertarian Tarl Warwick (Styxhexenhammer666).[xxxii] This would also help rekindle cultural and practical conditioning of the US population on the topic of civil defense. Although the United States has a long history of militias and home defense, it needs to better incorporate the new forms of information, cyber, and psychological warfare into its defense planning. The sophistication of already constructed cyber tools and programs enables persons with limited computer knowledge to contribute to cyber defense by creating cyber militias that could operate in parallel with state militias and the National Guard to bolster the federal level efforts. In this case, cyber militias could use people who do not typically go to war. The cyber militias could have volunteers from the elderly and retirement communities, giving them the chance to participate in national service without physical risk to themselves. For younger persons, cyber militias could be manned by interns and students earning their software, programming, or network engineering degrees for hands on training and experience. Some politicians have proposed a "National Digital Reserve Corps"[xxxiii] but the public should also consider forming local cyber auxiliaries to states' militia and defense forces. Regardless, having the public directly assist Taiwan's population in developing its civil defense capabilities will also help rekindle the discussion and consideration within the United States as well. Of course, the discussion on civil defense issues will require the civil population to have some understanding of the situation and the justifications for carrying out such actions. This means the United States would also need to re-evaluate how to bring back a common understanding of national civics which would require reforms in education.

Increasing the electorate's understanding and awareness of the potential national security threats and their various nefarious methods is a long-term project over a period of years. Decades of declining educational standards and public complacency about the safety of their place in the world requires a considerable amount of time to reverse. The main effort of improving the population's awareness of the true potential dangers of the world requires changes to Western education. The key advantage of the West over China is the innovative spirit that provides the superior dynamism allowing the West to adapt and overcome unforeseen challenges. The more the education expectations are lowered, the more this innovation advantage erodes. One of the principal lines of effort of the FBE in the wargame was to nudge the population into greater conformity by discouraging critical thinking and espousing mediocrity as virtuous. Anocracies thrive when the population doesn't understand anything beyond their immediate needs and desires. Helping the US avoid this calamity is a critical action in the current great power competition in the contemporary world.

There are three education themes the public should contemplate on how to best keep the West's future more secure. The first theme is regarding the West's current problem with credentials and authoritative persons. One consequence of the American public's complacency is to automatically defer to experts and authorities to solve problems so the public can carry on doing what they prefer doing without much thinking. It is an easy way of life and is perfectly summed up with the Homer Simpson slogan "Can't somebody else do it?"[xxxiv] This occurred slowly over the decades but consequently both official and proclaimed experts moved away from being experienced advisors providing options and perspectives to being gatekeepers and arbiters of knowledge. Credentials do not always guarantee objective expert advice and in certain situations and topics, many act more like a secular "priest class" that are faithfully consulted for solutions. Experts are often now treated more as oracles because people want easy answers while also feeling intellectually superior by being able to cite an "expert' to justify their own agendas while dismissing any contrarian views. This problem is exacerbated by many institutional organizations in medicine, media, technology, finance, and others that are incentivized to portray their agendas as the only proper solutions by referring to credentialled experts.[xxxv] This made it all easier as credentials became less valuable.

Since the 1990s, the US encouraged more and more people to get college degrees and sold this as the best way to get a high paying stable job. As time progressed, more and more jobs required degrees and licenses to work, but not every job is a profession requiring deep understanding of a subject matter. As more jobs required degrees, more varieties of degrees were created, including those of little practical value creating a booming business of diploma mills. Over time, the value of degrees and credentials in non-science, technology, engineering, or medical (STEM) fields diminished as everyone gets degrees, even for useless nonjobs.[xxxvi] The problem is the West treats all fields of study like STEM where there are clear definitive answers that are quantifiable. STEM fields regard academia possessing the apex of their knowledge because this is where most fundamental research is conducted and the most brilliant minds go to teach in their golden years. In STEM, the credentialling degrees are actually performing real-world training and hands-on work the moment students enter these fields which gives experts and students the necessary experience to understand their field. In the non-STEM fields, people only truly become experts when they gain experience in the real world outside an academic setting. In non-STEM, the credentialling schools and academia only provide the foundations of knowledge, not the apex, because truly understanding these fields can only come from real world experience. Non-STEM fields don't always have definitive answers, cannot be scientifically tested, or in some cases be quantifiably measured. Since there is no clear easy to define ways to evaluate the validity of experts in non-scientific fields, it is very easy for these credentialled experts to pontificate as if they factually know something can only be done a certain way. Unlike STEM, it is very rare to be able to disprove what an expert is stating as a solution because falsifying a premise can only occur after the proposed solution has been implemented. Even then, with no clear standards for non-STEM, many can skillfully spin failures as the result of something else. Blindly embracing credentials and experts without being properly challenged needs to change to avoid the mistake of allowing technocratic experts to be unquestioned advisors because some are promoted beyond their competency.

The easiest first step is to make credentials mean something again. Higher education has become less meaningful and experts less credible as a result of it.[xxxvii] Instead of encouraging everyone to go to college to get a degree regardless of the students' desired life choices, make the colleges revert back to centers of professional development. Instead, allow higher learning to specialize again where universities are for credentialling professionals while trade and tech schools provide easier to attain credentials for more hands-on work that is just as vital as the professions. By only encouraging a segment of the population to pursue advanced degrees, it incentivizes the academic world to improve quality as their market becomes smaller with more selective clientele. Narrowing the number of degrees to ones that yield positive results for most their students would compel academia, the think tanks, and other producers of experts to actually create high standards again. This also would encourage experts to properly criticize each other again as the "expert class" will become less saturated with fewer more competent members meaning organizations now have to compete with each other to get the best real experts available. Bringing back open proper debate between experts and their contrarians instead of dismissing them automatically as "misinformation" out of fear of losing grant money or reputation. Despite what many experts want to believe, a person doesn't have to be able to "lay an egg to smell a bad one." Poorly articulated and inconsistent positions, even ones embellished in technical jargon, can be identified by anyone who truly wants to scrutinize them. Even if laymen don't know the technical details, these people still comprehend consistency within a supportable argument. If an expert has an agenda, they must embellish or omit key points in the position which skeptical persons will notice. Allowing open debate that encourages experts to address concerns or counterarguments from both contrarian experts and amateur alike will keep experts accountable to a standard.[xxxviii] This is just the first theme to help improve the American competency predicament.

One consequence by the wargame's FBE' efforts and the foreign adversary's use of qi (indirect warfare) in the scenario was the degrading of societal competency within the targeted Western nation. By prioritizing conformity based on political indoctrination through cultural and educational propaganda, the FBE creates a pliant population that will acquiesce to the nudging towards autocratic rule. Loyalty to slogans, pontifications, and platitudes for a vague ideological promise of utopia requires making the population imbecilic by discouraging critical thinking. This was seen in Mao's China at the height of the Cultural Revolution and Pol Pot's Khmer Rouge. The trick for China's collaborating elites to successfully use this method of subverting the Western population to be more controllable is finding the proper balance of conformity while retaining sufficient competency to keep the society running. This is best accomplished with using a highly centralized public education system that directs all curriculum from early childhood to adulthood. Although this creates numerous inefficiencies, the system would provide sufficient feedback for the pro-autocrat elites to gauge how much indoctrination they can impose without costing them a functioning workforce. The second theme the public should contemplate is how to upgrade America's education to not only be more adaptable to the sophistication of modern economies but also to insulate the system from malicious subversion from rival states.

One solution is to adopt older ideas of education with the technological capabilities of the 21st Century. These technologies no longer require highly centralized education systems run by inflexible industrial age Weberian bureaucracies. Advanced communications technologies enable a variety of volunteer subject matter experts, enthusiasts, hobbyists, and others to give tailored presentations to classes for more substantive discourses on topics of learning. These volunteers would work with and be supervised by volunteer parents, grandparents, and highly enthusiastic professional teachers working within a commonly agreed upon confederated organization that enables maximum dynamism and efficiency. This could come in many guises including home-school associations, charter schools, or even company sponsored schools that pay for one or two years of education in exchange for internship work. There are likely many other forms this could take. To make these more efficient, these education cooperatives could adopt the older 20th Century concept of talent-tier placement education. This would create classes based on student course performance with academically gifted children given in-depth courses while those struggling will go through slower, more hands-on, methodical courses. These courses may highlight a student's deficiencies, but they will get the tailored education requirements they need to succeed and graduate.[xxxix] This far more effective and efficient than the current one size-fits all common curriculum of mediocrity that inhibits intellectually enthusiastic students because the course work is not stimulating and simultaneously keeping the poorest performing children disadvantaged because the course work is too poorly structured. Instead of the schools having courses adhere to simplified generic standards set by bureaucracies, the schooling system can survey the requirements and desired qualifications of universities, trade schools, and industries to tailor their curriculums to better integrate the knowledge given to students with the needs of the society. Each major industry has associations as well as university associations. These groups could publish annual desired skills, traits, and abilities for entry-level persons and each confederated school system can tailor their teaching plans accordingly based on societal needs and geographical considerations.

This system would be more secure because concerned parents and teachers would be directly watching the students without having to worry about adhering to highly centralized bureaucratic requirements that can be more easily subverted. Keeping accountability and supervision as localized as possible diminishes foreign misinformation and qi subversion. This would require active community participation, which admittedly doesn't exist in many parts of the West where they have deferred to the state for all educational solutions.

The third education theme to consider is what substantive information needs to be instilled in the public's learning to better prepare them against the prospective threats in the world. One important consideration as a solution is to have a common national standard for a national security focused civics curriculum. China and other gray-zone warfare adversaries rely heavily on the targeted country's population being ignorant of the threats of the world. If a population doesn't know its history or government, then they are easy to manipulate into turning against their own people. For the United States, having a civics curriculum focusing on three types of civic understanding: security in cyberspace, security in the physical space, and having a common baseline understanding of their nation to anchor everyone in common understanding would address most of these concerns.

The first dealing with security in cyberspace is to make sure everyone actually knows how computers work and the exploits that are common threats. This may seem redundant in modern times but as the younger generations are raised on smartphones, they have less understanding of how the supporting networks and computers actually work.[xl] People are savvy at the modern graphic user interfaces and the various applications of modern devices but don't necessarily know how search engines work, how malware works, or the basic technology fundamentals that were taught to the Gen-Xers and Millennials. After decades of living in the information age, phishing and bad passwords are still the main ways hackers get into systems and younger generations still carry on the tradition of bad security practices.[xli] Even if the United States curbed the number of people who use bad practices by only 10%, it would drastically increase the cost for adversaries like China in trying to exploit cyberspace. This threat is only being made worse by the "internet of things" coming online with 5G networks. Preparing generations for war in cyberspace is critical as this is the one domain, other than nuclear, where all citizens will be directly attacked.

The second type of civic understanding is teaching the now taboo subject of one of the main functions of government which is the ability to wage war. Teaching the fundamentals of what war is and why it functions in the way it does would drastically improve the public's civic awareness to make more deliberative decisions as an electorate. This doesn't mean teaching how to run a war but what war is and how it impacts a society. For American students, making high-school level students read the first two chapters of Clausewitz's book *On War*, sections of Sun Tzu's *Art of War*, sections of Liddel Hart's *Strategy*, and Admiral Mahan's *Influence of Sea Power upon History* would be more than sufficient. Other things that could be included might be gun safety courses which, like sexual education and prophylactics, would help people understand these weapons and tools to prevent mishandling and demystify them. Understanding weapons education would vary depending on the community's sentiments, but people forget this used be common in the United States before the 1970s.[xlii]

The third and final type of civic understanding is the political foundations of the nation itself. Understanding how and why the United States formed the type and characteristics of the government the Founding Fathers chose better orients citizens as to why society works in the way that it does. If one understands the society they are in, the more the person can adapt to it and with the added bonus of being less likely to be politically deceived. Although some would think focusing on the Founding Fathers is too myopic or narrow for helping understanding America's political context, consider the reality that all governments, both democratic and autocratic, all try to address the same challenges. All governments seek to solve issues of public order, societal integrity, and harmony with the only difference being what in society should be prioritized and to whom shall power be bestowed. So, if one studies the Founding Fathers and their arguments, one gets exposed to all manner of civil concepts and ideas. Reading Thomas Paine's *Common Sense*, various excerpts of the *Federalist Papers*, and some of the correspondence of Washington, Jefferson, Madison, Adams, and Hamilton would offer a good baseline. Of course, the final requirement would be to read the actual US *Constitution* verbatim without commentary helps ground people before they read or hear all the various academic commentaries.

One final consideration to consider alongside the study of the American political foundations is re-examining some elements of Enlightenment Thinkers. In many ways, the West is stuck in the aftereffects of the political philosophers of the Enlightenment Period where the West tries to fulfill the theoretical ideals of one or more of these thinkers. Although they advanced human thought on social and political concepts, they did not discover the definitive answers to mankind's societal problems. The West now has had several centuries of social experimentation with many elements of Enlightenment political theories and experiencing practical results. Since these are social theories, many argue they are not falsifiable like scientific theories. However, from these real-world experiences of social experimentation, it is time to acknowledge some of these theories have been disproven. Specifically, the theories of human nature and governance of Jean-Jacques Rousseau. Many know of Karl Marx, and a few know of Giovanni Gentile, but few in mainstream discussions link these persons' theories back to one of their philosophical grandfathers, Rousseau. Rousseau's concepts are the baseline for all utopian totalitarianism and yet despite over a century of perpetual failure when these ideas are implemented, his theories are still given equal legitimate consideration along with other political and economic philosophers of the same period. Rousseau should be studied because he is one of the few social and political philosophers definitely disproven because the Rousseauian-inspired totalitarians have used multiple societies as guinea pigs in their grand social experiments and each time failed to achieve the results promised by Rousseau's assertions. Acknowledging it is time to move on from perpetual failure to other ideas would be a tremendous positive advancement in human thinking.

All of these education reforms would make the United States considerably more difficult to subvert, divide, or manipulate into civil chaos. Holding experts to an accountable standard, improving the quality of experts, the quality of education, and instilling the real-world concerns of civic security all bring greater understanding to the public. Not everything suggested is politically palatable to all, but having the public continue to live in happy and blissful ignorance of the world around them only allows nightmarish disasters to germinate into unchallenged crises. No doubt some reforms will be compromised to cater to rivaling interest groups, but the American electorate needs to be included on understanding the threat from great power rivalry to help shape the institutions working on protecting the society to have a greater chance of success.

Inevitable Changes:

Finally, the electorate should be aware of changes that are inevitable. The only difference an aware electorate can make is how fast these changing transitions occur and how the disruption will impact on society. There are two subjects of national security relevance in particular that will shift how society operates in the future. The first is the West's plans for energy security and sustainment where real-world obstacles are destroying many policy and advocacy plans and assumptions. The second is the fate of professional news services and the dissemination of current events to the masses. Both are changing in unexpected ways and the electorate needs to be cognizant of this fact in order to help determine the final outcome of both.

Energy policy in the West for the past 30 years has invoked two rationales to justify its formulation: environmental degradation, and economic dependence on unreliable overseas sources. In the past 10 years, national security arose as a third rationale due to the increasingly fragmented division between the Western-led international system and the newly arising Tianxia-led imperium. Generally speaking, the policies have focused on alternative energy sources such as wind, solar, hydroelectric, and geothermal to ween the West and eventually the rest of the world off of fossil fuels. [xliii] These policies were driven by multiple groups including environmental activist organizations, politicians, academics, and subsidy seeking corporations in the hope that the West could accelerate the technological transition into an all-electrified society using non-gaseous emitting energy sources. However, in recent years objective reality is revealing major deficiencies in these grand schemes and that the people advocating for accelerating a rapid energy technology transformation rely far more on hope than actual technically feasible capabilities.

There are many projects, experiments, and innovations in the fields of energy generation and storage technologies that give humanity a glimmer of optimism for the future. For instance, Texas A&M University has been researching metal-free water-based battery electrodes that could potentially have a 1,000% greater storage capacity than current lithium-ion batteries.[xliv] Such a battery would potentially eliminate the West's dependence on lithium-ion batteries as well as drastically reduce the need to extract this valuable metal. There is, however, one small problem that applies to many green-energy technologies which is that it is not yet practical. Many technologies are still in stages of laboratory research, early prototyping, or are still too expensive to produce on an industrial scale. Then there are green technologies that are being manufactured but with glaring deficiencies that prevent them from being adopted by the mainstream market such as electric vehicles.

Electric vehicles (EV) are a critical component for plans of having an emissions-free economy which is why they are pushed by governments and activist organizations to artificially accelerate the West's transition to an all-electrified society. The problem is the enthusiasm from advocates is outpacing the practical implementation of these technologies. The EVs have overcome the older challenges of having a powerful motor, range, and road worthiness but these technological marvels are still incomplete. The biggest complaint from a consumer perspective is recharging times and the lack of recharge points to make EVs a suitable replacement for petrol-fueled vehicles, but few consider the implications of these complaints. Fast-charging batteries are still not a mature technology and the EV market is completely dependent on lithium-ion batteries to be viable. Lithium-ion batteries do not quickly charge and have physical limitations that restrict the applicability of EVs to only specific environmental conditions. Areas of extreme heat and cold directly affect the performance of these batteries. Cold places decrease the ionic conductivity of the battery by reducing its charge capacity which consequently reduces the EVs' range. Continuous exposure to high heat can drastically reduce the lithium-ion batteries' lifespan which leads to costly replacements in the range of thousands of dollars. [xlv] Although the odds of needing a replacement pack early are low, it is large enough of a risk to discourage many buyers.[xlvi]

Even if these challenges were overcome, the problem of installing more charge points for more EVs exposes the problem of inadequate infrastructure and resources to sustain such a transition. To make the majority of the population have EVs requires having adequate amounts of lithium, cobalt, and other critical minerals being churned out in adequate quantities in a timely manner. At current projections, the world industry would need to open an additional 300 new mines which further adds to more global pollution.[xlvii] This is not helped by the fact that many

226

elements of EVs are still more expensive than petrol-vehicles and this has encouraged insurance companies to scrap low-mileage EVs because it is cheaper than repairing them.[xlviii] Overcoming the resource issue will still not solve the other problem of building the additional necessary infrastructure to sustain a large number of EVs. A review of the Californian city of Palo Alto's effort to build EV infrastructure determined the need for 6-12,000 public ports and up to 26,000 residential ports. This requires modernization of the electrical distribution system designed in the mid-20th Century to handle far less demand and 95% of residential transformers need to be upgraded to handle the projected peak-load times and these are just the challenges in one city.[xlix] All of this is just supporting one element of an all-electrified society, but what about the crux of the West's energy policies, the power generation systems themselves?

There is an uncomfortable reality about wind and solar power systems from both a moral and security perspective that many in the West choose to ignore so they don't have to deal with the problem. The rate of construction and proliferation of these "green" power systems throughout the Western and Asiatic parts of the world are sustained by slavery and dependence on totalitarian economics. China supplies the majority of both raw materials and manufactured components of both solar and wind power systems accounting for 80% of the solar manufacturing market alone.[l] China uses its disregard for both the Earth and the well-being of humans to keep these products cheap in order to maintain its monopoly on renewable power.[li]

Chinese slave labor exploiting the Uyghurs and other minority groups of China accounts for over a third of the global supply for solar panel polysilicon.[lii] Slave labor is not limited to the solar industry or within the boundaries of China either. China's investments in Africa to extrapolate the critical rare earth elements and other metals used in solar and wind industries exceed any other country, but like all previous imperial ventures, the Chinese companies maximize profit at the expense of the locals. Chinese use of slave labor and brutal exploitation of locals, including children, to extract the critical materials for wind turbines as cheaply as possible while simultaneously ignoring any environmental safeguards is pervasive.

[liii], [liv] These mining operations use toxic chemicals and other metals such as arsenic as part of the extraction process and create waste byproducts that contaminate both soil and rivers. If the world continues to go forward with the renewable focused power systems, the demand for minerals and rare earths will grow exponentially leading to a surge of toxic runoff issues.[lv] This is likely to happen because there is another major problem for current green energy plans which is the number of resources required verses the amount of power being produced.

For whatever advantages solar and wind provide, these two types of power generation in terms of the material input required to generate power output are the most inefficient of all known methods of generating electricity. Both solar and wind require large volumes of acreage with numerous structures filled with copious amounts of critical minerals to make these systems function. All power generation systems have downsides. Fossil fuels produce air pollutants and gases but renewables require the most mineral extraction from the ground.[lvi] This problem is exacerbated by the fragility and needed rate of component replacements required for these systems which creates a large amount of waste and increases the risk of power interruption. One empirical example occurred in June 2023 in Scottsbluff, Nebraska where a solar array of over 14,000 solar panels with the potential of generating over 5 megawatts of power was destroyed by an intense hailstorm. It took the power company over six months to repair and replace the damaged elements to get it back to full working condition. [lvii] A separate statistical example for wind is 400,000 tons of turbine blades are projected to be decommissioned and disposed of annually by 2030. Although the studies point out this will have minimal impact on landfill usage and would still remain at low cost to replace these components, this is not the main security issue.[lviii] The high attrition rate means there will be continuous demand for far more raw materials and manufacturing production to sustain these power generation systems than for fossil fuel or nuclear power generation systems. These studies and researchers often mention various recycling and improvement methods for manufacturing but these often have a lot of caveats with the words "if", "could", and "should" in them which indicates more reliance on hope than practical implementation. For instance, the Siemens Energy Corporation, Germany's premier energy company, in June of 2023 confirmed their wind turbine production suffered severe quality and reliability problems that will take years to correct and require the German government to subsidize Siemens' mistakes for their wind industry to survive.[lix]

The West has committed itself to a very tight timeframe to implement its ideal renewable energy outcome that doesn't allow for factoring-in real-world disruptions like the Siemens problem or the number of new mines needed to meet renewable demands. Part of the reason this inflexible commitment exist is due to the information and influence campaigns of the CCP and its apologists.[lx] Keeping the West bound to a tight inflexible schedule prevents the West from finding alternative solutions and remain dependent on China. The added bonus from China's perspective is the West will more likely mismanage their energy policies that will damage their economies and undermine their governments' support with their electorates trying to keep to an unrealistic timeline for the sake of saving face. There is no better real-world example of this kind of failed Western energy policy than in Germany.

Germany is reputed to be a nation of innovators, hard workers, and having an industrious capability that makes it the economic center of Europe. Germany, like all nations, has its down sides and it seems Germany decided the way to keep their society successful was to offload all their bad traits into the German government. There is a quote, likely apocryphal, of Winston Churchill declaring "Americans will always do the right thing, after all other possibilities are exhausted". In this case, modern German governments seem to always do the wrong thing after exhausting every other possibility. From the German officers discussing classified material on an unsecured communications channel, allowing their military to decline to the point of being enfeebled, to simultaneously prop up their most likely security threat by economically tying the country to the autocratic Putin regime in Russia for years. [lxi], [lxii], [lxiii], [lxiv] Of all the miscalculations, the worst has been their mismanagement of their energy policy to the point it will neither accomplish its renewable energy goals nor keep their economy more secure.

The Germans for the last 10 years have been more enthusiastically committed to meeting their arbitrary climate and ecologically friendly energy goals than any other Western nation. So stubborn is the German government's commitment to these goals they effectively ignored any criticism, warning, or naysayer creating a cavalcade of energy chaos. Numerous miscalculations, refusal to admit mistakes, and continuously disregarding the fact that what is theoretically possible on paper doesn't mean it will work in practice has now, as of 2024, weakened Germany's energy security and environmental commitments.[lxv] Numerous examples of failure include the dismantling of old wind turbines in Lower Saxony without anything to replace them due to funding shortfalls as two thirds of an estimated 16 gigawatts of wind performance lost funding because of the costs.[lxvi] An estimated 10 gigawatts worth of solar panel modules in Germany will need early replacement due to poor quality back-sheets that increase the risk of electrocution as of September 2023.[lxvii] Shutting down their remaining nuclear reactors and stating Germany doesn't need them to deal with power deficiencies then simultaneously bring coal power plants back online to deal with unforeseen power shortages is a perfect policy of contradictions. [lxviii], [lxix] Shutting down nuclear power in the name of environmentalism while turning back on CO_2 and particulate emitting power plants that diminish their net-zero goals is self-defeating even if the German government doesn't comprehend it. This policy of coal usage still continues as their renewables cannot sustain their power requirements in the winter.[lxx] A more darkly humorous example of German government mismanagement occurred in 2022 when a wind farm was dismantled to expand one of its coal mines in North Rhine-Westphalia, Germany.[lxxi] On top of all this, some studies indicate Germany is at a high risk of chronic power shortages all the way through 2030.[lxxii] All of this demonstrates that a poorly considered energy policy without being scrutinized exposes a nation to potentially have an unreliable power grid while being simultaneously dependent on a foreign adversary. This is critical for an electorate to discuss when dealing with how to maintain energy sovereignty while delivering the energy required for the nation.

All of these points are to highlight the fact the American electorate is inevitably going to face three choices regarding its energy future. Much of the West's energy policies were driven by hype that was partially pushed by China and its desire to monopolize the West's energy production. This consequently overlooked some critical challenges like in Germany which has failed in keeping its environmental commitments, energy security, and energy dependability secure by blindly rushing forward into projects where only some parts are fully developed. The United States will likely face a similar dilemma soon and will have to readjust to avoid the mistakes of some of its European counterparts. The three key facets of modern energy policy are to achieve continuous reliable energy generation that minimally impacts the environment without the nation's energy being held hostage by rival nations. The electorate needs to understand and then decide which facet of energy policy is the most important to them and then demand that goal be pursued realistically. If the electorate wants to prioritize environmental protection while still getting electricity, then the electorate must accept that nuclear power will be a critical mainstay of any future "clean" energy grid.

There are two challenges in current clean energy efforts that mutually reinforce each other. The first is a purely renewable energy grid that has to be massively resourced and is area intensive. The sheer volume of wind turbines and solar arrays needed to match the power output of a single natural gas combined cycle turbine is immense. A new combined cycle gas turbine being built in Florida in 2023 generates 900-megawatts of power and generators of this type typically occupy between 20-40 acres.[lxxiii], [lxxiv] The average solar field generates 650-kilowatts of power per acre. [lxxv] This means that to generate the necessary 900,000-kilowatt equivalent to that of a natural gas plant would require on average 1,385 acres of land. This in itself would not be too terrible of a challenge but the Western nations also want to electrify the entire economy and infrastructure. This means new electricity demands including EV charge points, smart homes, electric boilers, electric heaters, stoves, replacing natural gas-powered infrastructure, data centers, and all the additional peripherals and appliances linked into the 5G "internet of things". There is no realistic way of building only solar and wind powered generation fast enough to support that scale of demand growth. This doesn't take into account the sheer amount of environmental damage that will be amplified in Africa and Asia mining and using Chinese-dominated industries manufacturing these power generation systems. Nuclear power has the greatest power density of any generation system available to mankind and will have to be a mainstream feature to sustain any major environmentally friendly economic transition. In the past few years, Western governments have been quietly acknowledging this reality already and are becoming more receptive to investing in nuclear power to support their efforts to reduce fossil fuels but this only becomes realistic if the electorate provides support.[lxxvi]

The electorate needs to be aware of the challenges of bringing in nuclear power and proposals to solve these challenges in order for them to decide on what policies to support. One of the most important reasons nuclear power is so costly in the United States is that planning and execution timelines set in building nuclear reactors are prone to disruption. Activist lawsuits filed under the National Environmental Policy Act can occur up to six years after a project has completed environmental reviews with many activists using near-religious zeal in disrupting nuclear developments. [lxxvii], [lxxviii] Also, changes in political support in election cycles will often protract and delay new reactors for years beyond the initially planned date of starting operations. Having a safety regulatory framework is crucial to ensure that only highly reliable designs are approved with high quality materials, but this framework must be consistent and stable. Constantly changing the regulations out of political whims or advocacy pressure creates uncertainty and additional costs as nuclear designs and construction must continuously change to comply.[lxxix] Such disruptions also mean there cannot be a means to create standardized designs which would allow for mass manufacture and ease of reproducibility since they could simply expedite the license review with an acknowledged design. A public weighing the pros and cons from all sides will be necessary for understanding this course of action of moving towards pollutant-free energy. From a security perspective, the United States still relies on adversaries for nuclear technology because it is cheaper to acquire these materials from less regulatory conscious Russia, yet it would still be easier than making a full break from dependence on China's renewable industries for the foreseeable future while still remaining solar and wind focused exclusively.[lxxx]

If the electorate, on the other hand, prioritizes national security and energy independence as quickly as possible, then it will require expansion of both shale oil and natural gas development and delaying environmental mandate dates. Fossil fuel infrastructure is well developed and North America provides ample petroleum and natural gas deposits for exploitation. The third option is to rely on hope that advanced technologies can soon escape the lab and become practical to implement on an industrial scale to keep on the current planned paths but the odds of this happening in a timely manner to sync with pledged net-zero emissions dates is very poor. No matter what the decision, a major change on this subject is inevitable as the demand and capability to meet that demand appear to be drifting further apart while China maintains considerable influence in the West's energy industry.

The final inevitable change the electorate needs to prepare for is the extinction of the news media industry in its current form. Many pundits, experts, and others are voicing their concerns that this is a critical cultural institution that is essential to Western society.[lxxxi] This concern is nonpartisan as this is voiced by all sides.[lxxxii] Many media outlets with histories of having national-level influence for decades are laying off more people amid shrinking subscriber bases such as the Washington Post.[lxxxiii] The fear, they claim, is that without a professional news and journalist industry, the American population will be awash in misinformation and susceptible to the influence of foreign adversaries and domestic threats. This is why some are advocating for tax incentives and subsidies to prop-up the declining professional news industry. The media's supporters often cite partisan political divisions are the source of the media's decline. While no doubt the intensity of the current American political divisions is accelerating the news media's decline but that alone is not the cause. The true cause of this industry's decline is that it's obsolete.

Even before the internet, the media was at best a mediocre institution looking out for the public good. There is still a nostalgia-derived blindness to the past refusing to accept that the media, whether authoritative or not, was always hit-or-miss in terms of reliable information. Many examples are already cited earlier in the chapter on FBE line of effort for information control, but it must be reiterated that the media has always been sloppy, susceptible to corruption, and advocating for its own interests at the cost of the public. Even when the media tries to be sincere in its reporting, it often gets details wrong and would rarely admit to mistakes. The notion put forward by the legacy media's proponents is that the industry is the critical vanguard to protect society against misinformation and nefarious influence is at best, a joke. Already previously cited was the New York Times knowingly misleading its readers on the glories of Stalin's Soviet Empire but on the flip side, Great Britain's largest newspaper, the Daily Mail, praised and condoned Adolf Hitler and the Nazis' system of government before the Second World War.[lxxxiv] Those despairing of the professional media's decline fear that social media, amateur journalists, podcasts, and forums will misinform, mischaracterize, sensationalize, mislead, slander, and manipulate the masses. The above verbs have been used against media organizations for over a century before the internet indicating the proportion of misinformation disseminated into the public will not change at all.

If somehow, there was a way to make news media more honest and dependable, it still could not be the idealized vanguard against misinformation the media's allies claim. Even if media corporations forgo sensationalism and other actions in the name of profit, these organizations remain too slow and cumbersome to deal with the current media environment. If a piece of nefarious false information was circulated through official channels and is overlooked, then that organization's credibility is diminished, especially if they don't publicly apologize and retract. Misinformation is easy to disseminate because there are no facts to check, no corroboration to be done, and no legal reviews because the deceivers acted either covertly or are able to evade legal actions. With so much information proliferated in such a short amount of time, the obsolete media will never react in an adequate amount of time. A.I. will not help with this either because detecting misinformation requires understanding context and contemporary A.I. doesn't think at all. A.I. only helps aggregate data and will likely only exacerbate the problem as these programs are easier to deceive than humans in this regard. Even so, all of this is predicated on the assumption that these media organizations are always honest, diligent, and incorruptible, which is only true in fiction.

Another argument to "save" the obsolete media is that the amateur media and online "influencers" will not provide substantive information on topics and issues creating more ignorance of the world. The only difference between the social media amateurs and professional media is the eloquence of phrasing of the misinformation being conveyed. Anyone who exclusively relies on the news media for their information about the world is, without exception, misinformed and does not know how the world truly works. There is no better word in the world to describe such a person than the word—sucker. Yes, the people and groups currently trending to replace the old media are no more reliable and are prone to the same temptations such as sensationalism, yellow journalism, deception, and agenda driven reporting yet these elements are providing a new positive development. Studies have shown younger generations do not trust media in almost any form, viewing them as deceptive, and take most of their news from social media.[lxxxv] On the face of this study, it can appear to be bad news but in fact it is good news. This is one of the few instances demonstrating that younger generations are using more critical thinking than the generations before them.

The younger generations are critically thinking more because they are aware they are informed by amateurs who are not shielded from well-funded and well-connected corporations. They also deal with deception daily in forms of phishing, publicity stunts, and sensationalist hoaxes just for daily entertainment. Before with the obsolete media, people would take what the news told them as mostly, if not completely true. People know social media is not authoritative nor professional and will take everything that is stated with proper suspicion. Furthermore, this democratized form of information sharing encourages the audience to actively participate and correct verifiably bad information. Audience participation, crowdfunding, and zealous know-it-alls create more systems of accountability than the obsolete media that built their empires through favors and dealings with economic and political power brokers. This new form of amateur media forces the audience to actually think critically and which over time people will get better at discriminating and detecting poor information sources. Of course, this isn't perfect and will still have the curse of echo chambers and manipulation but it is more easily correctable and the corruption more short-lived as more of the audience better understands what is going on.

There is no way to contain or eliminate misinformation. Misinformation is not constrained in the way as accurate information because misinformation always pleases its intended audience with confirmation bias and is not encumbered by reality. Any organization that tries to centrally mitigate misinformation would have to be completely accurate all of the time to avoid being discredited which is impossible. The best way to deal with misinformation is to expose it to the light of day and continuous scrutiny. Misinformation relies on the quick news cycle where the misinformation is conveyed with little questioning, sets the narrative, and then the news cycle moves on to another story. Keeping the misinformation in the public spotlight and in open debate will discredit the misinformation and the majority of the audience will realize what is accurate and what is misleading. Misinformation always has gaps in narrative and logic flow. If it remains under public scrutiny long enough, the gaps and contradictions become more apparent. Misinformation is faster but it is brittle compared to accurate information.

For all of these reasons, the old news media and the system that supported it are dying and it is inevitable at this point. Some will no doubt attempt to prolong its existence with additional funding, legal frameworks, and other efforts but all of this will only delay the inevitable. There is nothing of value being lost as the same weaknesses in information dissemination will remain, it's just happens more rapidly, but there is now a means to react to those weaknesses and have a chance to actually correct them. The electorate would best be prepared for this inevitable transition in information dissemination as they will be crucial in directly assisting in combating misinformation from the Tianxia imperium.

All for Your Consideration:

This book comprehensively laid out how a sophisticated adversary nation, like China, can launch the ultimate campaign in gray-zone warfare against the West without the risk of open warfare. The wargame also postulated the most optimal means of combating such a strategy if the West remained complacent to the point violent rebellion was the only recourse. All of this is intended to make the electorate more aware of the potential dangers in this complex and unstable geopolitical environment because Western governments cannot counter all of these gray-zone strategies without the public's active support. Not all things within the book are definitive or inevitable, but a cognizant public drastically reduces the risk of such events from occurring. All of this is for your reflection and consideration.

---

[i] Raymond Kua, Christian Curriden, Cortez A. Cooper III, et al, *Simulating Chinese Gray Zone Coercion of Taiwan* (Santa Monica, CA: RAND Corporation, June 22, 2023). https://www.rand.org/pubs/conf_proceedings/CFA2065-1.html

[ii] Edmund Burke, *Reflections on the Revolution* (Whithorn, UK: Anodos Books, 2019, originally 1790) Page: 14.

[iii] Ronald H. Linden, "Is the Chinese Dream Turning into a Chinese Nightmare for Beijing?" National Interest, April 3, 2023. https://www.rand.org/pubs/conf_proceedings/CFA2065-1.html

[iv] Government Report, *Military and Security Developments Involving the People's Republic of China: 2021* (Office of the Secretary of Defense: Washington DC, 2021) Page 17.

[v] Willy Wo-Lap Lam, "Much Cause but Little Recourse for Popular Discontent," Jamestown Foundation's China Brief, vol. 23, is. 22, December 1, 2023. https://jamestown.org/program/much-cause-but-little-recourse-for-popular-discontent/

[vi] Willy Wo-Lap Lam, "The National People's Congress Exposes Xi Jinping's Problems," Jamestown Foundation's China Brief, March 15, 2024. https://jamestown.org/program/the-national-peoples-congress-exposes-xi-jinpings-problems/

[vii] Sunny Cheung, "Decoding China's Dilemma: The Difficulties of Economic Reform," Jamestown Foundation's China Brief, vol. 23, is. 22, December 1, 2023. https://jamestown.org/program/decoding-chinas-dilemma-the-difficulties-of-economic-reform/

[viii] John Jay, "Federalist No. 4" Federalist Papers, November 7, 1787. https://guides.loc.gov/federalist-papers/text-1-10#s-lg-box-wrapper-25493265

[ix] Mark Medish moderator, David Rothkopf speaker, "Superclass: The Global Power Elite and the World They are Making," Interview at Carnegie Endowment for International Peace, April 9, 2008. https://carnegieendowment.org/files/0410_transcript_rothkopf_superclass.pdf

[x] Alessandra Scotto Di Santolo, "Verhofstadt's United States of Europe Dream DISMANTLED – 'LOSING Your Battle'" The Express, May 14, 2019. https://www.express.co.uk/news/world/1127020/European-elections-Guy-Verhofstadt-EU-Commission-Brexit-United-States-of-Europe

[xi] David M. Herszenhorn, "Commission President Calls to End Unanimity in EU Foreign Policy Decisions," Politico, June 20, 2022. https://www.politico.eu/article/commission-president-ursula-von-der-leyen-end-unanimity-eu-foreign-policy/

[xii] Maria Psara & Jorge Liboreiro, "EU Corruption Scandal: Eva Kaili Released from Prison and Put Under House Arrest," EuroNews, December 4, 2023. https://www.euronews.com/my-europe/2023/04/12/corruption-scandal-eva-kaili-released-from-prison-and-put-under-house-arrest-lawyer-says

[xiii] News Article, "World: Europe – EU Plunges into Crisis," BBC News, March 16, 1999. http://news.bbc.co.uk/2/hi/europe/297457.stm

[xiv] Jorge Liboreiro, "The EU has a New Deal to Achieve 'Tax Fairness'. This is How it Will Work," EuroNews, December 16, 2022. https://www.euronews.com/my-europe/2022/12/16/the-eu-has-a-new-deal-deal-to-achieve-tax-fairness-this-is-how-it-will-work

[xv] David Oakley, "EU Regulations Blamed for 'Swamping' Businesses," The Financial Times, February 2, 2016. https://www.ft.com/content/658bd8e0-c91d-11e5-be0b-b7ece4e953a0

[xvi] Carl Gahnberg, "New EU Telecom Rules will Leave Everyone Worse Off," Politico, March 27, 2023. https://www.politico.eu/article/new-eu-telecom-rules-will-leave-everyone-worse-off-internet-network/

[xvii] Francis de Vericourt, "Innovation in Europe is Falling Behind. What Can We Do to Catch Up?" EuroNews, March 13, 2024. https://www.euronews.com/next/2024/03/13/innovation-in-europe-is-falling-behind-what-can-we-do-to-catch-up

[xviii] Renee Corders, "Tackling the EU's 'Innovation Deficit'," Politico, June 7, 2000. https://www.politico.eu/article/tackling-the-eus-innovation-deficit/

[xix] Giancarlo Benelli, "What Are We Going to Do About Europe's Innovation," The Parliament Magazine, June 20, 2022. https://www.theparliamentmagazine.eu/news/article/what-are-we-going-to-do-about-europes-innovation-deficit.

[xx] News Report, "We Need a European Army, Says Jean-Claude Juncker," BBC News, March 9, 2015. https://www.bbc.com/news/world-europe-31796337

[xxi] Policy Study, *The European Security and Defence Policy: from the Helsinki Headline Goal to the EU Battlegroups*, European Parliament Archives, September 12, 2006. https://www.europarl.europa.eu/meetdocs/2009_2014/documents/sede/dv/sede030909noteesdp_/sede030909noteesdp_en.pdf

[xxii] Stephen M. Walt, "Why Europe Can't Get Its Military Act Together," Foreign Policy Magazine, February 21, 2024. https://foreignpolicy.com/2024/02/21/europe-military-trump-nato-eu-autonomy/

[xxiii] Ludwig Von Mises, *Human Action: A Treatise on Economics* (New Haven, CT: Yale University Press, 1949). https://mises.org/online-book/human-action/chapter-viii-human-society/4-ricardian-law-association

[xxiv] Michael Lind, "The Anglosphere Needs a Customs Union," National Interest, October 28, 2022. https://nationalinterest.org/feature/anglosphere-needs-customs-union-205531?page=0%2C1

[xxv] Jinghan Zeng, *The Chinese Communist Party's Capacity to Rule* (UK: Palgrave MacMillian: 2016) Pages 61-66, 77-79.

[xxvi] Gary Anderson, "Deterring China's Designs on Taiwan," National Interest, February 27, 2023. https://nationalinterest.org/feature/deterring-chinas-designs-taiwan-206254

[xxvii] Carl Forsling, "The Fundamental Flaw in US Plans to Defend Taiwan from A Chinese Assault," Task and Purpose, July 20, 2022. https://taskandpurpose.com/opinion/us-flaw-china-taiwan/

[xxviii] Charles KS Wu, Fang-Yu Chen, et al., "Are the Taiwanese People Willing to Fight China?" National Interest, January 13, 2023. https://nationalinterest.org/blog/buzz/are-taiwanese-people-willing-fight-china-206119

[xxix] Charles KS Wu, Yao-Yuan Yeh, et al., "Why NGOs are Boosting Support for Self-Defense in Taiwan," National Interest, February 22, 2023. https://nationalinterest.org/feature/why-ngos-are-boosting-support-self-defense-taiwan-206240

[xxx] Marco Ho Cheng-hui, "Civil Society Defense Initiatives," Jamestown Foundation China Brief, vol. 24, is. 4, February 16, 2024. https://jamestown.org/program/civil-society-defense-initiatives/

[xxxi] David Sacks, "Why China Would Struggle to Invade Taiwan," Council on Foreign Relations, January 10, 2024. https://www.cfr.org/article/why-china-would-struggle-invade-taiwan

[xxxii] Cindy Wang and Peter Martin, "Taiwan's Ability to Defend Against Chinese Invasion Questioned," The Japan Times, December 20, 2023. https://www.japantimes.co.jp/news/2023/12/20/asia-pacific/politics/taiwan-ability-china-invasion-question/

[xxxiii] Reference, "H.R. 162 – National Digital Reserve Corps Act", US Congress Record – 118th Congress, January 9, 2023. https://www.congress.gov/bill/118th-congress/house-bill/162/titles?s=1&r=68

[xxxiv] Reference, "Trash of the Titans," The Simpsons, season 9, episode 22. https://www.imdb.com/title/tt0701277/

[xxxv] Sydney Finkelstein, "The Problem with Relying on Experts," BBC, October 15, 2014. https://www.bbc.com/worklife/article/20141015-the-problem-with-experts

[xxxvi] Jon Marcus, "Critics Warn that Well-Meaning Reforms May be Lowering Standards," PBS, August 17, 2018. https://www.pbs.org/newshour/education/critics-warn-that-well-meaning-reforms-may-be-lowering-college-standards

[xxxvii] Megan Brenan, "America's Confidence in Higher Education Down Sharply," Gallup, July 11, 2023. https://news.gallup.com/poll/508352/americans-confidence-higher-education-down-sharply.aspx

[xxxviii] Julian Michael, Salsabila Mahdi, David Rein, et al. "Debate Helps Supervise Unreliable Experts," Cornell University, arXiv: 2311.08702, November 15, 2023. https://arxiv.org/abs/2311.08702

[xxxix] Stephen L. Chew, "Improving Classroom Performance by Challenging

[xl] Daniel Pfaltzgraf and Gary S. Insch, "Digitally Native, Yet Technologically Illiterate: Methods to Prepare Business Students to Create Versus Consume," Journal of Applied Business and Economics, col. 23, no. 2, May 11, 2021. https://articlegateway.com/index.php/JABE/article/view/4084

[xli] Jon Gold, "Email Phishing Still the Main Way for Hackers: Report," CSO Online, August 15, 2023. https://www.csoonline.com/article/649551/email-phishing-still-the-main-way-in-for-hackers-report.html

[xlii] Anna Sanders, "When Toting Guns in High School was Cool," NY Post, March 31, 2018. https://nypost.com/2018/03/31/when-toting-guns-in-high-school-was-cool/

[xliii] Kelly MacGregor, "Full Steam Ahead: Unearthing the Power of Geothermal," National Renewable Energy Laboratory, March 7, 2023. https://www.nrel.gov/news/features/2023/full-steam-ahead-unearthing-the-power-of-geothermal.html

[xliv] University News, "1,000% Difference: Major Storage Capacity in Water-Based Batteries Found," ScienceDaily, April 15, 2023. https://scitechdaily.com/1000-difference-major-storage-capacity-in-water-based-batteries-found/

[xlv] Shuai Ma, Modi Jiang, Peng Tao, et al., "Temperature Effect and Thermal Impact in Lithium-Ion Batteries: A Review," Progress in Natural Science: Materials International, vol. 28, is. 6, December 2018, p. 653-666. https://www.sciencedirect.com/science/article/pii/S1002007118307536#s0010

[xlvi] Perry Stern, "How Much Does it Cost to Replace an EV Battery?" US News and World Report, January 26, 2024. https://cars.usnews.com/cars-trucks/advice/ev-battery-replacement-cost

[xlvii] Christian Gralingen, "The EV Transition Is Harder Than Anyone Thinks," IEEE Spectrum, March 28, 2023. https://spectrum.ieee.org/the-ev-transition-explained-2659602311

[xlviii] Allen Zhong, "Fuel Costs of Electric Vehicles Overtake Gas-Powered Cars: Study," The Epoch Times, January 31, 2023. https://www.theepochtimes.com/business/fuel-costs-of-electric-vehicles-overtake-gas-powered-cars-study-5017783

[xlix] Robert Charette, "Can Power Grids Cope with Millions of EVs?" IEEE Spectrum, November 28, 2022. https://spectrum.ieee.org/the-ev-transition-explained-2658463709.

[l] Rizwan Choudhury, "China Becomes Solar Energy Superpower, Dominates 80% of the Supply Chain," Interesting Engineering, November 8, 2023. https://interestingengineering.com/innovation/china-becomes-solar-energy-superpower-dominates-80-of-supply-chain

[li] Edward White, "World's Biggest Solar Company Warns West Not to Cut Chinese Suppliers," Financial Times, February 15, 2024. https://www.ft.com/content/ba27f8d3-df06-4e2a-96b7-a8bbc06632a2

[lii] Alan Crawford and Laura Murphy, "Over-Exposed: Uyghur Region Exposure Assessment for Solar Industry Sourcing," Sheffield Hallam University – Helena Kennedy Centre for International Justice, November 2023. https://www.shu.ac.uk/-/media/home/research/helena-kennedy-centre/projects/over-exposed/crawford-murphy-et-al----over-exposed-xuar-assessment-aug-2023.pdf

[liii] Alexis Okeowo, "China's Bloody Frontier in Zambia," Pulitzer Center, May 15, 2013. https://pulitzercenter.org/projects/chinas-bloody-frontier-zambia

[liv] Congressional Hearing, "From Cobalt to Cars: How China Exploits Child and Forced Labor in the Congo," Congressional-Executive Commission on China, November 14, 2023. https://www.cecc.gov/events/hearings/from-cobalt-to-cars-how-china-exploits-child-and-forced-labor-in-the-congo

[lv] MG Macklin, CJ Thomas, et al. "Impacts of Metal Mining on River Systems: A Global Assessment," Science, vol. 381, is. 6664, p. 1345-1350. https://www.science.org/doi/10.1126/science.adg6704

[lvi] Report, *The Role of Critical Minerals in Clean Energy Transitions: Executive Summary*, International Energy Agency, May 2021. https://www.iea.org/reports/the-role-of-critical-minerals-in-clean-energy-transitions

[lvii] News Report, "Scottsbluff Community Solar Array Damaged in June 2023 Hailstorm is Back Online," Star Herald, January 8, 2024. https://starherald.com/news/local/business/development/scottsbluff-community-solar-array-damaged-in-june-2023-hailstorm-is-back-online/article_232bd84c-ae5c-11ee-87a6-0f4837caa473.html

[lviii] Aubryn Cooperman, "Wind Turbine Blade Material in the United States: Quantities, Costs, and End-of-Life Options," Resources, Conservation and Recycling, vol. 168, May 2021. https://www.sciencedirect.com/science/article/abs/pii/S092134492100046X

[lix] Sabine Wollrab, Maria Sheahan, and Christoph Steitz, "Siemens Energy's Shares Tumble as Wind Turbine Troubles Deepen," Reuters, June 23, 2023. https://www.reuters.com/business/energy/siemens-energy-ceo-setback-turbine-troubles-more-severe-than-thought-possible-2023-06-23/

[lx] Brett Christophers, "Capitalism Can't Solve Climate Change," Time, March 20, 2024. https://time.com/6958606/climate-change-transition-capitalism/

[lxi] Kirsten Grieshaber, "A German Military Officer Used an Unsecured Line for A Conference Call. Russia Hacked and Leaked It," AP News, March 5, 2024. https://apnews.com/article/germany-russia-ukraine-leaked-audio-taurus-98ba4fe85caf7d29902691f543a4dd04

[lxii] Daniel Darling, "Germany Faces Tall Task in Reversing Bundeswehr's Decline," Defense and Security Monitor, December 8, 2023. https://dsm.forecastinternational.com/2023/12/08/germany-faces-tall-task-in-reversing-bundeswehrs-decline/

[lxiii] Matthew Karnitschnig and Nette Nostlinger, "How Germany Inc. Played Russian Roulette — And Lost," Politico, April 13, 2022. https://www.politico.eu/article/germany-inc-played-russian-roulette-and-lost-ukraine-war-energy-gas-trade/

[lxiv] Melissa Eddy, "For German Firms, Ties to Russia Are Personal, Not Just Financial," NY Times, March 6, 2022. https://www.nytimes.com/2022/03/06/business/germany-russia-companies.html

[lxv] Jack Newman and Reuters, "Angela Merkel Says She Has NO Regrets Over Her Decision to Bind Germany to Russian Gas Which Has Now Led to Spiraling Inflation and Economic Chaos," Daily Mail October 14, 2022. https://www.dailymail.co.uk/news/article-11312461/Angela-Merkel-says-NO-regrets-decision-bind-Germany-Russian-gas.html

[lxvi] Andreas Demmig, "Allstedt in Lower Saxony, Dismantling of Wind Turbines After the Production Switch," Eike (Google English Translated), April 6, 2021. https://eike-klima-energie.eu/2021/04/06/allstedt-in-niedersachsen-abbau-von-windanlagen-nach-auslauf-der-foerderung/

[lxvii] Cornelia Lichner, "Weekend Read: A 10 GW Time Bomb," PV Magazine, September 9, 2023. https://www.pv-magazine.com/2023/09/09/weekend-read-a-10-gw-time-bomb/

[lxviii] News Report, "German Official Says Nuclear Would Do Little to Solve Gas Issue," Al Jazeera News, July 12, 2022. https://www.aljazeera.com/news/2022/7/12/german-says-nuclear-would-do-little-to-solve-gas-issue

[lxix] News Report, "Germany Due to Connect Coal Power Plants to Grid to Save Gas," Reuters, July 11, 2022. https://www.reuters.com/markets/commodities/germany-due-connect-coal-power-plants-grid-save-gas-sources-2022-07-11/

[lxx] News Report, "Germany Approves Bringing Coal-Fired Power Plants Back Online This Winter," Reuters, October 4, 2023. https://www.reuters.com/business/energy/germany-approves-bringing-coal-fired-power-plants-back-online-this-winter-2023-10-04/?taid=651d91ea74209d0001cd91b1

[lxxi] Mihajlo Vujasin, "Wind farm in Germany Is Being Dismantled to Expand Coal Mine," Balkan Green Energy News, October 25, 2022. https://balkangreenenergynews.com/wind-farm-in-germany-is-being-dismantled-to-expand-coal-mine/

[lxxii] Berit Hanna Czock, Hendrik Diers, and Dr. Philip Schnaars, "Supply Gaps in The Electricity Market Possible By 2030," Institute of Energy Economics at the University of Cologne (Google Translated into English), September 29, 2022. https://www.ewi.uni-koeln.de/de/aktuelles/versorgungssicherheit-bis-2030/

[lxxiii] News Report, "New Natural Gas-Fired Capacity Additions Expected to Total 8.6 Gigawatts In 2023," U.S. Energy Information Administration, October 16, 2023. https://www.eia.gov/todayinenergy/detail.php?id=60663

[lxxiv] Shannon Cuthrell, "$1.3B Combined-Cycle Natural Gas Plant Opens in Illinois," EEPower, August 28, 2023. https://eepower.com/news/1.3b-combined-cycle-natural-gas-plant-opens-in-illinois/#

[lxxv] Reference Page, "How Much Money Does 1 acre of Solar Panels Make?" PowMr.com, March 19, 2023. https://powmr.com/blogs/news/how-much-money-does-1-acre-of-solar-panels-make

[lxxvi] News Report, "Countries Launch Joint Declaration to Triple Nuclear Energy Capacity By 2050 At COP28." OECD Nuclear Energy Agency, December 2, 2023. https://www.oecd-nea.org/jcms/pl_88702/countries-launch-joint-declaration-to-triple-nuclear-energy-capacity-by-2050-at-cop28/

[lxxvii] Congressional Report, *Judicial Review and the National Environmental Policy Act of 1969.* Congressional Research Service, August 4, 2022. https://crsreports.congress.gov/product/pdf/R/R47205

[lxxviii] Mackenzie Shuman, "Should Diablo Canyon Stay Open? Keeping Nuclear Power Plant Running Is Illegal, Groups Say," The Tribune, January 18, 2023. https://archive.is/gP75X#selection-885.19-885.109

[lxxix] Report, *Nuclear Technology Development and Economics Unlocking Reductions in the Construction Costs of Nuclear: A Practical Guide for Stakeholders* (OECD: Nuclear Energy Agency, 2020): p. 61-65. https://www.oecd-nea.org/jcms/pl_30653/unlocking-reductions-in-the-construction-costs-of-nuclear?details=true

[lxxx] Andrea Stricker, "Ending Dependence on Russia's Nuclear Sector," National Interest, February 18, 2024. https://nationalinterest.org/feature/ending-dependence-russia%E2%80%99s-nuclear-sector-209488

[lxxxi] Paul Farhi, "Is American Journalism Headed Toward an 'Extinction-Level Event?" The Atlantic, January 30, 2024. https://www.theatlantic.com/ideas/archive/2024/01/media-layoffs-la-times/677285/

[lxxxii] Peter Laffin, "The Legacy Media's Downfall is a Tragedy, not a Triumph," Washington Examiner, June 28, 2023. https://www.washingtonexaminer.com/opinion/2569532/the-legacy-medias-downfall-is-a-tragedy-not-a-triumph/

[lxxxiii] David Folkenflik, "'The Washington Post' will Cut 240 Jobs Through Voluntary Buyouts," NPR, October 11, 2023. https://www.npr.org/2023/10/10/1204939842/the-washington-post-will-cut-240-jobs-through-voluntary-buyouts

[lxxxiv] Rober Philpot, "How Britain's Nazi-Loving Press Baron Made a Case for Hitler," The Times of Israel, August 5, 2018. https://www.timesofisrael.com/how-britains-nazi-loving-press-baron-made-the-case-for-hitler/

[lxxxv] Jacob Liedke and Jeffrey Gottfied, "U.S. Adults Under 30 Now Trust Information from Social Media Almost as Much as From National News Outlets," Pew Research Center, October 27, 2022. https://www.pewresearch.org/short-reads/2022/10/27/u-s-adults-under-30-now-trust-information-from-social-media-almost-as-much-as-from-national-news-outlets/

www.ingramcontent.com/pod-product-compliance
Lightning Source LLC
Chambersburg PA
CBHW081132020726
47504CB00010B/2056